The Wabash Trilogy

Other Books by William J. Palmer

NOVELS

The Detective and Mr. Dickens
The Highwayman and Mr. Dickens
The Hoydens and Mr. Dickens
The Dons and Mr. Dickens

FILM STUDIES

The Films of the Seventies: A Social History
The Films of the Eighties: A Social History
The Films of the Nineties: The Decade of Spin

LITERARY CRITICISM

The Fiction of John Fowles
Dickens and New Historicism

The Wabash Trilogy

The Wabash Baseball Blues
The Redneck Mafia
Civic Theater

William J. Palmer

Parlor Press
West Lafayette, Indiana
www.parlorpress.com

Parlor Press LLC, West Lafayette, Indiana 47906

Printed in the United States of America

SAN: 2 5 4 - 8 8 7 9

Library of Congress Cataloging-in-Publication Data

Palmer, William J., 1943-
 The Wabash trilogy : The Wabash baseball blues, The redneck mafia, Civic
theater / William J. Palmer.
   p. cm.
 ISBN 978-1-60235-164-6 (pbk. : acid-free paper)
 I. Title.
 PS3566.A547W33 2010
 813'.54--dc22
                            2009054341

Cover image © 2008 by Dori O'Connell. Used by permission.
Cover design by David Blakesley
Interior design by Kate Bouwens.

Printed on acid-free paper.

Parlor Press, LLC is an independent publisher of scholarly and trade
titles in print and multimedia formats. This book is available in paperback and ebook formats from Parlor Press on the World Wide
Web at http://www.parlorpress.com or through online and brick-and-
mortar bookstores. For submission information or to find out about
Parlor Press publications, write to Parlor Press, 816 Robinson St., West
Lafayette, Indiana, 47906, or e-mail editor@parlorpress.com.

This book is dedicated to Christy, Nancy and Jill,
my other trilogy.

My sincerest appreciation goes to David Blakesley,
Editor and Publisher of Parlor Press, and to his
assistant editor, Kate Bouwens, whose magic
transformed my novels into this book.
—WJP

Contents

The Wabash Baseball Blues

A Novel

William J. Palmer

1 Wabash

The Wabash flows past diamonds dust-lit on summer's nights, but in April 1976 the ballfields on the river's banks have not yet found their sparkle. Bicentennial America's pastime, or at least the softball version of it, has not yet come to life in the twin river towns of Wabash City and West Wabash. The river north of the twin towns is really two rivers converging, the Wabash and the smaller tributary (yet more famous in American history) the Tippecanoe.

Above the twin towns, the two rivers come together to form a dark V of verdant deltaland then flow south from the delta-V as one larger stream. Widening, it flows down past the softball fields and between the two hills upon which the twin towns perch. Atop the eastern hill in Wabash City sit the mansions of the captains of industry, the bankers, the merchants, the lawyers, the factory managers. On the hill in West Wabash sits the university. They strike a delicate and deceptive balance.

Entering the city limits of the twin towns, the Wabash first flows under the concrete New Bridge then past the crumbling stone pilings of the recently demolished Brown Street Bridge then under the bustling traffic of the Main Street Bridge to finally exit the twin towns through the skeletal portal of the rusty railroad bridge. For the twin towns the bridges seem like pulsing arteries, yet beneath them on the river banks are troubling signs of decay. On the west side below the railroad bridge sits a junkyard. In the spring in floodstage the river flows through the carcasses of junked cars just as desperate men flow through the whorehouses and strip joints of Wabash Avenue and Alabama Street on the east side of the river.

One wild wag from the university once called this whole area "the heart of the heart of the country" but in Bicentennial 1976 that poetic rhetoric may have gazed too high. On hot, humid summer evenings when the clouds dip low the air in the twin towns acquires a distinctive pungency closely akin to a huge hovering fart. Some blame this transient Wabash City smell on either the corn factoring plant or the pharmaceutical lab or the aluminum mill or the combination of all of the above. But in Bicentennial 1976 what all of the newly ecoconscious captains of industry most vehemently deny (for obvious reasons) is that the smell comes from the river which some suspect is the principal toilet for the dumping of their industrial effluents.

Atop the Ninth Street hill in Wabash City sits the turreted, columned, gabled, frescoed and stone-walled mansion of Justin Endreem, president of All-American Homes, the city's major industry and second largest (to the university) employer. Atop the State Street hill on the West Wabash side sits the grave stone prominences of the university buildings. West Wabash is a residential town where the professors live while Wabash City is a factory town where real people work and play and live.

But it is April in Bicentennial 1976, not summer quite yet, and looking across the river from the West Wabash hill the Wabash City ballfields look tragic in their defeat, pitiful in their emptiness. The backstops stand lonesome in the cold April sunshine. One backstop bends halfway over like a man who has just pulled the muscles in his back. The infields are like Dali deserts with gaping cracks opening in the hard, crusted dirt. The fields are lineless and littered with broken boards, tin cans, scraps of paper, used rubbers, dead branches and crushed McDonald's cups. The dugouts are racked and in ruins. Sprawling spider webs dotted with mummified sacks of spun death hang like waiting gladiator's nets in the corners. Pieces of the roofs have been torn off, scavenged to make winos' winter fires. Across the entry road an empty beer can rolls and comes to rest. Its embossed label in garish red, white and blue letters gazes up at the cold April sky and, after 200 years, independently declares, "AMERICA'S FINEST."

The unlined baseball fields need to be raked and manicured, their faces scrubbed and a comb run through their matted hair. It is ironic that in the spring when the river is so alive and swollen the ballfields are so dead.

But they always come back.

When the new season starts, almost instantly the ballfields become sleeker, their lines straight, the backstops, fences and foulpoles fixed, the dugouts, freshly painted, sparkling in the summer sun. The dull ballfields of April become summer diamonds. Just imagine looking down from the hill in West Wabash into a midsummer night's dream; say, to the evening of the third of July in '76, the eve of America's 200th birthday. You can see the shifting substance of the humid summer night. Halos of light hang purple in the thick air around the ballfield lights. The five light poles on diamond number one stand at attention to salute the American flag that flies ostentatiously from the flag pole on top of the concession stand directly behind home.

On the field the men stand still, pounding fists into gloves or crouching forward with hands spread open on their knees waiting for the pitch to trigger some oft-felt reflex that will send them, free of thought, lunging to their left or right or digging back for the fence or diving forward for a shoestring catch. They wear strangely schizo-phrenic uniforms. The bottoms are raggedy, but the tops are vulgarly opulent. Most of the players wear cut-offs (and proudly sport scabs on the sides of their knees) or blue jeans (usually torn at the knees from sliding). A few wear real baseball pants and thin oversocks that disappear like sideburns into their spikes. But all wear gaudy neon tops; softball jerseys that Liberace or Evil Kneival could feel at home in. And the names: ALL-AMERICAN HOMES in red, white and blue, SAMMY'S TAVERN, UNIVERSITY ELECTRONICS, KRIEG MOTORS, WABASH CITY ELEVATOR, DICK AND TONNA'S BAR AND GRILL, AMERICAN UNITED TRUST INSURANCE, BEN HUR VOLKSWAGEN, PEERLESS TRUCK-ING CO., POLICE, THE OLD GLORY BROKERAGE CO., THE MARS THEATER.

The men, standing still in anticipation, waiting for the pitch, kick-ing the dust in readiness as the hitter steps in, begin their meaningless formulaic chant as if the field were an open air church and they the ministers in a pagan summer ritual:

> Cmonbabynohitterpitchtoimbabeschuckitinthere-
> chucktoimbabychuckitin

> Cmonbabybringimtousmakeimhititcmonbabyyeahy-
> eahhesallourschucktoim

> Alrightattababygogetimmanaintnohittercmonbaby-
> hesourscmononetwothree.

The pitcher crouches, the hitter stands tense waiting for the lazy arc of the ball coming like a planet into his ken, revolving slowly in empty space through frozen time. Then, with the pounding thump of bat on paunchy ball, the players by suddenly remembered reflex churn in the sweaty summer dust and the evening moves electric out of fidgety stasis into confident balletic motion.

A winning team from a previous game lounges around the tail-gate of a rusty pickup, lying to each other as they replay the game, their women sipping slowly from pull tab cans and telling the children to go play on the swings. Teams waiting to play warm up languidly on the grass behind the dugouts or lean on their elbows on the low fences along the first and third baselines criticizing the teams on the field: "that dude runs like he's pregnant." In the stands the humidity oppresses the women, sluicing stickily against their teased and lacquered heads, over their short-shorted, bug-sprayed thighs. Sweat rolls down under their sleeveless blouses and out of the bottoms of their halter tops. Recession, depression, unemployment, no one thinks of those things here. Softball is cheap entertainment for a midsummer's night. American flag decals, the insignia of the Bicentennial, adorn most of the cars, wave from the rear windows of Volkswagens, Mazdas, Toyotas and Fiats, flutter on the tailgates of gun-racked pickups.

The players warming up turn and laugh, smile knowingly at one another, as a sleek, highly-polished black car rolls slowly through the parking lot behind the refreshment stand and parks on the river bank down by the boat launch. Its lights blink off with finality. No one gets out of the black car. It sits invisible and mysterious as if waiting for something or someone at the water's edge.

But in the heat of the July evening the games go on. Softball is a game where men who were once real ballplayers try to bring to life, in slow motion, a dream of the past, a dream of motion, prowess, and promise declining but not lost as they grow older.

But it isn't July yet. It's still April both up on the hill and down by the river. The ballfields on the bank are still empty and unlined. The river is still swollen and washes up high, over the boat launch and the bottom half of the parking lot. From up on the hill the view is still gray, not yet green, and the April wind is cold and drives one inside.

2 Gown and Town

"They're killing American literature! They're coming in the windows with new books! They don't even teach *Moby Dick* anymore!" The old professor's demented ravings held the English Department faculty meeting in thrall. His vision of the apocalypse was young professors no longer teaching books like *Beowulf* and *Moby Dick,* classical monster fare. Bill Franklin's tweed sportcoat itched at the wrists. ESCAPE, only a vague, remote hope, ricocheted around in his mind. It was an unseemly desire for a newly-minted Assistant Professor to nurture.

"They're teaching tripe! Like that Cuckoo's Nest thing! They're coming in the windows with these new books!

Bill Franklin looked over his shoulder at the bank of windows for reassurance. It came to him in a vision, the title for a new course, GREAT AMERICAN TRIPE. He looked at his watch. In only a few more hours, he could escape the coat and tie for a pair of jeans. Only one month after his thirtieth birthday, he saw himself squirming through thirty-five more years of insane faculty meetings like the one he was not paying attention to at the moment. In the hallway afterwards, fleeing the meeting and the noblesse oblige of the senior professors, he saw the semester's dream coed striding toward him. Curly blonde hair, wide prairie shoulders, her gauzy blouse winking open down the front, her skirt flowing over the shadows of long, smooth thighs.

"Hi, Professor Franklin," she smiled in passing.

Each semester he changed the coed, but his recurring daydream remained the same. She walked demurely into his office, carefully shutting the door behind her. She sank wearily into the broken-backed, cracked-leather easy chair and opened her thighs as she caught her breath. She never wore panties and the dark triangle between her legs always played a shadowy little game of peek-a-boo.

"Dr. Franklin, sir," she asked, conspiratorially resting a hand on his knee, "what can I do to get an A in the course?"

Except she never showed up. In his five years as a professor, she had never come; perhaps because dreams rarely do.

Bending over a convenient drinking fountain, Bill watched the tall, wide-shouldered blonde swing down the long hallway and disappear around a corner. Straightening out of his daydream, Bill marched toward his last class of the day. It would be filled with clear-eyed students who inexplicably believed all that he told them.

Two hours later, he steered the car up onto the bridge between West Wabash and Wabash City. Below, the Wabash flowed, spring-swollen and unconcerned. He had delivered his lecture on *The Great Gatsby* with grim intensity and had fled, when the bell rang, out into the cold April sunlight. Crossing the bridge, he looked north toward the dark V of rich deltaland above the twin towns. Turning south on Ninth Street and climbing the hill he passed the ante-bellum mansion of Justin Endreem, Wabash City's major industrialist. His destination was the big new discount store. He loosened his tie as he crossed the parking lot. The sale table in the middle of the store bristled with children's cowboy boots. He hunted until he found Danny's size. They were a full three dollars cheaper than anywhere else in town. He carried his prize to one of the long lines at the checkout registers. The line moved slowly. Five, ten minutes. Only one lady stood between him and escape.

The cashier took the woman's money, bagged her purchase.

Bill stepped forward with the cowboy boots, already pulling his wallet from his pocket.

The cashier looked at her watch, pulled a small plastic sign that read "CLOSED" out from under the counter, placed it nonchalantly on the rubber conveyor belt in front of Bill.

Then, as if the words were a recording being played in her chest cavity and piped out through her mouth, she said, without looking up: "Sorry sir, this line is closed. You'll have to get in another one."

"You can't do that."

"Sorry sir, this line is closed. You'll have to get in another one," the recording repeated as she started to walk away.

"Stop. I've been waiting fifteen minutes."

"Sorry sir, this line . . ." Her recorded voice trailed off as she walked away.

His eyes wild, Bill turned and flung his bargain boots high and hard back into the plastic and linoleum bowels of the store. The people standing docilely in line to pay the machines shrank from him as he started toward the door. Their aversion made him feel good about it. He began to feel fine when from afar back in the store came the sound of shattering glass and falling weight. It was probably the most un-American thing he had ever done, and in the Bicentennial year too.

Driving toward the bridge that crossed back into West Wabash, Bill passed the riverfront park. The softball fields, their skeletal backstops and gloomy dugouts, brooded on the river bank. The ballfields looked gray and empty, neglected. *But they always come back,* he thought, *dull April ballfields become summer diamonds.* It was the first sort-of-interesting, semi-poetic thought he'd had all day.

He pulled into the driveway and switched off the ignition. Martha's house loomed above as he sat in the car staring straight ahead at nothing. There was no escape. The house, which should have been the most satisfying symbol of his success, told him that. Large, high, it sat on a wide, treelined street in a staid old neighborhood. Young children like Danny and Grace played in almost every yard. Six months before, he had plunked down their savings for a downpayment. It was a real Indiana house. Its weatherbeaten boards (they'd probably have to aluminum side it) had roots reaching back a hundred years to trees that once flourished in forests in the river valley bottomland. They had considered buying one of the fancier All-American Homes. It would have been much easier to maintain. But none of the new neighborhoods had any trees where the children could climb and hide and build forts in shady, secret spots.

Martha Franklin greeted her husband at the back door: "I saw you drive in. Why were you just sitting out there?"

"Just resting a second."

"Is anything wrong?"

"No. No. Just tired."

"You didn't get a chance to look for those cowboy boots for Danny's birthday?" She presented it as a pointed question.

"I stopped on the way home. Size four right? There weren't any left."

Martha made a sour face.

They sat like mannequins at the dinner table. The children, Danny seven, Grace six, a boy and a girl, both all-american blonde, watched television through the door to the den as they ate.

"Did you decide about the summer job?" Martha asked carefully. "Are you going to take it?"

"Hell, I have to, don't I? They sure as hell aren't going to give me any summer teaching. Hell, we gotta eat, make the lousy payments on your lousy house."

"Don't start that again."

"Yeah, I'm gonna take the job."

They had notified him only two weeks before that no summer school teaching was available. He could have borrowed money to get them through the summer, but Martha balked at that idea. She decided that he should get a summer job to make the payments on her house. Out he'd gone in a flannel shirt to humbly submit applications at beer distributors, trucking terminals, and, of course, All-American Homes. On the forms, he never gave himself more than a high school education. He'd worked laborer jobs before, during grad school. He spent one interminable summer working for the highway department cleaning used condoms, beer cans, and dead dogs off of fourteen miles of desolate Ohio interstate. Two days after he applied, All-American Homes had called and offered him a summer job. He had called them from his office to accept that afternoon. As he hung up the phone, he had given up all hope of having a good summer.

"Oh, it won't be too bad," Martha said gaily, snapping him out of his reverie, "at least we won't have to pay off a lot of loans when you go back to school in the fall."

Martha fell asleep early on the couch to the drone of the television set. Lately, their sex life seemed regulated by the TV GUIDE. He and Martha had been married almost eight years. She had become like his tennis shoes, broken in, comfortable, almost too familiar, the tread worn so thin that when he tried to run he slipped, found himself ineffective. He groped for reasons for his unhappiness. He had everything he was supposed to have. His wife was pretty and he loved her (but regularly she fell asleep on the couch in front of the TV). His kids were healthy, happy, smart in school and flush with friends (yet they spent most of their waking hours watching television like robots). He was a good teacher (but nobody cared). He could still dream of his son playing baseball, running bases with long blonde hair flowing back off his face, whirling free in the joy of the basepaths. Or of his daughter rocketing down the slide at the swimming pool, the joy of freedom exploding from her sun-haloed face.

Death or violence had never really intruded into Bill's life. But un-invited whispers of impending disaster had threatened him in the winter months. In January, a small lump had appeared in Martha's breast. Surgery was decreed and for three days, they had lived in terror. Then Martha came down the hall on her back beaming from ear to ear The lump had only been a harmless water-filled cyst which the surgeon had popped like a balloon. New love had flowed briefly in as the stalled machine of their lives together had restarted.

In February, Danny had run a 104 temperature for two days. Kneeling on the hard tile floor beside the bathtub and sponging his hot listless little body, Bill felt a fear even greater than when Martha had been in the hospital. As Danny threatened to burn out, Bill saw only images of emptiness. One thought flogged his desperate con-sciousness: a man can replace a lost wife, perhaps, secretly, guiltily, even envision life with a new woman, but no man can ever replace his only son. He didn't sleep for two days. Finally, the fever broke and Danny woke up and smiled. "Hi Dad, "the little boy had said quizzi-cally as if surprised to see him.

Spring has to be better, Bill thought hopelessly.

3 All-American Homes

Like an insane wife, the All-American Homes factory was put away out of sight on the far side of the Wabash City hill. Through the huge doors at the back of the two-storey corrugated tin box, formless materials—wood, aluminum, miniature kitchen sinks, toilet bowls and stove tops, barrels of nails, screws, bolts and rivets, rolls of thin carpeting, tubs of pastel paints—enter. Through the huge bay doors at the front, they roll out as baby houses, mobile homes, module apartments and pre-cut bungalows.

The executive offices, housed in an afterthought wing off the main factory building, bulge like a tasteless remark The lower back part of the executive wing houses "the shop" where so-called "detail" work—cabinet making, register assembling, extrusion cutting and materials receiving—is done, mostly by women, cheap labor. High piles of lumber, sheet metal, pipe, wire and plastic bloom in the desert around the factory. Fork lifts and tow-motors prowl "the yard" as this industrial garden is called. In the back, the employee parking lot shimmers dustily in the unseasonal May heat.

Out in front stands a huge billboard beaming out over the two-lane blacktop that runs into Wabash City. The cherubic and glossy face of Justin Endreem smiles benevolently down from the billboard. Like satellites, trailers, houses and sparkling module buildings orbit around Justin's wizardly head as if tornado-tossed in Oz. His face is always freshly painted, and, around the top of his head, like a halo, curves the company's homey motto: FAMILIES GROW TOGETHER IN ALL-AMERICAN HOMES.

As Bill Franklin pulled into the All-American Homes parking lot, the sun stabbed off the silver sides of the main building, closing his eyes momentarily in pain. He had been instructed to report to the personnel manager, one Mr. C. Wallis,

"May I help you?" the secretary smiled.

"My name is Franklin and I was told to report here to start work today."

"Oh. Well what's your last name?"

"No. No. It's Bill. William Franklin. Franklin's my last name."

"Oh. OK. Will you please have a seat."

"Uh, yes, thank you."

He coughed awkwardly as he looked down the front of her blouse. She pressed the button on the intercom.

"A Mr. William Franklin is here Mr. Wallis. He says he was called in to start work today," she cooed into the brown vinyl box.

"Get his file," the box barked back.

"Yes sir," the girl said submissively to the box. She left the protection of her desk and walked to the file cabinets. Tall, long-legged, blonde hair flowing free to her shoulder blades, her blouse open two buttons from the top, a knee-length skirt shimmering on her thighs, the secretary bent from the waist to root in a bottom file drawer.

Bill coughed like a man being checked for a hernia.

"Franklin. Here it is," she straightened up.

"Mr. Wallis, all his forms seem to be here except the W-2," she said efficiently into the box.

"Good, have him fill it out, make sure he knows what he is declaring, then take him down to Washington."

"Don't I even have to see him?"

"Oh no, he's much too busy. Nobody hardly ever sees him. Anyway, he's fat and bald."

"Uh-huh."

"Are you married?" she asked pointblank.

"Uh . . . yes, no . . . uh yes . . . Why do you ask?"

"The W-2, your income tax deduction. We have to fill it out. Any kids?"

"Yes, two . . . but . . ." but she seemed uninterested in everything but filling in the numbers on the card.

As they walked the corridor to the stairway down to the factory floor, Bill asked her name.

The question startled her, as if it was something strange that people rarely asked.

"It's Rae Ann . . . Rae Ann Ross."

"That's a nice name. You have any deductions?"

"What?"

"Tax deductions. The W-2. Kids? Husband?"

"Oh . . . No . . . not anymore. Never had any kids. OK, here we are."

The fire door opened out onto a small landing one level above the interior expanse of All-American Homes. The roof arched like an airplane hanger. The factory sprawled out below.

The floor looked like a surreal mating of a railyard, a graveyard and junkyard. Tracks ran from the twelve-foot-high doors in the back to identical doors in the front. Rectangular aluminum frames ran on rubber tires along the tracks: the undercarriages of mobile homes. Between the tracks, like graves, were a series of rectangular pits. The pits, each about seven feet deep, allowed men to work under the carriages which moved along the tracks above from pit to pit, from one stage of the assembly to another. Between the pitted lines, either in large bins or in piles on the floor, all the components waited. Electrical sockets, window frame extrusion, registers, aluminum moldings, electrical wire: all the little things stored in bins. Colored aluminum in large rolls wound around eight-foot-high spools. Large table saws spaced at strategic points for cutting pipe and extrusion. Huge metal breakers for bending aluminum and shearing sheet metal. Along the floor between each line snaked the coiled black cords of the power tools: drills, screwdrivers, air wrenches, circular hand saws, planers, sanders, soldering irons. The assembly workers carried their power tools in leather holsters like old-time cowboys packing six-guns. The pits, the floor, the very air of the plant was choked with sawdust and the more dangerous metal shavings.

Rae Ann, waiting patiently, watching him with curiosity, broke the silence: "That's it. The pits. You'll get your fill of them once they teach you what to do."

"What do you mean?"

"Oh, I don't know. It just gets awful hot during the summer. I'm sure glad I don't work there anymore."

"You're kidding. You worked down there? Women work down there?"

"Sometimes, during the summer, when the men start going on vacations. If they get really short they pull some of the women out of the shop to do some of the jobs. I don't know which is worse."

"What's the shop?"

"You'll see. C'mon."

She led him down the open metal steps to the factory floor. They weaved through the chaos to a cage in the back of the building. A man sat at an old wooden desk in the cage working over some papers. A guitar leaned against the side of the desk.

"Hey Jim. Here's your new man," Rae Ann hailed the man. She handed over the clipboard she had carried down from the personnel office.

"This is Jim Washington. He's foreman for the mobile home lines," she informed Bill as she walked away.

"Man she does have a nice butt," the foreman said speculatively. Then, as if returning to reality: "I hope you last longer'n the last one they sent me. He got drunk the night he got his first paycheck. To-taled a cherry '71 Chevy. Still in the hospital. Lyin' there with his ass jammed up around his elbows."

This guy looks awful young to be a foreman, Bill thought.

Jim Washington was a young foreman because he could build any-thing, repair anything, read and add and subtract, get along pretty good with everybody, and had been working at All-American Homes since he was eighteen. He'd taken the job a week after graduation from Thomas Jefferson High School in Wabash City in 1966 because his ex-wife, whom he hadn't married yet, was knocked up. He'd done well on the job and after fighting with his wife for five miserable years, he'd divorced her. He was twenty-eight, a foreman, and looking at the yellow personnel sheet on the clipboard that Rae Ann had given him.

"William Franklin. You go by William or they call you Willy?"

That's different, Bill thought, *why not?"*

"Yeah, it's Willy," he answered, "I prefer it, Willy."

So he became Willy Franklin, whoever that was.

"I guess I better show you around. For a while you're gonna be a go-pher, doin' odd jobs, fillin' in, takin' care o' the bins, mebbe breakin' metal or poundin' storage boxes together. Then . . . well, we'll see."

Bill followed Washington through the chaotic maze of materials and tools.

"OK, in this first pit on a line we build the floor on a carriage, wor-kin' from both underneath and on top. Dick Adams, Willy Franklin," Bill nodded to the man holding a seven-foot-high piece of plywood upright with one hand and a hammer in the other. Nails bristled from where his grin should have been. "His brother Sam does toilets an' showers up at the other end," Washington added as they moved on.

"Underneath there, that's Duane Zenger. He don't talk much. Floors are plywood and sheet metal. When we git the floors done we use this same area ta throw up the walls an' roof. In the second pit on a line, we put in pipe and conduit. C'mon."

He followed Washington on like a man just fallen to earth from outer space.

"Don Devere," Washington pointed to a blocky man with thinning hair climbing out from under the shell of a mobile home. Holding a power drill with an eighteen inch bit in his hand, he looked like a spearfisherman emerging from a swimming pool.

"Don Devere, Willy Franklin."

Bill shook hands with the barrel-chested man.

Devere nodded "how are ya," picked up a piece of pipe and dove back into his pit.

Washington rambled on about water pipes and disposal pipes and shower pipes and which width was which.

Devere called: "Hey Jimmy, gimme that drill with the three-quarter by twenty-four inch bit in it since your just standin' there. When you gonna git me out of this hole an back on finishin' work?"

"When ya hit six hundred with a hundred an twenty RBI's. Here ya go . . . that the right one?"

Devere disappeared back under the trailer.

"You'll be workin' with all these guys off an' on dependin' on where we need ya at the time."

"Man, I don't know. I've never done any plumbing or electrical work. I really don't know too much about any of this stuff."

"No sweat. An idiot could throw this stuff together. Trailers are simple. Anybody can do it."

Washington worshipped the power tools. As he showed Bill a power drill or air wrench or sander, he would heft its weight, holding it like a priceless antique dueling pistol. Then he would pull the trigger, fire off a burst of rpm's in the air. He was in charge of five lines and had to get fifteen trailers out each week. Usually the only day he personally did any building work was Friday. On Friday, they all worked together on the upper end of the lines until number fifteen was out the door. When number fifteen rolled off the line and out to the holding lot, Washington always told his men to stop working and keep an eye on the executive stairway in case any of the fat cats came snooping around, unlikely as that possibility was since they all left at noon every Friday.

On finished Fridays, some of Washington's men slept in the pits under half-finished trailers. Others sat out on the loading dock drinking cokes, smoking cigarettes, and swapping stories. Anything went after number fifteen was wrapped, but nothing went until fifteen was done. A lightning storm once knocked out the power to the plant for three hours on Wednesday afternoon. It had been eerie, the quiet, no power tools whirring, only hammers and nails. But that storm made them pay on Friday. They didn't finish number fifteen until almost ten at night. Everybody cussed and bitched and Washington worked like a madman, but nobody left. About twenty minutes before fifteen was finished, Washington disappeared. "Where did Washington go?" somebody grunted. But when they opened the doors to roll fifteen out, he was sitting in the back of Devere's pickup truck with three cases of beer. "What took you guys so long?" he asked innocently. They all sat in the front parking lot and drank under the mindless eyes of Justin Endreem. Everybody thought Jimmy Washington was a good old boy. He was in charge of forty-five time cards.

"C'mon I'll show you the shop. It's over in the other building," Washington grinned. They had finished touring the mobile home lines. "You'll like this. Women work over here."

"What's the shop?"

"It's just more assembly lines. They make the little stuff They size extrusion for small windows and bang the frames together, hang those plastic louvers. They build cabinets for the kitchens. They assemble all the floor and wall registers. Shipping and Receiving's over here too."

Through the swinging doors, they ran head-on into an assembly line. It was a long conveyor belt about twelve inches wide with women lined up at three foot intervals all down its length on one side. On the other side were piles of steel parts which the women perpetually, like pendulums, reached across to grab.

"You know Rae Ann, that girl brought you down this morning? She used to work on that register line," Washington said softly.

Four years before, during his first month as a foreman, Jim Washington had met Rae Ann. Nothing like it had ever happened to him before or since. She had been working with the men that week on the mobile home lines. One afternoon, late, after everyone had left, Washington had been conscientiously, new foreman that he was, cleaning

up some paperwork in the cage when Rae Ann came back in the loading dock door. She had nodded silently as he swiveled around in his
chair and walked on without a word toward the lines. He found her
prowling inside an almost-finished trailer.

"Lose something?" he had asked.

She stared at him as if her voice didn't work. When she got it going,
her voice trembled as if trying not to crack: "I . . . I lost my rings. God,
he'll kill me."

She was crying. Tears rolled down her cheeks as she opened cabinets, looked frantically under resting power tools.

"Look, calm down, we'll find 'em. What were ya workin' on? Do
ya remember takin' em off?"

"It must have been this morning. I was puttin' those stainless steel
mouldings around the sink an I cut my hand. I went to the restroom
to wash off the blood."

"Maybe they're in the ladies room?"

"No. I took them off before I went."

"Well, they sure as hell ought to be here then." He went into the
small kitchen but there was no sign of any rings anywhere. A splotch
of blood had hardened on the stainless sink. "I wonder," he wondered,
looking down.

"Where you goin'?" she asked dejectedly.

"You'll see."

In a moment he was back with a pipe wrench. It took him all of two
minutes to open the pipes up. There, sitting high and dry in the virgin
pipe, were the rings, a silver wedding band and a diamond solitaire
engagement ring. They looked like put together they might be worth
eighty-five maybe a hundred dollars.

"Oh, you found them, thank you, oh thank you." Her arms went
around him. She was still crying and he could feel her breasts trembling in his chest as she sobbed in relief. "Oh thank you, he'd be so
mad. I never would have found them there." She burrowed deeper
into his arms still sobbing, "he would have beat me up." It was as if
she hadn't talked to anyone in days. "Oh thank you," she clung more
tightly to him as if afraid to let go.

Then, abruptly, she wasn't sobbing anymore. She didn't say anything. As she looked into his face she seemed very sad. Her arms
reached up around his neck and she kissed him full on the mouth.

He had forgotten where he was, that it was his first month as a foreman. Together, they sank to the floor. She made love to him desperately, appreciatively. He never knew what hit him.

"Man, we'd better git out of here," was all Washington, remembering that he was a new foreman, said when she was done.

"Yeah," she answered sadly, "but thank you, really."

He struggled comically to pull up his pants.

Her jeans had landed clear across the room. She picked them up, wiggled as she pulled them over her hips, retreived her panties and shoved them unceremoniously into her back pocket. "Thanks for findin' my rings," she said and left.

They passed each other three times the next day without speaking. The next week Rae Ann went back to the register line in the shop. Two months later, she was gone. All he could find out was that she and her husband had moved to Chicago.

Washington had never been able to figure it out, what it had meant. He had a bunch of theories. Maybe it was just her way of saying "thank you" for finding the rings. But she was so frenzied and so sad, as if it was something she had to do. Maybe it was revenge, a way to hurt her husband. Sometimes, he'd pretend that she had been attracted to him all along, desired him from afar until that opportunity presented itself. But he knew that was probably not it. Pretty soon, he stopped trying to figure it out. When she moved away, he tried to put it out of his mind. But the memory continued to haunt him.

Washington led Bill slowly along the assembly line, explaining each step in the making of the registers. "They don't always make registers, some days they put together kitchen and bathroom fans, some days door and cupboard latches."

While Washington talked, Bill studied the women. Their hands moved monotonously in the same repetitive pattern. They sweated like men. Most wore dark tee-shirts. Circles of sweat were formed under their armpits. Two had streaked hair pulled back in rubber-banded ponytails. One, with long blonde hair, wore a red, white and blue headband to keep her hair out of her face. One didn't have a bra on. Her dark green tee-shirt was tucked into her Levis. As she reached across for parts, her breasts moved, the nipples clearly outlined against the thin fabric. An old box radio blared Country and Western music from a shelf on the wall above the line and some of the women mouthed the words or bobbed their heads to the doggerel beats.

"Ellie." Washington greeted a tall girl with flowing auburn hair.

"Uh-huh," she answered, barely looking up from the line.

Washington led Bill on into the cabinet room. "Whitey, how ya doin'?" he greeted a beer-bellied man of about forty-five who was working on the door channels of a cabinet frame.

"Aw OK, I guess, these damn things git harder ta groove evry year. Those suits upstairs oughta start buyin' some good wood again like we usta have."

"How's that rag-arm?"

"Great. Can't wait for it ta start."

"This's Willy Franklin. He's new."

"Howdy. I'm Billy Joe Warren. These dummies call me Whitey."

Bill and Washington crossed back into the main factory building.

"Did he hurt his arm on the job?" Bill asked.

"Naw. He's our pitcher," Washington said. "That's the grand tour. You've seen the whole place 'cept the loading docks. That's where we all eat lunch on good days."

And so it began, Bill Franklin's summer at All-American Homes. One day during the first week, walking to his car at closing time, Bill spotted Rae Ann and Ellie, the girl Washington had spoken to on the assembly line. They were coming out of the office wing. He waved.

Now why the hell did I do that? he wondered. Rae Ann waved back gaily in the dust. *She can't be much more than twenty-five, twenty-seven,* he thought, *but eyes like thirty-five.* Rae Ann filled his thoughts as he drove home to Martha.

His first Friday on the job number thirteen was done by eleven-thirty in the morning. Fourteen and fifteen only needed the inside finishing work. All of Washington's people broke early for lunch. It was a sunny day and they carried their pails and bags out to the loading dock. Nobody was in a hurry to go back to work. They knew they had the afternoon knocked. Washington strummed on his guitar. The others drank cokes, threw their bags and cans in the black oil drum, soaked up the sun.

Bill sat against the overhead door smoking a cigarette. "Can you play any songs?" he asked Washington innocently.

Devere, also sitting smoking against the door, broke out laughing. "Shit man," he cackled, "he plays em, sings em, even writes some o' em. Hey Jimmy, let's do our duet for the rookie. Me an Jimmy wrote this one together Willy boy."

Groans rose spontaneously. But Devere prevailed. He and Washington launched into their version of *Home, Home On The Range:*

Its Aawwl Aamerican Homes,
Where the tow-motor roams,
Where the veneer and aluminum splay,
Where men seldom voice,
a complaint or a choice,
and tin houses keep rollin' away.

Home, home in your jeans,
In the pits with a trailer above.
The plant is all dark
So just for a lark
Won't you be my All-American love.

It was a lazy day and they all laughed as they headed back in to finish up.

About ten of five, Bill went over to the cage to ask Washington about his pay, when he could get it. As they were talking, the girl, Ellie, came in.

"You about ready?" she asked Washington.

Tall in her tee-shirt that tapered down into tight beltless Levis, Ellie ignored Bill. Her face, wide cheekbones and freckles over the top of her nose, carried a level, open steadiness, almost challenge. At least five-eight, maybe pushing five-ten, she seemed to explode into the room. Her face was animated, alive, not as it had been when Bill first saw her, semi-comatose, on the assembly line.

"Yeah, all finished," Washington answered. "Willy, meet Ellie. Say hello to Willy, darlin.'"

4 Rae Ann and Ellie

Rae Ann lived in an All-American Mobile Home in a trailer park on the outskirts of Wabash City. All-American Homes sold returned units to employees at a cut price and she had borrowed the money for the trailer from the company credit union. The trailer had been damaged in transit and sent back, sort of like Rae Ann herself.

Drifting in from work in the afternoons, she always sat down at the kitchen table to drink a glass of lemonade in the summer, a cup of hot chocolate in the winter. Alone, looking out the window at her neighbors' drab, tin roofs, she sipped slowly on her memories, cautiously tasted her dreams.

She had been steering clear of men since that dingy day in December when she had driven up through the dirty snow to Chicago to sign the final divorce papers. In the car driving back to Wabash City, she felt sorry for Wes's new girl. She couldn't believe that she had once found Wes exciting. She had lost her virginity to him on a blanket in the moonlight under the grassy bank by the sixth green of the University golf course up on the hill in West Wabash.

What a sex life, Rae Ann thought as the trailer houses, stretching in treeless rows along narrow streets, came back into focus through her window. I lost my virginity on a golf course and I did my adultery in the middle of a mobile home factory. She wondered at the strangeness of it all. She wasn't unconventional.

During the last two years of their marriage, Wes's presence had threatened every part of her life, even her most secret thoughts. She never would have cheated on him intentionally. But that one day, her whole world had just split open. Mr. Washington—she hadn't even known his first name then—had gone out of his way to help her. He saved her from a beating and somehow she had just ended up in his arms. Even on the floor of a half-finished trailer in the middle of the factory, it had felt right. She thought about it all the time. Since she had gotten back into All-American Homes with the secretary job, she saw Jimmy Washington almost every day. Her own trailer always struck her funny because it was exactly like the one they had made love in that day.

Every day for half an hour when she got home from work, Rae Ann sat behind her flowered curtains looking out over the cramped black-top of the tin trailer park. She thought about Ellie. Ellie was the only real friend she had made since coming back to Wabash City. And Ellie, it turned out, was dating Jimmy Washington. Sometimes Rae Ann would lie in bed in the darkness. As she touched herself, she would think about her and Washington that day years before and she would think about Ellie and Washington now and as she fondled herself toward release and sleep she would think about how she really liked Ellie but was gently jealous too and about how it was all so complicated.

Rae Ann had met Ellie the August before in the summer heat and dust of the All-American Homes parking lot. She remembered thinking what a pretty car it was, a baby blue Chevy Malibu with a white top. Ellie was sitting on the hood, her long auburn hair framing a face wet with sweat. She looked exhausted, forlorn. Rings of sweat darkly circled the armpits of her green tee-shirt. Rae Ann, bouncing out of an air-conditioned office, fresh and cool, said "hi."

Ellie said "sheeeit!"

"Is something the matter?"

"Car is bran new an it won't start."

"Can I help? Drop you someplace?"

"No, that's OK, this guy from the plant I date said he thought he could fix it."

The guy turned out to be Washington. He appeared behind Rae Ann carrying a set of jumper cables. She was embarrassed. She'd only been back working about a month and it was the first time she'd seen him outside of the factory.

"Hullo Mrs. Ross," Washington said awkwardly.

"Hi." Her mind flashed to the exact images which she knew with absolute certainty were simultaneously sparking in Washington's mind. "Well, I guess I'll be heading on home," she added, trying to escape gracefully.

"Wait a minute," Washington stopped her. "Since you're parked right here, why don't you start it up an let me jump Ellie's battery off your's."

"OK," Rae Ann consented agreeably.

"Super!" Ellie seemed to be regaining some enthusiasm for life.

"Baby Blue rides again," she shouted moments later when Washington made the final connection and her engine coughed to life.

Washington looked like he wanted to linger, perhaps to ask Ellie for a date, but Rae Ann scared him off. He disconnected his cables saying "that oughta do it" and fled.

Ellie slid over, stretched her head out of the window and called "thanks Jimmy, I'll see ya" after him.

He waved back indiscriminately as he moved off.

The two women turned to each other.

"He's a nice man," Rae Ann said, complimenting Ellie.

"Yeah, well, a, I'm Ellie Warren, a, thank you, Mrs. Ross, for lettin' us use your car ta git mine goin.'"

"Please call me Rae Ann. I hate that Mrs. Ross."

"What's your old man haveta say about that?"

"Nothin.' In a coupla months that Mrs. will be gone for good."

"You gettin' divorced?"

"Uh-huh."

"Look, I'm so goddamed hot I can't stand it. I'm gonna stop in a nice air-conditioned bar for a beer on the way home. You wanta come along?"

"Yes. I'd like that. It is hot."

"OK. Why don'tchoo just follow me."

They talked in the bar until almost seven-thirty and they had been friends ever since. In fact, Ellie was Rae Ann's only real friend in Wabash City. Ellie was twenty-two when Rae Ann first met her in the parking lot. Two weeks later, on a Saturday, they went swimming together at the pool in Ellie's apartment complex. Rae Ann had only seen Ellie at work, in jeans and tee-shirts, sweaty and tired. At the pool Ellie was something completely else. Tall, at least five-eight in her bare feet, with perfect long legs, in her bikini, she was overpowering. She had the legs of a movie star, not an assembly line laborer. Her hips were wide and her breasts high and firm.

"How come you're not married," Rae Ann finally asked after they'd known each other long enough for the question to be acceptable.

"Most men are a real crock o' shit," Ellie answered in her typical way.

Ellie refused to live in a trailer park even though it was the cheapest way to go in Wabash City. Instead, she had a cluttered one-bedroom basement apartment in the Old Boston complex just across the river in West Wabash. She picked her clothes up off the floor once a week to take to the laundromat. She hated the students who made up most of the population in the complex. All they seemed to do was lie around reading books and listening to their stereos. Not that Ellie thought working at All-American Homes was so great. When she wasn't working on the register line, she was wrestling with power tools on the assembly lines with the men. Behind her back, they loved to call her "the best screwer in the place."

5 Skywatch

The Tuesday of Bill Franklin's second week at All-American Homes, Washington popped the question.

"Hey Willy, you ever played any softball?"

Bill charged it like a slow roller: "I sure have. I played baseball every year since I was eight years old. I started playin' softball about ten years ago."

"OK look, Devere runs our team. We play in the city league, slow-pitch. We need an infielder. You ever played any infield?"

"Yeah, first and third."

"We got a first baseman. Third would be perfect . . . if you're good enough."

"Whadda you mean?"

"Ya gotta have a tryout. Devere has to decide."

"Uh-huh."

"Look, I'll grab Devere at lunchtime an meet ya on the loading dock. We'll talk."

"OK. I'll be there."

Tentative as it was, it was the first sign of acceptance that anyone in the factory had given.

When Bill walked out on the loading dock, Washington and Devere were already there, sitting with their legs dangling over the edge, unwrapping their sandwiches. He sat down next to Washington, awkwardly, not wanting to seem too eager.

"You remember Willy Franklin," Washington started it off with Devere.

"Yeah, he was cuttin' pipe for me one mornin.'"

"Devere's the manager o' that softball team I tol' ya 'bout this mornin.'"

"You played third before?" Devere didn't waste time with small-talk.

"Yeah. Both hardball and softball."

Devere turned to Washington and began discussing Bill's case as if Bill wasn't there: "He's gotta be better'n most o' the turkeys Wallis hires in here," turning back to Bill, "bunch o' eighteen-year-old kids can't hit their hat size an got all the smarts of a two-day old turd."

Bill laughed because he knew he was supposed to. It sure wasn't the way people talked up at the university.

"Yeah," Devere continued, "we sure could use a third baseman whose arm don't scatter like a thirty-ought-ten. We got practice to-night. Seven-thirty. If ya can make it, we'll give ya a tryout."

Thanks a lot! Bill thought.

"I'll be there," he said.

"The field's down there by the river next to that big 'ol tennis bub-ble."

Devere went back to work.

"Don't mind him, Willy, he takes it all pritty damn serious," Washington tried to reassure Bill as they walked back into the building, "see ya tonight."

Driving down the West Wabash hill from his wife's house on the way to practice that night, Bill remembered the first time he'd ever played softball. He had just turned eighteen and was still playing hard-ball. His senior season in high school ball had just ended and he went out to watch his dad's softball team from the steel plant play. One of their regular players didn't show up. "My boy's in the stands. He's a pretty good ballplayer. He could do it," his dad had said. He'd gone three for four and two of his three times on base his old man had knocked him in. After they won the game, driving home, his dad had said, "I'll tell ya Bill, if you were battin' two in front o' me evry game, I'd lead the league in RBI's." That summer was long gone and his dad had had a heart attack. Bill had played a lot of softball since but no game had ever excited him as much as that first one.

He dreamed of his own son growing up to play on the same team with him. Six years before, in grad school, he had played softball. Mar-tha was working that summer and he had taken Danny to every game. The little kid sat on the third baseline strapped into a blue plastic baby seat. He waved his arms and laughed each time the players flashed by him to score. *It's a good game,* Bill thought as he got out of the car in the dusty parking lot and headed for the diamond.

The backstop was bent halfway over on one side like a man who has just pulled all the muscles in his back. Two guys were working on it. Two others were painting in one of the dugouts. The garish red, white and blue label of a lonesome beer can sitting on the top rail of the bleachers caught Bill's eye as he walked past. "AMERICA'S FINEST" it read.

Devere was leaning against the fence near the backstop, chewing gum. "Hey Franklin, whatta ya say," he greeted Bill. He looked Bill all up and down like you would a hooker in a bar who had quoted either too high or too low a price. "Ain't ya got no spikes? Ya gonna play in tennis shoes?"

"Uh-huh. For now at least." He really didn't like Devere.

"You sure you've played third base before?"

Counterfeiting his most rational tone of voice, almost whispering as he tried to keep the anger out, he answered: "Look, Devere, I can play third. Just hit me a few, I'll show you." But no matter how hard he tried, Bill couldn't keep the edge off his voice.

"OK, hot shot," Devere spat back, "let's see what you can do."

Devere grabbed a bat and two balls and waddled up to home plate. Bill trotted out to third. He made Devere wait while he cleaned the area around the third base bag with his right foot. He did it automatically, a remembered reflex, a typical infielder's fetish to police the grounds before an inning starts, to throw or kick out all the obnoxious little pebbles that cause bad bounces into face, neck, shoulders, or worst of all, into base hits.

Devere saw what his third baseman was doing and approved. He waited. He hit the first ball as hard and as fast as he could right at Bill. It bounced twice, skipping on the hard, sun-baked dirt of the infield. Bill got no jump on the ball at all. He got his glove down and his feet in position but he had to short hop it, catch the ball on that sharp, second bounce right in front of his glove. The ball played him. As it came off that short hop, Bill's head shot up and away, the classic third baseman's fear reflex. His whole body flinched. His glove raised up, his knees splayed out, and the ball shot through his legs into left field.

"It's been almost two years," he yelled apologetically, embarrassed. "I'd forgotten what the shooting gallery was like," he finished lamely, trying to make it into a joke.

Devere didn't laugh.

"Try another,' Devere said grimly. He hit another screamer, hard and two steps to Bill's right.

Bill was there but he flinched again and the ground ball caromed off his ankle and spun crazily at his feet. As he lunged for it, he kicked it all the way to the pitcher's mound.

"Just what I need, a gunshy third baseman," Devere muttered under his breath. He walked part way up the line toward third base.

For a moment Bill thought Devere was coming after him with the bat.

"What the hell you think this is, a skywatch? Keep your head down. Look the ball into your glove. Ya can't make chicken salad outa chickenshit!"

"C'mon man, hit some more. I haven't had a glove on for awhile," Bill yelled back, fuming inside.

Devere slouched back to the plate muttering under his breath.

Bill caught the next grounder and the next, but he threw them both over the first baseman's head and into the dugout that was being painted.

"Hey, whoa, this is like bein' inside a pinball machine," one of the painters yelled, grinning. The other painter waved his white handkerchief from around the corner of the dugout.

"C'mon Skywatch! I can't have no third baseman with a scattergun arm. Ya don't have ta hurry those throws. On a hard-hit ball ya got all day the way the turkeys in this league run."

"Sure Coach," Bill said under his breath.

He hated Devere telling him how to play his position. But he knew he had better start catching and throwing the ball or he wouldn't even be playing on their team. He caught every ball after that and only threw one more away. He concentrated, made the plays, looked like a ballplayer albeit a rusty one. He didn't know whether he raised the level of his fielding out of fear or embarrassment or just plain anger at the arrogant SOB hitting balls at him like torpedos.

"OK, that's enough," Devere finally barked. "It's gettin' dark. Whitey'll be here tomorrow night an we'll hit," Devere said. That was it.

Jim Washington, sitting on the bottom row of the bleachers, braced Devere: "Well, how'd he do?"

"Not too bad. First time out. Ol' Skywatch here'll git better,"

"Skywatch? What's that?" Washington asked.

"This here's Skywatch, our new third baseman. He looks ta God for Deeevine Assistance on hard hit groun' balls. We'll cure him o' that."

Then Devere turned to Bill: "Howinthehell ya gonna play with that ratty piece o' Kotex you're pretendin' is a glove. Ya don't see Brooksie workin' with a piece o' junk like that, do ya? An ya better git yoreself a pair o' spikes too."

"Well, whatta ya think?" Washington cut in on Devere's lecture.

"I dunno. Hell, we came in third in the league last year an nobody hit the ball outa the infield the whole second half. We'll do OK if we hit."

He turned to Bill: " Sheeit, Skywatch, we had games last year . . ."

Turning back to Washington: "Remember that one against the Poeleece?"

Turning back to Bill: "We had games the whole team 'cludin' me turned into a bunch'a banjos. Softball's like a war. You gotta be 'gressive. You gotta attack that ball at the plate. You gotta charge them groun' balls."

Turning back to Washington: "Hell, we'll be OK if we hit."

The prospects for the season thus succinctly synopsized, they all headed for home: Devere, the bat bag slung rakishly over his shoulder, crossed the parking lot to his Ford pickup; Jimmy Washington gunned out in his bright yellow Chevy; and Willy "Skywatch" Franklin, the promising rookie third baseman, huffed away in his rusty Volkswagen.

The next day at work, they were all calling him "Skywatch." He'd never had a nickname before.

As the season progressed, he would also find he wasn't the only one who deserved that kind of nickname. Everybody was gunshy in one way or another. They all fought their personal fears. The first baseman, Zenger, hated to stretch for wild throws down the baseline into cannonballing baserunners. Devere, the catcher, got no joy out of blocking the plate on plays at home. The outfield fence terrified Hank Patrick, the centerfielder, which was probably why he ran into it at least once every game. The summer would not sparkle defensively. The action was in the batter's box and on the basepaths. As the summer would progress, Bill would come to realize that they all loved to hit. Defense was just something you did between those moments when you were taking your cuts and running the bases. They watched their batting averages like tycoons watched the stock quotations. All of them, to a man, were trapped into the electricity of offense, the spark of hitting, the flash of running and sliding, the perfect illumination of coming home.

Coming home from that first practice, knowing that he'd made it, Bill tried to visualize the season, the summer. He sensed that the baseball would be good, something that would free him from the torture of the factory, the boredom of his home.

Martha exploded that weekend. Out of his first paycheck, he spent thirty-five dollars on a new glove and a pair of spikes.

"God Bill, we're almost broke and you spend money on stuff like that," she whined, putting on her new swimsuit to take the kids to the pool.

He ignored her. It was a Rawlings glove like the one he'd used in American Legion ball when he was seventeen. He brought it home and spent an hour rubbing neatsfoot oil into the pocket. Then, he wrapped the fingers around a softball and tied the pocket tight with brown twine so that it could sit overnight and the pocket could form. He counted the days until the season started like a man scratching on a dungeon wall.

6 The Wives

"Why do you do it?" Martha asked as she rubbed her husband's aching shoulders after the second practice. "Why do you get so excited about playing softball?"

"Why not?" Bill avoided the question. "Get a little higher, no, higher, that's it, good, there."

"Why do you do it? You hurt all over."

"It's a good game. All the guys, when they were younger, played real baseball. You didn't even know me when I was a real ballplayer, did you? They're all trying ta find some kind of . . . some kind of joy, excitement, that they've lost."

"You're too old to be running around like a high school kid every night after working in a factory all day."

Bill jumped under her fingers as if she'd struck a nerve.

"Listen, I can handle it. I'm just a little sore. Everybody feels this way after the first coupla days. I'm just a little outa shape. Its something ta do besides just going ta that job evry day."

"If you want something to do, why don't you stay home with me and the kids in the evenings."

Molly Devere was older than Martha Franklin and more attuned to the loneliness of the long-distance softball season. She lived across town in an All-American modular home slabbed in a tract development behind the cement plant with her two daughters, one eleven and one thirteen, and Devere who visited briefly once a day at dinnertime. From five-thirty to six each day, Molly and her husband passed the same amenities back and forth with the meat and potatoes.

"Whud ya do today, babes?"

"Went over to the grocery an got the gas pedal on my car adjusted over at Harley's. Been sticking. Washed clothes this afternoon. You need a new pair of work pants. D'jew have a good day?"

"Can't have a good day at that crummy place. Put in toilet pipe on trailers all day. Boring. Hate it. Good ham. Like it. Got a ball game tonight. Probly go out for a few beers after. Don't wait up for me."

They exchanged the same monotonous round of clipped dinner-time conversation each night. Then bowling in the winter, softball all summer. Her lonesome evenings piled up like units rolling off the end of an assembly line, her dead days piled up into years and soon days and years would all pile up into an empty lifetime.

She had stopped going to the softball games years before when the girls had lost interest. From the beginning she had hated sitting down there by the river in the heat and dust, sweat running off her as the mosquitoes swarmed. Molly tried to get into the spirit of the softball. She tried to feel bad when they lost and excited when they won. But somehow softball never became an important part of her life. It was a flaw she carefully hid from her husband. She never felt at home in that "let's drink and brag" community that gathered around the backs of pickup trucks to drink beers after the games.

When the first baby came, she had hoped things would change. They did, briefly. Devere came straight home after games to see how "his little girl" was doing. But the novelty wore off quicker than rubber cleats. Soon Molly was spending her nights alone, and the nights piled up into years, and the years, ten of them, comprised their marriage. Molly was thirty-five and drowning.

She wondered anymore if she could bring herself to do anything. He was a good man, a good provider, a little gruff, but a good man. But he was never there and she didn't really love him anymore. Molly knew she wanted out but she didn't know where to look for an escape hatch. *Maybe I'll see if Devere'll let me get a job,* she thought.

7 The Opener

The season began dully like the dead sound of a rubber hammer on a floor joint of a mobile home. It rained hard for a half hour the late May afternoon of the first game. By seven-thirty the field was barely playable. Ground balls slithered through the muddy infield. The outfield grass, according to Washington after the first inning, was "slippery as shit."

Outfielders skated after fly balls. Spikes filled up fast and baserunners felt like Mafia victims in cement shoes. The white softball, virgin for a new season, after two batters was soaked, smudges of mud caked over the laces. Infielders' throws soared out into orbit over the first baseman's lunging glove. Baserunners fell down in the muck rounding the bags and dug frantic trenches as they tried to crawl back safely. Batters' feet went out from under them as they swung in the mire of the batters box.

Willy "Skywatch" Franklin remembered only flickering images of the game.

Pulling the new, unwashed jersey on, deciding it looked better hanging out rather than tucked into his cut-offs. Bright "Dodger blue" with red piping on the neck and sleeves, "All-American Homes" in big white letters across the front, like an American flag.

Reading the lineup card,
    Dickie Adams2B
    Willy Franklin 3B
    Don Devere C
    Jimmy Washington LF
    Hank PatrickCF
    Andy Stevenson SS
    Duane Zenger1B
    Joe Warren P
    Gil BlassRF
    Sam Unk SF

He was surprised Devere batted him so far up in the order, him a "rook." Devere's explanation: "Figure we'll just see you can go ta right field an move Dickie round ta third."

Devere's terse pep talk as they took the field: "Let's git these pricks!"

Whitey's comment when they gathered on the mound the first time after Devere sent it down to second and they'd flipped it around the infield: "OK, I want a steady stream of authentic baseball gibberish from you guys."

The first pitch.

The hitter tensing.

The ball revolving slowly.

The soft crunch of the bat.

The evening moving electric out of fidgety stasis into baseball motion.

Actually feeling the ball leave his bat the first time. Seeing it describe its lazy arc out toward right center. He flew out to the right fielder, a "can o' corn."

His first chance at third, one sharp "GLUMP" and it slid muckily into his glove, a slow-motion Sunday hop followed by an easy lob over to first as the hitter treaded water in the batters box.

Franklin got his first hit in the bottom of the third. Dickie Adams popped up to the second baseman to start the inning. Trudging out of the batters box to run it out hopelessly, Adams muttered at himself in disgust. So Bill came up with one out and nobody on. He hit the first pitch on a line right up the power alley in left center. The ball took one hop and skidded all the way to the fence. He'd hit it low enough and hard enough that they held him to a double. As he perched on second breathing hard, he basked in the voices from the dugout:

> "Super shot, Willy!"
> "Way ta hit, Skywatch!"
> "Good wood, Willy boy!"

He waved a clenched fist and grinned.

Two pitches later, Devere hit a sharp single to right and Bill took off as soon as he realized it was going to drop. He churned toward third thinking *hit the inside of the bag, the inside of the bag, hit the bag.*

As he crossed the third base bag the voices assaulted him at point-blank range. The whole team was up and screaming, at Bill, at the third base coach, at them both, at the essence of the moment itself:

"Score 'im!"
"Send 'im home! Send 'im home!"
"Go, Willy, Go!"

He dug down the line, full speed, no hesitation, swimming on the waves of their voices. It was a moment they had all created, like a work of art, together. He heard one voice louder, more insistent, more frenzied than all the rest, screaming from the on-deck circle:
"SCORE! SCORE! SCORE! SCORE!"
He beat the right fielder's weak throw by ten feet. It wasn't even close.
"Way ta fly, Willy," Washington nodded as Bill passed him on the way to the dugout.
Ah, to hit, to run, to field ground balls, perchance to dream, that's the stuff, Bill the English Professor might have been thinking as he fought to catch his breath on the bench.
Hot damn! Willy the ballplayer was thinking as he settled back to enjoy his first score of the season.
His second chance at third he fielded cleanly, going two steps to his left and dipping it out of the mud with his clean new glove. He took his time with the throw but the ball was slippery and it curved away from the first baseman a little. Zenger had to stretch a bit to get his glove on it, and he did, but after the ball was nestled safely in the webbing, it popped out.
He dropped it, Bill winced.
The runner was safe.
Zenger kicked the dirt, then looked up for forgiveness knowing full well that there is nothing an infielder hates more than a first baseman who drops a throw.
"No sweat, baby, we'll get em, that's OK, that's OK, c'mon let's turn a double now," Bill heard himself chattering.
Damn! Squeeze the ball over there! Bill was thinking.
The infield got more chewed up and the outfield got more slippery as the game careened on. "We shouldn't have to play in this shit," they bitched in unison in both dugouts between innings. But the field was

the same for both teams and the game stayed close. In the top of the seventh the other team scored three runs to go ahead. With men on first and second, Blass dove for a sinking line drive down the right field line. He landed in a mud puddle camouflaged by the grass and slid ten feet on his belly into foul territory, planing then going under as if he were body surfing. The ball went all the way to the fence and both runners scored. By the time Hank Patrick got there from center field to back up the play, the hitter was rounding third. If the ball had been dry and Patrick armed with a howitzer, he wouldn't have been able to cut the hitter down at the plate. That fluke inside-the-parker gave the other team a tenuous 9–7 lead with All-American Homes coming to bat in the bottom of the seventh.

Whitey Warren started it off. He had a major league beer gut, was forty-eight years old, and the only position he could play was pitcher, but he was a smart ballplayer. On a three-two count, he went with the pitch and punched a money single into right.

Blass, next up, got anxious. He topped a country club ground ball to the shortstop who forced Warren at second. Whitey went in standing up and caught the second baseman's throw in the shoulder. No double play.

Then, on the first pitch, Sammy Unk lined a sharp single to left and Adams was the winning run at the plate. He went for the first pitch and topped a slow roller to the first baseman for an easy force.

Unk and Blass were on second and third with two outs and the winning run was still at the plate in the person of Willy Franklin.

Why me? Bill thought.

All he wanted was a walk. Obligingly, the first two pitches arched deep. Then a strike. Bill suddenly awoke out of his paralysis, remembered where he was, realized that he was going to have to hit the ball, saw that there was no way this pitcher was going to walk him, let him off the hook. But the next pitch was outside for a ball. Three-one.

Maybe, Bill thought.

No way, he knew.

Then he saw it coming. The pitcher had piped one, grooved one. It was the perfect pitch, the one every hitter longs for all his life, desires to take downtown. The ball looked like the sun rising over the Wabash, hanging bright and motionless in the grey sky over the muddy land.

He popped it up meekly to the third baseman in foul territory.

They slunk off the field like lepers.

"What a lousy way ta start the season," was all Devere had to say as he dragged the bat bag across the muddy parking lot to his pickup. They had just lost the opening game to a team they should have beaten, should beat every time they play them. But what really pissed him off was that he had been looking forward to drinking after the game. No one had even mentioned it. *Those turkeys blow an easy game an I gotta spend the whole night listenin' ta my ol' lady talk 'bout what she's gonna pack in my lunch tomarra,* Devere brooded. He was not much of a romantic in regard to either his baseball or his marriage.

In Bill's car, on the way over the bridge to West Wabash, Martha knew better than to attempt consolation. The two kids were in the back looking out the windows.

"Ugh! Icky old Wabash. Daddy, is that like the kind of pollution they talk about in school?"

Bill, his mind occupied elsewhere, answered immediately, "yeah sweetie, I stunk up the whole town tonight."

8 Carla's Car

The first game was gone.

That team won't win half their games, Devere evaluated the victors. *I'm gonna go see Carla.*

Standing in the on-deck circle in the fifth inning twirling two bats, Devere had spotted the big black car gliding through the parking lot.

"Hey Jim," he'd yelled to Washington who was standing by the backstop waiting to lead off the inning, "Hey Jim, lookee there, huh."

Washington grinned as he caught sight of the shiny black car: "Well, now we know its really softball season. Back at the same old stand same as last year."

Later, in the dark parking lot, leaning in the shadows against the tailgate of the pickup, unlacing his spikes, the spectre of going home to his wife hanging over him, Devere remembered the black car. He swiveled around to check. It was still there, lights out, parked down in the corner of the lower lot against the murky backdrop of the moving river.

Carla was Wabash City's classiest and best equipped hooker. She specialized in truckers, cops and softball players, and operated out of her big shiny black car. She was the most mobile of small-town whores.

Devere had been there two years before on the first night she set up for business at the Riverfront Park. They had just finished playing and he was sitting on the tailgate of his pickup drinking beer when she drove up. She parked her big black Chevy Impala right by the fence along the left field line, got out and sat on the front of the car like a hood ornament.

"Man, will you look at that," Devere whispered in awe to Whitey or Jimmy or Hank or whoever he was drinking with at the time.

"She looks like an American flag with tits," someone said.

"Look at them goggles. She looks like a cross between Marilyn Monroe an Snoopy."

They all stared. The left fielder, center fielder and short fielder playing in the game stared. A simple fly ball could have gone for an inside-the-park homer. As she climbed up on the hood, one guy, staring, backed his car into the third base dugout. A father stood and stared, holding the drinking fountain on long after his kids had drunk their fill and gone away. The wives and girlfriends in the stands stared the hardest.

Unconcerned, she surveyed the scene, ignored the stares. She wore white vinyl calf-high hooker boots, a red vinyl mini-skirt that barely covered her hips, and a bright blue, sheer-silk, skin-tight halter top. With her haltered breasts bursting in air, her red, white and blue presence gave proof through the night that a revolution had begun in softball city.

And she wore goggles. Not glasses. Aviator goggles. Wrapped around the top of her face, they made her look like a Star Trek mermaid: the voluptuos body of a woman below, the eerie goggle-eyed appearance of a creature from outer space above. She didn't have to sit on the hood of her car long.

"Boy I'd like to meet that," Devere sighed.

"No way you could handle that. Man, that's a red white n' blue atom bomb jus sittin' there waitin' ta go off."

"You ain't man enough ta even go talk ta whatever that is."

On a dare, Devere found himself crossing the parking lot. He had held a special place in Carla's world ever since. He had been the first to break the ice, to tip into motion her softballing career in Wabash City.

"Hello there . . . That sure is a wild outfit you got on there," Devere, in his gaudy softball uniform, carrying his can of beer, greeted her cockily.

She ignored him.

"What the hell you dressed for anyway, the fourth of July?" he tried again, glancing nervously back over his shoulder at the guys by the pickup.

"I'm dressed for business, cowboy," she answered. Her goggles swiveled around to face him. She had no panties on and the vinyl miniskirt didn't hardly cover the tops of her thighs.

"How'd ya liketa be my first customer, cowboy?" she snapped his head up. "A free sample. Whatta ya say?"

Devere didn't know what to say. All he could envision was how good getting into the car with her would make him look to all those guys standing around his pickup watching.

"Yeah, sure, why not."

She flowed down off the hood and hooked her arm through his. As if he were some kind of big shot, she escorted him into the car, sat him down in the front seat and closed the door. Then she skipped around the back of the car, tweaking her red-vinyled butt. She drove off right past Devere's buddies.

As he walked toward Carla's car in the darkness, remembering how it had been the first time, Devere had to smile. He'd never forget the looks on their faces when she dropped him off back at the pickup. She'd rehearsed him on what to say. She'd demonstrated her wares and was breaking him in as a salesman.

"Hey, this is Carla. She's just new in town from Las Vegas. Say hello," he gloated. They crowded comically up to the rolled-down window, elbowing for a clear view.

"I hope I git to meet all you boys personal real soon," she had smiled up from under her opaque goggles. "You be sure an pass out my cards now," she instructed Devere just before she drove off.

"Who is she?"

"Whaddid she do to you?"

"She a hooker?"

"Whadja say to her?"

"Whadshee say ta you?"

"How come ya just went down there and parked?"

Their questions ricocheted around him. Savoring the moment, he loitered to the cab of the pickup, got a beer out of the cooler.

"That Carla, she's OK," he began. "She's a hooker, but she's the wildest one I ever seen. Here, 'for I forgit, she told me ta pass these cards around ta you guys. She saya she's gonna set up shop down there in the lower parkin' lot durin' the baseball games."

CARLA'S CAR
TAKE A RIDE
Inquire at speaker
in the front fender
or phone 743–6969

"She's got a mobile phone right inside that black Chevy."

"Ya mean she's gonna do all her business down there in that car?"

"Damn right. You ain't gonna beleeve what that thing looks like inside. It's like a damn space ship."

Carla's car was indeed like something out of Flash Gordon or a James Bond movie. Devere knew they'd never believe him.

"You're gonna hafta see it for yourselves," he told them," an you still ain't gonna bleeve it."

The car was unobtrusive enough on the outside. In tiny thin white script letters CARLA'S CAR was stenciled on both front fenders. On the right front fender just forward of the door was an inset white button which when pressed activated a speaking grill like the order-gobbling kind at drive-in restaurants. Attached to the rear bumper was a tall thin radio antenna.

But inside, the real science fiction began.

After identifying himself through the intercom in the fender, a customer entered a futuristic pleasure palace that no more resembled the interior of an automobile than Alice Cooper resembled Richard Nixon. At the touch of a button in a console mounted on the ceiling above the door on the driver's side, the seats reclined and raised to form a perfectly fitted divan that covered the whole interior area of the car. This small bed was upholstered all in white fur and precisely sculpted to the dimension of the car's interior. It was as if the push of a button opened a pipe through which waves of liquid ermine flowed. The fur seemed to pool into a placid unbroken surface upon which the space-age mermaid could sing her siren song. Another button triggered the descent of white, fur covered walls. Folding panels flowed down out of slots in the ceiling all around to cover the windows. They formed an enclosed, fur-lined womb. The largest panel curved down over the windshield and magically bonded to the top of the dashboard. Another button retracted the folding steering wheel. It disappeared like the loop of a lariat pulled by a sinking hand down into the white quicksand.

Another button made the surface of the bed undulate, a fur-gloved version of Magic-Fingers. Others controlled the lights. With a touch, Carla could dapple that white womb with pastel shafts or flood it with black light making bodies glow eerily and the white fur shimmer like molten mercury.

In the front dashboard was the music system and bar. Her cassette stereo piped Country and Western music. The bar had everything . . .

miniaturized. All the liquor bottles were airline size, holding one nice double shot. Tiny ice cubes rolled like dice out of the automatic ice-maker and into a glass at the touch of a button.

Carla could mix drinks with her toes. From the center of the bed, she could reach back with one foot into the square recess of the bar and grab one of the tiny bottles between her toes. Then she would pour the booze into the glass, press one button with her big toe for ice, another for water or mix, and pick up the glass between the balls of her feet, wrapping all her toes around it. She served her mixed drinks by simply swivelling around and sticking her full feet at her guest. She was so talented in so many ways.

Inside Carla's car, all sense of time and place vanished. A guy like Devere immediately forgot he was in a parked car in a dusty parking lot next to a dirty river.

As he approached the black car anchored in silence by the river, all of Devere's Carla-soft memories, from that first night in '74 on through the last two years, winked in his mind. Even his frustration at the opening game loss in the mud began to subside. He wondered if anybody was with her, if she was busy he'd have to wait. She had been busy that first year. The word spread fast. Guys from other teams would ask Devere: "Who was that masked woman?"

"I don't know but she'll put some silver bullets in your guns," he would answer.

For a while, she ran her business like a bowling alley—whole teams would reserve her for a night, signing up far in advance. But after that first summer and about a month of the next, the novelty began to wear off. She stayed on, but business wasn't nearly as good. She still had a group of loyal customers. Devere was good for about once every two weeks during the summer. In that second year, he noticed how she seemed to enjoy talking a while afterwards. He got in the habit, when they had time, of having a drink and shooting the breeze with her after she got through doing him.

Her car had become a familiar summer landmark. Warming up before games, whole teams would smile and point and laugh as they followed the slow glide of the sleek black Chevy through the lot between the diamonds and down the ramp to its regular parking place by the water. For three years, Carla's car had been an unchanging constant in Devere's mottled mind.

He pressed the button to activate the speaker in the fender. It crackled.

"Yo Carla."

"Who izz that? Wait a minute. Damn . . . who izz that?"

"It's Devere."

"Damn Devere. I knew I recognized that voice. Git the hell on in here."

She was giggling as if she was really glad to see him.

Only one thing about Carla had always bothered Devere. He'd never seen her face without the goggles. Nobody fooled with her goggles.

Out of habit, Devere bent down to pull off his boots as soon as he sat down in the front seat.

"You sure are muddy. You better take yore pants off right there too. Why they makin' you guys play on a field like that?"

He skimmed out of his pants and dropped them on top of his shoes and sweat socks on the floor. A layer of crumbled, caked mud had already gathered on the floor mat.

"Looks like you're takin' most o' that damn ballfield home with you tonight."

"Damn mud. We lost to a bunch o' idiots we should never lose to, never."

Out of habit, Devere pulled his legs up under him on the seat as Carla pressed the first button. They rode gently up and back as the interior of the car became wall-to-wall fur bed. The fur-lined panels slid down over the windows. Devere slid back over the soft fur until his head rested propped against the back wall. He lay on his back, legs open, in his uniform shirt and jock. He still had his baseball cap on. Carla knelt between his legs. She pulled the pink mohair sweater over her head slowly, being careful of the goggles and her hair-do. It had been almost nine months since he'd last seen her naked. She had left town in early September, right when the season ended. Her breasts were big enough and they stood out firm as she arched her back for effect and slowly drew the sweater over her head.

"Carla, hey, it's good ta see ya again."

She came into his arms, kissing him on the nose as if he were a small child: "Devere, baby, you're startin' the season right again."

"Like hell! We lost!"

"Not here, baby. Not here."

Devere looked into her innocent goggles and understood. "How ya been?" he inquired.

"OK. Ya miss me?"

"Yeah, ya could say that."

"I got twenty dollars tonight. Do what you can."

"You know I can't do you for that."

"Yeah, I know. I know."

"Whatta ya want?

"I dunno. Whatever's easiest."

"OK. How about either a handjob or a blowjob? They're clean, and you are one of my reg'lars."

"That's good, a blowjob. I haven't had one since you left in September."

" You're kiddin.' The way you love blowjobs. I really oughta talk to your wife."

"Oh yeah, that's what I need," and they both laughed.

That was what he liked about Carla. She talked to a guy like he was a person while she was doing him. Devere had been in the Alabama Street rattraps where the girls did their numbers like zombies. You walked in, got off, and you walked out. But Carla was different.

He relaxed and let her work, stroking the top of her head as her platinum hair spread across his lower belly.

"That was quick. Ya must not be gettin' much at home," she said moments later.

He didn't answer. All the frustration that losing the opener had built up was gone.

"Hey, ya wanta drink?"

"Yeah. Ya got time? A scotch an water."

"Hell, we can drink until somebody pushes the button."

She rolled over on her back beside him, propped the top half of her body up on her elbows and reached out with her feet to mix his drink. With her left hand she pushed the button for the stereo.

He sat up and reached for it when it was only half way there. It always made him nervous when she did her foot trick. He always thought she would spill it.

She took one sip from his glass and swished it around in her mouth like mouthwash.

"You have a good winter?"

"It was OK. Florida this time. Miami Beach was boring but Lauderdale an Daytona in February and March were beautiful. All those young college boys. Most of em didn't even know what ta ask for. They just wanted somethin' ta remember their vacation in Florida by."

"You glad to be back?"

"Yeah. Things are more relaxed around here. Lotta old friends been in already an I've only been back three days."

"Old friends" struck him kind of funny. *I guess we are old friends,* he thought.

"Hey look, I got myself a new toy. Gonna do wonders for business. Gonna make me a nationwide franchise."

Sitting up, she switched off the stereo and opened a door in the dash.

"It's a CB radio."

She pulled the mike out.

"Let's see if I can drum up any action."

She hit a switch: "Hey there, Humpty Dumpty's got her ears on here at the baseball diamond in Muddy River City. Any o' you rollin' dudes on sixty-five doin' any business tonight?"

The radio crackled a moment, then a slow-moving southern drawl oozed syrupy in answer: "Yooo humpty, good to heah yo voice agin. This heah's Captain America an ah'm pullin' a whole load o' textiles outa 'Lanta for the Windy City. GOT TWO GIT TWO GETHER TWO NIGHT! Ah'm gassed high an rollin' 'bout ten north o' Naptown. Like two check out yo seat covahs at that theah rest stop jus' past the forty-three turn off. Hey Hump, got me a pome ah scribbled after that last run-in we had. Listen up:

Humpty Dumpty pahks ba the wall,
Naht or day she's raddy ta ball.
Awl the king's hosses and awl the king's men,
Keep callin' ol' Hump aggen and aggen.

"Yew like that pome. Hell, ah'm the Shakespeare o' the fourlanes. Hey, this heah's Captain America sayin' see ya latuh tuhnight an ten-foah."

"Yo Captain, yore poetry's music ta my ears. We'll have ourselves a seat cover party 'bout 'leven-thirty. Watch out for the smokes. This is Humpty Dumpty sayin' ten-four."

"What in the hell was that about?" Devere had to ask as she put the mike away.

"I got lucky. I just set up a trick for later tonight, a trucker comin' up 65 from Atlanta. I got that little gem last fall just before I left for Florida. This little gizmo makes me a ten-four whore."

Suddenly the intercom crackled: "Hey Carla, its Johhny Tremaine out heah. I got thirty bucks. You got some time for me."

"Hey Tremaine, good to hear yore voice again," Carla answered, winking at Devere. "You bet I got time but you're gonna hafta give me 'bout five minutes. OK?"

"That's fine, fine, I'll be back," Tremaine assured her.

"Well Devere, its been nice but I gotta go back ta work. Here, let me wash you off. Can't send you home with lipstick on your dipstick."

She pushed the seat button and they were in a car again. It only took Devere a moment to get dressed. He paid her.

"Here, kiss me before ya go baby," Carla ran her hand around the back of his neck, "ya know, I really like talkin' with ya when ya come. Maybe we'll have more time next time." She kissed him goodbye. He knew it was all just a game. But still, Carla always relaxed him, made him feel better.

9 Post-game

They won the second game easily, 22–7 in five innings, because of the ten-run lead rule, and the third and fourth the same way before the hot weather of early June set in. Martha came with the kids to the early games and Bill drove to the late games alone. Driving across the bridge, he always looked out expectantly over the trees for the lights on the diamonds.

Ellie came to the games with Washington. Martha asked Bill "who is that striking tall girl that roots for your team?"

"Just a girl from the shop. Dates our left fielder, Jimmy Washington."

"I didn't know women worked there too. What is she? A secretary?"

"No, she works on the lines, sometimes even does the same stuff I do when we're shorthanded."

"Do many women work out there like that?"

"Some," Bill said, feigning disinterest.

"Oh," Martha paused, "well, the men must like that."

Her prissy tone put Bill off. *What the hell do you know*, he thought, *you never worked in a factory.*

The fifth game was at nine-thirty on a Friday night. Number fifteen rolled off the line at three-thirty and the team sat around on the loading dock talking about that night's game. Bill was amazed at how well they knew the other team. Devere and Whitey went over the hitters like Ford and Berra getting ready for the opener of the World Serious.

"Johnny Burgoyne's a dead pull hitter."

"So keep the ball inside with a lot o' arch. Make the first pitch a strike. Always takes the first pitch."

"What about the Arnold brothers."

"Matt'll be battin' third. He hits line drives to center so git a lot o' the arch on your pitches. Mebbe he'll pop some up."

"What about Benny?"

"Ya never know what that sonovabitch's gonna do. He can go ta either side anytime he wants. Pitch im inside. I'm sick o' seein' him hit those triples into the right field corner."

"How do you know all their names?" Bill, drinking a coke and listening, broke in.

"Those boys been playin' together in this league long as we have. They're a bunch o' good ol' boys, work at that big grain elevator over at Bristol. Names are right on the backs o' their uniforms."

"Are they good? I mean, can we beat em?"

"We been splittin' with em for years. Hell yes we can beat em. What a dumb question. Ya don't even go out there 'less ya know ya can beat em."

There were sixteen teams in the league but only four or five were really competitive, had a chance to win it all. All-American Homes had always done well, but they'd never won it all. Dick and Tonna's Bar from Bristol was always right up there. They'd won the city championship three years before. The Peerless Truckers—"those obnoxious pricks" Devere characterized them—had won it the last two years. The year before, Peerless had gone all the way to the state finals. Krieg Motors always picked up the jocks from the university who hung around Wabash City during the summer. They always beat people but they never won it all.

That Friday night, All-American homes played Dick and Tonna's.

The first really big game of the season, Bill thought as he drove acrosss the bridge, bending forward for the first magic glimpse of the ballpark lights.

Gotta git ahead o' them at the beginin', Devere told himself as his pickup bounced down the Wabash City hill toward the river.

"This is gonna be the toughest game we've had so far," Washington said to Ellie and Rae Ann, who sat next to him, drinking beer, in the front seat of his pickup.

"Well, it's a perfect night to play," Ellie said, shoving the beer can down between her thighs, tightening her denim cutoffs around it, rubbing the back of Washington's neck, "look at all those stars up there."

"I don't think I've ever been to a softball game," Rae Ann said. She was happy to be out on a Friday night, even if she was a third wheel.

"Well, this oughta be a good one," Washington answered. His thoughts were already on the field between the lines.

All-American Homes trailed 6–5 after five innings. Bill started off their half of the sixth with a hard groundball single in the hole between short and third. It felt good coming off his bat. Not like a groundball. More like a frozen rope line drive. Taking his turn at first, the solid feel of a base hit tingled in his hands and wrists.

"No outs Willy. Halfway on a fly ball. Gotta go on a grounder. Watch for the ball ta git by the catcher. It does, you tear ass. No outs now," Whitey yammered from the first base coach's box.

Devere looked at the first two pitches, a ball too deep and a strike that dropped down out of the sky across his back shoulder as if it were suspended on an invisible wire. He took the third pitch to right in a slow loop. It bounced momentarily away from the right fielder when it hit. The center fielder was right there to back up but Bill went around to third. He slid hard even though the throw was only halfway there when he hit the bag.

"You hotdog," Adams said with a grin from the third base coach's box, "give us some Pete Rose plastic hustle."

Nobody ever said anything nice to anyone else on the All-American Homes team. Sarcasm acknowledged a good play. Disbelief commented on a job well done. Every cleanly fielded groundball was shrugged off as a Sunday hop. Each diving catch was greeted by "you sure made a can o' corn look hard." A sharp single always drew a chorus of "banjo hit" from the dugout. A home run collected comments like "man, wind's really blowin' out tonight."

Washington, next up, took the first two pitches for balls, then fouled one off into the parking lot. The next one wasn't a bad pitch. It would've been a strike, but it didn't have that good high arch on it. Washington didn't even seem to swing hard. He admitted later that he was just trying to hit it out of the infield, tie up the game with a sacrifice fly. The ball exploded off his bat and was still halfway up the right center field light pole when it cleared the outfield fence.

Bill and Devere waited for Jimmy at home plate. The three trotted back to the dugout together.

"Man I wish I got fat pitches like that ta hit," Devere muttered.

In the first base stands behind the All-American Homes dugout, Ellie was glowing. Even as the ball was rising over the infield, she was jumping up. "It's gonna be a homer! It's gonna be a homer!" she yelled, jumping up and down and clapping her hands, her bra-less breasts bouncing.

The next three batters laid down and died. All-American Homes went out in the field with an 8–6 lead.

Whitey got them out one-two-four in the bottom of the sixth. The third batter, with two outs, drilled a triple that rolled all the way to the fence in right center between Patrick and Sammy Unk. But Benny Arnold, trying to go to right, lined out to Adams at second base and took them out of the inning.

Gil Blass singled to open the seventh but Sammy Unk hit a line shot right into their third baseman's glove. The snap throw doubled Blass off first with room to spare.

"Damn Gage didn't even know he'd caught the ball," Devere groused in the first base coaching box. "You got a Christmas present, Gage," he yelled across the diamond at Dick and Tonna's third baseman.

"Aw blow it out your ass, Devere," Gage yelled back. They seemed to be pretty good friends.

After Adams flew out weakly to the rover, the Homes team went back out for the bottom of the last inning with a skimpy two run lead.

They got the first out with no sweat, a lazy fly ball to Hank Patrick in center. The whole game Whitey had been making the boys from Dick and Tonna's look bad. They were overswinging on his high-arched pitches.

The second batter in the bottom of the seventh, Dick and Tonna's pitcher "Red" Coates, overswung even more savagely than the others. He topped the ball and hit a full-swinging bunt out in front of home plate. In the Wabash City Softball League, bunting was against the rules. The baselines were too short for the third basemen, pitchers and catchers to throw out baserunners. But Coates's version wasn't covered by the rule. The ball spun off his flailing bat and sauntered slowly down the third base line in fair territory. There was no chance of it darting foul as a proper acknowledgement that it had all been a mistake in the first place. Whitey, caught by surprise, froze on the mound. Bill, playing behind the third base bag, never had a chance. It was Devere's ball all the way. He was late getting out from behind the plate, but he pounced on the ball and raised up to fire. His throw hit the scrambling baserunner hard on the right shoulder about two steps in front of the bag. The ball glanced out into foul territory down the right field line and the baserunner was leveled as he crossed the bag. When Zenger turned to lumber after the errant ball, he tripped over Coates.

Their legs tangled up and Zenger joined Coates flat on his belly in the dust. Blass, playing right center, had a long run to the ball. By the time he got to it, Coates was rounding second on his way to third. Blass made a perfect throw to Bill covering third. The runner would've been out. But the ball hit Coates hard on the ankle on the fly, knocking him down. It caromed off crazily down the left field line with Jimmy Washington racing frantically after it. When Washington picked up the ball, he heard Bill screaming "home, home." In a blur, he saw that the baserunner was up and trying for the plate. Washington was right on the foul line in shallow left field. He had the strongest arm on the team. Coates was only halfway home when Washington uncorked his throw. It was a perfect throw, flat and hard, sizzling on a line right toward Devere's waiting glove. Except . . . It hit Coates squarely in the middle of the back, high up between the shoulder blades, about ten feet up the line from the plate. Hit him like an axe. Pitched him forward like a rag doll shot out of a catapult. Slid him across home plate on his face and belly like a side of beef on rollers as Devere scrambled to get out of the way.

Ellie, standing up, yelled: "What'n hell are you guys doin,' c'mon now."

Rae Ann, next to her, laughed at the slapstick comedy, the falling down, the getting up, of the little red-haired man's dash around the the bases.

"That's the shortest inside-the-park home run ever hit in this league," Devere spat at Coates.

"Throw had him nailed by five yards," Washington muttered to himself in left field.

Just don't hit the ball to me, was all Bill Franklin could think.

There was one out in the bottom of the seventh, the last inning, and that Mack Sennett home run had made the score 8–7 in favor of All-American Homes. They couldn't afford to give up another.

Ellie was bouncing up and down in the bleachers chanting, "C'mon you guys. Git em out. Git em out."

Rae Ann didn't exactly understand what was happening, why tension was building, why each play was suddenly so important. She was glad Ellie couldn't read her mind. It kept repeatedly violating the ninth commandment: *Thou shalt not covet your best friend's boyfriend.*

The next Dick and Tonna's batter, Easy Ed Hession, stepped into the batters box. He hit the ball on two quick hops to Bill at third and the ball appeared, as if by magic, in Zenger's mitt at first before the batter was even three quarters of the way down the base line. Somehow, as the ball had bounced innocently toward him in hard straightforward hops, Bill had forgotten his fear, his prayer for disengagement, his hope that the responsibility would fall to someone else. It was the kind of forgetting that American nineteen-year-olds learned in Viet Nam the first time they got ambushed in a rice paddy. As the ball bore down on him, Bill let his instincts take over. He made the play . . . mindlessly. It was a simple act of survival.

Two outs, bottom of the seventh, the score 8–7, and Bill prayed again, *God please don't let them hit it to me.*

Big Ed Burke, Dick and Tonna's number two hitter, lunged forward as Whitey's first pitch arched in. He was swinging for the fences all the way, trying to tie up the ballgame with just one swing. The result was ludicrous. Swinging like Ruth, he hit the ball like Toulouse Lautrec. Like Coates before, he topped the ball weakly out in front of the plate. It trickled up the first base line.

Another damn swingin' bunt, Devere cursed in his mind. But this time he was ready. Burke was a righthand hitter and Devere beat him out of the batters box, crossed the first base line in front of him going after the ball. It rolled tantalizingly out of reach in the no-man's land of the inner infield.

When Whitey saw what was happening, he stormed down off the mound toward the ball, lumbering slowly behind his gut.

Burke was out of the batters box and picking up momentum toward first base.

"Git away from it Whitey, it's mine," Devere screamed. He bore down on the ball which was entering the death throes of its puny bouncing. As he made his final lunge, his legs slipped out from under him. His whole body went down on top of the ball like a man trying to smother a live grenade. He had the ball in his hand but he was flat on his stomach in the dirt.

Burke was steamingdown the first base line.

Zenger waited stoically at first.

Devere fought to his knees and threw the ball. His throw nailed Burke by a step and a half.

"How'd he do that?" Rae Ann asked Ellie, "aren't they supposed to stand up to throw the ball?"

"Damn, honey, I don't know, but he got im out no matter how he did it an we won an that's one o' the toughest teams in the league, least that's what Jimmy said."

The whole team gathered around Devere who was still on his knees in the infield dust. They offered amazed congratulations. It had been a major league throw. A magic moment.

That's it, Devere thought.

The game was over. They'd won. They'd beaten Dick and Tonna's, were 4–1 in the league, and all alone in second place behind the Peerless Truckers. But there was still a long way to go, twenty more games. They'd see all those guys again—Gage, Coates, Burgoyne, the Arnold brothers, Hession, Big Eddie Burke—before the season was over.

"Nice play, catch," guys from Dick and Tonna's muttered grudgingly as they left the field.

In the parking lot Devere yelled to Washington who was walking with the girls, "hey Jimmy, you wanna go drinkin'?"

They all did.

"What about you Skywatch?" Devere yelled across to Bill.

"Yeah, why not?. Where you goin'?"

"The Pub. Toward downtown about two blocks. Right by the new bridge.

Whitey said he'd like to "tip a few" and Unk joined them, saying, "my old lady can't bitch, hell this is the first time I've gone drinkin' all season."

They descended on the bar like Huns. The lies flowed as swiftly as the beer.

"Man, that was a hell of a throw, but d'jew see that ball I hit in the sixth inning. That baby was still up in the lights when it went over the center field fence," Jimmy bragged.

Ellie and Rae Ann didn't say much as the men talked baseball. They listened, sipped beer and smoked while the men basked in the glow of having done something right, of having accomplished something important.

"Hey Skywatch, super play you made on that ground ball in the last inning there," Whitey said.

"Ya know, I hardly even saw it. It was pure luck. The ball just went into my glove like it had eyes. I don't even remember makin' the throw."

"Well it was a hell of a good time ta make a lucky play," Devere barked.

They talked quickly, darting from subject to subject, after the ball-game and the first few pitchers of beer were drained.

"I usedta work in a bar like this," Ellie said, "up by the university. Some kid just punched me in the face one night, so I quit."

"Yeah, I worked my way through college in bars," Bill put in, "one of the funniest lines I ever heard . . ."

"You never told me about any guy punchin' you," Washington said, looking sharply at Ellie. "You never asked. Hell, I ain't told you a lot o' things, honey," she grinned around the table.

Devere and Unk and Whitey got a good laugh out of Ellie's reply.

Bill went on with his story: "One night I was working in the bar. The place was packed an we got word that the ABC was in town. You know, the Alcoholic Beverage Control cops. Hell, we knew that probly half the kids in the place were underage an we'd all git hung if there was a raid, so me an the other guy who was waitin' on the tables started goin' around an tellin' evrybody there might be a raid an if they were underage they'd better take off. I'd gone to two tables an the next thing I know this guy's got his hand on my shoulder. He looked just like a college kid, twenty-one, jeans, a sweater, longish hair. Hell, he was an ABC cop. They'd been in the place all night. You know what he said when he grabbed me: 'Who the hell you think you are, Paul Revere?'"

"Ya know, I worked two months in a liquor store at night last winter," Sammy Unk started when Bill's laughs subsided, "one night, I'd been workin about two months, this guy came in an stuck me up. He had a gun. One o' those little ones where the barrel just comes out from between your fingers. I gave him evrything in the cash drawer. Hell, I woulda carried it out to his car for him if he'd wanted me to."

"You're married, aren'tcha?" Ellie asked Bill as Sammy paused a moment for a swig of beer.

"Yes I am."

"The cops caught the guy fifteen minutes after he left the store. The moron was wearin' an Army jacket with his own name on it. The whole time he was standin' there pointin' that gun at me I was readin' the name over the lefthand pocket on that Army jacket: GEORGE, GEORGE, GEORGE, over an over. The guy's name turned out ta be Rex George an he'd been home from Viet Nam about six months. I just told the cops his name an they went over to his house an he was sittin' there in the livin' room countin' the money. I was readin' his name the whole time. If he woulda realized it, he probly woulda shot me."

"Too bad he didn't," Whitey grinned, "maybe then we'd o' gotten a good outfielder."

"Nice talk Buffalo gut."

"You think that's stupid, you outta hear what Patrick did last fall," Jimmy started another story.

"This is the funniest damn thing you ever heard," Sammy nudged Bill, the newcomer.

"Hank was up in Michigan for the beginnin' o' deer season an he'd been out in the woods for two days an hadn't got a smell. Well he's drivin' down here, all pissed off 'cause he'd been shut out, an it's 'bout 'leven-thirty at night when all of a sudden this deer runs out in front of his car and he hits it. So he gits out an the deer's lyin' on the side o' the road an ol' Hank thinks *Man, I'm gonna take me some meat home after all.*"

"Yeah and he'd a'been braggin' about what a great hunter he was too," Devere cut in.

"Yeah, well anyhow, he puts the dead deer in his trunk an drives on in figurin' he'll dress it in his garage when he gits home. So he pulls in his driveway an goes ta git out his deer."

"You're not gonna believe this," Sammy nudged Bill again.

" 'Cept the deer ain't dead. Ol' Hank opened that trunk an that deer ran right over him. He said it was like it came out of a cannon. Knocked him on his ass an took off down the street. He said that thing was movin' so fast it was probly back in Michigan by mornin.'"

Bill and Rae Ann, the only ones who hadn't heard the story before, laughed hard while the others grinned at each other knowingly.

"God that's wild," Bill stammered.

"My ex-husband usedta go huntin' like that. But I think all he ever did was go up somewhere in the woods an get drunk," Rae Ann tried to add something to the conversation.

When she said it, Jimmy flinched, slapped by memory.

"That's the best kind o' huntin' trip if ya ask me," Devere said.

"Who asked you?" Whitey growled.

"D'jew hear about the kangaroo?" Devere continued, ignoring Whitey. "This kangaroo cornered two cops in an alley up in Chicago an beat the crap outa em."

"Aw c'mon," in chorus.

"I swear. I heard it on the radio."

"He's right. I heard it too," Rae Ann backed him up.

"Imagine those guys reporting in," Bill was intrigued by the possibilities of the story, "put out an all points bulletin on a kangaroo, wanted for resisting arrest, attacking a police officer and hopping through a red light."

After that story subsided, Rae Ann, still feeling her way in the conversation, asked: "Do any of the other guys on the team go drinkin' with you after the games?"

"Most everybody comes in here most o' the time. Specially when it's really hot and dusty out there," Devere answered. " 'Cept for Stevenson, he's our straight-arrow. I think he carries a bible around in his back pocket."

"C'mon, Johnny's a good guy."

"Good guy? He don't drink. He don't smoke. He goes ta church," Devere listed his sins. "I oughta fix him up with my ol' lady."

The more she listened, the more Devere reminded Rae Ann of her ex-husband Duane.

"He don't cuss. He don't argue with the umpires. He don't rag the guys on the other team. He don't do diddly."

"Hell, all he does is hit the hell outa the ball."

"Yeah, and I don't think he's missed more than one or two groundballs all year. I crowd the line at third 'cause I know he'll stop anything hit on the ground to my right."

"He had two hits again tonight."

"OK, he's a super hitter. I know that. But he's strange."

"Hey, maybe you oughta stop runnin' around so much an start goin' ta church. We could use a few more hits offa you."

Devere flipped Whitey off.

"I guess it just goes to show," Bill said, sounding like Confucius, "that you can shake a tree and forty cussin' drunks'll fall out but not many super hitters."

The whole exchange told Bill where he stood. He realized it was OK to be religious, even educated, as long as you could hit.

"I'd just liketa take him down ta see Carla some night," Devere was still talking about Stevenson, "just ta see what happened."

"Is Carla back workin' the ballpark?" Whitey asked.

"Yeah, haven't ya seen her down there?"

"She's got a new black car," Washington supplied, "an she's not there evry night. I've only seen her twice."

"Who's Carla?" Bill and Rae Ann, the newcomers, asked simultaneously.

The other four men laughed and Ellie glared at them.

"We'll just hafta introduce ol' Skywatch ta Carla some night after the game," Devere said, grinning at the others.

Ellie and Rae Ann went to the john.

"She's in there tellin' Rae Ann who Carla is right now," Jimmy speculated.

"The guy we had playin' third base last year," Devere changed the subject when the girls returned, "was a real crazy man."

"And stupid too," Jimmy put in.

"How come he's not playin' this year?" Bill asked.

"Hell, he got fired."

"Fired, hell, he's in jail."

"He usedta work out in the yard drivin' a towmotor."

"Seems he heard 'bout a whole stand o' walnut trees growin' out in the middle of a cornfield down by Gas City an he decided he was gonna rip some off an sell em. But it started rainin' while he an this buddy o' his were cuttin' down the trees. When they loaded em on the truck, the whole damn thing sank. They tried to git it out but the farmer musta heard em an called the sheriff 'cause the next thing they know a siren an a bubblegum machine's comin' down the highway next ta the field an they got no place ta go."

"He was a good hitter too," Devere summed it up, "strong as an ox, hit about seven or eight home runs."

"After they found out he was in jail, they checked out at the place an he'd been rippin' off lumber an copper pipe an stuff like that by the truckload. He'd just throw a few pieces in the back of his pickup evry day after work."

"You've really had some winners on this team," Ellie summed it up.

"The worst was that vice-president or whatever he was. Rutherford. That was his name," Jimmy shook his head. "He was 'bout forty-five an one o' the big wheels in sales or marketing or somethin' like that out at the place. All he ever talked about was his country club an his summer house up on Lake Freeman."

"He thought he could play baseball so he came out an was gonna be one o' the boys."

"Yeah," Devere picked up the story, "but we got lucky an he broke his ankle slidin' into third 'bout the sixth game. It never healed good enough for him ta play anymore."

"Still walks with a limp," Sammy added.

"You were happy the guy broke his ankle?" Bill asked.

"Damn right. Shouldn't o' been out there playin' in the first place," Devere answered. "He didn't belong with us an he just pushed his way in. I'm the one who runs the team, but he was a big wheel, so what am I supposed ta say?"

"That's part o' what's wrong with the whole damn city league," Jimmy added. "They let anybody play. There's some teams in this league oughta be in a home for the handicapped. I mean, we shouldn't even haveta go on the field with em."

Bill glanced across at Ellie and Rae Ann who seemed to be taking the universal team barbarism easily in stride.

"Baseball's the best game as fars I'm concerned," Devere was saying, "football's so borin' anymore."

As the talk meandered around him, Bill sipped slow and studied Rae Ann and Ellie. Rae Ann was better looking in her tall, classic, long-legged blondeness, but Ellie was somehow more substantial, more exciting. As tall as Rae Ann but bigger boned with large breasts and hips, Ellie had long, loose auburn hair that curled around her face. She had pricked his curiosity ever since his first day at All-American Homes.

She worked like a man and, one time when she cut herself, she cussed like a man. But beneath her toughness, she was obviously aware she was a woman and that men were looking at her. Bill found himself looking every chance he got.

But Ellie clearly was Jimmy Washington's property. Yet he always seemed tentative around Ellie, as if he didn't know quite what to say or as if he was a little afraid of her. He acted like a man with a secret he was afraid might get out.

"D'jew see that new movie *Rollerball?* Now that's a sport."

"I liked that movie *The Longest Yard*. Ellie an I went ta see that, where the convicts play football 'gainst the guards in the state pen. It was funny."

"Yeah, that was a wonderful movie. There's one woman in the movie an all she's good for is gittin' beat up by Burt Reynolds."

"C'mon, that was a good movie. You just didn't understand it. The guy was a leader an they won the football game with the guards. That was the important part."

"Jimmy, that was an el shitto movie an, believe me, I understood it perfectly. The guy had ta prove he was a man, first by beatin' up a girl, then by beatin' up on a bunch o' other men."

Jimmy didn't say another word, just went back to his beer. It was as if he was afraid to challenge her.

Bill couldn't pick up the signals between Ellie and Washington. By all outward signs, they were together. But Washington always seemed uncomfortable when Ellie was around.

Rae Ann, however, was even more of an enigma. Few at All-American Homes remembered her from when she'd worked there before. Those who thought they could, said she had changed completely. Talked different. Quieter. Prettier. Better dressed.

Washington never let on that he remembered her from before. A lot of people wondered if Rae Ann had any private life. On the dock one day, Sammy had speculated aloud about screwing her as he did about every woman he had ever met. "I don't think she likes men," Devere had muttered, thinly veiling his dark hint. In the world of Wabash City and All-American Homes every woman, unless she was fat or ugly or ineligible for humanity due to some other glaring deformity, had to have a man. Sexual symbiosis was a basic sign of normality.

The stories drew the men to the bars. The stories that night passed back and forth, mainly for the benefit of Bill and Rae Ann and Ellie, the newcomers. The stories were all twice-told, oft-told tales that would be told again to other people in other bars, and then told again by other people to still other people in yet other bars in other towns in other states until pretty soon all of America would have heard them. They were floating fictions that lived only to be expanded and embellished, shifting the shape of reality repeatedly. For the men in the bars, telling their stories was like throwing a man out at first from your knees or poling a home run or rounding third on the fly. Telling their stories made them feel real.

10 The Midseason Bicentennial Blues

The Wabash rolls past diamonds,
Dust-lit on a summer night.
And bats hit balls
Like summer squalls
Empty lives flashin' into flight.

Jimmy Washington sang his new song slowly, almost mournfully, his legs dangling over the side of the loading dock. The others—Devere, Willy, Hank, Whitey, Adams—sat in the sun in dirty tee-shirts and listened, drank cokes, sweltered in the dusty late afternoon.

America you're dyin,'

his voice whispered the chorus as he seemed to coax sobs out of the guitar,

Wasted by an arid drought,

as the dust shimmered in the parking lot and the humid sun rolled sweat down their foreheads,

On workin' lives
Of stunted size
The meanin' all thrown out.

Workin' men escape to softball
And beer and cigarettes,
And they come alive

When the games arrive
Set free with no regrets.

America you're dyin'
Your men just ain't machines
Who'll run all day
For empty pay
And give up all their dreams.

They dream of makin' the big leagues
As the slowpitch arches high
But that past dream ages
Like a book's turned pages
Trapped men slowly learnin' to die.

America you're dyin'
Wasted by an arid drought
Your workin' guys
Wear empty eyes
Not seein' what it's all about.

But the Wabash rolls past diamonds,
Dust-lit on a summer night.
And bats hit balls
Like summer squalls
Dull eyes flashin' into light.

He finished without a riff, the guitar just stopping.
"Hey Jim, that's a super song. I really like it," Bill broke the silence.
"That's my softball song."
"It's a hell of a lot more than just a softball song."
"Whaddaya call that song Jimmy?" Devere asked.
"That's The Wabash Baseball Blues."
"Man that's about our team, ain't it?" Devere demanded.
"Yeah, I guess it is." He said it with a strange resignation which Bill
had never seen clearly in any of them before.

The river sounded good in Washington's song, but in mid-June
the Wabash was nothing special. All the water from the spring thaw

had run through in late May and the Wabash didn't "roll" anymore. It limped along, turgid and brown like greasy-spoon coffee.

The Wabash that summer of '76 seemed always the same. The softball season got to be that way too. The games all started looking the same. The doldrums set in. In mid-June in the Wabash City Softball League nothing was happening with the All-American Homes team. Few of the games went beyond five innings. How exciting could softball be when Devere would win the coin flip—he was uncanny at winning the pre-game flips; he only lost three flips all year—and choose to bat first. They would bat around twice, score thirteen, fourteen, fifteen runs in the top of the first inning, and the game would be over before they even took the field. After they beat Dick and Tonna's on Devere's magical night, they had no trouble running their record up to 10–1. That is how they stood on the twentieth of June when they were scheduled to play the Peerless Truckers, the defending league champs.

Except for the Dick and Tonna's game, all they played during that ten-game stretch were rum-dums, cripples and college professors, refugees from old age, stoned-out hippies from the Community Center, and heavy-booted motorcycle jockeys from Sammy's Tavern. Like a marriage, the trick was to survive those kinds of games, those mid-season doldrums. It's a hard thing to do unless a team can find something to shake them up.

After the Dick and Tonna's game, very little was shaking for Bill Franklin. He and Martha met only in passing. Somehow, diabolically, on the nights he didn't have games, she had her bridge club or her yoga sessions. When he went to the bar with the team after a game, Martha was always in bed, sleeping like a corpse, when he got home. They talked between five-thirty and six each evening over dinner before Walter Cronkite came on. Their cryptic, staccato exchanges described equally boring days:

> He: How was your day, hon?
> She: Cleaned house this morning, laid in the sun awhile (dips into her salad then chews while she continues), then went to the grocery store, took the kids to the pool this afternoon.
> He: Uh-huh, uh-huh.
> She: Did you have a good day?
> He: In that place? You gotta be kiddin.' It sucks.

> She: Do you have to talk like that with the kids around?
> He: (ignoring her) . . . the only interesting thing about that place is the lunch breaks where we sit around and talk.
> She: About your precious softball, I suppose?

Their dinner exchanges were the equivalent of two strangers talking about the weather after having been introduced over the hors d'ouvres table at an academic cocktail party. They were polite, attentive, but not the least bit interested. They made love Saturday mornings behind locked doors while the children watched cartoons. They rarely kissed each other, and they hardly ever laughed. Alone almost continuously in those hot mid-summer days, Martha seemed to have lost her capacity to laugh. One Saturday afternoon while the children played in the backyard and Bill slouched in front of the baseball game-of-the-week in the den, she found herself trapped in the toilet.

"Bill, will you go upstairs and get me some toilet paper," she shouted in a whisper, knowing that the windows were open and not wanting to chance offending the neighbors.

"Whud ya say?" he answered, not moving.

"I need some toilet paper," in a louder whisper.

"What?"

"Go upstairs and get me some toilet paper," she screamed, infuriated that he forced her to let all the neighbors in on her predicament.

He caught the anger in her voice and went quickly. Returning, he leaned his head around the bathroom door and, looking down where she sat huddled and soiled, said, "here's some film for your brownie."

But she didn't laugh: "That's not funny, it's crude."

"C'mon Martha, what's wrong with you."

He had liked his joke. He stalked back to his baseball game and didn't speak to her the rest of the day. At the dinner party at Dean Dingle's house that night, they pretended to be happily married.

1976 was getting on everyone's nerves that summer. Everything had blossomed into red, white and blue. Girls at the municipal swimming pool wore Bicentennial swim suits and donuts dripped red, white and blue icing. Dogs peed on fire hydrants painted like Minutemen or Redcoats while motorists drew up at red, white and blue crosswalks. Bicentennial minutes, commercials for American history, interrupted the regular TV programming. To Bill's mind, only Johnny Carson had the right attitude. His Bicentennial half-minutes always began "Two hundred years ago today" and typically continued "Abigail Adams, her husband John out zealously campaigning for liberty and higher interest rates, was getting her cupcakes frosted by Roscoe Lytton-Parmenter, the Tory baker with the biggest spatula in town." A funeral home in a small Indiana town advertised red, white and blue caskets and called them "The Spirits of '76."

Only once the whole summer did Bill see, or rather hear, anything good coming out of the whole Bicentennial orgy. He and Martha were eating in an Italian restaurant that provided good live music to accompany their pizza. A jazz trio, imported all the way from Dayton, Ohio, was playing. The piano player, a Roy Meriweather, played a piece he had written for the United States Bicentennial celebration. He'd gotten a government grant to write it and he called it "Black Snow." It was a 21-movement jazz history of black people in America. For fifty minutes it soared in wild joy and moaned unnecessary loss. It had a kind of sacredness.

Through it all, the turgid Wabash flowed. It trickled through June with little happening on its brown, boring surface. Near the twin towns a junkyard festered on the banks of the river. Only the ball fields, as if resisting the river's influence, seemed clean, ordered, alive. Every summer evening the softball games echoed out into the bicentennial darkness that hung heavy over the river.

11 Ellie in the Afternoon

Ellie emitted her usual lovesounds as she and Jimmy Washington, just come from work, coiled on the floor of her apartment. A jagged slash of dull black grease hung on her cheek. Washington, below her on his back, gazed up in wonder at her utterly liberated, disoriented, face as she methodically rocked her way toward a climax to their monotonous day at All-American Homes. Her voice quickened, got raspy as she drew hard for breath. She moved herself faster and faster into some other private world. His eyes riveted on her ecstatic face as she jammed her hips forward against him again and again, her hands pressed down on the sides of his ribcage as if holding on desperately even as she was being swept away. Her face, dirty with grease, stretched tight. Her lips were parted, her head thrown back, her eyes blank, feeling rather than seeing. It was as if she had thrown off everything that could hold her down and was climbing, alone, hand over hand, upward, toward freedom, release, a kind of heaven that Washington couldn't enter, couldn't even visualize. Then she hung there in mid-air not even breathing. Her breath was held in suspension, until she emitted one last moaning "uuuhhhhhh" as she collapsed on top of him, finally drawing breath.

She didn't move for long moments. She curled into the contours of his body and lay still. Then, her lips kissed up the side of his neck to his ear: "Oh darlin,' darlin,' thank you. I love it when you let me do it that way." She seemed genuinely grateful, not just indulging in sexual sound effects.

"Uh-huh."

"What's wrong?"

"Nothin's wrong. Don't worry about it. Just relax."

"You didn't make it did you?"

She looked into his face. It was the first time she'd looked at him since they'd come through the door already undressing. "Oh damn, you didn't." Somehow she could see it in his face. "Don't worry dar-lin.'" She started moving slowly down, kissing over his chest.

"You don't understand," Washington stopped her with his hand behind her neck. "I like that way, but I wanna have it with you, at the same time."

"So what should I do, give you a countdown. Can't you see, when I'm like that I don't even know where I am."

Frustration crept into his voice, then petulance: "You always wanna be on top."

"Not always."

"Most of the time."

Suddenly Ellie was glaring at him, the streak of grease bulging like a bruise across her cheek. Instead of saying anything else she just pushed herself up off of him and stomped into the bathroom

Their time together had been going that way more and more often lately. They would be easy with each other, listening to music, laugh-ing, making love, and then all of a sudden they would be arguing. Washington had asked Ellie to marry him nearly two weeks before on the last day of May—and she hadn't answered him yet. "Man, that's heavy, ya gotta give me time ta think about that," she had stalled—and she hadn't mentioned it since.

When she came back and started dressing he tried to reason with her once again: "Can't you see. This is all screwed up. We should git married. At least live together. You wouldn't haveta work in that place anymore."

His frustration glared out of his face like broken neon.

She tried to pick up the shards of their mood.

"Marriage is a big step. Can't we just take some time and love each other?"

"What do I hafta say? For God's sake Ellie, I want ya ta marry me."

"No!" she flared. "You want me ta be waitin' for ya with dinner when ya come home from work. You want me cleanin' yore house. You want me ta spend all my time waitin' for ya ta come home so my life can start up."

"Aw the hell with it," Washington said, "we're gettin' nowhere."

"So what'duh ya want. Ya want me ta just say 'yes,' don'tcha? You think it's that simple, don'tcha?"

"C'mon, this is stupid. Let's go git somethin' ta eat. I got a game tonight."

"It's not stupid," she begged him to listen, "I do love you Jimmy. I know how you feel about me. But I just can't get married yet. Look at Devere. He goes ta that hooker evry week. You had to git divorced yourself."

"That was different. You're not like she was."

"How do you know? How do you know I won't become like she was?"

"I don't wanna talk about my ex-wife. C'mon, let's go eat. I got a game."

"The hell with your game! You listen ta me," and then she softened, "I do love you darlin,' but I just can't be tied down like that now. There's so many places I've never seen. I wanna see California an San Francisco an Dallas an Nashville."

"I could drive ya ta those places. We could see em."

"That's not it. I don't wanna go there on one-week vacations from All-American Homes. I just can't be tied down like that. I gotta git outa this town Jimmy. It's gittin' too familiar. It's gittin' ta be just like my daddy's farm was before I left. I used ta lay in the hayloft up in the top o' the barn an daydream. It was so comfortable an quiet. I could be so comfortable here. Marry you. Sit back an let ya support me. Just lay around for the rest o' my life."

"What's wrong with that?" "But I don't want that. Can'tcha see, darlin'? I want other things. Different things from what you want."

"I just wantcha livin' with me, that's all."

"No, that's not all. I think you want a lot more than that. I just can't marry ya, that's all."

Washington was up, pulling on his pants, his workshoes.

Her voice turned much softer, almost as if she were pleading with him: "I've just got ta be in some control. Can't you understand that? That's the way I feel about it. Ya can't have any kinda control over anything if you're married. I decided when I left the farm I didn't want ta be married. Maybe I'll change my mind when I git ta be thirty, thirty-five, but right now bein' married'd be like bein' in prison."

"Why did you say ya loved me then?"

"Because I do."

"Women, damn," he muttered, shaking his head. "I got a game," he said as he went out the door tucking in his shirt.

12 Molly in Mourning

As the middle weeks of June stretched out in the summer sun, Bill Franklin noticed changes in both Washington and Devere. Neither seemed very enthusiastic about anything. Washington had gone mute behind Bill in left field. In the first few games he had been constantly jabbering, ragging Whitey, accusing the infielders of blatant coward-ice in the face of ground balls, whipping hard flat throws to the bases after one-hop singles to left. Devere had quieted down too. He didn't growl, except occasionally when utter stupidity screamed for acknowl-edgement. *How could anyone get excited about playing the rum-drums we've been playing lately,* Bill wrote it all off reasonably. *The whole team needs something to shake them up.*

Devere had been visibly shaken already. Sitting innocently in the living room after dinner, watching the Bicentennial News, minding his own business, out of a clear blue sky Molly had hit him with it.

"Hon, you want a beer?"

"Unh-uh, I'm just gonna watch the news, take a look at the sports page."

"Hon . . . I, uh . . . I got a job today."

It took a second for him to believe what he was hearing.

"What did you say?" His voice was ugly and menacing.

"I got a job as a secretary at the Peerless Trucking Terminal."

"Peerless t-t-truck," he sputtered in disbelief. "You can't work for Peerless Truck!"

Molly had known all along that she was going to have to stand up for herself. She came out swinging: "Why can't I? Just why the hell can't I?"

"Cause they're a bunch o' pricks."

"Who is? Whaddo you know about Peerless Trucking."

"No. I'm talking about their softball team."

"Softball team? What does the softball have ta do with it?"

"We hate 'em!" His words came spilling out over each other "They've won the league two years in a row an they think they're the hottest peckers in the whole peckerwood. No wife o' mine's gonna work for them."

"How was I supposed ta know any of that? That's ridiculous. What does softball have to do with me gettin' a job. Well, dammit, I've got a job!"

"No you don't!"

"Yes I do! And I'm keepin' it."

Devere was surprised. She'd never stood up to him like that before. He just stared at her

"You're never home. Softball. Basketball. The bowling alley. The bar. God knows where. I don't hassle you. But I need something to fill up my time too. I need somethin.'"

Devere fumed.

Molly was just bored. Sitting at home alone in their house had become like a banishment from reality.

"What's so great about workin' in a truckin' terminal?" Devere screamed.

When she had first seen the place, Molly couldn't have answered Devere's question. Her interview had been terrifying. It had taken place right in the middle of the open freight office. Two other secretaries sat at their desks pretending to work but listening the whole time. Dock workers wandered in and out shouting questions and demands for invoices, bills of lading, shipping orders. The man who interviewed her was at least ten years younger than she, about 26 or 27, wearing a white shirt and tie but with his sleeves rolled up as if after washing his hands he'd forgotten to roll them back down. He chainsmoked cigarettes nervously.

He's so young, Molly thought.

When he'd asked her about her last job, she'd had to go back fifteen years to give him the name of a small mobile home parts supply company that no longer even existed. She'd been practicing on the small portable typewriter at home for three weeks before the interview but he'd sat her down in front of a huge IBM Selectric. She'd never used an electric before, much less one of those professional monstrosities. They'd had a little manual Smith-Corona with a carrying case at the place where she worked so many years before.

"Hadn't you better turn it on," the young man said when she tried to start typing and nothing happened. She could feel the two office girls in the background looking at each other. She pecked out a few sentences and the young man finally said, "that's fine," in what she thought was a rather resigned voice.

Then, looking at his watch, the young man, in a one-last-question tone, asked her, "why do you need a job?"

"Because my husband is temporarily disabled and I've got two daughters in school and he can't work and . . ." she lied, puting a slight quaver (which she'd practiced) into her voice, "and I just need a job."

It must have worked. Either he felt sorry for her or he just didn't want to waste any more time interviewing any other girls. He hired her. The place was ugly and dingy, filled with crude, loud men, men like her husband. All her co-workers in the freight office were at least ten years younger. But the idea and the place had grown more attractive in her mind, had come to seem more important. *It's a test,* she remembered thinking, *a survival test. And it's real.*

"What's so great about workin' in a truckin' terminal?" Devere screamed.

"It's not sittin' at home with nobody ta talk to, that's what. We don't hardly do anything together anymore except make love evry once in a while. Can'tcha see, I'm tryin' ta find somethin' ta do, somethin' worthwhile, 'stead o' sittin' around."

"What about me?"

"I was goin' through the picture album the other day. All the pictures are of me and the girls. That's cause you were runnin' the camera. But they were still true. You were never really there at any of those places with us. Nashville. Mammoth Cave. Brown County when we found all those covered bridges."

"What are you talkin' 'bout? You wouldn't evena gone on any o' those trips if I hadn'ta taken ya. Why do you haffta work? We don't need the money."

"You just don't understand any of it, do ya? You don't even know what I'm talkin' about do ya?"

That was when Devere made his mistake. He tried to reason with her. His conciliatory tone of voice encouraged her to keep up the fight, restored her illusion that she could break him down, bolstered her fragile hopes that he would compromise, even made her think that she could win. "What about the girls?" Devere demanded almost quietly, almost reasonably, "there won't be nobody here when they git home from school."

"They do everything for themselves."

"Ya can't just have em comin' to an empty house."

"Why not? They clean it up without me botherin' them. They make their own meals."

"They're gonna be bringin' boys in here."

"You're sick. It's just a job. Why should I haffta sit home alone all the time? Why?"

They looked at each other for a moment, in silence, in hatred.

"I'm takin' that job Devere."

"You call that man an tell him you're not gonna work for him."

"No, I'm takin' the job."

"You take that job an you're not gonna be livin' in this house." Devere had overcome his attempt to be reasonable. "You call that man or you git the hell out." He slammed the door as he left.

In Carla's car a half hour later, Devere was edgy and not responding.

"What the hell's wrong with you?" Carla finally looked up and braced him.

"I dunno. I guess my mind's just not payin' attention ta what you're doin.'"

"C'mon now. Somethin's wrong, honey, just relax. Carla's gonna take care of it." She kissed his neck, her hands on his hair.

"Carla's gonna make ya feel so good you're not even gonna think about what's got ya so uptight. Just relax, darlin,' just relax."

A few minutes later Carla brought him back to the real world of the car. "I'll betcha feel better now, don'tcha darlin'?" She got him a can of beer with her feet that he reached out to grab before it was even halfway there. "I'm a Bicentennial Queen," she laughed, "for the All-American price of five Washingtons, a Lincoln and one large Alexander Hamilton."

"You my dear," Devere held his beer can high, "have the real spirit of '76 . . ." and then chuckling, "that's twin thirty-eights."

Devere enjoyed his joke and Carla smiled. No other customers were clamoring for entrance into the Wabash City's four-wheeled pleasure dome. The goggles, though, always bothered Devere: "How come ya wear those goggles all the time?"

"Because I always have. They're parta my image."

"Image? Wouldn't ya liketa take em off?"

"Yeah, I'd liketa take em off," she answered, her voice getting wary, "but I ain't gonna . . . an don'tchoo get any cute ideas either or it'll be the last time you come through the door o' this car." "OK. OK. Take it easy. I was just curious about em, that's all."

But Devere's curiosity had put Carla on edge to the point where she didn't feel like doing much talking. Devere finished his beer and left, thinking *you can never tell what's goin' on inside a woman's head.* He walked through the dark up the embankment from the lower parking lot toward the lighted ballfields.

Molly had no idea where Devere had gone when he stomped out. She was pretty sure he'd gone to one of his bars somewhere and was sitting around laughing and drinking beer with a bunch of other men whose own wives were sitting home alone like her. One thing she did know, though, was that the next morning she would call the man at the Peerless Truck Terminal and tell him that she couldn't take the job. She opened a bottle of Gallo's Hearty Burgundy and drank it all before she went to bed.

13 Rae Ann Rising

The Liberty Bar was the first watering hole along the faded blacktop on the way from the All-American Homes factory into Wabash City. On the outside, it was a flattish, squarish, nauseous greenish building with a **LIQUOR/BEER/WINE** sign in red, white and blue neon hanging over the door. Its decor stood somewhere between the designations "BAR" and "COCKTAIL LOUNGE."

The bar area was pure Indiana neighborhood tavern. Old men lined up on the stools watched Dinah Shore on the color TV over the bar. They leaned on their elbows sipping beer amidst ash trays, salt shakers and hard-boiled egg shells. In the center of the room under one bare light bulb sat the pool table. Hoosier cowboys in hard-hats, crewcuts and engineer boots circled the table silently, beer in one hand, cue in the other, cigarette in the mouth. Others, in checked, long-sleeved flannel shirts hanging out and unbuttoned over soiled tee-shirts, loitered against the back wall mocking missed shots and drinking beer.

The other side of the room was more cocktail loungey. A few tables fronted five spacious booths against the back wall. The tables were imaginatively appointed with red, white, and blue checked table cloths and Mateus bottles festering with lumps of melted wax.

The booths, however, were more cosmopolitan and sophisticated in the rich brown newness of their buttoned naugahyde. Centered on the wall over each booth and left over from the fifties was a small jukebox with the buttons running up the middle between the selections.

Ellie and Rae Ann stopped at the Liberty right after work on a typically hot and humid June day. Ellie's dark green tee-shirt was stained with sweat in a circle around the armpits and at her waist where she tucked it into her jeans. Rae Ann looked fresh and dry as if ready to head out for a round of golf at the country club. She wore a tight, blue, wrap-around, denim, discount store skirt and a sleeveless white tank top. They sat in a booth in the far back corner working on a pitcher of beer. Ellie did most of the talking.

"He's gettin' too serious about it. He wants me ta marry him. What would I wanta git married for? Evrybody I know hates bein' married. Look at Devere. Evrytime I go ta one o' their games he takes off afterwards down ta that hooker. I just gotta let Jimmy go. I didn't mean for it ta git this way."

Rae Ann wanted to jump up and down, twist and shout. *Yea! Let him go!* she thought. But she tried to look serious.

"Why don'tcha break up with him," Rae Ann offered, trying to sound neutral, uninterested.

"Yeah, I should, just break it off clean."

Rae Ann started to squirm.

"He's really a good guy." Ellie went on, talking it through. "But he's gittin' so heavy. I don't wanna git married. I'm only twenty-four years old."

Rae Ann was ecstatic, so she frowned. Inside, she was exulting even as she sat quietly sympathizing with Ellie's dilemma.

Rae Ann felt guilty: *she's talking serious to me as a friend and all I can think of is getting into her boyfriend's pants.*

"But he's in love with me. I'm not in love with him. I don't even know what love is. I'm sure as hell not ready ta spend the rest o' my life livin' in this damn town with Jimmy no matter how good he is ta me."

"He's divorced, isn't he?" Rae Ann groped for something, anything, to say to camouflage her real feelings. "Why'd he git divorced in the first place?"

"I guess his wife was a real bitch, a nagger, wanted him comin' home after evry game, that sorta thing. That's probly what I'd end up like. He said that a coupla years ago he just decided he wanted ta see other women and his wife divorced him. He says he misses his kids. She moved em to Indianapolis."

"How long ago d'jew say that happened?" Rae Ann asked, wondering.

"Coupla years. I dunno. Just the other day after work he ast me ta marry him again an I laughed at him an said no like I've done before but this time he really got mad. He doesn't really say nothin' but I can usually tell. He just stomped out. I didn't even hafta cook him dinner."

"Well it's better that way than some o' the things Wes, my ex-husband, used ta do. When Wes got mad evrybody knew it. One time, he was workin' for the Volkswagen place then, he got so mad at me he punched out a windshield. Our car was broke down an Wes was drivin' the VW Bus that shuttled people when they'd left their cars ta git em fixed. After he'd dropped evrybody off, he picked me up 'cause I had ta go someplace. Ya know how those VW buses got no front end an those great big windshields ya sit right up against? Well we were comin' right down the main street hill, an we got ta arguin' about somethin' an the next thing he's screamin' at me an he punches his fist right through that windshield. His hand didn't really go all the way through I guess but the glass shattered out in all these little lines like a spider web. There was some man comin' up the hill in the other lane an you shoulda seen the look on his face when that windshield went all cracks. I was afraid ta look at Wes an the guy couldn't believe his eyes. Wes ended up tellin' his boss at the Volkswagen place that he'd hadta stop quick ta keep from hittin' a dog or a kid or somethin' an he hit his head real hard against it. His head sure was hard enough ta break a windshield. Ya know what he said ta me right after he did it? He said, 'now see what you made me do.' No way no man's ever gonna beat me up again, like Wes did," Rae Ann drew the moral of her story in the form of a declaration.

"Jimmy'd never lay a finger on a woman," Ellie said.

I know, Rae Ann thought, remembering the sympathy in his eyes that day he'd found her rings.

"Maybe that's what's wrong with him," Ellie went on, "he's so submissive. I can do anything I want with him. He just wants ta please me. We make love any way I want. But it gits sorta boring. Sometimes I even feel like I'd like him ta be rough like that jerk you were married to."

"Oh no you wouldn't."

Just then, two hoosier cowboys, come from the pool table, materialized next to Rae Ann and Ellie's booth. The short one had a beer gut, a two-day stubble of beard, a front tooth missing and wore boots caked with mud just off a construction job. The tall one sported a drooping Mexican-bandit mustache and wore a porkpie hat, the kind Fred MacMurray always wore on *My Three Sons.*

"Now what are you pritty little ladies talkin' 'bout so serious?" the Porkpie Hat crooned. "Oh, not much," Ellie answered looking straight at them. "Our kids. Our husbands. How quiet this bar was 'til you walked up."

"Now you know you ain't got no husband, honey," the Gaptooth grinned cavernously poking the Porkpie in the arm. "You wouldn't be in here you did."

"OOOKAY," Ellie hesitated only a second and then continued in slow measured tones, "how 'bout this? Fuck off you paunchy gap-toothed jerk an take your toothpick friend with ya."

"Hey, it's foul-mouthed Flo," the Porkpie tried to make a snappy retort, thinking that Ellie was just joking.

"No it ain't," Rae Ann spoke up like a trooper, "now why don't you guys just take a walk," she continued, trying to imitate Ellie's tough bravado.

The Liberty Bar lotharios slunk back to the pool table.

"By the flicks of our BICS we could tell they were hicks," Ellie laughed, lighting her cigarette with her disposable lighter. "Ya see, ya stay in Wabash City ya spend the rest o' your life fightin' off jerks like those two. We'd end up like Laverne and Shirley on that TV show."

"That's a funny show."

"Not if you're livin' it, it ain't."

But Rae Ann missed the sharp irony in Ellie's voice. She was think-ing of the possibility of Jimmy Washington being set free, being put back into circulation like a used car.

"Jimmy's really a good guy," Rae Ann said tentatively trying to calm the guilt she was feeling.

"Yeah, I know. Let's finish this beer an git out o' here," Ellie said as if she was bored with the whole problem. "Here's ta my declaration o' independence."

She's gonna let him go, Rae Ann hoped as they got up to leave.

"An I'll see you tonight with an illegal smile," twanged out of the jukebox as they crossed the room to the door past the Gaptooth and the Porkpie and the other pool-playing cowboys, past the old men dumping salt into their beers.

14 Bill "Willy" Wandering

Only nine o'clock and Martha was already asleep on the couch in the TV room. Two hours before, as he was reading the newspaper, she had said, "I'm glad you don't have a game tonight. It'll be nice to have a quiet evening at home for a change." But she dozed off watching reruns.

Bill wandered into the living room and turned off the lights to think. He wondered what it would be like going down under the Wabash with an aqualung. He envisioned finding all the old softballs that had been fouled into the river in the last twenty years. They would be all slimy and dirty, waterlogged and gone soft.

What the hell got me on that, he thought, depressed about how empty he knew the river probably was beneath its surface, depressed about how empty his life seemed. Except for the softball. The last three or four games had been boring, easy games. None had gone more than five innings. They'd gone drinking after a couple but nobody's heart had been into celebrating. What they all needed was an interesting ballgame with a good team like Dick and Tonna's. *Peerless Truck's comin' up next week,* Bill thought, maybe that's what we need to shake us up a little bit.

Everybody on the team was looking forward to the Peerless game. They all knew it would be the most important game at least of this part of the season.

Boy, there'll be some celebratin' in the bar we win that game, Bill speculated.

But the bar hadn't been quite the same lately either. Ellie and Rae Ann hadn't come to the last couple of games and Bill wondered why. For the first couple of weeks, they had come regularly to the games and gone drinking afterwards. He had come to look forward to them being a part of the group in the bar. Ellie scared him. She was so different from Rae Ann. He tried to imagine what each of them would be like in bed.

Martha had been talking casually about taking the kids to her parents' cottage on the lake in Michigan for a few weeks in July. Bill wished she'd do it, though he knew she rarely did anything on her own.

He would miss the kids but it would give him a chance to be alone for awhile, a chance to clear things up in his head. He hoped he would start loving her again. Those hopes swam in the shallows of his mind, but lurking deeper down in a murky darkness wriggled the real reasons he wanted her to go. He plunged down among the tentacles and snakes of his sexual imagination and found Ellie and Rae Ann leering at him there. That sudden plunge made him uncomfortable. He stirred. He looked at the luminescent dial of his watch. The slight movement pulled him back from the depths into the calmer, slower world of the surface. It was ten-thirty. He could barely hear the TV set still talking to itself in the other room. .

He got a beer and went back into the dark. He knew he was feeling sorry for himself like one of John Updike's failed jocks, but he didn't care. He remembered how much he used to love to play basketball. He was the only forward on the high school team who went to the middle on the fast break. He loved to get the ball just inside half-court, dribble once high and then one low dribble for rhythm before going up for a jump shot at the foul line. *If I had my way,* Bill thought, *I'd hang up there above the foul line forever, floating, like a hovering gunship, a pure shooter, suspended above it all, ready to pull the trigger on those beautiful Jerry West jump shots.* He hadn't played basketball once all winter.

He drifted back to that long lazy summer when he was fourteen years old playing on the Pony League baseball team that eventually went on to win the city and one game in the state championship tourney. He saw himself playing third base just inside the lines on that bright green July infield with the basepaths slightly wetted down to keep the dust from rising. *The only time I'm ever happy anymore is on the softball field,* he thought.

A sound from upstairs snapped his head up, jolted him out of his reverie. It was Danny walking in his sleep, bumping into things upstairs. Before Bill could get to him, the little boy rolled down the top four carpeted steps and came to rest on his side on the landing, still sound asleep. He lay there like a small curled animal. He never woke up as Bill carried him back to bed. As he stood over his son, the little boy's fragile, imperceptible breathing made Bill feel like he belonged for the first time all evening.

With Danny tucked in securely, he wandered back down the steps to the darkened living room. He pulled open the drapes on the front window and stared out into the blackness of the Indiana night. No cars passed. The single streetlight was out, probably picked off by some neighborhood kid throwing rocks. *This brooding alone in the dark is for the birds,* Bill thought, *I guess I better get Martha upstairs.*

As he walked into the TV room, Johnny Carson was doing that evening's Bicentennial half-minute. "Two hundred years ago today on a hill outside the small settlement of Charlottesville, Virginia, Thomas Jefferson was writing a confidential letter to the new barmaid at the village tavern, Loretta Lynn MacTavistock by name, who had caught his eye and smitten him all over his little body with her overflowing charms as he slobbered in his cups. When in the course of human events, Jefferson began, it becomes necessary for a Virginia gentleman to forget the high station which the Laws of Nature and of Nature's God entitles him, a decent respect to the opinions of mankind requires that we meet in the woods in mid-afternoon without my wife knowing. In other words, Loretta baby, I've got the hots for you, and I hold that truth to be self-evident that all men are endowed by their creator with certain unalienable Rights, that among these are Life, Liberty and the pursuit of the voluptuous barmaids who give their consent to the governor. And that's the way it was, two hundred years ago today, in the life of one of the soon-to-be Fathers of our country."

That's it, stick it to em Johnny, Bill silently applauded as he switched off the TV set.

15 Washington Crossing

Jimmy Washington loitered in the doorway to the loading dock two days before the game with Peerless Truck. At ten after five, the All-American Homes factory was almost deserted. Only a few cars, his included, still baked in the dusty parking lot. Five minutes earlier, he had furtively stepped back into the shadows when Ellie came trudging out of the side door of the shop. He had stayed hidden until she got into her blue and white Chevy and drove away. He had wanted to hail her, to smile and make it all up. But he had hesitated. Then she was gone.

Back over his shoulder in the dark, empty factory, the abandoned assembly lines stretched out like dry river beds to the doors on the far side of the building. Mobile homes in various stages of undress squatted over the pits. Despite Justin Endreem's reassuring smile on the billboard, Washington laughed ironically as his eye trailed over the abandoned shells. He couldn't understand why people paid good money to live in them. They were put together carefully enough. He saw to that. But when the finished numbers rolled out the door, they invariably clanked. They were tinny, cheap imitations of homes. Mass-produced and all identical, they were conceived by mechanical extensions of hands, birthed by unfeeling power tools incapable of any pride in creation. Unsuspecting Americans towed them away, set them down on slabs. They squatted with no foundations, no roots in the land, fragile shells that could easily be blown away by the first high wind.

He turned away from the ghostly lines back to his surveillance of the parking lot. Rae Ann's car was still there, parked near his own on the skinned dirt. He wanted to talk to someone about Ellie and there just wasn't anyone except Rae Ann. She was Ellie's best friend. He hoped that maybe she could help him out. But, as he leaned in the doorway, he still hadn't decided if he had enough nerve to actually talk to her alone. He kept thinking about that one time two years before. He never had figured that day out. It had been a day just like this one, a hot summer afternoon, everyone gone home, the plant dark. *I shouldn't do this,* he decided.

He went back to the cage to pick up his guitar. *I'll have a coupla beers an go home an work on some songs,* he planned for an empty evening. *Sure wish we had a game tonight.* As he jumped down off the loading dock and made for his car, Rae Ann bounced out of the side door of the office wing. It was perfect timing, almost as if she'd been waiting for him. In her short pink skirt, yellow sleeveless blouse and fluffy blonde hair, she looked like a sunbeam shimmering pastel over the surface of the desert. She looked fresh and new, airy, not sweaty and tired, head down and trudging as Ellie had looked coming out moments before. Washington didn't know what to do. He was caught in the open.

"Hi Jimmy," Rae Ann called, smiling and waving. "Got a game tonight?" The sunlight glittered and glanced in her blonde hair.

"Uh . . . hi," Washington stammered. "No, no game 'til Friday. That's Peerless Truck, the league champs."

"Oh, that's nice," she said rather blankly, clearly not realizing the tremendous import of that game. "How come you're so late today? I thought the lines shut down about quarter ta five? Ellie once said nobody gits out late when they work on your lines."

"Ellie said that? Yeah, well I had ta finish some paperwork in the cage. Time cards, stuff like that. Whuddare you doin' here so late?"

"Wallis, that . . . At ten minutes ta five, Wallis gave me four letters ta type that had ta go out today. Then he goes waltzin' out the door ta have cocktails at his club or lie in his swimmin' pool like a smelly old whale." She said it happily though, without any real rage or resentment. "Boy, it's good ta git outa that place," she finished.

"Well . . . a . . . how about . . . a . . . Does he do that often?"

"Make me stay late? Hey, that's bettern some o' the things he'd like me ta do. I could tell you some stories . . ." but she stopped in midsentence suggestively. "Anyway, I still gotta drop these things at the post office on the way home."

"The hell with his letters. How about . . . a . . . wouldjew liketa have a beer? I mean since we both been workin' overtime an all. We could stop at the Liberty."

To his surprise, she didn't hesitate at all: "I'd love to. that'd be great."

Rae Ann followed Jimmy down the blacktop to the Liberty Bar. As they pulled into the parking lot, they both scanned the parked cars looking for Ellie's blue Chevy.

Inside, Rae Ann didn't recognize anyone from All-American Homes. But, as they crossed by the pool table on the way to a booth, she spotted Gaptooth and Porkpie leaning against the wall in the shadows fondling their cues.

"Hey Jimmy, got a hot one there," the Porkpie sneered in the bantering, condescending tone men use in their strongholds to talk about women.

"Watch your mouth, Ferrlock, or I'll take it out on you on Friday night," Washington answered, taking no offense whatsoever at the Porkpie's comment on Rae Ann.

"You turkey's ain't got a chance. You'll be lucky ta last five innings with us," the Gaptooth shot back.

"Are they friends of yours?" Rae Ann asked in the booth.

"You kiddin'? They're obnoxious. They play for Peerless Truck."

"Whew, that's good. That stumpy, ugly one that looks like a gopher and his toothpick friend tried ta pick Ellie'n me up in here a coupla days ago. Ellie really told em off."

"Ellie's good at that," Washington answered.

The pitcher of beer, frost melting down the sides, came. They drank in silence too long. It became awkward, as if neither knew why they had come, what to talk about. Washington tried the absence of rain, the heat.

"It'd be nice if I could just lie around in the sun in a bikini gittin' a suntan," Rae Ann poured rushing words into the silent air between them, "like those women over in West Wabash, the college set. By the time we git outa work the sun's on the way down an all that's left is dust."

The awkward silence ebbed in again. Rae Ann tried the softball.

"Hell, we've won ten games in a row. The last five haven't even been close. Evrybody's hittin' good an we've been endin' all the games in five innings."

"Why five innings?"

"If you're ahead by ten runs after five, they end the game."

"Oh, that's nice."

The silence pooled around them.

"Seen Ellie lately?" Washington finally blurted out running right up against what was on both their minds. "How come you two haven't been comin' out ta our games lately?"

"Whuddoya mean? You two are goin' together. Aren't you?"

"Well, yeah, but . . ." he stopped and refilled their beer glasses in silence.

Rae Ann knew she was losing him. She knew that the only way she could salvage the whole situation was to jump, eyes open, right in.

"I'm sorry Jimmy. I shouldn't lie. Ellie told me you two were havin' trouble."

"What did she say?"

"Ellie said . . . well, she didn't exactly . . . I mean, she thought that you . . . ya know, I don't know if I should be tellin' you this."

"What?"

"Well she . . . a . . ." Her voice trailed off.

"Look, Rae Ann, I was . . . I was waitin' on purpose for ya ta come out today 'cause . . . well, 'cause I haven't seen Ellie for four days outside o' seein' her walkin' around the place durin' work and I . . . she don't wanna talk ta me . . ." The words picked up speed like a baserunner trying to stretch a single. "All I did was ask her ta git serious. I told her I was in love with her an she got all pissed off. I can't figger her out. I thought mebbe you could help me."

Rae Ann was taken by surprise. *Now he's like I was that day, asking for help.* But she still couldn't sell Ellie out. She didn't yet have the stomach for stabbing her best friend in the back.

"I think she's just scared," Rae Ann began cautiously, trying to forget that she wanted Washington for herself.

"Scared o' what?" he raised his voice. Quickly, he slunk back into silence when heads turned over by the pool table.

"I think she's just scared o' bein' tied down. She doesn't wanna git married 'cause . . . well, 'cause evrybody she knows . . . me, you . . . are divorced, have been messed up bein' married."

"She told ya I ast her ta marry me?"

"Uh-huh, she told me. But it's more than that too. Ellie's different," she almost said "from you and me" but she pulled the words back knowing they would be the beginning of the betrayal.

"Ellie's afraid she'll lose her freedom. She wants other things," she almost said from you and me again. "She wants ta go places, do other things."

"I know, I know, she told me all that. That's stupid. What, does she think I'm gonna put her in jail or somethin'?"

"Maybe."

"That's stupid. Maybe if I told her we'd go ta Nashville. I could try ta sell some o' my songs. I don't know."

Rae Ann wanted to scream "SHE DOESN'T LOVE YOU!" but instead she answered him in her best "Dear Abby" tone: "Maybe it's just not the time for you two ta be gittin' serious. Why don'tcha just try ta make it up with her? Let things ride for a while."

"Yeah, she'd probly like that," bitterness crept into his voice. "Like we'd never talked about anything."

Maybe he's smarter than I'm giving him credit for, Rae Ann thought. Then she realized she was going to do it, knew she was going to turn Benedict Arnold. "Look, we're outa beer. Let's git outa here. Why don't choo come over to my place. I'll cook ya dinner."

Startled fear flashed in Washington's face.

She couldn't believe she had actually said it. She almost wished she could pull the words back. He's gonna say "no" and laugh about me tomorrow on the loading dock with his baseball buddies.

"OK," Washington said, "that sounds great. Can I git some beer or somethin'?"

"No, no," she stuttered. "No, I've got plenty. Why don'tchoo just follow me over in your car."

"That's right, I don't even know where you live."

He knows exactly what I want, she thought as she pulled out of the Liberty Bar parking lot.

They parked their cars side by side on the small square apron of asphalt in front of her trailer. Inside she said, "why don'tchoo sit down an I'll git us a beer." Carrying the beer cans, she felt safe. She had him on her own ground where no one could see them. The awkward silence of the bar flowed back in. She had rehearsed her lines all the way home in the car. Her only fear was that Washington wouldn't follow the script. He was looking into his beer can saying nothing.

"Do you ever think about that day you found my rings," Rae Ann went directly to the heart of all that had been unspoken between them since they had met in the parking lot.

Washington's head snapped up like it was on a string.

"I . . . I think of what we did that day all the time."

"So do I, oh, so do I." Her words came faster than she could breathe them. "I don't care if Ellie goes back with you. I don't want Ellie to go back with you. Ever since she told me, I've wanted this to happen."

Her body began to react. She was on him in the chair, her mouth crushing down on his. The flimsy stuffed chair couldn't hold them. It tipped over sideways spilling them on the floor. Smiles came as they relaxed in each other's arms.

"We always end up on the damn floor," Rae Ann whispered. "You're not in love with Ellie. You've just gotten used to her."

They rolled against each other, their legs twining.

"You could get used to me so easy. God, so easy, so easy."

"I've thought about . . . had dreams about . . . that day so many times," Washington picked her up gently. "Where'n the hell's the bedroom," he asked, moving directly toward it as if she had answered him.

I jumped on you like a frog on a Junebug, she would describe it later. And she thought of all those lonely nights spent making love to herself. *No more. No more. Not tonight.*

It was a quarter to seven when Ellie pulled into Rae Ann's trailer park. She was hoping that Rae Ann would feel like taking in a movie, something called *Rancho Deluxe* that a couple of girls in the shop had been talking about. She hadn't called. She just took for granted that Rae Ann would be home alone as always. Then she saw the truck parked in front of Rae Ann's trailer. She recognized it immediately.

That didn't take long, she thought as she slammed on her brakes. She didn't know whether she was happy or sad. She wanted free of Washington. She wanted out of Wabash City. But she hadn't thought Rae Ann would jump so quick. *Maybe they're just talkin.' Tryin' ta figure out how ta git me an Jimmy back together,* she speculated momentarily before envisioning what she knew was really going on.

Ellie went to the movie alone, had trouble laughing. Afterwards, she went back to Rae Ann's. Washington's car was still there.

"Oh well, easy come, easy go," she said aloud in the emptiness of her car as she jammed the accelerator to the floor. Baby Blue fantailed angrily out of the trailer park's driveway.

16 A Peerless Game

On the night of the twentieth of June, the All-American Homes soft-ball team stood one game behind the Peerless Truckers in the Wabash City Softball League standings. They had won six straight since the Dick and Tonna's game. But the real taste of winning, of building something solid and worthwhile, had faded since then. They won easily, beating inferior teams, and the numbers accumulated like junk in the win column. The Dick and Tonna's game had been something special. They all saw the Peerless game as the same kind of opportunity, their chance to escape the midseason doldrums.

Coming over the bridge with Martha and the kids in the car, seeing the lights of the ballpark, Bill hoped everything would fall back into place, come together like pieces in a trailer.

Ellie and Rae Ann sat in the stands by the first base dugout. They hadn't been to a game in two weeks. But Ellie hadn't been surprised when Rae Ann, professing a newfound interest in softball, suggested they go that evening.

Martha Franklin joined Rae Ann and Ellie in the official All-American Homes cheering section. She had met them once before, in the dark parking lot after one of the earlier games. She didn't think they'd remember her, though she recognized them immediately.

"I'm Martha Franklin," she reintroduced herself.

"Hey, you're Willy's wife. How are ya?" Ellie greeted her.

Martha almost flinched at Ellie's twang. She recovered herself timidly: "I haven't been coming to the games lately but Bill . . . I guess the men on the team call him Willy . . . said this was the most important game of the year . . ."

"Hey honey, evrybody calls him Willy," Ellie smiled.

" . . . Sooo, I just had to pack up the kids and bring them out to see their superstar father play ball."

Neither Ellie nor Rae Ann acknowledged Martha's sarcasm.

"Should be a pritty excitin' game," Rae Ann filled what was be-coming an awkward silence, "from all the guys tell me."

Guys, my butt, Ellie thought. *One guy you been talkin' to in bed.*

"Oops, there they go," Martha started up as the children ran away toward the playground behind the centerfield fence. "I better keep an eye on them. See you later." She smiled halfheartedly up at Ellie and Rae Ann as she trailed off after the children.

The Homes team loitered in the first base dugout waiting for Peer-less to finish so they could take some infield. Washington and Frank-lin waved up at Ellie and Rae Ann. Whitey cracked his knuckles.

Patrick and Unk lined the bats up along the inside wall of the dug-out. Devere scribbled on the lineup card. Stevenson sat there saying nothing. Gil Blass leaned on the low fence talking to a bounteous girl who looked Mexican or Puerto Rican or some similar species of Span-ish, a rarity in Wabash City. All of them, except Blass, watched the Peerless team take ground balls. Peerless had fancy pin-stripe uniforms like the ones Dick and Tonna's wore. The players' names were stitched across the shoulders.

"Hey, listen up," Devere caught the dugout's attention. "Be 'spe-cially careful o' the Hill brothers. Herman, the centerfielder, hits the ball 'bout as far as any human bein' in the world or anyplace else. Har-ley lives under the illusion he's a speed merchant. He'll take the extra base, head for second, no hesitation at all. I truly hope you git a chance to cut that prick down," Devere said, looking straight at Washington. "Hank Ford, the pitcher, s'got a lot o' arch but not much spin. Just stay back in the box an wait. Then there's the two major league assholes. Lee Ferrlock, the one with the funny hat an the moustache at first, pokes the ball out into right field. Ya never know what Jack Morgan's gonna do. Stumpy little retard kin hit the ball out or go ta right."

"Which one's Morgan," Bill nudged Washington.

"The catcher," Jimmy answered grinning, "built kinda like Devere, ain't he?"

But Devere ignored him. Devere was all business. "These ain't the New York Yankees," he growled. "They got no monoply on this league."

They took the field for infield practice. It had been the most elo-quent pep-talk Devere had given all season.

In the stands, Ellie turned to Rae Ann sarcastically, "well, there go the stars."

She sounds sorta like Willy's wife, Rae Ann thought.

Just then, Rae Ann and Ellie heard a voice.

"Excuse me, but I couldn't help overhearin' you talkin' ta that other girl with the kids . . ."

It wasn't the dark, foriegn-looking girl in the straining blouse sitting near the dugout. The voice came from above and behind them in the bleachers.

"Uh, do you know this team that's out there now," the girl continued.

She looked and sounded like someone just come out of hiding, cobwebby, not used to being outdoors among people. But she was a pretty girl in a subdued kind of way. She didn't have the natural, flowing looks of a Rae Ann nor the dark fire of an Ellie. She was pretty in a plain, nondescript sort of way. She was dressed up dumpy in a tee shirt that was too big and a pair of baggy, faded blue jeans. She wore no makeup at all. Her skin looked scrubbed as if she were trying to play herself down to avoid any kind of striking, eye-catching effect. Her mousy brown hair was clipped short almost like a boy's. She seemed tentative, as if not used to making small talk with strangers. She just seemed uncomfortable like someone just out of prison.

"Do we know this team?" Ellie answered, friendly-like. "Honey, we know too damn much about this team for anybody's good."

"They your husbands?"

"You kiddin,'" Ellie barked back. "No way I'd . . . we'd . . . we'd be married ta any o' those losers."

"My name's Rae Ann an this is Ellie an we work out at All-American Homes with all the guys that play on the team," Rae Ann answered her straight out, not grinding any axes like Ellie was.

"My name's Vicky Hickman," the plain girl smiled at Rae Ann. "I'm new in town an I was just drivin' around an I saw all the lights an I thought I'd see what was goin' on."

"You work here in Wabash City?" Ellie asked.

"I'm lookin' for a job now. Like I said, I just got here. All those boys work for All-American Homes? Maybe I oughta look for a job out there. What's All-American Homes anyway?"

"It's a big factory. They make mobile homes an pre-cut an module houses," Rae Ann answered.

"They'll make any damn kind a home they can sell," Ellie added. "I'm surprised they don't make pre-fab doghouses."

"An all those boys on that team work out there?" Vicky seemed to want to turn that fact over in her mind again. "Which ones o' them are married?"

Rae Ann looked sideways at Ellie.

"Which one you interested in?" Ellie answered.

"What about that one there, over by the dugout?"

"Oh, he's married," Ellie answered. "That was his wife here with the two kids a little while ago."

"What about the big guy out there in the outfield, catchin' the ball now, that one."

"Oh, that's Washington, he ain't taken," Ellie said sadistically, not looking at Rae Ann.

"I thought you were still datin' Jimmy," Rae Ann came back.

"Nope," Ellie spat.

I have been, Rae Ann thought smugly.

"What about that one catchin' the balls at home plate?"

"Devere?" Ellie almost choked.

"He's sorta cute."

"Sweetie, you think he's cute then you need an eye exam."

"She just doesn't git along that good with Devere," Rae Ann explained. "Anyway, he's married."

"Oh yeah, his wife here?" the new girl asked, looking around.

"Uh-uh. I've never seen her."

"Well, I'll tell you girls one thing," Vicki summed up, "your team's sure a lot better lookin' than that team o' plug-uglies they're playin.'"

All Ellie and Rae Ann could do was laugh as, just at that moment, Gaptooth and Porkpie (as they called them), A.K.A. Morgan and Ferrlock, trotted across in front of them on the way to the drinking fountain.

Devere won the coin toss and chose to be home team. They all knew they had to hold Peerless in the first inning. If Peerless got five, eight, ten runs ahead right away, the game would be over. Good hitters swing differently when their team is far behind.

Ferrlock led off and poked a single out into right field. Then Harley Hill hit a sharp ground ball through the hole between Franklin and Stevenson, but Jimmy Washington came in fast and held Ferrlock at second. A big inning seemed to be building. Herman Hill batted third. When he hit the ball, Whitey, head up and swivelling on the pitcher's mound, thought *Oh no! I threw him a three-run homer.* But,

Hank Patrick caught it up against the center field fence for the first out. The Porkpie and Harley Hill advanced to third and second on the throw in. One out, but still a big inning building. Jack Morgan walked to the plate grinning between the gap in his front teeth.

Whaddaya say, beerbelly," Morgan greeted Devere at the plate.

"How's ol' Carla? You still spendin' all yore money on that whore-lady down by the river?"

"How'dya liketa eat that Louisville slugger yore holdin' there," Devere spat back.

At third, Bill Franklin, trying to concentrate, was tight as a guitar string. He knew an error would start up that big inning. Morgan ran the count to three and two, fouling two balls hard over the third base dugout.

"You're dead Stumpy, you might even strike out in slowpitch," Devere ragged him from behind the plate.

"You watch," Morgan spat back viciously.

The count, *three and two, three and two, three and two,* kept echoing in Bill's mind at third. He turned over the endless possibilities, the metaphors, present in a three-two pitch: a strike-out, a home run, a ground ball into a double play, a walk. Anything, or nothing, could happen.

Gaptooth waited murderously for the pitch.

Bill crouched jumpy at third.

"SAAWING!" Devere screamed as the pitch arched in high.

Swing he did. Gaptooth hit the ball right on the button.

The line drive crackled like summer lightning. Bill had no chance to move. The ball shot off the bat and then he was squeezing it. The cracking report, like a gunshot, echoed, even with the ball already buried in his glove. He stood paralyzed by the sharp, quick violence he had just conquered. He felt as if he'd caught a bullet. For long seconds the searing memory of that line drive hung in the air, like a tracer, a premonition of violence to come.

Then Bill heard his teammates yelling. Harley Hill had taken off for third at the crack of the bat. But, when Bill unexpectedly caught the ball, Harley had to turn quick and hustle back. Instead, he fell down in the basepath. Bill lobbed the ball over to Blass to double him off. Hot-rod Harley threw his hat down in the infield dust and kicked it. Morgan muttered something obscene as he trotted back to the dugout to pick up his tools of ignorance.

Martha Franklin, sitting on a picnic table in the darkness just beyond the centerfield fence, keeping an eye on the children playing on
the swings, saw Bill's great play from a distance, jumped to her feet,
and yelled "NICE ONE!" But nobody heard her way out there. As
Willy jogged across the infield toward the dugout, he heard Rae Ann
and Ellie yelling "NICE CATCH WILLY, WAY TA GO!" Vaguely, he
wondered why Martha wasn't sitting with them.

In the dugout, he received the accolades of his teammates:

"Merry Christmas and Happy Birthday to you."

"You got your eyes open yet Skywatch?"

"Nice catch, Horseshoes!"

All-American Homes half of the inning went quietly enough. They
got one run on hits by Washington and Devere sandwiched around a
weak assortment of piddling ground balls and high harmless outfield
flies.

Peerless went out one-two-three in the top of the second on two
deep flies to Washington in left and a sharp grounder to Stevenson at
short that he could have thrown over to first underhanded it had come
out so fast.

In the home half of the second, they got two more runs. Whitey
surprised them all. With Unk and Zenger on base, he hit a line drive
between the center and right fielder that rolled clear to the fence. Everybody had to grin as he struggled around the bases with his beerbelly bouncing and his legs churning. They led three to nothing, their
confidence building, when Peerless came to bat in the top of the third.

The first hitter chopped a ground ball over second that Stevenson miraculously flagged somewhere out in the suburbs between the
infield and farm country. His off-balance throw beat the runner by
a step. One out. The next two men, the rock bottom of the Peerless
batting order, got on base, both with looping Texas leaguers. Ferrlock
tried to dump another one into right field but Zenger, surprising them
all, moved semi-quick, jumped into the air and knocked it down. He
threw to Whitey covering first base and beat the loping Porkpie by two
steps. Two out, but runners still on second and third. Harley Hill singled hard to left and one runner scored. The third base coach, smart
enough not to test Washington's arm, held the second runner up. Hot-
rod Harley, true to form, tried for second and made it sliding. Devere
called time-out and waddled out to the mound to talk to Whitey.
They decided to put Hammerin' Herman Hill on, loading the bases.

"C'mon, git us out o' the inning," Devere rode Morgan from behind the plate.

"You watch beerbelly!"

Morgan pulled the first pitch on a rising line right over third base. It landed fair, bounced high past Washington who was digging hard, and rolled all the way to the left field fence. All three runners scored and Morgan came chugging around third base, "inside-the-parker" written desperately all over his straining face. Washington's throw beat him by five steps to the plate. Devere blocked the plate gleefully, waiting to make the tag. But Morgan never even thought about sliding. He ran full speed, elbows up like a pulling guard, right into the braced and crouching Devere. The two stumpy bodies crumpled in a mushroom cloud of dust. The umpire had no idea what to call. The explosion obliterated everything, all reason, all rule. Home had been blown up.

Devere, on his feet first, never hesitated. He fired the ball as hard as he could at Morgan who was still on the ground. Then, he aimed a kick hard at Morgan's stomach . . . but missed.

Morgan came up swinging. He caught Devere on the shoulder, knocking him down, then jumped on him, swinging with both fists. Morgan certainly had one advantage; he didn't have to worry about his teeth getting messed up in the fight.

Bill ran in from third with the best intentions. He was going to be the peacemaker. He would break it up so the game could go on. Coming down the line toward the flailing heap of Devere and Morgan, Bill ran into Ferrlock who kicked him on the leg.

He kicked me, Bill thought in amazement. It all registered very slowly as Bill stumbled out of the way of the Porkpie's roundhouse swings. A punch grazed his shoulder and brought him to the conscious realization that he ought to think seriously about becoming the other half of a fistfight. He ducked the next punch. The joy of violence, prohibited by his English professor life, flamed up somewhere inside him. It was a good feeling when he hit Porkpie in the mouth and knocked him flat on his ass.

Then it seemed as if all of Wabash City was into the fight. Half were swinging, kicking, rolling in the dust while the other half futilely tried to break it up.

In the first base stands, Ellie and Rae Ann jumped to their feet when the fight erupted.

"Hey, you see what he did? Whattare they doin'?" Ellie shouted. "They can't do that."

Rae Ann clenched both hands into fists over her mouth and seemed to be shrinking, tightening her body in fear.

The brawl whirled like a sluggish ballet, slow, rhythmic, punches landing and taking off. Ferrlock flailed for a moment on top of Bill, but Washington, in like the cavalry from left field, pulled him off and threw him three yards and a cloud of dust down the third base line. Devere and Morgan rolled in the dust, clawing at each other. Whitey stood over them, trying to get in a shot without hitting his own man.

Ellie and Rae Ann jumped down from the bleachers to stand against the low fence that closed off the field.

"Stop it Jimmy! Stop it! Break it up!" Rae Ann found herself yelling. It all reminded her of Wes.

"Hit 'im Devere! Hit 'im again Willy!" Ellie screamed. She remembered how much she had wished she was a man when that guy hit her in the bar.

"Wow, does this happen often?" the new girl, Vicki, standing next to Ellie and Rae Ann, asked.

Then suddenly it was over. The dust settled. The main combatants—Devere, Willy Franklin, and Whitey who had finally found someone to hit in the form of big Herman Hill—being held apart and dragged toward the dugouts by their teammates though still firing curses at the enemy across the infield.

"This game's over . . . cancelled," the umpire yelled, running for his car.

"Man, you can't do that. We're ahead," Gaptooth, forgetting the fight, screamed from the Peerless side.

"Man, git back here. You can't stop a game right in the middle," Devere wailed.

But the umpire, already in his car, the doors locked, the windows rolled up, was hearing none of it. Gaptooth, on foot, a bat in his hand, chased the umpire's fleeing car all the way to the road.

"We'll play you pricks again," Devere yelled over at the Peerless dugout.

Then the police car arrived and everyone left, grumbling. On the way across the parking lot, a cop asked Devere what happened. "I dunno. I missed it all," Devere answered, a dark bruise blueing up on his cheek.

Martha Franklin watched the fight from a distance, perched on her picnic table out behind center field. She saw her husband run right to the center of the action. While it was still going on, she gathered up her children and started in, shielding them like mothers do.

"D'jew see Willy hit that guy!" Ellie greeted Martha gleefully, caught up in the bloodlust.

Ellie's attitude, Ellie's calling her husband "Willy" again, offended Martha, set her off. "I think it's disgusting. They all ought to grow up for a change."

Bitch, Ellie thought.

"Hey honey, that fight ain't nothin' compared ta some I've seen," Vicki answered instead, endearing herself forever to Ellie who wanted someone in some way to tell Martha how stuck-up she sounded. "Men gotta have somethin' like a good fight evry once in a while ta let off all that bottled-up steam they got inside em."

In the car, Martha started right in on Bill: "Why did he have to hit that guy and start a big fight? Why? You can't tell me why."

"The bastard barreled him at the plate. It's a question of property rights."

"Property rights? For God's sake!"

What the hell's she so upset about, Bill thought, the pain still dull up and down his leg. He felt blood caking over his left eye.

"Why did you have to jump right in? That man you hit could sue us for everything we have, take the house away. He could charge you with assault."

"You see, I told ya it had ta do with property rights. I shoulda killed him, then he couldn't sue us."

Martha glared at him: "You didn't have to jump that man. You could have tried to break up the others."

"My God," Bill's voice flared, "he kicked me in the leg!"

"How can you be friendly with animals like that?"

"They're not animals. They're good people."

"Thugs."

"Will you git off it."

"God, look at your eye."

"It doesn't hurt a bit."

"You act like you're proud of it."

"Maybe I am."

"Bill, for God's sake, you're thirty-two years old. You've got a Ph.D. What are you doing getting in a brawl over something as stupid as baseball?"

"The whole team was in on it. I couldn't just stand there."

"If the whole team jumped off a bridge, I suppose you would too?"

"Probably. Why not?"

"It's so stupid. Children fight, not grown men."

"Why can't grown men be like children?"

"This is ridiculous. I can't talk to you."

"Then don't."

"This is crazy. Look, why don't you quit, the factory, the job, the team, the whole thing. We can make it through the rest of the summer on what you've made already."

"The season's only half over."

They pulled up the driveway and the kids scrambled out of the car toward the backyard swingset.

"I'm goin' out an have a few beers with the team," Willy said, not moving from behind the wheel.

"I knew you would. You never stay home anymore."

"Why the hell should I? Just ta watch you go ta sleep on the couch?" He left her standing alone in the driveway.

Most of the team was in the bar: Washington and Unk and Whitey and Adams and Patrick, Rae Ann and Ellie and a new girl all sitting around three tables pushed together.

"Hey Willy," came a chorus when he wandered in. "Hey Willy, how'd ya like that game?"

"Will ya look at that eye! I love it."

"Take no prisoners," Willy grinned as he dropped into an empty chair and reached for a beer glass. "You turkeys don't do that very often do ya? I hurt all over."

"Hey, you tore up on Ferrlock, Willy," Washington grinned from over next to Rae Ann.

That's strange, Bill thought. Ellie was sitting next to the new girl on the end down by Devere.

Devere was transfigured, almost human, laughing, smiling, having the best time of his life.

It must take a good violent evening to really make Devere feel good, Bill thought.

"Man, best fight we ever had durin' a game," Devere actually smiled.

Willy turned to Washington: "Man it felt good hittin' that jerk."

"Don't it though. Especially that Ferrlock. Nobody I'd rather see git knocked on his ass."

"Yeah, well thanks for pullin' him offa ma afterwards."

"Hey, don't thank me for that. Devere calls me his bodyguard. Evry time he gits in trouble inna bar, I gotta pull 'im out."

Everyone laughed except Rae Ann.

"Hey Willy, this here's Vicki Hickman," Devere made a loud formal introduction. "She has deeeeclared herself a new found fan of the magnificent All-American Homes softballers."

Vicki fit right in and seemed already to have been taken under Devere's wing. They bent to talk to each other as Bill settled back for his first breath since coming in. He panned around the table. Washington and Rae Ann were listening to Whitey's and Unk's and Patrick's stories out of All-American Homes's shadowy past. Ellie was drinking, looking on, but didn't seem tied to any single segment of the group.

"You 'member that time they had that golf outin' for everybody in the place."

"Yeah, the execatives 'cided they're gonna invite us lowlifes out ta play at their country club."

"Ya shoulda seen us. We loaded them golf carts up with beer an started down the first fairway like it was the Firecracker 400. You 'member that hill by the first tee? We came down that thing like Donny Allison an Richard Petty on the back straight."

"Lemme tell 'em 'bout Unk."

"OK. OK."

"The time we played nine holes we're all so drunk we don't care 'bout nothin.' Well the tenth tee's right behind the clubhouse. The restaurant, with all them tables outside like in France, sits right up there above it an ya gotta hit your tee shot over a lake ta the fairway. Unk hits three straight balls right in the damn lake. He's cussin' evry one o' em. All these rich ladies are up there eatin' away tryin' ta pretend they don't hear nothin.' An Unk is really pissed."

"An really hammered." Willy looked over at Ellie who seemed perfectly still and alone. She could have been listening to the golfing story on one side or to Devere and Vicki talking on the other. He pulled his eyes away before she could catch him spying.

"Yeah, we were all drunk. Anyway, Unk yells I HATE THIS GAME at the top o' his voice an gits all the ladies up in the peanut gallry chokin' on their watercress, then he jumps in one o' the carts an drives it full speed inta the lake, clubs, beer an all."

"Ya never saw three guys laugh so hard. I thought Washington was gonna fall in the lake with me just from laughin.'"

Willy looked at Ellie again. This time she caught him. She grinned ever so slightly into his face.

"Ya know what those morons were yellin' when I came up from underwater. They're yellin' GIT THE BEER, GIT THE BEER. I hadda dive for three sixpacks 'fore they'd let me outa the lake."

Ellie looked right at Willy almost as if she was trying to look through him, as if she was trying to look inside and see what he was thinking. Then she gave him that little twitch of a smile again and, startling him, winked.

Whitey galloped off on another story: "You 'member when we went ta see Eddie Feigner?"

"Eddie Faner?" Washington didn't remember at all.

"The King and his Court."

Washington remembered immediately.

"Who's the King and his Court?" Bill asked.

They looked at him in disgust.

"Only the best softball team ever ta play the game. There's four guys, an they play reglar ten-man teams."

"An kill em evry time."

"Eddie Feigner pitches from center field, fast pitch, an hardly anybody ever hits the ball."

"They had a first baseman covered that whole side o' the infield."

Ellie got up and went to the rest room. When she came back, she sat down in the empty chair next to Willy.

Another story spun out over the table.

When Ellie looked up, Washington, pretending to be listening to Whitey, was looking directly at her.

"Boy, that eye is startin' ta swell on ya," Ellie said to Willy, gently touching his temple just above what was becoming a major league shiner. "C'mon, I'll clean it up a little bit. Hey Jimmy," she yelled across the table, "ya still got that bandage kit in yore car?"

Washington flipped her the car keys. She caught them familiarly, as if she'd caught them many times before.

"Woo Woo," everybody whistled and crooned as they got up.

"She's gonna fix my eye," Bill explained lamely.

Outside, Ellie sat him on the hood of Washington's car and got the first-aid kit from under the front seat.

"How come you're not sittin' with Jimmy tonight," Bill asked as she worked on him with a piece of cotton.

"We're done. He was gittin' too serious."

"He's sittin' with Rae Ann."

"How perceptive of you to notice," she mocked. "Musta been love at first sight."

"Sorry. I was just wondering. Whoa, what is that stuff? It burns like hell."

"Merthiolate. Hold still," and then she was putting a butterfly ban-daid on the small cut she'd washed out above his eye.

"C'mon, let's go back in. They'll all be wonderin' what we been doin' out here so long," she ended with another twitchy wink.

Back inside, the stories spun. They drank and talked, weaving the fabric of friendship until two-thirty in the morning.

Washington drove off alone.

Rae Ann took Ellie home on the way.

Devere and Vicki Hickman drove off in the same direction in sepa-rate cars.

Bill headed the VW in the opposite direction from the rest, up over the bridge toward West Wabash. It was a clear night, the sky spangled with stars bicentennially. In the bar it had felt as if they were all to-gether. Even Devere had been congenial. And then there had been Ellie?

17 True Confessions

"Why on a Wednesday night? I got a game at nine."

Martha loaded the whole family in the car and pointed them toward Saint Thomas Catholic Church at six-thirty on a Wednesday night.

"The last game is just the reason you should go to confession."

"But on a Wednesday night?" Bill moaned. "I don't even get that excited about goin' there on Sundays."

"Communal confession is something new."

"Confession? New? Confession ruined my whole childhood."

They sat silent as he drove. It lasted two blissful blocks.

"Ya know, I don't wanna go to confession. I haven't gone to confession for five years. What am I gonna say? Why don't I just wait in the car?"

"You don't have anything to tell. God, that's priceless."

Martha had been yelling all week about the fight. Sunday afternoon during the Cubs game on television, she had started back in on him: "Why'd you hafta get into it? I couldn't believe it when I saw you."

"It was just something that happened. I had to get into it."

"Had to! Had to!"

Here she goes, Bill thought,

"Yeah, had to! No way you can understand that is there?"

"No, to tell you the truth. What if your son would have seen you acting that way?"

"What if he had! He's gonna hafta fight sometime."

"We didn't buy him guns to play with because we felt they fostered violence. We never let him watch violent shows or cartoons on television, then his own . . ."

"YOU didn't! YOU didn't! Not me. YOU! YOU!"

The church parking lot loomed up in front of them. He knew the fight, still festering in Martha's mind, was the reason she had dragged them all off to this communal confession nonsense.

"I guess I'm supposed to confess about the fight, huh hon?" he taunted her. "Bless me father for I have sinned. I punched a Peerless trucker."

Inside, it was relatively quiet until the priest did some biblical readings, paused briefly, then began to wheeze like an air-conditioner.

"God loves us all no matter how far astray we have wandered, no matter what evil we contemplate or commit, no matter . . ." the priest droned on. The church got hotter and muggier.

"Now let us turn to the person next to us and . . ." the air-conditioner whirred benignly.

"Shaking hands with your wife is stupid," Bill whispered as he shook hands with Martha.

"It's the kiss of peace."

"At the kiss of peace," Bill whispered to spite her, "every guy in this church oughta give the girl next to him a good feel."

"You're vulgar," she shrank from him as from a leper, "that's from working in that factory."

"Well, I suppose we could eat all the pages out o' my books this summer."

Bill's thoughts trailed off into gourmetic visions of Moby Dick Bourguignon, The American en Brocette, Crepes Gatsby or Huckleberry Finnan Haddie, Country Fried Dickens, Sartre on a Shingle.

The priest moved slowly, flicking his microphone cord out behind like a singer on the move in a Las Vegas showroom: "Each of you, if you wish, may now enter one of the confessionals and quickly tell one sin. Absolution will be personally dispensed."

They got up to join the lines. Martha explained it to the children.

As he waited, Bill tried to choose the one sin he wanted to admit. Impure thoughts would be good, his coed fantasies. Fighting, that would make Martha happy. Coveting my neighbor's mistress, he thought of Ellie. Then it was his turn and he still hadn't decided.

Inside the confessional, he was tongue-tied. It had been years. He didn't know whether they still did it the same way.

"Just tell me your sin," a whispering voice cajoled.

"I'm unhappy," Bill confessed.

"What are you unhappy about?" the voice asked, sounding cautious as if it wondered if Bill was joking.

"I thought you were only allowed one sin," Bill snapped back on pure reflex.

"But being unhappy isn't even a sin," the voice said.

In the car driving home, all quiet on the religious front, Bill didn't feel much better. He dropped them all off, put on his game shirt, picked up his glove and spikes, and headed for the ballpark. Pulling out of the driveway he started feeling better, transubstantiated, as if escaping the house, the church, for the green world between the white lines could change everything.

They won the game easily and went drinking afterwards. Ellie and Rae Ann weren't there but Vicki Hickman appeared and sat next to Devere at the table in the bar. When Bill got home at one in the morning, Martha was waiting.

"You're still awake," Bill, drunk, observed.

Martha turned on the bedside light. She was crying.

Her tears angered him. *I'm never gonna git to sleep now.*

"OK. So what's wrong?" he went right on the offensive.

"Oh Bill, I don't feel well. It's no good."

"Whaddaya mean?"

"I mean. I physically don't feel well."

Bill sank back into the pillow. The mattress, as old as their marriage, sagged under his weight. All he wanted to do was sleep, not listen to her problems.

"My stomach has hurt for a week. Things are all wrong between us. I just know it. We never talk anymore."

Bill realized that Martha was giving a speech she'd carefully rehearsed. His beer-dulled mind tried to follow it.

"We've gotta do something," she continued. "This is not a marriage. I can't take it anymore."

"How are we supposed ta have a marriage when you fall asleep on the couch evry night?"

She recoiled as if she'd been slapped hard in the face.

"I know it's partly my fault."

Partly! God why doesn't she let me go to sleep.

"But I'm gonna change things. I'm gonna start staying awake to watch TV with you and listen to music and we can drink beer together here at home. I'm gonna start crocheting afghans for Christmas presents and that'll keep my hands busy and keep me awake . . ."

Great, it'll be like watching TV with Madame DeFarge.

"Where are you getting all these ideas," Bill tried to divert her from the despair she seemed to have worked herself into.

"I've been thinking of a lot of things lately when you're not here, when you're working or playing softball or sitting in your bar drinking beer. We just don't seem to look forward to seeing each other any more. Maybe that's what being married ten years does."

"C'mon now hon, whaddaya talkin' about, that's not true," he tried to cajole her out of her despair and fear, her truth.

"I think we should go to a marriage counselor, to save our marriage."

"Save our marriage! You sound like it's goin' down for the third time."

"Bill. Hear me out. I think we should get away from each other for a while. Give ourselves both a chance to think about things."

"What are you talkin' about?" he was suddenly sober. "You're not talkin' about a separation, are you?"

"God no," Martha shuddered. "I thought I'd take up my parents' offer to use the cottage. They keep supplies, wood for the stove, toilet paper, all kinds of stuff in there year round."

"You wanna go way the hell up on some godforsaken lake in Michigan just because I haven't told ya how much I love ya for a coupla days?"

"You haven't told me you love me all summer. You haven't talked civilly to me for a week. I just think it's the thing to do. The kids, especially Danny, will love it. We'll stay up there a couple weeks. It'll give us both a chance to think things out."

"This is stupid. I'm goin' to sleep. We'll straighten all this out in the morning." He didn't know what else to say. She had surprised him. His head wasn't clear enough to cope with it all.

In the morning nothing had changed.

"We both need a break from marriage," she said.

"How long'll you be gone," Bill finally gave in.

"I dunno. Two weeks?" a note of uncertainty crept into her voice, as if she hadn't expected her plan to be approved. "After a while I'll call and we can talk."

"I really think this is nuts ya know," he got in one last dig.

Martha made preparations as if she and the children were going off on a crusade.

He's gonna miss us so much he'll be begging me to come back, Martha hoped as she drove away.

I think I'll have a beer, Bill thought, going back into the house. He looked at his watch. Eight A.M. Just time for one before I go to work.

18 A Whole New Ballgame

Devere and Vicki had been sleeping together since the night of the Peerless game.

When the bar closed and everyone else headed for home, Vicki asked him innocently enough: "I'm still thirsty. Anywhere ya can still git a beer this time o' night?"

"Only place you're gonna git a beer is outa a friendly icebox," Devere answered.

"I'm new here. This town really close down that tight?"

"Better bleeve it. I could use another beer myself."

"Well then, if you want another beer an I want another beer an I got a six-pack left in my fridgerator, I think, why don't we just go back ta my place an have another beer."

"Jesus lady, it's two-thirty in the morning."

"So what?"

"You're right."

The bulky pickup lumbered obediently along behind her little Volkswagen and stopped in front of a large three-story house on an old street just off the downtown business area.

"There must be six or eight apartments in this place," she whispered as they went through the front door. "I got one room an a coupla closets on the ground floor."

Her apartment was just as she'd described it, only the closets were the kitchen and the bathroom. Inside, it was as if she didn't have time for the usual amenities of courting. She sat Devere down on the couch, turned on the TV as if by some unconscious necessary reflex, found a Tugboat Annie movie, and went to get him a beer.

"COORS? Where'djew get these? You can't buy these in Wabash City," Devere reached for the can greedily.

"I just came in from out west. This is the last six-pack."

"At's a good beer," he said as she sat down on the couch next to him.

"Let's go to bed. We can finish these later," she whispered in his ear.

"I'm married ya know." Devere didn't state it out of any impulse to confession or noble aspiration toward candor or honesty in their relationship. His words were merely precautionary so she would know there wasn't ever going to be any relationship.

"Evrybody's married sometime or other," she answered cooly, shooing him off the couch so she could pull it out into a bed.

When Devere got home at four-thirty in the morning, Molly was asleep. He felt a little guilty. He'd never cheated on her before, except for Carla. But Carla was different, non-competitive, pro-ball rather than sandlot. He climbed into bed and snored off.

When he limped out of the shower the next morning, Molly was more interested in his bruised legs and chest and the puffy mouse that had come up like a blue-brown prune under his left eye than in what time he'd come in.

Two nights later, on Monday, Devere told Molly he had to go down to the bowling alley to help with the scheduling for the Fall league.

"It may take awhile," he told her in his best regretful voice, "so you don't hafta wait up."

His escape made, he drove straight to Vicki's. They made love slowly, and came together right on the button, surprising themselves. Afterwards, they talked a bit. Vicki told him that she'd grown up in Utah on a farm on the edge of the desert and went to college for a year in Las Vegas before deciding to head east in steps. Flagstaff. Gallup. Tulsa. St. Louis. Devere didn't understand much of it even though he listened patiently. "Hey, I gotta git home," was his contribution to the conversation as he pulled on his pants.

All-American Homes had a ballgame on Wednesday. Vicki hadn't been at the game but she showed up at the bar about eleven-thirty. At her apartment later, she and Devere tried to make it last as long as they could.

In Molly's bed, Devere couldn't sleep. In spite of his hard shell, Vicki was starting to get to him. She was so different. To Devere, she seemed like a dream, as if she had just appeared out of nowhere. But he wasn't about to start asking questions.

Molly might have asked some questions but she rarely thought about Devere. She was feeling better, tighter. She was sleeping better at night. After turning down the job at the truck terminal, she hadn't stopped looking for a way out of the house. She jogged in the park on sunny clear mornings, ran on the grass in her bare feet.

She followed the same route on her jog each day. Parking the car on the street, she would start out slowly, padding along the chainlink fencing of the baseball stadium where a proud red, white and blue banner proclaimed HOME OF THE 1976 COLT WORLD SERIES. Circling the always becalmed green duck pond, she would search for the one with the blue head, smooth as a Queen's gown, she called "National Velvet." Weaving through the tiny amusement park and the playground, she dreamed of when the girls were little and begged her to push them on the swings, pleaded for nickels to ride the merry-go-round. Around the big swimming pool where toddlers waded and mothers in two-piece suits read paperback novels on beach towels on the grass, she picked up the pace. She floated past the tennis courts where the four women, in jeans and tee shirts, their children sitting by the side or running across the court, played a laughing game almost every morning, hitting balls wildly every which way. She always waved as she went by, though she didn't know them.

Other than her jogging, Molly's routine had stayed much the same. She cleaned the house, read books from the supermarket, did Devere's laundry. She may have noticed that Devere was acting strange, but she didn't pay any attention. With the softball season getting on and him having to attend to other things that seemed to keep cropping up in the evenings, she didn't see that much of him. When he was home, he actually seemed pretty considerate. One night when they couldn't find anything good on TV he even asked her to play gin rummy. It didn't take much to make Molly feel needed.

19 Neon Feelings in Martha's House

Martha left on a Friday morning, the 29th of June. All-American Homes played that night. They won by fourteen runs in five innings over the team that had beaten them in the mud the first game of the season. After the game, Rae Ann and Washington never showed up at the bar. Unk came and went quickly, complaining "my ol' lady's been bitchin' 'bout evrythin' lately." Devere drank steadily for awhile but when Vicki wandered in about midnight, the two of them threw down a quick beer and left.

"The lovers," Ellie remarked in a jaundiced tone of voice, nodding toward the exiting Devere and Vicki.

Bill was the only one left to hear the remark. He tipped his glass to the gone couple and said, "different strokes."

And so it happened. They came together like one of those pre-cut, pre-fab houses where all the pieces fit. Ellie and Bill were just left alone. As soon as it happened, the idea of adultery pulsed neon in Bill's nerve-endings. Other impulses—guilt, fear—tiptoed like shadows through the back alleys of his mind.

"Don't you hafta go home to wifey too?" Ellie teased.

"Not tonight," Bill answered, "tonight I drink alone as long as I want."

"What about me?"

"Oh, I didn't mean for you to go. I mean . . . all I meant was that I'm gonna stay even if evrybody goes home. I don't hafta go home. I got nothin' to go home to."

Ellie was wary. She was afraid he was about to launch into one of those "my wife doesn't understand me" eulogies for a dead marriage. But his face, his voice, didn't seem maudlin. Rather, he sounded excited as well as a little puzzled.

"Ya mind if I drink with ya for a while then?"

"I'd love it. Why don't we grab one o' those booths. It'd be more comfortable."

"Hey. You really wanna git drunk? Why don't we go git somethin' ta eat? A sandwich?"

"OK. It's a date. I'll take you out to eat."

"What'll your wife say?" Ellie teased.

"She's two states away in the middle of nowhere for reasons still a mystery to me."

"That's nice," Ellie said offhandedly. "C'mon, we'll go over ta Rickey's Drive-In in Baby Blue. We can eat in the car. OK?"

"Fine. I git ta buy. OK?"

"Deal. let's go."

In the car at the drive-in, despite the open windows and continuous hissing and crackling of the bug-burning machine, silence hung awkwardly in the air between them. The food finished, they hung suspended in a "what next?" state. They both wanted exactly the same thing, to heed the pulse of their neon feelings.

Ellie didn't say a word.

Her silence terrified Bill.

"Would you liketa come over ta my house for a drink?" he heard himself say.

"I'd love to," Ellie exploded in a blazing neon smile. "I thought you'd never ask."

"You better let me pick up my car at The Pub on the way," he said as she pulled Baby Blue out of the drive-in parking lot.

She parked on the street in front of Martha's house while Bill pulled up the driveway to the back. She met him at the back door.

Inside, his first concern was that all the drapes were pulled, then he got two beers and carried them out to the living room.

She prowled the house, exploring.

He caught her looking into the hall closet.

"This is really a nice place," she said.

He pulled out records and placed them gingerly on the automatic changer.

Ellie seemed stunned by the bookcase. She stood anchored in front of it, her eyes running back and forth over the gaudy dust jackets. She had something in her hands that she played with nervously. "You read all these books?" she asked.

"Most of them."

"It'd take me a hundred years ta read all those books."

The music came on. Rita Coolidge. He turned out the light. A small table-lamp in the hall sent a weak, shadowy glow into the dark room. All the rest was soft darkness.

"I always listen to music in the dark," he explained self-consciously, as if asking for her approval. "I think you can hear it better that way, think better."

"It's nice here," she answered, sitting down on the floor, the dim glow from the hall lamp sending shadows playing over her blue-denim shirt. He sat down facing her. They looked like two Indians ready to pow-wow.

"What have you got there?" he asked, pointing toward her hands.

"Oh," she seemed startled, realizing for the first time that she had something in her hands. "I must have picked them up. It's a deck o' cards."

"The kids must have been playing with them in here."

The "what next?" silence descended again.

"Wanna play cards?"

"What?" he almost choked on the beer in his mouth.

"Cards. Wanna play? I know blackjack."

"Ok," he said warily, wondering if she was thinking the same thing he was thinking.

"Whattaya wanna play for?" her teasing tone returned.

"We gotta play for something?"

"Sure, ya always gotta play cards for somethin.'"

He didn't have any audible ideas.

"I'll play ya for your clothes," she decided.

"You kiddin'? Strip blackjack?" he asked, laughing nervously.

It's all a game anyway, he thought. *It has to happen sooner or later somehow.*

"Yeah, you chicken?" her teasing voice challenged him.

"Deal."

"He got a Queen up and a six down. "I'm good," he said.

"Whatduz that mean?" she asked puzzled.

"That means I don't want any more cards.'

This is gonna be a dream come true, he thought, visions of stripping her naked in—quickly he calculated the number of articles of clothing she had on, the panties being pure speculation—about seven hands.

"You sure ya know how to play the game?"

"Sure," she growled, hitting a five with a four then turning up the ten she had down. "Nineteen."

"Luck," he grumbled, flipping over his six.

"I think I'll take off my shoes an git more comfortable," she said, working on the laces of her sneakers.

"I thought the loser was supposed ta take something off?"

"Winner calls the shots, I said."

He got a three up and a jack down. "Hit it," he ordered, looking at her seven showing.

"That mean you want a card?"

"That's what it means."

She busted him with another jack.

"Whaddid you have?" he asked out of curiousity.

She had a six down.

"Shit," he said out loud.

She would have hit it too, he thought.

"OK. What next?"

"I think I'll take off my socks. I'd feel much better barefoot," she teased, stripping them off.

"You're throwing the whole game, aren't you?"

"We'll see."

She dealt him an eight up. She had a King showing.

He flipped a look at his down card. It was a nine. "I'm good," he said.

"I certainly hope so," she said giggling. "Whaddaya got?"

"Seventeen."

"Twenty," she laughed, flipping over a Queen. "Why don't you just take off your shoes."

He got a four up and a three down. She had a seven showing. She hit him with a seven, then busted him with an eight.

"OK. The socks. Now we're even. I wouldn't wanna take advantage of you."

"Does a blackjack pay double?" he asked.

"Does it usually?"

"Uh-huh."

"OK. Fine. Blackjack pays double."

She dealt him a jack of diamonds up. She had a deuce showing. His hole card was a six.

She hit the deuce with a nine, then a three, and flipped over the six she had down. "Twenty, can you beat that?"

"Are you kiddin'? You oughta go to Vegas," he said, wondering if he was ever going to win a hand.

"OK. I'll take the shirt next," she ordered.

It had all been very cute and coy so far, but she had him down to his pants and jock. He decided to get serious and beat her, strip her.

He got a nine up and an eight underneath and stuck.

She hit a seven with a ten and busted herself.

"Now you get some of your own medicine," he grinned sadistically, feeling the taste of winning for the first time., "the blouse, unbutton it from the top."

She undid the buttons slowly. She had no bra on. Her breasts folded out like two flowers blooming as she peeled the front petals of her blouse back over her shoulders. Her nipples stood out tight and hard as if they were straining toward him. The soft light from the hall played elusive shadows over her firm breasts.

You like them Willy? she thought.

He realized he was sitting there with his mouth open.

She dealt another hand, utterly unconcerned that she was now topless.

He had a King and a nine. He hoped she didn't have any panties on under her Levi's

She dealt herself the Ace of Spades up. It glared at him, black and phallic.

No way, Bill thought. "I'm good," he declared.

She turned over the black Jack of Spades she had underneath.

"Blackjack pays double," she reminded him, "that makes me the winner."

Bill was stunned. He'd lost.

"Ya know, I could strip ya naked. The winner in a strip blackjack game can do anything she wants with the loser. It's like slavery. I could order you ta do anythin.'"

"Where'd you git those rules?"

"I'm the winner. I just made 'em."

"OK You're the winner. What do you want me to do?" He knew he couldn't lose.

"Kiss me on the mouth Willy, before ya do anythin' else." She said it in a quiet, almost pleading voice, not the voice of a winner at all.

Bill did what she asked.

They woke up on Saturday curled naked in each other's arms on Martha's living room couch. Breakfast was cold milk and three-day-old store-bought donuts that he found in Martha's breadbox. While Ellie ate, he picked up the playing cards that were scattered all over the living room. They were all stuck together.

"Dumb Bicentennial cards," he grumbled. "I'm glad they're ruined. They've got red, white and blue Minutemen on them."

She started to giggle. "That's appropriate."

They made love again in Martha's big double bed upstairs.

Saturday afternoon dove and stretched and dozed languidly along. They swam in the pool at Ellie's apartment complex. Changing in her apartment, she stood naked and suntanned in front of him. She hesitated for a slow moment, for effect, before stepping into her two-piece bathing suit. Her suntan was like a bright light pulsing through fragile gauze curtains. The layered, changing browns of her tanned body served only as a background, a frame to the striking neon whiteness of her breasts, the flashing white V between her thighs. Lying next to Ellie in the sun on a fibrous nylon chaise-lounge, he watched the suntans move by. As he hung in the twilight world between waking and dreaming where reality blurs and dances, a suntan in a sheer lime-green bikini suddenly stopped beside him. His eyes were slowly working their way up when a disembodied voice from somewhere above that glorious hovering suntan suddenly snapped him awake.

"Why . . . hi Professor Franklin," the voice above the suntanned skin sang.

His head snapped up to the girl's face as if she had yanked him out of a trance. "Oh, hi there," he said stupidly.

Ellie started to giggle behind him.

"Do you remember me? I'm Heather. I was in your class last spring, the one where we read all those long novels."

"Yes . . . of course," he answered, trying to remember if he'd given her a B or a D, an A or a C.

Ellie sounded like she was coughing huskily. He knew she was merely camouflaging laughter.

"Well, it certainly is a beautiful day for sunbathing," he said awkwardly.

"Sure is," Heather trilled, "nice ta see ya."

Ellie's giggling was just starting to subside: "Oh hello Professor Franklin," she mimicked. "I'm Heather. You know, the one who gits A's for comin' ta your office for private conferences evry Wednesday afternoon."

"OK. OK."

"Sooooo nice ta see ya, Professor Franklin sir. Havin' a nice day by the pool with your girlfriend?"

"Will you stop it. Is that all that lives in this place is students? They're evrywhere."

"They're so boring. College boys keep comin' over whenever I'm lyin' in the sun. 'Hi, my name's Bruce. Do you live here in the Apartments?' They always say that, evry single one. Then when I tell em ta go away, they git these poor little hangdog hurt looks like I stole their last piece o' candy or somethin.'"

That Sunday, Ellie got out of Martha's bed and promised to cook Bill the best Sunday dinner he had ever eaten. They ate facing each other like two jaded debauchees out of one of Bill's thick eighteenth-century novels. After dinner, they sipped crème de menthe and Ellie fell asleep on the couch

When Bill got home after work Thursday afternoon, a letter waited:

> Hi Hon, it began tentatively, I miss you and I hope
> you miss me.

Small prickles of guilt tightened his mouth momentarily. He thought of Ellie who was meeting him at their game that night. It was the third of July; nobody had to work the next day or the weekend. He almost crumbled Martha's letter up without reading on:

> The children just love it here. Danny said he wanted
> to stay here forever.
>   We get up early and fish off the dock or go for a hike
> around the point or pick blueberries out in the woods.
> I usually sunbathe while the children play in the water.
> Monday they fell asleep on their beach towels and I
> went up around the point. I took my bathing suit off
> and laid on the grass by the lake without a stitch on for
> almost a half hour. It really felt good. I kept wondering
> if anyone would come along and catch me.

That ought to turn him on, Martha had hoped when she wrote it. *He'll be panting for me when I go back.*

She never did that, Bill doubted. Martha's letter conjured images of Ellie stepping out of her bikini in her apartment on Saturday afternoon.

20 July 4, 1976: A Midnight Ride With Don Devere

On the eve of America's 200th Birthday, on the evening of July third, All-American Homes played Dick and Tonna's bar in a late game. From five-thirty on when the earliest games started, the ballparks, playgrounds and parking lots were like a festival. Everyone was sampling the sweet freedom of the just-begun four-day holiday weekend. Children clamored around the concession stand. The players in their gaudy gameshirts galloped and slid and dove out on the diamond. Everyone felt joyful and free from the factories, the grain elevators, the garages, the bars, banks, drugstores and insurance offices for four long days. Waiting teams drank beer off the backs of rusty, flag-decaled pickups. About eight-thirty, early for her, Carla's black car glided slowly through the parking lot and down to the riverside. Many of her best customers, playing catch or drinking beer, smiled knowingly to themselves as she shimmered by like black velvet.

Bill got to the ballpark at nine-thirty, more than an hour before their game was supposed to start. Most of the team was there ahead of him.

"What are you guys doin' here so early?" Bill asked as he took the beer Jimmy Washington handed him.

"We got four days off," Devere answered for Washington, "four days away from our beloved All-American Homes. "

"Yeah, I was havin' trouble sittin' home too," Bill agreed.

Ellie and Rae Ann sat together on the hood of Washington's car sipping beers. Unk, Whitey and Patrick lolled on the grass. Zenger, Blass and Stevenson played pepper nearby. Around Devere's pickup, it was like a family picnic.

All-American Homes took the field feeling loose and confident.

Ellie and Rae Ann sat together in the stands, good friends again. Around eleven-fifteen, about halfway through the game, Vicki joined them.

It wasn't nearly as good a game as the first one with Dick and Tonna's. All-American Homes won 10–7 in the full seven innings. It was a well-played game, but when the Homes team needed a hit someone always got it or when the Homes team needed an out someone always made the play.

In the fifth, Willy "Skywatch" broke his nose on a ground ball hit sharply right at him, the kind he had been flinching on early in the season. He was looking it right into his glove when it hit a rock and jumped high into the middle of his face. Stevenson picked up the spinning ricochet and threw Big Eddie Burke out by two feet. Bill toppled like he'd been hit by an ax. When he came out of it about five seconds later, they were standing over him wondering.

"You OK, Willy?" Washington was just a blur above him.

"Yeah, I think so. Wha happened?"

"Bad hop."

"Man, you oughta see your face," Devere chortled. "You're gonna have a matched set o' major league shiners."

"Just so I don't hafta go through life lookin' like you," Bill tried to joke. It hurt to talk. His whole face burned. He tasted blood dripping down into his mouth.

He sat out the last two hitters that inning—the team played defense with only nine men—but he was scheduled to lead off the bottom of the fifth. Ellie was standing by the fence looking anxiously toward him when he walked off the field.

Alone in the dugout, waiting to hit, his vision going in and out of focus, his eyes watering and blood still dripping out his nose down over his lip, he grinned. *Skywatch my butt,* he thought.

"You gonna hit, Willy?" Devere's gruff voice snapped him back.

"Sure," Bill said, taking one last swipe at the blood on his face and grabbing a bat. He popped to the shortstop.

Two innings later, he got an assist on the last out of the game. He looked a hard hit ground ball into his glove and cut Sam Hession down with a perfect throw.

"Play, Willy," Whitey yelled from the pitcher's mound before the ball even got to Zenger.

"Nice play Skywatch," Devere nodded as they trotted to the dugout. "Didn't try ta catch that one with your face."

Bill's nose was numb but it didn't hurt anymore. The blood had stopped. He felt like celebrating. It had been a good game.

The good ol' boys from Dick and Tonna's yelled over:

"Whyintchoo guys come over an drink some beer. We got more'n we can handle tuhnight."

"Whereinhell'd 'jew git the keg?" Devere asked Eddie Burke as they gathered around a pickup and filled paper cups out of a shiny cold keg.

"Boda gits em free. Drives a truck for a beer distribbutter."

"Plays the worst right field in the league," Benny Arnold cut in, "but he brings the beer so we gotta keep sendin' him out there."

"You shore quick ta criticize, but you shore don't mind drinkin' my beer."

They all sat on the grass and drank, talked about their chances of beating Peerless. The girls sat silent, drinking the beer out of flimsy paper cups. The lights switched off on the ballfield. The parking lot emptied out. People started to drift away from the impromptu beer party on the grass.

The Arnold brothers left.

Eddie Burke complained he had to take his wife all the way down to Brown County early the next morning for a family reunion.

Then Boda had to leave.

"What are ya gonna do with all this beer?" Devere asked. "That keg's still half full."

"Shit, I dunno. It'll probly git poured out up at the place when I go in Tuesday mornin.' You guys wanna finish it?"

"Damn right. Shore as hell a lot better'n goin' to the bar an payin' for beer the whole rest o' the night."

"OK. Keep it. Make shore ya git the empty keg an the pump back ta me. I gotta 'count for all o' them"

They drank another fifteen minutes and Whitey and Unk took off. When Patrick wandered away, only Devere and Vicki, Jimmy and Rae Ann, and Bill and Ellie were left. It was still a hot night with only the slightest trace of a breeze to cool it. They all were content sitting in the darkness and drinking.

"Oh-ho say can you seeeee . . . By the dawn's early light," Devere bellowed out. He looked at his watch. "Damn, it's the fourth of Jewlye. I could sit here an drink for free all night 'til the starlights' last gleamin.'"

"Let's do it," Washington, feeling good, took Devere up on his offer. "Let's have us a fourth of Jewlye picnic right here."

"C'mon," Devere ordered, moving toward the keg, "let's carry this little beauty out ta center field. The city rentacops come round, they won't even know we're here."

"I got my guitar in the back seat. I'll git it."

"An git the bug spray out o' the the glove compartment," Rae Ann ordered, still not quite drunk enough to forget the reality of a Wabash City summer night.

"I got somethin' for this picnic better'n anything else," Ellie said. She was back from her car almost immediately carrying a crushproof Marlboro box. She opened it up and in the darkness they could barely see the tops of five of the tightest, brown-rolled, end-twisted joints in captivity.

"Those what I think they are?" Devere asked suspiciously.

"I never smoked marijuana," Bill confessed.

Rae Ann and Jimmy had both smoked it with Ellie before. Vicki didn't say anything. She had been like a sphinx all night, like she was uncomfortable or nervous.

"It's good stuff," Washington assured Devere. "You'll like it. It don't do anything beer don't do."

They lifted the keg over the outfield fence and camped around it in center field like Indians around a campfire. Devere filled the cups and Ellie lit the first joint. It passed slowly from hand to hand, mouth to mouth, like an ancient peace pipe might have, bringing them all together in the same breath.

Ellie's grass started to take hold in the musky heat. The words of Washington's baseball song and the soft sounds of his guitar, floated around them:

> The Wabash flows past diamonds
> Dust-lit on a summer night
> America you're dyin'
> Your men just ain't machines
> Who'll run all day for empty pay
> And give up all their dreams.

As the song mourned, Bill lay back flat. The center field grass curled cool around the bare skin of his neck. The pungent smell of the other grass curled in ringlets around his head. The stars floated straight up high above him. Ellie rolled over beside him, cradled her chin in the hollow of his shoulder, kissed his chest and neck. Her hand snaked softly up under his shirt and made little curls in the hair of his belly and chest. Her tongue licked in his mouth like a cool flame.

"Here's a new verse since the last time you guys heard this one," Washington announced:

> America's a dyin'
> The dream's become a joke
> And the green, green world
> With its flag unfurled
> 'S an illusion goin' up in smoke.

The dope was getting to all of them. Rae Ann, sitting crosslegged, ran her hand slowly up Jimmy's thigh as he sang. Vicki watched a detached smile creep into Devere's hard face as he lay with his head in her lap. She never said a word but dragged deeply on the moving joint as if she had done it many times before.

"This stuff is great. Where'd you git it?" Bill whispered into Ellie's ear between kisses.

"Yeah, where'd ya git this stuff?" Devere repeated.

"I git it from this kid from the university lives down the hall."

"Sing the 'bottom button' song," Rae Ann giggled to Jimmy.

"The what?" Ellie asked.

"I can't sing that."

"C'mon. Sing it," Rae Ann coaxed. "You guys aren't gonna bleeve this one. It's really funny."

"It's really dirty," Washington laughed.

"SING IT," they all ordered in unison.

Washington struck up a twangy-quick intro and, trying not to laugh, launched into it:

> I'd liketa be the bottom button on yore body suit
> Baby that would really be topnotch.
> Ridin' around all day
> Whether you're at work or play

Right in the middle o' yore crotch.

By the end of the first verse they were all laughing.

I'd liketa be the linin' in the cup o' yore brassear.
Baby that would really be a deal.
When you go walkin' down the street
Hittin' the sidewalk with yore laughin' feet
I'd be up there coppin' a feel.

By the end of the second verse, they had all found the rythme and were trying zanily to sing along.

"Here, let me do the next one," Rae Ann giggled through a mouthful of beer.

I'd liketa be the pockets on the rear o' yore blue jeans
Baby that would really be a gas.
When you're out walkin' on the beach
Out of evrybody's reach,
I'd be back there playin' with yore ass.

"That's it folks," Washington stopped.

"Wait a minute. I got one," Bill started him playing again.

I'd liketa be the elastic on yore halter top.
That'd be like eatin' at the Ritz.
When yore dressin' up at night,
Tyin' that top on tight,
I'd be right there snugglin' yore tits.

"Snugglin'?" Ellie mocked him, running her hand up under his shirt again.

They were all flying on the beer, the dope, the closeness of the summer night on the clean grass of the ballfield.

"Ya know what we are? We're groupies, reglar groupies," Vicki said.

"What the hell are groupies?" Devere demanded.

"They're the girls follow all the big rock stars around evrywhere," Bill answered.

"She's right. We're softball groupies," Ellie agreed.

"That's ridiculous," Vicki contradicted herself. "Who ever heard of softball groupies?"

As the joints circled around him, Bill's mind wandered. Ellie's hand moved up and down inside his shirt. He rolled closer to her. His hand moved slowly up under her tee shirt to her bare breast. Her nipple bloomed in his palm. Suddenly she went rigid all over, sat straight up, then began to curl as if in self-defense. Her arms reached down to circle her knees. Her whole body tucked into a protective ball.

"This is the newest song I got. I call it Ellie's Song," Washington had just said. His guitar struggled at an uneven melody somewhere between happy and sad. His voice started to sing in a half-quick, quizzical rhythm:

Ellie lives a laughin' life o' lovin' when she can,
Wanderin' through a tainted world lookin' for the right kinda man.
The dudes that she keeps runnin' into
Ain't worth a damn
Soooo, Ellie lives her laughin' life alone.

Ohhhh . . . Shee's . . . pullin' out in Baby Blue
Her white-topped Chevy Malibu
Lookin' for a loveland . . . off the beaten trail
An she an Baby Blue are gonna prevail.

Yeah . . . Ellie lives her laughin' life o' lovin' on the run,
Wonderin' if there's anyplace where life can still be fun.
But empty men keep droppin' into
Her sunshine odyssey

Soooo, Ellie lives her laughin' life alone.
Yeah . . . shee's . . . headin' out in Baby Blue
Lookin' for a new room with a view.
Sippin' slow on wine an ginger ale

An she an Baby Blue are gonna prevail.
And . . . Ellie lives her laughin' life o' lovin' on the move
Down backroads an highways, the rough ones an the smooth,
Tryin' ta find a place ta go
Where men are real an love can grow
Still . . . Ellie lives her laughin' life alone.

She's pullin' out in Baby Blue
Her white-topped Chevy Malibu
Lookin' for a loveland . . . off the beaten trail
An she an Baby Blue are gonna prevail.

All through Jimmy's song, Ellie never moved. She hung on every word. When it ended, she rolled against Bill and clung to him as if she were drowning and needed someone to buoy her up.

"Let's take this show on the road," Devere suggested about one-thirty in the morning. "It's the fourth of Jewlye. We'll have us an old-fashioned Indiana hayride."

"Where we gonna git hay this time o' night," Washington asked.

"Don't need hay . . . git those mattresses outa yore place an throw em in the back o' the truck."

"You're crazy," they choroused.

Fifteen minutes later Devere gunned the pickup north on the blacktop out of Wabash City. Vicki Hickman sat tight against him in the cab. Jimmy and Rae Ann, Ellie and Bill stretched out in the back bed as the pickup rocketed out of town.

It's the fourth of July. Independence Day, Bill thought as the stars streaked in dipping circles above him.

Ellie kissed him. Martha wasn't even in town.

As the stars wheeled by above, Rae Ann sank back into the luxuriance of the summer night and Jimmy's arms. Stoned in the back of a flying pickup in the dark of the Indiana night, she felt safe, as if she had finally come home.

They whirled through the Indiana countryside, through funny little towns with odd unexpected names whose only lights shined through tavern windows. Deltaville. The Oracle Bar in Delphi. Limping Sam's in Bippus. The One-Eyed Dog in Argos. Apple Eve's in Eden. They passed through tiny towns where the occasional flickering glow of a TV screen through the gauzy brown shroud of ageless dusty drapes was the only sign of life. Pee Roo (spelled Peru), Indiana. Columbus. Pulaski. Plymouth. Princeton. Trenton. Lafayette. They rolled past the Tippecanoe Battlefield where the Indians stood together and fell for the last time. West Point, Indiana. Madison, Indiana. Freedom, Indiana. Liberty Center (pronounced "Libtee"), New Libtee, Freelandville, and Yankeetown, Indiana. Mount Vernon and Monticello, Indiana. The Bunker Hill Air Force Base. Frankfurt, Indiana with a sign like a Flagg enlistment poster ordering "FOLLOW THE HOT

DOGS," the high school basketball team. They passed at least three Dew Drop Inns but not a single No-Tell Motel. In the cab, Devere and Vicki listened to the radio as they drank. Sam Cooke sang The Midnight Special. Dolly Parton did a country version of Mah Country Tis O' Thee and Ronee Blakley sobbed out We're Just Not Gonna Make It, Darlin.' Kingsland, Indiana. South Boston, Indiana. Lexington, Indiana. French Lick. New Harmony. Santa Claus. Young America, Indiana which in the darkness seemed an old run down place, stores boarded up, almost a ghost town.

Periodically Devere pulled to the side of some dark road, got out and filled his beer cup from the keg. Once he stopped and peed hard and long right under the raised tailgate. Rae Ann listened with a kind of wonder as his water seemed to splash unendingly down on the pavement.

"You always carry those things around like that?" Vicki asked, pointing to the rifle and shotgun locked in the gunrack behind their heads.

"I went huntin' last weekend an I just never took em out."

In the back in darkness, Bill and Ellie were sitting up with their backs to Washington and Rae Ann. Sitting inside the circle of his legs with her back against his stomach, her shoulder blades tucked into his chest, she received his kisses on the back of her neck under her hair. His hands caressed her taut breasts. He ran one hand down under the waistband of her jeans into her kinky hair. In the dull glow of a neon sign on the roof of a bar in some tiny Indiana town, she tilted her head back and looked up at him. She bared her teeth as his finger probed into her.

They stopped again for Devere to refill his cup. Washington and Bill got out to pee. Rae Ann ran off into some bushes. She started to moan in the darkness.

"What the hell's that?" Devere asked, zipping up.

"It's Rae Ann," Ellie answered with no particular concern.

"She gits funny when she smokes dope."

"She's ululating," Bill observed, giggling nonsensically.

"She's moanin' not peein' dumb ass," Devere corrected.

Washington and Ellie went and got Rae Ann, brought her back to the truck. Almost immediately, she fell asleep.

"Guess we better head back. It's almost four," Devere decided for them all.

Ellie curled up beside Rae Ann like a sister and soon fell asleep. Bill and Jimmy sat with their backs against the chained tail-gate silently drinking beer as Devere drove slowly back toward Wabash City.

In the cab, Vicki was asleep.

They came into Wabash City from the south on the blacktop that ran past the All-American Homes factory. They'd made almost a fifty mile circle north out of Wabash City and then east and then back.

Let's have us some target practice, inspiration clicked on in Devere's beer-blasted brain. He skidded the truck to a halt on the sandy strip of shoulder in front of All-American Homes.

"Let's have us some targit practice," Jimmy and Bill, groggy and burnt out in the back, heard Devere yelling almost before the truck stopped rolling.

The highway was deserted. The factory was plunged in brooding darkness. The only lights anywhere came from the dim spotlights that illuminated the company billboard.

"What are you doin'?" Vicki watched wide-eyed as Devere unlocked the gunrack and took down the shotgun and the rifle.

"You can't do that," Jimmy said languidly.

"Watch me," Devere laughed, loading both barrels.

Devere raised the gun toward the patronizing billboard and blew Justin Endreem's nose off.

"You guys want a shot?" Devere invited.

"Whoa, we gotta git outta here," Ellie yelled.

But Bill was out of the back and taking the shotgun from Devere. He blew a hole in old Justin's forehead. The kick from the twelve guage threw him back against the truck.

"You idiot, we gotta git outa here," Vicki screamed.

Rae Ann slept on.

Why not? Washington thought.

With both guns blazing, they peppered Justin Endreem and his static universe of tin satellites: trailers, pre-cut houses, module homes. As they fired and reloaded, fired and reloaded, they felt like the minutemen at Lexington and Concord must have felt. Little men behind trees firing at the enemy.

Ellie finally got them all back in the truck. Devere took off fast down the two-lane blacktop. His red taillights shrank to pinpoints in the black night.

21 July

July flowed calmly by.

Devere was in love.

Franklin was in heat.

Washington and Rae Ann started singing together.

For Carla, business at the ballpark was way off, but she was covering herself in other sectors of the community.

On nights alone Molly hooked a small rug for the bathroom and crocheted a shawl for her mother.

Ellie, after sleeping with Martha's husband, washed Martha's sheets in Martha's washer in Martha's basement.

Martha came back on the twelfth.

The factory steamed in the July heat.

All-American Homes smoked the hippies from the Community center on the eighth and buried American United Insurance on the tenth. They murdered the police on the fourteenth and blitzed Bill Krieg Motors on the eighteenth to run their record to 17–1, second best in the league.

Ellie and Rae Ann threw a party at Ellie's place after the game on the eighteenth. Bill showed up late but didn't leave until the next morning.

Then the rains came. They stayed like vacationing relatives for a full week. The second game with Peerless Truck was rained out.

The softball delivered them from the brutal furnace of hot July days. After the midnight ride and their sunrise Bicentennial firepower display, Washington, Franklin, and Devere played their best ball of the season. It was as if they had gotten all of the tension out of their systems. They played steadier, calmer, like the river flowing. But snags still slumbered beneath the placid surface.

"Where have you been?" Molly screamed when Devere rolled in at seven on the fourth of July.

"Out celebratin,'" he wheezed, his tongue thick.

"You can't do that to me. It's the fourth of July."

"Why can't I?"

"I wanted to have a picnic with the girls."

"Fine. This afternoon. I'm goin' ta bed."

All he does is live here, Molly thought.

"Hey Jim, ya see what those kids did ta the billboard?" Unk yelled to Washington the first day back after the long holiday weekend.

Washington hurried into the cage so nobody would see him laughing.

"Ya see that billboard?" Unk asked Devere.

"Lousy joovnile deelinquents," Devere tried to keep a straight face.

"Man, sumbuddy shur shot shit outa that billboard," Unk made smalltalk with Franklin on the loading dock at lunchtime.

"When's our next ballgame?" Bill answered.

Sam Unk was disappointed. He thought the billboard murder was a real conversation piece. But, nobody seemed interested.

However, Devere in love struck everyone funny. He treated Vicki like a fairy princess, a Snow White thrown among rough and homely dwarfs. In reality, she looked like Cinderella still in the ashes. Vicki never put on any makeup or set her hair. Her wardrobe tended toward sweatshirts and baggy jeans. But Devere didn't see any of that. Around Vicki, he was a frog turning into a prince; perhaps not a prince, but at least some kind of minor public official like a dog catcher.

Devere in love definitely struck everyone funny, except Devere. For him it was dead serious. In his mind he was working up the nerve to tell her he loved her, that he wanted to leave Molly and the kids and live with her.

Then the rains came and Vicki disappeared.

Molly suspected something was wrong in the days after her big fight with Devere on the fourth of July. She became certain something was wrong the night in mid-July when she told him over dinner about her job. She had started looking again out of anger at Devere's arrogant attitude toward her after his little all-night fourth of July episode. And she had gotten lucky. The personnel manager at the Great Lakes Rubber Co. had offered her a job because she was "just the right age" to greet visitors who came into the deep-pile carpeted offices. The first thing she did after the offer was made was check whether Great Lakes had a team in the Wabash City Softball League.

"I want to take a job at Great Lakes Rubber as a receptionist," she blurted out pointblank over dinner.

"Great Lakes Rubber. That's a big place. Why not? We could use some extra money," Devere said.

She wondered if he had heard her right. No argument. No ranting. No scoffing at her ability to work. No reaction at all. She was momentarily stunned. He didn't seem to care. She finally wondered if something was wrong at the Homes factory, if maybe he was afraid of being laid off. But whatever the reason for his change of heart, Molly wasn't about to argue. She was excited. She couldn't wait to start work.

Martha, after she got back from Michigan, fell far short, at least in Bill's estimation, of exciting. The main thing he held against her was her occupancy of Ellie's place in the bed. He did get excited by the twisted illegality of her first night home. As they made love, her crooning about how long it had been, he felt the excitement of committing adultery, of cheating on Ellie. Two nights later, Martha, just like before, fell asleep on the couch in front of the TV set.

At the party at Ellie's apartment after the Krieg Motors game, the singing group of Washington and Ross made their debut. Their harmonies were vivid and natural. They were together and on key. Even Devere, holding hands with Vicki like some teenager going steady, listened intently. A pony keg of beer squatted in the kitchen in a rusty metal tub. It sat on its throne of melting ice like some fat diety bowing sagaciously to each new supplicant. One group hovered around the keg, leaning against counters swapping stories. The other group lounged in the living room, sitting cross-legged on the floor or lying with their heads propped up against the sofa. No wives were there. The single guys on the team brought their girlfriends and the married men, except for Devere, came alone to drink. Ellie and Rae Ann served a huge batch of Sloppy Joes which disappeared almost as soon as they were put out.

Bill Franklin had gone home right after the game in hopes of persuading Martha to go to the party with him. He did it either out of guilt or out of curiousity. He was curious to see Martha and Ellie together in the same room.

"I've told you before, I have nothing in common with those people," Martha said.

"I'm too tired," Martha said.

"I've got to take the kids swimming tomorrow," Martha said.

"I'm going to bed," Martha finally said.

I should never even have come home, Bill thought.

He slammed the door behind him as he stalked out of the house.

He got to the party late. When he walked in, Ellie's eyes lit up.

"Hi darlin,'" Ellie whispered when they reached the kitchen out of earshot of the others. "How'd ya git rid of her?" Ellie continued.

"When she said she didn't wanna come, I just walked out."

The party meandered on until about two when only Rae Ann and Jimmy and Ellie and Bill were left.

"Look, I can clean up this mess in fifteen minutes if Bill'll give me a hand . . . so if you guys wanna take off, go ahead." Ellie knew that Rae Ann was hanging around only out of politeness.

"OK. Ya sure?" Rae Ann asked with meager enthusiasm as she and Washington fled.

Left alone with Bill, Ellie put a record on the stereo then turned out the lights as the music came on. It was soft music without words. They wrapped their arms around each other and swayed with the music in the tiniest of circles on the party-strewn shag rug, then kissed their way into the bedroom.

For Carla things hadn't been moving nearly so smoothly. Only one or two days a week was it worth her while to park down by the river below the ballfields. Many of her regular customers had just stopped coming. But Carla wasn't hurting for customers. She simply had to move around a bit more to get to them. The new CB kept her in touch with the boys out on the interstate and she spent a lot of time at night parked in a remote corner of the Wabash City Courthouse underground parking garage where the city police cars parked when they were off duty.

But the main thing in July was the softball . . . and the stories they told afterward. The night at Ellie's place, the lies flowed faster than the beer. Unk and Patrick and Whitey matched fishing stories. Whitey told about the time he and Hank Patrick were fishing in the Wildcat Creek:

"I hooked a trout as long as a ball bat."

"Wuz way too much fish for you," Patrick cut in.

"I musta fought that fish for five minutes before it got my line around a snag an got off. I cussed that fish all up and down the river."

"Wait'll ya hear what happened then."

"No more'n a half hour later we're still floatin' in 'bout the same spot when Hank here hooks into anuther big trout. Well he lands this beauty just as easy as pie . . ."

"Easy! I fought that thing fair an square for 'bout five minutes 'fore I got im in the boat."

"He lands it an it's the same fish I caught before. My hook an about ten feet o' line's still hangin' outa the side o' his mouth. I figured it was my fish 'cause I hooked im first. I tired im out."

"You lost the fish. I caught the fish. It's that simple."

"We musta argued 'bout five minutes 'bout whose fuckin' fish it is while I'm takin' the hooks out an hangin' the fish on the stringer."

"We'd also been drinkin' beer mosta the mornin' too."

"Anyway, ol Hank gits all pissed off an gives me a good push an I drop the whole stringer in the water an the current takes off with my fish."

"You're fish hell! It was my fish."

Unk topped that story with another fish story.

"I ever tell ya 'bout the time I caught the barracuda?" he started.

"There's no barracuda 'round here," Whitey cut in.

"Like hell, wuz that day. I wuz fishin' the Libteeville pools an I'd hiked down aroun' where that road runs between Libteeville and Americus comes down right along the creek."

"Yeah, I've fished those pools. Good spot," Whitey complimented Unk on his taste.

"Anyway, I got a fly rod an I ain't havin' much luck so's I'm just flippin' it out an pumpin' it back not payin' much attention ta anythin.' An that's when I hooked my barracuda."

"No way," Whitey disagreed, "just ain't none."

"I went into a cast an all of a sudden I'm flat on my back on the bank an my fly rod's clatterin' down the road. Hooked the radio antenna o' a Plymouth Barracuda on the back cast. Some big ol country boy got out just laughin' his ass off an carried the pieces o' my fly rod back ta me. 'Bet y'all never caught no Barracuda fore,' the kid said. An I ain't never caught one since," Unk laughed.

"The best huntin' story I ever heard happened when I was in the Marines out at Pendleton on the West Coast," Hank Patrick decided to get into the act. "Ya know how they cut yore hair in the Marines? Well, I mean, back in the sixties they cut yore hair so short evrybody's head was lookin' like a cue ball. Well there was this one maniac, for all

I know he might even o' been part Indian or sumpin,' who talked em into givin' im one o' them Mohawk or Mohican haircuts. One strip o' hair right up the middle o' his head."

Patrick paused for effect. The audience was hooked. No one could figure out how it was going to develop into a hunting story.

"Anyway, one evenin' we're all sittin' eatin' dinner in the mess hall, mindin' our own business, when that crazy Mohawk comes smashin' through the door stark naked with nuthin' on but a belt with a tom-myhawk in it an carryin' a bow an arra. He goes roarin' up to the slop table where all the pots o' food were still sittin' screamin' 'you ain't givin' me no more saltpeter,' an he shoots the mashed potatoes with his bow an arra. Then he pulls out the tommyhawk an starts hackin' at the meat loaf an the carrots. All the time screamin' at the top o' his lungs, 'You ain't feedin' me no more saltpeter.' They clapped im in a straight-jacket an section-eighted him right outa the Marines. Two weeks later they sent all o' us ta Nam. He wasn't so dumb."

Whitey told the deer in the car trunk story again, but nobody could top Patrick's hunting story and the talk drifted on to other things. At one point in the evening they reminisced about collecting bubblegum cards.

"D'jew ever have a Choo Choo Coleman?"

"You remember Coot Veal? Wayne Terwilliger?"

"How 'bout Johnny Berardino? He's a doctor on television in the afternoon."

"My favorite ballplayer was Richie Ashburn," Washington nomi-nated.

"Smokey Burgess," Devere cut in. "He was a catcher once 'til he couldn't git down no more. What a hitter!"

"Man, if he hit his weight he'd be a lifetime three hundred. He'd come out, pinch-hit a run-scorin' single, an go right back ta the hot dog an beer he'd set down on the bench."

"How 'bout Rip Repulski?"

"How 'bout a shortstop named Clyde Kluttz?"

"Ya know, one year I finally found a sucker. I traded a hundred an fifty o' my spare cards—Roseboro, Woody Held, two Bo Belinski's, a Fred Harris, a Brendan Boyd, a Sibby Sisty—ta git a Teddy Ballgame. Best baseball card I ever got. I think I still got it."

"Ya know. I always wanted a Teddy Ballgame card an I never got lucky enough," Bill Franklin said, almost tragically.

22 Rain on the River

It rained six days straight, the last week of July.

The second Peerless game, which would have been for the regular season title, was rained out.

Bill sat awake nights trying to figure out how to tell Martha he wanted a divorce that he didn't know if he really wanted.

Washington and Rae Ann talked about getting married.

Molly started work at Great Lakes Rubber wearing one of the five new outfits she had charged at the K'Mart.

Devere fell more in love. One night he told Vicki he wanted to move in with her. "I think I've fallen in love with ya," he said.

"Say what?"

"I'm gonna git divorced from Molly an I wanna move in an live with ya. I'm in love with ya."

"Right," Vicki coughed, almost choked.

Two days later she disappeared.

No explanation.

No warning.

She just flat out disappeared the night the two tall ships collided in Boston Harbor.

Not a trace.

She disappeared as if she'd been a visitor from another world and was called back.

When Vicki didn't show up in the bar the night the Peerless game was rained out, Devere stomped over to her house. He knocked at the door but got no answer. That night he drove around Wabash City for two hours looking for her car parked outside some bar or house or apartment building. He even checked the hospital, but she wasn't there.

Then he got scared. Fear struck in. At the back of the house he found her kitchen window and broke it with a brick from the garage.

132

When he got inside nothing was there. He tore from room to room like a man running bases. They were all empty. No furniture. No signs of life. Not a trace. It was as if she had never been there, as if he had just dreamed her.

Franklin's panic was different from Devere's. He wanted to disappear, leave all the confusion that kept him awake nights behind.

It wasn't that Martha was so bad. It was just that Ellie was so different, so much more exciting. He wasn't head over heels in love with her, but he certainly lusted after her, thought about her constantly. He dreamed of trips they could take together, worlds they could discover, things he could teach her. The only problem was he didn't trust her. She actually scared him sometimes. She was so independent.

He and Ellie had been sleeping together for about ten days when they got serious about it for the first time. They had gone out to a restaurant for dinner the night before Martha was scheduled to arrive back home from her lakeside sabbatical.

"I think I'll tell her," Ellie had giggled across the table with no warning.

Bill choked on his soup, burned his tongue and ended up coughing violently from the shock of the hot soup and the cold terror. "Sorry . . . went down the wrong pipe."

Ellie laughed at him silently from behind her eyes.

"We could meet her at the front door without any clothes on," Ellie teased, "and say 'SURPRISE . . . guess what we've been up to.'"

"What an excellent idea," he answered without enthusiasm.

"I'd be a great professor's wife," Ellie teased some more. "Wouldn't that be funny? After I flunked outa the university an all."

Yeah, really funny, Bill cringed as he thought of her at a West Wabash faculty cocktail party.

" . . . when I was in nursing school I usta look at all my professors, 'specially my English teacher who was this sorta middle-aged guy with a red beard, an wonder what they'd be like in bed. Oh, geez, we really oughta tell her," Ellie laughed.

"It's not funny," Bill snapped. Suddenly he was feeling enough love for her to actually consider the possibility. The idea of taking her into that academic crowd was ludicrous, as ludicrous as Martha swapping stories with the ballplayers in the bar.

I'm just using her, Bill accused himself, *using her to break the boredom. I use her because I'm unhappy and she makes me feel like I'm doing something about it.*

"It's not funny," Bill lowered his voice. "It's exactly . . . telling her about us . . . is exactly what I've been thinking about all week."

"What about your kids?" Ellie asked in a stunned voice.

"Yeah, they're a problem."

"Don't say anything to her yet," Ellie pleaded. "Let it ride for awhile . . . 'til we're both sure. OK?"

Bill was happy that Ellie let him off the hook so easily. The next day he greeted Martha with a lying homecoming smile.

All during that week of rain, Devere searched for Vicki. He drove past her apartment but nothing ever changed. He tracked down her landlord, but she hadn't had a lease and hadn't left any forwarding address. He moped and sulked around the house, talking little, pacing the rooms like a caged animal. When Molly would talk about her day at work, about how much weight she was losing, he would nod slowly, almost comatose. Molly knew something was wrong.

One night the rains came just before the All-American Homes ballgame was to start. Taking off his spikes in the pickup, Devere spotted Carla's car lurking black and shiny down by the river. *I could sure use a blowjob,* he thought.

"Where the hell ya been all summer," Carla's voice barked over the intercom.

"I been gittin' it for free," Devere barked back. "Now will you let me in outa the friggin' rain."

Inside the car, the seats moving, the fur flowing, the lights dimming blue and yellow and misty red, the music twanging, Devere apologized and told her his troubles. "The damn woman ran out on me an never said a word."

"You're better off payin' for it, honey," Carla advised. "That way it don't cost nearly so much."

Carla served him a beer with her feet and Devere talked on as she listened silently like a topless psychiatrist. Her dark goggles stared at him like the bulging eyes of some creature from another planet.

Outside, the rain fell slowly and steadily on the long black car.

The darkness gathered. Just a deeper shade of black in the general blackness of the summer night, invisible in the saturated dark, the river rose slowly and moved along more swiftly.

23 Molly Breaks Up a Ballgame

The rain stopped on July twenty-eighth and the All-American Homes softball team won their last two games of the regular season. Their record, 19–1, was second best in the league. They played their last regular season game on the second of August and won handily in five innings. After the game, most of the Homes players hung around to drink beer off the rear end of Devere's pickup and watch the Peerless Truckers dispatch the good old boys from Dick and Tonna's in a quick five innings. About half way through it, Devere said, "I ain't gonna watch those pricks play no more," and walked away down toward the parking lot.

That night, Molly got to the ballpark as the Peerless Truck-Dick and Tonna's game was going on.

She had been sitting home alone. Her daughters were at a slumber party at a friend's house and wouldn't be home until morning. And, if the last month or so was any indication, Devere wouldn't be coming in until three or four in the morning either. Sitting there alone, she had decided to hang the Bicentennial sampler with the eagle and the lightning bolts on it which she had just finished needlepointing. Devere had made her a frame the week before from some wood he had brought home from the Homes factory, but he hadn't gotten around to hanging it for her. Looking for the wire he always used to hang pictures took Molly down to the basement into Devere's workshop.

Searching for it, she opened cabinet doors and pulled out drawers. In the second drawer she found a grey plastic bag. Thinking that the wire might be coiled inside, she opened it. At first she didn't understand what she had found, then everything began to come clear.

When Molly pulled up in the darkness of the ballfield parking lot she was boiling with a vicious hatred for Devere. She had known for weeks that something was wrong. But not until she pulled open that drawer in his workbench had she considered that it might be another woman.

Molly had dumped out of the grey plastic bag two pairs of women's panties.

Sitting in her car in the darkness of the parking lot, Molly wondered what to say, how to tell her husband of seventeen years that she wanted a divorce, wanted her life back. She sat there trying to find the words, not really seeing anything but the luminescent halo of light diffused brightly out over the baseball diamond. Then she became more aware of the people on the field, the people loitering around the periphery, in the stands, at the concession booth, along the fences.

She spotted Devere's pickup and the team hanging around the tailgate.

She recognized them by their jerseys, the same one she had washed so many times. At first she didn't see Devere, but then she picked him out. She looked for the woman. One tall blonde girl seemed to be a part of the group. Molly watched closely for some telltale sign, an arm draped possessively around her neck, a hand brushing familiarly across her rear. Devere seemed to pay no attention whatsoever to the pretty blonde girl.

Then, as she watched, Devere did a strange thing. He walked away down into the darkness of the lower parking lot. At first Molly figured he had just gone down to the river to take a pee. But he didn't come back. Ten minutes passed. Still angry, she got out to investigate. She didn't want to walk down in the darkness by the river alone, so she decided to ask around at the ballfield. She moved toward the light confident that no one would recognize her as Devere's wife. She hadn't been to one of his games in years and, as far as she knew, she'd never met any of the men who played on his team.

The two mens' teams were just coming off and two womens' teams were getting ready to play when Molly approached the ballfield. Three or four of the All-American Homes players had drifted over carrying their beer cans to lean against the fence and watch the girls in their short-short uniforms warming up. The others, including the tall blonde girl, sat in the bleachers drinking their beers. Nobody seemed in much of a hurry to leave and nobody paid attention to Molly. She approached the men leaning against the fence drinking.

"Excuse me, do you know where I might find Don Devere?" she inquired timidly of a large man with a protruding belly.

"Devere's down in the parkin' lot. He'll be back in a minute," Whitey answered.

"Could you tell me where I could find him?"

"Look lady," Whitey began, but another voice cut in. "He's down in Carla's car," Bill Franklin blurted out to Whitey, throwing the words back over his shoulder like grains of salt, not even knowing who Whitey was talking to.

Molly said "thanks" quietly and moved away.

"What the hell you tell her 'bout Carla for?" Whitey growled at Bill. "She could be his wife or a plainclothes cop."

"You're dreamin,'" Bill scoffed and they all promptly forgot about it as the womens' game started.

Molly next approached the small group of All-American Homes people, which included the tall, pretty, blonde girl, sitting in the stands. Quietly she asked where she might find Devere.

Jimmy Washington, sitting next to Rae Ann when the woman walked up, recognized her almost immediately. He had met her years before when she used to drive Devere to work. He had never seen her at the ballpark before.

I wonder if it's some emergency, Washington thought in the split second of silence after the woman's question.

"OH he's . . ." Rae Ann started to answer.

"He's probly gone home by now," Washington cut in, smiling stiffly, obviously lying.

Molly took it all in and moved on.

"That's his wife," Washington whispered to Rae Ann.

"He's down with Carla, isn't he?"

"Yeah, I think so."

Molly tried once more on the opposite side of the diamond from where the All-American Homes people were gathered. She approached two men leaning against the fence drinking beer, smoking cigarettes and watching the womens' softball game. One of the men was short and stocky like Devere and the other was tall and thin and wore a dirty, floppy hat on his jutting head. Both had PEERLESS TRUCK printed across their backs.

"Excuse me. Have you ever heard of Carla's car? Could you tell me where it is?" she asked them timidly. She wasn't prepared for the overt hostility of their answers.

"Whadduyou know 'bout Carla's car?" Gaptooth barked.

"Yeah, whaddareya lookin' for Carla's car for?" Porkpie backed up his partner.

"I'm looking for my husband and I think . . ."

"Oh-hooo, her husband . . ." the Porkpie giggled.

"Ya know who Carla is?" Gaptooth asked, leering.

"No . . . I . . . I'm just . . ."

"Whoosier husband that yer lookin' for?"

"His name's Devere . . ." and she started to edge away. She wished she'd never approached them in the first place.

When the two men heard Devere's name, they both broke out laughing and poking each other in the ribs as if she had just delivered the punch line of a hilarious dirty joke.

"Yore lookin' for Devere . . . his wife . . . oh that's beeeyewwwtiful . . ." (poke) Gaptooth mumbled.

Their obvious enjoyment of the joke and her not seeing the humor in it pulled Molly up short, cut off her retreat.

"What's so funny?" she demanded.

"What's so funny? I'll tell ya what's so funny, lady," Gaptooth began with obvious relish, excited by the prospects of his coming revelation, "yore ol' man's probly right now shacked up in her car with the wildest hooker in Wabash City."

"It's the big ol black Ford parked down close ta the riverbank. That's ol Carla's car," the Porkpie added, savoring every graphic word.

Molly fled in horror.

"Hot damn, this's gonna be good," Gaptooth chortled.

"I wouldn't miss this for nothin," the Porkpie grunted.

After fleeing Gaptooth and Porkpie, Molly was even madder than she had been when she found Devere's little collection of panties.

She wanted to hurt Devere, humiliate him in front of all his friends. She wanted to kill him for all his lying, his ordering her around, his stealing of her life so he could make her a servant in his stainless steel kitchen. The more she thought about what those two obnoxious men with PEERLESS written on their shirts had said, the more enraged she became.

She found herself in the parking lot near Devere's pickup truck. It was abandoned in favor of the womens' softball game. In the back of the truck, behind the beer cooler, she spotted the bat bag, taped handles sticking out. She pulled out a heavy aluminum Richie Allen model, hefted it once with both hands and headed toward the river.

For long minutes in the darkness Molly watched the car. It just sat there. Occasionally it would move slightly, rock gently on its springs, the movement almost unnoticeable in the heavy, silent blackness. She wondered what the woman looked like, whether she was pretty in the face as Molly knew herself to be, whether she was thin and tall as Molly knew herself not to be. The speculations made her madder.

Molly moved closer, gripping the bat tighter.

She moved even closer. She was no more than two or three feet from the car.

She heard muffled voices, then a laugh. She couldn't be sure it was Devere. But somehow she knew it was. She felt herself going blind with rage. Another muffled laugh. She forgot who she was, where she was.

Inside the car, Carla was just taking a sip of Doctor Pepper, swishing it around in her mouth, when the roof fell in.

Outside, Molly had raised the Richie Allen bat high with both hands and brought it down hard right in the middle of the shiny black roof of the flawless sleek car. The roof crumpled like tinfoil. The sound of that first crashing blow echoed up over the ballfield like a Chinese gong.

When the first blow hit and the fur ceiling just above their heads sagged, Devere and Carla jumped hard against the rear wall. They tried to press themselves into the upholstery as their eyes froze on the smashed-in roof with its fur sagging down.

But Molly didn't stop at just one swing. She was hitting for the circuit. The fenders, the hood, the doors, she hammered at the car. She ran around it feverishly, setting her feet for each swing, taking her cuts, screaming "YOU BASTARD! YOU BASTARD!"

Inside, Carla and Devere jumped each time Molly's bat slammed into the car. The plush fur walls bounced and shook and buckled. The tiny liquor bottles flew around their feet like tracer bullets. Then Molly took out the windshield on the driver's side, splintering from top to bottom the thin, retractable interior wall that descended down over the glass.

When Devere saw the barrel-end of the ball bat come through that thin front partition, it finally registered that it was Molly.

Outside, Molly ran in mad circles around the car, smashing at the windows. She smashed and bashed and reveled in the power of her bat penetrating the soft skin of the car to that inner private world.

Inside, Carla and Devere scrambled to avoid the pounding bat. Their hands, arms and elbows covered their heads and necks from the firestorm of glass fragments and splinters of wood.

"Push those buttons for the doors," Devere screamed at Carla. "We gotta git outa here 'fore she kills us."

Devere came out of the car backwards and Molly caught him across the shoulder blades, her smoothest swing. She looked like Teddy Ballgame taking one downtown.

The shock of the blow staggered Devere, slammed him into the side of the demolished car. But she had connected with the strongest part of his body. The bunched biceps and layered shoulder muscles absorbed the power of her swing, made the bat THUD dully.

He ricocheted off the car and came up murderous.

Molly was already swinging again.

He wasn't quick enough. Her second swing caught him high on the right shoulder. It knocked him to the ground and hurt him.

She had him down and was moving to hit him again. *This time across the legs,* she thought, getting more and more rational with each swing.

"Don't hit him you bitch," Carla screamed from the doorway of her crumpled temple of love and money. "Don't hit him. I'll kill you for this."

The scream snapped Molly's head around, drew her attention from Devere to a new target. She ran at the topless blonde woman in the tight rubber goggles. Even as she ran she was swinging the bat from her heels.

Carla ducked.

Molly's bat slashed through the empty air as Carla hit the deck. Missing Carla, it smashed into the windshield on the passenger side and connected solidly on the doorpost. The impact ripped the bat out of Molly's hands.

Carla, the odds suddenly evened, came up off the ground and tackled Molly around the knees, wrestling her down. The two women, Carla topless in a short skirt, hooker boots and the everpresent goggles, Molly in a faded housedress that hung down over her knees, rolled in the gravel and dust, scratching and clawing at each other.

Molly was the larger and stronger. She fought to her knees and wound up for a full roundhouse swing at Carla. The punch caught Carla on the side of the head as she was coming up. It was a glancing blow that raked across the snaps of Carla's rubber goggles just behind her right temple. The snaps were smashed open and the goggles popped loose from Carla's face and hung in the tangle of her platinum blonde hair.

The punch didn't even slow Carla down. She jumped on Molly both fists flailing.

Molly tried to roll away, tried to get to her feet, knowing the smaller woman wouldn't have a chance in a standup battle.

But Carla held on, scratching at Molly's arms and body.

Molly felt her own dress rip all the way down the back. She panicked as her own clothes ripped away, leaving her as naked as the other woman. No longer was she trying for an advantage. She only wanted to escape the mess she found herself tangled in.

But Carla held on, cursing, clawing, pulling Molly's dress to pieces.

Molly tried desperately to claw her way out of the nightmare she had created. Her hand caught in Carla's hair. For a moment Molly thought the woman's whole head had yanked off in her hand. But it was only a wig. All of Carla's gaudy, primped, platinum-blonde hair had come off in Molly's hand like a birdnest ripped out of a tree. Molly flung it away into the darkness and struggled to her feet.

Carla suddenly stopped fighting and let go. It was as if, like Samson, all of her tenacity had resided in her wig.

Both women scrambled to their feet. Both realized how undressed they were. Devere was forgotten. Carla screamed staccato curses at Molly even as the sobs started to come.

Both women heard the voices approaching down the grassy bank from the ballfields.

Then the light came on and froze Carla and Molly in their tracks. From up on the bank, a high-powered flashlight shown down on them. Other shadows bobbed and bounced around the source of the light, whispering. A crowd had gathered.

Devere was picking himself up off the ground, holding his shoulder, pain pulling at his face.

Molly tried to cover up.

Carla tried to cover her face. She stood there in the unrelenting light, silent, ungoggled, dewigged in front of Devere.

"What are you doin' here?" Devere stared at Carla.

Carla didn't utter a sound. She stared helplessly at Devere. Carla's identity had fallen in shards around her and Vicki Hickman had emerged from the rubble.

"How could ya do that ta me? Just take off," Devere moaned as if ready to break down and cry. Molly was forgotten. "How could ya do that? I told ya I loved ya."

Washington came down off the bank into the circle of light. "C'mon, let's git outa here before the cops come," he said to Devere trying to pull him away from the two women. He pulled on Devere's throbbing shoulder.

Devere's whole body flinched, shrunk up, as much with the frustration of it all as with the pain. "Leave me alone,"he screamed, pulling away. Then, by pure reflex, he kicked Washington square in the balls.

Washington sank to his knees in a heap on the ground. "I told ya I loved ya," Devere blubbered, doubled over in pain, trying to reach out to Vicki. "Who are you anyway? I loved you."

Vicki, Carla, whoever she was, stared dumbly at Devere, then turned and ran off into the darkness toward the river.

"You whore," Molly screamed after her. Then she ran off too, hugging her arms around her.

Washington was on his knees on the ground puking up beer. "What'd ya do that for?" he coughed up between spasms of nausea.

"Turn that light off," Devere screamed up at the crowd.

"Get the hell outa here, all of ya," Washington, standing up next to Devere screamed up at the vultures on the bank. "It's none o' yore business. Turn the light out or I'll make you eat it."

Gaptooth switched off his flashlight and fled before Devere and Washington could make a move up the bank.

Rae Ann joined the two men next to the ruins of Carla's car.

"You go find Vicki an take care o' her," Washington ordered."Here's my car keys. I'll take care o' him."

Devere sank to the ground holding his shoulder. He moaned unintelligible phrases.

The next morning the ballfield looked the same as ever. The river flowed as turgid and brown as always. The sun glinted off the crumpled ruins of Carla's car. About one in the afternoon a wrecker towed away the remains and no signs whatever of the battle on the riverbank survived. Carla's friends in the police department made out a phony accident report. No charges were ever pressed. It was all as if none of it ever happened, sort of.

24 Unhealed Wounds and Playoff Games

It took Devere a full day and a half in bed in Washington's apartment to recover enough to go looking for revenge.

"What the hell'd ya do that for," he demanded of Molly on the phone before she even said "hello."

"Oh, it's you," she answered with studied disinterest.

"Yeah, it's me. Ya almost killed me."

"I saw a lawyer yesterday . . . I'm filing for divorce . . . I've been to the bank so don't try to draw the money out . . . The locks on the doors have been changed . . . You can get your things by calling my lawyer . . . Everything of yours is in the garage . . . including your little bag of playthings I found in the workbench . . . The lawyer made a list of all the things . . . Don't try to come near me . . . Don't try to come near the girls . . . If you do I will call the police."

Devere went back to bed feeling like he'd gone fifteen rounds with Muhammad Ali. He lay in bed confused. His incomprehension turned in his mind like an assassin polishing a bullet. He wondered how she'd found out he was with Carla. He wondered where Vicki or Carla or whoever she was had gone. He wanted her back because he had lost everything else. It was all just happening too fast for Devere.

When Washington got home from work, Devere shot questions at him.

Washington pretended to know just as little as Devere did: "I'm sittin' in the stands drinkin' beer an watchin' a ball game an she just showed up. Rae Ann an I didn't tell her nothin.' Afterwards, Rae Ann found Vicki sittin' on the ground bawlin' her head off. She took her back to the car an got some clothes on her then dropped her off at the entrance ta some trailer park out by the interstate."

Devere was getting madder and madder. He knew Washington was fixing the timecards at work, that the other guys were holding up his end. He still hurt all over. Every time he raised his arm a pain shot across his back. He went into work the next day anyway. He was looking for someone to blame, someone to lash out at as he couldn't at Molly with her lawyers and locks. First he asked Unk, then Patrick.

Whitey finally gave him a hint: "Willy said somethin,' you know . . . just kiddin' . . . 'bout Carla's car. But hell, we didn't know who she was an we never . . . I mean Willy . . . never told her where it was or what it looked like or nothin.'"

Bill "Willy" Franklin was just what Devere needed, a pigeon he felt no qualms about shooting down. *I never liked him from the beginnin,'* Devere decided, *even when he turned out ta be a good ballplayer.*

Devere found Willy putting up a wall on a dolly foundation on line number one just across from Washington's cage. Devere walked straight toward him. Willy looked up, the electric drill still spinning in his hand. He saw Devere coming. He smiled: "Hi Devere. How ya feelin'?" He put down the drill preparatory to taking a break for conversation. And took the punch high on his right cheekbone.

Devere's suckerpunch spun Willy around and sprawled him across a workbench on the other side of the aisle. Screwdrivers, hammers, powertools, nuts and bolts, clattered on the floor. He stood over Willy raging, murderous. From his cage, Washington saw Devere's unannounced punch and was on him before he could take another shot at Willy.

Willy sat stunned on the floor.

Washington held Devere in a squirming half-nelson.

"What the hell 'djew do that for?" Willy asked. He was still dazed.

"D'jew tell 'er? You told 'er I was in Carla's car, didnn ya?"

Washington held on tight as Willy got to his feet. Whitey, Unk, Patrick, and Zenger rushed up.

"I didn't know she was your wife. I didn't even turn around ta see who it was. I just heard Whitey ask if anybody'd seen Devere an I just sorta yelled over my shoulder that you were down in Carla's car. I didn't know the lady was crazy."

"You shore got a big mouth," Devere spat.

Willy ran cold water over his face but it didn't help much. Within minutes a blue-black thunderhead came up beside and under his right eye.

When Bill got home from work, Martha fastened on the black eye like a vulture. "What happened to you?" she demanded.

"Had some trouble at work," he answered, pushing by her.

"You had another fight," she followed him into the living room.

"No," his sarcasm sloshed, "I walked into a doorknob."

"Somebody hit you didn't they?"

"Just leave me alone."

After dinner, Martha came into the living room where Bill huddled in the shelter of his newspaper. The look of serious negotiations marched like a picket line across her eyes.

"I'm gonna talk to you . . . I've decided," she began. "You've been so moody lately . . . You stayed out all night that one night."

"I was just at a party drinking. I told you that."

"Bill, what's going on? You're so different. I've been thinking about it even before you came home all beat up."

"I'm not all beat up."

"I've thought about it for days and I'm gonna do it," talking more to herself than to him.

I wish she'd do it, whatever it is, pretty soon, and get it over with, Bill thought.

"I don't care if you don't say a word. I'm gonna tell you all the things I feel . . . I've been feeling . . . ever since last February and March. At least you'll know where I stand."

Bill knew he was trapped. From the TV-room he heard the sounds of the kids watching The Sonny and Cher Show. *I wonder if she would let me go if I told her I wanted to watch Sonny and Cher,* he speculated whimsically.

"Ever since you took that summer job . . . started playing softball with those men . . . you've been different, vulgar, not as nice to me . . . It's almost as if you don't live here anymore. You just stop here to eat and sleep between work and softball games."

"Look, the season, the job'll be over in two weeks. What's the big deal?"

"See, that's what I mean. You're different Bill. I thought things would be better when I got back from the lake. But they're worse."

"Better! You fell right asleep on the couch the second night back."

"Most nights you're not even home. You're out playing baseball or sitting in bars with your gross friends and those ridiculous factory girls."

Yeah, well your husband's gonna leave you for one o' those ridiculous factory girls, Bill wished he had the nerve to say out loud. Just then

Danny, his stomach bouncing out over the elastic waistband of his short summer pajamas, ran in from the TV-room: "Daddy, daddy, please come see. Sonny's dressed up like Benjamin Franklin and Cher's got on this great big dress that Sonny keeps climbin' down under like it's a playhouse."

"Danny, you go watch it. We'll be in in a little while," Martha ordered, tightlipped.

"This is stupid," Bill tried to escape, "let's just go watch TV."

"You listen to me right now," Martha snapped. "Since I've been back from the lake . . ." she stopped dead as if stalled.

"Since I've been back . . ." pause again, as if she was afraid to say what she was going to say.

"You've hardly touched me at all . . ." and she stopped as if she didn't know how to proceed, stopped dead, tears welling up.

Bill was starting to get curious. He'd never seen her so upset before. *She's sure got herself worked up,* he thought.

"Since I, since I, since I've . . ." she was stammering.

"Daddy, daddy, now Sonny's dressed up like Paul Revere and he keeps running into all these houses an Cher's in them with this long nightgown and a silly hat on her head an he keeps jumping in bed with her. Come an see. Come an see," Danny burst back in.

"GET OUT OF HERE!" Martha screamed at the little boy. "GET OUT! GET OUT!"

"Don't yell at him like that," Bill tried to divert her attention as the shattered child slunk back to the TV-room.

"Do you have another woman?"

The words bit into him like an axe.

"Since I've been back, you've been completely different. I know you Bill. Something's wrong. Is it another woman? I've got to know."

Her words were relentless. *How could she know,* he wondered, *how?* He stared at her, saying nothing, gathering his strength to lie convincingly.

"Where did you get a stupid idea like that? When'm I gonna have another woman? On my lunch hour from buildin' tin trailers?"

"But you don't act like you love me anymore," she whined.

She doesn't have any proof, he thought, relieved.

"How can you love someone who's always asleep on the couch or paintin' or naggin' about fixin' this, doin' that. You're right, I didn't miss you when you were at the lake." He paused, wielding his own axe.

"I didn't miss you at all 'cause it was the first peace an quiet from fixin' you're damn house I've had since we moved in."

"I promise I won't bug you about the house anymore." She was offering concessions he hadn't even sought.

"What about fallin' asleep evry night? What about sex?"

"I promise I'll stay awake. I'll do anything you want . . ." the words Bill thrived on, " . . . if we can just be like we used to be."

Bill knew he had turned their confrontation into victory with his counterpunching. He also knew they could never go back to being what they used to be to each other."I love you," the words rolled off his tongue convincingly like a man selling elixir off the back of a wagon.

Bill Franklin felt confident he could handle his wife; it was Devere he wasn't sure about. *No way he's gonna git away with that,* he vowed.

As Bill's temper stoked up, Devere was out looking for Vicki or Carla, whichever. The day after he punched Franklin, Devere skipped work. The first playoff game was that night and he didn't see any point in tiring himself. He prowled the town in the pickup, checking out the bodyshops, the glass suppliers, the repair shops. He cruised slowly through each of the three trailerparks out by the interstate but couldn't pick up her trail or any sign of the black car.

"What're ya doin' it for?" Washington asked. "She's a pro, a whore. Let 'er go."

"Watch it, Jimmy," Devere's temper flashed ugly. "It's my life. So she's a pro. Evrybody's a pro at somethin.' You don't like bein' a foreman. You'd rather be a songwriter. But you're a foreman anyway . . . evry damn day."

Washington didn't want to fight Devere, so he just let the subject drop.

Bill Franklin wasn't letting anything drop. He got to the ballpark late, only ten minutes before game-time. The All-American Homes team was warming up on the grass behind the third base dugout. Whitey was arching tall, motionless warm-up pitches to Devere who squatted with his back resting against the dugout. Bill walked straight toward Devere in measured steps as if they were being counted off by a second.

Washington saw Bill moving toward Devere, but was too far away to stop what he knew was going to happen.

"Git up Devere," Bill screamed from about four steps downrange.

As Devere started up, Bill swung. Devere's head dodged, but he took the punch on the shoulder which Molly had so effectively softened up. The pulsing waves of pain in the already sore shoulder sent Devere back down into the dirt.

Franklin stepped back to drink in the satisfaction of seeing Devere writhing on the ground. He stepped back further as Devere struggled to rise.

The others, Whitey who was closest, Washington and Unk and Patrick and Zenger who were playing pepper futher away, froze momentarily.

Devere rose slowly, holding the bad shoulder.

Bill was stunned. He had expected his punches to take the fight out of Devere, leave him crumpled in the dust sucking for air. Instead, Devere was standing straight up and looking him straight in the eye.

"I'm gonna kill yore ass," Devere growled and the two of them went down in the dirt rolling and clawing. Devere came up on top firmly intent on bludgeoning Franklin to death. Then, luckily for Franklin, Washington and the cavalry arrived and pulled Devere off.

"What the hell's wrong with you two. We got a ball game. You crazy?" Washington lectured them.

Devere held his shoulder, his face tangled in pain.

Franklin sulked.

"You OK?" Washington asked Devere.

"This damn wing was just startin' ta feel better again. Why'd d'jew hafta go beatin' on my bad shoulder." Devere seemed strangely blithe about it all, as if he had gained some respect for Franklin. "I'm just gonna hafta walk the ball out ta Whitey after each pitch tuhnight."

Though what Devere said wasn't all that funny, everyone laughed.

The Star Spangled Banner came on over the loud speaker. They raised the flag each night but they never played the anthem before any of the regular season games.

When Devere came up in the bottom of the first, Adams was already perched on third and Franklin was lounging on first, no outs.

The top of the first had gone smoothly for two outs until Washington charged in too quickly on a line drive single to left. The ball had dipped sharply in front of him and bounced crazily to the left off the concrete ripple of the outfield grass. The ball squirted all the way to the fence. By the time Washington chased it down and threw it in, the runner was prancing into third base. The next batter, Tom Sherman, the Southern States Insurance shortstop, burned a single on a straight line out into right field and Sid Grant scored easily. So, when Devere came up in the bottom of the first with no outs and two on, the Homes team was down a run.

Fat Billy Pickett threw up the first pitch. Devere let it go. He hit the second pitch weakly to center, a lazy looper that Elton Lee caught on the run coming in fast. Devere, holding his shoulder, trotted back to the dugout. Washington's long fly to Dave Jefferson presiding in center scored Adams on the tag. That was all the runs the Homes team got until the third.

Ellie and Rae Ann arrived in the top of the third when their men were in the field. There was one out and a man on first as they sat down in the bleachers on the third base side. Franklin had, just before the girls arrived, booted an easy grounder. It had come bouncing gaily down the third base line taking high hops and singing "I'm yours baby, catch me if you can." He couldn't. First he dropped the ball, lurching after it like a man chasing a chicken with a meat cleaver, then he threw it into the dirt in front of Zenger who barely managed to glove it as Bo Reegard flashed across the bag.

Ellie waved to Bill as she sat down.

The next batter hit a hard ground ball between short and third. It skittered across the hardpan of the infield. Franklin chopped two quick steps to his left and, keeping his balance, stretched to glove the ball. He came up throwing to second. Dickie Adams made a perfect pivot and his throw beat Big Barney Quantrill to the first base bag by half a step. What a difference the arrival of a few impressionable fans can make in a ballgame.

"Super play, Skywatch," Devere, forgetting everything, said as they poured into the dugout to take their cuts.

They were back together, ready to hit. They put the game away in the bottom of the third. Though they only scored four runs, the complexion of the game had changed with that double play. They got five more in the fourth and the umpire stopped it after they'd scored two more in the bottom of the fifth to make the score twelve to two.

In the top of the fifth something happened that buried the fight between Devere and Franklin, the bad feelings, in laughter. Elton Lee hit a line single to left and took a big turn at first base, bluffing toward second. Washington fielded the ball cleanly and, without hesitating, fired the ball all the way across behind the runner to Zenger who by some stroke of luck was paying attention. They had Lee hung up between first and second. They flipped the ball back and forth, toying with Lee who dodged and reversed frantically. They closed in. Lee made a sudden break back to first. Lee's headlong dive startled Adams. As soon as the ball left his hand, Adams knew he had thrown too hard for the short distance. The throw had the diving Lee beat easily, but Zenger couldn't get his glove up in time. The ball buried itself in Zenger's stomach with a WHOOSH. Lee scambled and clawed through the dust. Zenger's eyes bugged. His mouth flapped open and his false teeth popped out and clattered down onto Lee's chest in the dirt below.

"At first I thought ya were tryin' ta bite me," Lee told Zenger after the dust had cleared.

Adams, Stevenson, Franklin, Devere, and Whitey, the whole infield, were close to the play. They collapsed with laughter.

The All-American Homes Team was loose and they were past the first round.

Two nights later, on the weekend, the Homes team beat Krieg Motors 17–5 in an easy five innings, the balls jumping off their bats.

Three nights after that, they beat Dick and Tonna's in a tight knee-knocker. In the last of the seventh with two outs and the Homes team leading 6–5, Big Eddie Burke was on first. Benny Arnold hit a line shot right up the middle. Unk, playing rover, must have been pretty shallow because he took the ball on its first sharp bounce and fired as hard as he could to second where Stevenson was covering. The throw was too late but Big Eddie came charging down the basepath too fast and overran the bag. Stevenson slapped a tag on Burke's hip and the ball game was over. All-American Homes had made the finals. Only Peerless was left.

It was the night of the second playoff game that Devere showed Jimmy Washington his secret weapon. Devere was hobbling to the parking lot after the game, listing to one side and holding his bad shoulder. Washington plodded along beside him dragging the bat bag.

"Wait'll ya see what I got in the truck," Devere warned. "I'm gonna git her back tuhnight."

"What're you talkin' 'bout?" Washington mumbled. "Yore not still tryin' ta git that whore . . . I mean Vicki . . . or Carla . . . or whatever her name is . . . back, are ya?"

"Yep, an what I got in the truck's gonna do it."

"She's long gone by now. It's been almost a week. She knows she ain't never gonna be able ta git no more customers at the ballpark."

I just got a feelin' she's still aroun' an I gotta talk ta her if she is . . . git her ta come back."

"You're crazy. How ya gonna git a'hold 'o her? Hasn't been a sign o' her since that night."

"The same way evrybody else gits ahold o' her. With this little beauty," Devere said, pointing.

Hanging from the dashboard next to the steering wheel was a shiny new CB radio.

"I don't bleeve it," Washington worked to hold back his laughter. "What is this? Some kinda truckers' version o' Cinderella? You're gonna git her back with a CB radio? Ya gotta be kiddin.'"

"Yeah, well you watch."

"Ya know how to talk on one o' those things?"

"I been listenin' ta the damn thing for two nights now an I can't understand but half o' what they say. Strangest bunch o' people ya ever met. This one short-haul trucker outa Indianapolis with this real deep, gruff, scratchy voice answers ta the name o' Cookie Monster. Ya can only understand what they're sayin' 'bout half the time."

"How's this thing gonna find her?"

"She's got one. All I gotta do is call her sometime when she's listenin.' I tried this afternoon, but no luck. I'm gonna try right now."

"You're outa yore mind."

Devere twisted some knobs and the radio crackled. He smoothed out the dissonent popping and scratching by twirling some more knobs. Washington began to distinguish voices, words. Then Devere was ready.

"Breaker, Breaker," he started out, his voice cracking in embarrassment. "I got no idea what that means," he leaned out the door to whisper to Washington, "but they always say that 'fore they start talkin.'"

"Yo got Boss Tweed outa Newport heah . . . c'mon," the CB crackled.

"Ol Iron Burr outa Windyville's all hooked up heah too . . . c'mon."

"I don't want none o' you turkeys," Devere spat into his mike. "Hey Humpty Dumpty, you got yore ears on. If ya do, please say hello, it's the Catcher callin.'"

"Breaker, Breaker, hey Boss Tweed maker, when's this yokel gonna learn the vocal. Ten-foah . . . c'mon."

"Hey Burr, fer shur, he don't sing right but he ain't wrong neither. Ten-foah."

"Breaker Catcher, this is Humpty. I'll talk long as those eighteen-wheelers don't walk all over us pore little barefoot boys."

"I got her. I got her," Devere screamed at the top of his voice.

"What the hell you screamin' 'bout? Yore 'bout ta break my ears," Boss Tweed growled out of the radio.

"Man, flip that broadcast button off 'fore ya start screamin,'" Iron Burr pleaded.

"How ya doin' Catcher? Boy, you shur got one holy terror of an ol' lady," Humpty, Carla, Vicki, purred.

"Vicki, we gotta forgit 'bout all that. Please. I gotta talk ta ya."

"Forgit it. My car's runnin' but it still isn't right. It's gonna cost me eight hundred bucks ta git all those dents fixed. Ya know what I gotta do for that eight hundred bucks?"

"Breaker, break. C'mon you hot dogs start talkin' right on those lil' barefooters or I'm gonna start cuttin' me some coaxials an doin' some bandy toe-stompin,'" Iron Burr cut in, obviously offended.

"That's a big ten-foah," Boss Tweed added.

"I don't beeleeve this," Washington turned away in hilarious disbelief.

"You guysback off. I'm tryin' ta git my girl back here," Devere barked.

The romance of it all must have gotten to Iron Burr and Boss Tweed because they didn't interrupt anymore.

"Devere, you're crazy. What d'ya want?" Vicki's voice, softer, came over the radio.

"Honey, I wantcha back. I wanna marry ya. Why dintcha tell me who ya were, are? I don't care. I love ya."

"Hey Baby Buggy, home on channel nine, you're not gonna bleeve this one," an unknown voice cut in on Devere.

"Devere, that's ridiculous even talkin' about. It's a bad idea. I'm a professional lady. Nothing like that's never gonna work."

"Vicki, listen ta me."

"Can't Devere. Listen baby, you take care y'hear. I'm goin' south in a coupla days an I won't be back. Maybe I'll head back ta Vegas or Shakytown. Ya know, you're OK Catcher, I'm glad I knew ya. Gotta put the pedal to the metal now baby. Here's my last big ten-foah," and her voice crackled and went dead.

"Wait! Come back! Come Back!" Devere screamed into his mike.

"Breaker Boss maker. You bleeve that?" Iron Burr chortled.

"That's gotta be some kinda put-on," Boss Tweed answered. "Tenfoah."

Devere sat there for long minutes. He tried again to raise her but he got no answer.

Washington never said a word. He watched silently as Devere slid the brand new CB radio out of its hanging bracket, ripping loose the wires as he tore the whole assembly away from the dash. He watched as Devere carried the shiny new radio behind the truck and placed it tenderly in the dirt of the parking lot. He fought to suppress his laughter as Devere beat the silent radio into tiny pieces with an aluminum ball bat. He cracked up when Devere drove over the remains three times with the truck before roaring away.

25 Ellie Belts Her Barnstormin' Blues While Rae Ann Sings Her Siren Song

Bill Franklin agonized through the playoffs, but not about the softball. The softball stayed pretty much the same. They were playing good and they knew they were playing good. They went out expecting to win. That could all change in the final with Peerless, but through the early playoff games the softball made few demands. It was the women that were Bill's problem.

He was being especially nice to Martha, telling her he loved her, praising lavishly her meals, even hanging shelves in her house's den. But one hot afternoon, after work, he met Ellie in the All-American Homes parking lot and took her straight to bed.

It had been more than two weeks since the party, the night they had spent together, and they fell on each other like piranhas. When Bill arrived home sweaty, he told Martha he'd been forced to work late to repair a butane line that had broken just before quitting time.

"What's butane?" she had asked.

"Poison gas," he answered gravely.

He felt like he was caught in a rundown between third and home, constantly changing direction, trying to avoid the inevitable while hoping for an error that would let him go home. At times he felt good about Martha. They had been together so long, were so used to each other. To stay with her seemed the right, safe thing to do.

But he was always thinking about Ellie. He fantasized of their life together after he dumped Martha. Yet he knew they were going nowhere. He knew he should end it. But he didn't know how. And he didn't really want to. Ellie was like a cold beer at the end of a hard, hot day's work; something to look forward to, something that gave you the heart to go on with the drudgery of living. He got a beer out of the icebox.

After the second playoff game, when the others went to the bar, Bill and Ellie headed for her apartment. They didn't talk as they undressed. Bill was tired from work, from the game. He wasn't sure he even wanted to make love, but he knew he had to. They couldn't miss an opportunity. They made love methodically. They might as well have been on the Monkey Island at the zoo. Bill came quickly and collapsed. Ellie didn't get off at all.

"This isn't really working, is it?" Ellie finally said after long minutes of silence.

"I guess not," Bill had to agree.

The silence brooded around them.

"It isn't any way for two people ta try ta love each other," Bill agreed.

"Yeah, that's the problem. I think in a desperate kinda way we really do love each other," Ellie said as if she regretted it.

"For three weeks I been tryin' ta figure out some way ta tell my wife I'm in love with another woman."

"You haven't told her, have ya?"

"I'd hafta tell her I didn't love her anymore, didn't love the kids. But I still do. But I love you too. I just can't figure it all out."

"No need ta figure anything out. You may think ya do, but you don't really wanna leave your wife an kids."

"Ellie . . . I do love you. Those two weeks when Martha was gone . . . I've never been happier in my life. Everything was perfect."

"Sure, it was beautiful, 'cause we were free, we were honest and in love with each other. But now she's back Bill. Your family's back. We can't go on like this. You can't love somebody once a week sneakin' behind the barn. That's for high school kids just learnin.'"

"I can do it. I can leave her. It's all just happenin' so fast. I haven't been able ta figure out how ta do it."

"I don't wantcha ta do it."

Ellie's face suddenly went hard. Her words snapped Bill's head back like a punch.

"What?"

"I don't wantchata leave her, your kids. I don't wanna be the cause o' that kinda stuff. I been thinkin' about it for a long time . . . long before I even met you. I'm gonna leave. I gotta git outa this town."

She's going to end it, he thought. His relief threatened to show itself.

"That stuff, settlin' down, stayin' home, kids, house, cookin.' That's OK for some people, for someone like Rae Ann mebbe. But not for me. I'm only twenty-four years old. I'd go outa my gourd. You'd hate me."

"I could leave her . . . I could," Bill insisted doggedly. "I couldn't hate you. I wanna live with you, like those two weeks when Martha was gone."

"It just can't ever be like that again. Can't you see? I wanna leave now while I'm still in love with you, so I can remember how special you were to me, how special we were together for a little while during a long hot summer. I really do love ya Bill . . . in my fashion."

Man, I almost sound like I mean all this, Ellie thought.

"We had our time. It's done. I'm leavin' Wabash City. I handed in my two weeks notice at the Homes factory yesterday."

The words of Jimmy's song—

> Ellie lives her laughin' life of lovin' on the run
> Wonderin' if there's anyplace where life can still be
> fun.
> But empty men keep droppin' into
> Her sunshine odyssey
> Sooo, Ellie lives her laughin' life alone.

—ran in Bill's mind. It was as if Washington had been trying to warn him.

But during the playoff week Ellie wasn't the only one that had her songs. Rae Ann was singing too. After the third playoff game, Rae Ann invited the temporary roommates, Devere and Washington, back to her place for a home-cooked meal, spaghetti she'd been simmering all afternoon. While they were eating, Ellie called to see how the game had come out.

"I just couldn't make it tuhnight," Ellie answered.

"They won," Rae Ann announced proudly. "Now we're in the finals against Peerless at five-thirty Saturday night."

"That's good. I'm glad. Thanks."

"Hey wait a minute. Look, Jimmy an Devere an I are sittin' here drinkin' beer. Why dontcha come over?"

"Well, hell, why not?" Ellie accepted knowing she wouldn't be seeing much more of Rae Ann who had gotten to be, in one short summer, the best friend she had ever had.

When Ellie got to Rae Ann's, the spaghetti was still hot and she had some. Then they all just sat back in the living room to drink beer.

"Should we play it for em?" Jimmy asked Rae Ann.

"Why not," she consented. "It's a demo tape Jimmy an I made ta enter in the Grand Ole Opry talent hunt contest they have evry year. Costs fifty dollars for a fifteen minute tape but when Jimmy got done puttin' all the tracks together an evrything we thought it sounded good enough ta enter. The grand prize is twenty-five thousand dollars an a contract ta appear at the Grand Ole Opry down in Nashville."

It started with the Kris Kristofferson-Rita Coolidge song, "The Things I Might Have Been." But it wasn't Jimmy Washington strumming his guitar and singing on the loading dock. It sounded like three or four guitars plus a bass playing behind his soft mournful voice. Then Rae Ann's high flashing voice came in like the sun bursting through even while the rain is still falling.

It was a professional job. Washington had recorded the four different tracks seperately and then, using borrowed equipment, mixed them. "That's me on all three o' those guitars, an I stole the bass part right off Kristofferson's own album."

Jimmy and Rae Ann did the second song in harmony, their voices sensually caressing and twining like lovers alone stroking each other:

I like the way your sparklin' earrings lay

Against your skin so brown

An I wanna sleep with you in the desert tonight

With a billion stars all aroun.'

"Wow Rae, I didn't know you could sing like that," Ellie whispered in wonder.

"I'd never sung anything in my life 'til I started singin' with Jimmy," Rae Ann whispered back as her other, recorded, voice filled the room.

The last song on the tape was "Ellie's Song," the one Washington had written. *They've made it,* Ellie thought, *and all I'm doin' is hittin' the road.*

Rae Ann was saying, "we decided ta use this one 'cause even if they don't like us mebbe someone might like Jimmy's song" when Ellie got up and ran out the door. By the time they got outside, Baby Blue was fantailing down the street. It had happened so fast nobody had noticed Ellie's tears.

26 Uphill Battle

Since that opening loss in the mud in May, the All-American Homes softball team had waged an uphill fight for the city league championship. They had won every game since that first one, the slippery fluke, even though a couple had been rained out and the game with Peerless Truck had ended right in its midsection. Now it had all come down to one game against Peerless Truck. If All-American Homes won, they garnered bragging rights in every bar in the city for the whole winter. If they lost, it had all been a waste of time, like playing a game, any game, without keeping score. On the evening of the fifteenth of August at the Riverfront ballpark the All-American Homes team came to play. They wanted Peerless Truck. They had fought their way to the top through the humid summer heat and the thickening dust. All that was left was the Peerless game.

The All-American Homes ballplayers started drifting into the ballpark about five, a half-hour before the championship game was scheduled to begin. The Homes team took some slow-motion infield. The outfielders gloved a few lazy fly balls. It was twenty after five and no one from Peerless had shown up.

""They're probly havin' battin' practice over at Kennedy Park," Devere speculated.

The umpire arrived. The city parks and recreation director was there to personally keep score and present the trophy. Five-thirty sounded on a downtown whistle. The umpire called for the captains for the coin flip. No one from Peerless Truck was there.

"We'll give em ten minutes," the umpire said, "then it's a forfeit."

But no one came.

"They might be playin' in the state tournament this weekend an couldn't git back," a spectator said to Washington as they all stood helplessly around the dugout. "The state's down in Indianapolis an if they won their afternoon game, they'd hafta play again tonight. They'd never be able ta make this game."

"Those Peerless pricks knew this was gonna happen," Devere spat the words out like they tasted bad, "an they never said a goddam word." He looked genuinely murderous as he stared out in disbelief at the empty ballfield.

"Well, looks like it's a forfeit fellas. You're the new city champs," the umpire said.

"City championship game an they don't show up," Devere sputtered as if he were going to explode.

"Hey, we won," Franklin tried to break the gloom.

Nobody seemed interested.

"Won? We didn't even play," Washington countered.

"But we're still city champs," Franklin tried again.

"I'd liketa go find them down in Indianapolis an kill em," Devere said dead serious.

"Hey, why's evrybody so down. We are the city champs, aren't we?"

"Why don'tcha just shut up," Whitey told Bill politely.

Washington had brought a bottle of cheap champagne that he had planned on sneaking up and pouring over Devere's head after they won the city title, like Reggie Jackson had done to that stuffed shirt Bowie Kuhn. When he saw the champagne sitting there in the ice chest in the back seat, it angered him. He grabbed the bottle and threw it hard against the back of the dugout. It shattered, cracking like a gun shot.

"What the hell was that?" Devere emerged from his murderous muttering, startled.

"That was our victory celebration," Washington spat.

As they slunk away from the ballpark, the whole season seemed to crumble around them. They had struggled through the long season like explorers climbing a mountain and had come out on top in a junkyard. No one felt like going home to brag about the victory. Some didn't even have homes to go to. They felt cheated out of something they had earned.

In the Sunday paper, section C, page one, a headline bragged:

PEERLESS TRUCKING SECOND IN STATE SOFTBALL
Lose to South Bend in State Tourney Final

Nowhere was there any mention of the City League champions. Nowhere any mention of All-American Homes' 23–1 season record.

27 A Laugh Among The Ruins

October in the Wabash Valley is the best month of the year. The colors of the trees on the hills and in the lowland copses, even along the city streets, flash and flow into each other. The air tastes of change, the thick humid oppression of summer chased off by snapping breezes. The speckled sunlight, twice filtered, first through high wispy clouds like dirty gauze, then through the phantom filaments of swirling dust particles, beats down cool and welcome, hospitable, no longer able or inclined to burn. The air is thick but sharp, brightly burnished and shining like dull bronze buffed up. Quiet timid days, like leaves trembling then circling slowly down, pile up unobtrusively until all the ground has been covered and the year has been stripped bare leaving only the skeletons of summer dreams to simper as the winds of winter gather.

October in the twin towns on the Wabash is when the past stands the most substantial: in the fallen leaves, the plundered fields, the burning hills that all summer brooded a deep forest green. The fall, the fragile Cheyenne autumn, the lush Indian summer that once softened the faces of the Ouiabache braves who dipped their blades into the smooth running waters of the Wabash, is a momentary spurt of life, a thrust forward against the current, as the colors of the world emerge out of the dust and heat of summer. That's why the World Series is always in October.

Bill Franklin loved to walk the campus in the fall, mostly to look at the girls, the healthy, cornfed, summer-seasoned coeds back from the farms and fields of rural Indiana, but also to breathe the fall air, smell and taste the fallen past. One crisp afternoon, he crossed the campus and walked down the hill to the riverbank. The river, which in August had petered out like the baseball season, was no longer a muddy brown trickle. It was up and flowing, nourished by the quick-hitting thunder showers of September that almost every day had plunged down the valley like halfbacks hitting holes in the stadium on the west end of campus.

Straight across, on the Wabash City side, the empty ballfields sat brown and dusty and still. With the bases gone, the lines rubbed out, the diamonds teetered on the verge of rust. The barrenness of the ball-fields made Bill turn away, drove him back inside to the reality of his classroom. He had only one more class to teach, then he would ride his bicycle home through the heavy October air to a five-o'clock drink on the patio with Martha and a stringy pot roast with carrots clinging like barnacles for dinner.

Sure wish I had a ballgame tonight, Bill thought as he walked the straight and narrow lines of the quadrangle.

It had been almost two months since Bill Franklin's last day at All-American Homes in the shimmering heat of August. But that last day, something, really not a very big thing, had happened and it stuck in his mind like a tattoo. That whole last day Bill had kept think-ing about what a good season, what an exciting summer it had been, despite everything, despite even the fight with Devere, the forfeit of the championship game. He had felt sad that last day, sad because he knew he'd never play ball with them again, not next summer, not ever. He knew he'd never come back to the mobile home factory. He never belonged there in the first place.

Purposely, that last day, he sat next to Washington on the load-ing dock at lunch. When Devere joined them, Bill even felt a kind of thorny kinship for him, the kind he had felt as a kid for his high school football coach who had screamed and cussed and tortured and humili-ated them to the point that they went out and won ten straight games, went undefeated, just so they could spit in his face, backed by over-whelming evidence, the fact that they weren't the "cowards" he had ac-cused them of being all through the season. But nobody had ever said anything. Somehow, when they had accepted the trophies, everything had been forgotten. It was that afternoon of the last day at the Homes factory that the thing happened that stuck so vividly in Bill's mind.

Washington had yelled for Bill and Devere to help load a special-ordered mobile home on a truck for delivery. It was an extra-plush, ac-cessory-glutted module that some millionaire must have ordered to use for a hunting cabin in his private woods or a ski lodge on his private mountain or a beach house on his private lake. Washington needed some hands to steady it as the loading crane hoisted it onto the truck. Devere and Bill happened to be within earshot.

Out in the dust, the crane stood waiting like the long arm of the law. The super-deluxe mobile home, the very best that All-American Homes could produce, sat next to an oversized flat-bed trailer. Four shorter steel cables, all converging into one thick cable, hung down from the towering arm of the crane. Under the supervision of the crane operator they secured the cables to the corners of the premier All-American Home. The unrepaired eyes on the billboard looked on. The crane operator climbed into his cab. The cables tightened. The plush palace of a mobile home began to rise, inch by inch, slowly, a foot at a time.

Then it happened.

It couldn't have been more than fifteen feet off the ground when the cable on one of the corners snapped. The hanging trailer at first just sagged slowly at the one corner. But then another corner came loose and the whole thing crashed to the ground. It didn't fall far. Or fast. But when that ideal All-American Home hit, it disintegrated as if it was a fragile house of cards. Joints broke. Plastic shattered and split. Pipes burst jagged and thrust out from beneath the rubble. Siding crumbled and walls cracked and fell. Then the dust rose in a small comic cloud over the pile of junk in the barren parking lot. Only moments before, it had seemed so solid, All-American's finest mobile home.

Washington looked at Bill.

Bill and Jimmy looked at Devere.

They all momentarily looked at each other.

Then, simultaneously, they started to laugh. A mere giggle at first, then louder, harder, leaning against each other as they laughed. Laughter was the only possible response, the only action that made any sense.

From an upstairs window, Ellie and Rae Ann watched the whole thing. It was Ellie's last day of work and she had gone up to Rae Ann's desk to fill out the final forms, say goodbye to All-American Homes once and for all. As they stood at the window watching Devere and Washington and Franklin and then the house coming down and disintegrating into rubble, they didn't know how to react.

"You bleeve that?" Ellie finally blurted out.

"Wow!" Rae Ann breathed in pure amaze. "What are they doin'?"

"Looks like they're chokin.'"

"I hope they're OK."

"Oh they're OK," Ellie reassured her, "ain't no way you're gonna put a dent in those guys."

As Bill Franklin walked the campus in the drugged October air, he thought about the two months since the season had ended. He had spent them sitting in Martha's house trying to convince himself that the long evenings spent watching her crochet afghans were important. He had spent them in the classroom hovering like a scarecrow over the innocent scrubbed faces of the children of the middle class. One of his first days back at the university that fall semester, he had assigned, as a bad joke, to his composition class the topic "How I Spent My Summer Vacation." They had all groaned and then bent their heads to write the in-class theme and the sour taste of winning a championship on a forfeit had swirled up into his consciousness.

Back in the classroom, looking out at the fading October afternoon, Bill felt better. The class was Introduction to Fiction and he liked the books. His memories began to fade into the pages of F. Scott Fitzgerald. But that one memory kept coming back, he and Jimmy Washington, whom he hadn't seen since, and Devere standing there laughing with each other as that mobile home crumpled into tinny matchsticks.

How they had laughed. Rocking horse laughs. The three of them standing there laughing with each other.

The Redneck Mafia

William J. Palmer

Inspired in part by some true incidents and a major historical event, nonetheless the characters and plots of this novel are wholly fictional.

Part One

The Hamlet

Death of a Salesman

The red "VACANCY" sign blinked off and on in the driveway of *The Crossroads Inn* in Newport, Kentucky just across the river from Cincinnati. 1977, early March, and Bill O'Neill had been staying at *The Crossroads* upwards of twenty years. He pulled in at about six-fifteen, his black Chevy loaded with samples in both the back seat and the trunk. Like Willie Loman, he was a traveling salesman, baby furniture. He liked *The Crossroads*. It was cheap, but the sheets were clean. It was close to Cincinnati. And there were other entertainments to be enjoyed in the small town of Newport.

He checked in to *The Crossroads*. They knew him there. He stopped in the bar for a Scotch before he drove the Chevy around back to his room. The barman he liked, Eddie, a gray-haired guy about his age, 48, but black, wasn't working. Too bad, but he had the drink anyway. When he got to his room, he picked up the phone and made his call through the office switchboard. Forty minutes later, the woman parked and climbed up the stairs to Bill O'Neill's second floor room. They were getting to be old friends. She was an ex- stripper he had been introduced to by Eddie the barman just about two years before. She was careful because she worked freelance and only kept a small number of regular tricks. And, like the motel's sheets, she was clean.

When she left, an hour and a half later, she dallied to fix her eye makeup and lipstick in her rear-view mirror. As she pulled out of the back lot, she glanced up and saw what looked like two men going into Bill O'Neill's room. *That's strange,* she thought, but shrugged it off.

When the motel room door flew open with a crash, Bill O'Neill was sitting on the bed watching *The Mary Tyler Moore Show* in his underwear. His head jerked toward the door in surprise. He saw a brief flash of metallic light as the two men raised their hands toward him.

"What the . . . ?"

When the first bullet hit him, he died instantly. The other three bullets were the killers' bow to thoroughness. Unfortunately, they had just murdered the wrong man.

"It ain't him."

"What the . . ."

They ran out the door and down the steps without remorse or analysis. The question of who they had shot never crossed their minds.

Tim Mounce was an eighteen-year-old busboy working four-to-midnight in *The Crossroads Inn* bar and coffee shop. About nine o'clock each night his job was to circle the parking lot with a pad and pencil and write down all the license plate numbers of the cars and trucks parked in front of the motel room doors and out along the edges of the lot.

In the summer this chore was a nice cigarette break. In January and February it was a freezing pain in the ass. This night was one of the first warm ones of the year. Tim had only jotted down four numbers from the front row of rooms when he heard the tires squeal and the gray pickup truck sped by him. He remembered that as the truck rushed by a cigarette flew out of the window and bounced on the pavement of the parking lot sending off a shower of sparks. He caught just the briefest glimpse of the license plate, white, 79, the first two numbers. For some reason he wrote them down, then went on about his business. He never noticed the open door of the second floor room or the wavering blue glimmer from the TV set.

It was a trucker leaving early the next morning who finally looked into the room with the open door, then ran down in a panic to report what he saw to the night manager in the office. By then Bill O'Neill had been dead for almost nine hours, and no one had even noticed.

At the night manager's call, two detectives from the Newport Police Department came to investigate. One was middle-aged and slovenly, his gut hanging over his belt at about twelve-pack a day level. The other seemed young and eager. The older cop didn't care and the younger didn't seem to know what questions to ask. Lyle Gaines, the night manager, tried to help them as much as he could. But they were out of their depth. They might as well have been garbage men. They took out the body in a plastic bag and cleaned up the room after they dusted it for prints and took some pictures. Lyle rented it that next night to a young couple from Atlanta driving north.

Dial M for Murder

The phone rang in Megan O'Neill's apartment in Columbus, Ohio a little after noon. Megan was sitting at the kitchen table studying for an accounting exam.

The two detectives, the beer belly and the rookie, had gone through the murdered guy's wallet, luggage and clothes. First they found his name and address in the wallet but when they called the number in Akron, Ohio, nobody answered. Then they found his salesman's address book. Megan's was the only O'Neill name in it.

Hello.

Is this Megan O'Neill?

Yes.

Is your husband William Michael O'Neill of Akron, Ohio?

Husband?

Brother?

Try father. What is this? Who are you?

This is Detective James Mayes of the Newport, Kentucky police department.

What is it? Has my dad been arrested?

Miss O'Neill, I've got some bad. . . .

O my god! He's hurt, isn't he? Did he have an accident. I told him not to drive when he's too tired.

Miss O'Neill, I'm sorry, but your father is dead.

Dead. O my God!

And that was the moment when Megan O'Neill's schoolgirl life came to an end. She didn't faint, collapse sobbing, nothing like that. She just sat there holding the phone, paralyzed, her throat tightening up, her mind scorched clear across its surface, burned off into the charred blackness of incomprehension.

Miss O'Neill. Are you there?

She couldn't make her throat work to answer. Her father's smile, his kind eyes, the pride and love in his face when he saw her, his excitement at her ballgames: these images whirled in her mind as if she was looking into a kaleidoscope filled with the spinning fragments of her father's face.

Miss O'Neill. Are you OK? Miss O'Neill.

The voice of death, that policeman somewhere in Kentucky, prodded her out of her paralysis of disbelief.

On the other end of the phone line, Officer Mayes, the rookie detective, didn't know what to do. He'd never made a call like this before.

How did my father die, officer?

Ma'am, he was shot four times in his motel room.

What? That's not funny!

Miss O'Neill, it's true.

You're serious, aren't you?

Yes, ma'am.

Strange the things one thinks of in times of stress. *Why does he keep calling me "ma'am?" I'm not old enough.*

Again, a long silent pause. She was utterly confused. *No one would ever want to shoot my dad,*

Give me that.

The beer-bellied older cop plucked the phone out of Detective Mayes's hand.

Miss O'Neill, if you are Mr. William Michael O'Neill's only relative, you will need to come here to the Newport, Kentucky city morgue to identify and claim the body of your father. Just ask for Detective Mayes or Detective Gropper. The morgue and police department are both in the same building. We can give you the name of a mortician who can help you with the arrangements, transport, coffin, those kinds of things. We will need a day or so to investigate the body. Since it is a murder investigation there will be a partial autopsy. If you could come on Monday, we should be ready to release the body.

Yes, alright.

It was one of the longest weekends Megan O'Neill had ever spent. She told her two roommates what had happened and they gasped, holding their mouths as she had. She looked at the smiling pictures of her father on her bedroom dresser and she still didn't believe it. Then she started to cry. The sobs wracked her body so hard that her room-mates wanted to take her to Urgent Care.

Then the reality started to set in. An orphan, completely alone in the world. No one to call when she needed to talk. Then anger. How could he do this to her, leave her all alone like this? What kind of an animal would shoot her dad? He had never hurt a soul. Why would anyone want to hurt him? It had to be a mistake. Yes, maybe it wasn't really him. Maybe someone had stolen his wallet. Denial. Maybe he wasn't really dead. She couldn't stand it. She couldn't make it through the weekend. Sunday morning she got in the car and drove to New-port, Kentucky.

At the police station, Megan asked for Officer Mayes and luckily he was on duty.

Miss O'Neill, James Mayes. I'm sorry about your father.

I'm sorry I'm here a day early, but I couldn't wait any longer. I have to know. I don't think it's him. No one would shoot him. He's a sales-man.

What did he sell?

Baby furniture, toys.

Yes, we found that stuff in his Chevy.

Can I see the body?

Yes. We're done with it. Here, this way.

They climbed up two flights of steps to the morgue. Somehow she thought they should have gone down. It should have been in the base-ment. It was a small room, very cold. A stainless steel table sat in the middle of the floor grooved with run-off channels around its edges. One wall had three drawers like an oversized file cabinet, except each drawer had a heavy pull-back clasp instead of ordinary handles. Young officer Mayes opened the middle drawer and pulled it out just one-third of the way so that only the head, covered by a yellow sheet, was exhumed.

Are you OK to look?

Megan nodded her head quickly. She just wanted to know one way or the other.

He pulled back the sheet.

Her hand went to her mouth involuntarily as if to stifle a scream that never escaped her throat. It was her dad, her sweet dad who cheered at her games, who used to buy her ice cream in the evenings, who always kidded her about her boyfriends. It was him, gray, frozen, what seemed a huge hole ringed in black blood through his cheek on the right side of what had once been his sweet, loving, smiling face. Her throat clenched up again and she staggered backwards from the partially opened drawer. She banged into the steel table. It was on wheels and careened off into the wall with a clang of metal. She felt the policeman's hands on her shoulders trying to steady her and she struck out at him in anger, slapping at his face and shoulders with both hands.

It's him, dammit. Yes, it's him. It's him.

She stopped flailing at the frightened cop finally, realized where she was, what she was doing.

I'm sorry. I didn't mean to hit you. It's not your fault.

But driving back to Columbus the next day after all the arrangements had been made, anger started to set in and she began to wonder just whose fault it was?

Look Back In Anger

Meg O'Neill's grief, and confusion, festered into a throbbing anger. It took almost three days to bury her father, to get the body to Akron, to endure the well-meaning condolences of her mother's and father's circle of friends. She stood in the cold and rain as they lowered her father into the grave next to her mother. He was only forty-eight years old. Her mom had only been forty-six when she died of cancer. It seemed so unfair. Through it all her anger grew. She was building a strong, hard hate for whoever made this stupid mistake.

After the funeral, she went back to her family's home, but it wasn't a home anymore, just an empty house. She tried to sleep there that night, but she was so alone that she heard every creak and rustle in the floors and walls. She tossed and turned, then sat bolt upright out of her half-sleep when she saw her mother and father walking toward her out of the mirror. Then she was staring at herself and she realized that the only place they existed now was in the mirror of her mind. At six AM she was in the car driving south toward Columbus and school, but the anger still burned inside her.

Some stupid jerk, some retarded hit man, made a mistake and killed my father.

As she drove, the anger built, fueled by memories of the things she and her dad had done. He loved to play catch with her, and go out to the field and hit her ground balls. He'd swing the bat and hit the grounders with only his right hand and wear a glove on his left so that when she fielded the ball she'd have someone to throw to. He'd be out on the road trying to sell things all day, but when he came home all he wanted to do was play with her or watch her play her games.

When she got to Columbus on Interstate 71, she never stopped. Her anger kept driving her south to Newport. Her anger was so strong that she knew she couldn't just go back to school, to studying and going to class and going out to the bars on weekends. She had to find out what had happened. If she didn't, she felt that all of her feelings would just burn up, and the whole twenty-two years of her life, all the memories of her mom and dad, would just go up in flames and turn to ashes as if they had never been real. She had to do something and driving to Newport, Kentucky, was all she could think to do. Her anger burned like a fire smoldering in her throat and chest. She suddenly looked down and the speedometer was on ninety-five miles an hour. She let off the gas and tried to swallow.

When she got to Newport, the first thing she did was drive past the motel where it had happened, *The Crossroads Inn,* but she didn't pull in. She wasn't ready for that yet. She couldn't think with this anger burning inside her. She drove on to the police station.

It was a Thursday afternoon and both of the investigators, detectives Mayes and Gropper, were on duty. As she waited for them to answer the desk sergeant's page, she tried to think of how she could explain why she was here. When the older, fat one showed up eating a large sandwich with mayonnaise smeared on his face, it made her anger flame up again. She forgot all she had rehearsed to say. The younger one was polite. The older one seemed totally disinterested.

Miss O'Neill. You're back. What can we do for you?

Have you found out why my father was shot in that motel?

No, we haven't, Miss O'Neill. The investigation is ongoing.

Now look, honey, the fat one interrupted.

He said it with his mouth full and that angered Meg even more. Her voice went tight and sharp.

Don't call me honey. What does ongoing mean? What are you two *doing?* What have you found out?

It's police business, Miss O'Neill.

No. It's my business. The murdered man in your ongoing investigation is, was, oh damn, my, my . . . father.

She hadn't wanted to cry. but to her surprise her tears got it done. The young one started to talk and the fat one walked away in disgust.

We've talked to people at the motel. The night clerk didn't see anything. Your father made one phone call. We're checking it out. The fingerprints from the room haven't come back yet.

It's been almost six days. How long does it take to check these things out?

Miss, we've got other ongoing cases.

Jimmy.

The older cop wandered back.

Jimmy, that's enough. We're working on it, Miss. We'll let you know when we find something out.

She left the police station in a daze. They didn't even care. A murder, some kind of gang assassination right in their small little Kentucky town, and they didn't seem to care. What other cases could be as important in this small town? From talking to them, she knew that those two Newport police detectives had no idea what had happened that night at *The Crossroads Inn,* and probably were never going to find out.

From a pay phone in the gas station, Megan called her roommate in Columbus and told her that she wouldn't be back to school for a few days. Then she called the lawyer in Akron, a friend of her dad's, and told him where she was. He advised her against staying there. Get on with your life, his cliché angered her. Those rudimentary logistics attended to, she drove straight to *The Crossroads Inn* and got a room.

It's a run-down, cheap motel, she thought as she carried her bag into her room. *Why would he stay here? To cut down on expenses? Habit? Location? Certainly not amenities. Relationships? Did he know people here?*

Long Day's Journey Into Night

It had been a long day for Meg O'Neill what with the driving, the anger, the frustration with those two cops. She took a nap in her clothes on the bed in the room as soon as she checked into *The Crossroads Inn*. At about seven, she awoke and went down to the bar. It was almost empty, a nuzzling couple in a booth against the wall.

Can you make me a Long Island ice tea? She asked the bartender.

No problem.

He was a middle-aged black man, about her dad's age.

When he came back with the drink, she came right out with it because she really didn't know any other way to go about it.

My father was murdered in this motel last Thursday night.

Oh. Yes. I wasn't workin' that night.

Oh, I'd hoped maybe . . . well.

Long silent pause between them. But the bartender did not retreat. She sipped.

I read about it in the paper. I knew your father. He was a nice quiet man. He'd been staying here regularly for years, about once a month, when he worked in Cincy across the bridge. Scotch and water.

Do you have any idea why this happened?

Awful strange. I thought that when I read about it. Why do a hit on a travelling salesman?

Megan. My name is Meg O'Neill.

She extended her hand across the bar to him.

Eddie. Eddie Wells. I'm sorry about your father.

You said 'a hit.'

Yeah. Had to be. I heard from the night manager, Lyle, they broke in and shot him. Didn't rob him or take anything. Just bang, bang, bang.

I'd like to talk to Lyle. When does he come to work?

Eight.

Silent pause again. Long sip of her sweet brown drink. Eddie pours himself a cup of coffee, turns back to her.

Why are you doin' this?

What?

Bein' here. Askin' around like this.

I don't know.

Silent pause. Both sip.

Got to be some reason.

It all made me mad. I think it was a mistake. No one has any reason to shoot my dad. For god's sake, he was a baby furniture salesman!

I know. I know. I think you're right.

You said you knew my dad.

Only here, over a drink. He wasn't a drinker. One, at the most two, scotch and waters. Or maybe one before he went out to dinner and one before he went to bed. We'd talk a little. This place is not very busy during the week. Mostly sports. Baseball. He liked the Indians. I follow the Reds. I remember him sayin', my daughter plays baseball.

Softball.

Yeah, softball.

But Meg had started crying again and didn't hear. He passed her a cocktail napkin and after a minute she got herself back together.

Sorry.

It's OK. OK. Fatherly

She tried to regain her focus.

Can you tell me anything about his stays here before? Has anyone around here mentioned anything about that night? Anything unusual.

Suddenly Eddie the bartender clammed up. He finished his coffee and looked for somewhere to escape to, but there was nowhere for him to go. The couple in the booth had left. There was nobody else in the bar.

Miss, I don't think this is a good idea. Askin' these questions. Shouldn't you let the police handle this?

The police. Right. They're like *Car 54 Where Are You?*

Eddie had to laugh at that. You got that right.

Meg pushed her empty glass at him.

One more, I need help sleeping.

Poor Kid, Eddie couldn't help thinking as he made her a second drink. You're pretty much right about these Newport cops, he said when he brought it back to her.

Have they been here?

Yeah. They talked to Lyle, that's all. He was workin' that night. I just told 'em I wasn't here and that was it. Those Newport cops though, you never know about them. Best be careful around Newport here, miss. There's a lotta things goin' on aren't what they seem. I just don't think it's a good idea askin' a lot of questions around. There's murder involved here. I'd hate to see you get yourself hurt.

What do you mean?

Look, Miss O'Neill, you might find out some things you don't want to know.

What do you mean? About my father?

Maybe. About this whole thing. It could be real dangerous. Best leave it alone.

What do you know about my father?

Miss, please.

Tell me. I need to know.

Your father was a lonely man since your mother died. He told me about her. I helped him. There is a woman I know that he got to be friends with. I sort of introduced them. Lyle said he called her that night.

My dad and a woman, here?

She's a prostitute, miss.

The bartender had been very right about one thing. Meg had just found out something she didn't want to know.

The Night Manager

Eddie the bartender had been right about one other thing. Lyle Gaines, the night clerk, was a nice guy. He was also a fairly obvious homosexual. He spoke openly to Meg, who was feeling good, talkative, from her two Long Islands in the bar. She introduced herself and told him what Eddie had told her. That ice broken, she asked him what he knew about the night that her father had been killed.

He checked in at 6:37. At 7:21 he placed a phone call to this number (and Lyle wrote it down for her). I'm guessing that is the lady in question.

He didn't question her or try to put her off. He seemed almost eager to help.

Have the police been here?

Yes they have. They were so rude. They treat everyone like dirt.

Did you give them this number?

I had to.

They never said anything to me about it.

I'm not surprised. Those two did not strike me as, shall we say, rocket scientists.

Do you remember anything else about that night?

I don't, but you might talk to one of our young busboys. He might have seen something. He was out in the parking lot that night. He's in the café, the cute one with the long brown hair.

The Catcher in the Rye

Meg found Tim Mounce, the busboy, in the kitchen. He had a base-ball cap on, turned backwards. She was really getting tired and the drinks were beginning to make her head spin. She introduced herself and asked if she could talk to him about that night. He looked about eighteen and seemed eager to talk to her.

Let's go out back. I can smoke out there.

On the way through the bar he grabbed a half-full bottle of Coca-Cola out of Eddie's cooler. The bartender watched them go out the back exit with a sad look on his face but without a word (as if he knew that all of this was going to come to no good).

Lyle, the night manager, said that you were out in the parking lot the night that my father was murdered.

Yeah, I was.

Did you see anything, anything?

I don't know, mebbe. I didn't think anything about it at the time (he lit up his cigarette).

What. Tell me.

I was checking license plates. They make me do it every night. I write 'em down.

License plate numbers?

Yeah.

You write them all down?

Yeah.

What did you see?

A pick-up truck. Gray or silver, I think. Squealed its tires peeling out of the back parking lot.

Did you see who was in it?

No. It went by so fast it almost hit me.

I wrote down part of the license number though. I don't know why. I think it was an Indiana plate. Ask Lyle, he keeps those lists.

Did you see anything else?

Nope.

Thanks.

Hey, you want a cigarette? Stay a while. It's a pretty nice night for March.

I can't. Gotta go. I don't smoke. I don't feel so well. Good night (and she fled).

In her room Megan threw up twice, which was unusual because she had drunk more than two Long Islands before.

Main Street

Megan slept late and surprisingly well. That long day before of driving, and thinking, and finally questioning, had exhausted her. When she woke up, after ten, she took a long, hot shower, as if trying to wash the reality of her dad's death away. She wanted to see Lyle's license plate list. She wanted to call the prostitute's number that Lyle had given her (and the police). But at eleven-thirty in the morning all she wanted was to get away from *The Crossroads Inn* for awhile.

She pulled out of the parking lot and spotted the golden arches in the distance. Coffee. *The Crossroads Inn* was at a crossroads, a major intersection between Interstate 71 and State Highway 9. After her coffee and cardboard breakfast, she needed gas.

What's that big building up at the top of that hill? she asked the gas station attendant.

Across the highway?

Yes.

Oh that's Southgate, and that's the night club, been there forever. It's the fanciest place around these parts on weekends. Sure beats all that trash downtown.

Downtown?

Downtown Newport.

Which way is that?

Just turn right out that driveway, and then left, at the first light, that's Main, takes you right through downtown. Guess that's why they calls it Main, HAW!

Megan found downtown Newport, Kentucky pretty funny. After she drove through it once, she turned around and drove back through it again in disbelief. Then she parked her car and walked up one side of Main and back the other, all the while playing a word game in her mind, searching for the one perfect word to describe this dirty little town: tawdry, sleazy, horny, raunchy, kinky, scummy, sordid, honky-

tonk, glitzy (hardly), trashy, dirty (maybe that was best)—dirty in a
lot of different ways. Main Street was a crazy quilt of bars, restaurants,
strip joints, massage parlors, peep shows, arcades, drug stores, a store-
front church, a gas station on a corner, a *Burger King,* a convenience
store dominated by cigarette signs, a bail bonds office, a pawn shop
with the classic three balls over the door and a chain link fence pulled
down over the window, assorted coffee shops, and a mom and pop
grocery store. Meg thought the names and the signs were hilarious. *La
Madame's,* very French, "The Prettiest Girls on the Strip—25 Show
Girls." *The Brass Bull Show Lounge,* "Girls Galore." *Dillinger's Lounge*
with the black silhouettes of Tommy Guns framing "Girls, Girls,
Girls" on the garish sign. The Newport "strip" certainly lived up to its
name. *Lurid,* maybe that was the word she wanted. One thing nagged
at Megan's mind as she walked around Newport, taking it all in, what
Eddie the bartender had said: *things aren't always what they seem.*

She got back into her car. She had planned to stop at the police station to ask the two detectives if they had called the prostitute's phone
number, but for some reason she just decided against it. Instead, she
fled dirty little sex-obsessed Newport, Kentucky, crossed over the
bridge into Cincinnati and went to a movie, *Taxi Driver.* It didn't
cheer her up. The Robert DeNiro character reminded her of her dad,
so alone and lonely, attracted to a prostitute.

Lord of the Rings

When Meg got back to the motel, about four, she sat on the bed with its nubby white chenille spread, tucked her legs under her, and stared at the phone. Deep breath, dial the number, no idea what to say. Surprise. Picked up on the other end after only two rings.

Hello. . . . Hello?

Meg couldn't think of how to begin, so she hastily hung up. The woman's voice wasn't intimidating or anything. She didn't sound like a prostitute. After rehearsing opening lines for almost a half hour, Meg dialed again.

Hello.

Yes. Hello. I was given your number by Eddie, the bartender at *The Crossroads Inn*. I wanted, well, I wanted to see, uh, meet. . . .

Honey, Eddie should know better. I don't do girls. Sorry. Hang up, but not angry, just matter of fact.

Third time's a charm, Meg hoped as she re-dialed.

Hello (annoyed).

Look, please don't hang up. My name is Megan O'Neill. My dad was murdered at *The Crossroads Inn* last Thursday night. The night clerk said he called this number. I don't know your name. I'm sorry.

The woman on the other end was momentarily silenced by the urgency in Meg's voice, but she didn't hang up.

It's Mary Al. . . . It's Sheila. I read about it in the paper. I'm sorry.

The paper? You mean the police haven't contacted you?

No. I thought they would.

What is going on in this town? Meg thought.

Could I. . . . talk to you? About my father. Did you see him that night? I'll pay you. Your . . . your regular fee. Tonight? Could you come here to the motel and we could talk? I'll pay you for your time.

Look honey . . .

Meg sensed that the woman was getting ready to hang up.

Please, please talk to me. This is all some terrible mistake. I know it.

I'm sorry honey, but I can't get involved in this. This is murder. And I'm a working girl. Your dad was a nice guy. I'm sorry that he got killed, but I can't. . . .

You were there that night, weren't you? Oh please, help me. He was all I had . . .

The woman on the other end of the line could hear the tears in Megan's voice. She hesitated, but she didn't hang up. Look, I've got two dates tonight. Should be done about midnight. I'll come by *The Crossroads* then. What's your room number?

One-oh-nine. Oh thank you.

I shouldn't be doing this, but your dad was an OK guy. He told me about your mother dying. I'll be there.

Hang up.

Meg collapsed back on the bed and the sobs wracked her chest. *I've got to stop this stupid crying* she thought when the fit was over. *It hurts too much.*

Alice in Wonderland

Mary Alice Martin became Sheila Shepherd at night. Sheila was the name all of her customers knew her by. She was not inexpensive. She charged one hundred and fifty dollars for a half-and half (oral sex and a straight fuck on a one hour time limit). She had a price list for more exotic sex acts (or more time). She did straight blow jobs and she considered dog style and reverse cowgirl straight sex. She also did anal but it was twice the price. She actually liked to dance for her customers. She had started out as a stripper and carried a small jam box in her car with some great dance tapes. Sometimes the stripping and dancing really made her job easier. All men dream of doing a stripper.

She was careful in picking her clients and never infringed on any downtown pimp's or madame's turf. Her greatest fear was working for someone else. Her business was good enough that she had been able to stop stripping.

As for her regulars, she actually liked some of them. Bill O'Neill had been in that category. No risk there. Need. She could make him feel good for a while. *I'm a naked physical therapist,* she would chuckle to herself after a good trick with one of her likeable regulars. She actually had a kind of specialty. Seven of her regulars were wheelchair-bound, paralyzed, and she was really good with them.

The Wizard of Oz

The crying jag that talking on the phone to Sheila, her dad's hooker, sent Megan off on ultimately dropped her into sleep. When she woke up, her tears were dried and it was almost eight o'clock. She decided to risk a burger in *The Crossroads Inn* café. Instead she had the night's special, meat loaf and mashed potatoes, and it reminded her of her mom. Tim the busboy was working the café. There was hardly anybody eating so they had time to talk.

When Lyle comes in, I'm going to talk to him about those license plate lists, see if he still has the one for that night. If he does, would you go over it with me?

Sure.

Maybe the two of us going over it will help you remember something about that night?

Maybe.

Meg had the feeling that Tim would probably do anything she wanted him to do.

Lyle went on duty as the night manager at eight. Meg was waiting for him.

Miss O'Neill. Hello. What can I do for you?

Hi. I was hoping you could help me. Tim the busboy said that he makes a list of all the license plates in the parking lot every night.

Yes. It's a house rule.

Why do you do that?

The owners, they're lawyers, tell us to do it. In case there are problems, I guess.

Problems?

Oh. Like damage to the rooms. Or theft, or. . . . Oh, really worst scenario (and he patted the back of her hand in a very sisterly way), if someone should die in one of the rooms. I guess they want the license numbers in case they have to go to court.

Do you still have the list from last Thursday night, the night my father was . . . ?

Here, here, he consoled her, patting her hand again. Yes, I'm sure I do. Each night I just toss the busboy's list in a file folder. They're all dated.

He disappeared behind a partition and returned almost instantly holding a fat file folder bulging with scraps of paper. But even in the short time he was gone, something else had occurred to Meg.

Didn't the police ask for these lists?

No, they never did. They asked for the registration cards for that night, and I made them copies on the copy machine. Most of the cards have license numbers on them, but not all. You would absolutely be amazed at how many people in America don't know their own license number.

It took him about ten seconds of rummaging in the folder to find the list in question.

Here it is, last Thursday, March 2nd. We were pretty full that night. He handed over the list to her, then took it back. Maybe I should make a copy of it for you, then you can just take it with you.

Again he disappeared behind his partition. His comings and goings were beginning to remind her of the Wizard of Oz.

Remembrance of Things Past

Back in the café, Meg caught Tim the busboy's eye. He scurried over like a puppy chasing a colorful ball of yarn.

Lyle gave me the list for that night. Could you look at it with me?

Sure. It's no big deal. Just a bunch of numbers. (But suddenly a bulb went on in Tim's eager face.) Wait a minute. Remember I told you about the pick-up that squealed out that night. I wrote part of the license plate down. I remember doin' it. Let me see that.

He grabbed the photocopy out of her hand and slid into an empty booth.

Here it is. I wrote it off to the side. See, here.

She slid into the booth with him, moving him over with her hips so she would have room to sit on the naugahyde. She sensed him tense up as she did it.

There, 79 white. That's what I wrote.

Yes. 79 white. What does it mean?

79 white. That's all I could get. The first two numbers and white is the color of the license plate.

What state has white plates?

Either Indiana or Colorado.

Wow. Do you know the colors of all the states?

She made herself sound very impressed. He beamed.

Yeah. Most of 'em. You see a lot of Indiana plates down here. It's just over the border. That's gotta be an Indiana plate 'cause their first two numbers are always separated from the other numbers by a smaller letter. See, there's a full Indiana number He pointed to about his tenth notation down the list—36E7714I. See. I always put the first letter of the state after the number. See all the Os for Ohio and Ks for Kentucky. There's another I for Indiana, and another one there, and there and there and there.

It turned out there were tons of I's for Indiana on the list.

Why are the first two letters separated from the others on the Indiana license plates?

Again he beamed, and moved closer to her in the booth so that their thighs were lightly touching.

It's probably the county the plate was issued in. Some states put the county name right on the plate. Others have a number code, like Indiana.

Wow. That's cool. You know everything about license plates, don't you?

His eyes went wide as she took his hand that had been pointing to the list. She looked him full in the face seductively.

Would you come out in the parking lot with me, walk around, show me where you saw the pick-up peel out, show me how you write down the license numbers?

Sure. Absolutely. Just let me tell the cook I'm goin' out for a cigarette.

She waited for him outside the door to the lobby under the red-blinking "Vacancy" sign. She didn't wait long. The first thing he did was light up a cigarette when he got outside. It was a cool windless night and the smoke hung over them like a cartoonist's bubble.

Do you do it the same way every night, writing the numbers down I mean?

Pretty much.

Here (and she held up the list from the night her father had been murdered), how did you write these numbers down that night (and they both looked at the list in the blinking red light)?

He took the list and started to walk with it like a pirate pacing off a treasure map.

These first four numbers were parked along here, see, and then just as I got to the corner of the building the pick-up came tearing out of the back, there (he pointed), and that's when I wrote down that number, the partial.

OK, where were you standing when the truck almost hit you?

He walked to a spot looking down the length of the motel's two-storey front wing. The smaller two-storey back wing stretched across the back of the parking lot.

Here.

And where did it come from?

There (and he pointed straight down the front wing).

And where is room 236?

There (and he pointed the same way again), on the second floor.

Then they could have been parked by my father's room?

Yeah (he thought about it), probably by the stairway at the end of the row.

OK.

She took a moment to think about it. If it was a mistake, then they were after someone else, in another room, but probably close by her father's room. The guy they wanted would have his car parked along the row.

You go to Ohio State, don't you?

Uh-huh.

I'm savin' up money to go to college. Probably UK or Louisville.

Yeah, great. When you went down this row, did you write the numbers down in sequence?

Un-uh. Not in straight sequence. Some cars are parked along the building, some are parked out in the lot in a row. I go sort of right/left as I walk.

Show me.

He took back the list and started walking.

The first number would be parked here (and he pointed to a parking slot on his right up against the building) and this next one might be out there (and he nodded to his left, one row away from the building).

So you usually alternate there then there as you walk down the aisle.

Yeah, I guess.

She took the list out of his hand once again and started walking down the two-storey row of motel rooms, her head moving from left to right as she passed each parking space, counting, until she came to an abrupt halt.

What? What are ya doin"?

That's my dad's license number (she pointed). He was parked right here.

They both stared silently at the space, then Meg's eyes tracked up to the second storey of the motel wing. Room 236 was up and over one door to the left.

The car was parked here, and his room was right there (she was thinking aloud).

OK, so what?

Then one of these license plates parked around this space could have been the guy these shooters were really after.

OK. Yeah, cool.

She paced off down to the end of the parking aisle, counting off license plate numbers right and left as she went. She planted her thumb on what she thought would be the last possible number on that row.

C'mon, let's get back to the café. I need a pen or pencil.

Tim was visibly disappointed.

Back in the booth in the café, a pencil found on the counter by the cash register, Meg was busily circling license plate numbers. There were 10 possible numbers parked in the vicinity of the rooms at the end of the wing. There were two from Indiana, three from Ohio, three from Kentucky, a Georgia and a West Virginia.

Next it was back to Lyle at the front desk. He found her the registration cards from that night. She matched up the license numbers with the room numbers. Lyle made her copies of all the cards for the occupied rooms at that end of the wing. But not all the cards had the license plate numbers written in.

If they don't know or can't remember, we don't make a big deal of it.

Only one of the Indiana license plate numbers matched a number written in on a card. The other Indiana license plate number, the one that didn't have a match, was Indiana 79E4216.

The Heart Is a Lonely Hunter

It was only nine o'clock when Meg got back to her room. She spread the registration cards out on the bed and put the list of license plate numbers right in the middle of them. The number 79 license prefix seemed to pulse at her like the red "Vacancy" sign over the motel entrance.

She made a note to call the next morning whoever in Indiana is in charge of license plates to find out what that 79 meant. It had to be some kind of prefix. She felt like she was trying to break some sort of code.

She studied the cards. Some were brimming with information, every line filled in, every number provided, every question (address, employer, make of car) answered. A couple of the cards offered little or no information. One had "John Smith" written on the name line. A couple left almost all the information blank. Meg took her questions back down to Lyle in the office.

Lyle, how come some of these cards aren't filled out completely?

People just aren't very creative. They don't lie very well.

What does that mean?

The people who fill the cards out completely are people who have nothing to hide or are telling the truth. If they leave a blank, it's because they just can't remember. The people who don't fill out the blanks on the cards are people who don't want anyone to know about them, who have something to hide.

What?

Well, that's pretty obvious now isn't it? This *is* a motel. Sex, of course. They're shacking up. They're having an afternoon affair with Mrs. Robinson. That sort of thing.

What about this one (and she held up her copy of the "John Smith" card)?

John Smith. We get a lot of those. Let's see (he pulled out the original of that card and turned it over). Hello. Look at this.

What?

The copies he had made for her only showed the fronts of the cards.

Your John Smith paid for the first night in cash. Then, this is sort of interesting, he never checked out. We didn't know he'd vacated the room until the maid knocked in the afternoon. The day manager checked the room and it had clearly been vacated.

How do you know that?

It's all here in these marks on the back. It's a motel-keeper's shorthand, a code.

John Smith was in room 240. My father was in room 236.

That's only two rooms away. The odd numbers are on the first floor, the evens on the second.

Lyle shuffled through the originals of the ten cards that Meg had copied, checking the backs of them.

Only two people didn't formally check out last Friday. See, that's this checkmark and the time. That's when they came in to the office in the morning to sign their credit card slips and drop off their keys. This John Smith was no problem because he'd already prepaid in cash.

And the other one was my father.

The End of the Affair

By 9:45 Meg had pried all the information out of Lyle that he possessed. She thought of going into the bar and having one of Eddie's Long Islands, but ruled that out. She wanted to stay alert for what was still ahead this evening.

The knock on the door came early, about eleven thirty, and woke Meg out of a full doze. Johnny Carson was just starting his monologue on the TV when she let Sheila Shepherd in.

Her father's prostitute was neither as attractive nor as slutty as Meg had imagined. She was actually a bit on the plump side though tall. She had dyed red hair and was wearing a rather ordinary tan raincoat of the London Fog sort. If she was a prostitute she certainly covered it up pretty well.

She is not near as pretty as mom Meg thought.

Hi, I'm Megan O'Neill. Can I take your coat?

No. No. I'll leave it on. I won't be here that long.

She probably doesn't want me to see the trashy prostitute's outfit she's wearing.

I'm really sorry about your father. He was a nice, quiet, gentle man. Did you know him . . . well?

For about two years. He would call me when he got into town. I would always fit him into my schedule. Oh honey, this is horrible (and the woman broke down in tears and had to sit down on the bed).

The last thing Meg had imagined happening was that she would end up consoling her father's hooker. The woman seemed sincere and honestly sad.

Oh honey, I'm sorry. I vowed I wouldn't do this. It's all some kind of stupid mistake. I liked your daddy. He adored you. He told me.

Now it was Meg's turn to cry.

How ridiculous, she thought as the tears coursed down her face, *me and my father's whore sitting on a bed in a cheap motel room mourning his death.*

I . . . I just wanted to talk to you. Were you here that night?

Yes. I was here. He called me and I came over. About eight-thirty, I guess. I had a later date, uh, client, but I fit your father in first. It took . . . I, uh, left about ten, I guess. God, this is embarrassing. I never thought I'd be talking to one of their daughters.

It's OK. I understand. Meg wanted her to keep talking.

I really don't know anything. When I was leaving I looked up at his room. Sometimes he'd stand in the doorway and wave. I thought I saw two men going in, or maybe they were just walking along the walkway. I don't know. I was driving off. That's it. I'm sorry. He was a nice man. He didn't deserve this. This is crazy.

You said on the phone the police never questioned you?

Meg's question stopped Sheila Shepherd's flight, her hand on the doorknob.

No. I haven't talked to them.

They haven't called you? Interviewed you?

No.

But they have your number.

They do?

The night manager said he gave it to them.

Damn!

But they've had it for days. They should have called you by now.

Those dimwits probably lost it.

Meg had to think about this for a minute. Everyone—Eddie the bartender, Lyle the night manager, this Sheila person—all seemed to hold the same low opinion of the Newport police force.

It's been almost a week. Why do you think they haven't called you?

Lazy. Stupid. Too busy taking bribes. Who knows?

They don't seem to be doing anything. It's a murder!

Honey, the cops around here. They're not real cops. Everybody pays them. The strip joints. The gambling rooms. The bookies. Newport's a regular little sin city. Why do you think you see so many Ohio license plates over here? Cincinnati loves Newport. We're her red light, gambling, sin district, and we're even in another state.

But they've got to investigate murder, don't they?

Why?

Because . . . because . . . it's a murder.

Look honey, all they're interested in is keeping their payoffs coming. They're probably trying to bury this murder.

Bury?

Something like this is bad publicity. They've got a good thing going. They don't want anybody asking questions. All they want is this whole thing to disappear.

I can't believe they haven't even questioned you, the last one to see him alive.

They might come around, try to scare me off. I'll just tell them the truth. I did him and left. They'll love it. What they want is dead-ends. They'll nod solemnly and warn me to quit my life of sin or they'll lock me up. Not for whoring, but for not paying them.

Meg stared wide-eyed as the woman spat out this utterly cynical version of the operation of Newport, Kentucky justice. She felt the anger starting to burn in her throat again, the helpless anger.

Sorry, honey, but that's just how it is around here. I've already said too much. I gotta go. I'm really sorry about your dad. There's just nothing you or I can do about it.

Then she was gone.

Tender Is the Night

After Sheila the prostitute left, Meg just sat stone still on the bed staring at the gray blankness of the closed door. Her throat was constricted and dry as if she had swallowed ashes. She was just getting up to get a glass of water from the bathroom when someone knocked on the door.

She's back. She remembered something else. Meg leapt to the door and opened it without thinking.

Want to have a beer? I brought a whole six-pack. Look. Eighteen ouncers. Pabst Blue Ribbon. What da ya say?

Tim Mounce, lovestruck busboy, stood outside her doorway with his ever-present cigarette in one hand and six red, white and blue cans suspended from plastic in his other.

She gaped at him in disbelief.

I, I, I thought you might feel like a beer.

His voice was friendly, begging. She could see the excitement in his eyes, hear the nervousness in his stammer.

God, I'd love one.

She couldn't believe what she was saying, doing. *Not even a week since her father was murdered. Inviting this stranger into her motel room. She'd just spent a half hour talking to a hooker. A whole evening playing detective trying to solve a murder no one else, especially the police, seemed to care about.*

He came awkwardly into the room, held the six-pack out to her with one hand as if it was a bouquet of flowers.

She was the one who closed the door behind him, who pulled the first beer out of its plastic harness and popped its top, who chugged a third of it hungrily as he looked on in amazement, not yet quite believing what was happening to him.

I saw your light was still on and I thought you might like a beer.

How did you know my room number?

She finished her first beer and reached for a second. He hadn't even opened one yet. He suddenly went tongue-tied.

You got it off the card when Lyle wasn't looking, didn't you?

Well, yes.

She sat down on the bed and drank some more

He sat down in the only chair by the little round table and finally opened himself a beer. He put his cigarette out in the ashtray and immediately lit another one.

They drank silently, sizing each other up. His imagination running wild. Her imagination guiltily rationalizing.

He helped me and he deserves a reward. I can make this the happiest night of this young guy's life. I sound like that Mrs. Robinson in that old movie. I'm only three or four years older than he is. It will help me sleep.

They didn't have much to talk about.

How do you like Ohio State? he asked.

Is Columbus a party town?

Is college hard? I'm saving up to go.

Can, can I, can I kiss you?

He hadn't even finished his beer before Meg had him undressed and into bed. He was sort of clumsy and scared, much less experienced than her.

She began taking birth control pills when she was a freshman at Ohio State. Her roommate in the dorm that first year had told her about how to go to an OB-GYN and get a prescription for them. She hadn't told her dad. Her mom had just died, and she wouldn't have told him anyhow. She had been an athlete in high school and she tried to keep in shape. She worked out with weights and ran at least three times a week. She was very conscious of her body, watched it, took care of it, used it. But she loved to party, to drink. When she drank she took risks. Her roommates thought she got too crazy. But most of the people she knew never took any risks, just studied for classes, dated high school boys from home. Meg sometimes slept with boys who just happened to be in the right place at the right time. Tim Mounce fit the bill this time.

She felt so old, so alone in the world. She was only twenty-two but already an orphan. This boy was eighteen, only a few years younger, but she felt ancient, experienced, exploitative.

Lying next to him on the motel bed her breath coming in shallow gasps, the anger began to burn at her throat again. He was lighting up a cigarette. The smoke hung over the bed. She realized that this anger wasn't going to go away.

You gotta go. That was great. You gotta go, she told him.

She hustled him out of the motel room, her anger mixed with shame. She stood against the closed door in relief when he was gone, cooling down.

Yes! She exhaled. *He left the beer.*

The Heart of the Heart
of the Country

Good morning, Indiana Bureau of Motor Vehicles. Here to help.

Yes. Hello. I wonder if you could help me.

Yes?

What does the number 79 as the first two numbers of an Indiana license plate mean?

That is the county number. Let's see. Yes, Tippecanoe. Tippecanoe county. County seat: Wabash City.

Great. Could you tell me whose name is registered to Indiana license plate number 79E4216.

Who is this?

My name is Megan O'Neill.

I'm sorry, but unless you are inquiring in some official capacity, Miss O'Neill, we are not allowed to give out that information.

Yes. I understand. Thank you.

After she hung up, Meg could have kicked herself. *I should have told them I was a detective on the Newport Police Department,* she thought. *That might have worked.*

The more she thought about it though, the more she thought they would have asked for more identification than just her work, probably some identification number of some sort. But she had gotten the most important information. Wabash City, Indiana: where in god's name was that?

She ran out to her car and got out the road atlas. She traced the route with her forefinger on the map. Out of Newport and Cincinnati on Interstate 74 to Indianapolis, then Interstate 65 to Wabash City which was almost in the middle between Indianapolis and Chicago in northwestern Indiana. On the map it looked like the Wabash River ran right through the middle of the town.

Back in the motel, she decided to try to call some of the people on the registration cards that Lyle, the night manager, had given her, the people whose rooms had been in the vicinity of her father's the night he was murdered.

She had eight cards with names and numbers listed. At the first two numbers she dialed, she got no answer. At the third, a work number, a man answered.

Hello. Is this James Stockton?

Yes.

I wonder if I could ask you a question about your stay at *The Crossroads Inn* in Newport, Kentucky, last Thursday night, a week ago.

Who is this?

This time Meg was ready, rehearsed.

This is Detective Mayes of the Newport Police Department.

OK. What can I do for you?

Could you tell me your business in Newport at *The Crossroads Inn* that night?

Why? I was on a consulting trip to Cincinnati. Why are you calling me?

Because a man was murdered in the motel that night and I wondered if you saw or heard anything that might help us in our investigation.

No. I didn't. I was out all evening and didn't get in until almost two AM.

Meg dialed all the numbers with about equal success.

One man, when she asked about his business at *The Crossroads Inn,* growled "None of your business!" and hung up.

On another call, after listening to her set up, a man said with annoyance: "What is this? Dawn, is that you?"

Meg was able to eliminate four of the cards, but no one heard or saw anything, had any sort of information to give her.

The further into this dead end she got, the more convinced she became that the two license numbers from Wabash City, Indiana were her best bet.

She checked out of the motel early at about nine thirty. Lyle wasn't on the front desk. She wanted to get away before Tim arrived for work.

As she was getting a cup of coffee in the café though, she saw Eddie carrying a box into the dark bar area. She followed him in and thanked him for helping her.

I talked to Sheila Shepherd.

Who?

Sheila. The woman you recommended to my dad.

Oh yeah. Sheila. Sheila's OK. She doesn't do dope like most of them.

Yeah, Sheila's OK.

Then Eddie went fatherly.

Look, Miss, you need to be really careful in what you're doin.' Before you talk to people you need to know who they really are. Somebody killed your daddy. If somebody thinks you're getting' close to findin' out who did that, they're liable to kill you.

On the Road

Why am I doing this? Meg O'Neill thought as she drove north on Interstate 71 toward Columbus. She had almost taken Interstate 74 to that Wabash City, Indiana, but she decided it was too soon. As Eddie had advised, she needed to take some time to think about what she was doing. It was anger that was driving her she realized. Anger at the stupidity of this whole mistake, anger at the monsters who had killed her father and left her totally alone in the world, anger at the police who didn't even seem to care, anger at God for letting her mother die and her father be killed. All those angers burned inside her like red-hot coals, but as she drove out of Newport, through Cincinnati, and north into the wooded hills of southern Ohio that anger began to bank and cool. *Why am I doing this?* she asked herself. Anger wasn't a very good reason.

She was just starting the first quarter of her senior year at Ohio State. If she was going to pursue this, she would have to drop out of school. Her dad would hate that. But she could go back to school anytime. Her major in Political Science could certainly wait. It wasn't going to get her a job anyway.

She would need to get some money together if she was going to drop out and go to Wabash City. She was sure she could get a tuition refund from the university. She'd plead personal problems. It would be hard for anyone to argue with that. She would have to get one of her roommates to drive back down to Kentucky with her and drive her dad's car back. She had left it in the impound lot at the police department. Then she could sell the car and that would generate some more cash. She knew her dad had some life insurance and maybe some retirement money, but it wouldn't be much because most of his money had been eaten up when her mom had been dying, and then he'd had to pay for her college. The lawyer in Akron would take care of that but it would probably take a while. And then there was the house. If she sold it then she would not only be totally alone in the world, but she'd be homeless, have no place to go, no center.

As she drove she thought of all of these things, but each new thought fanned the flames of her anger, burned in her chest like unexamined injustice. She didn't want to torch her whole life to try to find whoever killed her father, but she didn't really have any choice. She pulled off into a rest area. She sat in the car and cried, deep sobs wracking her body for long minutes. But the tears streaming down her face did no good. They couldn't put out the angry fire that had burned off her whole past life and was sending her on the road to Wabash City.

Goodbye Columbus

It took Meg two weeks to get up the nerve to actually get in the car and take the road to Wabash City, Indiana. Since returning to school from her amateur spasm of detective work in Newport, Kentucky, she had been paralyzed. Back at Ohio State, she hadn't gone to a single class. She'd started drinking beer in the mornings. She would sit at the kitchen table in the apartment sipping beer and watching soap operas. *Funny,* she thought, *none of the plots or the people on the soaps are anywhere near as messed up as me and my life.* She felt so totally alone.

Her roommates dutifully worried about her. They'd come in from classes or dates and find her sitting by herself at the kitchen table. They had all been close, happy, carefree friends until this happened.

Are you OK?

Oh sure, I'm great.

Pretty soon they stopped asking, which was what she wanted anyway. She felt like some burned-out hag dumped into the middle of their schoolgirl lives.

But despite her paralysis, her anger didn't go away. She couldn't drink it away or brood it away or cry it away. That's why she finally made her move.

As she drove under the hokey green gateway arch on the Ohio/Indiana state line, she remembered Eddie's warning that poking around in the ashes of all this desolation could be tricky, even dangerous. He had warned her to go slowly, to find out what and who she was dealing with. She was driving to Wabash City with her eyes wide open. The shooters may have killed her father by mistake, but if they found out who she was they would have no trouble killing her by design.

Driving toward Indianapolis, Meg thought of all the things she had vowed she'd never do. She had made her own personal list like this woman who was always driving did in a novel she had read in one of her English classes. When she stopped to think about it though, most of the things she'd vowed she'd never do she'd already done. So she made a new list with one item: She would never forget her mom and dad. But that list wasn't long enough. One more item had to be added because it kept burning away like a hot coal in her mind. She had to find out who murdered her dad, and why.

Changing Places

Tim Mounce changed busboy jobs no more than three weeks after Megan O'Neill left Newport.

Damn, she was cool, that Megan, he kept thinking, *that college girl whose daddy got shot at The Crossroads.* He fantasized about her.

He got a job at the fancy nightclub up on the hill in Southgate, still busing tables, but it paid more and was a lot busier, not nearly as boring as *The Crossroads.* And the scenery was terrific. The women in the nightclub were all dressed up like Julie Christie or Faye Dunaway and he got to watch big name entertainment on the weekends like Steve Lawrence and Edie Gorme or Ricky Nelson, the travelin' man. He thought about saving up his money and calling Megan up at Ohio State and inviting her out to dinner with all the fancy people at the nightclub.

To celebrate his new job, Tim Mounce bought himself a brand new Zippo lighter. He found it came in handy for lighting customers' cigarettes at the club.

A Moveable Feast

Twenty Six Miles Across the Sea
Santa Catalina Is A'Waitin' For Me

John Davidson, TV star, romantic crooner, all-around All-American sex symbol was Mayor of Catalina Island for New Year's Day, 1977. He looked and felt ridiculous sitting in a golf cart decorated as a snow sleigh flanked by two starlets in bright red bikinis trimmed in white fur wearing Santa Claus hats, holding a microphone and mouthing the Catalina Island song while the L.A. TV-news and newspaper cameras shot away.

Why am I doing this? John Davidson thought.

Ten minutes later, in the midst of posing for flash pictures and signing autographs for every gawking tourist in bermuda shorts, crew-necked polo shirts, and floppy hats on the Catalina Island pier, he grabbed his publicist by the cashmere coat sleeve and asked, in all seriousness, why am I doing this?

Because you're John Davidson and you've got to meet the people, press the flesh.

Part Two

The Town

A River Runs Through It

In April the Wabash, swollen with the winter's melted snow and the spring rains, runs high and fast through the twin towns of Wabash City and West Wabash. An access road runs along the river past the softball fields and the boat launch and through the thin line of woods that borders the golf course. This dirt road is like a shady tunnel in the spring with leaves popping out on the trees on the river side and the golf course greening up on the other side. It is a great place for lovers to walk holding hands and for everyone to jog and ride bikes.

The Gilbeys were a nice young couple who in the spring of 1977 had just treated themselves to fancy new matching thick-tired fifteen-speed mountain bikes. They were trying them out for the first time on that road along the river when Winnie Gilbey ran over the arm sticking out of the bushes at the side of the road. Her husband Tom poked the corpse out of the bushes with a big stick he found. There were burn marks on the naked man's skin and he had been shot in the head. Animals had been at him.

The black and white Wabash City Police cruisers were the first to arrive and those officers had the Gilbeys pretty much calmed down and the crime scene cordoned off by the time the two detectives got there. Mal Rogers, the thick, muscular black one, prowled the scene and meditated on the body while his Lieutenant talked to the Gilbeys. The two of them met at the body after they let the shaken Gilbeys go home.

He was tortured then executed. It looks like a mob hit to me, Mal didn't mince his words.

Mob hit? We don't have any mob. This isn't Chicago, Mal.

I know. But it's like a small town crime wave, and it's all being run out of that garage by those redneck pricks.

You're probably right, the Lieutenant's voice was placating.

I know I'm right, and I can't catch them doing it, Mal's voice was more urgent, insistent.

They'll make a mistake, Mal. Just be patient.

Look, Lieutenant, there's no problem with my patience. The problem is I'm the only one paying any attention to them. I can't watch them 24 hours a day. I need help. There's four of them. They've got the garage, the strip joint, the boxing club. They probably do business in all three. If you could just give me a couple of men to stake them out, or an undercover.

An undercover? he actually chuckled. This isn't *Serpico* or *Baretta*.

I know that. But I can't get inside their dealing. All the drugs in the county are coming out of that garage.

I just don't have the men to give you.

Look, Lieutenant, I'm black. You know I can't get close to these rednecks.

I know that. But these investigations are new to us. That's why I gave it to you. You're from Chicago. We didn't used to have much in the way of drugs down here.

Oh, there's always been drugs down here, trust me. It just hasn't been organized like I think these guys have got it organized.

Maybe you're right.

And they're not just selling to college kids. And they're not just selling grass. They're moving cocaine too. It's the latest thing. And they're selling it to rich people, influential people, bankers, lawyers.

Just be patient, something will happen.

Sorry Lieutenant, but it just doesn't work that way. You've gotta make something happen.

You may be right, but I can't give you more men.

Terrific. I'll just stick with my lame undercover at the boxing club.

What's that?

I joined those freaks' boxing club. No harm in getting a good workout while I'm keeping an eye on them.

The Godfather

Jerry McDonald pulled out of the car dealership onto the 52 Bypass in his brand new red 1976 Corvette. He took the first right on Kossuth Street heading into Wabash City. Hardly any traffic. A sleepy Tuesday afternoon. He was smiling as he pulled up to the light at 26th Street.

But the car behind him didn't stop soon enough. Jerry actually glanced in the rear-view mirror a split second before the big dark car hit the rear-end of his shiny new 'Vette. The concussion threw him forward into the steering wheel and banged his forehead on the low slanted windshield. It hurt, but all Jerry could think about was his shiny new car.

Unhinged, Jerry scrambled out, cursing, and bent down in angry mourning over the damage. The 'Vette's rear-end was crumpled like a candy wrapper. Raising up from the devastation, he turned to confront the idiot driver who had just rear-ended him.

The dark brown Bonneville had backed up after the collision. A woman was driving, but the passenger, a man, was getting out.

Poor Jerry wasn't seeing very clearly. Fueled by the disappointment that his brand new Corvette wasn't going to make it into the country club parking lot that afternoon, or to his favorite tavern where all his friends went for happy hour, or to the singles bar where he wanted to end up that night, his hitherto self-contained cursing, as he turned, escalated into a blind rant against the offending driver.

But poor dumb Jerry never finished that curse. The man, all six-feet-two of him in a squarish two hundred and twenty pound frame, who had emerged in dark sunglasses from the offending car in jeans, hit him so hard in the face that his jaw broke with an audible crack.

Jerry crumpled like his car's fender.

The man who had delivered the single punch stood over him, waiting.

Jerry stared up into the coldest unwavering gray-blue eyes he had ever seen.

Do you know who I am?

No answer. Fear growing out of the pain beginning to throb in Jerry's face.

I'm Joe Ted Smale. If I hear one word from the sheriffs or the insurance company or some fucking lawyer about this, I will hurt you so bad this here will seem like a kiss.

With that warning, J.T. Smale returned to the Bonneville, pushed his wife across the seat, got in and drove away.

Lucky Jim

James Winfield was a prominent banker in Wabash City. His office took up the whole corner of the fifth floor of the Wabash Bank and Trust building on the corner of Main and Second Streets. His desk sat in the large corner window overlooking the Main Street bridge, the primary crossover artery to West Wabash, the university town on the other side of the river. Big Jim Winfield could sit at his desk and watch everyone entering or leaving Wabash City. And Big Jim probably knew most of the people in the cars crossing the bridge below. He was forty-two and had been with the bank almost twenty years. He had worked his way up from newly hired graduate of the state university across the river through the loan department to Vice-President to President of the whole operation in 1974.

With a phone call, Big Jim could OK sweetheart auto loans for the hottest new basketball recruit or put together partnership financing for a new upscale wooded subdivision. He owned a Cadillac Sedan DeVille and he was a tennis fanatic. In December of 1976, he had opened his own tennis club, two genuine clay courts under a hot-air-inflated polystyrene bubble right by the river next to the city softball fields. In fact, playing his regular afternoon tennis game was where Belfry Smale found him on a blustery afternoon in early March 1977.

Belfry Smale, the second oldest of the four Smale brothers, was not that good a friend of Big Jim Winfield. But he was the supplier of the primo marijuana that Big Jim freely handed out to his country club buddies in their golf carts on the weekends, and smoked with his tennis partners in the private owner's locker room of the bubble after tennis games, and shared with his hip dinner guests after the final course was served at his house on the hill.

But Belfry had never liked him or any of his country club friends. Lately Big Jim had been demanding a larger quantity of grass as well as the new drug of choice, cocaine, and had not paid up for almost three weeks. In the family business, Belfry's specialty was collections, and Big Jim had become a rather sensitive collection problem.

He's out of hand, Belfry told J.T.

Just calm down. He's got a lot of friends. He's like, very visible, and a good customer.

He owes us twelve thousand dollars.

That much? How did that happen?

I gave the stuff to him. He always paid up on time before. He'd call. I'd deliver it where he said. He'd send the money over by a bank messenger. But he made two big buys in a row and he never paid. I've called him twice. He calls me back and says he'll get it to me. It hasn't come. It's been three weeks, a week since the last call.

Maybe you should go have a talk with him.

That's what I thought.

Belfry and J.T. worked very well together because they trusted each other and they spoke each other's language. That trust had developed out of years of beating the hell out of each other when they were growing up. For about ten years between the time they were five until they were in high school they would fight each other at the cock of a sideways look or the uttering of an unconsidered word or the slightest touch or bump or push or the most barely perceived slight or omission or intrusion on one or the other's property or space. If Belfry would even look at a girl that J.T. fancied, they'd be rolling on the ground. If J.T. even touched the hot rod that Belfry was working on, they'd be throwing things at each other in the garage. J.T. was bigger and stronger, but Belfry had a blind temper that was downright dangerous.

By the time they got to high school, the two of them were so tough they realized that together they could do anything they wanted and nobody could stand up to them. So they started working together, beating the hell out of anyone who got in their way. They especially like messing with guys on the football team, big guys who thought they were tough. J.T. and Belfry were together the formidable brains and brawn of the Smale family, like one person in two bodies. They had made the Smale family the closest thing to organized crime in rural Indiana. Around Wabash City, thanks to a cocky young newspaper reporter who gave them the title "The Redneck Mafia," they had a bad reputation. That reporter summarily moved to another paper on the west coast shortly after going three sparring rounds with Belfry and J.T. in the ring of the Wabash City Boxing Club on south Third

Street, They had no problem with the "Redneck" part of that title, it was the association with the Italians that they didn't like. The Smale family was right out of that movie *Deliverance,* and proud of it. They even lived down by the river.

Belfry was never one to let grass grow under his feet or go unpaid for. When J.T. agreed that they ought to have a talk with Big Jim Winfield, Belfry went looking for him right away. He was never very subtle when it came to overdue collections. His first stop was Big Jim's office on the fifth floor of the bank building.

The Bank President's personal secretary said that Mr. Winfield was not in.

Belfry had to stop himself from admiring Big Jim's good taste in secretaries to ask where he was.

The good looking secretary professed not to know.

Belfry, ever impatient, yanked her by the wrist into Winfield's office, shoved her roughly backwards onto Winfield's desk in the window, held her down and pulled her skirt up around her waist and her panties down to her knees, forced his hand between her legs and entered her with his thumb, told her if she made any loud sound he would kill her, then moved his thumb slowly in and out of her as he asked her again where Big Jim was.

At the tennis bubble. He plays every afternoon.

Now that wasn't so hard was it, he smiled disarmingly at her.

Sure enough, Big Jim was in the middle of a fierce game of tennis when Belfry walked into the high bubble at 3:30. Belfry walked to the side of the court and waved.

When Big Jim saw Belfry, he was startled, stopped dead in his tracks, and lost the point they were contending to a weak forehand down the line.

Hey. How ya doin'? I'll be right with you. Just let me finish this game.

With that, Belfry pulled out the .38 that he always wore in the shoulder holster under his flannel shirt and, pointing it straight up over his head without breaking eye contact, shot a large tearing hole through the double-layered polystyrene roof of the tennis bubble. He just wasn't in the mood to wait.

The hot air whooshed out of the inflated bubble with a sound like a jet airplane taking off, and the whole concave roof began to sag down toward the tennis players.

Sounded like a huge Buffalo fart, Belfry would later describe it hilariously to J.T. and Hump.

Big Jim's tennis opponent took one look at Belfry, one look at the deflating roof above his head, dropped his expensive metal racket right in the middle of the court, and ran for his life.

When he was gone, Belfry walked to the discarded racket (one of those fancy teardrop Head models that Arthur Ashe had made so popular), picked it up, stepped carefully over the net, and hit Big Jim Winfield as hard as he could in the face with the taut strings. It was the most powerful forehand of the day.

Big Jim flopped onto his back in the top-dressed clay flapping like a fish in the bottom of a boat. He would wear the tight grid of the racket strings indented in his face for the next ten days when he would only be available to his friends and business associates by phone. The roof of the bubble continued to deflate down on him.

Twelve thousand dollars in cash at the boxing club by noon tomorrow, Belfry discarded the racket with a sideways toss and walked out.

Big Jim lay on the ground for a long moment holding his face, but then realized that he had to move. The rubber ceiling was sagging fast, bearing down like the Goodyear blimp coming in for a landing right on top of him. When he got back to his office with a towel wrapped around his head so that no one would see the grid of tight lines caked with dried blood etched in his face, his private secretary of four years (who he had been sleeping with) had quit.

The tennis bubble wasn't the only Wabash City landmark that Belfry Smale deflated that day.

Deliverance

Humphrey Smale was the third of the four Smale brothers of Wabash City.

In the spring of 1977 he had been out of the state prison at Pendleton for almost two years but still had that ghostly pallor of the convict. He'd been in there for three years and it certainly hadn't reformed him.

Hump Smale had always been scrawny and slow. He did what his brothers told him to do to the best of his limited abilities, like taking the fall for J.T.'s first marijuana operation. That had put him in the joint for three years. There he had become the sort of grim predator that J.T. sometimes found useful.

Everybody knew that something was wrong with Hump. All you had to do was look at his slack jaw and his vacant eyes and you knew that the electrical connections in his tangled cerebral cortex had somehow short-circuited. But it was worse than that. Sometimes when Hump had drunk too much or when some hooker didn't satisfy his twisted demands or someone looked at him in a way he didn't like he would explode in anger as if a switch in his damaged brain had been tripped and it had blown a fuse.

It was common knowledge in Wabash City that Hump Smale wasn't smart enough to piss out of a boat and hit water. But no one ever laughed at him or taunted him because they were afraid of his two big brothers. But all you had to do was look at Hump Smale and you could tell that he wasn't wired right.

J.T. and Belfry took care of their little brother because he was family and because sometimes they found it useful to have someone who would do exactly what they told him to do (even if it meant going to jail for three years) and was very much at home with hogs. They let him hang around and be a big shot at *Tippers*, one of the owners, but they didn't let him sit in on any of the business or strategy meetings in the back room of the boxing club. Hump didn't care about the box-ing club anyway. All he wanted to do was sit at the bar in *Tippers* and drink beer, ogle the girls, and, when he was lucky, every once in a while when one of the dancers would be late for work a couple of nights in a row, or would show up drunk or high, or wanted some coke but couldn't pay for it, his brothers would give her to him for a night, tell him he could do anything he wanted to her except kill her, and he took them at their word. A night with Hump usually straightened out the most rebellious stripper's act.

Hump was their on-going project. His biggest problem was playing with matches. In grade school the other boys had called him "Freddy the firebug" when his brothers were out of earshot. One time he'd set a guy's car on fire right in the Jeff High School parking lot. That's why Hump loved Halloween so much. All those nice piles of dry leaves in the street that he could set off with just a flick of a cigarette out of his car window. He'd sit in the car and watch them burn, throwing flames and sparks high in the air with little kids dressed like ghosts and devils and princesses and cowboys and Indians holding their parents' hands trying to pick their way around the flames and falling ash. Then he would move on to the next neighborhood and start another fire.

Bang the Drum Slowly

Wesley Smale was the youngest of the four Smale brothers, only twenty-five, thirteen years younger than his oldest brother J.T. He was the baby in the family and the only one who made any pretense of maintaining a visible means of support. J.T., Belfry and Hump all hung around the auto-repair garage on Center Street that they had inherited from their father, but there hadn't been a car repaired there in seven years although a lot of customers went in and out through its two bays in the course of a normal day.

Wes managed the *Wabash City Gymnasium and Boxing Club* right around the corner from the family garage on Third Street. The only Smale brother to go out for sports in high school, he had turned into a pretty good wrestler in the 160–170 lb. class. He had worked construction right out of high school and had saved up some money. When he had gone to J.T. in the winter of 1973 when all the construction jobs were shut down and told him his idea, J.T. had liked the sound of it so much that he immediately threw in with Wes as (what he called himself then) a "silent partner." But J.T. and Belfry and Hump didn't stay silent for very long.

Wes's idea was to take the money he'd saved up, and rent a building, and build a gym for guys who were serious about working out and wrestling and boxing. When J.T. insisted on becoming Wes's partner in the venture, J.T. also insisted that they buy the building, that it be three times as large as Wes had envisioned, and that two rooms in the back be private, a sort of family clubhouse where the brothers could go to relax without being disturbed. Wesley didn't really like J.T. taking over his idea so wholeheartedly, but it had worked out well. Wesley had his own business and it was not only pretty much legit, but it became very successful. Wes had really not imagined how many guys there were around who liked to lift and work out and wrestle and box after a full day's work. He also hadn't really imagined the auxiliary uses his older brothers would find for the gym and boxing club.

As J.T. put it, the club was where he and Belfry did all their "negotiations." Those negotiations generally took the form of late-night sessions in the gym putting the target of their "negotiations" in the ring with both of them and beating him senseless with boxing gloves on. The first time Wes saw them do this, he couldn't believe his eyes. The second time it happened, he protested to J.T. in the strongest possible way.

J.T., you're bringin' people here against their will and beating the crap out of 'em.

Relax little brother. Belfry and I wear gloves. It's boxing. It's a sport.

Sport! No way! It's two to one in the ring.

Sometimes we just gotta send these guys a message. They get hurt, we just mark it down to sport.

You know I don't really wanna be part of you guys's business. I told you that.

I know. I understand that, Wes. Just relax. The cops haven't ever been here, have they? You run a good club here. The boxing team for the neighborhood kids, good stuff. It's good publicity for our family. Everybody thinks the Smales are a bunch of pricks.

J.T.'s solution to Wes's reservations about this particular use of one of the family businesses was to tell Wes to go have a beer with Hump at the family strip joint next door, and he and Belfry would join them when the "negotiation" was over.

C'mon J.T., Marcy doesn't want me goin' to no strip joint.

What? You listen to her?

No, but you're gonna kill one of these guys you bring in here sooner or later. One of 'em's gonna have a heart attack or you're gonna hit one of 'em too hard. Then the cops'll come after me. Close the gym.

Little brother, little brother. Everything's gonna be fine. Relax.

But Wesley couldn't relax, and he couldn't say no to his older brothers who had always been good to him, taken care of him, and he just couldn't seem to avoid the family business that kept closing in on him.

But Wes was his own worst enemy. When he broke his collarbone it made everything clearer. The city softball fields were built right on the river bank behind the corn factoring plant. Wes sponsored a team from the gym made up of his customers, and played right field. In a game the summer before, he had been on first base with one out when the ball was hit on the ground to the second baseman. Wes didn't get down fast enough going into second base and when the opposing shortstop came across the bag, took the flip, and made the double-play relay to first, the throw hit Wes hard in the middle of the chest.

He's out. He's out. Interference, the shortstop yelled at the umpire and pointed at the runner on first who had hit the ground ball.

Getting hit in the chest like that really hurt and Wes's whole chest and right shoulder had gone numb. The pain really pissed Wes off, but when the umpire called it a double-play, it pissed Wes off even more. He cussed the shortstop for throwing at him.

The shortstop was starting to run off the field, but he turned around and laughed when Wes cussed him.

What happened next was sort of like when that river in Cleveland, Ohio caught on fire and burned down one of its own bridges.

Wes ran at the laughing shortstop and threw the first punch, but it never hit its target. The punch just sort of hung in mid-air when the motion cracked Wes's already bruised and numb collarbone.

The punch just hung out there as if it was on a leash and Wes collapsed on the ground with the new pain. The shortstop laughed at him again. In the ambulance going to the hospital, he was still cursing the player who threw at him.

Later, when Belfry showed up, Wes joked, I'm the only man in Wabash City who has figured out a way to break his own collarbone.

Still later that night the shortstop came out of a bar in West Wabash and the three Smale brothers were sitting in his car. The guy was a grad student in the Political Science department at the university. They took him to the gym in the back of Belfry's pick-up truck with duct tape over his mouth.

Still later that night, they dumped him back at his car in the deserted parking lot with three broken ribs, two swollen testicles, and a crushed hand, his right, his throwing hand.

The Prairie

The tractors, twelve of them, were lined up three deep on the blacktop lot of the John Deere dealership in Battlefield, a small town eight miles north of Wabash City.

Three-thirty AM. No moon.

Hump drove one of the semi tractor-trailer trucks and Wes, unwillingly but unable to say "no" to his older brothers, drove the other. They backed the trucks into the wide driveway of the John Deere store. It was a small town. There was no night watchman.

While Wes and Hump pulled down the ramps of their trailers, J.T. and Belfry jump-wired the brand new tractors and drove them into the trucks, two to each trailer. Six minutes later the two trucks were on I65 South on the way to Kentucky.

The next night Hump and Belfry broke into a large farm supply store on the south side of Wabash City. It had a cheap burglar alarm that they were able to disable by cutting one wire. They filled up their pick-up with 16 brand new chainsaws.

Two nights after that Hump, Belfry and J.T. pulled up to the hog barn of the Wilson farm at 1175 County Road 800 South. This time J.T. drove the big pick-up truck and acted as the lookout. Belfry wrestled the chute out of the covered trailer they were pulling, and Hump, the pig specialist, herded twenty of farmer Wilson's fattest market hogs out of the barn and into the truck. The next morning all the farmer found was a trail of manure leading from the open barn door to where the truck had been parked. Even as he scratched his head and cussed, his hogs were being slaughtered in Illinois 74 miles to the west. But those little forays into rural thievery were not the backbone of the Smale's family business.

The Burnt-Out Case

In December Mal Rogers had gone to the Wabash City Police Department and asked if he could go through any files they had pertaining to drug investigations. He never mentioned the Smales because he saw no reason to advertise that he was looking into them. He could just hear some friend of theirs on the force or some cop they had in their pocket saying, "there's some State Police Investigator, a black guy, poking around in your business."

All the woman file clerk, a civilian, could come up with were three cardboard boxes of file folders most of which contained the paperwork on college students arrested for clumsily smoking grass. It only took him an afternoon to go through them. There was surprisingly little on the Smale brothers, only three files on an investigation five years before that had resulted in Humphrey Smale being sentenced to three years in the state penitentiary for dealing marijuana. Nothing since. It was as though the Wabash City cops had just decided to leave the Smale family alone once they sent Humphrey away.

But what Mal Rogers did find in those files were the yellow sheets on three of the Smale brothers. Wesley didn't have one.

The yellow sheets made for some sparse but interesting reading.

Belfry's was the most consistent. Three different arrests for assault, but the complainant's never appeared in court and the charges were always dropped.

J.T. had been arrested twice. Once for car theft when he was eighteen and once for a home invasion. He got off on a first offense suspended sentence on the car theft and the complaint was dropped on the home invasion when he swore that he had just gotten the wrong house when he was drunk. The complainant never appeared in court for that one either.

Humphrey's was the longest. He seemed to get caught for everything, all pretty minor stuff: public intoxication, indecent exposure, shoplifting, breaking and entering, carrying a concealed weapon, disturbing the peace, possession. Mostly misdemeanor stuff that his lawyer got him off on, all except for the dealing marijuana case that had sent him to Pendleton for three years. That one had never even gone to trial. His previously quite competent lawyer had pled him into jail.

There wasn't a single mark on any of the yellow sheets since Humphrey Smale had been sent up in 1972.

Strange, Mal thought. *The State Police have more on these guys than that.*

The State Police had gotten interested in the Smale brothers and their garage as the result of a routine traffic stop on the Interstate in October 1976. The car was speeding and had a Kentucky license plate. It was driven by two suspiciously incoherent Spanish guys (they turned out to be Colombians) who turned out to be high on cocaine. When the patrolmen searched the car, they found over two hundred pounds of coke under the back seat and in the spare tire wheel well. The mules pled "no comprende anglais," sat it out in the county jail for a week until the sheriff figured out a way to get rid of them by giving them to the INS. The immigration officers from Indianapolis deported them to Colombia on the next plane out and they were most probably greeted in Cali by a death squad who killed them as soon as they cleared the airport for losing all that dope, more than two million worth. Problem solved and cheaply. But the real find in that traffic stop was an envelope in the glove compartment with addresses scrawled on it in Chicago, Illinois, Wabash City, Indiana, Indianapolis, Indiana, Cincinnati, Ohio, and Newport, Kentucky. The Colombians, evidently, were running the interstates from Kentucky to Chicago. The address in Wabash City just happened to be J.T. Smale's garage on South Third Street. That was when Mal's captain told him to start looking into the Smale family business.

Mal Rogers had been watching the Smale brothers ever since. But after three months, his investigation was going nowhere. He had lists: license plates and names of people who frequented the garage, places the different brothers frequented, names of frequent companions of the brothers, time tables of how the brothers usually spent their days, their weeks. What Mal had was a folder full of disconnected information that really added up to nothing (especially in a court of law). He was a good investigator, but he was stalled. He needed something to take the investigation to the next level. He needed a break. That's when he decided to start working out. at the Smales' Third Street gym. He had walked in off the street one day, paid his fifty bucks for a membership (he couldn't believe that the youngest Smale brother actually took it), and started working out. He registered under a phony name and never asked the State Police for reimbursement, never discussed his (sort of) undercover operation with his Lieutenant.

In fact, he enjoyed the gym. When he was lifting or doing sit-ups or jumping rope, he forgot about how lonely his life was. He had always taken care of himself. At 35 he was in pretty good shape so he was able to pull it off. He was the only black guy in the gym, and he got a few double-takes, but nobody bothered him. He'd spar with somebody if they asked him. He got to know three or four guys that way. He was on speaking terms with the youngest Smale brother, Wesley. And then one day the two older brothers walked in together and saw him working on the heavy bag.

He stopped them dead in their tracks.

Wes was behind the counter when J.T. and Belfry came in. They hustled him off to the closed rooms in the back.

Mal stopped pounding his personal version of his ex-wife's new white husband and tried to listen. He thought he heard brief shouting, but it was muffled. A minute later young Wes walked out red in the face. The two older brothers never came out. Mal just finished his workout, showered and left. He didn't want the other two brothers to get too close a look at him. When he left, he drove down the alley behind the gym and noted that there was indeed a back exit door right across the alley from the parking lot of the strip joint.

He didn't know if he had been made as a cop or if the older Smale brothers just hated blacks. For once he hoped that racism was the reason.

Herself Surprised

Unemployed, Ginevra Boland, Big Jim Winfield's former private secretary, sat drinking vodka and tonic at the bar in *The Knickerbocker
Saloon* on Fifth Street in Wabash City at three in the afternoon when
what should have been her worst nightmare walked in. Belfry Smale.

Belfry smiled and walked right up to her as she sat perched on her
bar stool.

Ginevra blew smoke in his face.

Their eyes locked and about sixteen different emotions coursed like
electrical current between them.

Belfry didn't apologize.

Ginevra never flinched.

It was all pure lust, fear, hot anger, curiosity, pride, and revenge
that caused their confusion. Neither love nor romance had anything to
do with it. Their silently looking at each other in the smoky afternoon
of that dim bar was both sick and perverted and they both knew it and
neither one of them backed down.

I wanted to see you under a little better circumstances.

What's that? You wanna bend me over the bar and finger-rape me
again.

Rape?

It was a rape.

More like coppin' a feel. I'd say.

You'd be wrong.

OK. Look. I was a little rough. But I didn't have time to, to . . .
mess with a secretary who was lyin' to me. That's over. OK?

Not over for me.

Look. Give me a break. What are you gonna do? Go to the cops?
They won't do nothin.' Don't you think you're overreactin' a little bit.
Quittin' your job.

How do you know that?

Big Jim told me. He wants you to come back to work.

That's not why he wants me to come back to work.

Whatever.

What's with you and Jim Winfield?

We're back on speakin' terms. Actually, I asked him where I could find you. He said here.

I'm not a barfly. I just didn't have anything to do this afternoon.

Fine. Can I buy you another drink?

No.

Great. You're pissed. I was a little rough. I was in a hurry. I wasn't payin' attention to who I was dealin' with. By the time I figured out how beautiful you were, well, I was already doin' things the wrong way.

Ya got that right.

Why did you quit? Because I scared you?

No. I didn't want to work for him anymore anyway. You were just the last straw.

How come?

I just decided I didn't need all the aggravation that job was causing. I was sick of lying to everybody who came into the office, protecting that pig. He's out of hand. I want away from him.

He wants you back.

Of course he does.

They looked at each other a long moment and he understood.

OK. I'll get you a job. You still want to be a secretary? Or you willing to branch out?

Well I don't want to be a strip dancer or a hooker if that's what you mean?

He laughed, ordered a beer, sat next to her on a bar stool, relaxed a bit, got cozy.

Look Geneva.

It's Ginevra, but my friends call me Ginny.

A week later, same bar, different company, her girlfriend Sandy.

New job, new guy, you're just a little movin' on machine these days, aren't you honey?

I don't know about that, but I'm sure glad to be out of that bank and away from Jim. Today was only my first day of work, but I think I'm gonna like the place. My guy got it for me. Called in a favor.

Who cares! A job's a job. I've worked at about seven different hair salons in Wabash City and they all stink. Who's the guy?

You're gonna laugh at his name.

What?

His name's Belfry, Belfry. . . .

Omigod! Sandy cut her off.

What?

Omigod, you're dating Belfry Smale, aren't you?

OK, yes. I know who he is.

You don't know who he is. If you did, you wouldn't be going near him.

OK, he's different but. . . .

Different? Ginny, he's a major gangster. I know he beats people up. Everybody says he kills people.

How do you know? That's probably just all beauty shop talk.

Gin, I went to school with him at Jeff. He's a monster, a criminal. I've seen him in action. He enjoys hurting people. How bad is it? Are you sleeping with him?

Maybe.

Maybe! You are, aren't you?

Look, I've gotta go. Her drink only half drunk, Ginevra gathered up her things—cigarettes, lighter, keys—off of the table, sorry she had ever mentioned his name.

But her friend Sandy reached across the table and grabbed her wrist. Ginny, look, you're playing with fire. What do you think you're doing? He's a Smale.

Beauty and the Beast

Oh honey, you are too much. Belfry's eyes were glassy and his breath was coming in fast gulps as he sank back into the pillows of Ginevra's bed.

We seem to have it pretty together, Ginevra collapsed her cheek against his shoulder, all muscle and thick, and ran her finger down the center of his chest hair glistening with moisture.

I'd say together hits the nail on the head that time.

For Ginevra, it was hard to get too romantic about Belfry Smale because everyone she knew was warning her off of him. But she was having a good time and, for an ignorant redneck, he was treating her OK. He seemed guilty about them having gotten off on the wrong foot. She told him about all her friends' warnings and he just laughed them off.

Things get blown up lots bigger than they are, Belfry tried to explain. In a small town like this, rumors are like hard-ons. They have a life of their own.

With Belfry the sex was great, strenuous and hard with a mean edge that really turned her on. Everyone was warning her off of him, but they didn't know why she was with him in the first place. She liked the danger of it, the excitement.

Cat in the Rain

Coming out of Indianapolis on Interstate 65, the road north to Wabash City, Meg spotted a girl about her own age holding a sign and hitchhiking. It was raining steadily, a cold March rain. The girl had on jeans and a winter parka with a hood, and her sign said "Wabash City."

In her side-view mirror she watched the hitchhiker run up to the car. The young woman looked like a drowned rat. When the hitchhiker got to the car, she didn't get right in. She stopped and looked Meg over, checked the back seat.

Oh, hi, the hitchhiker finally said.

Hi, I'm going to Wabash City.

That's great.

The hitchhiker scrambled in.

Oh, it's nice and warm in here. I'm pretty wet, but I'm really cold.

You can take that wet thing off and throw it in the back seat if you want. Do you live in Wabash City?

No. I go to school there. Do you?

No. I mean no, I don't live there or go to school there.

The hitchhiker gave Meg a blank look and an awkward silence settled over the car as the windows steamed up.

In fact, I've never been to Wabash City.

It's a college town mostly.

Like it?

Yeah, it's OK. It's got what I want, but it sure isn't easy.

What do you mean?

I want to be an engineer, but there aren't many women studying engineering.

Engineering. I'll bet that's hard.

Are you out of school?

You could say that, I guess. I went to Ohio State until I got in the car this morning.

What do you mean?

I guess I'm dropping out, at least for a while. It's a long story.

Actually, it turned out to be a pretty short story the way Meg laid out the facts for her hitchhiker.

Oh, I'm so sorry, the other woman seemed genuinely upset. Why are you going to Wabash City? I mean, if you've never been there, don't have people there?

I think the men who shot my father live there.

You do. Wow. How did you find that out?

Meg spent some more time filling her in on the facts gathered in her amateur detective work. It was the first time she'd told this stuff to anyone. This girl being a stranger made it easier somehow.

That's wild. It's like detective work isn't it, like Perry Mason or Columbo?

Meg laughed, I guess.

You've got that license number. What if you do find them?

I don't know. I guess I'll go to the police, but the ones in Newport, Kentucky, sure didn't seem to care about any of this. Nobody cares, except me, and then the tears started running down her face. Oh, I'm sorry. I hate this, she apologized to the stranger.

They rode silently for a moment. It took Meg a couple of miles to calm down.

My name is Megan O'Neill, by the way, Meg.

I'm Jesse, Jess, everybody calls me Jess, Jess Mittermeier.

Sorry. Sorry about all this. I didn't mean to dump all my stuff on you like that. It just was sorta nice telling it all to a total stranger. How long had you been standing back there in the rain?

About twenty minutes. My mom dropped me off on her lunch hour. She's divorced. She'd drive me up there, but she has to work. That's a pretty good spot. It usually doesn't take that long. It's the rain. People can't see you so well in the rain, don't want to stop 'cause they're afraid of getting hit from behind. Two guys stopped but I didn't get in with them. One was a trucker in a big sleeper rig. I don't take rides from guys? One tried to rape me once when I was hitchhiking.

Oh my god. And you still hitch?

It was sort of funny actually. He came on to me while he was driving, his hand on my knee, but then he pulled off the interstate onto this little country road. He tore my blouse right off. Somehow I convinced him it would be better if we got out of the car and did it on the ground. He was a fat traveling salesman. Once I got him out of the car everything was OK. I kicked the crap out of him.

What?

Yeah, it was funny. He never knew what hit him. I've studied kick-boxing since I was a sophomore in high school. I've got a great kick-boxing class in Wabash City. Thai guy. Has a studio in a loft up above an auto parts store.

What's it like in Wabash City?

Pretty quiet really, or at least it seems that way.

What do you mean?

Being at the university you don't really see that much of it. Wabash City is really two cities.

How's that?

Well, the university's in West Wabash and that's all students and faculty, pretty quiet. But across the river in Wabash City it's different.

What's the housing like in Wabash City? Am I gonna have trouble finding a cheap place to rent? Where should I look to live?

Could be a problem. Most everything's taken 'cause school is in session. I'm looking for a roommate actually. Mine just left.

In the middle of the semester?

Yeah.

I guess that's what I did to my roommates back in Columbus.

Yeah.

Why did she leave? Flunk out?

No.

Why then?

We broke up.

You mean you two didn't get along?

No, we broke up.

Broke up?

I'm a lesbian.

Oh.

Sooo, I've got half an apartment without a roommate. But I don't suppose you'd want to live with a lesbian.

Well I . . . I hadn't really. . . .

Most straight girls don't. They're scared, I guess.

They are?

I think they think it's sort of like trying to go to sleep with a rat or a bat in the house.

I hate rats.

Most people hate lesbians.

I've never known a lesbian.

You probably have, you just don't know it. Lesbians tend to lay low, but that's changing.

It is?

Yeah, if you're a lesbian, you don't have to be a bull dyke or a lipstick lesbian anymore. You can be a lesbian and just act normal like other people.

Uh-huh.

You're welcome to stay with me. You have your own room. It's fifty a week.

OK. But just for a while, 'til I see if I'm gonna even stay.

Jess's apartment was in an old house on Pierce Street in the Village right next to the campus in West Wabash. It was a sprawling, four-storey monstrosity, decrepit, falling down, a large porch with sagging railings on the front, rotting gables on the roof, it had once been a home for a large family but now was broken up into four apartments. It was also right next to a student bar, *The Stabilizer.*

Nice name for a bar, Meg thought, and it was the first place she stopped after she unpacked. Jess had classes to go to, studying to do. Meg explored the town, sat at the bar at *The Stabilizer,* took two days to get up enough nerve to go to the police station across the river in Wabash City.

The police were polite, though not all that interested.

My car got hit in a parking lot, Meg had rehearsed this part over and over. I was just coming out of the grocery store and I heard the sound of the car hitting mine. I ran over and the car was taking off, but I got most of its license number. Here it is. She had the whole number but she decided to hold back the last digit to make her story sound more authentic.

Usually the insurance claims adjuster runs a number like this or the reporting officer at the scene. Did you file a police report?

No. I didn't. I was late for class yesterday and, well, officer (and she tried her best to sound scared and young and confused), I just didn't know what to do. It was all so frustrating and my whole rear fender is dented.

Now, Miss, calm down. I'm sorry, but we don't usually give out private license numbers to the general public.

I called my insurance company in Columbus, Ohio, and the insurance man said that if I could follow up on the numbers over here it would really help things along.

But we just don't . . .

Oh officer, couldn't you just help me with this? My insurance man said it might take weeks to get one of their people to check this out.

The policeman was wavering.

Meg concentrated really hard. She thought of her dad lying cold and gray on that slab in that sleazy little Kentucky town. The tears began to roll down her cheeks.

The policeman buckled.

Miss, it's OK. You just sit down over there and I'll see what I can do.

Five minutes later, the officer was back.

Meg dabbed at her eyes for effect, but to her surprise the police officer's whole attitude had changed.

Sorry Miss, my watch captain said that we are not allowed to give out that information to the general public. You'll have to ask your insurance adjuster to call the BMV (Bureau of Motor Vehicles) in Indianapolis for that information.

Thank you, officer. Meg could barely hide her disappointment as she left.

It almost worked, she thought, *and I've still got the West Wabash and the University Police to try it on.*

Outside, unlocking her car door, Meg's hopes for success in her little charade momentarily re-ignited when the desk officer came running out of the police station in hot pursuit.

Miss O'Neill, Miss O'Neill, here's an accident report form for you to fill out and send in. There's a place for your insurance company's address. When we get it, we'll send them a copy.

Oh, thank you officer. How helpful.

When that desk sergeant reentered the building after Meg had driven off, his watch captain was waiting in the hallway just inside the door.

You were right, the desk sergeant reported, no dents in the fenders of her car. She was lying.

Unsuccessful on her first attempt, Meg, the very same day, tried her hit and run insurance story on the cop on the desk at the West Wabash Police Department up the hill from the university. He made her fill out a form, a police report, and asked for the name of her insurance company and her agent.

She gave them the company and made up a name for the agent. Then, she broke into tears. I can't believe he hit my car and just drove off right in front of me.

Five minutes later, while she was still dabbing at her eyes, the West Wabash desk officer was back. To Meg's delight, he gave her four numbers and four names neatly lettered on a piece of white memo-size paper:

79e 4211	D. Seybold
79e 4214	M. Yetman
79e 4216	J. Ferris
79e 4219	S. Hughes

The Street

The phone on Mal Rogers' desk at the State Police Post rang four then five times before anyone picked it up, and that was only a coincidence because the radio operator happened to be walking by.

Mal, Mal Rogers? This is. . . .

No, he's not here.

Could you take a message?

Right.

Ask him to call Captain Steve Russell at Wabash City PD. Thanks.

Mal got the message the next morning when he reported for his shift. It was scribbled on a scrap of paper and stuck in the corner of the blotter on his desk. He could designate what shifts he wanted to work, but he usually worked days, got off at five, then went for his workout at the Third Street gym.

Steve, Mal Rogers at the State Police Post.

Yeah, Mal, how are ya?

OK. I got a message that you called.

I did. Yes I did. Something strange here I thought might, or might not, who knows, be of interest to you. I hear you are the State Police's narcotics man these days.

Yeah, I am.

Yesterday this young girl, looks like a student, comes in with a license number trying to hustle an ID out of our desk sergeant. Tells him it's the number of a hit and run that dented her fender in the Payless parking lot. But the desk sergeant brought it to me and we ran it. One of the possibles that came up was registered to that dead drug dealer Ferris that couple found down on the river trail. We didn't give the girl that information, and when she left I sent my desk officer out after her on a pretext to get a look at her car. No dents.

I guess that's interesting. You make anything of it?

Just seemed like a strange coincidence to me. That guy gettin' hit like he did and then this student comin' snoopin' around and his name comes up.

It does seem like more than a coincidence.

I don't know what to do with it, but I thought you might be interested.

Did you get the girl's name and license number?

Yeah, it's an Ohio Plate. Here it is. Megan O'Neill, Akron, Ohio, POD 649.

Thanks Steve, I appreciate it. And Mal hung up.

He called me because he doesn't want to touch this Ferris murder, afraid it might get too close to his own favorite little family of drug dealers. Mal sat in the stiff-backed chair at his desk thinking it over for a good five minutes after he hung up. *He figures the Smales killed Ferris cause he was trying to horn in on their drug business, and the Wabash City PD want to leave the Smales alone.*

He checked both the city and the campus phone directory. No listing.

Finally he decided to do it the hard way, but it wasn't really that hard.

It took him a day and a half of cruising the streets around campus to find her car (with that distinctive out of state POD license plate) parked in front of a big, dilapidated, wood house on Pierce Street. He only had to watch the car for about an hour and a half before she put in an appearance.

Stranger in a Strange Land

Mal Rogers knew how to run a drug investigation. That's why the Indiana State Police had hired him (that and the fact that his black face looked good nestled in among all those white crew-cuts in the group picture in the lobby of the police post). The one thing he knew for sure about running a drug investigation was that it would never go any further than dealers and mules if you didn't have someone on the inside, undercover.

The drug world moved to a rhythm, slow to fast to superfly, off-the-scale, outtasight, megahigh like a Jimi Hendrix guitar riff. The drug world moved from the slow-waiting for the product to become available to the careful seduction of transportation and distributing it to the suppliers to the turned-on-excitement of its hitting the streets to the out-of-control orgasmic high of supply, the stony buzz and ecstatic hum of being able to toke up or shoot up or snort up or cook up anytime you want. In the rhythm of the drug world, high times were better than love, more energizing than victory, more satisfying than sex. Mal Rogers had learned to move with the rhythm of the drug world as an undercover cop in Chicago. Mal Rogers knew how to run a drug investigation alright, but what he hadn't known was how much harder it would be in the country than it had been in the city.

But an undercover is an undercover, he decided. *They won't give me someone who'll fit in, I'll do it myself.*

The Importance of Being Earnest

Friday afternoon. Megan had been in Wabash City almost five days. Jess's classes for the week were done.

I really need a beer. What a week!

Tests? Homework?

Just everything.

They were sitting in a booth in *The Stabilizer*, four-thirty in the afternoon. Students were just starting to straggle in from their classes.

What have you been doing? Any luck?

Wabash City police wouldn't run the numbers for me.

That's too bad.

But the West Wabash cops did. He gave me four numbers.

Alright!

The one I wanted is registered to a J. Ferris.

Do you have an address?

No. They didn't give me an address. I'm gonna look in the phone book.

Hey, let's do it. They've got one behind the bar.

No. Not yet. Let's just enjoy a couple o' beers.

You're not hot to find this Ferris guy who just happened to be in Newport, Kentucky, the night your father was murdered?

Yes, but not now. All I think about is this stuff. Not this weekend. It's stopped raining. I wanna get away from it for a day or two.

Gotcha.

They drank for a long moment in silence.

Hey look, I've gotta study almost all weekend for my midterms, but there's this thing tomorrow night . . . I was gonna go but . . .

But what?

Well, before that bitch left me, we were. . . .

You oughta try finishing a sentence.

Sorry, I. . . .

Meg was starting to find it sort of funny. Jess had gotten so nervous all of a sudden, tongue-tied.

This thing tomorrow night, what is it?

The Counter Culture Prom.

What is that?

It's like a high school prom. (Meg delivering another eyebrow-raising, amused look) No really. (Even Jess had to giggle at Meg's scrunched-up face) We even rent prom dresses to wear.

You're kidding.

No. Honest. It's cool. It's a mock prom for all the freaks in West Wabash and Wabash City. You wanna go with me?

Let me get this straight. You want me to be your date at a dress-up prom for freaks.

Well, yeah, sort of. Not really a date. I mean you're straight. Not really freaks. Well, not all freaks. I mean not deformed, just different, mostly politically different, well culturally too, well pretty much physically also, you know, tattoos and pierced ears and stuff like that.

For some reason, Meg absolutely cracked up at Jess's earnestness, nervousness. She couldn't keep herself from laughing. Pretty soon Jess had to laugh too.

No really, it's cool, a lotta fun. It's all sponsored by this great band, Mary Jane-A-Go-Go and the Kreemettes.

Kreemettes? You've got to be kidding.

No. Really. They're three chick singers in prom dresses. They're great.

You're serious.

Yeah, it's a great party. Lesbians can go there to party, dance, and nobody cares. Why don't you go with me?

Is it all lesbians?

No. It's all kinds of people. Mostly hippies or hippie wannabes. Lot of counter culture types from back in the sixties. Gays, musicians, dopers, professors, freaks, pottery people, people with tattoos. It's fun. C'mon, why don't you go?

But I'm straight.

So.

People will think I'm a lesbian.

So what. You don't know any of them.
You're right.
So you'll go?
Yeah, why not?
Alright!

The Old Curiosity Shop

On Saturday, Jess had to study Quantum Mechanics (*whatever that is,* Meg thought), so she dispatched Meg to Amused Clothing, the local nearly new, second-hand costume rental and old clothes store, to rent a couple of dishy prom dresses.

Everybody in town has been in here looking at these things, the clerk (whose ears were pierced and ringed so many times that you could hang a shower curtain across his face) warned, hope you find some that fit.

Meg got lucky. She found two that came close, one blue and one the ugliest purple ever dyed.

She needed shoes too, and got them at K-Mart.

For a couple of hours she actually forgot about her father's murderer.

She was driving back to Pierce Street when she saw a sign that read "THE HAIRMAN—WALK INS WELCOME." She stopped and treated herself to a haircut.

She never noticed the black man in the dirty white Dodge Dart who followed her everywhere she went.

When she got back to the apartment, Jess thought the purple number was just divine. Go figure.

We both need tiaras, silver ones. There's a Woolworth's down on the square in Wabash City. They should have tiaras. Oh please, Meg.

So she was off to Woolworth's which did indeed have tiaras.

Mal followed along like a pull-toy, but was beginning to wonder why.

The Great Gatsby

The Counter Culture Prom was a party right out of the hippie version of *The Great Gatsby*. Mary Jane-A-Go-Go and the Kreemettes held it out in the woods on the banks of the Wabash in a flat-roofed rental building owned by the Fraternal Order of Elks. The building was called the Old Elks Club because the Elks had built a new clubhouse in town for the herd to graze in. Now the Old Elks Club was just rented out for functions like the Counter Culture Prom. Of course, if any of the Elks ever saw the people, the costumes, or the goings on in and about their old clubhouse, their antlers would probably rotate. It sat in a nice grove of trees at the top of a grassy bank that swept gently down to the river. Prom night turned out to be one of the first nice nights of Spring, clear, with a Hunter's Moon shining on the river, and a heaven full of stars.

The building had been turned into a loopy fairyland right out of a sixties rock-n-roll hop. Magic lanterns swung on strings in the trees outside. Inside, suspended over the dance floor, a huge faceted revolving crystal ball twirled slowly, sending out shards of light that peppered the room with white pinpoints.

When Jess and Meg got there, the prom was in full swing. The band was wailing "I can't get no . . . Satisfaction." Everyone was dancing. Couples in grotesque tuxedos (pink and purple and black and white with plaid cummerbunds and fluorescent lapels) and frilly prom dresses gyrated to the sexual beat of the Stones. All manner of couples—straight couples, male couples, female couples, men in prom dresses dancing with women in motorcycle boots and leather jackets, women in top hats and tails dancing with men in exquisite beaded flapper dresses—packed the dance floor. Right in front of the stage and the band, four punks, mostly men, all with multi-colored, fluorescent mohawks and mega-pierced ears with strings of paper clips hanging to their shoulders, boogied to the band's beat, imitating the

Temptations. In the middle of the dance floor, a circle of prom queens twirled their crinoline poofed dresses to the wailing of the Kreemettes. People were out on the lawns walking hand in hand, fondling each other, wrapped in lewd and luxurious embraces under the trees, on blankets on the grass, down by the river bank. Smoke, the sweet smell of marijuana, hung in the air like body powder on a stripper.

Wow, I know that smell.

Do you do grass?

I have.

I do it every chance I get. Trouble is I can't afford it so I've got to depend on a little help from my friends as John Lennon would say.

Any of those friends here tonight?

Oh yeah.

They went inside, wrestling their flowing dresses through the narrow door like two belles out of *Gone With the Wind*. Screwdrivers and Bloody Marys in plastic cups mixed in large ice-filled trash cans near the stage seemed the evening's cocktail of choice. It was a trashily elegant affair.

Meg loved to dance. She started out dancing with Jess. *Everybody thinks I'm a lesbian,* she was sure. But pretty soon Jess had drifted away into the crowd on the dance floor and Meg found herself dancing with about ten other girls in prom dresses—*they're probably all lesbians too* she wondered—to the hottest new song of the growing disco craze, the Bee Gee's *Stayin' Alive.* It was exhilarating. Just moving with the beat. So free. So unconventional.

Meg had a great time dancing, but when the band switched to a slow song she refilled her screwdriver and went looking for Jess. She found her out on the lawn sitting on a blanket with a gaudy blonde. They were drinking and sharing a joint. When she sat down, the blonde glanced quickly at Jess for confirmation and, at Jess's nod, passed Meg the joint. Meg drew the sweet smoke deep into her lungs and held it.

Wow.

This is Meg, my new roommate.

I'm Jackie.

Hi.

Jackie's a stripper.

Hi Meg, and Jackie took her hand.

Settle down, she's straight.

What a shame.

The joint went around again.

A stripper?

Yeah, actually dancer. Topless go-go-girl. Exotic dancer. Whatever. I work at the *OK Corral.*

The OK Corral?

It's West Wabash's only strip joint. Lot better than the ones in Wabash City. I've worked there too. *OK Corral* is easier to deal with. Bunch of drunk and horny fraternity boys from the university. They come in to ride the mechanical bull and look at us when the college girls are playin' hard to get.

Mechanical bull?

Oh yeah. It's the latest craze. Sometimes I think the bull turns those boys on more than naked dancers do.

A stripper, wow.

Meg could see why Jackie would be a successful stripper. When Jackie leaned across the blanket to pass the joint, Meg could look straight down the front of her low-cut prom dress. Wow twice.

Jackie looked up and caught her in the act of admiring that impressive cleavage.

You sure she's straight? Jackie joked to Jess.

Yeah, she's straight.

Aren't these puppies great? Jackie laughed at Meg. Paid for them with my student loan my sophomore year right before I flunked out. I could have been one of those Silver Twins, you know, the twirlers, but I stopped goin' to classes.

They're really great! Meg's voice was dreamily awestruck.

I'm not sure she is that straight, Jess joked back.

Wow. This stuff goes straight to the back of your head.

Yeah. It's primo. Too bad it's the last of it.

How come? Jess asked, passing the roach back to Jackie.

Did you read about that dead body they found down on the bike trail?

Yeah, I guess so.

That was my guy.

Your boyfriend fell off his bike and died. Omigod!

Jess and Jackie looked at Meg as if she was a martian.

Boyfriend? Jackie stared.

Fell off his bike? Jess squinted.

Meg really wasn't thinking very straight. The grass had gone to her head.

Not a boyfriend, Jackie's voice was filled with utter disdain. I don't do guys, remember. Unless, of course, they pay outrageously.

She and Jess got a good laugh out of that.

No, he was my grass connection. Now I probably gotta go back to those pricks in Wabash City I used to work for to get it.

Wasn't he murdered? Jess was just making conversation.

Probably. He *was* a drug dealer.

What was his name again?

John Ferris. He was at *The OK Corral* every night. He loved dancers.

John Ferris, did you say? Even through her dope fog, that name caught Meg's attention.

Yeah, John Ferris.

Suddenly Meg's grass-muddled mind came crystal clear.

It took Jess a moment longer, but she recognized the name too.

You say he was murdered?

That's what I'm guessin.' All the paper said was they found his body under mysterious circumstances down on the bike path by the river. There's an ongoing investigation. He's dead. That's it. No more dope from Johnny. The girls at the *OK* are really missing him.

Why's that?

He had a lot of money and he loved dancers. Especially young ones. He was real hetero . . . and kink-key.

Did he fuck the strippers?

Oh yeah.

Regularly?

Oh yeah.

And he's dead?

Yeah, must of really pissed somebody off.

What do you mean, Ferris must have pissed somebody off?

Well, he's dead, isn't he? He was only about thirty. He didn't die of old age.

Pissed somebody off how?

Jess, your friend here's got a lot of questions. You sure she's not a narc?

No. She's cool. Somebody murdered her father.

No way!

Yeah.

Not Ferris though.

Why?

He wasn't a violent type. He joked around, smiled a lot, you know. He never beat up any of the girls. He wasn't a rapist. He liked the performance aspect of sex. That's why he liked dancers so much. He liked a good show before he fucked.

What kind of show?

He liked to take dancers home with him, sometimes two at a time, for private parties. He liked to make us do weird stuff. Dancers with dildoes hanging out of our holes or with bags over our heads. He liked us to expose ourselves and masturbate for him. He smoked cigars and he liked to stick them up into our pussies before he'd light up. Said it made 'em taste better. Most of the girls liked him—lesbians, straights, college girls—he treated us good. Paid us good in either money or dope.

And you bought dope from him?

Not really. He gave it to me. I was, like, his choreographer. Now I gotta find a new supplier.

Is that so hard?

For me it is, maybe.

Why might it be hard for you to get dope, Jackie?

Meg's voice was quiet and intent, directly opposite the high-on-grass banter of Jess and Jackie. The whole turn of this conversation on the moonlit, starlit, lanternlit lawn had cleared her head.

First of all, because I don't want to pay for it, and second, 'cause there's no way I'm goin' back to work for those dope dealin' psychos over on the other side.

Psychos?

Oh, Jess, listen to that. *Moon River.* How about a dance?

Yes, I'd love it. Jess sounded like some lovestruck schoolgirl.

But . . .

See you later, Meg.

They were holding hands as they moved toward the music.

Could I talk to you some more, Jackie? Later?

Sorry honey, gotta go, gotta dance.

Jackie, I need to talk to you.

Sorry honey, I still gotta go to work tonight. Late shift with the buckin' bronco. Nice meetin' you.

But. . . .

Jesus, she's oppressive, Jackie whispered to Jess as soon as they were out of Meg's earshot.

She's trying to find out who killed her father.

What do I know about that? Why is she askin' me so many questions?

I think she's just trying to understand how this place works. She's only been here a few days. She must think you know stuff that can help her.

Look Jess, I gotta go to work at eleven. I just stopped in here for a few giggles and a real dance or two before all the bumpin' and grindin' starts. C'mon, let's dance. It's *Moon River*. Can't dance to this in *The OK Corral*.

The dance floor was crowded for the slow song. The two women in prom dresses swaying slowly to the familiar love song in a close embrace were not unusual. Then, about half way through, they stopped moving. In the ricocheting light of the revolving crystal ball, they kissed long and deeply.

Look honey, I'll talk to her on a break, then maybe you could, well.
. . .

A Fringe of Leaves

As a dancer, Jackie was a hard worker. Up on the stage at *The OK Corral,* in a tiny g-string and a pair of cowgirl boots, Jackie worked the crowd in a variety of eye-catching ways. Bathed in overhead theatrical light that alternately washed over her naked body in changing red and yellow and blue waves or strobed stark white down upon her, Jackie spun, climbed, danced with and hung from the thin pole that vertically bisected the stage. Jackie's hair was blonde on her head, but the hair that stuck up out of the top of her tiny g-string in a nicely trimmed square was jet black. She was dancing to *I'm Your Boogie Man* by K.C. & The Sunshine Band when Jess and Meg came in.

The front of the stage was stacked with college boys perched on stools drinking beer, smoking cigarettes and waving dollar bills at her. They loved her because for each dollar she collected she would go to her knees right in front of them and pull out her g-string so that they could look right down into it as they deposited their money. They loved her because she would shake her pointed tits for them, bend over and slap them in the face with them, pull them up to her mouth and suck her own erect nipples. They loved her because she would bend over with her legs apart, spread her ass with both hands, and spank herself so that the red mark of her handprint lingered on her white skin. Dollar bills formed a fringe all around her waist.

Jess and Meg, still in their prom dresses, sat in the shadows at a side table watching Jackie work. They had left the Counter Culture Prom at midnight. In the car driving home Jess had suggested they stop at *The OK Corral* for a beer. It was right down the State Street hill from their house. It sat back against the hill beside a greasy spoon diner appropriately named *The Triple XXX.*

Meg jumped at the idea.

Both Meg and Jess had ulterior motives.

They drew some strange glances from the men when they walked in, either because there weren't but two other women customers in the place or because of their prom dresses, but the men's attention quickly reverted to the stage and left them alone.

They took a table in the dark against the wall and ordered two beers. From this vantage point they watched Jackie dance and work the men around the edge of the stage.

Meg's gaze roamed the room fascinated by the ritual of voyeuristic lust being played out before her.

Jess couldn't take her eyes off of Jackie.

I've never been to one of these places before. Meg tried to make conversation and break the concentration of Jess's lust.

I love comin' here. It's really hot. This is my fourth time. This is where I met Jackie. I came here on a dare. But I liked it. You think guys like lookin' at naked women! What they don't know is most of these dancers are lesbians, like Jackie. I love lookin' at these women dance naked. This place turns me on.

Wow.

OK. I'm drunk and I'm high and I talk too much. That was probably a whole lot more information than you wanted to hear, right?

No. I . . . I just. . . .

After her dance ended, Jackie came down off the stage and circulated through the tables trolling for tips. Behind a thin partition, the hoots of the college boys riding the mechanical bull periodically punctuated the low buzz of the between-the-acts showroom. She spotted Jess's and Meg's prom dresses first, then squinted into the darkness to make sure it was them. When she got to the table next to theirs, she tipped them a wink, put her hands on the table top where two white shirt, tie and pocket protector science nerds were sitting, hung her hard tits down so that her nipples touched their napkins, and cooed: If you guys would like to tip me, I'll let you stick it into my itty bitty, teeny weenie bikini.

Man girl, you sound like that Brian Hyland song, one of the pocket protector types belched as he fished his dollar bill out of his fat wallet.

Jackie glanced over at Meg and Jess, rolled her eyes like Johnny Carson.

You boys havin' a good time tonight?

Oh yeah, they leered down her g-string as they took turns tucking.

Alright then.

Yeah, we're in for the Engineering Conference at the university.

Well good for you.

A moment later, a new dancer took the stage and Jackie got a break.

Strip dancer etiquette, she explained as she sat down with Jess and Meg. We don't work the tables while another girl is on the stage.

Looks like you're having a good night, Jess flicked one of the crisper dollar bills tucked into the hip of Jackie's g-string.

I've already emptied my bootie belt five times in two songs plus intermissions. Jackie pulled bills out of her g-string, counting them. I'll bet I make two hundred and fifty bucks tonight. Whoa, there's a five. That guy must really be in love with me.

Or at least parts of you, Jess teased.

Meg was finding it more than awkward, almost surreal, sitting at this table in a prom dress with a ninety percent naked woman totally surrounded by drunken horny men. Jackie's breasts were truly amazing. They pointed straight out like torpedoes. Even more amazing was Jackie's total lack of awareness of them, or of her nakedness in general. She sat calmly counting her money, making sure as she neatly piled up the bills that all of the presidents were facing the same way. Ah, Capitalism.

Jackie, do you mind if I ask you some things?

Sure, go ahead. What things?

About getting drugs from John Ferris. About why somebody might have wanted to kill him.

Shoot.

How long have you known this John Ferris? How long have you been getting dope from him?

About three months. It was a sweetheart deal.

Only three months?

Yeah, since I've been working here. I used to work at another joint on the other side of the river, *Tippers*.

Tippers?

That's what they call it.

Why did you change? Better money?

Not really. I think because I hated the guys who owned that other place. Scary.

Were you doing drugs over there?

Yeah, when I got 'em for free. Mostly grass. A little coke once in a while. They gave the stuff to you, but believe me, they made you pay.

Scary guys. I quit and came over here. Told them I was going back to school.

That's when you met Ferris, when you started working here?

Yeah, some of the girls introduced me to him that first week. We went to his place and partied, down by the university power plant. Nice apartment. Right by the railroad tracks though. Every once in a while a train would come by and the whole house would shake.

He gave you dope?

Yeah, that's when I had to tell him I was a lez. He was hittin' on me. He gave me the dope, but he was also willing to pay me for sex. I thought about it.

Why didn't you?

'Cause that's what got me in trouble on the other side with those other guys. Once you sell it to 'em they think they own you.

Who were those other guys? They were dope dealers too?

Yeah. The Smale brothers. They're a piece of work they are. One of 'em is so retarded you gotta be careful he doesn't drool on you.

And this Ferris was different?

Yeah. He gave me primo grass. I like grass. It relaxes me for dancing.

Boy I can understand that, Meg thought, sweeping her gaze out over the shadowy, smoke-draped room filled with drunken men leaning into the stage drawn as if to a flame.

Where are you gonna get your grass now that he's gone? Jess broke into what was becoming almost an interrogation by Meg.

I don't know. Something will turn up. These college kids gotta get their dope from someone. Maybe I'll have to go back to the Smales.

To work at *Tippers?*

No. I like it here. Younger crowd. Safer.

Why then?

They're the only other ones I know who sell dope around here.

But you said they were scary, that they gave you dope but they made you pay.

Jackie made a quick nervous turn to Jess. You sure she's not a narc? She's not, trust me.

Why did you say they were scary?

I saw some things that scared me, OK?

What do you mean 'they made you pay?' You said they gave you free dope.

Girls who worked for them had to work private parties for their friends, their customers. It was out of control. It made me nervous.

What did you see?

People. Important people. Bad stuff. Hey, sorry, gotta go. Her song's over. Gotta work the tables. Manager's giving me the eye.

Jackie, thanks, I appreciate it.

Hey, no problem. Jackie took her outstretched hand and shook it as if they had just closed some sort of business deal.

Jackie was moving off into the crowd, but she turned back at the last moment.

Jess, are you going to stick around? We close at two.

Yes, yes I am (eagerly). Meg's going home but I'm staying.

It was the first Meg had heard of it.

The Mysterious Stranger

Hey, yeah, I'll tip ya, a drunk black guy sitting alone at a table flagged her on the way to the dressing room. He waved a five spot seductively in his hand so she stopped, but then he popped the question. Those girls you were sitting with over there, the ones in the funny dresses, they friends of yours?

He startled Jackie with his question. The customers at the tables didn't usually ask questions.

No, they're not.

I think they are.

He reached into his pocket and changed the five to a ten.

No, they're not. You wanna tip me or not?

Hey, don't get nervous (but he still hadn't tipped her). I just like the looks of that brown-haired one in the white dress. Thought you might know her name, might introduce me.

Do I look like a dating service? She snarled as she turned on her heel.

Our Town

Driving home from *The OK Corral,* fighting her way out of that silly prom dress, brushing her teeth and getting ready for bed, Meg mulled over all the things she had learned from Jackie. She wanted to talk them over with Jess, but Jess never came home.

Ferris drug dealer strippers Smale brothers drug dealers strippers Ferris dead drug dealer. She finally dropped off into a troubled sleep. Questions. Answers. Dreams. Her father surrounded by strippers. Shadowy figures moving in and out of the darkness. A sudden explosion of white light. Gunshot. No. Light streaming through her window. Sunlight. Meg was jolted out of sleep by a beaming spring morning.

She dawdled over her coffee, waiting expectantly for Jess to show. Finally, Jess stumbled in. Meg's first impulse was to ask her where she'd been, but she already knew and she didn't want to sound like someone's mother.

Hi.

Hey.

Hey, that was fun last night. I really had a good time.

Yeah, the Prom is somethin,' isn't it?

Actually, if someone asked, I'm not sure I'd know how to describe the Counter Culture Prom (for just a moment a pall of sadness spread across Meg's consciousness when she realized that there wasn't anyone to ask).

Suddenly, tears were streaming down her face.

Oh honey, what is it? What's wrong?

Oh, I'm so sorry. I don't want to do this. I just can't help it. I'm so sorry.

It's OK. OK. OK.

It took long minutes for Meg to regain control of herself, to stop her shoulders from quaking.

I'm sorry. Sometimes I just feel so old and so alone.

It's OK. You ought to be crying, maybe a lot more, the stuff that's been comin' down on you lately. It's OK.

I like your friend Jackie. She doesn't have a drug problem, does she?

I don't think so. She does like her grass, but she says she doesn't buy it.

What did you think about all that drug dealer stuff?

I didn't like it.

I thought about it for a long time before I fell asleep last night.

And?

This Ferris's car was at the motel in Kentucky that night. Then he turns up dead. I think he was the one that was supposed to be killed, not my dad.

I think you need to be careful, Meg.

You're the second person who's told me that.

Who was the first?

Oh, just a bartender at that motel in Kentucky.

Why did he say to be careful?

Because things aren't always what they seem, people have double lives.

He was right. I think Jackie's right too.

How so?

This seems like a little cornfield college town, but there's all kinds of stuff goin' on beneath the surface. Like this Ferris guy.

But every town's like that. Every college has drugs. Every town has strip bars.

Did you know that someone's following you, asking about you?

What?

A black guy.

What?

A black guy was asking Jackie about you last night after she left our table. He said he just liked the looks of you and wanted Jackie to introduce him.

Who was he?

Don't know. Jackie thought he might be a cop.

Why would a cop be following me?

You're suspicious? He knows what you're doing? How should I know?

How can he know what I'm doing? Nobody knows what I'm doing except me and you and now Jackie.

Look, I gotta go to the library. I've got a horrendous week.

Yes, I know, but . . .

I've got two exams in the next three days. Look, be careful. Wednesday we'll go out, beers, pizza. Honest, I gotta go study.

You say a black guy?

Yeah, bye.

A cop, Jackie said?

Maybe. Who knows? and Jess was gone.

In Our Time

Wes, dammit, what is Muhammed Ali doin' workin' out in our gym?

He is not Muhammed Ali, J.T., he's just a guy.

A black guy.

So what.

So what! Wes, he's black. What if he brings all his friends in here?

He hasn't yet. How many black guys you think there are in Wabash City outside of the students at the university? He paid his money, cash on the barrelhead.

Wes, dammit, why do you haveta be so different.

Different? I'm different cause I don't want to spend the rest of my life in jail? I'm different cause my brothers won't leave me alone, keep callin' me to drive trucks late at night cause they can't trust anybody else, won't let me run the business I built up from the ground the way I wanta run it? He's black. So what? All he's doin' is workin' out. He's been here three weeks. This is the first time you've seen him. Let it go.

OK, Wes, look, we got the CYO Boys Club boxers, we got the Golden Gloves team, we got a bunch of guys who've been workin' out here since we opened, and now we got this Ubangi.

Belfry laughed at that. His older and younger brothers arguing amused him.

What's the big deal? Wes turned to Belfry hoping for some support. Bad idea.

We ain't never had none of his kind in here, Belfry agreed with J.T.

We don't want none of his kind in here, J.T. agreed with Belfry.

Well too damn bad, because he's here and he isn't causing any problems.

Belfry seemed to have lost interest after that.

C'mon J.T. he's not causing anybody any harm. He's just a guy who likes to box and workout. Let it go. This guy's serious. You oughta see the workouts he does. He looks like he's been around boxing gyms all his life. He keeps to himself.

Of course he does. He's the only black guy in the gym.

No. He concentrates. Skips rope, heavy bag, light bag, and he spars with guys, white guys. Nobody cares he's black except you. Leave him be. He's just a guy who likes boxing.

We'll see how much he likes it when I get done with him.

If you girls are done whinin' at each other, I'm goin' over to the joint and have a quiet beer, Belfry, bored, announced

J.T. ignored Belfry.

His kind don't come down here, Wes, never have.

Look J.T., it's the seventies. Those days are over.

Not on 3rd Street and Wabash Avenue they ain't.

Hey J.T., Belfry hooted, it's the seventies and our little brother's a liberal.

The Big Money

Wink Tyler was looking for a Chevy Camaro. He and his brother had a customer in South Bend who would pay them six-thousand dollars for a fresh one. Camaros were about the hottest cars going these days, especially among street and rod freaks. His brother Bobby had sent him out to look for it, given him exact instructions; had to be either a '75 or '76, hardtop (no T-tops), with the big engine not the phony economy six. Wink had been cruising the streets of Wabash City for two days, car shopping. They called him Wink because he had a slow left eye, but his fingers were fast. He could hotwire any make of car in 30 seconds.

Wink settled on a red '76. He would steal the Camaro in the morning and have it in South Bend in a garage being spray painted with primer before its former owner took his morning coffee break. His brother would be happy.

Bobby Tyler was the brains of the operation. Wink was the wheelman who stole the cars and drove them wherever Bobby told him to. Their chop tools were totally portable so sometimes they used the garages in town, other times barns out in the country that they'd borrow for a couple of days from friends. And then there were the special orders that came along once in a while through Bobby Tyler's grapevine. They were a good payday for very little work, a lot less labor than filling up a semi-trailer with chop parts.

Bobby and Wink Tyler had met John Ferris in the strip joint on the west side near the university. Ferris was a high roller from Chicago, and they'd stolen a really strange (for Wabash City) car for him, a Porsche. Wink had gone all the way to St. Louis to get it because the Ferris guy stressed that he wanted it from far, far out of town. The Porsche had been silver, but they painted it black for him. Ferris had really liked their work and had enlisted them in his growing drug dealing business at the university. Wink and Bobby had become his pick-up and delivery men. They ran the interstate between Wabash City and Kentucky, transporting grass under tarps in the back of their pick-up.

Ferris had paid them well, but then he had ended up dead.

Who you think killed Ferris, Bob? Wink brought the subject up as they sat at the bar in *The Squirrel Cage* nursing longnecks.

I dunno.

He musta really pissed someone off.

Yeah, they shot him in the head.

What are we gonna do now?

I don't know. It's too bad.

He paid good.

Look, Wink, he's dead. No more deliveries or pickups for us.

Yeah, no more cash.

On that note the Tyler brothers took a long moment to stare into their beers.

Bet it was those Smales, Wink broke their silence.

Mebbe. Could've been them, or somebody from that shithole down in Kentucky he sends us to.

Why would they kill him?

Who?

Those people you just said, in Kentucky.

How the hell should I know?

But they wouldn't just kill him, would they?

Mebbe he ripped them off or didn't pay 'em. This was a hit.

Not the Smales then?

Mebbe the Smales.

Why the Smales?

Cause he was sellin' dope in Wabash City.

Well, the Smales sell dope.

His brother's dimness was starting to try Bobby Tyler's patience.

Of course they do, that's why they killed him. Those pricks think they're the only ones who should ever sell dope in this town.

Too bad about Johnny Ferris. He was OK for a city boy.

Hey Wink, Bobby decided to try to cheer his dimwitted brother up.

What?

Would you rather steal cars or sell dope?

I sorta like stealin' cars.

We could make more money sellin' dope.

We could?

Yeah, and we know where Ferris got his dope, from that place down in Kentucky.

I guess.

The Redneck Mafia

After the Counter Culture Prom, Meg didn't even see Jess until late Sunday afternoon, and then Jess was off to the library to study for her tests. Then Meg hardly saw her for three days while Jess was taking her tests. Then it was nine-thirty Wednesday night and Jess burst into the apartment from the rainy street as if she had just escaped from prison.

I'm done! Man do I need a drink. I'm starved. All I've had is peanut butter crackers out of vending machines in the library the last three days. Come on. Let's go next door.

Meg did a quick translation. 'Done' were her exams. Real food such as burgers was required. 'Next door' was *The Stabilizer* bar.

Wow, this place is crowded for a Wednesday night, Meg noticed as they entered.

Yeah, I think Wednesday is softball night. *The Stabilizer* has a men's team.

I played coed softball during summers at home.

These guys play slowpitch down by the river.

The softball players in their garish polyester uniforms and their carefully molded baseball caps were gathered at the bar.

Meg and Jess found an empty booth in the back under the TV set.

Half an hour later, halfway through a pitcher and right in the middle of their cheeseburgers, two softball players slid into their booth.

Hi girls.

Meg and Jess, both hands wrapped around their burgers, just stared at the intruders.

What's this? Jess finally finished chewing enough to ask.

Nothin.' Nothin.' The short one with the comical gap between his front teeth evidently was their spokesman.

The other softball player didn't have on a baseball cap. Instead he wore a ridiculous-looking floppy porkpie hat made out of what looked like brown canvas. It had probably once been white.

Those guys at the bar just dared us to come over here and talk to you.

You two aren't on *The Stabilizer* team.

No. *Peerless Truck.* We were playin' *The Stabilizer* tonight but we got rained out.

Well boys, Jess was warming to the exchange, why don't you two just go back to your buddies at the bar and tell them to . . .

No wait, Meg stopped her.

Jess stared at Meg in disbelief: You wanna talk to these guys?

Sure. Why not? Hey guys, and Meg motioned to the two softballers to lean into her, let's talk real serious for a few minutes and you'll win your bet from those guys at the bar, Meg smiled at them like a coiled snake.

Jess stared at Meg as if she was an alien. Those guys at the bar told you we were a couple of lesbians, didn't they? Jess snapped.

Well we're not, Meg cut her off. I played softball. Tell me, do you guys ever smoke dope?

Well sure, yeah. You mean marijuana, right? Some. Yeah.

Jess rolled her eyes in disgust.

You got any? Meg pursued her line of questioning.

You mean marijuana?

Yeah, you got any grass? You know where I can get any?

Well no.

Wait a minute, I do, the porkpie hat lurched into the conversation.

You do?

Good. Where would that be?

I hear you can get it down on Wabash Avenue at the Smale's garage.

What's the Smale's garage?

The Smale brothers own a garage, auto repair, you know. There are gas pumps out in front, but they haven't worked in years.

Why?

They pump more dope out o' that garage than they ever pumped gas.

Who are the Smale brothers?

Man, you *are* new in town.

Yes, I am. Would they sell me some dope?

Listen girls, and to their great surprise Gaptooth really had turned serious, you don't want to mess with the Smales. They're really bad news. Stay out of Smale Hollow.

Smale Hollow? What's that?

Wabash Avenue. That's what everybody calls it. The Smales run that whole neighborhood, own most of the place.

What do you mean? What do they own?

They own the garage, but they also own the strip joint, *Tippers*. They own the 3rd Street gym right behind the strip bar. They all got houses down there. The old lady, Ma Smale, even runs the concession stand at the softball field. That's why they call it Smale Hollow. It's their place.

Sounds like they own a lot of stuff.

Don't get me wrong, honey, sellin' dope is their main business.

Would they sell dope to me?

Who knows? Maybe. You two aren't female cops, are ya?

No, we're not (Jess just couldn't hold off any longer), we're lesbians.

The two softball players laughed nervously.

No, we are, really. Lesbians.

Now it was Meg's turn to smile nervously.

No you're not.

Yes we are, Meg backed Jess, but you can go back to your softball buddies at the bar and tell them you dated us up for later if that's what it takes to win your bet.

They said we were lesbians, didn't they?

Yeah, they did.

I knew it.

Gaptooth and Porkpie slunk off back to the bar like two wounded weasels.

These Smale brothers must be the same guys that Jackie was talkin' about, Megan was really thinking out loud. She said they were scary. From all the stuff they own and do, they sound like Wabash City's little ole' redneck mafia.

The Awakening

The next day Megan bugged Jess all morning to let her call Jackie.

Call her before noon, Jess warned, and she's liable to come after you with a gun.

Both boobs blazing? Meg laughed

They are sort of like guns, aren't they?

They are truly amazing.

When Jess finally caved in and called, Jackie answered the phone sleepily.

Hi Jackie, it's me Jess.

Hi sweetie. That was really great last weekend.

Yes, it was wonderful.

I meant to call, but there's this Engineering Conference at the university and the *Corral* has been busier than a whorehouse on dollar day. I've been working 'til three every morning. We have to get together again soon.

I'd like that.

So would I. I am so sick of being pawed by drunken, smelly, smoky, horny men.

Hey Jackie, look, Meg wants to talk to you, ask you somethin.'

OoooKay, Jackie's voice slowed, sounded suspicious, not really pleased.

Jess, feeling guilty, handed the phone to Meg.

Hi Jackie.

Hey.

Are the Smale brothers the same guys you were talking about last weekend, the ones you used to work for, the scary drug dealers?

Yeah, why?

We were talking to some guys in a bar. They said the Smales were the main drug dealers in town.

So?

Well, do you think they might have murdered John Ferris?

Whoa girl!

I know, it's sort of wild gangster stuff, but if somebody wanted to kill Ferris, you've got to think the Smales would be right up there on the list.

OK, maybe, but you don't want to mess with the Smales. (Jackie was the second person who had said those exact words by way of a warning.) They're more than scary, they're evil. At the strip bar once I saw them hold a girl down and let the retarded brother set her hair on fire when she didn't pay up right away for some coke.

Is there any way I could find out more about them? Could you . . . ?

Whoa, no way. I'm stayin' as far away from the Smales as I can.

Do you have any ideas about how I could get close to them?

No. None. Nada. Put Jess on.

Hi. It's me.

Look, sweetie, tell your straight friend she's in over her head. These guys are sick perverts. They'll rape her, beat her up, kill her if they think she's spying on them. They'll think she's a cop.

She's trying to find out who killed her father and she's come this far. I don't think she's going to stop now. Can't you think of any way you can help her?

No. The best thing she can do is stay away from the Smales. That's the best advice I can give her and the best she'll ever get.

I don't think that's what she wants to hear.

For god's sake, why don't you two sorority girls just go get jobs dancing at *Tippers?* You'll get to know the Smale brothers real fast and real close that way. They love fresh meat.

Terrific.

What did she say? Meg asked after Jess had hung up.

She won't help you. She said to stay away from the Smales. She said there's no way to get close to them. She said they're evil and dangerous.

I guess I'm just going to have to go over to their garage and convince them to sell me some dope. See if I can get to know them that way.

You won't learn anything that way. You'll be just another customer. Jackie says the two of us might as well go get jobs dancing naked at *Tippers* for all the good spying on the Smales will do.

What?

Meg looked at Jess and Jess couldn't believe what she saw in Meg's eyes.

What did you say? Meg pressed.

Oh no.

What did you say?

It was just a joke Jackie made. You can't be serious.

Why not? It's a great idea. I could see things they might not want anyone to see.

It's a terrible idea. Meg, they're dangerous. Maybe they kill people. And you're not a strip dancer.

No, but Jackie is. She could teach me. Call her back.

No way. Look, you need to be careful, Meg.

You're the second person who's told me that.

Who was the first?

A bartender in Kentucky.

Meg and Jess just looked at each other, a silent standoff.

The hard knock on their door made them both almost jump out of their skins. They looked at each other, questioning, hesitating. Jess made the first move toward the door. When she opened it, there was a black man standing there holding up a badge for her inspection. Megan stared at it over Jess' shoulder.

Mal Rogers. Indiana State Police, the man identified himself.

Hello, Jess said.

The policeman ignored her and looked at Megan as if he already had her in handcuffs. Miss O'Neil, we need to talk.

I haven't done anything.

I didn't say you had. You seem interested in the same people I'm interested in.

What do you mean?

John Ferris, the dead dealer. I also know your father was murdered in Kentucky.

How do you know? How did you find me? You have no right to follow me.

I know a lot of things. I've checked you out. All this has something to do with the murder of your father down in Kentucky. I've been following you for a week.

Then Meg did a curious thing.

You wanna come in for a cup of coffee?

Yeah. That's a good idea.

They brought him in and sat him down and then they all just looked at each other.

All we've got is instant. It'll take a minute for the water to boil, Jess broke the awkward silence.

I know. I live alone.

The three of them, sitting at the kitchen table, their mugs expectant with instant coffee, waited.

Why are you following me around? Meg finally asked

You've managed to make yourself part of an ongoing investigation.

I don't want to be part of your investigation.

I know. You've got your own investigation going, don't you?

What do you mean?

Look, Miss O'Neill, this may seem like a quiet little place, a medium-sized midwestern town with a nice river running through it, but it really isn't. It's just like everywhere else. There's all kinds of stuff going on beneath the surface. There's bad guys doing evil things. It's no place for amateurs. I'll take mine black.

Jess had gotten up to tend to the teapot that had started to whistle, leaving Meg and the cop confronting each other at the table.

You've got a black eye, Meg changed the subject rather transparently. How did you get that?

Boxing.

Boxing?

That's part of the investigation too. Now look. . . .

No, you look. Don't tell me to stop doing whatever I'm doing because I'm not going to stop.

Jess poured the steaming water into all of their cups, handed them spoons, and sat back down. She didn't say anything. She was sort of a referee between them.

Miss O'Neill, I'm a Special Investigator for the Indiana State Police and my area of concentration is on interstate transportation of controlled substances, drugs. My concentration at this particular State Police post is on those that we suspect are the biggest local drug dealers.

And that would be John Ferris and the Smales.

Right.

But with Ferris turning up dead . . .

Yes, that leaves the whole market to the Smale family.

That is what it has taken me the last two weeks to figure out.

That's fine, but I want you to stop.

I can't.

You must.

I can't because I think the Smales killed my father by mistake when they were trying to kill John Ferris.

And that's what brought you to Wabash City, looking for Ferris who was already dead before you got here?

Yes, I guess.

No, what brought you here was trying to understand the bad luck of your father being dead, trying to figure out how it happened and why.

OK.

OK. So you've figured it out. Now you need to get out of here and leave the Smales to the professionals. They're dangerous. Maybe they killed your father. There's just nothing more you can do.

Oh, there's a lot more I can do! A lot more than the police in Newport, Kentucky, or Wabash City, Indiana, want to do as far as I can tell. Don't tell me to leave it to the professionals!

Look. I've been working on the Smale brothers for six months. I've been going undercover to their gym for almost two.

Jess couldn't believe her ears: They sent a black cop undercover? There's only about a hundred black people in the whole city.

I admit I stick out like a sore dick.

Not the way I would have put it, but . . .

They didn't exactly send me undercover. I decided to go under on my own. I told Wes Smale, who runs the gym, that I worked at the university in financial aids.

I've decided to go undercover too, Meg wrenched Mal's attention back from Jess.

No you haven't, Jess corrected her forcefully.

Yes I have.

You undercover? How? Mal Rogers reasserted his authority.

As a dancer at *Tippers*. The Smales own it too.

I know what the Smales own.

This is crazy, Jess couldn't believe what she was hearing.

Miss O'Neill, your friend's right. You can't go undercover at *Tippers*. You're a college girl not a stripper.

No, you're wrong. I'm what they want. I'm what they advertise for, young naked women. I'm doing it.

Both Jess and the State Police cop tried to dissuade her.

Your father would hate this idea, Jess argued.

My father was murdered and no one seems to care.

It's dangerous in so many ways. You'll be naked on stage. They use the dancers as prostitutes. If they find out who you are, they'll kill you. No way, the cop argued.

You can't stop me from seeking employment.

Employment! You're not a strip dancer.

It looks like you're not much of a boxer.

He had to laugh at that. He got up and fixed himself another cup of instant coffee.

They'll laugh you right out of the place.

You think I'm so ugly?

No, but . . .

I'm in pretty good shape. If I start working out and stop drinking beer, I'll tighten up in two weeks.

That's not what I mean.

So, what?

You're not a dancer. Can you even dance?

Yes I can dance. I love to dance.

This is hardly that disco stuff everybody's doing now.

Jackie can teach me.

Who's Jackie?

A friend of mine, Jess interrupted. She's a dancer over here at *The OK Corral.*

Is she the one who gave you this crazy idea?

Meg and Jess looked at each other and for the first time realized that Jackie's offhand joke had somehow turned into reality.

Look. Give it up, Mal ordered sternly but without much confidence.

I'm gonna do it. OK?

Fine. You're going to get a job at *Tippers* as a dancer. How?

I'll get Jackie to teach me some dances. I'll buy some sexy underwear.

What if this Jackie won't do it?

You'll ask her, won't you Jess?

Jess rolled her eyes sarcastically.

OK, here's how it will be. You'll be all alone, naked, with men who think you're a slut, who expect you to act like a slut, who expect all the things from you that they get from the other sluts. They'll expect you to do drugs. They'll try to turn you out as a whore to their customers. I mean, honey, this isn't just a job where you go in there and dance for a couple of hours and then go home.

Mal's speech was the first thing that had brought Meg up short.

The dancers are all druggies, prostitutes. You don't think those dollar bills they collect on stage are the reason they dance naked. They make more money offstage I'll bet, or they work for their drug habit.

And most of them are lesbians, Jess added.

What?

Lesbians. We'll be Lesbians.

We'll? Meg stared at Jess.

Yeah, you and me. That'll be our story.

What story? The cop turned his attention to Jess.

The two of us will be college students and lesbian lovers who need the money to pay our college tuition, or our rent, or something like that, our bills.

Jess, you don't have to . . .

No, this can work. We tell them we're lesbians and that'll keep them from hitting on us. Whenever they're around, we make a show of touching each other. It'll really turn them off.

Jess, no, you don't want to dance naked.

Actually, that sorta sounds like the fun part.

Terrific, now I've got to worry about both of you.

You sound like my father, and you've only known us for an hour.

You two sound like a father's worst nightmare.

I can kinda be your lesbian bodyguard.

Can either one of you act like a lesbian?

I am a lesbian.

That shut Mal up.

Do you think you can pretend to be my lesbian lover?

That shut Meg up.

Geez! Mal stood up shaking his head.

Well, I guess if I can dance naked in a room of drunken men, I can probably pretend I'm a lesbian.

So there you are, and Jess turned to Mal, she won't be alone. I'll be her bodyguard.

Great. That oughta keep her safe.

I'm a kickboxer.

Terrific, little Orphan Annie teams up with the lesbian Bruce Lee to go dance naked. You two oughta write a novel.

They all laughed, nervously, but then, an awkward quiet settled over the table. They sat there with the cold reality of what they were planning turning their coffee to ice.

We've got to go slow with this. I'm going to be both of your bodyguards, but we need some time to set this up, Mal finally committed to the craziness. Two weeks. OK.

Good, I can get ahead in my classes.

Good, I can get in better shape, though I don't think I can grow better boobs in two weeks. A joke, OK, a joke.

Mal didn't laugh. He hated the whole idea. I'll start going to the strip club after my workouts, establish myself as a regular customer. It's right next to the gym. I'll order club soda and watch the girls. I'll be a health nut who gets horny after his workouts.

Meg and Jess realized that he was rehearsing his cover story out loud, not really for them, but for himself, to try it on for size.

And we have to get with Jackie, learn how to be strip dancers.

This is like being thrown into an episode of The Mod Squad, Mal Rogers thought as he walked out to his car, *and that makes me fucking Linc Hayes.*

Little Women

You're gonna do what!

You heard me.

Strip dancers! You two? Jackie couldn't help but laugh.

We're going to get a job there so that I can spy on the Smale brothers. I think they're the ones who killed my father.

Why you? Jackie turned to Jess.

I'm going to be her lesbian lover.

But you're my lesbian lover.

We figure if we can do this lesbian act they won't push the prostitution aspects too hard with us.

You're gonna have to fight off the other dancers.

OK, we'll deal with that.

They might want you to put on shows.

We'll see.

You'll have to be convincing.

That's her problem, Jess laughed. I know I can pull it off.

They'll expect you to do drugs.

We'll do some grass to keep them happy.

Jackie looked first at Jess, shaking her head slowly, then turned to Meg, serious, almost maternal. Strip dancer, lesbian, doper, listen college girl you're gonna have to take your fantasy life to a whole new level.

I know. That's why I need your help.

Terrific! What, you want me to teach you to be a lesbian?

They all laughed.

No, can you teach us to strip and dance?

You want me to teach you to dance naked in front of men?

Yeah.

Hey, the stripping and the dancing are easy. I can teach you that. It's doing it for a room full of men that's hard. Not everybody can do it.

Well, Meg looked at Jess, I guess we won't know until we give it a try.

You sure you want to do this?

Both of them nodded "yes."

O-O-O-Kay then. No better time to start. Take your clothes off.

You mean right now? Meg stepped back as if she had been unexpectedly burned.

Hey, you're the one who wants to be a stripper. If you're afraid to strip right now for me, well, let's just say it don't get any easier out in public.

Meg and Jess started to undress. Meg's short-sleeved pullover was up and over her head in one motion. Jess's jeans were around her ankles after a quick pull on the zipper and a firm push over her hips.

No. No. No. Whoa. Wait a minute. Start over. When you strip for a man or men, you don't just rip off your clothes. You gotta do it slow. Tease 'em. Men are all perverts, peepers. They like to watch women take off their clothes nice and slow and dirty. They like to think their eyes own our bodies.

Start over. That's it. Take it up over your tits real slow. Then stop. Touch yourself. Play with your nipples. Men love that. They love to watch women play with themselves.

Now, both of you, pull your jeans down real slow over your ass. That's it, now stop and bend over. Now pull your panties up into your cracks. That's it. OK. Whoa, you're makin' me hot. Now kick your jeans off.

They stood before her in just their bras and panties.

I'll tell you, we gotta get you two some good underwear. Those Tidy Whities ain't gonna cut it at *Tippers*. You gotta start wearin' french cuts and thongs, red, purple and black. This must be what nuns look like in their underwear. Take those ugly things off.

Whoa. Slow. Slow down. Don't just drop your panties. Work them down slow, roll them slowly over your hips so they can see your pussy hair. Then show 'em your little goody. Now, bend over as you turn around and work your panties down slow over your ass. Spread your thighs so your panties catch on them. Slap yourself on the butt. Hard enough so it leaves a red handprint. Slowly drop your panties to your ankles and kick them off. Then turn around, and there you are in all your butt naked glory. OK, pull'em up and try it again.

They both pulled their panties up then bent over and slowly pulled them down again, before spanking themselves.

Meg couldn't believe that she was actually doing, or trying to do, what Jackie demanded.

Jess was totally aroused, exposing herself to Jackie, stripping just for her.

That's better, but even slower, Jackie was getting into it, coaching. There's two reasons men go to strip clubs. They're all pigs, and their little wives aren't very imaginative. Their wives are boring and they want women who are sluts.

Oh great, are these dance lessons or slut lessons?

Both. It's not easy to be a slut, you know.

Meg laughed out loud at that.

It isn't. A slut is these perv's fantasy. Think of it that way. You gotta be some hillbilly's or lawyer's or professor's or frat boy's fantasy. They want women who are sluts, who like sex, who like to show off their bodies, who are dirty and aggressive, maybe dominant, or whores they can give orders to. Hell, they tuck a lousy buck and we show 'em our cunts. You know how women read those Harlequin Romance novels? Well that's what we are for these assholes.

They stood in front of her stark naked. Meg crossed her arms over her breasts protectively. Jess just stood with her hands on her hips looking smugly at Jackie.

Jackie was overheated; they could both tell.

Okay, well. Jackie put both hands to her face and tried to press the blush out of her cheeks with her fingertips. We've got you out of your clothes. Remember, when you're taking it off there's no hurry. Do it slow and dirty. Wiggle it. Spread it. Tease them. They're perverts. They think you're their private dancing girl even if there's forty other guys in the room.

Jackie took a moment to slow down her breathing.

When you're on stage, you'll be wearing a net g-string. You can't take it off, but you can move it around. You'll need to learn to manipulate it. It's no problem in the back. It's just a thin string. They can see your whole ass. But you gotta practice moving the front pouch around so you can flash the customers your snatch.

Man, Meg finally said something, do all the strippers talk like that, those words.

All the ones I know. Whaddaya want us to say? Vagina? Rectum?

No, but . . .

But what! That's how the girls talk backstage. Get used to it. This is a dirty business. Don't think you're not goin' to get dirty doin' it.

But, but . . . that's how men talk.

This is like talkin' to Mary Tyler Moore, Jackie threw up her hands.

They're just words, Jess cut in.

'Topless!' Just that word on a sign gives men hard-ons. It's only a word, but men don't think with their minds. They're all peeping Toms and you're Lady Godiva, except every man in town is looking and they're all hoping you'll get it on with the horse.

Geez Jackie! Even Jess was grossed.

It's true, Jackie defended herself. All those guys around the stage at *Tippers* or the *OK* screamin' for you to take it all off, show 'em your ass, are all husbands and fathers and brothers. They've just come from their daughter's gymnastic meet or their sister's softball game or their prissy little wives. They come here to treat you like slutty whores because they can't have them. That's who you're dancin' for.

That's pretty sick.

But it's true. Men are perverts.

That shut Meg up, but Jackie wasn't done with her.

Look, don't take this personal Meg, but you gotta start doin' sit-ups and leg lifts. Your cookies are hangin' out and you need to tighten your thighs. Jess, you look good, tight. The kickboxing, eh? But you both need to watch what you eat. You'll keep the weight off because the dancin' itself is good exercise, but you gotta eat energy foods right before you go to work, carbs, spaghetti, pizza, that kinda stuff. You need some energy to get through long nights of dancin' and gettin' pawed.

For the next hour, while the music played and she taught them dance steps then whole routines, Jackie kept them naked, wouldn't even let them put on a robe.

You gotta be comfortable with yourself naked, she lectured. You gotta like being naked with all those men, and women too. Women come to titty bars to look at you too you know. Right Jess? And they both laughed. You're gonna be the only naked person in a crowded room where everyone else has their clothes on, all lookin' only at you, bright lights on you. You better do your sit-ups.

She worked them out naked for an hour and a half every day for the next week. Meg did her exercises, her sit-ups and leg lifts, and became a temporary vegetarian. Usually, when they were finished, Jess would hurry off to class or lab or the library and Jackie would hang around for a while to finish a cup of coffee with Meg. Two days Jess and Jackie left together with Jess carrying her backpack full of books. Meg doubted that she went straight to the library to study though.

One day, after Jess had left for class, Meg asked Jackie a funny question.

Am I getting any good at this? Do you think men'll want to see me naked? Am I fat?

Jackie really laughed at that one: Don't you worry, honey. They're gonna love seein' you naked.

But I don't feel like a strip dancer. I don't like talking like a strip dancer. They're gonna know.

You're right.

I am?

Absolutely. The only way you'll ever succeed as a dancer is if you treat it like a business. You're a self-employed business woman. Like those golfers, Palmer and Nicklaus, who are makin' so much money. You make good tips, then the house is happy with you. You wanna make good tips? Then make the men around the edge of the stage want to fuck you. I told you, it's not easy to be a slut.

Meg laughed. It was such a funny conversation between two women.

Sluts say 'yes,' Jackie warmed to her subject. Men don't want to fuck a woman who says 'no' half the time. They want women who want to have sex with them. Women who want to show off their bodies. Men get sick of begging for it from these pampered, self-satisfied Barbie dolls they're married to. They want women who have "FUCK ME" written all over them.

You make it sound like men are all perverted monsters.

Well they are.

My dad wasn't like that.

He wasn't?

Meg thought of the prostitute in Newport, the last person who had seen him alive.

Wake up girl, who *are* you? Jackie scoffed. Doris Day?

At the end of the week, Meg popped another important question: Jackie, how do we go about getting this job anyway?

Believe me, honey, you'll have no trouble gettin' this job. At your age, are you kiddin'? These strip joints are dyin' for young meat like you two. They'll snap you up.

I think she means, Jess continued Meg's thought, how do we get hired? How do we do it? Just go over there?

Yeah, just go in and say you heard they were hirin' dancers. See what happens.

What will happen?

Hell, I don't know. They might want an audition. Somebody will surely want to see the goods.

What kind of audition?

Who knows?

Haven't you auditioned?

Not for a long time. I've got experience, you don't.

Does it make a difference?

Twenty-two-year-old new meat like you two, probably not.

If we audition, what will they want us to do?

It depends. If they put you up on stage you'll be fine. They'll just want you to strip and dance. If one of the brothers takes you into the back office for your audition, be careful.

Will it be bad?

It could be. It depends on which brother it is.

Two days later, they were in Meg's car in the parking lot of *Tippers*. Jackie had done their make-up that morning, heavy on the blue around the eyes.

You sure you want to do this?

Yeah, I'm sure.

Let's go.

It was two-thirty on a late April Friday afternoon and, surprisingly, *Tippers* already had about ten buck-tucking customers when Meg and Jess walked through the door. There was a dancer on stage, a naked blonde with large hanging breasts and a rather prominent roll of fat around her waist. Another woman, in nothing but a bra and panties covered by a wispy see-through wrap, sat smoking and sipping on a glass of brown liquid at the end of the bar.

Probably coke, Meg thought, *it's a little early for seven and sevens.*

The customers, all men (*on their lunch hours,* Jess wondered, *or just getting some skin before they go home to the wife and kids for the week-end?*) all sat at the counter built into the edge of the stage ("*up close and personal" like they say on the Olympics,* Meg thought). It was dim in the large room. *She looks old,* Meg thought as she watched the naked dancer on the stage.

'C'mon, let's go, Jess nudged Meg, who had frozen just inside the doorway. Over there, the bar.

They approached the bartender who was reading a newspaper. One large man sat at the bar just biting into a steak sandwich out of a bag from *Steak and Shake* down the street.

Hi (in unison, smiling).

Girls, the bartender checked them out looking sideways from his newspaper, you old enough to be in here?

Yes, we are. In fact, we'd like to work here, Jess piped right up. Meg was having trouble finding her voice.

Work?

As dancers.

Oh yeah, right (and he turned to the man eating the sandwich). J.T., for you, (before going back to his paper).

The large man, in mid-chomp on the steak sandwich, turned and took them in from head to toe as he chewed. Not a word. Grease from the sandwich ran slowly out of the side of his mouth and down his chin. He lunged for a napkin in the bag and wiped himself.

What do you want?

His voice was deep and mean and he looked much more interested in the sandwich than in them.

Jess flinched right up against Meg, her arms going up around Meg's shoulder, one hand coming to rest right next to Meg's right breast (Meg couldn't tell if Jess's move was true startled fright from the sound of the man's voice or just part of the lesbian act they had planned but had never rehearsed).

Jobs, Jess answered (Meg hadn't yet said a word since entering the club). We're dancers.

You're lickers, aren't ya?

What?

Lickers. Lezzies.

Jess looked wide-eyed at Meg and didn't say anything right away, just moved her hands in a circle around Meg's shoulder. That was when Meg knew that Jess was putting on the act for the man.

Yes, we are.

I knew it. I'll bet you're college girls too, aren't ya?

Yes.

Fuckin' college girl lezzie strippers. I love America. Can she talk?

He nodded at Meg as he took another bite of his sandwich.

We're good dancers, mister. Meg, in a wavering little girl voice that was only half acting, ventured her first words.

The man's mouth was full and after he'd chewed for a long minute and took a sip from his long-neck beer bottle he looked them up and down again, then he looked at his sandwich.

You're strip dancers?

Yes.

You got any experience?

Hesitant silence. Jess was looking daggers at Meg.

I do (Jess finally spoke up), but she doesn't.

Where have you got experience?

Fort Wayne.

OK, and she's got none?

I've been teachin' her. We got our tapes all made up and we've been practicing routines.

Yeah, I'll bet you two dance naked together a lot.

The sandwich seemed to be burning a hole in his hand.

OK, usually I'd wanna go into the office and see what you little sluts have to offer, but you look OK. I'll give you a shot. It's Friday. Can you work tonight? We'll be packed. We'll see what you can do.

Yeah. Yes. Almost in unison.

Good, you start at six. Be here at five-thirty. I got some rules we gotta go over.

We'll be here, Jess stuck out her hand to shake on the deal, but his face was already back into his sandwich.

In what seemed only a second they were out the door. Meg couldn't believe how quickly it had all happened.

We're in, but this Little Miss Deer in the Headlights act has got to stop.

I know. I'm so sorry. I froze. It just wasn't what I'd expected.

Yeah, I expected it to be like . . . well, like one of those letters out of *Penthouse* magazine. The strip joint casting couch.

I think your lesbian act worked.

Maybe, but I think we were saved by a steak sandwich.

Terms of Endearment

As J.T. finished his steak sandwich, his brother Belfry was even more sensually engaged. His eyes were glassy and his breath was coming in fast gulps as he sank back into the pillows of Ginevra's bed. Ginevra collapsed her cheek against his shoulder, all muscle and thick, and ran her forefinger down the center of his chest hair glistening with moisture. For Ginevra it had been hard to get too romantic about Belfry Smale because everyone had been so intent upon warning her off. She burrowed into him, satisfied. Gangster, animal, drug dealer, thief, everyone had a different level of dislike for or fear of her new boyfriend. But she was having a good time and he was treating her well, showing her respect. She told him about all her friends' warnings and he just laughed them off. Don't listen to them, forget it, he was saying, but he wasn't denying anything. Still, he took her to the nicest places in town, to *Ten West* the new restaurant at the top of the National Bank building, the steak house out on the bypass by the interstate, and when they'd walk through the restaurant to their table men in coats and ties, leisure suits and turtlenecks, would wave to them, stand up to shake Belfry's hand as they passed, then lean in to their mousy little wives and whisper something that would invariably draw a shocked look. Belfry was even talking about the two of them taking off for a weekend in Chicago or even Las Vegas by plane. None of the guys she had ever dated between high school and secretarial school had ever talked about going out of town. A lot of Wabash City boys' idea of a romantic date was a moonlight ride on the tractor and prickly sex in the hayloft of the barn. Belfry had plenty of money, plenty of friends, and what looked like plenty of power, and the sex was great. In her mind, her girlfriends shouldn't be fearful for her; they should be envious, and she suspected some of them were. When she got the emerald necklace, she knew they were.

Wes Smale, on the other hand, wasn't nearly as satisfied as his two older brothers. He felt helpless like he was up to his waist in quicksand. It had taken a long time to dawn on him that he'd never had a chance. He had gotten married, left his construction job and opened the boxing club with an optimistic, ambitious view of the world and his future in it, but he'd never had a chance. No way was he ever going to escape the fact that J.T. and Belfry were his big brothers. No way was he just going to walk away from the family business when there were so many crimes to commit and so much money still to be laundered. That was what the Smale auto-repair garage, *Tippers* strip club, and the boxing gymnasium were really all about. J.T. was running drug money through all three of them faster than grease through a duck.

But lately it had gotten worse. For one thing, J.T. had started working out again, saying he wanted to get back in shape. *For what?* Wes had no idea. J.T. had taken to showing up about two in the afternoon and doing a pretty heavy workout with the weights, the bags, the bike, jumping rope, and even sparring a few rounds if he could get somebody to get in the ring and let him chase them around and pummel them for a while.

For another thing, J.T. seemed to have adopted the back room of the gym for his office away from his office in the family garage. He and Belfry met there almost every day in the late afternoon. 'The daily staff meeting of the Smale Drug Company' was what Wes's wife, Ginny, called it. From her he certainly wasn't hearing the same sort of terms of endearment that Belfry was hearing from Ginevra.

Aw hon, they just need someplace to relax, have a beer, sure, maybe go over the day's business.

Yeah, but the day's business is dealing drugs.

That's not all they do.

Oh, sorry, I forgot. There's also the pig rustling and the tractor theft and the general burglary and bribery and beating up of the low-life population of Wabash City.

Aw, hon, what am I gonna do? Wes really did feel helpless and his wife wasn't helping out any.

The boxing gym has done well. We've saved up some money. Tell Joe Ted you want to buy out his share and you don't want him and Belfry meeting there anymore.

Yeah, right. I can't do that.

Why not?

Because they're my brothers.

But Wes, you told me you'd walk away, get out of this family madness before you go to prison like Hump did and J.T. and Belfry will real soon. Wes, they're your brothers. Talk to them. Tell them you want out.

I will. I will. But not right now. Somethin's goin' on.

What is it?

I don't know. Maybe the cops are watchin' them.

See. There. That's why you've gotta get out, cut the gym's ties with them.

I can't. Not now.

You can't do it soon enough for me.

But if J.T. and Belfry were satisfied and Wesley was unsatisfied and anxious, Hump Smale was happy. He felt like J.T. and Belfry were giving him more responsibility. He had a new car that Belfry had gotten for him, and J.T. would send him out to drive the country roads of the county and the two neighboring counties to look for pig farms they could easily get a truck in and out of in the middle of the night. Their little pig stealing sideline was profitable and if Hump found what he thought was a good place, either Belfry or J.T. or both of his brothers would ride out there with him to take a look at it. Then they'd all go drink beer. That was the part Hump liked best.

They also encouraged him to hang around *Tippers,* which didn't take a lot of encouragement since he loved to watch the strippers. His job was to keep an eye on the bartender and make sure he wasn't stealing from them. Whether Hump was smart enough to even know if the bartender was stealing occurred to J.T. and Belfry, but they let it go figuring that the bartender at least wouldn't steal as much if Hump was always hanging around the bar watching him.

Besides that, Hump felt good about himself because the coke-addict dancer Rhonda was giving him sexual favors every time she needed some nose candy. So Hump Smale was happy. He just didn't have a clue.

Hump wasn't the only one keeping an eye on things at *Tippers.* Mal had started frequenting the strip bar behind the boxing gym. He'd stop in there for a beer after his evening workout.

If those two crazy white college girls are gonna work here, he reasoned, *I need to establish myself.*

He'd sit at the bar, have a beer or two, nurse them, and watch the white women take off their clothes. Just as at the gym, he was the only black guy in the place. On the weekends, when it was crowded, a few black guys came in, usually college students in a group with a bunch of white kids.

No black strippers, he noticed. *All white women.* A couple looked like they might be students like Meg and Jesse. *What a way to work your way through college,* he thought.

But most were hard and looked well-traveled, in their thirties. When they danced you could tell how bored they were, their eyes blank, like robots, as if they weren't really there. The younger ones seemed to enjoy it more, were at least a little more energetic, smiled down at the men waving their dollar bills along the edge of the stage.

The bartender noticed him after his third or fourth time sitting at the bar, sipping his beers, watching the girls. Mal would sit his gym bag on the bar stool next to him. It served as his ticket of entry, explained why he was there in this white redneck strip joint in this white redneck section of town.

You a boxer?

Yeah, I work out next door.

Uh-huh. Budweiser?

Right.

Sense and Sensibility

Mal had just finished skipping rope and doing sit-ups, the way he always loosened up before hitting the light and heavy bags. He was leaning on the edge of the raised ring, watching two guys spar, catching his breath.

Wanna spar a few rounds?

He had expected to turn around and see some eighteen-year-old kid with sideburns, one of the Golden Glovers, or some older amateur like himself, panting, sweaty, trying to work himself into shape, doing the asking. But when he turned to the voice, he was looking right at J.T. Smale.

Either my undercover's working, or he knows who I am.

Sure, why not? After these guys?

Yeah.

I'm Duane, Duane Brown.

All the while Mal was looking J.T. Smale over, playing dumb as if he didn't know who he was.

J.T., J.T. Smale. But he didn't stick out his hand to shake Mal's.

Why does he wanna box me? Mal asked himself. *Does he know I'm a cop? Has he spotted me tailing him? Has somebody tipped him off?* The one motive that never occurred to Mal was the most obvious one.

We're not quite the same class, weight class. You look like a heavyweight, Mal tried to make smalltalk.

Man, you can say that again, J.T. smiled disarmingly and patted his belly.

OK, a couple of rounds.

Good.

Let's get the stuff on.

Oh, we gotta use all that stuff?

Oh yeah. It's sparring. You never spar without the headgear and the pillow gloves.

Mal didn't even wait for an answer, just headed for the equipment locker on the wall. *What is this? He knows you gotta wear headgear. Why's he want me in the ring?*

He flipped a leather headgear to J.T.

They strapped the headgear on, got one of the guys coming out of the ring to help them lace up the gloves.

Time for us, willya? Mal cleared it with the boxer who had laced them up. Ring the bell at two minutes. OK? And Mal turned to J.T. for approval.

I usually do three minutes.

No problem, Mal agreed easily, but it didn't bode well.

This wasn't going to be Marques of Queensbury. Mal was pretty sure of that. *Why's he want me in the ring?* Mal kept thinking.

They climbed through the ropes. J.T. Smale grabbed the top rope and flexed his knees twice.

Mal windmilled both his arms, danced twice on his toes.

They turned and faced each other.

Are you ready for this?

I don't know.

Earlier, you sure didn't seem ready for it. You hardly said a word when we were in there before.

I know. I was scared. I didn't think I'd be, but that is a scary place. So dark and all those men . . . in the afternoon.

It'll be worse tonight.

5:15. Jess and Meg in the car driving back to *Tippers.* They had their reel-to-reel tapes, driving rock and roll like *Shake your Booty* by KC and the Sunshine Band for hard grinding, and disco tunes like *You Should Be Dancing* by the Bee Gees for prancing the stage, and even a slow song like Streisand's *Evergreen* for caressing yourself for the customers late in the evening when things slowed down. They had their suitcases with their g-strings and panties and bras and see-through body sheathes and leather pants and silky flared bell bottoms, costumes whose only function was to be taken off. They had their make-up cases filled with eye-shadow, body makeup and tampons.

Honey, are you ready for this? Jess asked her again.

Yes, I hope so.

Look, you've got to get rid of that deer caught in the headlights look. This is just a job. It's different, but it's just a job. You got that.

OK. I'll be fine.

You better be. They'll know something's wrong if you're a total stiff on stage.

OK, let's go.

They walked across the parking lot, but Meg stopped Jess at the door.

What is your problem?

What if they think I'm ugly, not worth looking at naked? What if they don't pay any attention to me?

Look, honey, they'll love you. You're pretty and you'll be naked. They're gonna want to fuck you in sick and twisted ways. Are you happy now?

Oh god.

Hon, be cool. Smile. We gotta have fun with this. It's the only way we'll get through it. If you're having fun dancing for them, it'll show and they'll love you. Smile. Laugh. Tease. All the stuff Jackie taught us. We gotta have personality. I'll go first. Just watch and see how I do. You know you're a big chicken, don't you?

OK, let's go. And they walked through the door of *Tippers* like Dorothy and Toto entering Oz.

They were drawing a small crowd, sweaty men in dull trunks and sleeveless shirts drifting in from the dim corners of the gym to lean their elbows on the edge of the ring and watch.

What's J.T. gonna do to the black dude? Mal figured they all were thinking. And that's when it hit him. *That's why he's got me in the ring. Because I'm black.* He felt a strange sense of relief. *Not because he knows I'm a cop. Not because I'm undercover. Just because he's a redneck racist asshole and he wants to drive me out of his white hillbilly world.*

Mal smiled inwardly. He could deal with this. He turned his back on his white opponent for just a second, went to the ropes and flexed his knees, looked around at all the white faces gathering just below him around the edge of the ring to watch.

They're here to watch the white guy beat up on the black guy.

He liked being closed inside the ropes. It was a real boxing ring, elevated like a stage. He bounced twice, feeling the give in the floor, sending the message of motion and speed to his legs and toes.

J.T. Smale was waiting for him in the center of the ring.

As he turned from the ropes and the corner post, from the faces of the men around the edge, he realized that the ring was a closed little world. He could get angry and it was what you were supposed to do. He moved quickly to the center of the ring, ready.

True to her word, Jess went first. The boss, J.T. Smale, had taken them into the back office when they first got there, but not for any monkey business. The lesbian cover seemed to be working, at least with him.

You get paid minimum wage. $2.10 an hour.

I get fifty percent of all your tips. Don't try to hide anything. You push any bill up your cunt, I'll know about it, and first I'll go get it, and then I'll make you pay more. You work the tables for ten minutes after every dance until the next dancer comes on. You sit at a table with customers when the other girls are dancing, get 'em to buy you a drink. Don't worry, it'll be ice tea. My bartender makes all the collections. When your g-string's filled up you take the money to him. He puts it in an envelope with your name on it and we make the split at the end of the night. He'll also tote up how many drinks you sell. You get a dollar for each drink. You get credit if a guy buys you a drink and for every other drink he buys on that round, except beers. You get nothing for beers. Umbrella drinks are more expensive. They're the ones we want you to sell. We'll see how you do. There's other ways you can make money afterhours too, but we'll see how you do first. He said it all in a bored monotone. It was a speech he had recited many times.

Jess went first.

Hey boys, you're in for a treat now, the disk jockey at the upholstered table next to the stage announced. The next two dancers are new meat, college girls taking it all off for the first time.

The bartender had shown them to the dressing room and introduced them to the two girls who were there. One, Janey, was totally naked smoking a cigarette. The other, Jennifer, was topless with a red leather miniskirt on. He just walked in on them without knocking. More than anything, that told Meg what to expect when she came to work. The bartender wasted few words.

That's Janey. This is Jennifer. Dawn is on stage dancing now. This is . . .

Jesse.

Megan.

Hi. Hello.

There's lockers for your stuff. The girls'll show you the john, where to put on make-up. Give your music to the disk jockey. His name's Mike. You go on in fifteen minutes.

That was it.

It was more like an ugly locker room than a dressing room. A chaos of make-up cans and tubes on a long table with three cracked mirrors and wooden stools was hardly luxurious. The lockers were metal, and dented, and looked like they came from a junior high school in the fifties.

Here's the beautiful Jesse . . .

Jess went first.

They had time to smoke a joint together in the dressing room before Jess went on. It was good grass. Jackie had gotten it for them. The two other girls had joined in without even asking, just reaching for it as they passed it around. When they finished the joint it was time for Jess to go on.

Break a leg, Jess.

What?

That's something we always said in the plays in high school for good luck.

This is a long way from high school plays, hon. Well, here goes nothing.

Meg cracked the door of the dressing room so she could see the stage.

. . . the beautiful Jesse. . . .

Jesse went first, and she really did well. The men around the stage were hooting and clapping for her from the minute she came up out of the darkness and into the neon light. Meg watched her every move. They had both picked their costumes for symbolic value and had brought three apiece. They had decided on the college coed fantasy to begin with, and Jesse was a cheerleader. As she pranced the stage and then unzipped her black and gold cheerleader's top all the way to her waist, letting its corners hang and her bobbing breasts play peek-a-boo with its edges, the customers clapped and whistled. Smoke swirled in the neon light that swooped and slashed over her body as she discarded her top, put her hands behind her head, and shook her tits at the men in front of her. Meg, alone, giggled.

Jesse went first, and she really did well. Meg, watching from the wings, envied her true grit, her ability not to be afraid, her grace under the rapacious eyes of all the men around the stage devouring her nakedness. Nothing seemed to faze her. As Jesse danced, she had a smug smile on her face the whole time as if she was harboring some secret those men shouting and waving dollar bills at her could never understand.

Jess quickly shed the cheerleader's short skirt and was all but naked now, moving from man to man all around the half-circle edge of the stage, taking a stance in front of each of them, feet apart, hips open, thrusting her hips hard at each one, all the while playing with her g-string, flashing them fleeting glimpses of her blonde pubic hair, gathering the sheer fabric of the front of the g-string and pulling it tight up between the lips of her sex, working it up and down. The men were going wild, clapping for her, shouting things that Meg couldn't hear.

Jesse was doing so well. She was working the floor now, on all fours and wriggling her naked rear end right under the noses of the men seated on the edge of the stage.

They touched gloves—*that's the last sign of sportsmanship we'll see here,* Mal was certain—and as soon as Mal dropped his hands J.T. hit him hard in the face with a right cross. It seemed to come out of nowhere, fast. He wasn't ready at all. He felt a concussive flash of pain right in the middle of his face. He was already dazed. He got his hands up.

The next punch, before he could backpedal, was a low lunging hook, not as fast or unannounced as the first suckerpunch, but heavy. He ducked his shoulder and caught it with his elbow, and he still hadn't thrown a punch.

He moved backward fast, clearing his head from that first punch to the face, the disembodied heads of the men lined up along the edge of the ring, like a fence of skulls, careening past and falling away.

J. T. Smale lumbered after him as he backed into a corner, then realizing that was no place to be, Mal jumped sideways clumsily to avoid the bull rush. That sudden spastic sideways lurch seemed to surprise J.T., who actually went by into the corner, bulling so hard that he couldn't stop his momentum.

As he went by, Mal clubbed him on the side of his head by the earhole of the helmet with a wild right. It was an ugly, ungraceful, unpremeditated punch, but it connected solidly and got Mal into the fight. He felt it in his hand inside the big glove, in his forearm, in his shoulder, and it felt good, got him started.

J.T. actually stumbled into the ropes around the cornerpost and turned quickly back, his gloves coming up, but Mal was gone.

Mal backpedaled all the way to the other side of the ring, both hands up now, bookending his temples. He bounced on his toes, watching J.T. come up out of the corner.

J.T. made another wild rush across the ring. This time Mal waited for him like a bullfighter, and when he was almost on him stepped out on his left foot and tapped him with a quick jab to the forehead as he went by.

He's not a boxer, Mal knew, *a puncher, a slugger. You can't let him hit you.*

Mal backed away and watched as J. T. Smale's head came up to look for him after that quick jab. There was no fear or pain in J.T.'s face, no confusion in his eyes at all. Perhaps after feeling two very different punches the big man was growing wary. He didn't make another wild rush. He stopped, pounded his gloves together once, bared his teeth, and started boring in.

For the rest of the round he just kept coming relentlessly forward, his chin on his chest, trying to sock, to pound, to thump.

Mal moved. Backpedaling, sliding, weaving, ducking, he tried to fend off the big man with jabs. He'd snap off one, two, then back off and skip away, away from the murderous uppercuts and hooks that J.T. kept trying to land.

Once Mal tripped over his own foot as he tried to go sideways too quickly and J.T., slogging in, caught him with a heavy right that glanced off his shoulder right into his chin. Even on the ricochet like that, the punch staggered him, made his knees buckle.

And then J.T. was on him. No jabs. A puncher not a boxer. Right, right, right, three so fast Mal couldn't back away, stumble away, run away.

The round seemed like it was lasting forever. The rights hammered into his shoulders and arms. In horror, Mal realized that he was backed into a corner and the pile-driving punches weren't going to stop. He needed the bell. Time seemed stretched so far out it would never snap back.

J.T. bore in, all body hook and uppercut, but Mal wrestled him into a clinch and, using the big man's own body for leverage, pushed off and spun himself off of the cornerpost and out into the center of the ring.

But he hurt. The heavy pounding he had taken in the corner made his shoulders burn, his knees wobble. He realized that this whole time he'd never even hurt the big man who was still advancing on him. 'A good big man always beats a good little man' was the age-old ring axiom. He needed the bell, needed time to regroup. But he didn't get it, not yet.

Coming in, coming in, clumsy, flatfooted, with a look of cheerful viciousness on his face, both hands held low, J.T. was daring him to step in and punch to his face, inviting him in so he could get him in close where he could punish him.

The bell finally rang.

Thank God, finally, Mal relaxed.

The punch exploded square into his face, a straight hard right, rang his bell good, knocked him straight backward across the ring.

J.T. kept coming, wanting to finish him off, but the bell, ringing urgently three more times, made him back off.

Sorry man, didn't hear it, Mal caught the words out of a strange haze that seemed to have settled all around the edges of the ring.

He sagged against the ropes.

You OK man? The timekeeper, who had rung the bell, asked.

He looked down at the man standing below him on the floor. He couldn't make him out. His vision still wasn't clear, haze still drifting around the edges of his sight.

Hey, you OK? That was great.

This time the words were coming from a different direction, inside the ring, on his level, J.T. Smale's vicious voice.

He turned in off the ropes he had bent over looking down and, as his head came up, his vision snapped back in. There, right next to him, was the big man, grinning like a hulking bear eager to bite off his head, grinning smugly like every southern cop who'd ever beat a black man senseless with an axe handle.

Yeah. OK. Great.

Go another?

Sure.

And he saw the meanness blossom in the big man's face, the vicious relish of getting another chance to punish him.

Alright!

Gotta get some water.

Leaning over the water fountain, punching the bar with the big training gloves, bathing his face in the cool water, drinking deep, Mal marveled at the miraculous recovery he was making. There was blood in the water swirling into the drain. He looked into one of the full-length shadow boxing mirrors and saw his lip was split, but the blood was already drying under the influence of the cold water.

Prick hit me after the bell.

So what! What did you expect? He's trying to drop you, humiliate you, hurt you, force you out of his white gym. Good news is he doesn't know you're a cop. This can work for you. You hang with him, you survive this, you get lucky and even hurt him a little bit, then maybe you get his respect, then he leaves you alone and your undercover is set. If he's not paying attention to you, you can pay all the attention you want to him.

How he had climbed down out of the ring and made it across the gym floor to the water fountain he didn't really know, but the water had cleared his head and he was thinking straight again. He grabbed a towel off a bench along the wall.

It's all about firepower. He formed a plan. *He's got it. I don't.*

He sat down on the bench.

But I've gotta hit him. I can't just run away. He's big and he's strong but he's slow and clumsy, slow and clumsy. Gotta get up. Go back in.

J.T., grinning viciously, raised the rope up for him to duck under, welcomed him hungrily back into the ring.

When Jesse came down off the stage, she made a beeline straight for Meg in the dressing room doorway.

Oh man, it's a trip, she was breathing heavily as she came up. It is so cool. Damn, it's a trip. She tossed Meg her outfit, whirled on her heel, and went back into the club stark naked except for her g-string to work the tables for tips.

I'm next, Meg thought. She knew there would be a few minutes while the girls worked the tables for tips, did private dances for individual customers in the shadows along the walls.

She sat down in front of the mirror to check herself one last time. She hardly recognized the heavily eye-shadowed, bright-red-lipsticked slut staring back at her. She had on her sorority girl outfit, a plaid miniskirt with a tight black sweater top and a bright red (to match her lips) ribbon choker around her neck. It was one of the three costumes she'd made up for the night. No shoes. It would be easier to dance barefoot, at least the first time.

OK, I'm ready.

She went to the door.

OK boys, here's our second virgin (at least for dancing) of the night, the disk jockey shouted. Let's hear it for Megan, the sweetheart of Sigma Chi.

Omigod, I've really gotta do this.

You're gonna get through this with your legs, Mal told himself as the bell rang for a second round and he and the big man came out and circled each other warily. You gotta hit him, let him know you're here. You just can't let him pummel you, turn you into a punching bag, or worse, make you run away the whole round.

Mal *stepped* out on his left foot to jab, once, twice. He snapped two quick lefts to the big man's head, just standing there flatfooted, his hands coming up too slow to block them.

Mal skipped away from a looping right hand, then ducked into the opening it left and hit the big man right over the heart with a straight sharp left.

J.T. swatted at him like he was an annoying insect.

But Mal was gaining confidence. He had hit the big man three times to two misses. Though no visible damage had been done, he had the good feeling of hitting him in his hands.

Show him some moves, Mal thought, *cross him, carry the fight to him.*

What he didn't realize was that he was getting greedy and it was too early in the round and J.T. wasn't as dumb, flatfooted and slow as he looked.

Mal moved quickly around J.T. He felt like he was dancing on a stage for a lineup of severed heads. He feinted to J.T.'s body, making the big man drop his hands the slightest bit, then quickly crossed him with a straight hard right to the jaw that actually buckled his knees and knocked him backwards.

Mal liked that punch, thought he had the big man in trouble, moved in to smack him again. Big mistake.

The big man lashed out with a vicious uppercut that slashed into Mal's chest and caromed up under Mal's chin. That uppercut's momentum carried him up under Mal's weak reaction jab and into a clinch. J.T. was headlocking him with his left arm and clubbing him brutally in the head with his right fist, thunk, thunk against the leather helmet.

There was no referee to break the two fighters out of the clinch.

Mal flailed aimlessly at J.T.'s stomach, trying to escape the wrestling hold. He twisted away, but as he went the big man butted him hard with his head under the chin.

Mal tried to dance away, but the punishment he had taken in the clinch slowed him. Eager to press his advantage, the big man made another wild bull rush like he did in the first sparring round. This time Mal wasn't quick enough to get out of the way and the slow looping rights as J.T. came in nailed him, pounded him, drove him backwards into the ropes, made the muscles of his shoulders and chest burn.

His only salvation came as he bounced off the ropes. Twisting to the side, he caught the big man with a short hard jab to the cheekbone that stung him, gave Mal a precious moment to escape his charge. That jab snapped J.T.'s head sideways, but didn't seem to faze him. He stood straight up, wiped his nose with his right glove, and began to move in again.

Mal stood his ground. He didn't know why, but he did. It surprised the big man, who hesitated, and Mal hit him with his best left-right combination, the left licking at his face like a flyswatter, the straight right, short, compact, slamming into his chin like a rolled up newspaper. The two quick artful punches in combination momentarily startled the big man, but they didn't hurt him.

That's when Mal realized that the best he could expect from this brutal exercise in initiation was to merely survive.

J.T. Smale began again. Moving in, coming forward, throwing long slow punches that glanced off Mal's bobbing headgear or were fended off by Mal's blocking gloves. When he came with the right,

Mal took it on the shoulder. The big man was a hooker and his left jab didn't have much pop. The right was a problem.

He only gets me if I make a mistake, Mal knew. And immediately he made one.

Backing up from a clumsy right hook that missed completely, Mal went too far and hit the ropes midway between the two corner posts. With a kind of slingshot or rubber band effect, he recoiled the slightest bit off the heavy ropes looking away for just a split second to see where he was, and came back right into J.T.'s arms who had chosen that moment to make another flailing rush.

Like an eager lover, J.T. wrapped him in a clinch and pounded away at his kidneys. Thump, thump, thump, the punches hitting his body sounded like a helicopter coming down. He would pee blood for two days.

Mal twisted frantically and broke loose, but as they came out of the clinch the big man caught him with another uppercut, up under his chin, grazing his adam's apple and burying in the underside of his face.

The punch made him go limp, turned his legs to taffy, spun him out of the clinch and down to his knees in the corner. It was the hardest he had ever been hit in this ordeal and it took all of the dance out of him. He was hurt. He was hurt and the big man was standing over him, waiting, grinning probably but Mal couldn't see that, standing ready to finish him off.

Mercifully, this time the bell rang and he stayed on his knees, half expecting Smale to hit him while he was down there on the floor like he had after the bell rang in the first round. The big man hulked over him, waiting.

He pulled himself up the ropes to the cornerpost then fully onto his feet. His head was clearing though his eyes were watering from the concussion of that last punch and the sweat was running off him like he'd just climbed out of a lake.

Hey, good round. How bout it? One more?

No, Mal thought, *no way.*

Man, I'm not used to these long rounds.

C'mon just one more. We're just getting warmed up.

But if I can make it through one more round, he gauged the rewards, *everybody in this gym, maybe even J.T. Smale will respect me. This undercover is knocked.*

OK. But this is the last.

OK. Good.

Let's hear it for Megan, the sweetheart of Sigma Chi.

As she walked up the steps to the stage, the disk jockey's patter was pretty funny. She hadn't told him to say that. *But if the shoe fits,* she thought. *'Have fun,'* she remembered Jess's advice as she reached the top step and moved into the careening neon light. *'Be a slut'* she could hear Jackie lecturing.

As she strutted slowly to center stage, she tried to find Jesse in the audience, but all she could see were the men gathered around the edge. Beyond them, all was simply a pool of darkness. For a long moment it was strangely quiet.

Damn, this one's a baby, she heard one man say close by.

We'll see about that, a stab of determination pierced her mind as the music began.

I can't get no . . . satisfaction.

She had chosen it for her first dance because it was quite simply the sexiest song she knew. She had always loved to dance to it in the disco bars and at the college parties. Those places seemed like far off memories of some other life.

She started slow, rotating her hips to the music and playing with the buttons down the front of her tight sorority girl sweater. She popped the top one open, then the second, and the third, until they could all see the tops of her breasts. Then she went into her Prance, back and forth across the stage.That's when the fear and butterflies started to fly away.

I can do this. I can handle this.

What she hadn't expected was the men talking to her as she danced.

They screamed filthy things. They shouted romantic things. They begged her to do things. They yelled compliments and degrading insults.

The music began to pick up and she shed her sweater. She went into another slow prance, caressing her nipples as she went. The men sitting and standing around the edge of the stage were already waving their dollar bills in the air. She strutted the stage stopping four times to proudly display her toplessness to four different sections of hollering men. Arriving back at center stage, she dropped to her knees, *the Blow Job position* Jackie called it, stretched her arms straight out to her sides as if courting crucifixion, and shimmied her breasts fast and hard for all the hungry men around the edge of the stage.

On her knees, she scuttled across the stage, shaking her boobs until they were right in the faces of the gesturing, arm-waving men. Her erect nipples, moving fast and hard to the panting beat of the Stones, gyrated mere inches from their open mouths.

Jesse was right. This truly is a trip. It seemed as if time had slowed down. "No, no, no," Mick Jagger crooned. Prancing forward, she collected her first buck, snatching it from a middle-aged hillbilly in a blue denim shirt. As a thank you, she brazenly grabbed him by the ears, buried his face in her cleavage, and shimmied her nipples across the cornfield stubble of his day-old beard. She went all around the stage, dancing for their dollar bills. By the time she had made the circuit, they were in a cheering frenzy.

She almost laughed as she pranced. Being half-naked in front of them was giving her a rush, a feeling of power that she liked, that was actually sort of funny. *Men are so easy,* she thought. *It's time to get out of this skirt.*

She was starting to think like a strip dancer, minding her mechanics, making her money. The funny thing was, she wasn't embarrassed at all.

She hooked her thumbs under the waistband of her green, brown and red kilt. She played with the top of the kilt with her thumbs, moving it around on her hips, pulling it out away from her body, turning around with her back to them and pushing it down quickly again and again over her hips to give them some peek-a-boo glimpses of the crack at the top of her ass.

Turning back to them, she withdrew her thumbs and, grabbing the itchy woolen fabric of the kilt, she flashed them her panties (or rather the silken front panel of her green g-string). Then, never missing a beat, doing a quick hop-pivot on her toes, she turned her back and flashed them her bare ass with just the thin green string of her panties running up her crack. Bending over, she wiggled her ass at them. Turning around, she jiggled her bare tits at them.

Then she was on all fours, doggie style, crawling around in front of them, the kilt up around her waist, ber bare butt thrust in the air. Then she was back on her feet thrusting her hips, unbuttoning the kilt from the front, unwrapping it to flash them her green panties, slowly drawing it back and forth across her ass like a bath towel, pulling it up between her legs and humping it with deep knee bends, finally casting it aside to join her sweater as trash strewn across the stage.

She went through all the moves that Jackie had taught them, all the positions. She worked the stage one section at a time. It was all so logical, so geographical, simply moving from one country to the next, exposing new parts of the landscape as she went, journeying from one piece of private property to the next, selling them off and moving on, an adventure in real estate. She strutted the stage to The Rolling Stones. She was starting to feel her own heat. She pulled up at a new section of the stage. *New meat,* she thought. *Her* new meat now.

She bent over in front of them and went down to the floor. They howled with joy. She crawled in a circle like a tigress as they tucked their bucks. She laughed at the men arrogantly and tossed her hair as she pranced away and then returned to go to her knees to collect yet another buck.

Moving to the final section of the floor, she remembered the pole. She had completely forgotten its existence in the excitement of all the men. *Fuck the pole,* Jackie had taught her. *Be really slutty when you fuck the pole,* Jackie had stressed. *Just think one thing. It's a big cock. Lick it, jack it off with your hands, wrap your legs around it and hump it slow and hard.* As she moved against the pole, she felt all shimmery and liquid and slick. The pulsing lights seemed to caress her body like hundreds of hands. She felt like she was flowing with sex, whoring herself for each dollar bill she collected in her frail money belt.

Down off the pole, she pranced from one man to another collecting dollar bills in front, behind, tucked all the way up the string in back. All the men were yelling for more. She went down on her back and spread her legs for them, only this time she stretched her legs straight up in the air as if she was riding a bicycle upside down, totally exposing herself to them all. Rocking back down onto her back, she put her hands behind her knees and pulled them up until they were around her ears and then she spread them apart. The pervs around the edge of the stage went wild.

Her song was coming to an end and she knew she had to get off the stage. But she was so high. She had done it. She couldn't believe it. She was picking up the money and waving it back at them. Her g-string was crammed full of bills. She pranced back and forth. The song was almost done. The last note. She threw her arms in the air and dollar bills cascaded down over her.

Climbing down out of the ring, walking to the water cooler, drinking, clearing his head, coming back to the ring for that last round, the whole time he could feel their eyes tracking him, all the good old white boys lined up along the edge of the ring watching him, wondering if he would go back in. The big man, J.T., was already back up there, white and sweaty, waiting.

I make it through this round, I'm so far undercover I'm out the other side, Mal suddenly realized he wasn't really doing this to solidify his undercover, to gain this thug's respect, to infiltrate their little redneck mafia. He was doing it because he could box. He could stay with this thug, maybe even hurt him, that would prove he was a pretty good boxer, but more important might gain him respect in the gym.

J.T. was grinning down at him, wondering if he had the guts to climb back up for this last dance.

Mal ascended the narrow steps and climbed through the ropes.

They touched gloves for the last round, and, surprisingly, this time they both backed up and circled, wary, both looking like boxers rather than a bull and a ballet dancer.

Maybe he's not as fresh as I think he is, a spark of hope ignited in Mal's bruised mind. He decided to take the fight to the big man. He stepped out on his left foot and snapped two quick jabs into J.T.'s downturned forehead. No effect whatsoever.

Mal danced left, circling, jabbing, two, three, four. But he knew they were harmless punches, not hurting the big man at all, like insect bites. Mal was on his toes, but his legs were tired and his arms weary. He kept jabbing with his left, but they weren't real punches, just taps, as if delivered with a single finger not a fist.

The big man, still holding his hands low, unconcerned about his head it seemed, kept boring in, throwing hooks to Mal's body, missing almost all.

Mal would backpedal then jab, backpedal and then jab from the side when the big man moved in. But they were all harmless punches, doing no good. He wanted more.

Mal planted and tried a combination, quick jab to the chest, lower than the others, followed by a short punishing right directly into the center of J.T.'s face. It connected. It felt like it tagged him. But J.T. shook it off like it never happened and Mal couldn't get out of his reach fast enough. He never saw the right uppercut that hammered into his ribs left unprotected by the right to the head. It almost caved him in. It knocked him back on his heels and stood him straight up like a heavy bag suspended from the ceiling.

The big man knew he had hurt him and followed up, lashed out with a rain of punishing hooks and straight lefts driving him back into the ropes. He drilled Mal in the stomach with another right upper-cut then bashed the sides of his head with lefts and rights. They were bouncing off his upraised gloves and off the sides of his headgear but Mal could still feel their power, the pounding as they landed.

Mal's legs weren't working right. He was stumbling against the ropes. Arm-weary, it was all he could do to keep his gloves up to pro-tect his face. He slid sideways along the ropes, the big man still bat-tering at him.

Gotta hit him. Gotta get him off me. Gotta hit him.

He lashed out with a right that somehow, miraculously, slipped the big man's gloves and got in around the side of his chin, momentarily caught him off balance, snapped his head back even if it didn't hurt him much.

To Mal's great surprise, the big man, startled, backed off, hesitated, and Mal was able to roll away, get off the ropes, stumble sideways out of reach.

It was as if that one punch, the right to the face that had got Mal free, angered J.T. Smale. The big man lashed out with a fury, rushed in, windmilling punches. Mal managed to block most of the punches in this barrage with his gloves. Then Mal hit him again with a short sharp right. It exploded out of his shoulder and into the big man's face even as Mal was backing up.

Again, that punch surprised J.T. Smale, stopped him, rocked him back on his heels and turned off his wild swings long enough for Mal to retreat all the way to the other side of the ring.

As they faced each other across the ring, Mal realized that there wasn't much bounce left in either of their steps. They measured each other, but now they were both moving as if in slow motion.

Mal flicked a left jab to the big man's face, barely brushing it. J.T. wheeled a slow uppercut at Mal's ribs, missing awkwardly. They cir-cled each other. Mal jab. J.T. hook. Jab. Hook. Each breathing hard. Each moving slow. Sweat rolling off them as if they were boxing in the rain.

At what point does getting hit start to feel good? Mal thought. He felt his breath coming in shorter bursts, his legs suddenly didn't feel so heavy. He actually bounced on his toes, trying to send a body message to J.T. Smale: *"You're not gonna take me out, redneck. You're not gonna use me for your punching bag today."*

And then the round just ended, anti-climax, over without him even begging it to be so. He had survived, and the big man glared at him as if he couldn't believe his eyes.

Mal could taste the blood in his mouth even as he spoke: Hey, great workout. Thanks for the work.

Yeah, good workout, J.T. Smale growled.

Mal politely held the top rope up for the big man to crawl through.

Meg and Jess danced five more times that Friday night. They only had three different costumes so they went through their wardrobes twice.

Jess followed her cheerleader outfit with a white prom dress that fell away to a black bra and sheer black g-string, and danced out of it to *Tonight's the Night* by Rod Stewart followed up by *Shake Your Booty* by K.C. and the Sunshine Band. Her third dance outfit she liked to call her bull dyke special. I got it right out of my closet, she laughed to Meg the first time they had spread their costumes out on the bed to show each other. The outfit consisted of a studded black leather motorcycle jacket, a black Harley-Davidson motorcycle hat with a plastic peak that looked like it had been stolen right off of Marlon Brando, and the same black bra and g-string panties she had worn with her white prom dress. When she danced to Boz Scaggs' *Lowdown* and Cliff Richards' *Devil Woman,* it really seemed to confuse the redneck drunks around the edge of the stage.

Meg followed her sorority girl sweater set with a frilly black silk negligee that she swirled and stepped out of to *I'd Really Love To See You Tonight* by England Dan and John Ford Coley, and followed up with *You Should Be Dancing* by the Bee Gees. Her third outfit was utterly simple, white shorts, a white university tee shirt cut-off just above her navel, and a white headband, workout clothes, plus a red g-string you could see through the white shorts, trashy. They were perfect. She fast danced to *Car Wash* by Rose Royce. When she took off the headband and shook out her hair, she made a big deal of pulling it up around her thigh like a garter which gave the pervs around the stage another handy place to tuck their bucks.

They went through each of their outfits and their songs twice, but the customers didn't seem to notice. Meg estimated that the buck-tuckers around the stage turned over about every two hours or four times over the course of the busy night. As the night wore on though, the place just kept getting more and more crowded. She had to empty the dollar bills out of her g-string in the middle of dances or about every five minutes when she was working the tables. By around midnight everyone she met when she stopped at a table wanted her to sit down and have a drink so they could slobber over her up close. There were even some women scattered around the room at some of the tables, none around the stage. They had come in with their boyfriends she guessed, even as she was wondering why. Then there was one whole table full of sorority girls. Probably here on a dare, Meg said to Jess. Maybe they're checking it out 'cause they're thinking of working here.

They're lesbians, Jesse cued her to the obvious. My leather jacket outfit really got to them. They couldn't wait to buy me a drink at the table. One of them came right out and asked me if I was gay. I didn't think I was gonna get hit on by chicks here. This isn't half as bad as I thought it would be.

Some of the drunken men tried to carry on conversations with Meg and asked her stupid questions like "What are you majoring in? I'm thinking of changing mine." Or "How do you stay awake in class if you're up this late dancing?"

She thought she did real well carrying on conversations like the sorority girl that they all thought she was.

One wit asked her "how did you get into dancing?" as if it was a job like accounting or selling dresses.

She decided to answer him truthfully: It was my father's fault.

The jerk's eyes went wide. She could almost see his mind racing with dirty pictures.

That cockeyed truth gave her a pang of guilt. *God, mom and dad would both hate me doing this,* she thought as she sat on the filthy toilet behind the curtain in the dressing room. After midnight she felt as if the iced tea was shooting through her so fast that she was drinking it from a fire hose. *But one of these Smale bastards might have killed him* she buried her guilt in anger and determination. *If you're gonna play, you gotta pay* she remembered one of her dad's favorite sports cliches. He knew them all, she remembered fondly as she changed for her next dance. *You can't make chicken salad out of chicken shit. You can't make the club in the tub.* She missed him and it hurt to think about him.

Learning to strip dance from Jackie had taken her mind off the waves of sadness that would wash over her whenever she was alone. Actually being on stage and performing successfully was a rush that she had never imagined would take her over so completely. She was somebody new and different. Never ever could she, would she, have done this if her mother and father had been alive. When Meg was alone, she always thought of her mom and dad. Her life was immersed in loss. She hated being alone.

Thank god for Jess, she thought, *such a serious flake.* She wondered what it would be like to be a man, if she would feel so empty and lonely. She wondered what it would be like to be a man and make love to Jess, not be alone, or let Jess make love to her. *Which one of them would be the man? Would one of them have to be the man? Couldn't they both just be lovers trying to please each other, love the other?*

She wondered all these things quizzically, comically, giggling at the ideas. She was curious, but she couldn't help but giggle at the prospect. The whole thought was so unlike her. She'd always enjoyed boys. But she was so alone and down. And Jess was so different. *So fearless.* Most of the time Meg felt afraid of her shadow. Only her anger drove her on, angry because someone had killed her dad and God had stolen her mom. She wondered what it would be like to be a man, if she'd be able to shoot a gun if the time came and she ever got a chance.

When she came down off the stage, she knew that her life would never be the same again. *Big deal,* she thought, *every damn thing that happens to me, every damn decision I make totally changes things from the overprotected little schoolgirl life I had before. I took off the right clothes in that dance.*

When she came down off the stage, Jess was waiting for her with open arms. They were both stark naked, hugging like a couple of sorority sisters at a prom.

God, you were sensational.

Jess kept hugging her, both of them hot and sweaty, cigarette smoke forming a haze around them.

What about you? I never could have done it if you hadn't gone first.

Didn't I tell you it was a trip? Jesse finally stopped hugging but kept hold of her hand.

I've never felt like that before, being up there with the lights, and all of them yelling at you. Thank god for Jackie telling us what to do.

God, you were great. Jess had calmed down.

They liked us, didn't they?

Mal was in the audience that first Friday night that Jess and Meg debuted at *Tippers*. He couldn't believe his eyes how good they were. *That Jackie is quite a teacher,* he thought. *She oughta be a professor at that university. A doctor of stripology.*

I've gotta make sure they don't do anything too stupid.

Dr. Jekyll and Mr. Hyde

You wanna know something about the Smales?

What's that?

What do you mean?

They don't even know we exist.

Or they think we're just there to entertain them.

Since they began at *Tippers,* Mal had taken to joining Meg and Jess after quitting time in their apartment kitchen on Pierce Street for a beer and a post-mortem.

They don't think anybody is smart enough or tough enough or crazy enough to get inside their organization and all three of us are in, or close, Mal agreed.

They think we're just a couple of money-hungry lesbian college girls. They know no woman cop would do what we do night after night in that place, wouldn't do it the first time, Jess nodded across the table at Mal and Meg.

The police chief could never explain it to the city fathers. Yes, Mayor, I sent Sergeant Mary off to shake it every night as part of our ongoing investigation.

Oh yeah. The newspaper would love that, Meg laughed.

They just think I'm some crazy black dude who doesn't know better than to hang out in their lily-white boxing gym.

Actually, I'm really liking the money. Rents not the ongoing problem it always is and I'm thinking of saving for a trip to San Francisco this summer, Jess chimed in.

Terrific. Doctor Jekyll and Ms. Hyde. Engineer by day, stripper by night, Meg taunted her.

Sounds to me like you're gonna be disappointed when this undercover gig ends, Mal turned serious.

Hey, it's not so bad. Except for the threat of cancer from the toxic cloud of smoke we dance in, Jess shot back.

Which is turning my hair dirty yellow, by the way.

Look you two. Something's gonna break. I give this operation one, two more weeks at the most. OK?

They haven't asked us to do anything extra yet. That's gotta come, Jess got serious.

You're gonna have to deal with it when it happens, Mal picked up on her tone.

Boy, tell me about it, Meg thought. *They kill my dad, somebody kills my dad, maybe them. And it changes my whole life, splits it in half. Now I'm two different people. Like I've got a real life and a secret life.*

You know, sometimes you just go away, don't you? You haven't heard a word we've said.

What?

Mal had to laugh at the two of them. The fact of the matter was they were still two flaky college kids.

Officer Mal here says we need a signal if the Smales turn us out for any extracurricular activities. If they tell us ahead of time, we call him immediately.

No names, just a time and a place, or a day and a time, so I can be waiting outside this strip joint to tail you. If there's no warning, you gotta get a note to me. If I'm in the strip joint when it happens, I need a note on a napkin, or some kind of a high sign when you're working the tables.

What if they don't tell us where we're going?

I'll follow you, but I gotta know. Be careful, you can't just go places without backup.

Hey Mal, it's *Mod Squad.* You need to get some of those neat bell-bottom pants.

Yeah, I'll do that.

The hard part is, Meg decided, *not to let your secret life take over your real life.* Her problem was, though, that her real life didn't really exist anymore.

Innocents Abroad

At the end of the night, after the last dance ended and the last drunks were herded out, the lights were turned on and the true squalor of *Tippers* emerged. The boss, J.T., and some little skinny guy in a leisure suit who had been sitting at the bar drinking and smoking cigarettes since about midnight, and the bartender, and the girls (the six dancers and the waitress) all gathered at the cash register on the bar for their payout. In the course of the night, each time they would empty their g-string of bills, the bartender would count out the money, write the total on a slip of paper twice, make them initial it twice, tear it in half and give one piece to them, the other piece going into the cash register. At the end of the night, the girls totaled their slips, the bartender to-taled his, and if the totals matched to everyone's satisfaction they split fifty-fifty. This Friday night, everybody made a lot of money. The bar-tender, or J.T. if he was there as he was this night, did the math, made the payouts. He did the regular girls first, making the new girls wait their turn. When he finally got to Jess and Meg, he was interrupted by the little skinny guy who had been sitting at the bar with him.

Hey, I'll take care of these two. the skinny little weasel in the brown leisure suit with the cigarette dangling from his lips told J.T. who just shrugged, but got a strange little grin on his face.

C'mon girls, we'll go into the office to make this split, the skinny smoker ordered.

Meg caught that grin followed by a suppressed laugh pass between J.T. Smale and the bartender.

Meg's and Jess's eyes met. *Oh-oh, here it comes,* they both knew instinctively what the other was thinking. They both remembered Jackie's warning about being asked into the office by one of the Smale brothers.

C'mon now girls, he put his leisure suited arms around both their waists and ushered them toward the door of the office, I'm Humphrey Smale, one of the owners. I don't think we've been introduced.

This is Hump, the slobbering idiot Jackie warned us about, Meg thought.

Once inside the office, he closed the door behind them.

You girls are really good, he exuded smarm. Hard to believe you're amateurs, college girls, you done so well on the stage.

We've been practicin' at home.

Is that so?

Yeah, we need the money.

What's your names?

I'm Jesse and this is Megan.

Hump and Jess were carrying on this cat and mouse conversation, but he never took his eyes off of Meg. He had a dark bird of prey look in his eyes.

Great. What's the matter there, Megan? Cat got your tongue? And he reached out and touched her face, grabbed her chin with his fingers and thumb not too roughly. You look like a scared bird. His voice was still smarmy, cajoling, as he moved his hand along her face, but then his voice went hard and ugly. I won't hurt you, you little whore, or maybe I will.

Hey, leave her alone, Jess cut in.

What are you, her mother?

C'mon man, it's late. We both been up there dancin' for dollars since six o'clock.

Shut up! Like a snake, his hand darted from Meg's face to her wrist and pulled her across the room to the desk. Your silent little friend here is gonna get down on her knees and suck my cock.

Meg was in the throes of a four-alarm panic. Her eyes, wide and scared, begged Jess for help, rescue.

Hey, man, Jess actually managed to counterfeit a laugh, your buddies didn't tell you, did they?

What?

Jess, dropping the leather motorcycle costume that she was holding in her hands, took two quick steps across the room and with both hands caressed Meg's bare bottom underneath the short knit kilt that Meg had put on while they waited for the settlement. Looking Hump Smale right in the eye and smiling seductively—Your buddies didn't tell you about us did they?—Jess moved in close behind Meg, rubbed against her from behind, reached around with both hands and lasciviously fondled her breasts through the short tight fuzzy sweater that made up her sorority girl outfit.

Suddenly it was Hump Smale's turn to be the deer caught in the headlights.

Or do you wanna watch us? Is that it?

Slowly Jess turned Meg toward her . . .

It was taking a long moment for Hump Smales's inbred little mind to understand.

. . . and kissed her full on the lips.

You jerk! Hump Smale went charging out of the office toward J.T. You prick! They're a couple of dykes!

But Jess didn't stop kissing Meg when Hump Smale fled, and Meg found herself kissing her back, opening her mouth and accepting Jess's eager tongue.

When Jess and Meg rejoined them at the bar, J.T. Smale and the bartender were doubled over in laughter while Hump was on his way out the door.

You think maybe you could pay us now?

It was all the two men could do to subdue their laughter.

It doesn't take much to entertain these guys, Meg thought.

Sure thing, honey. Give 'em a ten dollar bonus, he ordered the bartender. You girls did a good job tonight.

I guess we did, Jess smiled as they collected their money, a hundred and eighty-five dollars for her and two-twenty for Meg.

Later, in the car driving home, Jess waved her wad of bills at Meg. I don't know if we're naked dancing whores or undercover snoops, but whatever we are it sure pays well.

Here, you take mine, and Meg tried to give Jess her wad of money.

No way, babe. You worked hard for that.

But you don't even have to be here with me. Take it. Use it for school.

No. It's OK. You earned it. Buy me dinner tomorrow.

Before we come back to work?

Yeah.

Sorry about freezing up like that in there. He scared me.

Yeah, I know. Those are scary guys.

They don't scare you.

Oh yes they do.

You didn't freeze up like I did.

The only thing that got me through it is I've been wanting to kiss you for weeks.

They both laughed.

It was a joke, sort of.

But Meg knew that Jess was more than half serious, and Jess knew that Meg had kissed her back. Both of them knew that it was something that was probably going to happen again.

The Heart of the Matter

A week into their dancing at the strip bar and Mal Rogers was already thinking that his college girls/strippers were becoming a dead end. Nothing was happening with their undercover.

You're two college girls pretending to be strippers . . .

Pretending pretty well I'd say, Meg gave him a wide-eyed look that mocked all the fatherly concern in his voice.

Yeah, right, and nothing's happening but a bunch of bucks being tucked.

Best money I've ever made at any of the jobs I've had since I've been in college in Wabash City. Jess gave him one of those "What is your problem?" looks.

Later, after Jess had gone off to study, Mal and Meg sat across from each other at the kitchen table.

Why are you doing this?

I need to find out if they did it or not, killed my dad.

You think he'd want you taking these kinds of chances, doing what you're doing?

Meg didn't answer.

Look, this is not some movie or crime novel, some hillbilly *Godfather*. This is real and you could get hurt.

They did it. I know it. I need to find out.

So what do you do when you find out?

Either I'll be very disappointed or the Smales will be very sorry.

You'll testify against them?

Of course I will . . . if it comes to that.

What does that mean?

You know that movie *Death Wish* from a coupla years ago. I saw it on TV last night after I got home from *Tippers*.

Death Wish? This is not a movie.

That's what I wanna do. Make someone pay for killing my dad. You can't just forget about something like this. Those cops in Kentucky. They didn't even care. They just wanted to forget the whole thing.

Great. So that makes you the great avenger.

No, and she smiled at him, no, it makes me a dancer in a two-bit, low-life strip joint trying to find out what happened.

Great. So what does that make me?

I don't know Mal. Probably the same thing you've always been, a cop trying to find out what happened.

Midweek at *Tippers*. Pretty slow night. Twelve thirty, already getting ready to close, nobody left to close for, no sign of a late bachelor party stumbling in. J.T. Smale alone on a bar stool sipping at a beer. Closing time. Settle up time. Jesse not working tonight because she has a test tomorrow morning.

It's Megan, isn't it?

She breathed in so hard at his voice that it shut her throat for just a second. He was standing right behind her. She turned to look at him. He was big and wide and grinning. Her breasts were naked under the skimpy open wrap. She crossed her arms protectively over them as she looked up at him.

Meg, call me Meg.

OK. Meg.

Silence between them. She was aware of him looking down at her naked breasts.

You're the best dancer in this place, ya know.

Thanks. I work at it.

The customers like you.

I know. That's the idea.

Too bad you're a licker. Where's your girlfriend?

She's got a test tomorrow. Who says I'm a . . . lesbian?

You did.

No. My friend Jess did.

Ooookay.

And sometimes I am.

Ooho, you go both ways.

You go at all?

Yeah. Right.

Nothing happened that night. J.T. just walked away and Meg headed for the dressing room, half expecting him to follow her.

Once Upon A Time in the West

Meg had seen his ugly, shaggy-eyebrowed, sleazy-goateed, ferret face in a TV commercial and that was what had steered her into his store. 'Ol' Ron just loves to sell guns' he had cajoled in the most honey-dripping of redneck drawls on the TV. Now she was looking at him across the counter and he looked like Dr. Frankenstein's demented servant Igor in that crazy Mel Brooks movie she'd watched on late night TV.

For a young woman who wants to defend herself, this is the perfect gun. It's small and light and fits easily into a lady's purse.

He might as well have been selling cosmetics or hairbrushes.

But this little twenty-five's best feature is how easily the safety comes off. Here, it's right in front of the trigger guard. You just run your finger over it on the way to the trigger and it's ready to fire.

She nodded, thinking what a wonderful thing it was to switch off safety so easily, to be ready to kill with just the gentlest flick of a finger.

And if you buy this little gun, honey, there's so much more.

Him calling her honey, this sleazy little rodent, made her wretch internally. But she smiled appreciatively, gave him all her attention, the same false way she did with all the guys who bought her for a ten-dollar table dance at *Tippers*.

For only twenty dollars, we'll teach you how to shoot it and set you up a practice schedule at our own shooting range right here in the back of the store.

That's great. I'll take it. She was sick of listening to this weasel talk.

Two days in a row she shot on Ol' Ron's Range.

That's enough practice, she thought. The little gun was starting to feel good in her hand.

How much is one of those double barreled shotguns? Meg asked.

Ol' Ron's eyes lit up.

Two nights later when Meg came down off the stage, she pretended she could hardly breathe. I've gotta get some air, she told the bartender.

That excused her from working the tables right away. It bought her at least twenty minutes.

She had bought a dark army trenchcoat at the surplus store at Five Points that afternoon. It was long and buttoned all the way up, covered her from her neck to her ankles.

Perfect for going out back for a cigarette on breaks, she had told Jess when she brought it home. I can be stark naked under this coat and nobody'd ever know.

Terrific, Jess had been reading and showed little interest in Meg's latest thrift store purchase.

In the dressing room she grabbed the trenchcoat, not even bothering to put on a bra, and told Jess, who was dancing next and in the act of putting lipstick on her nipples, that she was going out in the parking lot to get some air. Jess gave her a wave as she went out the back door.

Outside, Meg didn't loiter in the parking lot. It took her two minutes to drive down Wabash Avenue to J.T. Smale's house. The other thing the new trenchcoat did so well besides cover her up was conceal the whole length of the shotgun she had bought from Ol' Ron.

Meg amazed herself at how coolly she was thinking. She had gotten the idea while lying in bed two nights before after Mal Rogers had left their house. Sitting at the kitchen table drinking beer with her, he had complained that their undercover jobs at the strip joint weren't producing any results. He had argued that if nothing happened in one more week they should give it up. That was when Jess complained about giving up such a good income for part-time night work.

But after Mal had left, lying in bed thinking about it, the TV on, Meg had to agree with him. Nothing much was happening. Something had to be done to shake things up. That was when she got the idea for the trenchcoat and the shotgun. She was watching an old western on TV at the time.

She pulled the car down the street in the dark away from the only streetlight on the block. She walked toward the Smale house with the shotgun concealed under her long coat, its metallic barrels cold against her bare thighs. Mal had shown them where J.T. lived.

The house was on an alley with a big yard. It was dark, nobody was out on the street. She walked past the house and turned down the alley. In the darkness of J.T. Smale's backyard, she stood on her tiptoes to look in a lighted window. It was the kitchen she was looking into, spying on Smale's wife making something at the stove.

She went around the side of the house, keeping to the shadows, and looked in another lighted window—the living room, empty.

She climbed up on the front porch from the side, unbuttoned the coat down the front, and emptied both barrels of the shotgun through the front door.

The recoil knocked her backwards and it was all she could do to keep herself from falling down the front steps. She ran to her car and was inside before anyone came out into the street. No one came out of the Smale house. A neighbor across the street came out on his front porch, looked around, went back in.

Meg drove two blocks with her lights off, then turned right toward downtown Wabash City. She went around four blocks, turned right two more times, before parking in the same space she had left only a grand total of twelve minutes before. She got out and went back in the dressing room door.

A minute later, topless, Meg re-entered the showroom of the club. The second table she approached offered to buy a table-dance.

Can't do it, honey, 'til after this dancer's done. But if you'll buy me a drink I'll hang around 'til then.

Sure thing, lil' darlin.' Come on over here and sit yore pretty self down.

It was only after she had sat down with the two good old boys— they looked like farmers—that she really thought about what she had just done. Jess was dancing on the stage above her.

That ought to shake things up a little.

She looked around. Mal had not yet taken up his regular stool at the bar. It wasn't very busy. There were about seven or eight guys sitting along the edge of the stage and two other tables besides hers were occupied.

The farmers were trying to make conversation as they stared at her chest. You shore are a pretty young gal. You really go to the college?

She watched the youngest Smale brother come in the front door, cross the room to the bar, and pull at the idiot brother's shoulder. Then the two of them rushed out together. She couldn't help the grin that bloomed on her face.

Yore a happy little thing, aren't ya? the fat farmer clucked. You really like yore job, dontcha?

Boy, I shore do, honey, she mimicked his illiterate cornpone drawl. Nine PM.

Mal just coming out of the locker room at the boxing gym.

I'll get a beer at the strip joint, he was thinking. *The girls are working tonight.*

He hated to admit it, but he really liked watching them strip. Seeing them naked excited him—*Big deal,* he thought, *it excites every guy in the joint*—because he also saw them with their clothes on, in their house, in the light of day. But in the dark, spying on them through a haze of smoke from the back of the crowded showroom, he possessed information about them that all the other lusting men in the room didn't have. That's why he felt like a peeping tom, a pervert, when he enjoyed watching them dance, because he knew them, like a father or a big brother, and it was sick.

But it excited him.

They were working into their second week on the job. As undercovers go, it was going fine. No problems. All of them were getting used to it, falling into a sort of routine. No results though. Unless being taken for granted was a result, which for an undercover operation it was.

He was just coming out of the door of the locker room, his hair still wet from the shower, when J.T. and Belfry Smale burst out of the door of the back office in so big a hurry that they didn't even see him off to the side.

First time a black man has ever been invisible in this neighborhood, Mal thought.

The other brother was behind the counter.

Wes, get Hump next door and tell him to meet us at my house. It was an order. J.T. wasn't asking and the younger brother Wes did what he was told.

J.T. and Belfry ran out the front door.

Something's up, Mal thought.

He waited a minute, then followed them out. They were gone but he knew where they were going. He drove down Third Street, turned left to J.T. Smale's house on Wabash Avenue and drove by slow. It was dark so no one could see his black face inside his car. He drove to the end of the block, turned around and came back. He parked on the opposite side of the street and sank down into his usual surveillance position. It looked like J.T. Smale's front door was off the hinges and had a big hole in it.

Hillbillies, Mal thought.

We were back in the kitchen, thank God, Cindy Smale was going back and forth between sobs and anger when J.T. and Belfry got there. I was makin' Joni a toasted cheese sandwich 'cause she'd just got home from basketball practice. The girls practice at six this week after the boys.

OK, hon, it's OK. Tell me what happened. Did you see anybody?

No. They shot through the door from the outside. God it was loud, like a bomb going off.

I know. You're OK? Joni's OK?

If we'd been in the living room . . .

I know. I know. We'll take care of this.

Outside.

Mal, from the car, watched the two brothers talking animatedly on the front porch.

Who did this to my house?

Who's stupid enough or crazy enough to do this?

My house, judas priest, Cindy and Joni inside.

J.T., man, I don't know.

You pissed anybody off lately?

No. No more than usual.

Who? Who?

The Tylers. Some friend of that Ferris. The cops, I don't know.

Ferris didn't have any friends. He wasn't from around here. The Tylers aren't that stupid, are they?

They're two-bit car thieves.

You think they're tryin' to move into dope?

I don't think so. They're ignorant rednecks.

Yeah. Just like us.

Look, Belfry, who did this to my house? Find out. OK? Find out, then I'll take care of it myself.

Mal sank down lower in the front seat as the car roared up, slammed on its brakes in front of the house, and spat Hump Smale out.

What happened? Hump ran across the yard to the porch and spotted the hole in the front door.

Somebody shot J.T.'s front door with a shotgun.

That's pretty stupid.

No lie.

Who did it? Let's git 'em.

We don't know.

You don't know? That really seemed to stump poor Hump. The idea that there was something his two brothers didn't know or hadn't figured out was hard for him to swallow. They'd always told him exactly what was going on, told him exactly what they wanted him to do.

Well, when you know you tell me and I'll kill whoever it is.

You got it, Hump, and Belfry and J. T. broke out laughing.

The Sound and the Fury

J.T. and Belfry picked up Wink Tyler coming out of *The Squirrel Cage Bar* at Sixth and Salem about two AM. They hadn't brought Hump along because he talked too much when he was drunk and J.T. didn't know how far he was going to have to go with Wink Tyler. Wink's pick-up was parked right outside the back door of *The Squirrel Cage* and J.T. and Belfry were parked across the street, so Wink was into his truck and the lights were on before they could make a move on him.

Follow him, Belfry.

He's probably just goin' home.

Fine. If he turns down Wabash Avenue, block him at the blinker light. I wanna talk to him.

Sure enough, that's the direction Wink Tyler headed. He lived in a falling down rathole next to the sewage treatment plant on the far south side of Smale Hollow, south of the *Ralston Purina* plant, south of *The Log Cabin Inn,* a good mile south of the Smales' places and the garage.

When Wink Tyler eased to a stop at the red blinker light on Wabash Avenue right before St. Ann's Church, Belfry in his big new Chevy Caprice, pulled up beside him, then tried to pull around him and block the intersection. But he wasn't quite fast enough. Wink saw who it was, spotted J.T. through the side window as the big Chevy tried to cut him off. He looked at J.T. for a long moment with a big "What the hell?" stare on his face, then jammed his rusty old pick-up into reverse and took off.

Now Wink may have been as dumb as a dried-up cow patty, but he was an accomplished car thief and one hell of a driver. Beyond that, his rusty old pick-up was deceptive. He'd been tooling it up for fifteen years and, while its rocker panels may have been almost gone, its engine still had a lot of souped-up pop. He accelerated fast in reverse for about a hundred yards then hit the brakes hard as he spun the steering wheel. The old truck came around on a dime and he floored it north on Wabash Avenue before J.T. and Belfry had even gotten turned around.

At the eight-story bank building, Wabash City's only skyscraper, he dug a hard right, skidding in his panic, ran the light on the Courthouse Square, and cut sharply to the left on Fourth Street.

That's a miracle, he thought. *Right through the middle of downtown and never saw a cop.*

He's headin' out into the county, J.T. coached Belfry. Take it easy through town. We'll catch him.

When Wink hit Ninth Street Road, he floored the pick-up until the engine wailed. He knew it was a straight shot all the way to Battleground, and he thought he could outrun them.

We lost him.

No, we haven't.

He's gone.

He's a dumb whorehoppin' hillbilly. He's headin' straight out of town into the county.

Terrific. There's plenty of places to hide in the county.

Here. Comin' up. Turn on Ninth Street and open it up. You'll catch him, I'm tellin' ya. He's too fuckin' dumb to get away.

Halfway to Battleground, Wink Tyler was just starting to feel safe when he spotted the big car in his rear-view mirror, headlights coming up fast.

Belfry had the big Chevy cranked to 105 by the time they caught up to Wink Tyler's puny little pick-up. It was a basic Indiana two-lane blacktop so Belfry throttled down and hitched the big Chevy right to the rusty pick-up's back bumper. They were both still doing 85.

Don't you even think I'm gonna hit him with this car.

OK. OK. J.T. already had his black .38 snub in his hand. Pull up beside.

What are you gonna do?

Pull up beside him.

Belfry did as he was told. He knew that tone of J.T.'s voice. *He gonna shoot him?* he feared the worst.

J.T. shot out the left rear tire on Wink Tyler's truck.

J.T. Smale had meant the shooting out of Wink Tyler's truck tire as a conciliating measure. After all, he could have just shot Wink in the head through the driver's side window. But he shot out the tire because he sincerely wanted to stop the fleeing truck and talk to the panicked Wink. Unfortunately, shooting out the rear tire proved much more effective than J.T. expected it to be.

The tire blew. The truck ducked and swerved. The front tires hit the edge of the drainage ditch, then imbedded in the bank on the other side of the ditch. Coming to such an abrupt stop like that threw the truck's rear end straight up in the air and over.

Wink's truck rolled first up over the embankment, then twice end over end in the muddy cornfield before dipping over on its side for one more flat roll in the rich black dirt.

Inside the truck, Wink was batted around like a pinball, swatted and bounced until dead. His neck was broken on the first roll up over the embankment. Luckily, he was already dead when his head smashed the windshield and his pride and joy NASCAR gear shift impaled in his groin. The truck ended up on its top in the middle of the cornfield a good thirty yards off the road. He ended up with his broken body half out the driver's side window, his open eyes staring peacefully up at the stars.

When J.T. and Belfry got to him, he was long gone.

Damn, Belfry stared down at the body. He's dead.

No lie! J.T. screamed.

Don't git all pissed off at me. You shot the tire.

I know.

Let's git outta here.

Damn, I wanted to ask him why they shot into my house.

Too late now. Let's go.

Back in the car, into the first side road away from the accident, still nobody had seen them or heard anything; no sirens yet, no flashing cop lights.

It sure wasn't supposed to happen this way.

I know. We're lucky nobody saw it.

Lucky?

Not so lucky for Wink.

Mebbe they'll think it was an accident.

If they don't check the rear tire too close.

Now we're gonna have to deal with Bobby Tyler.

Yeah, we're the first ones he'll figure for this.

Yeah. We're the first ones everyone figures for everything.

Saturday Night & Sunday Morning

3:30 AM. on a busy Saturday night and Sunday morning.

Non-stop buck tuckers at *Tippers* from nine o'clock on. Meg was slap-happy. Too many dances, too much tea, too many groping rednecks, too much stale beer breath. She just wanted to go home. She knew she wouldn't sleep. She was too wired on caffeine and dollar bills. More than two hundred bucks tonight. She was topless in her g-string. No point in putting her stage costume back on before she went into the dressing room because she'd just take it right back off. The other girls were the only ones left in the place. Jess had worked with Meg all of Friday night, but had begged off for the second half of this Saturday. She had worked 'til midnight, but then either she had a test to study for or she was meeting Jackie. She hadn't told and Meg hadn't asked, though Meg's money was on a late date with Jackie. She still marveled at how quickly she had gotten used to Jess and Jackie sleeping together. It didn't even seem unnatural to her. None of this did anymore. She was just waiting in line for her money when J.T. and Belfry Smale walked in. On a bee-line, they walked right past the girls and went straight to the cooler behind the bar for beers like they needed them badly.

Something's up, Meg thought

I'm goin.' See you tomorrow, she heard Belfry Smale tell his brother as she retreated to the dressing room.

When she came out, the showroom of *Tippers* was deserted. The other girls were all leaving with her.

Who's closing up? She remembered thinking.

J.T. was sitting against the hood of his car drinking a beer when she came through the back door into the parking lot.

Yo, college girl, wait a minute. I wanna talk to you.

Omigod, he knows who I am. He knows I'm watching him, trying to catch him for killing my dad. He thinks I'm a cop like Mal. He thinks I'm working for the cops. He's going to get me alone and kill me. All the other girls are getting in their cars. Omigod, Meg's mind raced.

Hold on a minute while I lock the place up. He left her standing in the parking lot as he went back into the strip joint to switch off the last lights, left her standing alone, waiting, the other girls pulling out in their cars, almost four in the morning. She wanted to run, wanted to hide, pull the covers over her head and make this whole nightmare that was her life go away. He came back out, locked the back door from the outside. When he turned to her, he didn't look like he was going to kill her. He was grinning.

You have a good night tonight?

Yeah, it was really busy, crowded and steady.

How much you make?

I don't know. I haven't counted it. Over two hundred, I guess.

That *is* good. That means I had a good night too.

Yeah, I guess so. But you always have a good night.

Hey, whattaya say? Let's celebrate both our good nights, party a little bit. Huh?

That's when it dawned upon her. He hadn't discovered her game. He didn't know who she was other than some college girl/stripper. A wave of relief swept over her. Her fear drained away like floodwater going back to the river. *All he wants to do is hit on me.*

Oh, I oughtta get home. It's almost four. I gotta get some sleep.

You can sleep all day tomorrow. It's Sunday.

Yeah. I know, but . . .

He was up close to her now.

Her arms were crossed over her breasts protectively.

He reached out and ran one finger of his right hand along her upper arm to her shoulder.

You said you weren't a lesbian, that you like men too. Let's party a little tonight. How about it? A coupla drinks, some grass. Whaddaya say?

The grass would relax me, smooth things out.

She couldn't believe what she was saying. *You can't do this,* she told herself, but she was already in too deep. *You can't do this. It's sick. He could have killed dad.* She looked around for Mal, for Mal's car. No sign that he was watching her. She didn't know whether she was looking for him out of fear or out of shame.

That's it babe. C'mon, I know this perfect place.

She followed him like a lamb to the silent slaughter.

Mal had gone home, actually gotten into bed, but he hadn't been able to sleep. He couldn't stop thinking about his college girl undercovers, worrying about them. He knew he wasn't going to sleep. He got up. Two thirty. He thought of watching some TV as he pulled on his pants, but he reached for his shoes. He was going back out. It was what he knew he was going to do all along. He parked outside the strip joint on the street that ran alongside its parking lot, but he didn't go in. Three o'clock now. The lot was almost empty, just three or four cars left, one of them Megan's. He could see the whole parking lot and the back door of the club.

Can't be many customers left in there, he thought. *They should be closing it up soon.*

He didn't have to wait long. A couple of the girls came straggling out, got in their cars and drove off.

Another stripper came out. Mal recognized her, the big bottle blonde with the appendix scar. No Meg yet.

Then it all got strange.

J.T. Smale came through the back door with a long-neck beer bottle in his hand. He leaned up against the rear gate of his pick-up and drank.

Mal automatically sank lower into his seat in the car, full surveillance position, red alert. He watched in horror as Meg came out the back door of the strip club and walked right into J.T. Smale's ambush.

She stopped dead when she saw him waiting for her, retreated a step.

They talked for long minutes, then J.T. went back inside.

Good, she dusted him off, Mal expected her to head for her car, get away.

But she didn't go. She loitered there by the back door, looking guiltily around. Then Smale was back, taking her by the hand, pulling her after him.

Mal felt a five-alarm panic building inside his chest, his heart pounding. He watched them cross the parking lot, cross the street about forty yards behind his car, and go in the back door of the boxing club.

As soon as the door closed, Mal was up and out of the car. He flattened himself in the very darkest shadow against the wall of the boxing club, under a window, listening. He waited at least five minutes, but he couldn't hear a thing. The lights gradually came on inside, their dim glow seeping out through the dirty window above him like blood.

He knew he couldn't stay there. All he needed was some Wabash City cop to drive by, patrolling the neighborhood, or worse, one of J.T.'s brothers to show up and see him, but he couldn't leave her alone in there.

Back in the car, he settled in to wait. Sick and tormented thoughts raked across the surface of his mind. Bloody and perverse visions alternated in the dark theater inside his head.

It was almost five when she came out and ran to her car.

His whole body relaxed like a spring uncoiling. He watched her drive away. He didn't think she'd seen his car.

J.T. Smale came out a few minutes later. As he crossed the gravel parking lot, Mal drew his gun out of the holster in the small of his back and levelled it at J.T. as he walked.

I could take you out right now, you prick, Mal whispered.

Alice Through the Looking Glass Again

To her surprise, J.T. didn't lead her to his car or pick-up truck, didn't drive her off to some sleazy motel room. Instead, he took her hand and led her across the parking lot and the alley. Using the same ring of keys he had used to lock up the strip bar, he unlocked the back door to the boxing club and pulled her through into the darkness. Inside, instead of turning on the lights, he pushed her back against the closed door and kissed her hard on the lips, then around her neck and up the side of her face.

I never kissed a licker before, he laughed in her ear. You taste good.

She didn't say anything because she was scared and ashamed. It was too late to say anything, no way out. She had let it go too far and now he had her. She was a stripper, a whore who danced naked for men who paid her. No way she could get away with shyness or reluctance.

Let's just keep the fact that you're not really a licker between you and me, J.T. whispered in a voice that made Meg feel dirty.

Why? Meg tried to make conversation as he pressed against her. It was her attempt to stave off what she knew was inevitable.

'Cause that's how I want it, his hand was up inside her sweater. Everybody thinks you're a lezzie. They won't suspect that we're . . . well.

Well what? She decided to challenge him.

Why not? she thought. *If I can't get out of sleeping with him, I might as well push him a little, make him work.*

Well . . . interested in each other.

Interested . . .

He was kissing her again. Kissing her mouth was his way of shutting her up, cutting off her words, questions. He wanted her. He was going to have her. They both knew that.

You want everybody to think I'm a lesbian, she pushed him away, walked a few steps into the dark boxing club, your brothers, your little wife, right?

He walked after her. His white Cheshire Cat teeth were grinning in the dark.

Maybe. So what?

Yeah. So what.

You wanna smoke some grass? You wanna beer?

Absolutely. What is this place?

It's my brother's boxing gym.

Oh yeah, cool. *That's very college girl,* she thought.

It's a sweaty dump.

Terrific.

But its close and I wanted to be alone with you tonight. He flipped a light switch, but nothing happened. The lights have to warm up before they come on, he explained.

You bring all your girls here? The other dancers?

I never brought anybody here. You're the first one. I like the idea of being with a lesbian.

But I'm not a lesbian.

You said you are sometimes.

Yeah, right, sometimes.

You've got a great body and you can really dance. I been watchin' you. He was rolling a joint as he talked. She knew that every single word he uttered was a lie.

Yeah, you and most of the rednecks in Wabash City. In case you haven't noticed, I'm up on that stage to be watched.

I know. You're very watchable. He grinned at her like a snake as he lit the twisted brown cigarette.

Sweet smoke. Drawn in then exhaled in a thin curling stream. No puff. No cloud. Just that thin stream of sweet smoke coming out of his mouth.

Here, he handed it over to her.

She drew deep, kept it in, let it spread its heavy fingers into the recesses of her lungs. *He may be the one who killed dad.* She took another deep drag. She wanted the dope to work really well tonight, take her away, lighten everything up. *It's just sex she tried to tell herself.* She passed the joint back over to him. *You've turned yourself into a whore anyway.*

He handed her a beer in return, taken from a cooler beneath a glass-topped counter that looked like a reception or sales desk. Lights were coming on, but not many. She could see the outline of what looked like a stage in the middle of the big room.

She drank from the nice cold beer, took back the joint for more sweet smoke. What looked like a stage was the boxing ring. Beer in one hand, smoking the joint in the other, she circled the ring, walking slowly. She handed the joint back to J.T. who was following her. The grass emboldened her. She kept moving, leading him, taunting him.

C'mon, you wanna fight? C'mon. She turned and shadow boxed at him, then ran up the steps and ducked between the ropes into the ring. In the center of the ring she danced on her toes, throwing shadow punches at him as he circled around her, that wolfish grin on his face, his hands full of beer and marijuana.

He took one last drag, one last sip, dropped the roach into the beer can, sat it down on the edge of the ring.

You wanna box, eh, little lesbian? You wanna box?

He circled around her, his hands up in front of his face like a boxer, but open not clenched in fists. He flicked out and tapped her shadow-boxing fists with his open hands. He moved faster around her, tapping the sides of her head, her hair, then her chin lightly with his open fingertips, caressing her face lightly with his flashing hands, his shadow punches.

She wasn't fast enough. She couldn't block him. She couldn't evade his flicking caresses. He moved around her, tapping, touching, caressing her face, laughing at her futile efforts to slip his punches.

Then suddenly he moved in on her. His arms locked her in a clinch and his mouth devoured hers.

Boxing's good, his voice was husky and sexed up tight, but I'd rather wrestle.

He had her clenched tight in his arms, his mouth molesting her face, her neck. His hands moved down to press her body into his. The time had come. No more shadow boxing.

He pulled her down in the center of the ring, but he didn't seem intent yet on totally subduing her, forcing her.

But he won't have to, she thought. *I knew what was going to happen. I'm letting him. I'm undercover. I have to give up myself to live out my cover self. This is just part of the job. Oh, I'm so sick. He killed my dad.*

His hands were on her jeans, unbuttoning the waist button, pulling unsuccessfully at the zipper. He stopped in frustration, stood up over her.

Take your clothes off. He didn't say it as an order at all, more as a request, asking. He stripped his own shirt off, worked at his jeans.

Maybe he didn't kill my dad. She was pulling her sweater over her head, unhooking her bra.

He was faster, already naked, moving in on her. She backed away, trying to get out of her jeans. But they bunched at her ankles, tripping her, toppling her over onto the floor of the boxing ring.

She lay on the floor, pulling at the jeans bunched around her ankles like the cement shoes mafia gangsters gave their enemies in movies.

He stood directly over her, menacing, waiting for her to untangle herself.

She pulled the jeans off finally, kicked them away across the ring just like she did when discarding a piece of clothing onstage.

Take off your panties.

This time it was an order. Urgent, impatient.

Then he was upon her. He was really big, unbelievably strong, heavy on top of her. *He could kill me in a minute if he wanted to,* she almost felt relieved that what he was going to do wouldn't kill her.

Then the strangest thing happened She could feel the floor of the boxing ring actually moving beneath them. It gave and moved with her, gently accomodated her body, absorbed his blows from above.

Then it was over, his final brutal spasms subsiding, the moving floor coming to rest.

Thank god for the grass, she thought. *It made it not so bad.* She felt grateful for the giving floor. It hadn't hurt that much.

She wasn't even surprised at herself. Somehow, somewhere, deep down inside herself, she knew that she might do this, might do anything, once she let herself dive into this sick, night world that had killed her father.

The Third Man

Meg was onstage, dancing on her knees, naked except for her g-string, near the end of her two-song set, when she saw them make their way through the dim smoky room and take a table close to the stage. Friday night but still early, nine, *Tippers* hardly half full.

J.T. and Belfry caught her eye, but then she recognized the third man.

Omigod, she instinctively brought her hand to her face even as her breath caught in her throat.

Omigod, what's he dong here? She panicked even as she kept dancing.

It was the fat police detective from Newport, Kentucky—she couldn't remember his name—sitting there at the ringside table with J.T. and Belfry Smale. Lieutenant Grouper or Gomer or Groper, no Gropper, that was it, the one who was supposed to be investigating her father's murder.

What's he doing here? And with them? Her second song had ended and she was gathering up her skimpy costume strewn across the stage.

All three men were smoking cigars. Gropper the cop had his sport coat unbuttoned, his tie loosened, and was patting the sides of his protruding gut like a man who had just finished off a twenty ounce porterhouse. He was obviously enjoying himself, fed and fat and ready for some female flesh.

Meg crossed behind them and emptied out her dollar bills on the bar. The bartender counted them, wrote it down on her tab. She didn't know what to do next.

Her eyes scanned the room, but she knew Mal wasn't there yet. Too early. It would be another hour before he would arrive to keep an eye on her and Jess. She knew she had to work the tables for the next ten minutes until Jess, up next, started dancing.

She wanted to eavesdrop on them, hear what the fat cop from Kentucky had to do with the Smales.

No problem, just work the tables around them for some good long tip dances. Hell, you can even flirt with J.T. while you're doing it. Better yet, get the rubes at the table next to them to buy you a drink then just sit down and listen.

She decided that the better part of valor was to keep on the move, not risk the Kentucky cop recognizing her.

Hell, she reasoned, *he's only seen me twice, sure wouldn't expect to run into me naked and dancing in a strip joint. And what guy ever looks at a stripper's face anyway.* But she had recognized him right away. No reason he couldn't do the same.

Somehow, all of a sudden, hearing what those three men sitting at the table smoking their cigars were saying blazed up as the culmination of everything she'd been doing since her dad had been murdered. She knew she had to get as close to them as she could, hear as much of what they were saying as she could hear.

Hey, this is why I'm undercover, she scolded away her hesitation and plunged into the smoky shadows of the room.

Hi guys. Having a good time? How about a table dance?

You really a college girl like that disc jockey said?

Yeah, I am. What about a table dance? she smiled at them.

How much?

Just five.

They looked at each other, laughed, and started throwing dollar bills in the middle of the table.

Here, I got the extra, one of the four young guys crowed. They could have been college boys or farm boys or construction laborers. It didn't make any difference to Meg. Their table was right next to the one she wanted to listen in on, and they were about to get the table dance of their life, and at a discount.

As she danced, she caught J.T.'s eye at the next table and winked at him. *He probably wishes he could have me right now.* But he quickly lost interest in her and went back to his conversation with his brother and the fat cop.

This was a good idea comin' up here, getting' away, she heard Gropper saying to Belfry Smale.

Hell, it's always good to get outa town an chase a little strange, ain't it?

You got that right. Great steak dinner.

Yeah, Stiney's can burn a steak.

When do we get some sweet young stuff dancin' up there?

There's one dancin' right behind ya right now dummie, Belfry laughed.

With that, Gropper spun around in his chair and looked right at Megan.

She was still dancing around the table and hadn't started to work on any of the four young guys individually yet. She managed to keep her back to Gropper until he turned back to the Smales.

Man, that's nice young stuff.

Meg hooked her leg over the lap of the young guy seated closest to Gropper and looked right at J.T. as she did it.

You say the greasers sent you up here to see us, J.T.'s voice was impatient, as if grown bored with Gropper and Belfry's byplay. Run it by me again. What's goin' on.

They're a tight lipped bunch o' spics. I'm hired help. They hire me to run errands, clean up after them down there.

Meg leaned over to the most enthusiastic of the guys at the table and whispered in his ear: If you buy me a drink, I'll sit here and talk a few minutes.

Whoa, baby, call the waitress. You are my kind of cowgirl.

Well alright cowboy, and Meg commandeered a chair from a nearby table. She gave the waitress the high sign to come over, then parked her chair right next to her new found sugar daddy, but more importantly backed it right up against the back of Gropper's chair, and settled in to listen.

All I know is they're expectin' somethin' big this week. Big enough to send me on the road in person rather than usin' the phones. You're my second stop. Indy last night, then Gary tomorrow, then Chicago.

A shipment?

What else?

Grass? Coke? What?

I don't know. They wouldn't tell me. But I don't think they'd be this excited over just pot.

No. No, they've always got that.

Meg's drink came. She sipped the tea hard through the straw. It was as if trying to eavesdrop on J.T.'s table had dried her up, parched her throat from tension. The cowboy's rough hand had already started to wander.

She leaned in to his ear and putting on her best slut voice purred: Oh honey, let me enjoy my drink here a minute. I've been working hard all night. You're the first guy has given me a chance to sit down.

How much? Belfry quizzed Gropper.

They told me to tell everyone "as much as they could handle."

Handle? J.T. joined the interrogation.

As much as you can buy. You know the price. Figure it out.

J.T. just stared at Gropper. Meg saw the surprised look on J.T.'s face when she got up to rub the shoulders of the other three yokels at her table.

C'mon guys, let's have some fun. All I'm doin' is delivering the invitations. The spics said to be in Newport next weekend, ready to deal.

That's Memorial Day weekend, Belfry sounded like he was wounded. We go to the 500 in Indy.

One of the yokels was getting an extra long shoulder rub, because it gave Meg a perfect angle to watch the faces of J.T. and Belfry through the smoky dimness as they talked to the crooked cop from Newport.

J.T. looked at Belfry as if he had just pissed in the middle of the table.

Tell them we'll be there.

But the 500.

Shut up!

It'll be a big weekend in Newport, Gropper tried to console Belfry. The town'll be packed. Everybody from three states will be in there to party.

The music started up and Jesse took the stage to dance.

Meg sat down again back to back with Gropper, but it was too loud and she couldn't hear a thing. She took one last sip on the straw of her tea, set the glass down on the table, stood up, brushed a chaste kiss across the cheek of the cowboy who had bought her the drink, grabbed the bills from the table, and fled for the safety of the dancers' dressing room.

Five minutes later, in her trench coat and high heels, she crossed the gravel parking lot of the strip club and found Mal's car parked on the street beside the boxing gym. She left her note under the driver's side windshield wiper: "Our place. 3. Imp."

J.T. was momentarily distracted from the conversation at the table as Meg, done entertaining a group of guys at the next table, walked past on her way to the dressing room.

You guys oughta make a weekend of it, Gropper was saying.

What the hell was that? Belfry, who didn't miss much, had caught the byplay between Meg and J.T.

What?

You bangin' that cherry little college girl?

J.T. ignored him and turned back to Gropper. OK. Look, what's the deal? Exactly.

No exactly. I'm just carryin' an invitation to you a week ahead of time.

OK, so what exactly is the invitation?

Next Saturday, deals are gonna be made. The spics are giving you a week's notice to get your act together, including transportation back here, and they'll give you all you can handle.

Meaning all we can pay cash for.

You got it.

No advance against sales?

No.

Now Belfry was getting bored by the businesslike turn of the conversation between Gropper and his older brother. The music had started up and another dancer had come on, another college girl like that other one. They all looked the same to Belfry. He liked older women, more experienced, sicker. His mind wandered momentarily as he watched the dancer on stage. *I'll go to Ginevra's place tonight as soon as we're done with this Kentucky fat ass.*

Really. You guys oughta make a weekend of it down in Newport. Bring your ladies down with you. Do your deal on Saturday, then party Saturday night. Dinner. A night club. Dancing. Hey.

J.T. laughed at his enthusiasm.

Hey, I'll bet Ginevra'd like a weekend out of town, Belfry thought.

Come on down. I'll take care of you guys.

You sure as hell owe me one, Belfry pointed at him with his long neck.

I know. I know. That's one of the reasons I wanna make it up to you. The kid feels as bad about that as I do.

Hey, forget it, Belfry waved him off with the beer bottle.

Think about it, Gropper's concentration was back on J.T.

We'll be there, J.T. decided on the spot.

You won't regret it. Hey, look at her. Damn you got some good young stuff in this joint.

Something Happened

OK, what is so important that you're leaving notes on my car?

I had to talk to you tonight.

You *never* leave a note on a car.

I didn't know if I'd be able to give you the message in the club. J.T. and his brother were there all night. J.T. watches me. He likes me. I didn't want him to see me talking to you. Especially after you two fought.

Undercovers just don't do stuff like that. Anybody walking down the street can take that note off the windshield and read it.

I made it really little.

Terrific!

What I wrote wouldn't mean anything to anyone but you.

OK. OK. Enough.

They were a strange burnt-out threesome at 3AM in the morning—The Mod Squad, hair-dos wilted and sleep deprived.

Meg was sprawled on the couch in a pair of brown flannel pajamas drinking a beer, totally unaware of how tired she looked.

Jesse wasn't much better, slumped in the apartment's one overstuffed easy chair which was probably older than she was. She wasn't drinking. All she wanted to do was go to bed. She was so tired that she wasn't even that curious.

Mal had turned around one of the straight kitchen chairs and was sitting at the dinette, his beer on the table, his arms draped over the back, looking at the sorry sight of the two of them.

Like spontaneous combustion, Meg just burst out crying. She started with her face just disintegrating around her lips and in two seconds tears were rolling like boulders down her cheeks.

Oh I'm sorry. Forget it. I didn't mean to make such a big deal of it, Mal hated women crying.

No, no, that's not it. I don't know why I'm doing this. I hate crying. It's so . . . so . . . weak.

Meg, are you OK? Jesse moved to the couch and put her arms around her roommate, motherly.

Listen, Megan, we can stop this undercover deal right now. You won't ever have to go back there.

No! she sat straight up. No! that's why I had to talk to you tonight. Something's happened. We're finally getting somewhere.

Mal looked at Jesse. Jess nodded in support of Meg.

What? Mal was suddenly curious.

For the next five minutes Meg told Mal and Jess everything: about Gropper, about J.T.'s and Belfry's reaction to him, every word that passed between them. The whole story of the evening came in a powerful stream like a fire hose opening up full blast. Meg amazed herself. She seemed to remember everything down to the smallest detail, every word. After she started talking, Mal had to slow her down. He took out a small pocket notebook and wrote things in it. When she finished, she just sank back on the couch in a kind of shock. She couldn't believe how clear every important moment of that evening had been in her consciousness, her memory.

He invited them to come down to Newport, Kentucky, next weekend to buy dope? Mal wanted to be absolutely sure.

Yes, that's what it sounded like. A lot of dope. All they could handle.

It's Memorial Day weekend. He told them to come down there and party, right?

Yes.

What else did he say about that? Tell me again.

He said he'd take care of them.

Then Belfry Smale jumped in?

Yeah, J.T.'s brother said "you better, you owe me one" or something like that.

So what was that all about?

Maybe it was just payback for them getting Rhonda to go home with him, Jess cut in, bored with listening to Mal quiz Meg.

Maybe. I don't know.

What'd he say then?

He said, "Sorry about that" I think. Oh god, Mal, I'm sorry. I can't think. It was so clear a minute ago, now I can't seem to remember anything.

OK. OK. It's been a long night. Let me think about this. I'll be here about noon. We'll figure out what we're gonna do.

The next morning Meg was up much earlier than she normally would be after a long late night at *Tippers*. She sat at the dinette drinking coffee, trying to figure it out, this Newport cop just showing up like that.

Jess was dead to the world, buried under her enormous blue flowered comforter on the sofa.

As promised, Mal showed up at noon.

Meg had noticed how tired he had been looking lately. A good night's sleep seemed to have done him good. He was almost cheerful. She gave him coffee.

I'm going down there this afternoon to check it out.

Newport?

Yeah.

Wait 'til tomorrow, I'll go with you.

No. I wanna be down there on a Saturday night. See how this so called Sin City works.

Why?

Because I'm gonna follow J.T. and Belfry down there next weekend when they make their buy, then I'm gonna have the Highway Patrol stop them in Indiana when they're driving it back up here.

You're going to do this all by yourself?

It's the only way.

Why?

Look, the only way we get these pricks is to catch them in a drug deal, catch them on the road with the stuff in their possession. That's why I want to go down there, so I can get used to the place, so I can follow them next weekend.

You won't have to follow them.

What are you talking about?

I'm going to be with them.

At that, Jess came bolting back to consciousness, sat straight upright.

What did you say? Mal couldn't believe his ears either.

I'm gonna get J.T. Smale to make me his date for the weekend in Newport.

What the . . .

Meg, what are you talking about?

He likes me. He'll take me. You don't think he's gonna take his wife, do you?

No way. I'm handling this alone and as soon as they get across the state line we'll nail them.

You can't stop me, Mal. You want a drug dealer. I want the men who murdered my father. Same goal, different game. If he asks me, I'm going to be there.

Don't Meg. It's too dangerous. Mother Jesse was back in the land of the living.

You're sleeping with him, aren't you? Mal thought it, didn't mean to say it, but did.

It was the way that Mal said it—"You're sleeping with him, aren't you?"—that set off the alarms in Meg's head. Not fatherly, as she so often thought he treated her, though he was only ten years older. Jealous almost, accusing, as if he felt betrayed.

What?

Jess stared at the two of them wide-eyed.

You heard me.

Yes, I heard you, but it's none of your business.

Damn, I should have lied right away, denied it. Now they know, Meg realized.

None of my business! You, you. . . . He didn't finish, didn't say whatever he was going to say, call her whatever he was about to call her, because he realized how much damage it would do. He fought to gain control of himself, but he couldn't . . . completely. He tried to fix it, calm his voice.

None of my business? You're my undercover. I'm running you, supposed to be protecting you, guarding you, and you're sleeping with the enemy.

Mal, I had too. It was the only way to make the undercover credible. I dance naked in a roomful of men.

But this is different.

No it's not. It's all part of the game, the play, the theater of the real.

Jess felt like the only spectator at a tennis match being played with a hand grenade. When was it going to go off and blow them all up? The three of them had become like this weird family, her and Mal as father and mother to this wild child, and now it all seemed to be coming apart as families always do. Or maybe Mal was right; he and she were just Meg's bodyguards. Or maybe it was much more complex than that . . . for both of them. She too had heard that hurt and pain in Mal's voice, that jealousy.

Dammit Meg, you don't sleep with your target. You're my undercover. You're supposed to work it the way I say.

You don't own me, Mal. I had to make a decision right then, on the spot.

It was the wrong decision.

No way. It got me all the way inside. Now he trusts me totally. Don't you see? We've got him, and his brothers, their whole operation.

This undercover's over. You two aren't going back to that strip joint.

Yes I am! Meg glared at him as if she wanted to fight him, strike out at him.

No Meg, he could be the man who murdered your father.

Meg's fierce glare fractured into a thousand shards of pain. The tears came back, tracing jagged furrows down across her broken face.

Meg, I'm sorry, I'm sorry, Mal was up out of his turned-around chair crossing to her on the couch. His hands went to her shoulders first to steady her as she shook with sobs, then he pulled her to him and wrapped her protectively in his arms.

Oh, we're all so unstable, Jess thought.

Meg was crying so hard that she didn't even realize that she was in Mal's arms. When she did, she pushed him away.

The silence came down on all three of them like a shroud.

Hey, look, Jess felt like a boxing referee, things just got a little carried away. You two need to talk to each other, not fight with each other.

Mal and Meg looked at each other.

Look, I'm not trying to own you, but what you did, what you're doing, is really dangerous. It's my job to keep you from getting hurt, Mal broke the silence.

Your job?

Yeah.

This has all been dangerous from the very beginning and I was hurt as much as anybody could ever be hurt before we even started this undercover.

I know, I know. But now it's getting out of control.

No it's not. We're just getting closer. Mal, we're almost there. We've almost got these monsters. Can't you see?

OK. OK. But I hate what it's come to.

I know. But it's almost over. OK?

OK.

Meg was done crying. She wiped her face. But she couldn't wipe out of her mind what she had heard in Mal's voice, the hurt, the jealous anger. She hadn't seen that coming.

Are you really going down to Newport today? Jess broke the awkward silence, changed the subject.

Yeah, and I've gotta get going soon. I want to be there by six so I can get everything done I want to do.

Stay at *The Crossroads Inn*. That's where it all happened.

I know. I've thought this all out.

Talk to the bartender there. Eddie. He's. . . . He's . . . well, he's black too. A good guy. He'll give you straight answers. He was a friend of my father's. He'll remember me.

I'll do it.

Then Mal and Meg just looked at each other as if they didn't know where to go next.

You've got to promise me you won't do anything . . . he realized he had to choose his words carefully with her because she was like a bomb trip-wired to go off . . . anything that will get you in trouble tonight. I won't be there.

I know. I promise. He thinks I've got my period this weekend. That was my 'get out of jail' card.

Going All the Way

As soon as Belfry untied Ginevra, he asked her if she would go away for the weekend with him.

Why not? Where?

Newport, Kentucky.

Kentucky? What's down there?

We've got some business there. Some people down there owe us, so we thought we'd mix the business with some pleasure.

And I'm the pleasure?

Baby, you're always the pleasure. Belfry assured her.

You said "we've" got business in Kentucky. J.T.'s going too?

Yeah.

His wife?

No.

He's going alone.

No.

She looked at him over her shoulder, not understanding.

I think he's taking one of the girls from *Tippers*. I don't know.

Oh great! The Smale brothers take their bimbos to Kentucky for a sex weekend.

No. It's not like that. You're not a bimbo. This'll be nice. First class. Nice hotels. Night clubs. A holiday weekend.

In Kentucky?

Yeah.

But Ginevra knew better. She didn't buy anything that Belfry said, yet she couldn't say "no" to him. Between them it was all about the sex, the danger. She forced him to tell her what he made the whores from the strip joint do when he got them alone, then she forced him to make her do those things. She taunted him to treat her like one of his dope slaves. She pushed him further and further, turning his domination into a sexual heat that she utterly controlled, which he neither understood or questioned. For Ginevra, Belfry was the unsuspecting vehicle of her flight from the boredom of life in Wabash City,

Sure, I'll go. But it better be fun and different.

Meg plotted for two days. She decided she had to sleep with him again, then catch him offguard right after they'd done it, manipulate him into inviting her to go along. She even wrote down and rehearsed her lines:

Oh baby, that was sooo good. You make me feel so good. We've gotta find some place to really make love, in a bed, in a nice hotel, someplace like that. That was going to be her come on to get him to ask her to go to Newport for the weekend. But when the time came, she never even had to say a word.

Monday nights were always really slow at *Tippers*. The club was closed on Sundays and few people went out in Wabash City on Monday nights. That was why Jess never worked Monday nights. She took all her Sundays and Mondays to study.

J.T. showed up at about eleven thirty Monday night and closed the place down at midnight. He was waiting for Meg when she came out of the dressing room. She was hoping he would be. She had stalled to be last so that they'd be all alone when she came out. She had calculated right. He was standing in the semi-darkness just outside the dressing room door.

When Meg came out and saw him, she looked around, checking to see if anyone was still there.

They're all gone, his voice, quiet and husky, came out of the shadows.

Good, and she was in his arms in an instant.

They kissed deep and hard, his hands all over her

This time she did him right there in the club like she was taking a stud horse out for a ride, on a sturdy straight-backed chair from one of the tables right in the middle of the showroom floor. When he was done with her, she tried to get her head together to deliver her lines. But she never had to say a word.

Hey, my brother Belfry and I are going down to Newport, Kentucky, for Memorial Day weekend, to party. He's taking his girlfriend. You wanna go with me? We can do this in a bed.

She tried to play it cool, hide her excitement. What about work? It's a big weekend.

Hey, I own the joint, remember.

What the hell is in Kentucky?

✗

Seventy thousand worth, J.T. sat across from Belfry at the poker table in the back room of the boxing gym. That's how much I wanna buy.

That's a lot o' coke.

They were both drinking from long neck bottles.

Can you put that much cash together by Friday?

Yeah. We've got it. I'll have to empty a few piggy banks.

Yeah right.

Hundreds?

Gotta be. I want 'em to fit in as small a package as we can get.

Belfry saw himself haunting every bank in the county making withdrawals from scattered accounts, changing bills, putting together their stake.No problem, he gave J.T. the assurance he required.

Hey, this buy is gonna make us a load o' money.

If the weight's right, the same those spics have always given us, I figure it adds up to about three-quarters of a million bucks when I get done sellin' it.

Hey, brother, we'll make this deal Saturday morning and we'll party like Elvis and Johnny Cash Saturday night.

Alright! Wait'll you meet the woman I'm takin' down there. Her name's Ginevra. She's the wildest damn cowgirl you've ever seen.

I'm takin' that college girl dancer from the place.

Hello? No little wifey this trip (taunting), no romantic weekend getaway?

That's none o' yore business.

Hey, easy firedog, like I care if you're bangin' this little jailbait college piece behind your old lady's back.

How's this? We'll go down there in Billy Keirce's limo. That big ol' Cadillac with the huge fins. He'll give me one of his boys to drive. It's got leather seats and a refrigerator even.

They sat back and contemplated the beauty of the plan for a long minute.

What about Hump? Belfry asked. You know he'll wanna go.

He ain't goin.' It's too big a deal.

What do we tell him?

We don't tell him anything. I'll handle Hump. You get that money put together.

No problem. Then we party like Elvis.

Look, me and Belfry are goin' out of town for the whole weekend on business. I need you to take care of things here in town while we're gone.

Where you goin'?

Kentucky.

Kentucky?

Yes, Kentucky. On business.

OK, Kentucky.

Look, Hump, pay attention. It's a big holiday weekend. I need you to stay straight and take care of things here while we're gone. OK?

OK. OK.

There'll be a lot o' business at *Tippers*. The bartenders will help you out, but you gotta watch over things.

OK. I'll stay there all night.

Friday and Saturday.

OK. Both nights.

And don't drink too much. You gotta stay sharp. You'll be in charge.

Hey, I'll be in charge, J.T. No problem.

Yeah, right, J.T. thought as Hump went back to his beer at the bar.

Underworld

Driving south toward Kentucky, Mal tried to distract himself. He turned the radio up loud, but after fifty miles he lost his Wabash City station and all he could find was Country and Western, redneck music. He stopped at a gas station for coca cola and snacks, but he couldn't distract himself by eating either. He thought about boxing, fantasized about entering the Golden Gloves next year, but even that didn't work.

Nothing he did could keep him from worrying about this Smale undercover, this crazy white college girl. She had him totally confused. He was starting to feel funny around her. He sat in the dark and watched her strip almost every night. He had coffee with her in her bathrobe in her apartment most early afternoons. He realized that he looked forward to seeing her. Waited for her, eagerly, to take the stage in the strip club. She'd even given him a key to the apartment so he wouldn't wake her up when he came in. He made her coffee when she woke up in the afternoons. *But I'm not in love with her,* he thought, *I can't be.*

He checked into *The Crossroads Inn* in Newport, Kentucky, about six and hit the bar about six thirty. It was empty. A black man, Eddie the bartender he was pretty sure, was slicing lemons.

Hi. Are you Eddie?

The bartender blinked when he looked up from his work and saw Mal. But just a blink, not startled, or at least not letting on.

Yes I am. Do I know you?

No. Sorry. No you don't.

What would you like?

A beer. Bud's fine.

Eddie only needed two steps to reach the cooler and pull Mal out a long neck. He popped the top with a church key he kept in the pocket of his apron.

Thanks. Do you remember Bill O'Neill?

Bill O'Neill?

Traveling salesman got himself murdered here about two months ago.

What did you say your name was?

I didn't.

Oh, and he turned his back and walked down to the other end of the bar as far away from Mal as he could get.

Mal took one sip, then followed Eddie down to where he had buried his head in a newspaper.

OK. I'm Mal Rogers and I'm Indiana State Police. I'm friends with this O'Neill's daughter, Meg. She told me to talk to you.

You don't look like a cop.

I take that as a compliment.

Around here most of the cops are fat and crooked, Eddie looked around when he said it, making sure the bar was still empty.

Mal laughed.

Eddie went back to his paper, uneasy, as if he'd said too much.

Meg O'Neill said you were a stand-up guy, that you'd talk to me.

About what? The murder? I wasn't here that night. She knows that. I don't know anything about it.

I know. I know. Hey, relax. I just need somebody to tell me what's goin' on down here, how Newport works. She thought you'd help me.

OK. Shoot. But let's get it done before this place starts fillin' up.

Mal looked around. He'd been there ten minutes and not a soul had disturbed them.

Doesn't seem much danger of that.

Yeah, right, Eddie actually almost laughed. What do you want to know?

Do you know a Newport cop named Gropper? Fat, grey hair.

Yeah, yeah, he's one of them, one of the boys.

Boys?

Yeah, one of the insiders. He works for the powers that be.

Powers that be?

Whoever's got the money to buy off the cops.

He's on the take?

Oh yeah.

How long?

Since the first day he got his badge.

What do you know about him?

On the strip they call him Groper because he likes to take out his protection fees from the strip joints and whorehouses in trade. Gropper the Groper.

He was supposed to be the investigating officer on the O'Neill murder.

He couldn't investigate his own hemorrhoids.

Are all the cops like Gropper?

The cops, the politicians, they're all on the take. Hell, even the county health department. There's restaurants where the cockroaches in the kitchen are bigger than some of the cooks.

You'll have to tell me where *not* to get dinner tonight.

They both laughed.

Newport's like this little hillbilly sin city across the river from this respectable Midwestern metropolis. Eddie was warming to the subject thanks to his bar still being empty.

Metropolis?

Yeah, like in Batman. Cincinnati. Gotham City. Metropolis.

Fine.

Newport is Cincy's red light district, gambling den, drug connection, all rolled into one. It's perfect. It's got a river and a state line between itself and its urban crime. Nobody in Ohio cares what goes on in Kentucky.

If I was coming down here for a big holiday weekend of partying, like next weekend, where would I go for a high end good time?

Sure not here! Eddie laughed.

I can see that.

Depends on what kind of partying you want. If you want whores, you go to *Marty's Golden Corral*. It looks like a strip joint on the outside but it's the fanciest whore house in town. You want gambling, you go to the Chinaman's down on Main Street and talk yourself into the basement, *The Dragon Inn*. You want dinner, dancing, fancy entertainment, you go to the night club up on the hill in Southgate.

Mal wrote them all down. He meant to check them each out before the night was over. He had high hopes that Eddie was right and he really didn't look like a cop.

What about drugs?

What about them?

Where are they? Who sells them?

They're everywhere. I think they're what makes the whole place cook. They're the fire that provides the heat for everything else. For all I know, the mayor's a dealer.

C'mon, who runs the dope?

I don't know, but there's a lot of it around, and it never seems to dry up.

You know anything about a gang of Columbians here who deal dope?

Whoa. Now you're getting into the bad boys. Colombians, Mexicans, Puerto Ricans, there's all kinds of Spanish speaking gangsters in Newport. I can't tell them apart. In my book they're all evil.

Great.

Hey, I just sell drinks. Really, I try to stay clear of the really evil stuff that happens around here. Like Mr. O'Neill.

I guess I can understand that.

I'm not sure you do. You know, America seems like this quiet harmless place, especially here in the midwest, like Cincinnati or a small town like Newport, but underneath everything there's all this ugly stuff going on. New York and Chicago have got nothing on us.

I'm afraid you're right.

So am I.

Hey thanks. That's what I needed. Here, keep the change.

But Eddie pushed the ten back across the bar to Mal.

It's OK man. I liked that little white girl's dad. I was sorry he got shot. I think it was all a mistake.

I'm afraid you're right.

The Crack-Up

It was a long and tiring time for Bobby Tyler, mainly because he had to think a lot more than he was used to thinking.

Bobby had buried his brother Wink a week ago Monday, then proceeded to drink himself into a stupor for three days as his way of mourning. Then he had spent Thursday sleeping his bender off. Over the weekend he started in with all that tiring thinking.

Wink would never roll his truck and kill himself, he was too good a wheel-man was the thought that started Bobby Tyler thinking. *So how did it really happen?*

Sitting in a back booth by himself in *The Squirrel Cage*, Bobby Tyler pondered that mystery the better part of the weekend. Then he went looking for answers.

First he drove out into the country toward Battleground and found the place where it happened. He'd gone out there the morning they'd notified him they'd found Wink's body. By the time he'd gotten there, they were towing the remains of Wink's truck away on a flatbed trailer and Wink's body had already been removed to the morgue. All that was left for him to look at were some skidmarks off the blacktop and a line of deep muddy wounds in the jet-black earth of the plowed field. They'd told him that from the looks of things Wink's truck had left the road at a pretty high speed and rolled over about four times. Now, back at the crash site a week later, you couldn't hardly tell that anything had ever happened there. Rain had washed away all the blood and smoothed out the wounded earth. Returning to the scene of the accident hadn't eased Bobby Tyler's tortured thought process at all.

Next he went and talked to the county sheriffs who had gone to the wreck and seen his brother's body. They both were convinced it was just another accident.

He was just driving too fast and lost it, Sergeant Walker assured Bobby.

He'd been drinking, Sergeant Higgins added.

But their certainty didn't ease Bobby Tyler's mind either. *He was a professional wheel-man drunk or sober,* he told himself but not the sheriffs.

Can I see the truck? Bobby asked. See if any of my brother's things are still in it?

Sure. No problem. In fact, in another week they'll release it to you. The sheriff was trying to be helpful.

Or buy it from you for junk if you don't want it, the other sheriff put in his two cents.

Bobby Tyler caught up with what was left of brother Wink's rusty pick-up in the county impound lot behind a chain-link fence on South River Road. The sign on the fence read:

TIPPECANOE SHERIFF'S DEPT.
Private Property
Keep Out

The chain and padlock on the gate were crusted in rust. The two sheriffs who had led him down there in their brown cruiser opened it up for him, told him to lock it when he was done. Then they left. *Probably in a hurry to get to the donut shop,* he thought.

'Tippecanoe and Tyler Too' popped into Bobby's mind when he saw that sign hanging on the rusty fence. He had always hated that old saying, especially because it had his name in it and he didn't have a clue what it meant.

"Sheriff's Impound Lot" was just a fancy name for a junkyard. Surrounded by a rusty chain-link fence, it was nothing but a square field, not very big, piled three high in wrecked cars, on the river side of the South River Road. Because the Wabash periodically flooded it, rust had almost totally taken over every single wreck in that automobile graveyard.

Wink's truck was easy to find. Having been there only about a week, it wasn't nearly as rusty as the others. It was piled upside down on top of two rusted hulks about twenty yards from the entrance gate.

Bobby Tyler climbed up to Wink's truck so he could get a good look at it. Because it had been piled upside down on top of the heap, when Bobby got up there he sat down on the dented gas tank with his legs straddling the twisted transmission shaft. The pick-up's tires stuck straight up in the air like the legs of a dead horse. Three of the tires were actually pretty much all in one piece while the fourth was all ripped and torn apart. That was what first caught Bobby Tyler's attention.

It just didn't look right to him. *How come that tire's all wrecked?* he wondered.

He looked closely at the other three tires. None of them looked like that.

A blowout at high speed would roll a truck he knew, *but what would cause a blowout like this that would tear the whole tire apart?*

Puzzled, stumped, confused, thinking about it so hard it hurt his head, Bobby Tyler climbed down off his brother's truck, locked the gate behind him, drove to *The Squirrel Cage* and got some beer to ease the pain of all his heavy thinking. By the time he'd spent two hours drinking beer and thinking about it in *The Squirrel Cage,* he thought he knew what happened the night Wink died.

He figured that Wink was running from somebody who was chasing him and the only way they could get him to stop was to shoot his tire out. *That's why he crashed. They shot that tire that was so torn up. But who?* That didn't take Bobby Tyler nearly as long to figure out. *Has to be the Smales,* he convinced himself. *They killed Wink!*

Far From the Madding Crowd

Tuesday night, early Wednesday morning.

Tippers, midweek, not busy at all. Meg actually got home early. She'd barely had time to open a beer before someone was knocking at her door.

You must have followed me home.

I was right behind you.

I saw you in the club, but I thought you took off a long time ago, went home to bed.

I decided to wait in the car.

Wait?

You can only watch women strip for so long, Mal avoided her question.

That's not the way most men think.

I just didn't feel like sitting in there anymore. It makes me. . . . His voice just trailed off.

Beer?

Yeah, that'd be good.

If you didn't want to sit in there watching us dance, why didn't you just go home?

Where's Jesse? She didn't work tonight. He tried to change the subject.

Probably studying. I don't know. Why did you wait around, sit in a parked car waiting for me to finish?

This was unusual. Mal was usually so decisive, always seemed to have an answer, a plan, even if she and Jess didn't like it. This night she could sense his uncertainty.

He didn't say anything. He didn't answer the direct demand of her question. He just sipped at his beer and tried not to look at her. It got awkward again.

He went to the front window and looked out through the blinds. He came back to the dinette table, turned a chair around and sat down, putting a small wall up between them. Real awkward.

Did you want to talk to me about something?

Yeah. I think so.

What is his problem? C'mon, spit it out. She felt like a schoolteacher trying to pry information out of a first grader. She changed the subject.

What did you think of Newport, Kentucky?

It's a dump. He didn't have any trouble answering that question.

She laughed. The awkwardness was broken. They were themselves again. Doesn't take long to figure that out, does it?

No.

Where'd you go?

I did it by the book. Checked into *The Crossroads,* talked with Eddie the bartender . . .

Nice man.

. . . then I went downtown and walked around. What a dump. A lot of people are paying off a lot of people to let that honky-tonk slum stay in business.

No lie.

I drove out to the big night club by the highway too. Now that's pretty nice. Huge place up on a hill.

That's probably where I'll be next Saturday night, Meg saw her chance to break the news to Mal. She knew exactly how he would react.

Aw Meg, you did it, didn't you?

No. I didn't. I didn't have to do a thing. He just asked me. I had my lines all rehearsed to get him to invite me, but I didn't have to say a thing.

That's what I wanted to talk to you about. Please don't go down there with him this weekend. Meg, it's a major drug deal. It'll be dangerous. You could get caught in the crossfire.

That's why you waited tonight? You should of just gone home to bed.

I waited last night too.

The silence that fell between them this time totally redefined their earlier awkwardness.

Mal's head hung over the back of the wooden chair, his eyes glued to the ugly reddish-green linoleum of the floor.

Oh Mal, she came around behind him, set her beer down on the table, put her hands on his shoulders.

Meg, it's just too dangerous. I don't want you to get hurt. Don't go down there with him. I can't sleep at night until I know you, and Jess, are home safe.

Oh Mal, that's so sweet, and she forced him to turn around on the chair and face her, but I've gotta go. We've just come too far with this whole undercover thing not to see it through. Someone in this whole crowd of crooks killed my father. I just can't stop now.

He just looked up at her, didn't say a thing, but that look burned straight through her. For some reason she sat down on his lap, straddled him on that kitchen chair. She put her hands to the sides of his face and kissed him hard on the lips.

He kissed her back, hungrily.

When the kiss was over, he gently encircled her with his arms, slowly, tentatively, and pulled her close, as if he wanted to feel in his body her skin, her warmth. He held her silent for a long moment until she twisted her head away and kissed him again long and deeply.

Are you crazy? He breathed, barely audible, breathless, in her ear.

What?

You're kissing me.

Really, are you sure? punctuated with a little laugh.

This is . . . this is . . .

What *is* your problem? You don't like me kissing you?

No. No. But I'm the wrong color.

Geez, how could I have missed that.

I'm ten years older than you. I'm old enough . . .

Don't say it, and she stopped his mouth with another kiss. Mmmm, chocolate. She kissed him again as if tasting him. Mmmmm, old chocolate.

Even as he was kissing her back, he was starting to worry, wondering what had happened to make his most secret fantasy come true. Despite wanting her so bad that he couldn't stop kissing her, he felt like he was betraying some unspoken trust that went with his job or his age or something else he didn't understand. She had him totally confused.

Oh Meg (he could smell the powder she put on her body when she danced), what are we doing?

I don't know about you, but I think I'm putting the make on you.

Because you want me to let you go to Kentucky this weekend?

Hey, news flash Mal, you got no say in either that or this, and she kissed him again, hard, urgent, her body pressing.

He stood up, her still clinging to him.

She wrapped her legs around him as he shuffled toward the couch.

You know, she gave that tiny little laugh again, I think I really am putting the make on you and I think we're gonna make love no matter how old or racist you are.

Racist?

Hey, you started it, not me.

Standing above the couch, her legs wrapped tight around him, they kissed so long and deeply that all reality seemed to burn away leaving them alone in a super-heated world where all their senses seemed totally captured by the feel, the taste, the touch and the smell of the other.

The key grated in the lock of the outside door like metal rasping across a blackboard.

The door opened, then closed quietly.

Mal and Meg jumped away from each other as if they'd been burned.

Hi guys. What's up?

Jesse came through the door, dropped her backpack full of books on the dinette table, headed to the fridge for a beer. She didn't seem to notice the sheepish looks on their faces, their guilty retreat from each other, the awkward silence that her question caused.

Damn, I wish I'd been dancing tonight. This hydraulics class is just kicking my butt.

You didn't miss much.

I can see that. What are you here for Mal?

For Jess, it was just a simple offhand question, but from the look on Mal's face you'd think that Perry Mason had just asked him if he'd murdered the Mayor and the City Council and thrown their bodies in the Wabash.

Nothing. Nothing. He protested way too much.

Mal is concerned about my going down to Newport, Kentucky, this weekend with J.T. Smale.

What? If Jess's mouth had been full of beer, it would have been all over the table. You did it, didn't you? You got him to invite you down there, didn't you?

No. Actually I didn't have to do a thing. He just asked me of his own free will.

Jesse stared across the table at her in disbelief.

Mal was leaning against the fridge, sipping on a new beer, trying to regain his composure.

Meg, I think Mal's right. Jess stopped pacing and got serious. It's too dangerous. Let Mal and the State Police handle it. It's your undercover work that set this all up. Now let them handle it. You've done your part. They'll go to prison thanks to you.

I've already told him I'd go.

Don't do it.

He'd know something wasn't right.

Meg, listen to Mal. Neither of us want you to go. Doesn't that mean anything?

You're not my parents. She looked from one of them to the other. I don't have anybody to answer to, remember? I'm going.

I gotta go. Mal had to get out of there. He could hardly breathe. This whole thing had gotten away from him, had taken on a life of its own. I'll talk to you tomorrow.

After Mal was gone, Jess stayed at the table. They just sat looking at each other.

Meg began to cry, not one of her sudden torrents of sobs, but just quiet tears as if they were all she had left to help her.

Something had changed. Jess could sense it. Their little family had somehow redefined itself. She didn't quite know how, but she sensed that suddenly things were different between them all.

Meg, I wish you wouldn't do it. These guys are monsters. If they think you're spying on their business, they'll kill you without a thought. Please don't.

I have to. I've got to finish this.

I know. And Jess got up to come and sit next to her on the couch. But, honey, I'm scared. Then she looked at Meg for a long moment, her hand on top of Meg's hand in Meg's lap. I love you. I don't want you to get hurt.

I can't be hurt anymore than I already am.

You could be dead.

But, can't you see, I can't ever be alive until all this is settled.

Oh honey, and Jess's arms were around her, pulling her close, like a mother or lover, neither of them knew which or cared.

They held each other tightly, Meg crying, Jess stroking her back, her hair.

Would it be so bad, so wrong?

What?

You and me. Together.

Tonight it wouldn't be so bad at all.

Come to bed with me, in my room. We won't make love. We'll just be together. Like friends are supposed to be.

I don't know.

I promise I won't talk about this weekend thing anymore.

OK, and Meg was wiping her eyes, actually sort of smiling at her.

I'll tell you, I'm gonna miss the money from the dancing though.

You could keep doing it, somewhere else.

Yeah, right, the only reason I did it in the first place was because I wanted to be your lesbian lover.

Terrific. I thought it was because you wanted to be my bodyguard.

Well, that too. I *am* the female Bruce Lee, you know.

Uh huh.

Seriously, I wish I could go with you down there this weekend. You're going to need eyes in the back of your head.

I thought we weren't going to talk about that.

No. Sorry. C'mon, let's go to bed.

Breakfast of Champions

John Davidson thought he was in Cleveland, Ohio. He actually had to walk across the hotel room to the calendar that his publicist gave to him every Sunday to check. It was a Friday morning in May and they hadn't gotten into the hotel until three A.M. after what seemed an interminable bus ride from, he checked the calendar again, Pittsburgh.

He looked out his hotel room window. He seemed to be about forty floors up in the air looking right down on downtown Cleveland. The cigarette and alcohol haze began to lift from around his brain. This tour had been going on for a month, a combination of college campuses and night clubs. They had two buses that transported him, the orchestra and the gear. His bedroom in the lead bus was comfortable, even spacious, but he couldn't sleep in it. When he was on tour he always drank and smoked too much.

From the fortieth floor it looked like a really nice day in Cleveland. He found his watch on the night stand beside the bed—almost noon. He looked out the window again. The sun seemed to be shining brightly.

He picked up the phone on the desk and dialed the hotel operator, asked to be connected to his publicist's room.

Jake, good morning.

Yeah, who, oh John, hello, hi, he had obviously awakened him out of a sound sleep.

Jake, it's a gorgeous spring day. I've gotta get out.

Yeah, right, get out.

Could you set it up so that I could play golf this afternoon before I have to go to the gig?

Yeah, sure, where are we?

Cleveland.Cleveland, right. Give me an hour. Golf, you say.

Yeah, and see if you can get me someone to play with.

Part Three

The Mansion

Couples

Billy Kierce's black Cadillac limo was probably the fanciest car in Wabash City. When J.T. Smale (with two days notice) asked Billy if he could have it (with a driver) for the whole Memorial Day weekend, it was a done deal. After all, J.T. had helped Billy buy it. Billy was one of the neighborhood guys who had hung out with the Smales since high school.

Listen, you only speak when they speak to you, y'hear. When you're on the road, drivin', keep the curtains to the back pulled. Anything you hear, anything that goes on in the back, you ignore. I don't care what's happenin' back there, you just keep drivin' and do what you're told. You sleep in the limo. You're on call for these guys every minute all weekend. Got it? Billy gave his twenty-year-old nephew Ernie his driving orders.

Ernie knew better than to complain, not because he was afraid of his uncle, but because he knew who he was driving for that weekend. Everybody in the neighborhood knew that you did what you were told around the Smales.

J.T. and Belfry loaded the luggage into the trunk of the limo. The two girls watched as their suitcases went in. One a beat-up brownish plaid square old-fashioned monstrosity, the other a newer baby blue plastic hard-shell, both heavy.

What've you girls got in these things, J.T. complained, laughing, as he hefted Ginevra's blue hard-shell into the trunk. We're only goin' away for two days.

Young Ernie packed the four other bags in. Two seemed the right weight but the other two felt like they were empty. Then he reached for the brand new vinyl briefcase sitting on the ground to throw it in on top.

No, Belfry Smale stopped him. That goes inside with me.

Brother, lighten up. Go ahead, put it in, J.T. ordered young Ernie. This is a holiday weekend, Belfry boy, and the party starts as soon as we close ourselves into the back seat of this limo. So lighten up. Don't worry so much. It'll be safe in the trunk.

Belfry just shrugged, but couldn't help wonder how his older brother could let a case packed tight with hundred dollar bills to the tune of seventy thousand dollars out of his sight.

The drive down to Kentucky was a rolling party. Neither Meg nor Ginevra had ever been in a limo before and the interior of that long black Caddy was leather luxurious. The drinks of the day were beer and tequila sunrises poured out of the bar that opened in the back of the driver's compartment.

The girls got to know each other.

As per his uncle's orders, Ernie kept the curtains closed. He got no complaints on the music he played on the radio. He switched between a romantic, easy listening station and Country and Western, but the couples in the back didn't seem to care.

They left Wabash City about two on that Friday afternoon and got through Indy with no problem. The 500 race wasn't until Sunday. When they got to Newport, Kentucky, Ernie spoke for the second time on the four-hour trip to ask for directions. The first time he'd said two words, "yes ma'am," when one of the women had asked if they could stop to go to a ladies' room.

J.T. directed him to a brand new Holiday Inn in a little town called Southgate, one exit on the highway past Newport.

One of our friends down here said this was the best place to stay, J.T. explained to Meg and Ginevra.

On the way there, they drove past *The Crossroads Inn* and a river of memories flowed through Meg's mind in a brief glimpse.

The rooms in the new motel were clean and the beds were big, only one in each of the adjoining rooms.

You girls make yourselves comfortable, J.T. leered at them. We'll be right back. Gotta make some phone calls.

Meg noticed that he and Belfry took the briefcase with them when they left.

Little Big Man

By Friday Bobby Tyler had fanned the flames of his hatred so hot that he was ready to move on the Smales.

He did two spoons of coke in the parking lot outside of *Tippers* before he went in, some of the last stuff left over from the days when ol' Johnny Ferris would give him and Wink all they wanted. *This is for both Wink and Ferris too,* Bobby decided as he put a fresh clip into his big old service forty-five and got out of the truck.

It was about eleven and the strippers were doing table dances all around the room when he came through the door. He was high and wired and heavily armed, but he had no intention of doing anything inside the club in the middle of that crowd of witnesses. For now he just wanted to find the Smales, fix on his targets like they used to tell him in training camp before he went to Vietnam.

He stopped inside the door to see if any of the Smale brothers were there. He scanned the room the way he used to check the perimeter of a camp at night. The only Smale he saw was Hump sitting at the bar.

He hesitated a minute, trying to decide whether he should go in or not. *Hump's a moron,* he thought and that's what decided him. *Maybe he can tell me where his brothers are.*

Hey Hump, business looks good, Bobby went right up to the bar and sat down next to him.

Yeah, business looks good. Hump was confused. What are you doing here? You and your brother never come in here.

My brother's dead, remember?

Oh yeah. Sorry. I forgot. I heard about that.

Where's J.T.?

Not here.

You all alone tonight?

Yeah, I am.

Bobby couldn't believe that J.T. and Belfry Smale had left Hump alone and in charge of their business.

They comin' in later?

You want somethin' with 'em?

No. No. I'm just out havin' a few beers.

Three hours later, Hump was poring over the directions J.T. had written down on a piece of paper for him.

1. Help settle with the dancers.
2. Help turn off all the lights, empty the trash and make sure nothing is left that could start a fire.
3. Do a final check to make sure all the doors to the club are locked.

Hump followed the directions perfectly.

Hump checked the front door. Locked.

He came back for one last check on the back door. *Can't be too careful,* Hump took his responsibility seriously. *Locked.* That was when Bobby Tyler stuck his gun right in the middle of Hump's back. When Hump started to turn around, Bobby jabbed him hard with the gun right in the middle of his spine.

Ow!

Hump, you moron. Get in your car and drive.

At the body shop, Bobby handcuffed Hump to the hanging chain of a block and tackle and raised his hands over his head until Hump was on tiptoe. Then he punched him as hard as he could in the stomach, so hard it spun him all the way around.

Ow! Hump puked beer all over himself.

That was for my brother. This is for John Ferris.

And he hit Hump again, hard, in the face.

Ahhh! When Hump's head snapped back, he looked at Bobby wide-eyed as if he were totally clueless why this was happening to him. His lip was split and he was bleeding from the mouth. His eyes screamed out confusion.

Bobby just stared at him, waiting, trying to control himself and keep from beating him to death right there on the spot.

Who's John Ferris? Hump finally asked through the blood and split lip.

That's when it dawned on Bobby Tyler. Hump Smale didn't know shit, had no clue what was going on in Wabash City or with his brothers' dealings.

Where's your brothers? Where's J.T. and Belfry? I'll beat it out of you, you fuck, and he raised his fist.

No, don't hit me. They're not here.

Where are they?

They went to Kentucky for the weekend.

Kentucky. What's in Kentucky?

They took girls with them. In Billy Keirce's limo.

Girls? Limo?

One of the dancers.

Where in Kentucky?

I don't know. Hump was just starting to realize that he was talking too much. Unfortunately, that realization was written all over his weasel face.

I think you do, and Bobby hit him again hard in the kidneys as he spun around on the block and tackle.

Where are they?

Newport. Newport, Kentucky.

Why are they down there?

I don't know. For the holiday weekend. I don't know.

Suddenly, Bobby Tyler was tired. Four in the morning. He'd been drinking all week. All that thinking about his dead brother, the Smales, revenge. Looking at Hump Smale, he realized there was probably nothing more to get out of him. He felt too tired to even hit him again. He lowered Hump to the ground and just left him hanging there. He had to think and he was too tired to do it. He moved to the ratty old couch against the wall and fell asleep almost right away.

The next morning they were halfway to Kentucky in Bobby Tyler's pick-up truck before Hump Smale woke up.

After lying on the cold garage floor all night while Bobby slept, Hump was like a passed-out drunk when Bobby put him in the truck. He left Hump in handcuffs and tied wire around Hump's neck and pulled it tight to a rib in the truck wall behind the seat. Hump could hardly move and he quickly fell asleep.

When Hump Smale woke up, he had no idea where he was or what they were doing.

We're goin' to Newport, Kentucky, to see your butt-hole brothers, Bobby Tyler informed him.

Good. They'll fix you, Hump spit back at him like some kid in a schoolyard.

Bobby Tyler just laughed.

Where would a bunch of partiers in an out-of-town limo go tonight in Newport? Bobby Tyler asked the attendant at the gas station.

Probably wouldn't go nowhere in Newport.

Whattaya mean?

All the limos from Cincy tonight will be headin' straight for South-gate.

What's Southgate?

There's a big ol' nightclub there. Dinner, dancin,' big name enter-tainment. That's where the limos go after they cross the river.

You seen a black Caddy limo drivin' around? Indiana plates? You gassed one up?

Nope.

How do you get to this Southgate?

Babylon Revisited

Wow, that's the first time we've done it in a bed, J.T. hooted when he was finished.

I think I like it better in the boxing ring, Meg counterfeited enthusiasm and naughtiness.

J.T. just laughed: I like wherever I can get you, baby. And he laid back on the pillows very pleased with himself. You gotta admit, this ain't bad.

Not bad, no, not bad at all.

Now don't you go to sleep on me, girl.

Aw c'mon, just a little nap. This is so cool, not havin' to work at *Tippers* all weekend.

OK, but tonight we're goin' gamblin.' Put on your good luck shoes.

Gambling? You'll have to show me how. I've never been gambling before.

Don't worry about that. You'll love it. Then tomorrow you can sleep in 'til noon if you want. Me and Belfry got some business to take care of tomorrow morning. Then tomorrow night we're goin' to a nightclub. See John Davidson. Front row table.

No problem there, Meg laughed. I'll bet I could sleep even later than that.

That night Meg found the gambling boring, but Ginevra seemed to really enjoy it. They found themselves in a smoky basement underneath a Chinese restaurant called *The Dragon Inn*. It was like a huge cave that seemed to wind and spread out beneath the city of Newport like some kind of ancient catacomb. For an underworld, it was actually pretty nice. It had wood floors and dim lights and the ever-present green felt of the gambling tables.

It was the idea of just throwing money down on a table and watching someone take it away that really put Meg off. Her dad would have hated it. For Ginevra, that seemed to be the attraction. She seemed to enjoy throwing money away. Meg hung out on Ginevra's shoulder most of the night, watching her bet on the crap table, the roulette table, finally settle down to play blackjack.

How much have you lost? Meg asked her toward the end of the evening.

Who knows? It's Belfry's money. He just gave it to me and told me to go have fun. He and his brother are over on the crap table.

When they got back to the motel that night, J.T. asked her how she did.

I didn't really play too much. I won a couple of times. Here's the money back you gave me.

No. No. Keep it. Buy yourself something. I figured you'd lose it all anyway. And he rolled over laughing, fell asleep, and was soon snoring loudly.

Meg wasn't as lucky. It was almost five AM before she dozed off. She never heard J.T. go out Saturday morning. When she woke up it was almost noon, the sun was bright, the bed was warm, and she felt like she'd been J.T. Smales' whore all her life.

Hearing noises, Meg knocked on Ginevra's door.

C'mon in, honey. This is great. I made coffee. There's a coffee pot right here in the room. I gotta have coffee when I first get up.

Meg liked Ginevra. She was very direct. She had all sorts of questions.

How long have you been, uh, dating, I mean, J.T.'s girl?

Not long. Couple of weeks. Since I started working at the club.

I've been dating Belfry since March.

Do you find them scary?

Yeah, but exciting too.

Yeah, I know what you mean. Sure not boring.

What's stripping, dancing at a club like that, like?

The money's great. Sure beats waitressing. It's a good job. Different. For just a moment Meg wondered if Ginevra had been told to ask her all these questions. But they were just girl-type questions. Nothing really revealing.

Can you ever forget that you're naked in front of all those men?

Oh yeah. You've got to. You know what I do? Sometimes I pretend I'm at a beach party, dancing to a band in a little teeny bathing suit.

They both giggled at that.

J.T. and Belfry came back about one-thirty. They found Meg and Ginevra eating breakfast in the motel coffee shop. Meg had showered and done her hair and makeup.

What a waste of time that was, Meg thought as she and J.T. went back to bed for the afternoon.

J.T. and Belfry really got dressed up for Saturday night, their big night on the town. Polished boots, tapered boot-leg pants, sports jackets and ties. J.T. had a fancy Western cut jacket on, a grey tweed with a light beige suede yoke across the shoulders. Belfry's jacket was more tailored, a wide-whale blue corduroy. J.T. had on a Western string tie with a turquoise inlaid medallion for a knot. Again, Belfry had a regular necktie on, red against his dark blue shirt. J.T. looked like a dressed-up cowboy. Belfry looked like what he was, a gangster.

You two get out of here, Ginevra shooed them out of the motel rooms. Come back in a half hour and we'll be unbelievably beautiful.

Tomorrow morning we get the hell out of here early, J.T. reassured Belfry in the bar.

Good, I wanna get this stuff back to Wabash City.

Those suitcases with the fake bottoms are a great idea.

Hey, that's what you pay me for brother.

When they got back to the rooms, the connecting door to Belfry and Ginevra's room was closed and Ginevra yelled, "You can't come in yet," when Belfry knocked.

Why not?

Just sit down. It's a surprise.

When the door opened finally, they were treated to a fashion show.

Ginevra, followed by Meg, paraded out, then back and forth in front of them like two models on a runway in Paris. Ginevra had on the most beautiful black cocktail dress Meg had ever seen. Cut just below the knee, it had a plunging V-neck and really neat fringed long sleeves. Meg's dress was Chinese style, slit up both sides to mid-thigh. She had bought it to go to a Spring dance last year at Ohio State with a fraternity boy whose name she couldn't even remember. It had a black background with a white floral print overlayed on it.

Whoa. Look at you two.

Oh baby!

J.T. and Belfry were duly impressed.

What are we gonna do tonight? Ginevra never seemed to run out of questions.

You'll see.

What? Is it a secret?

We've got friends down here. They're gonna take care of us. You girls'll like where we're goin' tonight.

The fashion show was fun, Meg thought as they got in the limo, *but really strange, almost as if they were normal people playing dress up.*

The Good Soldier

Jess couldn't help but worry.

Meg had taken off for Kentucky.

Before he'd left, Mal had told her not to go to work at the strip club that night because the undercover operation was officially over.

She could have put in the whole weekend studying for her Hydraulics exam, but she just couldn't concentrate.

Maybe she was worried about Meg (and Mal).

Maybe she was feeling left out and treated like a weak child.

Maybe she just had basic problems with authority.

Mal had ordered her to stay put in Wabash City, so she decided to do just the opposite.

Before she hit the interstate for Kentucky, she stopped at Jackie's and borrowed a brunette wig.

As Jess drove south in Meg's car, John Davidson was finishing his part of the sound check. The orchestra still had to finish theirs. He made his way through the deserted kitchen to a door that opened out to the back of the building. It was really a nice setting for this nightclub, perched high up on a hill with a wide grassy lawn all around it. Outside, sitting against the back wall, smoking, was a young man. *A club worker* John Davidson assumed as he came through the door.

Mr. Davidson, the young smoker jumped to his feet.

Hi. Hi there. I didn't mean to startle you.

Hey. No problem. I was just having a smoke, taking a break.

Could I borrow one of those from you?

Sure. Of course. Help yourself, and Tim Mounce handed his pack over, scrambled in his pockets for his lighter.

They smoked silently in the late afternoon sunshine.

What do you do here?

I'm a busboy.

That's work, especially in such a big place.

Aw, it's not that bad. I'm saving up for college.

Hey, that's great. Thanks for the cigarette.

No problem. Have a good show tonight.

Thanks.

Deliverance

Bobby Tyler and Hump Smale had been sitting in the car in *The Beverly Hills Supper Club* parking lot for almost an hour before the black Cadillac limo with the Indiana plates pulled up to the front door to unload.

There they are! Bobby Tyler couldn't hide his excitement.

That's Billy Kierce's limo alright. Hump was dying for a cigarette.

The two of them watched as J.T., Belfry and the two girls got out. Hump wanted to yell for help at the top of his voice so that his two brothers would come and get him, but he knew it wouldn't do any good, would just piss Bobby Tyler off more. They were parked way too far from the front door where the limo had pulled up, and out of just a cracked window his voice would never carry that far.

We're goin' in there, Bobby Tyler was making up his plan as he went along.

Can't you take these cuffs off? Hump whined.

No.

People'll see 'em if we go in there. They won't let us in. I'm tellin' ya. Besides, it's hard as hell to smoke a cigarette with these things on. Gimme a break.

OK, and he unlocked Hump's handcuffs, but we ain't goin' in the front door anyway. I need to see what's goin' on before I go against your brothers by myself.

Where are we goin' then?

We'll find another way in, then you and I will join them at their table. That oughta be a nice surprise. Then we'll all be together and I'll find out which one o' you killed my brother.

A one-lane driveway from the parking lot curved slightly downhill around the side of the brightly lit nightclub. Bobby Tyler, prodding Hump Smale in the back with his gun, decided to see where it went. It dead-ended at a loading dock on the lowest level of the building.

When Bobby tried the door next to the overhead door of the loading dock, he found it open and pushed Hump in.

They were in the huge whitewashed basement of the nightclub. It was a long, wide, low-ceilinged open area studded with the load-bearing columns that held up the building. It was also a disorganized cluttered mess, a storage dump for everything the nightclub wanted to keep out of sight.

All along one wall were industrial size washers, dryers, sinks, troughs, a fork-lift, pallets with bundles of table cloths and cloth napkins and uniforms piled up. Cleaning materials—mops, wheeled buckets, plastic drums—were strewn about the floor and leaned against the columns. The aisles between the columns were filled with wheeled laundry hampers, large canvas baskets filled with dirty linens. Way down at the other end from where they entered was the furnace and a whole wall of electrical boxes. Cardboard boxes filled with all sorts of restaurant supplies stacked to the ceiling lined the whole length of another wall.

We're in, Bobby Tyler informed Hump Smale as they stood inside the door and took in the cluttered, low-ceilinged room.

This basement was deserted. Everyone was upstairs working.

Bobby waved his gun at Hump to move.

Hump was just happy he wasn't poking him in the back with it anymore. His hands were loose, he was smoking a cigarette, and there wasn't a soul around in this basement.

This is my best chance, Hump got his first brave thought.

They explored the basement.

Here, stop. Bobby waved the gun at Hump.

Hump flipped his cigarette into a nearby aluminum sanitary sink. He heard it 'hiss' out as it hit the wet drain. But it gave him an idea. He looked around. There were laundry hampers everywhere. Bottles of liquid cleaners sat under the sinks.

He lit another cigarette. He flicked his lighter on and off two, three times. *This is perfect,* he thought.

The plan blossomed inside his limited mind like a spiky weed. He'd start a fire in one of the hampers. That would distract Bobby. Then he'd go for the gun. A simple plan, the best Hump Smale could do.

Bobby Tyler leaned over a pallet of white linen bundles.

Hump dropped his lit cigarette into a hamper of dirty laundry, and quickly lit another.

Hey, look at this, Bobby turned and held up what looked like a white jacket.

What is it?

A busboy's or bartender's jacket. Put it on. They'll think we work here. He handed it to Hump.

When Bobby turned back to get one for himself, Hump dropped another cigarette into another hamper of dirty laundry. Bobby only took his eyes off Hump for a split second, but Hump's timing was good and Bobby never saw him flick it.

Hump lit another cigarette. He loved to light fires. He couldn't wait for the moment when they would flare up.

Put it on, Bobby ordered.

They both dressed themselves as bartenders or busboys or waiters.

Hey, Bobby was proud of their disguise, this is great. Now nobody'll stop us or ask who we are.

The first hamper burst into flames behind him.

What the . . . Bobby ran to the hamper for a closer look.

Then the second hamper flared up off to his side.

You son of a bitch, he turned to his prisoner, but Hump was already charging him. Instinctively, Bobby pulled the trigger.

Hump Smale lurched backward like he'd been hit by a ball bat, went to his knees, then collapsed on his back on the floor.

The flames were leaping from the two hampers.

A small flower of bright red was growing in the center of the stark white jacket that covered Hump Smale's chest.

Bobby panicked. He ran for the loading dock door where they'd come in. When he got to his car, he realized that whatever he had been doing was finished. He got in and drove away.

It took long minutes for Hump Smale to die. He lay on his back holding his chest like the little Dutch boy, trying to stop the warm flow out of the hole in his body. Looking up at the low ceiling of that basement, he caught sight of his fire spreading.

It was the perfect fire.

Fire burns upward. That was one of the few things Hump Smale knew and understood. The dirty sheets and the towels, the table linens, the waste paper, the cleaning materials, all the fuel stored in that basement also seemed to understand that full well.

Hump hadn't even meant to start a big fire, just a couple of baskets flaring up as a diversion. But the whole place had gone up like tinder and now that it was burning it was beautiful. Lying on the floor with Bobby Tyler's bullet burning in his chest, that fire spreading, licking upward along the walls, flowing across the ceiling was the most beautiful thing he'd ever seen, his finest creation.

Hump Smale felt he was going to die an artist. *This is where I belong,* he thought as the bullet burned in his chest and the flames closed in fast all around him.

The House of Mirth

No. That's alright. I'll park it myself, the young limo driver waved off the parking attendant at the front entrance to *The Beverly Hills Supper Club* as he opened the door for his riders.

What a cool place, Meg said to everyone else as they got out of the big black limo. It was a warm May night and the girls weren't even wearing wraps. *The Beverly Hills Supper Club* sat at the top of a high grassy hill at the end of a long winding drive underneath the arc of a sky-patrolling spotlight and a full hunter's moon.

Look, just like Hollywood and the movies, Ginevra pointed up at the spotlight moving across the night sky.

Yeah, nice place. J.T. seemed distracted as he climbed out. You stay with the car, kid, he warned their driver in a threatening growl. Don't let it out of your sight.

Yes, sir.

Inside, the club was a fairyland. Light, like the sparkle off of diamonds, twinkling from crystal chandeliers, gave a romantic glimmer to every room. Each table was candlelit sending soft flutters of light up into the air to meet the darting sparkles of the crystal. In every room (and there were many smaller dining rooms off the large main showroom) the low candlelight sent out a lush, sexy aura around the couples dining at the tables.

The Smale party, J.T. announced to the maitre'd at the small podium in the archway to the main showroom.

Gropper better have done this right or I'll kill him, Belfry whispered to J.T. as the black tie'd maitre'd consulted his list.

Yes Mr. Smale, right this way please, and he led the four of them in a parade all the way to the front of the dining room to a table flush up against the low stage. The girls turned a lot of heads as they passed through the room. It made Ginevra feel awfully good about the black V-necked dress she had picked out for this night.

Hey, Gropper did us pretty good, Belfry nudged J.T. as the tuxedoed maitre'd seated the ladies.

Yeah, he said he'd set us up. Great table.

What's the show? Ginevra asked when they were all seated.

John Davidson, the white-gloved maitre'd informed them before he receded back into the middle class sections of the room.

John Davidson, wow, did you hear that?

Oh, he is soooo handsome.

Who the . . . who's John Davidson? Belfry asked.

Oh you know, the TV star, the singer. You've seen him.

The fan magazines say he's the new Troy Donahue.

Who's the old Troy Donahue? J.T. laughed with a wink to Belfry.

Ginevra looked at Meg with disgust for the two redneck hicks sitting at their table.

So, Belfry tried to appease her, this John Davidson's a pretty big deal for Kentucky?

I'd say so. Ginevra laughed at his ignorance.

I think he'll put on a really good show. Meg resorted to her sunshine Barbie act to edge away from Ginevra's disdain.

Hey, let's eat. J.T. changed the subject much more abruptly.

It wasn't much of a menu. Only four choices. Steak. Chicken. Pork chops. Shrimp. The men ordered steak. Ginevra, ever adventurous, ordered the shrimp. Meg got the chicken. They all got a foil-wrapped baked potato and some green beans that looked like they'd been sitting in lukewarm water in the kitchen since Christmas. J.T. ordered two bottles of Lambrusco to drink with their meal.

Oh, the bubbles always go to my nose, Ginevra giggled.

Meg wished she could be having the carefree good time that Ginevra was.

Meg's first big surprise of the evening came when she finished eating and a busboy showed up to clear their table.

Here ma'am, allow me, she heard a voice at her elbow and looked right up into the beaming face of Tim, the busboy from *The Crossroads Inn* that she had met what seemed so long ago in such an innocent time.

Omigod, she didn't know whether she said it out loud or to herself or if anyone heard her.

The busboy had clearly already recognized her and was flashing her an ear-to-ear Cheshire Cat grin.

Hey, he whispered, how's it goin'?

Meg quickly turned her head away from the others and put her finger to her lips in a silencing gesture.

Thank god! Smart boy, she inhaled in relief as he took her meaning right away, straightened up and left with the dishes.

It was almost nine by the time they finished eating and Ginevra gave Meg the high sign to accompany her to the ladies room.

Time to powder my nose, Ginevra bent over and said louder than she needed to in Belfry's ear.

Yeah right, Belfry gave a little tight-lipped laugh as he answered, as if there was some inside joke they were sharing.

Isn't this place something? Ginevra raved as they stood in front of the mirrors in the ladies room.

Megan's Inferno

Meg was halfway to the table, weaving through the huge room behind Ginevra, when she saw them. Two men had joined their table. *Pulled up chairs from adjoining tables and sat down,* she guessed. They were smiling and talking to J.T. and Belfry.

Ginevra, hey, I've gotta go back to the rest room. Be right back. Meg turned and fled.

When she reached the safety of one of the arches into a smaller side dining room she stopped and looked back. Ginevra was just sitting down. Introductions were being made. Meg was sure the men hadn't seen her. She didn't know what to do.

Hey honey, where you goin'?

The voice sounded familiar, then unmistakable. When she turned to it though, she was looking right into the rhinestone dotted eyeglasses of an outrageously curly big-haired brunette.

What are you doing here?

No idea.

No idea. What does that mean?

I just thought you might need me here. I am your kickboxing dyke bodyguard, you know. Have been ever since we started this undercover stuff.

Where did you get that fright wig? Meg had to smile at Jess's get-up.

Jackie. You like it? I do. Always wanted to be one of those curly-haired Barbie dolls.

Jess, I'm in trouble. I've gotta go back there. Those two cops from here know me, and they're sitting at our table.

You smell something?

It's probably just the cigarette smoke. I've gotta go back there. They'll recognize me.

Maybe they won't. Maybe they'll leave.

I can only stay so long.

Why don't we just get out of here? Mal's in the bar. I saw him. Let him handle these guys.

But then I'll never find out who killed my dad. I'm so close.

What are you gonna do?

If they recognize me, I'm just going to confront them with it.

They'll kill you.

Not in this room in the middle of a thousand people eating dinner. Not in front of John Davidson.

Ooh, John Davidson. Really?

Really.

So you're going back to the table? Bad idea.

I know. Maybe they won't remember me. I look different. It's been two months.

Look. The band's playing now. Wait 'til Davidson comes on. Then they'll be looking at the stage. You can keep your hand up to your face. Maybe the lights will be down lower. Maybe they won't recognize you.

Let's hope.

I'll be watching. I'll try to get closer.

Meg left her standing there.

✗

Mal had never let Meg out of his sight from the moment she left Wabash City in the limo with the Smales.

He followed them to the motel, sat in the car in the parking lot when they checked into the room. Staked the room out all night, drinking coffee, reading a newspaper, having dirty thoughts, finally falling asleep in the wee hours against his will. He wanted this under-cover over, this crazy schoolgirl safe.

A headlined story in that day's newspaper—

> DRUGS AFFLICT NATION'S HEARTLAND
> Report Names 43 Operations

—caught his attention like an omen or a warning that it was time to close up shop on this one, get the girl out safe before the Smales got suspicious and started looking around them. "The report, which named 43 drug-trafficking organizations ranging from the Medellin cartel to the Hell's Angels motorcycle gang, divulged information only on completed investigations and prosecutions, not ongoing projects" the newspaper story read. *I wonder if we're one of those 'ongoing projects.'*

Saturday morning when the Smales left together Mal decided to follow them. He stayed well back. It was really a small town without much morning traffic. He had binoculars and could spy on them from a distance. The suitcases and the briefcase were the tip-off. They went into the normal looking house on the suburban street with the Smales. When the brothers came out, they were minus the briefcase. The driver pulled into the garage and helped them get the bags out of the trunk, but couldn't close the garage door because the limo was too long. *These guys are a piece of work,* was all that Mal could think, *but as soon as they cross the Indiana line with that dope, I got 'em.*

That night he followed them to the nightclub. He waited a good ten minutes before he followed them in. Their table sure wasn't hard to find. It was right in front of the stage. He found a seat at the bar in an adjacent room where he could see their table through an arched doorway. He nursed two beers for an hour while he watched them eat and two other men joined their table.

Smokiest bar I ever drank in, he thought as the show began on the stage.

Meg took Jess's advice. She hid out in the ladies room for five, then ten, minutes. Nobody came looking for her. When she came out, John Davidson was just being introduced. The lights had been dimmed and the room was smoky. *Maybe Jess's plan will work,* Meg hoped as she made her way through the room to their table.

John Davidson moved quietly into his first song: *There's a kind of hush (all over the world) tonight.*

The audience was suitably hushed.

Meg tried to sneak up on the table, sit down without anyone realizing she had returned.

Jess was right. The lights were dim. Smoke seemed to hang thicker than usual in the air. Everyone at the table was listening to the famous singer. Meg thought she might actually go unrecognized.

But just as she sat down the young cop, Mayes, turned and looked at her, nodded, turned back to the stage, then turned and looked back at her again. He'd recognized her. She knew he had.

But he didn't do anything right away, just turned back to the stage, thinking through the possibilities, wondering what she was doing here.

John Davidson sang on.

Meg caught movement out of the corner of her eye and spotted Jess sitting down in an empty chair two tables away.

Mayes, the younger cop, leaned forward and whispered in Gropper's ear. The fat cop evidently didn't hear him clearly because he cupped his ear and motioned for the young to cop to say it again.

For lovers in love, John Davidson crooned.

Gropper's head snapped around and looked straight at Meg.

He turned quickly away, reached out and grabbed Belfry by the shoulder. What's she doing here? he demanded loudly.

She's J.T.'s girl, Belfry had been startled by Gropper's tone.

The people at the next table were "shushing" them.

Now everyone was looking at her—J.T., Ginevra, all of them.

Meg's hand moved into the purse in her lap and wrapped around the small handgun she had brought with her but had never fired except on the range.

The whole table was looking at her.

Even John Davidson had mysteriously stopped singing.

What's wrong? J.T. asked.

What's she doing here? Gropper demanded, pointing at Meg.

She's my date. She works for me at the club, a dancer.

More 'shushing' from the tables around them.

But John Davidson wasn't even singing.

Tim Mounce, the busboy, had walked onto the stage and taken the microphone out of the hands of the famous singer.

Her old man's the guy who got killed by mistake. Gropper was trying to make Belfry understand.

What are you talking about?

The girl. Her name's O'Neill. Her father's the guy that got hit by mistake.

Ladies and Gentlemen, please stay calm, Tim was speaking into the microphone from the stage.

Meg, what's he talking about? J.T. seemed really slow on the pickup.

My God, she's got a gun, Meg heard one of the 'shushers' from the next table shout and realized that her hand was out of her purse and the small gun was moving in a slow arc from one to another of the men across the table from her.

. . . . we have a minor fire in the dining room. We ask you to get up and move slowly toward the exits in the rear.

Who killed my father? Meg was screaming at them.

All four of the men stared at her, at the gun, in disbelief.

WHO KILLED MY FATHER?

FIRE! FIRE!

Everyone around them was screaming, then moving, moving frantically.

For some reason the band started playing again. John Davidson had the microphone back.

Meg, now cool it. Give me that, and J.T. was moving around the table toward her.

Smoke seemed to be flooding into the room out of the walls, gathering up around the crystal chandeliers.

Meg pointed the gun at J.T. and he stopped moving toward her.

Don't panic people. Move slowly to the exits in the rear.

Jesus, this place is on fire. We gotta get outa here, Ginevra implored the others at the table.

WHO KILLED MY FATHER?

DAMMIT MEG, GIVE ME . . . J.T.'s voice trailed off. Meg had shot him in the chest.

It was an accident. She hadn't meant to shoot J.T. His sudden move toward her had startled her. The gun had just gone off. Accidentally.

J.T. staggered backwards, then just sat down in a chair next to the table, holding his chest, looking up at Meg in disbelief. All the others stood like they were paralyzed, staring at her.

All around them people were running for the exits, running up against each other, running over each other.

For some reason, the band was playing again and John Davidson was speaking, not singing, into the microphone.

Through the crowd, for just a moment, Meg saw Mal's face, trying to fight his way through the panicked people, trying to get to her side.

When she turned back, Belfry was moving, coming around the table, lunging for her gun. He grabbed it, tore it out of her hand.

But just as he got it from her, out of the corner of her eye Meg saw a swift movement. Jesse kicked him square in the face.

Jess's high kick knocked Belfry straight backward onto the table. The table broke under his sudden weight sending glasses, plates, wine bottles, silverware all cascading to the floor. Meg's gun flew out of his hand and off into the chaos of the room.

Meg felt Mal beside her, Jess on her other side. She found her voice. Ginevra and the two Newport cops, stunned, were still standing behind the broken table looking at her. Belfry lay, momentarily subdued, on the floor.

WHO KILLED MY FATHER? Meg screamed at them again.

Silence.

Smoke clotted around them.

J.T. made sick gurgling sounds in the chair, holding his chest.

Smoke moved like waves up around the chandeliers still brightly lit.

Then most of the lights went out.

The music suddenly went dead. The musicians were getting up to leave.

John Davidson was still at the microphone. Tim the busboy was still next to him, feeding him directions.

Stay calm, John Davidson implored. Come up to the stage. There is an exit here behind the stage.

WHO KILLED MY FATHER?

It was as if this last repetition of Meg's question slapped Gropper and Mayes into action. In uncanny synchronization, they both went for their guns.

Don't do it! Mal was next to her. His police special .38 extended at arms' length and held in both hands was aimed right at the two Newport cops.

Mal's shouted order stopped the young policeman, Mayes, right in the act of drawing his gun, but it didn't stop Gropper. His gun came out and was coming up when Mal dropped him with one shot to his stomach.

Gropper catapulted backward like he'd been kicked by a horse.

Mal stood stock still, his gun steady in both hands, in the middle of the total confusion of the room.

Young Mayes looked down at his partner writhing on the floor with a bullet in his belly, looked back at Mal's gun leveled right on him, looked around at the mob of people running, screaming, fighting to escape, and wisely decided not to draw his gun.

Tim Mounce was down off the stage, at their table.

Follow me. Follow me, he was shouting at them. This way. This way. You can get out.

Decision time.

Belfry was up on his feet, but he no longer was coming after Meg. He was standing over, staring down at his dying older brother.

Both Mal and Jesse grabbed Meg by the arms, pulled her toward the stage in the wake of the busboy's orders.

Mayes saw his chance. He turned and ran. Mal let him go, holstered his gun. Mayes disappeared into the crowd and the thickening smoke.

The busboy was shouting 'Follow me. Follow me,' and they did. But Mal suddenly dropped Meg's arm and went back for Ginevra who was standing as still as if she'd been turned into a pillar of salt. Smoke was all around them. Ginevra was in shock. She acted as if she didn't even know where she was.

❧

Belfry was unaware of the others, unaware of them running away, unaware of the smoke and the sudden heat, unaware of the chaos all around, the people screaming. His eyes narrowed to a close tunnel of vision through which all he could see was J.T. His brother was sitting in front of him on a chair, holding his chest and looking up at him. Strange gurgling sounds struggled out of J.T.'s mouth as if he was trying to tell him something important.

Belfry went down on one knee next to J.T. and leaned in close to hear what his older brother was trying to say. Only dull clogged sounds were coming out of J.T.'s mouth on a sudden torrent of blood.

J.T. suddenly toppled straight forward off of the chair. Belfry tried to catch him, break his fall, but J.T.'s weight sprawled them both out flat on the floor. It took Belfry a minute to get his brother turned over and J.T.'s head cradled in his arms, but by then it was too late. J.T. stared wide-eyed up with that unmistakable blank look of the dead.

Belfry realized it was over. There was nothing more he could do. He came out of the strange trance he'd gone into when he first saw J.T. looking up at him, begging for help. The smoke was heavy around him, choking thick.

WHO KILLED MY FATHER? For some reason that woman's accusing screams echoed in Belfry's mind.

That bitch killed him, Belfry eased his dead brother out of his arms and laid him out gently on the floor.

Then Belfry was up and moving, looking for a way out.

❧

This way. C'mon, follow me. Meg's busboy from *The Crossroads Inn* was leading her and the others through the thickening smoke and the now blistering heat. C'mon. Hurry up. This way, he begged them.

He led them right up on the stage at the front of the room.

The orchestra was gone, but John Davidson was still at the microphone that still seemed to be working just fine. Come to my voice, Davidson was crooning. There's a way out.

Tim had Meg by the wrist and the others were all around her, following. Suddenly, all the lights went out. He led them across the stage and back through the wings to a line of people crowding frantically through an open door.

There, he pointed, it goes out. He shook Meg as if she was a child and he was trying to get her attention. Then he turned away from her and was gone, disappearing back into the smoke and the dark.

They struggled, Jess holding Meg by the arm, Mal pulling the catatonic Ginevra along, but they finally made it to the backstage exit door.

When Meg staggered through the open door and burst into the cool, clean air of the outside it was like running and jumping into a clear, fresh lake.

Other people streamed out behind them. The line of people in front of them who had pushed their way through the door dispersed as soon as they hit the open air, broke into fragments and fled, running as fast as they could across the grassy lawn trying to get as far away from the building as possible as if it was an airplane about to explode.

Mal and Jess and Meg and Ginevra stayed together until they were about fifty yards out into the grass, but then Mal stopped, thinking. They all turned back to look at the building.

They were on the back side of *The Beverly Hills Supper Club* on a flat, wide grassy lawn that ran to a steep wooded hill that flowed down to the highway below. Smoke was streaming out of open windows along the back of the building and out of the exit door they had just come through. A few people were still straggling out of that open door. One of the last to escape through the door was Tim the busboy pulling John Davidson, the Hollywood star, behind him by the lapels of his sport coat. Fifteen yards from the door both of them collapsed, gasping on the grass.

True Confessions

Look, stay here. Don't move. I gotta be able to find you. I gotta go. It was as if Mal realized he couldn't just sit down and gasp for air with the others. He had to go back to being a cop.

Where are you going? Meg grabbed the tail of his coat.

I gotta get around in front where all the people are coming out.

Stay here.

No. There's still Belfry Smale and that young cop to deal with. And the dope.

Don't go. Let's stay together.

Meg, I can't. Look, you and Jess watch that back door. See if either Belfry Smale or the young cop come out that way. I'm pretty sure J.T. and the fat cop didn't make it.

This whole place is going to burn down and people are going to die in there, aren't they?

A lot of people, I'm afraid. Look, and he pointed to Ginevra, take care of her too, whoever she is. I gotta go.

While the back of *The Beverly Hills Supper Club* had opened out into a grassy green field of fresh air and the exhilaration of survival, the front of *The Beverly Hills Supper Club* was closed down into dangerous chaos. The front door opened right into the huge parking lot whose every space was filled with the cars of the Memorial Day partiers. When Mal ran out from behind the burning building, not only was the parking lot jammed with cars but it was also crowded with people, gasping for air, throwing up, many of them collapsed on the ground, men and women alike holding each other close, sobbing in fear and pain, trying to help others, help themselves, trying to get away, flee, survive. It was the chaos of a bombed city in wartime, a London or a Pearl Harbor. When he came around the corner of the building, it was all spread out in front of him.

He stopped and took it all in. He scanned the parking lot. He felt remarkably calm, focused, considering all that had happened so quickly. He knew exactly what he was looking for—the limo he had watched them all arrive in. It was parked at the very edge of the parking lot near the mouth of the entrance drive that wound down the hill in a line of seven or eight other limos of various shapes and colors. The drivers, all in black coats, white shirts and black neckties, were huddled together near the head of the line of limos, all looking at the fire, all waiting to see if their passengers would make it out. Two of them were actually smoking cigarettes even though the air hung heavy with smoke.

But even as Mal picked out the Smale's limo, third in the line, pointed downhill, out of the corner of his eye he saw a running man burst out of the milling crowd around the open entrance doors of the night club.

No mistaking him. It was Belfry Smale. He ran focused on only one destination—the limo and the coke.

When he saw him coming, Billy Keirce's nephew, Belfry's driver, broke away from the huddle of the other limo drivers and ran to meet him beside the long black Cadillac.

Mr. Smale, thank God, you made it out. Where are the others?

Quick. Gimme the keys. The keys. I gotta git in the trunk.

Sure. Sure Mr. Smale, and the kid handed them over.

Belfry opened the trunk. The suitcases were there. He closed the trunk, turned back to the kid and hit him as hard as he could in the face.

The blow knocked Ernie head over heels and when he looked up Belfry Smale was already in the driver's seat and the big Caddy was roaring to life. Ernie felt for his nose but already knew it was broken. Blood, all warm and sticky, greeted his hand when it reached his face. He watched as his Uncle's black limo peeled out of the line of parked limos, scattered the huddle of limo drivers, and disappeared over the hill down the entrance driveway.

It all happened right in front of Mal—Belfry punching the limo driver, the limo careening off down the driveway. He started to run toward the action but he'd only gone about twenty yards when the limo disappeared over the hill.

He kept running across the outer edge of the parking lot and out onto the crest of the hill that extended down to the highway below.

He picked up the headlights of Belfry's limo racing down the winding drive, narrowly missing a collision with a fire truck trying to make a turn into the driveway at the bottom, then racing on the flat out Monmouth Street to the light where it intersected with the highway.

All Mal could do was stand and watch Belfry's flight. At the light, Belfry didn't continue straight on into Newport from Southgate. He turned right onto the highway, headed for Indiana.

You've got it with you, don't you? Mal knew. *That's why you checked out the trunk before you took off.*

Meg suddenly got up and left Jesse and Ginevra sitting on the grass. She crossed to where Tim Mounce was sitting, trying to recover like everyone else.

He was coughing and breathing in fresh air in large gulps when she sat down. John Davidson had been sitting with him, but his orchestra members had gathered around him, moved him off a bit. A newspaper reporter was already accosting Davidson. Tim was left alone.

You OK?

Yeah. Yeah. Too much smoke.

You saved my life, our lives, and she swept her eyes across the grass and the little cluster of people like themselves, recovering from the smoke, watching in awe as the building burned before their eyes. You must have led forty or fifty people out of the fire.

I was just the guy who knew where the back door was.

But you kept going back.

You were the only one I knew I had to get out. You and Mr. Davidson. He's a really nice guy, you know, for a Hollywood star and all.

You went back for me?

Yes.

Thanks.

Hey. That night with you, I'll never forget that night.

But . . . I, we. . . .

You were all my dreams come true.

Wow.

There he is. This young man right here. He's your hero. John Davidson, with two eager reporters in tow, interrupted them. He saved all these peoples' lives, and the movie star swept his arm across the whole grassy hillside, then reached down and pulled Tim Mounce to his feet. He's the young man I was telling you about. He led us all out of the fire.

But I didn't really . . . I just . . . I, Tim was badly flustered. A flash camera went off in his face.

You see there, and John Davidson, with another sweep of his arm, directed the attention of the reporters back to the fire. He saved all our lives. He was the last one out of that burning building.

I was? Tim Mounce sounded like Gomer Pyle.

That's right, a black Cadillac limousine, license number 79 E 4169. That's right, Tippecanoe County, Indiana.

Mal called from his own unmarked State Police car talking across the state line to a dispatcher in Lawrenceburg, Indiana and watching the nightclub burn right in front of his eyes. Bright orange flames were starting to dart out around the edges of the roof. Two fire engines had arrived and he could hear the sirens of others on their way, fighting their way up the winding driveway to the top of the hill.

He should enter Indiana on highway . . . Mal stopped to consult the roadmap spread out in his lap . . . highway 52 out of Covington, Kentucky. He's got a whole trunkload of cocaine and he's headed for Wabash City, Indiana. I don't care where you stop him, but make damn sure you stop him and get that dope. Oh yeah, he's dangerous. Go in with guns drawn and waste him if he blinks.

When he got off the radio, Mal just sat there, exhausted, relieved, so glad it was over with and he was done.

This undercover was shaky from the beginning, he thought. *Thank god those kids made it through alright. Thank god it's done.*

But he was wrong.

In front of him refugees from the fire were wandering over the parking lot. Many were dazed and shaken, sobbing and sick. Others were tending to the sick and injured stretched out like war wounded on the hard blacktop. It looked like the aftermath of a bomb going off. The supper club was now burning full blast. Fire engines ringed its front, pouring long streams of water on it to no avail. The heat came across the parking lot in waves.

This is like being in hell, Mal thought.

He started moving back toward where he had left Meg and Jess. Then, he saw the Newport cop, the young one. He didn't even know his name. The young cop was sitting against the rear tire of a car gasping for breath. Mal almost walked right by him.

The cop didn't see him.

It wasn't over yet. This was still a loose end.

You. Get up, Mal ordered. He had him covered with his police special.

It took Mayes a long moment just to clear his eyes and figure out where the voice that was ordering him up was coming from.

When he saw Mal's gun, he obeyed and got up.

Up against the car. Mal cuffed his hands behind his back.

Move. Mal marched him back behind the building to where he had left Meg and Jess.

Look what I found.

The three women had been sitting on the grass watching the smoke billow out of the rear exit of the building, the flames licking blue-orange around the edges of the roof.

When Mal arrived with his prisoner, they all stood up.

Belfry got away. He took the limo and booked. But their little playmate here was catching his breath when I found him.

Mayes stood sullen and silent.

Ginevra didn't react at all to the news of Belfry Smale's escape. She was still glassy-eyed and confused.

He knows, Meg took a step forward. He knows who killed my father. She slapped the prisoner hard in the face. Her voice was husky, either from all the smoke she had breathed in or from all the hate and confusion she was feeling.

Meg. Don't. Mal stepped between them.

He knows. Make him tell Mal, please. End it. Her voice was determined even though she was pleading.

Mal looked at her. Her eyes never wandered as she waited for his answer. He thought of all they'd been through, all that she'd done undercover to get them to this place, so close to the end.

Not here, he decided. There's too many people around. Over there. Over the crest of the hill. You'll talk to us over there, he pushed Mayes hard in the back with the barrel of his pistol to get him moving. Mal kept pushing him until they were halfway down the hill. The three women followed like mourners at a funeral.

Last March, in the motel room, who killed the wrong guy?

Mayes' face was just a black shadow in the darkness of the hill. He didn't say a word.

Last chance to do it easy, Mal coaxed him. Who killed the guy in the motel room?

I don't know, the black shadow spat at them.

Mal laughed. He'd really had enough of this case. He wanted it over with too. That was what he was thinking when he laughed again and slapped the dark shadow of Mayes' face hard with his gun. The blow knocked him to his knees in the sooty grass. Mal hit him again, this time with his open hand.

Tell me, Mal stood over him screaming. Tell me or I shoot you right here!

Mal slapped him once more before the crooked cop started to talk.

OK. OK, Gropper and that Belfry brother did the guy in the motel room. It was a mistake. They wanted to hit some drug dealer from Indiana they'd come down here after. It was all a mistake.

You're cops. What kind of a place is this? This time Mal went to his knees, grabbed the bent over shadow by the lapels of his coat, and shook him hard backwards.

The violent twisting knocked Mayes over and rolled him down the hill.

Mal chased after him like an animal.

The three women scurried behind like a lynch mob.

Don't. Don't hit me again.

You crooked little punk! Mal was on top of him, his gun pressed into his neck.

Don't kill me. Don't kill me. Mayes pleaded for his life.

What happened? Suddenly Mal's voice was no longer insane, murderous.

It was all Gropper, Gropper. He'd been working for the drug gangs for two years. He was cuttin' me in. Mayes' voice was terror-stricken. It was a mistake, he begged.

Who made the mistake?

I did. I did. His voice was shaking with fear.

What happened? Mal pressed the gun barrel harder into Mayes's throat, then let up on the pressure so he could talk. Mal was back in control (that is if he had ever really been out of control).

I was watchin' the motel. We didn't know if the guy was there or not. But there was a car we thought was his parked there. They'd told me the guy loved whores so when I saw the hooker go up to the room I figured that was the guy. So I called Gropper and they came over. When the whore left, they went in shootin' and it was the wrong guy, the wrong guy.

There, you happy now? Mal said it softly to Meg, not angrily, not judgmental, not sarcastic, just quietly.

Yes.

The Fire Next Time

165 people died in *The Beverly Hills Supper Club* fire. Many of the bodies were never identified. Belfry Smale crossed the Ohio-Kentucky line on Route 52 for Indianapolis at about 11:30 on that Saturday night. If you wouldn't have known, you would have probably thought it was just another black limousine driving some rich guys to Indianapolis for the next morning's 500 mile race. Thanks to Mal Rogers, the Indiana State Police knew better.

An unmarked highway patrol car picked up the limo as soon as it crossed the line and trailed it for about twenty miles until it was well into Indiana and surrounded by nothing but cornfields. Then the chase began.

Belfry had settled down since he'd been driving. He was obeying the speed limits, trying to keep as low a profile as he could in the big black limo.

When the unmarked car pulled up behind him and turned on its blinker lights and siren, Belfry, without hesitation, ran.

The Indiana State Police chased him up 52 at speeds reaching over a hundred miles an hour. But the limo, though it had a powerful engine, was big and bulky and slow. The highway patrol cars were much sleeker and faster. They ran the limo down within twenty miles. When Belfry refused to pull over, they took turns pulling up beside him and trying to shoot out his tires. It took three passes before one of the troopers was able to hit his target.

Belfry knew what his inept pursuers were trying to do, but it didn't make any difference. He kept going anyway, speeding up whenever he could but unable to shake them, looking for some turn to take, some way to escape, but not seeing anything promising. Every time he glanced over his shoulder at them, it seemed like another police car had joined the chase. When they shot out his tire, it almost came as a relief.

When the tire blew out, the limo careened right, left the road, almost jumped a ditch but caught its front tires on the ditch's grassy rim. When the tires caught, the limo's rear end pitched straight up in the air, cartwheeled over the front of the car, and sent the large black coffin of steel and leather and plastic and rubber into a series of end over end rolls that ended with it coming to rest on its top in a cornfield just before it burst into flame and sent a pillar of fire up into the night sky.

Civic Theatre

William J. Palmer

1 Trailer Park Nights

The Wabash flows past a trailer park just north of the twin towns. The trailer park sits just east of the historic battleground where Tecumseh and his Indian army made their last stand. But most of the people in it "don't know much about history" as that old song sang. In the summer of 1987 at least two residents of the Tippecanoe Trailer Park had a much more personal history on their minds.

"I'm a college graduate and I'm living in a trailer park!" Lori Martin screamed. She never let her husband finish delivering his customary getting-home-from-work-late apology. At one in the morning on a ninety-degree August night, her frustrated scream escaped through the open windows of space 87 and fled angrily down the corridor of pastel aluminum toward the open cornfields at the end of the moonlit gravel street.

"Take it easy hon, I had to work late. Then some of us went out to play softball. What's wrong with you tonight?"

She'd heard it all before, only this time she didn't want to hear it anymore. "I told you, but you don't listen."

"Hon, what's wrong? Have you been drinking?"

"I'll tell you what's wrong. Damn right I've been drinkin.' Ever since some motorcycle cowboy came staggering down the street and banged on my door yellin' 'Hey little blondie, hear your husband works late every night. You want some company, little blondie?' and he stands on our porch drinkin' beer before he takes a piss on the side of our trailer and lurches off to wake up the rest of the trailer park. Damn right I've been drinkin'! Damn right there's somethin' wrong!"

"I'm sorry . . ." but she cut him off again.

"Don't tell me you're sorry. That's not good enough. I'm a college graduate and I'm living in a trailer park," she repeated herself, not hearing the slips and slurs in her speech. "Lori, you're drunk. Keep your voice down. Neighbors can hear you all up and down the street."

"Neighbors. You call them neighbors. One of them wanted to screw your wife tonight."

He knew he couldn't just do nothing. Her screaming was starting to embarrass him. "Shut up!" He didn't scream it, but he said it so sharply and angrily that he might as well have. He started closing the windows even though the heat hung in the air like the sides of a ditch waiting to cave in.

Lori Martin was twenty-six years old, a brunette who dyed her hair blonde because she had never liked her dark hair, never thought it matched her fair skin. Her eyes were an active grey-green heightened by green-tinted contact lenses. She was of average height, rather slim with smallish, quite average breasts. But there was nothing average about her face. It was perfectly angled in the long, clean vertical lines of intelligent movie actresses like Meryl Streep. She had always wanted to be an actress, but had ended up a legal secretary. Though she had majored in Theater at the university in West Wabash, when she graduated she hadn't had the courage to go off by herself to some big city like New York or Chicago or L.A. Her parents had applauded her level-headedness. In moments alone though (which now that she worked days and her husband worked evenings every night) she wondered if she should have taken the chance, tried to be an actress.

Instead, she got her legal secretary's certification.

"Please don't marry him," her mother had pleaded when Eddie popped the question. "Marry a boy who wants to work in a bank like your father, or better yet, somebody in the hotel business." Her mother loved to go to St. Louis and stay in nice hotels with buffet brunches that served champagne. "Or someone who wants to sell baby furniture. Everybody wants a baby these days."

They had both been twenty-three when they followed the purple tuxedos and hot pink bridesmaids' frocks down the aisle. Her mother cried all through the wedding and, by the time they moved to the trailer park in Wabash City a week later, after a too-short honeymoon in a nice hotel with a Buffet Brunch in St. Louis, all of her mother's friends were worried that if the woman didn't stop crying soon she would end up dried out like a raisin.

"I'm trying to talk to you," she was still drunk and depressed and screaming. "Don't just stand there staring out the window like I'm not here. I am here and I want you here when I'm here." She knew she wasn't making much sense. It was the three-quarters of a bottle of wine talking. She had sat alone all evening, waiting up, getting angrier and angrier and lonelier and lonelier. "We haven't made love for a week and then you just rolled over and went to sleep before anything even happened for me."

"God, you're like a nymphomaniac lately," he tried to defend himself.

"What? WHAT?" Her eyes started to bulge and it looked like her ears might pop off from the pressure. "Nympho . . . nympho . . . nymphomaniac," she was sputtering with anger. "I'll show you nymphomaniac. I'll do every guy in this trailer park if you're not interested anymore."

"That's crazy. My fault, bad choice of words. I just meant that I'm so tired when I get home from work."

"Not too tired to play softball. Not too tired to drink beer. I'm tired too. Tired of waiting up for you to drag yourself back here." she was crying now, and not screaming anymore. "Tired of feeling like I'm all alone and my husband doesn't care enough to make love to me. I'm tired too, damn you."

"Honey, I'm sorry."

You haven't listened to one word I've said, have you? You don't even know what I'm talking about, do you? I've got no life. All I do is sit here alone with the cats. I should have thanked that drunk for pissing on the side of our trailer. It's the only human contact I had all night."

"Honey, you've got to give me some time. I can get us outa this place."

"I've got no life. Can't you see that? Don't 'honey' me." and she slammed into the bedroom, but came right back out, not finished, burning with rage. "You wanna know how I spend my trailer park nights. I can't go out for a walk because I'm terrified of the sleazeballs and motorcycle gang bangers who are our neighbors. Do you know how dangerous it is to live in a trailer park? Think about it. Every time a tornado touches down it's in a trailer park. Whenever they discover toxic chemicals it's in trailer park water. When lightning strikes it strikes trailer parks. There are more motorcycles per trailer park than there are in Harley dealerships. How many houses can you fry eggs on in the summer? How many houses can be rocked by two drunks? How many houses have bathrooms where the door hits your knees? I'm sick of it." As she raced through this litany, she felt as if her whole life was caving in on her. As she came to the end, her voice started to slow and quaver and words were replaced with deep gasping sobs as the tears poured from her eyes and soaked her perfect face.

"Hon, take it easy. It's not that bad. This is only temporary. We'll get out of here as soon as we can."

He's not even listening to me, she thought. *He's just trying to calm me down, talk me out of what I feel. He could care less.* That realization cooled her panic and desperation. Her sobs stopped with one deep breath. Her anger returned, but was no longer hot and directed at herself and her life. Now it was cold and detached and hateful and directed right at her husband.

"You're right. It's not so bad. A tornado hasn't hit us yet! I'm done with sitting here talking to the cats and waiting for the neighbors to get done pissing on our porch."

2 Think Rich

That was how it all started.

I've got to do something, Lori decided. It was as if her cramped space, her cramped marriage, her cramped life had caved in and she was suffocating. She knew she had to dig herself out. Not out of the marriage. She wasn't ready for that yet. But out of the loneliness and boredom and fear of those empty trailer park nights.

A week after the blow-up, she saw the ad. On break at the law office, sitting in the small back room drinking her ten o'clock coffee, fingering the day-old newspaper on the table, it jumped out at her. "CIVIC THEATER" read the logo;" The Philadelphia Story" announced the title; "Audition" stated the business; "Needed: Women ages 15 to 60, men ages 25 to 70." It was as if some guardian angel had left it sitting there for her. It had been more than five years since she'd been in a play, but already she was feeling the old excitement.

She copied down the audition time and place, and the phone number to call for information. The next day she signed out a script. Two days later, after reading the script three times, after checking out the public library's videotape copy of the movie that had been made from the play, after reading lines aloud in front of a mirror as her old acting professor had taught her, she sat nervously waiting for the audition to begin.

There weren't many people there. Two older men, both with mustaches, one handlebarred and greyish blond, one clipped businesslike and greyish black, loitered in the back of the theater, chatting like old friends. An older woman with short grey hair sat alone in the middle of the theater. Four younger men, all late twenties to early thirties, all different (black hair, blond, long, short and yuppiefied), sat in a clump in the front row. One tall thin guy who, she remembered the movie version, actually looked like Jimmy Stewart and really seemed to know his way around the theater was conversing with the director.

Six other women besides herself, were scattered around in the first three rows of theater seats. Three were high school girls, no older than seventeen (although she would find out later that one was twenty-two), and clearly trying out for the little sister role which she had no interest in. The others, two college girls, one a striking brunette with long naturally wavy hair, the other a dishwater blonde, chewing gum, who didn't seem to be taking it all very seriously, who perhaps had just come along to give moral support to her gorgeous friend, sat to her right. To her left, perched up on the back of a seat reading her script, was a woman in her thirties with short dark hair, a laughing face, and a curvy athletic body accentuated by the short-shorts she was wearing. Lori pegged her for the kind of woman that movie or theater reviewers always referred to as "bouncy" or "perky" like Debbie Reynolds or Nellie in South Pacific.

As Lori surveyed the competition, she wondered how the other women were sizing her up. *Let's see, cold, blonde ice-maiden with no tits, but a very Katharine Hepburn type face. They've got to be looking at me as someone auditioning for the role of Tracy,* she thought. *Omigod!* It was honestly the first time she had really thought of herself in that role.

There were two parts in the play that Lori was interested in, but she'd really only targeted one. Nobody knew her in Wabash City or in this theater group. Nobody knew how good an actress she was, how dependable she would be, so she figured there was no way she would get the lead role of Tracy, the spoiled Philadelphia heiress/divorcee. The role of Liz, the photographer, was the one she had her eye on. There weren't all that many lines to it, but it was a bouncy, perky role that, if done right, could be a scene-stealer. *'Bouncy,' 'perky,'* she heard herself thinking and immediately glanced over at the woman with the short, dark hair who was laughing with the tall skinny guy who seemed to know everybody and looked like Jimmy Stewart. *Damn! They all know her. She's perfect for Liz. She's got the part. Damn!* That was when the first thought of reading seriously for the part of Tracy Lord entered her mind, a full two minutes before the audition began. *What an amateur!* she wanted to smack herself. *You should have paid more attention to how you look, to what part you fit better. It's Tracy, not Liz. Good luck, dummy!*

The last minute or two before an acting audition had always been Lori's time of greatest self-doubt. She found herself caught in a tug-of-war between small anxiety and competitiveness. The dryness in her mouth was there. The tightness around her eyes and up to her hairline was beginning to flex. She could feel her back teeth starting to grind, her jaw tensing. *Breathe,* she told herself, *relax the way you were taught, open your mouth and breathe slowly with your jaw slack, draw on your inner emotions, your motives for being here, for exposing yourself like this, for taking this risk. You want out of the house, out of that trailer park at night. You want to meet some new people. You want to have something that's yours to do.*

She closed her eyes, slid down in the theater seat and let her head fall back until her neck touched the seatback. She stopped thinking about Lori Martin and started thinking about Tracy Lord. Her competitiveness began to overpower her anxiety. She was thinking like an actress instead of some twinkie feeling sorry for herself because her husband wasn't paying any attention to her and strangers were pissing on her porch.

When she opened her eyes, she saw the director getting up to start the audition. She hoped she wouldn't be the first to read. She hoped she'd get to read more than once, get the chance to try different things with the lines, with the character. *No way you're going to get the lead part in the first play you do with these people,* her anxiety got in one last poke.

"Everybody, thank you for coming." The director, when she stood up, proved a much bigger woman than she had appeared when sitting behind the table. Her voice was an actress' voice and, though she wasn't booming, it filled up the theater. "Do you all have scripts?" When the nods stopped, she said "Good" and went on. "It will be a simple audition procedure. We will read scenes in different combinations of actors. Everyone will get more than one chance. We'll stay at it until every actor has done all he or she wants. This is just the first audition session. There will be others, but we hope to have a cast by next week."

She paused a moment, thinking.

"Oh, yes, I forgot. I'm Marge Coleman and this," Raising her arms up in a priestly hieratic gesture, "is *The Philadelphia Story.*" She paused a moment and swept the theater with her gaze. "Just one thing before we begin the audition. I want you all to think rich, old inherited rich, not Yuppie rich. These characters are Philadelphia Main Liners and being rich is second nature to them. O.K., let's go."

This woman director seemed competent enough even if she had forgotten to introduce herself. Lori guessed that she was in her late fifties and about thirty pounds overweight. The woman reminded her of the Army Sergeant in that Goldie Hawn movie *Private Benjamin,* someone with a tough craggy face and a lot of weight to throw around.

The first people chosen to read were the gorgeous wavy-haired brunette for the role of Tracy and the tall skinny guy who looked like Jimmy Stewart and strutted around as if he knew that he already had the part of Mike, the reporter. It turned out he was quite good and, much to Lori's delight, the brunette was terrible. She looked good, but she read with little expression and she never moved. On the stage, it was as if she was made of wood, like one of those dummies that comedians sit on their laps. Lori was tempted to laugh, not at the other woman, but at her own anxiety about competing with her. It was really getting funny. The woman was as stationary as a stump. The two were doing the drunk scene in Act II. The Jimmy Stewart clone was staggering around the stage slurring his words while the woman was standing utterly still as if planted. Marge the director mercifully cut it off after two pages.

Next, the "bouncy, perky" woman with the black hair was summoned to do the character of Liz, the photographer, once again with Jimmy Stewart. She was excellent, alive, bright, with a clear voice that projected every word. *She's perfect for that part,* Lori knew as soon as the woman started moving around the stage pretending to snap pictures. The director didn't let this scene go on very long. There was no need.

Next she called for a Dexter and two of the men raised their hands. The one with dark hair in the conventional blue blazer jumped right up. The chunky blonde guy in the dirty sweat shirt and sneakers with toe-holes slouched to his feet.

Who the hell does he think he is, Marlon Brando? Lori thought.

The director chose the blue-blazered Yuppie. The Methodical lump subsided back into his seat. It was the scene in the beginning of Act II where the sarcastic Dexter reads the riot act to Tracy. The director chose the gum-chewing dishwater blonde to do Tracy. The woman snapped her gum one last time, took it out of her mouth, deposited it on the arm of the theater seat, and went onstage.

Think rich! Lori remembered the director saying. *Boy, that's rich!* she also remembered the trailer park.

This scene had to be done twice, once for each of the men, and each version was a comedy of errors. The dark-haired blazer had a slight lisp and hesitated on particular sounds so that his sentences came out sounding as if he was constantly slipping gears. Pauses would come at unplanned places and then the real pauses would seem as eccentric as the lisp pauses. The ditzy blonde really wasn't that bad. She read well and moved adequately. It was just that she looked like a slut trying to do Katharine Hepburn. She also had a Hoosier accent that seemed to twang in rhythm with the dark-haired blazer's lisp. This version of the scene was a real linguistic video game. Each sentence, no matter who was speaking it, got blown to pieces before it could get across the screen of the stage. The words, the characters, came out sounding like a cross between Grand Ole Opry and speech therapy class.

The second version of the scene was better. The slutty blonde must have been nervous working with the lisper because she slowed her reading down a bit and her hillbilly twang wasn't so noticeable. The sweatshirt and sneakered Dexter was a bayer. He bayed each of his sentences by drawing out the consonant sounds at the ends of the words he wanted to stress. If, dressed like Marlon Brando in *Streetcar* as he was, he was a method actor, his method was "full moon houndog." As the scene unfolded, he bayed the dishwater ditz all the way across the stage. As he would bay a line of rebuke at her, she would take a step back and he would take a step forward to stay within baying distance. "Ohh, nooo, I couldn't doooo thatttt," he bayed and she backed up. "Youooooo got drunk," he bayed, "and climbed out on the roooof," she backed, "and stood there naaaaaaked," he howled, "with your arms out to the moooon," she jumped, "wailing like a bansheeee," he bayed her almost into the wings. Again, mercifully, the director stopped the scene before the two of them ended up out on the railroad tracks in the street in front of the building.

The guy wasn't Dexter. Dexter is a rich, handsome yachtsman with charm and a sarcastic sense of humor. This guy looked like a thug and delivered his lines like a bloodhound. The dishwater ditz wasn't Tracy either. Tracy, with her egotistic arrogance, wouldn't back off from anyone. She would counterattack. Lori hoped she'd get the chance to audition opposite this baying Dexter. She knew exactly what she'd do. She'd start tapping him in the chest with her forefinger until *he* backed up, then she'd back off until her next line and back him up again.

"Oh, now Lori, Lori Martin," the director was calling her name, "for Liz or Tracy. Which one do you want to do?"

Lori stood up and smoothed back her hair. *Be in control from the very beginning,* she gave herself one last bit of coaching. "Yes, Tracy," she answered, moving onto the stage, tapping her little blue book against her hand expectantly.

"Dexter," the director was already calling people by their character names, "why don't you stay up there and we'll do this scene again with this new Tracy." She had drawn the bayer. It was her chance to see if her aggressive Tracy, her chest-tapping Tracy, worked. They began the scene and she never retreated a step.

Marge "the Barge" Coleman, for that is what everyone called her behind her back, leaned sideways to tall, thin, Jimmy Stewart loo-kalike John Collins and whispered, "My God, she really looks like Katharine Hepburn sort of, doesn't she? She's not as tall as I'd like, but her face is perfect, aristocratic. Certainly not like that bimbo that just read."

"Her posture is no good," Collins whispered. "She stoops at the shoulders and she speaks with her head down. If she's going to be the one, we're going to have to completely redesign her posture."

"But that first girl is so gorgeous, so regal."

"For God's sake, Marge, she can't talk."

"But can't you see what we could do with her in a strapless evening gown."

"Do you really want to try to teach that moron to act? She can't walk and read at the same time. This one has the cool, blonde looks and has clearly acted before. She has a good voice. She seems serious, as if she really wants the part. If only she didn't stoop."

"And so far she's really all we've got. The second girl looks like she belongs either in a strip joint or on a pig farm."

The whispering broke off as Lori tapped the bayer in the chest one more time.

"You're being too aggressive, dear. She would never be poking at him like that. She'd have her nose up in the air, looking over his head with disdain. This is the Philadelphia Main Line, not the Cosby Show," Marge cut off their combat.

She never corrected either of the first two girls, Lori thought, why is she just criticizing my interpretation? Because she hates me, first came to mind. *Because I'm the only one of the three that interests her,* came second. Lori liked that better.

"O.K., let's take a five-minute break. I want to get my notes together and then we'll go on. Don't anyone leave. We've got a number of scenes I want to do," the director announced.

Lori took a seat in the corner of the theater by herself. She had come on pretty strong in her first scene. Too strong, it seemed, judging from the director's reaction, but they had paid attention to her. She had to change her character, but how? The woman had said "nose in the air."

O.K., if she wants stuck up, Lori thought, *I'll give her stuck up.*

She thumbed through the script. Tracy is on stage most of Act I with her mother, her little sister, with Mike and Liz, the reporter and photographer. Act II is where all the big dramatic scenes are: the confrontation with Dexter that she had already done, the romantic scene with George her fiance, the shouting match with her father, the drunk scene. She was sure one of those scenes would come next.

When they all came back from the break, the director began by auditioning the three high school girls with the older woman. Playing the role of Mrs. Lord, the woman was excellent, as if she had spent her whole life playing a rich matron helping fill out wedding invitations. She flitted and twittered around the stage like some middle-aged Munchkin. But Lori didn't pay too much attention. She sat alone brooding about how she was going to play Tracy.

It's going to be the drunk scene, I know it, she was certain.

She was wrong.

"Ah, Lori, I'd like you to do the scene on page 62 with Larry. Your finger pointing will be much more appropriate here than it was with Dexter in that other scene," the director announced. Larry, it turned out, was the more conservative of the two older men, the one with the clipped, businesslike mustache as opposed to the tall, thin, handlebarred man.

Omigod, what scene is that, Lori scrambled for page 62. She didn't even remember the scene. *This whole audition is going all wrong,* she feared. The scene was a good one for her, though. The actor, Larry, was clearly an old hand, forceful yet dignified, and Lori simply reacted to his lines. At one point, she actually put her hands on her hips and got right into his face as she had seen Whitey Herzog, the manager of her beloved St. Louis Cardinals, do to umpires so many times.

Next, the handlebarred older man, whose name was Harvey, did a short funny scene with each of the three high school girls.

He is a real ham, Lori thought as she watched him stomp around the stage mugging and throwing up his hands in frustration at the younger generation.

Next both Harvey and Larry, playing the lecherous Uncle Willy Tracy and the philandering Seth Lord, did a short funny picture-taking scene with Miss Perky & Bouncy playing Liz, the photographer.

Boy, she's got that part, Lori was absolutely sure.

"Where's John Collins?" the director swivelled her head like a spotlight scanning for an escaped prisoner.

"I think he's in the shop talking to Ernie about the set," handlebarred Harvey ventured.

"Go get him," the director barked.

When the Jimmy Stewart lookalike reappeared, Marge said, "I want to do the drunk scene with all three Tracys."

"And I don't even drink!" the tall skinny actor rolled his eyes.

"I do," mischievous handlebarred Harvey intoned from the darkness of the theater seats, "and sometime soon I hope."

"Shut up, Harvey," the director barked, not amused.

No sense of humor there, Lori thought.

The gorgeous, wavy-haired moron went first and was, if anything, worse than she had been earlier. She read the words in a monotone flatter than the Indiana landscape accompanied by no perceptible indication she was drunk.

The dishwater ditz went next and acted the scene as if it was second nature. She either was born to play a drunk or had a great deal of acquired experience.

God, could she really do Tracy? With those looks and that hillbilly voice? All of Lori's self-doubt caved in upon her. *I've got to do it better than she did,* Lori knew, *she's the competition. But I've got to do it different from her. She's playing a bar drunk. Tracy is an occasional cocktail party drunk. I've got to play it more sophisticated, more 'I'm not drunk. I'm too cool to ever get drunk. How dare you accuse me of being drunk. Why is the room spinning?'* Lori knew, all of a sudden, that her Tracy was right and this other woman's Tracy was not Philadelphia Main Line. When she took the stage, she was Tracy Lord wandering around in a champagne haze in the early morning hours before her wedding.

"Today is Wednesday. We will call you, certainly by Friday, either to tell you that you got a part, that you didn't get a part, or that we would like you to audition again sometime later in the week," Marge the director brought the audition to a close. "Thank you all for coming."

As the actors filed out of the theater, the director snapped for the handlebarred actor named Harvey and the Jimmy Stewart lookalike to stay.

John Collins was an architect in real life. He was the major set designer for the Wabash City Civic Theater and, young as he was, only 29, he was also a member of the Board of Directors and, therefore, rather a force in the theater group. Harvey Winkins was one of the older veterans of Civic Theater. He had been acting for Civic before there even was a theater, when they used to put on the plays in the 20-seat, folding-chair warehouse room on Ninth Street.

Marge the Barge assembled her braintrust. "I see two major problems," she began. She needed ideas from these other members of the inner circle. Before any auditions had ever been held, a number of the parts in *The Philadelphia Story* had already been cast. "Neither of the Dexters are any good. The hippie or whatever he is we could maybe use for a minor role, the brother maybe. But the other guy is dreadful. We need someone the women in the audience are going to want to put their hands on, someone light and playful and easy." She paused, but no one said anything, though both men knew they were expected to come up with a solution.

"The other problem is the three Tracys. I'm not happy with any of them. The pretty brunette acts retarded on stage. The skinny bleach blonde sounds like Dolly Parton and looks like a barfly hooker. The little blonde is clearly the best actress, but she just doesn't look like Tracy Lord. She's too short and she stoops. She's not regal enough. I want to see if we can find someone better. If not, she's going to be a project."

Driving home to the trailer park, and then sitting on the couch with her glass of wine not watching TV, Lori thought that she had won the part. *I was better than those other two. I look more like the character,* she tried to convince herself.

"Hello little blondie" that drunken shout from outside her door broke her reverie.

"I've called the police and complained to the park manager about you already. They know who you are," she was furious and she screamed at that drunken slob through her locked door. "Call the police about this, little blondie," and once again she heard the sound of a hard stream of water bouncing tinnily off the face of her aluminum screen door.

Eddie wandered in about one, uninterested in sex. She had failed to mention that she was trying out for a play. She had left the script and the videotape lying right out in plain view, but he hadn't noticed.

The call came on Friday at about 5:15, right after Lori got home from work.

"Hello . . . is this Lori Martin? This is Marge Coleman, director of *The Philadelphia Story*."

Lori breathed in hard. *She's going to ding me,* was Lori's first negative thought, *it's in her voice.*

"We're seriously considering you for the role of Tracy, but we would like you to come back on Sunday and do one more reading. It's such a big part, we just have to be sure. You understand?"

"Uh, sure, yes, Sunday, what time?" The call took about half a minute.

This means she doesn't really like me. She's looking for someone else for Tracy, but as a last resort she'll use me. She's not sure and she wants another look. She hates me, but she's desperate. She can't make up her mind between me and that hillbilly, the doubts caved in on her mind for hours, suffocating all the confidence she had felt after the first audition. *I was the best of all those Tracys,* she was still sure, *but she doesn't know me. She doesn't like me. She doesn't want me.* There were so many possibilities.

Finally, after four glasses of wine, Lori decided to show up at the callback, to prepare for it, to have the scenes worked out just the way she wanted to read them. *I'll be so good, so Tracy, so nose-in-the-air rich, she won't have any choice.*

3 Cary Grant Ain't Bad!

More and more Bill Franklin found himself wishing that he were someone else, somewhere else, in another time. Unfortunately, he was stuck in Wabash City.

I'm forty-two years old and I've never been so bored in my life, he had been thinking off and on all summer. Those three months had been like pulling a load of logs.

His softball team had lost almost all its games in a league suddenly filled with young kids who could hit the ball farther, run faster, throw harder than any he'd run into going back fifteen years to the glory days with All American Homes. He hadn't gotten any summer classes at the university. He had taught three summers in a row while Martha was finishing her degree, but the English department priority system had eliminated him this time around. He had tried to write another Spencer Knuckle novel, but had given it up about fifteen pages in. "The thought of going back to Spencer Knuckle makes me want to puke," he had screamed at Martha one late night back in May after getting drunk on beer.

He had plodded through the summer, playing golf almost every day and going to the movies a couple nights a week when he wasn't playing softball. The only writing he'd done was the movie reviews for the *Wabash City Journal.* He was proud of his weekly column which had been running for almost two years, even if it appeared in a medium with the disposability of a condom. Now August, with its dog-day heat and its humidity closing over you like a ditch caving in, seemed almost welcome. August meant getting back to work soon, meant not having to look at blank pages, empty hours, his boring life.

Martha had her job. She went to it early in the morning feeling good about herself.

He'd spent the whole summer doing nothing. *What a waste,* he thought as the phone began to ring.

In the other room he heard Martha stirring to answer the phone. He had left her softly snoring on the couch to the lullaby of the television. Since their daughter Christy had gone away to college, the evenings had become lonely vigils, him watching Martha sleep. He was actually glad when the telephone jangled her off the couch.

I'm bored because life has become so comfortable, he thought. Their house on the quiet street near the university with its books and plants and cool basement *was* comfortable. Christy going away to college and doing well, then coming home for the summer to work as a waitress and live in an apartment with two twin girlfriends *was* comfortable. His job of seventeen years teaching Dickens, creative writing, and film at the university *was* comfortable. His income as a professor added to the royalties he still received from his four Spencer Knuckle detective novels added to the little the newspaper paid him for his movie column plus Martha's new salary as a businesswoman *was* more than comfortable for Wabash City. *All too damn comfortable!* Even though he played golf, softball, ran every other day and only watched the Cubs games on TV, he still felt like a couch potato at life. The boredom of seventeen years in the same town with the same wife at the same university had paralyzed him. He saw himself becoming like one of the old professors who roamed the halls in the smiling vacancy of senility talking about their hemorrhoids and flashing their bibliographies of published works as an epitaph to a career gone south with their brain cells.

"Hello," Martha mumbled into the phone in the other room.

"Yes, he's here, hang on,"

Who the hell is calling me at this time on a Sunday night? he wondered. He was lying on his back on the sofa with all the lights turned out listening to a fifties rock and roll tape turned down so low that Little Richard sounded as if he was wearing a muzzle and Elvis sounded as if he was baying through marshmallows.

"Bill . . . it's for you," Martha called from the other room. Ten years ago she would have yelled "it's for you, honey," with a lilt in her voice, but all of their little gestures of affection had faded into the flatness of the Indiana landscape.

"I'll be right there, honey," he answered to spite her.

Martha was already back on her couch with her eyes starting to glaze. He bent quickly and turned down the volume on the TV as he passed by. She didn't even notice. The phone lay coiled like a snake on the garden-flowered upholstery of the chair.

"Hello," Bill tried to inject some small tone of cheerfulness, but he couldn't muster much enthusiasm.

"Bill, it's probably been two years since we last played golf, but this is Harvey Winkins," that "hail-fellow-well-met" voice booming through the phone line caught him by surprise, but was much more familiar than it thought.

Harvey Winkins. Nice guy. Great chipper and putter. About ten years older than me. Had meant to call him back to play some more golf together. Probably wants a game tomorrow, Bill flipped through the pertinent mental file cards.

"Harvey, how are you? Of course I remember. How's your golf game?"

"Oh, it's fine, we ought to play sometime." There was a momentary, almost awkward pause. "But that's not why I'm calling."

For the first time all evening, Bill was semi-interested. *All we have in common is golf,* he thought, *what the hell's this guy up to?*

"What's up, Harvey?" Bill really tried to sound interested.

"Civic Theater is doing *The Philadelphia Story* for the first play of this year's season," Harvey launched into his sales pitch.

That's right, Harvey is an actor, Bill remembered.

"And we've been casting the play this week."

"Oh?" Bill felt he ought to say something to fill the dead line when Harvey paused. "That's a good one, and a super movie. I'll bet I've seen the movie version seven or eight times."

"Good, then maybe you'll be interested."

"In what?"

"We've been trying to cast the lead roles for two auditions and we're really having trouble finding someone to play Dexter."

"That's the Cary Grant part, isn't it?"

"That's right, C. K. Dexter Haven, millionaire yachtsman, witty bon vivant," Harvey paused.

He probably got my department mixed up, Bill speculated, *thinks I'm in the Theater Department, not the English Department. Wants me to recommend an actor for the part.*

When Bill still didn't say anything, Harvey pushed on. "It's a good part, a funny romantic part, and Marge Coleman, the director, was in a literature workshop you taught at the university last year, and she reads your column in *The Wabash Journal* every week, and she thinks you'd be perfect for the part, and when she mentioned your name I remembered playing golf with you, and I agreed with her right away, so she asked me to give you a call and ask you if maybe you might consider doing an audition for it. We both think you'd be perfect."

Harvey was certainly an experienced actor because he didn't take a single breath as he spun out this whole speech.

It was all so absurd that Bill didn't think before he spoke. "You must be out of your mind," he laughed into the telephone, "I haven't been in a play, onstage, since high school."

"Didn't you get that 'Best Teacher in the Humanities' award a couple years ago? You're on stage every day," Harvey persisted.

"You're serious about this?" Bill still couldn't quite believe what he was hearing.

"Very serious. Marge is a good Director and calling you is her idea. She's sold on you for the part. Of course, you'd have to read, everybody does, but she thinks you'll be perfect."

Bill glanced quickly at Martha, motionless on the couch. Maybe what he did next he did out of spite. Maybe, as the receiver pressed against his ear, he realized that this phone conversation could be an opportunity. Or maybe it was just a case of his ego suddenly blowing up so big that it cut off the oxygen to his brain.

"Gee, I don't know, Harvey."

"It sounds like you're considering it," Harvey cajoled.

"Boy, I don't know, Harvey. It's been so long since I've done any stage acting." Maybe it was just some instinctive caution that was making him move so slowly.

"Marge is a good director and rehearses hard. Believe me, by opening night you'll be prepared," Harvey's voice was more controlled, "and besides, she's seen you in action in public lectures and you are her pick for the part."

"Well," Bill was almost ready to jump, "it is a nice play. And I've seen the movie version." He still hesitated. "You really want me to play the Cary Grant part?" It wasn't really a question, just his ego musing out loud.

"Why don't I just come by and drop off the script? I'm at the theater now and it's right on my way home."

"You know, it really sounds like fun, Harvey. And the Cary Grant part, that's wild. It's really tempting."

"Man, Bill, does it always take you this long to make up your mind?" Harvey said it laughingly. "Hell, Reagan decided to attack

Granada in less time than we've been on the phone and his brain has been in mothballs since 1975," Harvey joked. "Just let me drop off the script. You'll have a great time."

"O.K." Bill finally did what he'd known he was going to do all along. He glanced guiltily over at Martha. "O.K., I'll give it a try. But I hope it's going to be a real audition. If I'm terrible, you guys don't hesitate to kick me out."

"Don't worry. You'll be great. I'll be by in about ten minutes."

"O.K. Hey, this is wild."

"Outstanding."

Are you crazy? Can you really do this? he asked himself with the dead phone buzzing in his head.

"Ooo uzz at" Martha chewed the words like taffy.

"Just an old buddy. Asked me to be in a play."

"Azz nice," she turned over.

Didn't hear a word I said, Bill knew.

In what seemed like only minutes, the doorbell rang and Harvey Winkins, tall, thin, matched luggage packed under his half-mad eyes, stood grinning on the front porch with the little blue book extended in his hand like a passport to some exotic place.

"Read it. It's a fun play and you've got a scene-stealing part," Harvey was all enthusiasm and welcome-to-the-inner-circle cameraderie.

As they stood in the front hall exchanging audition time and place and other pleasantries, Harvey never stopped staring at him as if taking his measurements for a bust.

Only when Harvey walked off the porch and left Bill standing with the script in his hand did Bill realize just how badly he wanted to be someone else and, *God knows, Cary Grant ain't bad.*

4 The Waiting Room

The home of the Wabash City Civic Theater is commonly known as the Depot Theater. Wabash City is one of those towns that still has active railroad tracks running down the center of some of its main streets. A Railroad Relocation Plan is in the works and has been for almost five years. The Depot Theater sits on the corner of Fifth and Ferry streets one block off Wabash City's town square where the domed, stone courthouse squats like a bulbous toad. One of Wabash City's three active train tracks runs right down the middle of Fifth Street within ten yards of the theater's front door. Thus, there is a reason for the theater's nickname. The square, two story, flat-roofed stone building is the old Monon/Chesapeake and Ohio Railroad station. Built in 1901 of stone quarried right in the county, its historical restoration as a theater in the mid-seventies saved it from the demolition ball. Behind it sits a modern one-story garage-like structure with a metal overhead door filling one-half its facade and an ordinary door and window with the words "CIVIC THEATER OFFICE" stenciled on both occupying the other side of the cement block facade.

About ten freight trains that never stop trundle down the middle of Fifth Street every day with no real pattern to their comings and goings. They disrupt everything in the town, pile up long lines of traffic all the way back across the Wabash River bridges, but they could care less. The AMTRAK passenger train between Indianapolis and Chicago is much more regular and much less arrogant toward the scheme of things in Wabash City. Every morning about 8:30 as Thelma Parkins is opening the theater box-office for the day's sales, and every night early in the second act (or, if a play isn't in performance, about 9:30) the AMTRAK clatters and rumbles down Fifth Street. It never stops at the old depot anymore—instead, it lets passengers off in the middle of the street in front of the hotel—but the train's sound, its closeness ˎ as it passes, serves as a reminder of the building's past. Even in the eighties, despite the sand-blast that has made its stone facade look as if it was just quarried yesterday and the modern light fixtures inside the lobby which seem to fire beams of laser light out through its high Victorian casements, it still is unmistakably a railroad station. The regular passing of the AMTRAK out front is a reminder of how for eighty-some years this building was Wabash City's jumping off place to a wider world.

Its waiting room is now a carpeted lobby and art gallery for hangings of local painters and photographers. Its ticket counters are now a concession stand and coat check room. Its baggage and freight bay is now a 160-seat theater. But it still has that functional, anticipatory air about it that every railroad station in America had at the turn of the twentieth century. In fact, turning a railway depot into a theater is, when you come to think of it, rather appropriate. Both are waiting rooms where people sit in anticipation of setting off on a journey into some new, as yet undiscovered, world, points of departure where ordinary people muster the courage to climb onto that train, or sit down in that theater, or walk onto that stage and leave the past behind.

There is history in the Depot Theater and in the Civic Theater group itself. The Fifth Street Depot in its heyday from the turn of the century right up to the sixties hosted history on a regular basis. Presidents and all sorts of other American royalty whistle-stopped their way through her. Teddy Roosevelt stopped for ten minutes to wave his hat and fire a gun in the air in 1904. Woodrow Wilson, Herbert Hoover, Robert Taft, F.D.R., Adlai Stevenson, John Kennedy and George McGovern all made similar whistlestops. Legend has it that Kennedy actually got off the train, went in and bought a Coke in 1959. An apocryphal story exists about how James Dean sat up all night in the waiting room in 1950 before a kindly postal clerk loaned him enough money to purchase train fare to Chicago, and how two years later a letter of thanks with a money order of a thousand dollars arrived for that old clerk who had died in the meanwhile. But nobody saw the letter or the money order or James Dean, so it is all just a story and not really history.

But the theater group has a real recorded history; in fact, it has an actual in-resident historian. Thelma Parkins wears the hats of office manager, ticket seller, board meeting caterer, art show hanger, concession stand boss, coat check clerk, maintenance crew supervisor, set design commissioner, advertising executive, program designer, usher procurer, thermostat controller, door opener and, of course, historian and building protector. Since the early eighties her history of the Wabash City Civic Theater has transported itself from the bulging folders of old flyers and programs, which she has collected in the file cabinet behind her desk, to the neat shelf of videotapes under the window which are propped against Thelma's potted geranium. But besides the programs and lobby cards and videotaped performances there is another history that Thelma has not yet written down; call it an oral history, a gossipy humorous history of all that has gone on behind the scenes and in the private backstage life of the Civic Theater since Thelma has been there.

One of her favorite stories is about how they got the money to make the down payment on the Depot property and then actually completed the restoration and outfitting of the theater which opened in 1978. It centers on an actress named Jeanine Foley who when they were worried about getting the large bank loan for the renovation of the theater took it upon herself to seduce and sleep with the president of the Wabash City Bank and Trust for three months until the loan was signed, sealed and delivered. Thelma still liked to refer to Jeanine's as the most profitable performance ever put on by any Civic Theater actor.

Another of Thelma's favorite stories is about the first nude performance at the Wabash City Civic Theater. It took place way back in the fifties. In those days the plays were being put on using the stage of the local burlesque house on nights when the usual attractions weren't working. One night, one of the strippers, who was holding over until the next weekend and using for her living quarters the Burly-Q's upstairs dressing room, got drunk and high on reefer and, hearing all the people downstairs in the theater, figured it was just another working night. Civic Theater was doing *Hamlet* that evening and there was a pretty full house. The minister of the Episcopal Church with his wife and the Bishop of the Catholic Diocese, whose residence up at the top of the Sixth Street hill was one of the most impressive houses in Wabash City, were there and sitting very close to the stage. The play had just started when, as the tormented and angry ghost of Hamlet's father made his entrance from stage right, Martina La Muff came bouncing onstage from the left wing shedding evening gown and gloves and sequined underthings as she came. Nobody paid any attention to the ghost who kept trying to deliver his lines as Martina wriggled out of her clothes. It didn't seem to bother her that the only accompaniment was the dirge-like beating of a single drum. She went right into her bump and grind as she got down to her pasties and G-string, and pretty soon both the ghost and the drummer, realizing there was no way that Shakespeare's language could compete with those tassels rotating in different directions at high speed, packed it in. A couple of ushers finally got her off the stage, but in doing so were booed roundly by a number of the theatergoers (who in Shakespeare's day would have been called "groundlings"). "It was said," Thelma always ended this story, "that the Episcopal minister and his wife stomped out scandalized, but that the Catholic Bishop, an old Irishman named McGuckin, gleefully applauded Miss La Muff's performance and thereafter delighted in telling various of his parishoners at whose houses he was known to share a glass of Irish whiskey occasionally that the Wabash City Civic Theater's performance of *Hamlet* was surely the most revealing version of that play he had ever attended."

Thelma was also fond of reminiscing about the performance of *South Pacific* in 1969 when the Civic Theater was using the high school auditorium. That was the year the stage had been invaded by the hippies from the university who were constantly looking for ways to shock the town, which had rather complacently ignored their sit-ins, teach-ins and love-ins. This was a real favorite of Thelma's because she had herself been onstage in the role of one of the chorus of nurses who stood around and harmonized in support of Nellie Forbush's numbers. "I'll never forget it as long as I live," Thelma told the story gleefully. "The Sea-Bees were all on one side of the stage and the Nurses were all on the other and Melba, who was the wife of the president of All-American Homes, was playing Nellie. She was washing that man right out of her hair at center stage when about ten hippies, both boys and girls, came onstage stark naked. Melba had a towel over her head so she had no idea what was going on, but everybody else was just stunned. Nobody said a word. The naked hippies all surrounded Melba at center stage, who is still dancing around with the towel over her head singing 'I'm gonna wash that man right outa my hair.' But pretty soon she bumps into one of the hippie boys and she realizes that something is screwy. But she's still got the towel over her head and she just sort of instinctively reaches out to see what she has run into and her hand grabs that hippie boy right in the worst possible place."

"Got him right by the dick," Harvey always leaned to whoever was closest and gleefully dug that person in the ribs.

"When she got the towel off her head and saw this whole group of naked intruders onstage and realized what she had in her hand, Melba just came apart and ran off the stage screaming. They had to cancel the rest of the performances of *South Pacific,* and Melba never tried out for a Civic Theater part again."

"You wouldn't believe the look on her face when she saw what she had in her hand," Harvey always delighted in adding.

Recently at cast parties, Thelma's stories had gotten more gossipy and she seemed to enjoy telling about things that happened offstage or backstage more than she did the onstage events of Civic Theater history. One such story happened in the winter of 1973 when Civic Theater was using the elementary school gym for their performances of *Irma La Douce.* After the opening night's performances, there had been champagne in the dressing room to be followed by a cast party at the home of Harvey Winkins. Two of the chorus girls, dressed as Parisian hookers, got in one of their cars in costume to drive from the theater to the party. One was a thirty-year-old wife of a university professor who was separated from her husband and the other was a twenty-four-year-old daughter of a local, very rich and community-involved, realtor. Needless to say, they got a flat tire in the middle of the Wabash City bridge and weren't out of their car more than thirty seconds when help arrived in the form of two farmers from Delphi in a pickup who had driven into Wabash City to see if they could find something to do. The story goes, as Thelma tells it, that Barbara and Melanie got their tire fixed, made eighty dollars apiece and showed up at the party only an hour and a half late giggling like schoolgirls and dying to tell the other women in the cast about their little adventure. But that wasn't the end of it. It seems like Barbara and Melanie's crowing to the other chorus girls, four of whom were married and housewives, got to be sort of a challenge among the female cast members. There were two weekends of performances left for the play and rumor has it that on each of those nights, in pairs, in costumes, members of the Wabash City Civic Theater cast of *Irma La Douce* had automobile breakdowns on the entrance ramp to the bridge over to West Wabash. The story has it that none had any trouble getting gentlemanly assistance and one girl, a thirty-four-year-old housewife with three kids and a husband who was an insurance salesman, claimed to have made one hundred and fifty dollars from a jewelry salesman who said he passed through town once a month. One pair of girls, a single twenty-two-year-old nurse from the clinic and a twenty- eight-year-old manager of a home health-care provider, had to break down on the bridge twice on their night. The first time they broke down, they were only out of the car about a minute and a half when a Wabash City Police car, all bubblegum machine and flashing lights, manned by two officers, pulled up to help them. Actresses to their garters, the two hookers explained in their most demure, good-citizen style that despite the way they were dressed they were members of the cast of a Civic Theater play and their car had stalled and they were on their way home and they were sure it would start up soon. The officers obligingly waited, lights pulsing full tilt, chatting up the two girls until, lo! and behold, Marjorie the nurse did indeed get it started and pulled away. But the two girls were disappointed. They wanted to have their story to tell to the others in the women's dressing room before the Sunday afternoon matinee. They decided to turn around, circle back across the bridge and try it again. This time, they were no sooner out of their car than the same police car pulled up behind them, except that this time there were no lights flashing. Marjorie and Eileen couldn't believe their eyes. They were sure they were about to be carted off to jail and booked for prostitution. But the two Wabash City cops clearly had something very different in mind that ended up involving a secluded park on the river bank, handcuffs, and a twelve-pack of Pabst Blue Ribbon. The two girls knew they couldn't charge money for their little adventure as the others had, but they came up with something better. Telling the story in the dressing room at the matinee the following afternoon, they both produced a live bullet from a police revolver. "Those boys sure weren't shootin' blanks," Eileen bragged.

"Actresses are always supposed to stay in character onstage," Thelma always finished this particular saga reflectively, "but that group really stayed in character the whole run of the play."

Thelma's stories about past productions always portrayed the Civic Theater as a waiting room, an empty stage waiting to be brought to life. As regularly as trains stopped at the Fifth Street Depot from 1901 to 1965, actors and directors and stage managers and set builders and prop people have met and pursued each other and made love and betrayed and buoyed each other's spirits by playing the depot game of departure into another world. Begun right after World War II, the Wabash City Civic Theater group was thirty-one years old in 1978 when it finally got its own theater in the old railroad station.

5 Lori and Tracy

As Lori drove toward the Depot Theater for her call-back audition, she knew that this time she had to be Tracy Lord. She had chosen her richest looking dress, off-white and flowing around the knees and thighs with a high, stiff waist below a lacy, peek-a-boo top.

But is it right for Tracy? she wondered as she drove through the summer tunnel of sycamore and oak and elm that arched over the River Road and enclosed her in a deep cool shade. *How is Tracy different from me?* she asked herself as she glided along the wooded river bank. *Tracy is younger, but she's already been divorced. She's made a mess of one marriage and now she's ready to get dragged into another without the slightest idea of why she's doing it. She's just like me, caught in the marriage-go-round. Every time she gets drunk on champagne she strips down and goes looking for a man. I always get horny when I'm drunk too. She's a rich bitch who wants men to pay attention to her because she's smart. She's a princess all the way. But who the hell am I?*

Driving across the bridge and turning right onto Fifth Street, all the time Lori was thinking about how she wasn't really anybody, about how in her own life she had just been an actress playing a role. Her play was a long-run hit. *Lori Martin, Obedient Wife.* Sure, it was job security for which every actor longs, but it gave one absolutely no space in which to grow. Her first major complaint in this theater of her life was that she hated her dressing room. Her second major complaint was that she was the only actor in *Lori Martin, Obedient Wife* who was required to give a real performance. All her leading man had to do was play himself. The role had become almost second nature and, as she pulled into the Depot Theater parking lot, she realized that she had never experimented with it, never played it for any different effect.

She parked, switched off the ignition and deposited the keys in her bag, but she didn't get out from behind the wheel. She sat there staring at the stage door. *I've got to get this part,* she told herself. Ever since that first competitive reading she had been counting on this part to solve all of her problems. She was counting on it to take her mind off of where she lived. She was counting on it to give her a new role to play with a wider cast of characters. She wanted to escape into another life . . . in Philadelphia . . . perfect. She remembered the epitaph on W. C. Fields' gravestone: "On the whole, I'd rather be in Philadelphia."

The play, Tracy, was a chance to just disappear into somebody else's life, somebody else's much more elegant house, with somebody else's men. *Men.* She thought on that for a couple of seconds. She loved the attentions of men.

Going through the stage door, she started counting how many men Tracy had circling her like satellites. Sitting in the theater waiting for the second audition to begin, she continued to shop amongst Tracy's men. *Let's see, there's Dexter. I can't believe they're going to pick either of those two guys to play him. They were both wrong. He's lighter than air, funny, playful, smart, a millionaire yachtsman, a sarcastic romantic. There's George, my husband to be. Nobody even tried out for his part last time. There's Mike. That tall skinny guy has that part nailed down,* she thought, and, sure enough, when she scanned the theater, she found him sitting with the director. So far, only one actor seemed set and she wasn't the least bit attracted to him.

Think Tracy, she tried to bring herself back to reality. *Think rich.*

6 Crossing the Bar

The moment he got into the car to drive to the Depot Theater for the audition, Bill felt as if he had been set free. As he drove across the Wabash River bridge, he looked downstream. The water was low and in places the brown bottom poked up through the turgid muddy surface. *When everything slows down and stops moving,* he thought, *all the dirty, ugly things that are hidden underneath push their way up.*

That is what the boredom of the summer had done. He had grown more unhappy with Martha, with her nightly falling asleep on the couch, with her widening sexlessness. But Bill was smart enough to blame his dissatisfaction with Martha upon his own moodiness, his dissatisfaction with himself. This time, however, his restlessness seemed closer to the surface, as if his life was drying up and the ugly bottom of his loss of possibility was being exposed.

For days, since he had gotten what, in his secret mind, he now referred to as his "Cary Grant phone call," he had been sexually obsessed, caught in a frenzy of horniness that he could only ascribe to "getting into his character." He had made love to Martha twice in those three days, a modern record. Once he had actually charmed her out of half-sleep by seductively sneaking up to her on the couch and whispering, "Joody, Joody, Joody, I want your boody." What was even more astonishing was that she had bought his corny imitation and awakened to his hot little fondlings. He was actually starting to believe that he *was* Cary Grant.

I wonder if normal people think in metaphors like novelists do, Bill thought as he started down the exit ramp from the bridge. *Do I really see the world differently from normal people? Do they look at a dirty river and see themselves? Hell no, they look at television and think they see themselves.*

As he came down off the bridge and the exposed river receded behind, he admitted to himself that he was doing it because Dexter, the Cary Grant character in the play, was only thirty-two years old. The biggest snag to poke its ugly snout up through the surface of his summer had been his fortieth birthday. That snag had stove him in. Forty years old. "More than halfway to Hawaii," his doctor had said when Mike passed his physical in July. But somehow being pronounced healthy hadn't made him feel any better about himself. This make-believe world where a forty-year-old man could become a thirty-two-year-old man looked much better than the real world in which he lived. What if the illusion became the reality? Where would he choose to reside? In the three days Bill had been waiting for this audition, all the things that had made him so unhappy all summer had poked up through the surface of his complacency. What he wanted now was to open a dam of new experiences and submerge them all again.

I must be crazy, he felt panic as he walked toward the stage door. *I haven't been in a play for twenty years. There will be people in here all looking at me, listening to me. What have I gotten myself into?*

When he entered the theater, his very first thought was to look at the women, and he did.

7 First Magic

Marge the director prowled the theater preparing for the final audition. She checked off the names of those who had arrived, arranged chairs on the bare stage, brooded over the script in consultation with good ol' Harvey Winkins. Every time the stage door opened, she swiveled in expectation.

Lori took it all in from her seat in the front row on the side. She sensed that this wasn't just another open audition. It had all the markings of a "by invitation only" affair. Marge huddled in the back row in the corner with the dark haired, "bouncy and perky" actress who had read for the Liz part at Lori's first audition. Lori couldn't hear what they were talking about . . . and it's a good thing. The two continued animatedly for long minutes.

"Sunny just won't take the lead part," Marge, in a conspiratorial whisper, summarized to Harvey her tete-a-tete with the brunette. "She wants to do Liz. She says she just doesn't have time to learn and rehearse a role as big as Tracy. I'm tempted to not even give her Liz," Marge ended with a growl.

"Let's not get vindictive now, sweetie," Harvey tried to mollify her. "Andrea is here. Maybe she could do it. Don't get all upset."

"Why the hell not?" Marge hissed. "If I don't get a good Tracy, this whole play is in the dumper. Andrea is too fucking fat."

Harvey recoiled as if he'd been slapped.

Lori watched it all, but didn't understand. The dishwater blonde hillbilly was there for another try just as Lori had expected. There was also one new woman who hadn't been at Lori's other audition. This new competition looked five to ten years older than Lori and quite a few pounds heavier.

They're going to have to use a lot of makeup to convince anyone that she is Tracy Lord, Lori thought. *She must be trying out for some other part.*

This new woman was attractive in a bulging way, and had long, shiny, brown hair that looked like you could do absolutely anything with it. The creature seemed quite comfortable in the theater, and greeted the Director by her first name.

They're going to give it to her, Lori thought, insecurity caving in upon her, but it also pissed her off. *The hell with their ringers,* she rebelled, *I'm gonna do this part, and I'm gonna do it the way I prepared it, and let's just see if their ringer can do better.*

Lori's eyes swept the theater. Harvey Winkins with his handlebar mustache waxed stiffly erect sat whispering with the director in the front row seats at center stage. Miss "Bouncy and Perky" sat under her dark helmet of short hair eight rows behind the three conspirators in the corner of the same center section. Sam Wilcox, the other older actor, was sitting alone poring over his script. John Collins, the tall skinny comedian who already had the role of Mike nailed down, was sitting on the opposite side of the stage from Lori, chatting up the two high school girls who were back to audition for the part of the little sister. There were two other men wandering about, but Lori was pretty sure they weren't actors. She figured they were somehow involved with the theater itself. They were up in the soundbooth and down on the stage and up on the light trestles above the stage. One was tall and thin, in overalls with a metal tape measure clipped to his hip, the other short and bearing a close resemblance to the mole in *The Wind in the Willows,* Lori's favorite children's book.

What are they waiting for? Lori wondered.

Everyone seemed just marking time. She knew that the longer she sat the more nervous she would get.

When the tall, slightly greying man in the light summer slacks and the white shirt unbuttoned at the neck opened the stage door and looked curiously in, almost all the eyes in the room turned toward him. Marge's face broke into an angelic smile as if a great load had been lifted from her shoulders. Harvey Winkins popped up like a toy soldier out of a box.

The man is awfully good looking; the thought was in Lori's mind before she had any chance to suppress it. She tried to figure out how old he was. His body, his face, both looked younger than the longish, greying hair that was brushed in a smooth wave back from his forehead and covered his ears and neck. *With hair that long, he's a professor at the university,* she decided. She realized she was staring as his eyes met hers. Quickly, guiltily, she looked away. *His eyes are blue,* she couldn't believe she was being such a schoolgirl sap, *and he's at least forty, and he looked straight at me.* Lori pretended to be consulting her script. She wondered if this new man was still looking at her. *He's Dexter,* Lori thought wildly as Harvey Winkins bustled across the stage to shake the hand of this newcomer standing just inside the doorway looking hesitantly around.

Lori looked up. *He's not one of them,* she thought. *He hasn't been here before. He's looking around at the place for the first time just like I did. He must be forty. He's at least fifteen years older than me, but, except for the grey hair, he doesn't really look it.*

When Bill entered the theater, he didn't really know what to do so he stood for a long moment just inside the door looking around. Everyone was looking at him. His first thought was to look at the women, and he did. The most interesting one was a little blonde whose eyes had met his momentarily when he first came through the door. She had quickly, *almost guiltily* he thought, looked away.

She is really pretty, he thought. *What great cheekbones.*

She was sitting, turning the pages in her little blue script, so he couldn't really get much of a look at her body. Like a train out on Fifth Street, his old buddy Harvey Winkins bore down upon him with out-stretched hand, pulling along a heavy-set, hatchet-faced woman.

"I don't know if you remember me," Marge brushed Harvey Winkins aside as if he were a tall piece of lint, "but I was a member of one of your workshops at the university last year. Marge Coleman," she offered her hand. "I teach English at Lincoln High School."

"When you're not directing plays," Bill smiled as he took her hand. "It's good to meet you. I'm flattered you thought of me for this part."

He's got a great smile and he's smooth, Lori thought as she eavesdropped. *He talks and moves with manners and class.*

Evidently, this new man's arrival was what all had been waiting for because the audition began immediately. Bill looked around and once again noticed the little blonde sitting by herself on the side near where he had entered. He decided to sit near her, to get a closer look.

Omigod, he's going to sit down next to me, Lori had to look right at him as he walked toward her.

"Hi," he smiled, but said no more. He didn't introduce himself as he had to the others and he didn't sit down right next to her. He took the seat two away from her and stretched out his legs to watch as Marge the director called the audition to order.

"OK, let's start," Marge's gravel voice demanded their attention. "You all got callbacks because you were the best at the earlier auditions. I'll tell you that some of the roles in the play are cast while others are wide open. This will be the last audition session and we plan to have a cast set by Wednesday. Now, if any of you has any doubts as to whether you can make the five nights a week and some Sunday afternoons rehearsal commitment, should you get the part, now is the time to raise them with me."

She paused, but nobody seemed to want to say anything before the whole group so she went on: "OK, if you have any questions about the rehearsal schedule, see me after audition today. Now, one last thing, as we read these scenes today, remember 'Think rich!' These people are classy, sophisticated, witty, but they are also pampered and spoiled and sneaky and lecherous and catty. I want everyone to take five minutes in silence. Put your hands up next to your eyes so that there are no distractions from the sides. Now, for five minutes, think of nothing but who your character is, how she thinks, what she feels, how she talks and moves, what she wants people to think of her. Get in character!"

Lori noticed that all Marge kept saying was 'she' and wondered: *Is the role of Tracy really the only one being auditioned here today?*

Bill had read the play twice since Harvey dropped the script off, but as the silence closed around him and all the people put on their imaginary blinders all he could think of was Cary Grant, how he had talked and moved in the movie. He had probably seen *The Philadelphia Story* ten times, the last being the evening before when he had borrowed the videotape from the Wabash City Public Library.

I don't know how to act, Bill knew. *All I can do is pretend I'm Cary Grant.* He tried to think of Cary Grant: *he talks fast, clipped, with his hands in his pockets and a smirk as if he's always ready to spring a joke. He's the one who livens everything up so he's got to be fast and witty.*

Lori had her hands up next to her face, but she was finding it difficult to concentrate. She sneaked a quick peek at the new man sitting down from her. His hands weren't up and he was smiling to himself.

He looks like a nice man, she thought. *What a doofus. You saw this guy for the first time about five minutes ago.* She had to get her mind back on Tracy. *Tracy thinks that when she goes to the bathroom she pees fresh-squeezed orange juice,* Lori giggled to herself. *That's it, loosen up.*

She tried to remember the breathing exercises that the acting teacher had taught her in college. *She walks around a room as if she expects everyone to do whatever she wants. She's stuck-up, but she's so smart and beautiful that she can get away with it.* Lori had done all this backgrounding before, at home alone with her script while her husband was at work. *She is a control freak. When she's in a room, she expects to be the center of attention. But she has soft spots. She doesn't really show them, but they are there. She wants a man to love her because she looks at men as possessions. Like her horse or her car. This wedding is a big deal because it gives her a chance to show off her latest acquisition. That's her problem,* Lori thought, *she's not capable of love yet. She's only capable of shopping.* Lori grinned behind her blinders, sneaked a peek at the older man. *Shopping is not too shabby,* Lori thought. *If I had Tracy's money, I'd be a power shopper.*

"OK, let's go," the harsh voice of the director shook Lori out of her little reverie, "we'll start about a third of the way into Act Two where Tracy is on the veranda with Mike and Dexter intrudes with the boat."

She paused. "OK, John Collins, you play Mike" (but he was already onstage), "and Bill Franklin, you play Dexter. Now, all we need is a Tracy." Again she paused as if making a decision, which Lori suspected she wasn't making at all. "Let's start with Sondra as Tracy," and with that she sat down, crossed her arms and waited, godlike, for the world she had set in motion to begin to talk.

Well, here goes nothing, Bill thought as he got up and took the stage next to the tall, skinny young man whose name he hadn't caught when the director said it.

No coddling. Not even any introductions. She probably figures this is the only time some of us will probably ever see each other. Just turn to page such and such and start acting. Is she kidding? There are about ten people here I don't even know.

His name is Bill, Lori filed it as she watched him and the dishwater blonde hillbilly take the stage together. John is Mike and Bill is Dexter.

Bill knew the scene, Dexter's first big speech. Dexter is hardly in Act One at all, except to make an entrance at the end. But this first scene of Act Two is his big confrontation with Tracy where he really chews her out for being shallow and arrogant.

The director (he had already forgotten her name) directed him to enter down the left-hand aisle of the theater right out of the audience and start talking to Mike and Tracy, who were standing center stage. This first Tracy was a rather tall and rangy girl with a terrible dye job.

"Hello," Dexter said as he wheeled down the aisle and onto the stage.

"Hello. Fannsey seein' yooo heah," Tracy answered, holding her blue script up close to her face and not looking at him.

My God, she sounds like Hee Haw, Bill thought.

Sitting front row left, Lori's hand involuntarily came up to her mouth as that twangy hillbilly accent mangled the words of this Philadelphia Main Line debutante. She would never have laughed out loud at a fellow actor, but she was afraid that her face would give her away.

"Orrnnge juice? Certainly," Dexter insinuated himself into the breakfast conversation.

"Hold it!" the director stopped them only three lines into the scene. "Now, Dexter," (Bill momentarily wondered who she was talking to, then realized that it was to him, his character), "You're a rich Philadelphia Main Line yachtsman and you slurred the word 'Orrnnge' as if you were some Hoosier farmer out in a cornfield. It's 'ore-ange.' Pronounce the words clearly, distinctly and haughtily as befits your verrry high claaass Ivy League education," she intoned the last with a snootiness that could well have been Philadelphia Main Line.

Me, Bill thought, *what about her?* he sneaked a quick glance at the dishwater blonde hillbilly. *She said her lines like Ma Kettle.*

"Ore-ange," Dexter pronounced it snootily, "right."

"OK, let's start it again and remember who you are," from her seat in the front row the director waved them backwards. This time, she let them read about two pages before she stopped the scene.

"OK, Sondra, thank you; now let's try another Tracy," again Marge the Barge gave them that stage hesitation accompanied by a finger to the chin as if she were making a decision. "Andrea, why don't you try it next."

The only part that is being auditioned here is Tracy, Lori knew it. *The two men are perfect. They are already cast. It's just the three of us she is looking at, how we look with them.* She felt a brief surge of confidence. She knew she was better than her first competition, Miss Bottle Blonde with the backwoods twang.

"Now, Dexter," the Director turned to the men as the second Tracy, the older pudgy woman with the gorgeous brown hair, took the stage, "you are just reading. Move around onstage. Try acting it rather than just reading it."

She's right, Bill thought, *I'm too tight. Loosen up. Look at the other actors when you read the lines. Pretend you're on the patio of a mansion in Philadelphia. Loosen up.*

"Hello," Dexter smiles mischievously as he intrudes on his ex-wife's *tete-a-tete* with the magazine writer.

"Hell-(pause)-O," Tracy is irritated. "Fawnsey seee-ing you HERE!" Tracy comes down hard on the last word to show how angry she is at her ex-husband's invasion of her privacy.

She's good, Lori could see it right away. *She got about three effects into that line. She's good.*

"Ore-ange juice? Certainly," Dexter raises his eyebrows at Tracy as he picks up the imaginary glass, salutes her with it, and takes a sip.

"Much better, Dexter," purred Marge the Barge from the front row.

It sure is better, Lori thought as she watched them read on into the scene. She glanced across at the dishwater blonde hillbilly just to see if she could gauge some reaction, but that spacehead wasn't even paying attention. She had out an emery board and was blithely filing away at one of her nails.

"Andrea is doing a good job with Tracy," Harvey Winkins whispered seductively in Marge the Barge's ear.

"Andrea is too damn old and too damn fat," Marge growled behind her hand. "We shouldn't be wasting her time. Three men want to marry Tracy in this play because she's young, beautiful, headstrong and witty. All Andrea is is witty. I'm sorry I let you talk me into calling her. God knows what your motives were."

Bill was getting into reading Dexter's part, starting to play with it, thinking about inflecting different words.

"OK, that's enough. Thank you, Andrea, you're a doll. Good job." Then, turning once again to Mike: "Now, Dexter, remember, you're never serious about anything. You've always got a twinkle in your eye. Everything is a joke to you, until you get to the middle of this scene and you suddenly get serious with Tracy." Giving him no chance to answer, the director waved the little blonde onstage. "OK, Lori, sorry to have kept you waiting," she said it so carelessly that everybody in the theater knew she didn't mean it.

Lori took the stage not knowing where she stood. She knew she was better than the hillbilly Tracy, but she wasn't so sure about the second

Tracy. She was pretty sure that woman wasn't right for the part, yet she was a good actress, delivered the lines with authority. *I've just got to be better, Lori was determined.*

"Hello," Dexter smiled his mischievous smile.

"Hell-OOO," she drew it out more than had the second Tracy.

"FAN-seee seeing YOU! here," Lori delivered the line with a haughty sarcasm that was very different from the threatened anger the second Tracy had put into her version of the line.

"Ore-ange juice? Certainly," she's the prettiest of all of them, Bill thought as Dexter picked up the glass and jauntily saluted his ex-wife. The director let them go on for another page before she stopped them.

"That was pretty good," the director, again, said it as if she didn't mean it, "but it was just a rehearsal. Now let's do the real thing. Tracy, throw your shoulders back and stick your nose up in the air like the spoiled society girl that you are. Dexter, remember, it's all a put-on until you get Tracy alone, then it turns serious. OK, let's go. From Dexter's entrance."

"All of this 'ore-ange' juice is going to sour my stomach," Bill joked as he went back up the aisle to make his entrance. The director didn't laugh.

The scene began as it had five times before, but this time it was different. Perhaps it was the director telling them they were doing it for real, or perhaps it was just that they had done it or watched it done so many times that it had become familiar, or perhaps they each alone decided that there was some chemistry there. Whatever was the reason, this time it was different. As he smirked at Tracy and pronounced "Ore-ange" just so, Bill Franklin playing Cary Grant playing C. K. Dexter Haven felt the magic for the first time.

He hadn't been onstage for years, yet he sensed what was happening. The actor is suddenly transported out of himself, as if on a mystic wind, into a new existence. He magically re-creates himself.

Bill touched the magic, became Dexter. He looked at Tracy and wanted her, to kiss her, to touch her, but he couldn't. All he could do was joke with her and it made him sarcastic, comically cruel. "I thought all writers drank to excess, and beat their wives," Dexter smiled slyly. "I expect that at one time I secretly wanted to be a writer," he raised a comic eyebrow in Tracy's direction.

Bill felt the magic and it was like wearing an elegant suit and soft shoes and walking on Gatsby's lawn toward a golden girl in a flowing dress. In a lifetime one doesn't get many magical moments—brief spots of time when you are exactly where you want to be doing exactly what you want to do—feeling all the excitement that you so rarely feel in the reality of everyday life. The magic is a fleeting thing that whimsically comes and tenderly goes, but once one feels it one longs for it, and spends the rest of one's life pursuing it. As he looked into Tracy's eyes, he was in love. As she stormed at him for his interference, she made him angry. As he pleaded with her to look before she leaped, he felt the frustration of a man losing the woman he loves. In the midst of the magic, Dexter emerged a full-blown character in Bill's mind.

Lori felt the magic too. As the Tracy she had been thinking and plotting with for days came alive within her, she knew that she was going to get the part. She was tempted to reach out and slap Dexter, or turn and touch his arm, or collapse and cry at the terrible things he was saying. She felt terribly confused and she knew instinctively that was how Tracy would feel. That was the magic of it. *I wonder what it would be like being married to him,* she thought, but she didn't really know whether she was looking at Dexter, whom she knew so well, or some man named Bill, who had walked into her life only half an hour before.

The magic comes and goes, but once it touches an actor, it leaves an impression. It isn't an exterior impression like a dent in a fender, but rather a brush-stroke across the imagination. Actors get that rare magical opportunity to re-imagine themselves and then, for as long as the run, flesh out and grow into that creature of their imagination. Like God they can create angels, like Victor Frankenstein they can create monsters, or, if they are good and dedicated and imaginative, they can create real people that their audiences will remember. The magic that Bill and Lori and John Collins were feeling was not even the most special magic that an actor can feel. Only during a performance when you become the person in dress and space and time and you soar in the certainty that you are doing the part exactly as it ought to be done, and the audience is coming along with you for the ride, does the magic totally take over.

"They look quite good together," Harvey leaned and whispered into Marge's ear. "They would make an attractive couple."

She's the best look and she's a good actress, Marge resigned herself to it. "What choice do we have?" she hissed. "Sunny won't take the part because she's too lazy. Andrea is too fat. The other one sounds like

Dolly Parton. This one looks just like Hepburn and can act. Dammit, if only she didn't stoop! I'm going to have to teach the little dope posture."

"OK, that's good," Marge ceased whispering to Harvey and cut off the scene. "In fact, that's very good. Let's take a short break. If you're going to smoke, please step outside. When we come back we'll read the younger actresses for the sister Dinah and then perhaps do one or two more scenes."

When she stopped the scene, the magic died away, but it left an afterglow, a warmth toward the others who had been co-conspirators in the moment. Bill looked at John Collins and they smiled together. They were friends though they hadn't yet even been introduced. Bill glanced shyly at the little blonde. He didn't even know her name, yet he was already drawn to her. She looked back at him and smiled and gave a quick little nod of her head. He realized that it was a "thank you" for helping her give a good performance. It was sort of awkward, the three of them still standing there in the center of the stage as if they didn't want to break the spell.

"Well, that was fun, a good read," Collins was just making small talk as he wandered off the stage. Bill was left there alone with the young woman.

"We've not been introduced," he began, *oh God, you sure sound like an old fart,* so formal, loosen up, "I'm Bill Franklin," and he stuck out his hand.

"I'm Lori, Lori Martin," she took his hand and didn't shake it, just held it for a second. "I recognized your face from the newspaper. I read your column on the movies."

"Oh, great," Bill liked her already. Much to his surprise she followed him offstage.

"Have you done much acting before?" she asked.

He laughed. "I haven't been in a play since high school. Somehow Harvey and this director got the idea I would be good in this part. What is the director's name anyway? I'm terrible. I forgot her name as soon as she introduced herself."

"It's Marge something."

Bill realized that he hadn't forgotten Lori's name. "How about you, Lori?" he tried her name out to see how it sounded. "Have you done much of this? You seem comfortable up there."

"I was a theater major in college. But it's been three years. Now I'm a legal secretary," she finished sort of lamely.

The others were drifting back into the theater. This time, when they sat back down, Mike didn't leave a seat between them. She didn't seem to think anything of his sitting next to her.

I'm glad he's not one of their regulars, Lori thought. *It's nice to know that there is someone else who isn't an insider.* She noticed that the overweight, older Tracy was gone. *Did they tell her she wasn't right or did she just have to leave?* she wondered. The dishwater hillbilly was still there.

The rest of the audition was clearly for the two high school girls for the role of Tracy's smart-aleck little sister Dinah. They were both cute and enthusiastic. One read with the hillbilly, the other read with Lori, then they switched and did the same scene a second time.

As Bill sat in the audience he could not take his eyes off Lori onstage. *You're building this into a premature fantasy,* he cautioned himself, *she may not even get the part.* But she was a good actress and got better, more relaxed, with each successive scene. *She's really pretty,* he thought. *She could pass as a short version of Katharine Hepburn.* And then the building started to shake.

The nine o'clock AMTRAC was rumbling down the middle of Fifth Street right outside the front door of the theater.

"It always shows up right in the middle of the second act," Marge the Barge announced.

It's too bad they don't do a play with an earthquake in it, Bill chuckled to himself.

Marge seemed to take the train's passage as an omen that the audition should be over. She cut it off and announced that final casting would be done in the next two days and that everyone would get a phone call whether they were chosen for a part or not.

That was it.

As quickly as the magic had come, it had been drowned out by the rattle and rumble of the passing train.

"Dexter, I mean Bill, could I see you for a moment before you leave?" the director wasn't really asking.

He wondered what she and Harvey wanted with him. He really wanted to walk Lori out to the parking lot, but the best he could do was say "Good luck. I thought you did a really good job," as she was gathering her things to leave.

"Thanks," she answered, "it was nice to meet you." She looked tired, washed out, as if she had used up all her energy. He didn't have anything else to say and she just walked away. It chagrined him that she had said "It was nice to meet you" as if they were never going to see each other again. He didn't know that the only reason she had said it that way was because, in her exhaustion, pessimism had flooded over her and she was absolutely certain that she was not going to get the part.

The braintrust was waiting for him. There seemed to be something delicate on their minds. Marge the Barge beat around the bush for a moment before she popped the question. "Bill, we've decided that we want to do this play realistically, in period costume, in real thirties style. We don't think it will modernize very well." She hesitated, carefully culling her words. "Would you mind getting a short thirties haircut?"

Bill smiled. *So that's all it is.* "No problem," he laughed. "I haven't had short hair since the early sixties. It will be different."

"But that's not quite all," good ol' Harvey stepped timidly into the conversation. "Since you're one of the play's romantic leads, we sort of, ah, hoped that, ah, you might be open to getting your hair dyed, just to get rid of the gray."

Bill almost laughed out loud at what Harvey thought was such a touchy subject. "Are you kidding?" he grinned. "For years I've been looking for an excuse to dye my hair."

8 Act One: Don't Stoop.

She had been sitting in the trailer watching television with the cat in her lap since six thirty, waiting for the phone to ring. She was sure that the director's casting call would come tonight. *Life won't stop if I don't get the part.* Her job kept her plenty busy. *Maybe Eddie would start paying more attention to her.*

But, most of all, she wanted to be Tracy for a while. She wanted to be rich and have three different men falling all over themselves to get at her. Finally, at fifteen minutes to nine, the phone rang. Time seemed to slow to the languor of the cat's walk.

"Hello."

"Hello, is this Lori Martin?"

"Yes, it is."

"Marge Coleman, Lori. Congratulations, we want you to do the part of Tracy in the play. It's an awfully big part, but we think you can do it and do it well."

Nothing.

"Uh, Lori—hello?"

Nothing.

"Lori?"

"Whooooooosh." Lori had drawn in her breath and held it for a long moment when she heard the words she had so hoped to hear. To Marge it sounded like a plane taking off. "Alllllllrightttt!" Lori couldn't help herself, had to shout it out, and in the process almost blew out Marge's eardrums.

"Oh, I'm sorry. I didn't mean to scream in your ear. But that's just such great . . . I mean, I'm really pleased to get the part, I mean, I'm excited about, it's great, I mean, it's really neat, I'm happy, you know."

"Well, that's nice. I'm glad you're happy," Marge said, her ear still ringing. "First rehearsal tomorrow night at seven," and she hung up in self-defense probably.

Lori dropped the phone, then dropped the cat that she had forgotten was under her arm, and whose eyes were bugging out from being squeezed in Lori's heedless grip. The cat was stunned and not moving too well, and Lori stepped on him as she began dancing around the room chanting: "I got it. I'm Tracy. I got it. I'm Tracy." The cat watched wide-eyed. Then Lori ran to the mirror on the wall. For some reason, she had to look closely at herself, to see if she could find Katharine Hepburn in her own bright blue eyes and high cheekbones and dyed blonde hair. The cat tilted its head as if saying: "How dare you choke me, drop me and step on me! May you ever be ugly!"

Lori liked the way she looked. *Baby, you're gonna be beautiful on stage*, she thought, and when she turned to the cat he seemed to agree. Eddie was at work, but she had to tell him. To her delight, he answered. The cat, jealous, moving better, lunged up onto the couch and cuddled into the curve of her thigh.

"Honey, I got the part, I got the part, Tracy, the part I wanted in that play, I got it, I got it," in her excitement her voice going a mile a minute.

"Hey, that's great babe, gotta go, we're busy," and he left her standing there with a dead phone and a numb cat. No goodbye. No pause to realize how excited she was. No passion for her happiness. He just hung her up. She pushed the cat away violently and crossed her arms in a pout.

That shit, she thought.

The cat sat on the other end of the couch in a state of stunned alert.

The ten minutes in the car from the trailer park to the theater downtown was, from the very beginning, a time of anticipation for Lori. It was the ten minutes when she stopped being Lori Martin and started being Tracy Lord. Those ten minutes were her passage through the looking-glass of identity.

As she pulled out of the trailer park entrance and onto the four-lane bypass around Wabash City, she always tried to imagine that her rusty Pontiac was a shiny Cadillac with a chauffeur cruising down the Philadelphia Main Line. As she drove through the sleepy, tree-lined neighborhoods of West Wabash, she tried to think like Tracy Lord, envision the gorgeous clothes in Tracy's closet, the comfort of Tracy's huge bedroom, the servants who came every time Tracy pulled a bell-cord next to her bed.

As she crossed the Wabash River bridge into Wabash City, nearing the theater, she would say a few lines out loud, working to catch the tone and feel of Tracy's voice, the confidence, the haughtiness, the lilt of money tripping off Tracy's tongue.

As she pulled into the parking lot the evening of that first rehearsal, the theater suddenly looked different than when she had come for her auditions. No longer was it a place to fear. Now it was hers, her mansion where she would speak and people would listen, where she would appear and all eyes would turn to her, where she was the star, the owner of the center stage.

As she got out of her car, which was, after all, only a rusty Pontiac, she slowly realized what she had gotten herself into. The whole play was on her shoulders and she had to produce. It wasn't just a case of "oh, goody, I get to pretend to be a rich girl." She had to stop and take a deep breath, standing there by her car, as that chill of responsibility passed over her.

It was, perhaps, by some unpredictable magic that just at that moment Dexter pulled into the parking lot and waved. For some reason she waited while he parked so that she could walk in with him.

Bill's drive to the theater had been freighted more with curiosity than anything else. His call from the director the evening before had been mere *pro forma.* She and good ol' Harvey Winkins had made it clear at the end of the audition that he had the part. While all the other readers were asked to turn in their scripts, Harvey had motioned for him to keep his. They had, after all, called to recruit him. And, actually, he had read pretty well. He had not reached the point where he was curious about who his character was, and he hadn't yet started to worry about what he had gotten himself into. He was curious, however, about who had gotten the other parts. He knew that Harvey Winkins was going to do Uncle Willie because Harvey had already let that slip. He presumed that Collins, the tall skinny kid, was going to be Mike, the Jimmy Stewart character in the movie. In truth, the part that he was really curious about was the starring role of Tracy Lord. All of his big scenes were with her.

That little blonde with the great cheekbones ought to get it, he was pretty sure as he drove across the Wabash river bridge. *I wonder if she's married or is a student . . . if she likes older men,* he chuckled as he bounced along the Fifth Street tracks toward the theater. He had felt a strange new sort of excitement on the stage reading that scene with Tracy at the audition. As he pulled into the theater parking lot, his first question was immediately answered. The little, high-cheekboned blonde was just getting out of her car. Instinctively he waved, and she waved back. Then she waited while he parked so that they could walk into the theater together.

"Congratulations," he smiled, "you must have gotten the starring role."

"Yes, I did. It's so many lines."

Bill smiled easily and said exactly the right thing: "Yes, but I think you'll be terrific in that part. After the audition on Sunday I was sure it was going to be you." For some reason just talking to this woman so much younger was making him jittery.

"Well, I wish I had been as sure of it as you were," she confessed as they walked across the parking lot.

Almost the whole cast was already there when they walked through the stage door together. *The theater must be one of the few places where people get to work early*, Bill thought. We're right on time and everyone else is here already.

Most of the cast were seated in the audience seats on the right side of the theater. There were only a hundred and sixty seats in the whole place and the cast took up about ten percent of them. While most of the cast waited on the right, the director and her braintrust, Harvey Winkins and John Collins, sat apart from them at exact stage center in the front row with their heads together in unmistakeable conspiracy. Every time he came into the theater, Bill would notice how the actors would always put space between themselves and the director in the way that labor kept apart from management.

What Lori noticed when they came through the stage door was the way that all the heads in the room turned toward her. A tremor of self-consciousness darted through her. *They're thinking: "so she's the one; she better be good,"* she thought. *They're probably all wondering how much they're going to have to cover for me, whether I can memorize all those lines, whether I'm experienced enough to do the role that has to carry the play.* As these thoughts raced through her mind, she stumbled over nothing and almost fell on her face. Bill grabbed her arm and steadied her. No one said anything, but it certainly wasn't a star's entrance.

"Thanks," she whispered to him after they were seated, "I'm not always that clumsy."

"OK, I think everyone is here," the director boomed the rehearsal into session. "Finally we've got a full cast. I want to start by having everyone introduce themselves, tell which character they're playing and say one sentence about their character." She nodded to Harvey Winkins to begin.

"I am Harvey Winkins, ham actor extraordinaire," he said it with a wonderful upper class pretentiousness, "and, though, as you can all see, still a very clean young man, I play Uncle Willie Tracy, who is a very dirty old man because, really, no one has ever heard of a dirty young man, though I wager there are plenty around," and finishing off with a neat little W. C. Fields imitation, "I was one once meself when I was younger."

Everyone giggled. Harvey had set the playful tone for all of their short comments.

"My name is Sarah Cunningham, but everyone calls me 'Sunny.' God knows why. I play Liz the photographer and I think she's one of those girls who has always got a wisecrack handy. She has a great sense of humor and (glaring at Uncle Willy) in the play, she takes a pinch well."

"I'm John Collins and I play Mike, the magazine writer, who drinks too much and talks too fast and is pretty much confused by everything in the world of this play, which makes me pretty well typecast."

"John is also an architect," Marge cut in, "and has done the set design for the play."

Bill noticed how the tall, skinny actor/set designer beamed.

"My name is Lori Martin," her uncertain voice began, "and, and I'm Tracy Lord." She was much more serious than the others had been. "Tracy is a spoiled brat, but I like her because she's smart enough to realize that just being rich and pretty isn't enough. Her problem is that she doesn't know if she's capable of really loving someone. She wants to be in love, but she just doesn't know how to go about it."

Marge, who hadn't been all that amused by the flippancy of Harvey and Sunny and John Collins, nodded in approval at Lori's seriousness.

Lori wished she could think of something witty to say as the others had, but she couldn't, so she just repeated what she had been thinking in the car on the way to the theater.

"I'm Bill Franklin and I really like the name C. K. Dexter Haven. It's right out of *The Great Gatsby*. I'll bet I've seen the movie of *The Philadelphia Story* fifteen times and to get the chance to play Dexter is really going to be fun. I like the guy. He does all the things I'd like to do. Hell, he's a millionaire who is a sporty dresser, races sailboats and chases beautiful women. What a great part!" Bill said it all with an easy smile, which he hoped hid his nervousness. His enthusiasm was genuine; it surprised even him.

The rest of the players introduced themselves and offered their little character sketches, most of them making a joke at their character's expense. The dishwater blonde with the hillbilly accent who had read for the part of Tracy opposite Lori had gotten the part of the maid and it didn't seem to make any difference to her. She introduced herself as Wanda Grobaski and laughed, "Ah'm gonna spend the next eight weeks cartin' round all you rich folks' dirty dishes."

The last woman to introduce herself had a great name. "I'm Barb Dwyer," she began and then paused for everyone to absorb it. "My mom and dad had a weird sense of humor. Anyway, I'm not an actor. I'm the costume lady and I'll be dressing all of you. The only reason I do this thankless job," she laughed, "is that it gives me completely free access to the men's dressing room." Bill could not help thinking that she meant it. He caught John Collins and Sunny Cunningham exchanging what he interpreted to be a knowing look.

Through all of this, Marge was not amused. "In the next week, I want you to totally background your characters. Take them seriously." Harvey raised his eyebrows and rolled his eyes at Sam Wilcox who had the part of Seth, Tracy's philandering father. "Forget who you really are and pretend you are your character. Try to act and think as your character would."

It's the first night of rehearsals, Bill thought, *and she's tighter than a ballerina's butt.*

"Acting is all a question of identity," Marge seemed to be just warming up. "You've got to give up your own for the next eight weeks. This new self, your character, may be somewhat like you or may not be, but, whatever the case, you have to stop being you." She suddenly pointed at Lori. "Tracy! You are not a legal secretary. You don't live in a midwestern college town. You *are* Tracy Lord and you've got to walk and talk and think like her all of the time."

Lori had been startled by Marge's singling her out. *Why me?*

"I'm absolutely serious," perhaps the director noticed the suppressed grin starting to crinkle the edges of John Collins' eyes or the hand over Harvey's mouth that covered the grin he couldn't suppress. "I want you all to remake yourselves in the image of your character. That certainly shouldn't be hard for some of you," and she glared in Harvey's direction. Her sarcasm, though heavy, was the first sign of any sense of humor that Marge had let slip.

"Now, I don't want you to take this personally, but I am never going to call you by your real names. To me you are the characters in the play. I could care less about your real lives outside the play. As far as I'm concerned this is 1939 and we're in Philadelphia and you are Tracy and Mike and Dexter and you, you old scoundrel," (everyone thought she said it affectionately) "are Uncle Willy."

With that, she distributed cast lists with phone numbers and the rehearsal schedule. "Since we are rehearsing by Acts rather than by French scenes, and because this play is an ensemble piece," she explained, "the whole cast will have to be here for every rehearsal. I realize that in one or two instances there will be unavoidable absences. Please let me know about any rehearsals that you must miss."

Are you kidding me? Bill was looking at the rehearsal schedule. Every single weekday night for six weeks. *How nice, she's given us Labor Day off.* He glanced quickly at Lori who was also studying the rehearsal schedule. *We're going to spend a lot of time together in the next six weeks*, Bill thought. Without warning, Lori looked up into his eyes, caught him looking, smiled weakly.

"Looks like every night except weekends," he, out of a slight embarrassment, tried to fill the air between them with words. "We might as well become our characters; we're not going to have time to be ourselves."

She laughed and nodded in agreement.

"OK," Marge barked, "let's do a read through of the first act. Tomorrow night we'll block it. But tonight we'll just read to get timing and inflection on our lines. Let's do it on stage. Bring chairs if you want or do it on your feet."

Those onstage at the beginning of Act I either carried up folding chairs or just walked onstage holding their little blue script books. The play opens with Tracy, her mother and her smart-mouthed little sister sorting wedding presents. Then, the various family members and guests start arriving for the wedding the next day. As the act progresses, one by one all the characters come onstage until there is a throng bustling around Tracy. Dexter is the second to last character to go onstage in Act I. He doesn't enter until about a minute before the first act curtain.

Because he wasn't due on stage for at least thirty minutes, Bill sat in the audience listening to the others read their lines. He closed his eyes and tried to imagine them all dressed up in a Philadelphia Main Line mansion. He saw high pillars and rolling lawns and sculpted bushes. He saw rich Oriental carpets and latticed windows and fresh flowers and silver trays and original oil paintings and servants in morning coats and starched dresses.

Sitting at home alone reading the play, it hadn't seemed nearly as funny as it was now as he listened to them read it aloud and play off of each other's voices.

The actress who played Margaret, Tracy's mother, and who opens the play, was marvelous as she read her lines with an uppity snottiness that was just right. The high school girl who got the little sister part was cute and lively. Tracy was feeling her way with her lines.

She seems a bit tentative, Bill thought.

The director caught it too. She was on Lori, Tracy, from the very first page of the read-through: "Now Tracy, hit that first word much harder" and "Tracy, remember you're rich and spoiled and used to having your own way; you don't ask for things, you demand things" and "Tracy (irritation creeping into her voice), please hold your head up when you speak; remember you're an aristocrat!" When Uncle Willie came on stage, it was immediately clear that Harvey knew exactly how to steal a scene. He did his lines in a high patrician accent that was hilarious.

He is going to steal the show, Bill was absolutely certain. *These people are good. They are bringing things to their parts I had never imagined when I was reading the play at home. This really is a funny play. They're bringing it to life.*

As he listened to them read their lines, his mind began to wander. He was nowhere near being Dexter yet. He had already forgotten the director's direction to forget their real selves and become their characters. He began planning how he would write this up if he were a novelist (which he was). *I'd call it "Civic Theater,"* he thought. Perhaps he'd start it as an English novel with that strong sense of place that Dickens and John Fowles always have: "The eighty-year-old railway station sits on the corner of Fifth Street like a solemn border guard who expects everyone to stop and present their papers. But now the only papers that get presented are theater tickets." *No, too stodgy and conventional. It will be a novel about people, not about a building.* He began again in a more existential vein: "William Franklin was sick of being himself. He wanted to slough his boring middle-class skin for some new identity. When the phone rang on Sunday evening, how was he to know that it was his second skin calling?" *Yikes,* Bill cringed, *it's the metaphoric mixmaster.*

"Dexter," Marge's whisper so startled him out of his dream world that his head snapped back and almost hit her in the face. She was directly behind him, leaning over and whispering in his ear. Her breath smelled like fast-food french fries. "I want you to make your entrance at the end of Act I down the aisle from the lobby right through the audience. You've got about two pages. Try it." He made his entrance and read his few lines with a smile . . . and nobody said a word.

They read Act I through a second time and Bill resumed his seat in the audience waiting to make his entrance. By the time they were a third of the way through the act, he realized that the director wasn't directing anyone but Tracy. In fact, in a semi-controlled voice, she was harping at the young woman, stopping and restarting her at least once every page.

I know why she's doing it, Bill thought, *but is this kid going to be able to stand up to this kind of pressure for six weeks? Tracy is the play, but the Director is pounding her awfully hard for the first night.*

Marge stopped Tracy again and asked for a different reading. "And Tracy, you've always got to remember that you're rich and beautiful and athletic and haughty. Throw your shoulders back and always keep your head up, like a confident princess," the director kept her voice low and under control.

Then it was time to make his entrance and deliver his little flippant lines at the end of Act I. And then it was over, their first rehearsal.

"That was good, excellent. Tracy, I could see you starting to get the character in that second runthrough. Tomorrow night we'll block Act I. Get on your lines. By next week, I want everyone off book for Act I." But before she dismissed the whole cast she asked, "Tracy, Mike, Dexter, could you stay over just a bit longer. There is one more thing we must do." All of the others filed out, leaving Lori, John Collins and Bill alone with the director.

In the course of the evening, most of which he had spent observing, Bill had consistently found himself focusing on Lori, on how she delivered her lines, but mostly on how she looked and moved. From the darkened audience seats, he had the ideal voyeur's vantage. He could look at Lori, her hair, her face, her body, without running the risk of her catching him as she had earlier. Now, as he stood next to her on the stage waiting for whatever the director wanted, he had the insane urge to massage her neck and shoulders the way he used to do for Martha when she would come home exhausted after a long and tiring day. Lori looked worn out by the exertions of the rehearsal, but Bill knew he couldn't touch her like that. She would certainly take it wrong. He jammed his hands into his pockets as Lori turned and whispered, "What do you suppose this is?"

Strangely tongue-tied, he just shrugged.

"OK, you three," Marge was smiling as if she was in on some private joke, "I always like to get this out of the way early in the rehearsals. My actors usually thank me because it takes the tension out of what is often an awkward situation."

She paused briefly and Bill and Lori glanced quizzically at each other. John Collins just stood there with a moronic grin on his face.

"At different points in the play, both Dexter and Mike, who are both in love with Tracy, have rather intimate scenes with her. In the drunk scene, Tracy and Mike kiss passionately a number of times."

Suddenly, Lori knew what was coming. The color was starting to rise in her cheeks. *You're damn right I feel awkward about it, kissing a stranger,* Lori thought.

"I've always found that actors are much more comfortable if they get that first kiss between strangers out of the way in private without the whole cast watching. Tracy," she paused for effect, "first I want you and Mike to kiss, and then it's you and Dexter. You two," she turned to the two men, "I want you to take her in your arms when you kiss."

I'm going to get to touch her after all, Bill who was really Dexter exalted as if his prayers had been answered. But to his surprise, instead of feeling sexual excitement, he immediately felt a mixture of guilt and anxiety. "It's a dirty job, but somebody has to do it," he laughed it off with a wisecrack.

Sure glad I brushed my teeth before rehearsal, was all that popped into Lori's mind.

Collins had his handkerchief out and was vigorously wiping his forehead and lips.

They all hesitated. Lori seemed the most flustered, as well she should be.

All of this is going too fast, Lori suddenly felt spooked. *I didn't think I'd have to deal with this for a couple of weeks.* She just stood there. Nobody was moving to take her in his arms.

"Oh, c'mon John," Marge broke the awkward silence. "You spent most of the last act of *Little Footsteps* kissing Sunny. You go first. This ought to be fun. Don't you people ever have fantasies of kissing strangers?"

Lori turned to John Collins. Waited.

He moved tentatively to her.

"You are Mike Connors, hot-shot reporter, and Tracy Lord, the prettiest girl on the Main Line, and you're both drunk," Marge coached.

John put his hands on Lori's shoulders and drew her to him. He was a good six inches taller than she and had to stoop to meet her mouth. She raised her face to meet his stoop, but her hands forgot to do anything and hung at her sides like a couple of limp mackerel. They kissed gingerly, tightlipped as a seminarian and a nun.

"Good Gawd," Marge laughed, swooping down upon them before they could separate, "you kiss like two people terrified of mono." She quickly took Collins' hands and moved them off Lori's shoulders down first to Lori's hips and then around to encircle her back. Quickly she guided Lori's dead-fish hands up around John Collins' neck. "You kiss like a couple of mannequins, stiff, cold, you gotta be able to do better than that," she chided them. "OK, now—look at each other; hold that eye contact. Smile at each other. Now, move your bodies together. Now, kiss each other as if you mean it." She was like a drill instructor going by the numbers, but she got results. It was a much better kiss this time.

"Not bad," Marge laughed, "the things I have to do to get actors to act natural. OK, Dexter, now it's your turn."

Bill was determined that he wasn't going to be the shrinking violet. He started out with a joke—"Hey, this is great. Kissing a beautiful woman who isn't your wife and it's all legal"—and moved over beside Lori. But when he got right up to her, all of a sudden it didn't seem so easy. *I really want to kiss her,* he thought, *and I want her to kiss me back.* He felt a sexual arousal beginning that he did not want her to feel when she was in his arms. He tried to remember the commands, by the numbers, that the director had given when Collins had kissed her.

Lori had to laugh at herself after John Collins moved away from her. *That wasn't bad at all,* she thought. *That's the first guy other than Eddie that you've kissed in years. Hey, this is kinda nice. I could get into this.* She turned to Dexter, who had moved to her side. She raised her face toward his. They were a good foot apart so she moved closer, but he took a small step back. *He's scared like I was,* she thought. She looked into his eyes and smiled and reached both hands up around his neck.

Bill felt her hands touch his neck and he knew that he had to do something. *You're Dexter,* he thought in desperation, *you were married to her.* His arms seemed to move in slow motion, but he felt the smooth fabric of her blouse as they encircled her. He looked down into her face and she smiled up at him as she pulled on his neck, and her lips came up to his. He could feel her body moving close against him and in a flash he thought, *Omigod, now she knows for sure this is real for me.*

She was kissing him hard and he had no choice but to respond. Her mouth was moving on his, not open, but alive, brushing and pressing his lips, turning in between his lips, meeting and holding his lips until the surfaces of their lips fit together like the petals of a flower. They didn't stop kissing for a long moment.

As they held that first kiss, the floor and the walls began to shake. The whole building began to shudder in that rhythmic, growling way that it did every night right around nine thirty. As they broke off from that first kiss, the Amtrak was in full rumble down the middle of Fifth Street in front of the theater.

Bill still had Lori in his arms as the building shook. He didn't know where they came from, but the words spilled out of his mouth. "Did the earth move for you, too?" he said it aloud in a stage whisper so that everyone could hear it.

They all cracked up except for Lori, who stepped a quick step back as if she didn't get it right away, before joining in with the others. "And it still is!" she laughed.

9 Taking Good Measure

The second rehearsal was slow getting started. The actors were all there on time at seven, lounging in the audience seats, making the first efforts to get acquainted with small talk. When Bill came in, John Collins and Marge were onstage pointing and measuring by eye the set design and the placing of furniture. Sunny, Harvey Winkins, and Wanda, the dishwater hillbilly, formed a cosy trio in the third row. Harvey seemed to be regaling them with some raconteur's anecdote which ended with a guffaw and two giggles on the line, "but have you ever met a dirty young man, I said." Stoic Sam Wilcox sat in front of this jolly group eavesdropping as he pretended to study his lines. The two high school girls sat in the front row, and seemed pleased and eager when Bill noticed their existence by smiling and saying "hi." Lori sat by herself at the other end of the front row and Bill hesitated only a moment, then went and sat down next to her.

"Why, Dexter, what are *you* doing here?" she grinned in a mock stage whisper.

He was quick to catch the spirit of her greeting: "Oh, I just dropped in to break up your wedding, my dear. I do hope you don't mind."

Before they really had a chance to talk, Barb Dwyer appeared out of the wings. She stopped just onstage near the back and peered out at the actors as if making some sort of fateful selection. As the woman stared down from the back of the stage, Bill caught another knowing look, like the one he had seen the night before when the woman introduced herself, passing between Sunny and John Collins.

What is it about this woman, Bill thought. *Every time she appears someone raises an eyebrow.*

In everything but her eyes and her breasts, Barb Dwyer was pretty average. She was neither short nor tall. Her hair was dark and neither long nor chopped. She looked to be in her late thirties and neither slim nor turning to heaviness. Her shape, however, though devoid

of prominent curves of voluptuousness below the waist, was distin-
guished by a major curve of voluptuousness above the waist. She was
wearing jeans that were neither tight nor loose and a loose-fitting but
certainly not baggy sweater. Her face had neither a distinctive beauty
in its complexion and configuration nor any sort of ethnic exoticism
in her nose or mouth or cheekbones. She was really a quite average-
looking woman, someone you really wouldn't glance at twice if she
was coming down an escalator opposite you, until you looked into her
eyes. Barb Dwyer's eyes, like her breasts, somehow seemed bigger than
the rest of her. It wasn't just the bigness of her eyes, but the hunger in
them. It was hard to look steadily into Barb Dwyer's eyes because they
were so demanding.

Much to Bill's surprise, Barb Dwyer came straight downstage to a
position directly in front of where he and Lori were sitting.

"Now, let's see," Barb Dwyer's eyes, like spotlights in a prison
movie, pinned Bill against the back of his theater seat, "you're Dexter,
aren't you? I've got some super ideas for how I'm going to dress you.
Could you come down to the dressing room? I need to get your measurements."

The woman's eyes made him nervous. *Maybe she is the Svengali of
the theater group,* he thought.

The dressing room area wasn't much. The staircase up to the stage
was but one of the five doorways or portals that opened off the small
square dressing hall. One doorway, hung with a heavy metal door,
led outside to a narrow stairwell that climbed up a grey concrete wall
to the parking lot. In this stairwell the actors smoked their nervous
cigarettes between exits and entrances. Of the other three doorways,
only one had a door. That was the bathroom. The other two doorless
portals opened into identically configured long narrow rooms. One
side of each room consisted of a waist-high counter topped by a wall-
to-wall mirror, while the other side was an open closet with a long pole
for hanging clothes extending its full length at eye-level. These were
the mens' and womens' dressing rooms.

As they reached the bottom of the stairs, Barb Dwyer started to
talk in a soft babble. That sound of her voice, their aloneness in that
basement, made Bill feel as if he had entered her "domaine."

"Oh, I just think you're going to love the ideas I've got for dressing
you in this play. You're the big romantic heartthrob. After all, Cary
Grant did play your role in the movie," her rhythmic voice had an al-

most mesmerizing effect, "so we have to make you look rich and classy and sexy. I've decided basically on three costumes. The first two will be casual and the last more formal. But the key to your personality will be the grey argyle socks. They will be the perfect touch."

Later, thinking about it, Bill would realize that he let her maneuver him into position with a lilting soliloquy about argyle socks.

"Your first costume will be a yachting outfit. Blue blazer, grey slacks, grey argyle socks. Your second will be a cardigan sweater, some tighter, sportier slacks, and those grey argyle socks, and your third will be this beautiful grey silk suit which will match those argyle socks beautifully. It is an authentic thirties suit with pleated, cuffed pants. I picked it up in a garage sale just last week. And, it goes perfectly with the argyle socks." The flow of her language gently carried him into what he presumed was the men's dressing room. There was a tape measure and a clipboard with pen, tools of the costume lady's trade, lying on the counter beneath the wall of mirrors. With a soft squeeze of his arm, Barb Dwyer stood him still even as she bubbled on about argyle socks. Once she got her tape measure in her hand, however, she went straight for his crotch.

For some reason she needed to measure both his inseams. But it was the way she did it that snapped him out of his trance. Her hand was literally cupping his crotch as she took the first inseam measurement. She ran the tape measure between her fingers, than flattened her whole palm up against his crotch. When he flinched and looked down in alarm at what she was doing, she laughed merrily up at him and explained, "I get a much more accurate measurement this way. If I'm going to get the pants properly form-fitting, I have to get the numbers exactly right."

He was acutely uncomfortable. He wondered just exactly what she was measuring.

"You know, I've found that a lot of men's legs are of different lengths," she talked wide-eyed up at him as if nothing out of the ordinary were happening at all. But something very out of the ordinary was happening. Bill was acutely aware of it and, if Barb Dwyer didn't finish her inseam measurement pretty quickly, he was certain that she would be aware of it too. "Just relax, Dexter," she hadn't finished soon enough, in fact seemed to be rechecking her measurements, "after all, everyone knows that there is no such thing as modesty in theater."

"I just haven't been in theater very long," he said rather lamely.

"Now, turn around and let me get the rest of your measurements in back," she ordered in that soft, unconcerned voice of hers. He breathed a sigh of relief, but he shouldn't have. She was behind him now and all of the measurements she was taking seemed to originate from his derriere. With her open hand flattening the tape measure against his buns, she extended it up to his shirt collar and then to each of his armpits in turn.

"I get much more accurate measurements this way," she once again assured him. "Are you married? Have any kids?" Her voice was so deceptive in its soft evenness that it took a second for him to realize that he had been asked direct questions.

"Why—yes," he stammered. "I have a daughter in college."

"How nice," Barb Dwyer burbled on, "kids are great," and she was up close behind him taking first his neck measurement, then his chest, then going down to her knees and deftly spinning him around with her fingertips on his hips to face her as she took his waist size. "My folks had three kids," she never stopped talking in that rhythmic sing-song, "besides me. My real name is Barbara Jean Dwyer, although everybody likes to make a joke out of my name. My mom and dad and all my brothers and sisters call me BJ," and she looked straight up at him with those wonderful wide eyes and he had never felt so uncomfortable in his life. "It's almost as much of a joke with them as Barb Dwyer is with everybody else," she chuckled.

She was so disarming, and yet he felt as if he were being molested. *She is either totally oblivious to what she is saying and doing as she goes on with her incessant talking, or she is putting the make on me in a not very subtle way.* He decided that she knew exactly what she was doing and had, in fact, done it many times before. That realization made him even more uncomfortable.

"Where's Dexter?" Marge's gravelly voice echoed down the stairwell from the stage above. "Dexter, we need you up here . . . now."

"I guess I've got to go," Bill moved out of the bondage of her tape measure.

"Oh, that's OK," Barb Dwyer purred. "I've gotten everything I wanted for now. You're just going to love the clothes I'm going to put on you."

"Yes, I'm sure I will. I'll love them, yes I will," Bill stammered as he backed out of the doorless dressing room and fled.

Everyone was onstage when he virtually exploded out of the wings. All heads turned at his abrupt entrance. It wasn't until Barb Dwyer emerged behind him with her tape measure draped around her neck and her benign smile hanging beneath those wide, hungry eyes that there was any discernible reaction. As if on a well-rehearsed cue, Marge, John Collins and Harvey Winkins exchanged knowing looks. Sunny's hand leapt to her mouth to stifle a giggle.

I've been set up, Bill immediately suspected, *or at least nobody bothered to warn me.* It would not be until Friday night when most of the cast would retire to a bar that, under interrogation, Bill would get the full Barb Dwyer story from John Collins.

"Man, I've never been measured by any tailor like that," Bill would laugh after his third beer. "And you guys all knew about it. I saw the looks on your faces when we came up from the dressing room."

"Came up, you shot up those steps like she was after you with a gun" Harvey Winkins poked the needle at him.

"Well, I was a bit startled."

"Startled, man . . . you were in full flight," Collins joined in.

"So what is the deal with her? Does she just like feeling up guys?" Bill didn't realize how stupid his question sounded.

"To tell you the truth," Harvey struck his best Polonian tone, "being measured for my costumes by Barb Dwyer is always one of the true high points of any Civic Theater play I do." Then, standing and emoting to the bar like a Shakespearean actor in a Western saloon, Harvey, raising his glass, proclaimed: "You have not lived until you have been inseamed by Barb Dwyer."

"She's really a very sweet, quiet woman," Collins' eyes twinkled "nothing at all like what one might expect from her name. The only problem is that all of that quiet sweetness is just camouflage for her perpetual horniness."

"She loves men," Sunny cut in. "The only reason she does these plays is to meet new men."

"Not to put too much of an emphasis upon it," Polonius emoted over his beer, "but I would say that she is somewhat of a closet, make that dressing room, nymphomaniac."

But that second night Bill was grateful to Marge for barking them all back to the business of the rehearsal. She was describing the way the stage would be furnished and, at her direction, John Collins was folding and placing chairs and boxes to simulate the set furniture. Bill tried to melt into the crowd of attentive actors while simultaneously moving as far away as possible from Barb Dwyer. Collins got the simulated furniture set—three chairs together equaled a couch, wooden boxes on each side of the stage were a coffee table and a desk, another folding chair up stage left an easy chair, while various chairs arranged down front and center were the porch furniture. Only then did Marge take center stage to deliver another speech to her actors.

"Tonight we are going to try to get Act One blocked," she began. "We're going to read through it, but I'll be giving you each move, each mark to hit, on every line, and I want you to take accurate penciled notes in your scripts. Use pencil because there will definitely be changes."

Bill turned to Lori, "What does blocking mean?" He didn't have a clue. The only way he'd ever heard the term used was on the football field in high school. He'd never understood his blocking assignments then, either.

"Blocking is the movements the actors make on stage, plus the places they take when they're standing still," Lori whispered.

Bill nodded as if he understood.

"This blocking is not going to be easy," Marge was warming to her lecture. "We have a large cast and the play, especially Acts One and Three, is almost completely ensemble acting. You are going to have to be absolutely precise to keep from stepping on each other, and from backing into the furniture. The set is going to be cluttered most of the time, not so much with furniture as with people. This whole play is based upon dialogue exchanges between three or more people. I'm going to want triangles, remember . . . triangles, that means always move into triangular positions downstage to upstage to downstage from stage right to left. Three is the magic number in this play. Always think in triangles."

Bill leaned close to Lori and whispered, "what is she talking about? What is downstage to upstage?"

Lori raised her hand to her mouth and whispered demurely behind it: "Upstage is toward the back, down is toward the front."

Across the stage, John Collins whispered "What is this triangle stuff?" in Harvey Winkins' ear.

"How should I know?" was the immediate rejoinder. "Either humor her or ignore her. I don't think it much matters which."

"Remember, cast, I must have my triangles."

Though he had no idea what she meant, somehow Bill suspected that "triangles" could become the catch phrase of the play.

"Before we start the blocking, I want to take a few minutes for a last emphasis upon each of your characters . . ."

Boy, she sure likes to give speeches, Lori thought.

What a pompous old bat! Bill was thinking as he smiled attentively.

"I've made a list of the single most important motivations of each character. These are one-word associations that each of you should always keep uppermost in your minds."

"Terrific, right along with triangles," Collins whispered seductively in Sunny's ear. In answer, she hit him hard in his pigeon chest with her fist. He coughed and recoiled.

Marge paused to glance his way with disdain.

"OK. Here are each of your character keys. Tracy, regal and vulnerable. Dexter, mischievous. Mike Connor, puzzled and drunk. Uncle Willie, lecherous. Liz, sarcastic. Seth, philandering."

She's giving every character a little name tag to wear, Bill thought. He didn't realize how before the play was over he would thank her for it. Those little tags would be the one thing he would fall back upon when he got in trouble onstage.

Because Dexter didn't make his first entrance until near the end of Act One, Mike was able to sit in the audience and watch the director block the set. It was slow work and the word for the Act and the evening was "congestion."

As Bill watched the Director and actors inch their way from line to line and move to move, he began to acquire a respect for how intricate a mechanism a play is. They worked for more than an hour before Marge called a break. The blocking hadn't arrived at Dexter's entrance yet, so all Bill had done was sit.

"Stick around for this," Harvey leaned over and whispered as the actors came offstage. The word passed quickly to the others and no one went out right away.

Collins loitered onstage, then yelled up into the rafters where someone had been clunking around most of the evening, "Hey, Ernie, why don't you get Thurman and we'll go over the set design. I think I've got it figured out."

"OK," came a voice out of the upper darkness, "he's over in the prop shop. I'll git 'im."

In a few minutes Ernie, the tall, thin one, and Thurman, the short one with the gap between his front teeth, appeared out of the wings. Ernie had a retractable metal tape measure in his hand and Thurman had a pencil and clipboard. Marge joined Collins onstage for this set design conference with Civic Theater's two head carpenters.

Lori, got a drink of water and wandered over to sit down next to Bill. Neither of them knew what was going on. Later they, like everyone else in the cast, would get used to John Collins' perpetual practical jokes. It was as if Collins was possessed, driven by a need to stage absurdity just to see how normal human beings would react to it. His practical jokes were a kind of guerilla theater, the principles of the stage applied to the chaos of real life.

"Ernie, Thurman, I think we've got it figured out," and Collins nodded in acknowledgement of Marge as his collaborator. "We want the stage to end right here," he pointed downstage, "which will be the end of the house and the beginning of the patio. We'd like the stage to be faced with a three-foot-high brick wall."

"No problem; we can do that," Ernie nodded amiably.

"I'd like real bricks and mortar so it has that look of depth and solidity," Collins added as if merely tossing off a second thought.

"Real bricks! Are you nuts?" Thurman, who had been quietly taking notes on his clip board, erupted. "We're not gonna build a real brick wall!"

"Now Thurman, calm down," Ernie chuckled.

"Use that brick plasterboard left over from two plays ago if ya ask me," Thurman muttered as the whole group moved downstage.

"Now here is where the rake will end and the brick wall will be," Collins was pointing as Thurman, still scribbling on his clipboard, continued to mutter.

"Now, right here I want to put a window box with a complete bay window frame and a flower box with real flowers."

"No problem; we can do that."

"No, we can't," Thurman was turning apoplectic. "You know how long it's gonna take to build a whole bay window? How are you gonna keep real flowers alive? By the end of a performance they'll be dead as a doornail."

"Now here," both Collins and Ernie ignored Thurman, "is where we'll put the fountain."

"Fountain? What fountain? There wuz nothin' in the set design you gave us about no fountain," Thurman's face was reddening like a burner on a stove.

"Now calm down, Thurman," the ever-docile Ernie only made it worse, "let's hear the man out."

"Calm down. Hear 'im out," the shorter man sputtered.

"If we could, we'd like the fountain to look like marble," Collins went blithely on, "and the water should shoot straight up in the air in thin streams to a point just below the ceiling, but it can't splash the audience."

"We could do that. That'd be fun to see," Ernie was really getting caught up in the romance of this magical set that he was going to build.

"Fun? No way. We can't do that. Fun? Are you nuts? We can't plumb no fountain right in the middle of the stage. Shoot to the ceiling. Absolutely not!"

"Great," Collins moved up to the back of the stage, utterly ignoring Thurman's gap-toothed protests. Ernie followed as if hypnotized by the grand plan. "Now right here," Collins was standing at stage rear in the center, "we'll cut a large square out of the carpeting and put down a marble floor."

"Ya don't mean real marble, do ya?" It was the first questioning of any kind that had yet surfaced in Ernie's trusting soul.

"Has to be," Collins said it with a straight face, "we need that marble sound to echo through the theater when people walk on it."

"Well, real marble's sorta hard to get," the first doubts were creeping into Ernie's mind.

"We can't git no marble. We can't build no brick walls. We can't plumb no fountains. We can't do none o' this. This is crazy." Thurman was spitting out the words violently.

John Collins ignored both Ernie's mild protest and Thurman's fulminations. He went right on with the rendering of his vision. "Now right here, directly behind the marble floor section, I want a formal mantlepiece that also looks like marble. We don't have to get any sound out of it though, so it doesn't have to be real. Next to it I want two marble pillars sculpted at the top which reach all the way to the ceiling. Then, over here I want a full wet bar with cold water and ice cubes so that Uncle Willie can make drinks."

"What the hell's wrong with the seltzer bottles we always use," Thurman erupted again.

"Now wait a minute, Thurman," Ernie had this anticipation in his voice, this excited look in his eye, "this could be the best set we ever built, a set where everything works, nobody's ever built a set like this."

"And we can't neither. We might's well try to build Rome in a day. We can't do all this stuff in four weeks. You NUTS??"

It was the challenge, the romance of the vision that had Ernie beguiled. Set builders could be artists too, could take their job every bit as seriously as the actors took theirs. Collins had mesmerized Ernie into embracing this romantic vision of the ultimate Philadelphia Main Line mansion. Unfortunately, there was no way Thurman was going to enter that romantic dream. If Ernie wanted to be a visionary artist with his head in the clouds, that was fine. But Thurman was the ultimate realist built like a gap-toothed fire-plug, and there was no way he was going to stand still while they pissed all this nonsense on him. Ernie and Thurman were romance and reality walking around.

"Now," Collins wasn't letting up, "over here, just offstage, we're going to have to build a stable for the horses . . ."

Ernie was actually considering it when it finally dawned on Thurman what was going on. "Wait a minute," the little gap-toothed man threw down his clipboard. "You bastard! It's all a put-on, isn't it? Ernie, it's a joke," an almost tragic note of protectiveness had crept into Thurman's voice, as if he didn't want Ernie's high hopes to be dashed. "It's a put-on, Ernie. Damn flaky actors have got us agin."

"I knew that," Ernie said lamely. "Hell, I figured that all along, Thurm. I was just tryin' to see how long it'd take you to git it."

Collins collapsed in laughter into a folding chair. He looked to be approaching jokegasm.

Marge was laughing right along with him like a real human being.

It was another full hour before the blocking arrived at Dexter's entrance. By that time he was ready to charge onstage as if it were San Juan Hill. For Bill, that first night of slow blocking would set his attitude toward Act One for the whole rest of the play. He hated when they had to rehearse Act One. He realized that all he wanted was to get Dexter onstage. He knew he had a good entrance, but he hated waiting around to make it.

The blocking of the end of Act One turned out to be almost as funny as Collins' practical joke. Absolutely the whole cast, including the maid, was onstage, and it was like the proverbial Chinese fire drill. Everyone was delivering lines rapid-fire while simultaneously trying to get offstage. Dexter and Tracy were circling each other warily. George, Tracy's husband-to-be the next day, was utterly annoyed at Dexter's crashing of his wedding party. Mrs. Lord was appalled at Dexter's bad form. Little sister Dinah thought Dexter was great and couldn't get close enough to him. Uncle Willie just wanted to have a drink with Dexter. Connor the writer and Liz the photographer didn't have the slightest idea what was going on. And Dexter was just sailing back and forth spraying everyone, particularly George, with wisecracks. But if the characters were confused, the actors were utterly lost. They were bumping into each other, delivering lines to the wrong person, exiting the wrong doors, or trying to exit and having no place to go. There was so much confusion that when the director finally got everyone offstage, she breathed a great sigh of relief just at the moment when Seth, the philandering father, comes onstage to deliver the curtain line of the act. The only problem was that there was no one left onstage to whom he could deliver his line. Marge the Barge had to re-do the whole fire-drill exit to keep Tracy within hearing range of Seth. It was eleven fifteen before rehearsal broke up.

Lori was exhausted. Bill watched her walk offstage when the director called an end to it and just slide slowly down into a theater seat like she was sliding into a warm tub. He went and sat next to her for the director's final notes. Marge the Barge spent ten more minutes telling everyone where the problems were in Act One. Most of that time was spent talking directly to Lori, pointing out things that Tracy had to do, places where Tracy had to arrive exactly on cue. Bill realized that the real pressure in this play was upon Tracy. Lori had twice as many lines as anyone else and controlled all the other actors' movements. Bill knew there was abundant reason for the director to be concentrating so fully on Tracy. He just wondered how long Lori would be able to stay afloat amid the constant buffeting of Marge the Barge's criticism. He was tempted to ask Lori if she wanted to go have a drink. He wanted to tell her how good he thought she was in the part. He wanted to tell her how pretty he thought she looked onstage. But she looked so exhausted, and he was afraid she'd take it wrong. He was just too uncertain of what he was up to, and so he didn't say a word. Everyone was tired and they had all had more than enough rehearsal for one night.

As they all trudged wearily out, Bill tried to make a joke. In his best suave Dexter voice he said to Uncle Willie and Seth, "I think I'll stay in character. I'm going to go home and be mischievous."

"Capital idea," Uncle Willie shot back. "I'm going home and drink and letch."

"I guess I'll just have to go home and philander," Seth grinned.

"You do your philandering at home?" Uncle Willie was aghast. "How utterly convenient. I've never thought of that."

Lori, who was listening in, could manage only a weak smile for all of them as they passed out of the theater. "I can be vulnerable without even trying," she said in a small voice when they all were out of earshot.

10 Couples

On Thursday night of that first week of rehearsal, Marge had set a meeting in the theater for her production staff: Collins who had designed the set, his set builders, the prop people, the costumers, the sound and light designers. As a result, the cast didn't have to present themselves until eight o'clock. After three days of eating dinner and immediately climbing into his car to drive across the bridge to the theater, Bill was actually sitting down on the couch after gorging on Martha's spaghetti with white clam sauce, his favorite. She had made it especially for him. He shared the couch with his first set of freshman papers. The university had been in session for almost ten days. He had started working on these first papers that afternoon. Martha was doing the dishes in the kitchen, so he decided to knock off a few more papers before leaving for the theater. Since they were all new freshmen, he had asked them to write a short essay on the book they had learned the most from in high school.

"What are you laughing at?" Martha asked, drying her hands on a dishtowel as she came in from the kitchen.

"God, here's another great one," Bill was still chuckling. "I wish over the years I'd kept a journal or a list of these great screw-ups these kids make in these freshman papers."

"What is it?" She sat above him on the arm of the couch looking down at the student paper he was holding.

"This is great. He's writing on . . . this is great . . . on *The Organ of the Species,* and in the first paragraph he tells how Darwin's researches were supported by Queen Victoria, get this, who sat on the thorn of England for sixty-three years."

"What was that great one you got a couple of years ago? About Plato, no Socrates . . ."

"Socrates dies of an overdose of wedlock."

They both laughed. They didn't spend much time together anymore. He had plenty of time. She was the one who usually wasn't there. Exactly the opposite of when they were younger and he was just starting out in academia and she was always home alone with the kids. He taught only two courses a semester at the university now and spent most of his time home alone writing while she worked her eight-to-five job across the river. In the evenings, tired from her job, she usually fell asleep in front of the TV. It was sort of nice having a moment to laugh together again. To prolong her laughter he remembered some of his other favorites.

"Remember the kid who got the Bible all wrong? He said Solomon had 500 wives and 500 porcupines."

And her laughter flowed back like a gentle wave. "You're enjoying this play, aren't you?" she gently changed the subject. "You seem happier these days."

"I do?" Her change of subject was too studied not to have been rehearsed. *She's curious,* he guessed.

"Yes, you do" and she slid down into his lap off the arm of the couch, "in fact, you're almost glowing with it, like the cat who swallowed the canary."

"I am having fun," he said it tentatively as if it was the first time he had really tasted the idea. "It's so different. I haven't really done much yet. Mostly I sit and watch. I've only got about twenty lines at the very end of Act One."

"I can tell you're enjoying it," she actually seemed happy for him. "You're so much more . . . relaxed, I guess."

"Now what does that mean?"

"Well, you're just not so quiet. You don't look at me as if you hate me when I lie down on the couch in the TV room. For a couple of weeks there, after softball ended, I thought you were going to lose it sitting around the house in the evening."

"I'm enjoying it so far, I guess," he suddenly felt this strange possessiveness about the play, that it was his and she was prying. He had meant to say more, tell her how insecure he felt in the company of all those actors who had spent so much time onstage, tell her how seriously they took it, tell her how intimidated he felt about all the lines he had to memorize, but he held back. *I'm not going to whine like she does about her job,* he thought. Yet he knew that was being unfair. She had no hidden agenda. She was just curious about the play. She was trying to sustain a conversation, something they rarely did anymore.

"What do you mean 'I guess'?" she had caught the hesitation in his voice.

"They're just all so good, I guess. I mean, they're comfortable on-stage, and they take it so seriously."

She laughed.

Then, she said the worst thing she could possibly have said: "Oh hon, it's only acting; it's not heart surgery. You can do it as well as any of those people."

She said it to console him, like a coach giving a pep-talk to an over-matched team, but all it did was annoy him. He hated the patronizing tone of "it's only acting."

You're right, sure, but I can still take it seriously, can't I? he spit the words at her inside his mind.

"No, you're right, it sure ain't heart surgery," he said weakly, rolling her gently off his lap onto the student papers spread over the couch. "I gotta go."

It was only twenty after seven and he knew he'd be early to the theater, but he wanted out of there, away from her. She had an uncomprehending smile on her face. She had enjoyed their little talk, hadn't a clue how angry she had made him.

"When you come in, maybe we can fool around with *The Organ of the Species*," she leered in what she surely thought was utter lewdness.

All it did was irritate him more.

Yeah, right, you'll be dead on the couch snoring like an asthmatic yo-deler.

"I'll probably be late," was all he said, ducking out the door.

As soon as the screendoor bounced shut behind, guilt surged over him.

He knew immediately that there was no reason to feel so defensive toward her. She hadn't done a thing. She was just trying to be nice, show interest. She loved him. They'd been together most of their lives. Maybe that was the problem.

Lori's right hand was stroking the cat curled up next to her on the couch. Her left clutched the already dog-eared little blue script in which her nose was buried. Eddie sat at the dinette table only five feet away eating fried chicken with his fingers out of a red, white and blue bucket and guzzling diet cola in an equally patriotic can. His beard was filling up with grease, but he didn't seem to mind.

Lori actually enjoyed memorizing her lines. They shut out the real world of the trailer park. She would focus her eyes on the lines, read them through two or three times, then close her eyes and drift away on the words, her lips repeating them in an almost inaudible whisper. Her inner eyes, her imagination, saw Tracy, who always looked like the young Katharine Hepburn, saying those words. What she found when she opened her eyes is that the imagined world of her inner vision tended to hang on for a while, had the power, even though her eyes were wide open, to blur over her surroundings, take over her life and world . . . until she was finally jolted back to reality.

"You sure look goofy with your eyes closed and your mouth moving and no sounds coming out," Eddie broke her concentration.

When she looked over at him, he was holding a half-eaten chicken part in his hand and grinning at her with a large piece of chicken skin hanging in his beard.

"I look goofy!" She didn't mean her tone to be sharp, but it was, and it wiped that greasy grin right off his face. "You look like Fidel Castro chowing down at some red-neck Mississippi truck stop."

"Oh hey, exxx-scoooose me for sitting here dining on the lovingly prepared home-cooked meal my stage actress wife has served to her hard-working husband."

Lori frowned, wanted to say something, but didn't. She smiled instead, then laughed, tried to be playful though she didn't mean it. "You seem to be enjoying it," she teased, *you greasy pig,* she finished the sentence undercover in her mind.

She didn't want to fight with him right before she went to the theater. She wanted to keep her two worlds separate so that one didn't distract her in the other. She knew that was going to be hard. So far she had kept her home life, her real life, off the stage, but she hadn't been nearly as successful going in the other direction. At home she couldn't keep her nose out of her script; she seemed obsessed with learning her lines. At work, she was constantly thinking of the play, drifting off into Philadelphia daydreams of Tracy and Dexter spending money and living their elegant life.

"You're really into this play gig, aren't you. I mean, it sure seems like a lot of work when you're not getting paid."

Why did she always feel like he was sneering at her, as if what she was doing was stupid and pointless.

"These people don't even think about money or how many hours they're putting in. It's fun. It rewards you in all kinds of ways."

"Like, what do you do down there every night?"

This wasn't flip or patronizing. She sensed that he was really curious, maybe even interested. He wasn't such a bad guy . . . husband. She didn't know why he ticked her off so much lately. They'd been together so long.

"We rehearse."

"I know that. But what's it like? I mean, is it like play practice in high school? I was in that one play, remember, *South Pacific,* a seabee, all we did was play grabass and try to sneak into the girls' dressing room."

"It's not too hard to sneak into the girls' dressing room at Civic," she gave a short, quick laugh. "There's no door on it."

"Oh really?"

"There's none on the men's either," she teased.

"Why you slut! You didn't tell me this theater gig was so kinky," he was having fun with this. They were kidding around with each other the way they always used to. This was the Eddie she liked, the guy so loose he could make everybody in the room laugh.

"It's not kinky. I don't think anybody even looks in the dressing rooms."

"The hell they don't!"

"Oh, you would," their friendly teasing was starting to take on an edge. "You're a pig . . . and a peeper."

"Get real, hon! Unless those guys you're hanging out with are all gay, and half of 'em probably are, you trying to tell me they're not gonna look if they get a chance to see my wife standing there in nothing but her panties."

"Oh, c'mon . . ."

"By the way, out of consideration for me," and he was really teasing her now, overplaying his utter mortification at the looseness of his wife, "please don't wear those red crotchless jobbies I gave you for our last anniversary. I'm very partial to those.

She had to strike back. Though this seemed just a carefree bit of teasing byplay, she knew it was more serious. He was going to laugh at or criticize anything she said about the theater. His question—"Like, what do you do down there every night?"—had simply been a trigger for his ever-present mockery. She decided to really shake him up, but to do it with a straight face, deadly serious.

"You're not going to believe what she made us do at the end of rehearsal that first night."

"What's that?" she had his attention, but that mocking grin was lurking in his face.

"God, it was so embarrassing." She actually leaned forward toward him and lowered her voice as if confiding a secret sin: "She sent everyone home except me and we had to practice kissing."

His eyebrows went up slightly as his eyes widened: "You were kissing the director?"

"What? No! She's a woman. Yuck!"

"So who were you kissing?"

"Two men actually."

"Oh great," and she suddenly realized that he wasn't mocking her anymore. She wished she hadn't started it, "now you're taking on two men at a time."

"They're both really nice guys," she said it primly, knowing that she really wanted to make him jealous.

He reacted predictably, fled back into his armor of mocking condescension: "Oh, I'll bet they are. Did you slip 'em some tongue?" he tried to convince her he was joking.

"You're a disgusting sicko."

To that, he did his ever-popular Groucho Marx imitation, waggling an imaginary cigar in the fingers of his right hand and jerking his eyebrows lewdly up and down. "Did I ever tell you how Sir Francis Drake circumcized the world with a 100-foot clipper."

"I gotta go."

"Hey, don't have too much fun at kissing practice tonight."

"We're only into the first act. There isn't any kissing until the end of Act Two."

"Who are these two guys anyway?"

He was trying to sound just mildly curious, but she could tell she had really gotten to him. The strange thing was that it made her feel good, as if she was exercising some power over him. She felt exultant. She wanted to hurt him for not paying enough attention to her, for not taking her to bed as much as he used to.

"John Collins is our age. He plays Mike the reporter in the play. He's really the only one I kiss, at the end of the drunk scene in Act Two. The other one is Bill Franklin. He plays my ex-husband, Dexter. I think he's about forty. We never kiss in the play at all."

"So what did he do? Pay the director to get in on kissing practice? Or does she just keep him after rehearsal to punish him?"

"Oh, so it's punishment to kiss me? It must be, because you sure as hell hardly ever do it anymore," she said it sweetly but hoped it castrated him.

"Terrific, is this some more of your nymphomaniac paranoia coming out."

The cat shrank away as if it could feel the hate pulsing in the air.

"I gotta go. I can't be late. I'm in every scene so they can't start 'til I get there."

"One guy's twenty six and this old guy is forty. How could he be your ex-husband? He's too old," he wasn't really talking to her, just sort of thinking it over out loud.

"He doesn't look that old. His hair's grey, but they're gonna dye it. In fact, he's really good looking. That's why he's got the lead in the play," and making her best moron face she finished by saying "DUH" with feeling.

"Oh, I suppose that means I could never have a lead in a play."

"What?" She couldn't believe what he had said. It was so childish. "Oh, not at all. You could be in this play. You could be the gardener who cuts the grass and cleans the pool."

"And don't forget, peeps into the girls' dressing room."

In the car, driving toward Wabash City, she tried to think about Tracy, to get into character, but she couldn't. She wanted to kick herself. She hated what she'd just done to Eddie, baited him. He didn't deserve that, but then she didn't deserve the way he treated her either. He didn't like to see her having fun unless he was in charge of it. And the look on his face when she'd mentioned the kissing . . . well. She grinned evilly in the darkness of the car.

By the time she drove up on to the Wabash River bridge, she had calmed down and felt ready to let Tracy take over. By the middle of the bridge, she was sitting up straighter, her nose was in the air, and she was ready to start firing wisecracks to the left and the right. Tracy never let a man get the best of her in a war of words. Maybe more of Tracy was becoming part of her than even she had realized.

When she walked into the theater, a feeling of warmth closed around her, like being in a home you really liked, not some trailer. Her smile bloomed under those terrific cheekbones as she greeted them with a "hi guys" with feeling.

Rehearsal ran late, and by the time Bill got home Martha was long gone to bed. He got a beer and thought about grading some papers.

Sitting on the couch amidst his freshman papers, he remembered the conversation about student bloopers earlier in the evening. *"Socrates died of an overdose of wedlock,"* he remembered. Martha was right; he should have written down all the funny things like that over the years, collected them. And that was what gave him the idea. The idea was that he really was enjoying this play. He liked it and, who knows, there might be a novel in it someday.

The idea was that, unlike those fifteen years of hilarious student bloopers, he ought to write this experience down. After all, he reasoned, that was one of the things he supposedly did for a living.

The idea was that, like Hemingway going to war, or Fitzgerald going to Europe, or Updike going to play golf at the club, he was doing something that someday might be worth writing about and he ought to remember it the way it was so that later he could turn it into the way he wanted it to be.

After all, you are a writer, he reminded himself. *You weren't much of a father or a husband, and you can't make the long throw from third base anymore, but you can write.* Lately, nothing else had touched his life powerfully enough to make him want to risk the prison sentence of writing a novel. Until this play.

The idea was to keep a journal, write the experience down as it happened so that if it turned out to have any meaning maybe he could turn it into a novel later.

Ironically, the more he thought about it, the less enthralled with the idea he was. *Do I really want to ruin this whole experience, the fun I'm having, by writing about it?*

He decided that he did.

He found a pen in the junk drawer in the kitchen, put on a Dexter Gordon record, and settled back into the couch to write. *Hey, Dexter Gordon and Dexter Haven,* he thought, *just two cats jammin' 'round midnight.*

Tonight was the fourth rehearsal. He decided to start on the first day of rehearsals and catch it up to the present, then every night he could make that day's entry in the journal.

> Monday, Sept. 2
> The first rehearsal. Everybody sitting in the theater waiting to start. Little blue scripts in everybody's hot little hands. The little blonde with the high cheekbones sitting on one side. She's Tracy. She's the one I thought it would be. She's slim and blonde and really pretty. Everyone knows that she's the one who has got to carry the play. Maybe that's why nobody is sitting near her. Cast meeting first. Handouts: phone numbers, rehearsal schedule—ouch! Every weeknight for six weeks. We all introduce ourselves to the group, give our idea of our character (in the play, that is). We read through the first act. Some of the actors and actresses are actually reading in their character voices. The play sure is different, a lot funnier, listening to them read it, than it was when I was home alone in the living room reading it by myself. I guess it's like sex; it works better with someone else. The director seems very professional. She is really concentrating on Tracy from the very beginning. That's smart. Tracy is the show. This director is going to run a tight ship. This is going to be fun, I think. Oh yeah, I kissed the leading lady after rehearsal. The director made me do it.
>
> Tuesday, Sept. 3
> Block Act One. I don't even know what that means. Lori, the girl who plays Tracy, tells me. We build a set with square boxes. It's a living room/patio set, indoor/outdoor. The director's word for the night is "congestion." There are a lot of people in this play and we all seem to be bumping into and stepping on each other. Director says she wants "triangles." Nobody knows what the hell that means. I'm impressed at the professionalism of all of this, both director and actors.

Wednesday, Sept. 4
Director is always on Tracy. I hope Lori, who is really
the only one in the cast I've gotten to know, can hold
up under the pressure. I like her. She's really serious
about this. All I do is sit around. I don't come on until
nearly the end of Act One.

Thursday, Sept. 5
Tonight, the night I got the idea to start this journal. God I'm tired. We rehearsed our butts off tonight,
working Act One over and over. Not me really. I only
have that one scene at the end of the act. I spent most
of the night out in the theater lobby with the other
actors—nobody uses the word "actress," everybody is
an "actor" no matter the gender. Actually, I enjoyed
it, gave me a chance to talk with some of the others. I
have a feeling that before this is over we'll all be pretty
comfortable with each other. Martha was in bed when
I got home. I'm up drinking and listening to music.

There, he thought, *now I've got a real journal going, like Gide or
Conrad. I just have to stick with it, make sure I do it every night after
rehearsal.* The summer before—*Or maybe it was two summers ago?* he
tried to remember—he had read a biography of Albert Camus. Camus
had written in a journal almost every day of his life. A friend, every
Christmas, gave Camus little leatherbound notebooks in which to
write, and Camus did. *He loved theater,* Bill thought, *so did Dickens.
Both of them were constantly organizing and acting in and directing amateur plays.* He dragged himself up to bed, happy to be in such good
company.

11 The Old Magic

"Did'joo hear about the three young plastic surgeons . . ."

"No, but I think we're about to."

" . . . who set up a chain of franchise clinics in the parking lots of shopping malls?"

"No, Harvey dear, we didn't."

"They called them Jiffy Boob."

"Alll-rightt!"

"I like that one. Usually his jokes take forever and aren't that funny."

"I'm going to call my husband and see if he'll join us. He gets off work at eleven. Where's the phone here?"

"Down that hall, sweetie, by the ladies room."

"OK, have you guys heard about the drink of the future?"

"OK, I'll bite. What's the drink of the future, John?"

"It's a combination of prune juice and that stuff the astronauts take on the space shuttle. Guaranteed to fight off colds and keep you loose. It's called Prune Tang."

"Sounds suspiciously like something we used to hunt in the Army."

"They let you in the Army?"

"I'd hate to be in the space shuttle when that Prune Tang kicked in."

"You could make a fortune selling that stuff in south Florida where we go on vacation. I've never seen so many tight-assed old farts in my life."

"You know who needs a good shot of Prune Tang?"

"Who?"

"Marge the Barge. Maybe she'd loosen up and let us act a little."

"Aw hell, it's only the first week. That'll come."

"Back off guys, here she comes."

"Oh god, I am so glad the first week is over." Marge lowered herself into the chair that Lori had been sitting in. "Have you ordered yet? I want to buy the first round. You people have worked so hard this week. We've really made progress."

"Bravo, bravo. Encore. You're right."

"Oh Harvey."

"But dear, I was visibly moved."

Lori returned from her phone call somewhat crestfallen, only to find Marge sitting in her chair.

Bill jumped up to get a chair from another table and pushed it in next to his.

"We'd like two pitchers of beer."

"Light or regular?"

"One of each."

"I'd like a Jack and water. Only supporting actors drink beer."

"Then bring him a near beer."

They were sitting at the big round table in the front window of *The Hoosier Saloon* on Fifth Street in downtown Wabash City only two blocks from the theater. Most of the cast were there, except, of course, the high school girls. Actually, Marge had suggested they all go out for drinks after Friday night rehearsal, and Harvey Winkins and John Collins had organized this expedition across the Fifth Street railroad tracks. Marge was no dummy. It had been a long week and she had driven them hard. But everyone felt pretty good about the work so far (which she knew they wouldn't feel good about every week on this play). She wanted to get her actors together outside the theater, get them comfortable with each other. She knew it would pay off onstage later.

Pretty smart, Bill thought later as he was writing his journal entry, *there is probably no place other than theater where total strangers must get in touch with each others' emotions more quickly.*

The Hoosier Saloon billed itself as "the oldest bar in Indiana" on its front awning. "Est. 1871" was also written there, which made it 127 years old. Inside waited a quiet classy bar, unlike the majority of bars in Wabash City and West Wabash. Wabash City bars tended to the smoky, red-neck, twanging, Country and Western, pool table set while West Wabash bars opted for the stand-up, packed wall-to-wall, deafening post-rock-n-roll, sloppy, beer-splashing, college student Yuppies. For some reason, *The Hoosier Saloon* had decided to stay small and intimate. Smoky jazz played over the sound system, but never intruded, always just floated in the background. Green and white checked tablecloths and flickering candles inside tinted vases graced the small tables. It was a dining car room, long and narrow from front door to back wall. Its dimensions seemed perfectly suited for coupling on each time a train rumbled down the middle of Fifth Street ten feet from the front windows (or for meeting prior to that other kind of coupling). The solid polished mahogany bar wore a gleaming brass rail as it stood all along one wall staring impassively back at the whole room out of its full-length expanse of mirror.

The mirror was playful. The Tiffany lamps mounted on the opposite wall winked in it. The mirror was flirtatious. It boldly reflected the poster size pictures of Marilyn Monroe, Katherine Hepburn, Lauren Bacall, and Bette Davis hung at intervals along the opposite wall. The mirror was discreet. Every night it looked down non-judgemental upon couples talking and touching, upon seductions and angry rejections, upon adulterous assignations and dangerous liaisons.

The waitress wore a black leather mini-skirt, a white blouse under a black cardigan sweater, a formal red bow tie, and a pair of world class legs. It was a nice quiet bar where people could talk without fear of being assaulted either by the sound system or the patrons. Lori took a quick look around when she returned from the pay telephone and while Bill was scrambling for another chair. She liked the idea of a man jumping up to serve her. God knows, Eddie never did! The drinks arrived soon after she sat down just as a freight train bumped rhythmically down Fifth Street setting all the glasses rattling.

"I told my husband your 'Jiffy Boob' joke and he laughed," Lori confided in Harvey Winkins.

Bill and Lori were sitting next to each other with John Collins next to Lori, then good ol' Harvey, then Thelma who had been in the theater taking measurements for the set builders and who never turned down a chance for a drink, then Marge the Barge next to her, then Sam Wilcox who hadn't said a word and rarely did sitting next to Bill to complete the circle.

"Is he going to join us?" Bill asked Lori more out of politeness than any desire to meet her husband.

"He said he'd try. He gets off work at eleven. But he probably won't come." she said almost wistfully.

For some reason that he couldn't explain, Bill momentarily hoped that her husband didn't show up.

"Are you going to call your wife?"

"Are you kidding?" Bill counterfeited a laugh as he bent his head to read his watch in the darkness. "It's a quarter to eleven. She's probably been asleep for two hours."

I wonder why she asked? Bill thought, feeling his imagination straining toward overactive.

Meanwhile, Ol' Harv was reaching across in front of John Collins to take Lori's hand.

"My husband wanted to know if we'd had anymore kissing practice this evening," she had just announced sort of , half-sarcastically

"My dear Tracy," Ol' Harv took her hand, gazed longingly into her eyes, and pronounced in his most love-stricken voice, "I am always more than happy to run lines with you, but I am also quite willing to take on the added burden of rehearsing your kissing, and excellent kissing I'm sure it is, any time you so desire."

"I'll bet you are!" Marge laughed.

"Hey, that's my job!" Collins feigned combativeness.

"Aha, Winkins is willin,'" Bill arched an eyebrow and quipped. He felt he had said something quite witty, but not a soul caught his Dickensian allusion. Actually, his speaking up was really a cover because as soon as she had mentioned the kissing practice he had felt himself starting to redden in the darkness. *She's fifteen years younger than you,* he tried to warn himself.

Lori handled the whole situation with great aplomb. "Why Uncle Willie," she withdrew her hand from his and pressed it to her pursed mouth dramatically in mock shock, "I do think that your child molesting tendencies are once again rearing their ugly little heads."

"And their lips and hands and whatever other little heads they rear," Collins cut in with his best Groucho Marx eyebrow flutters and imaginary cigar waggles.

Harvey retreated with a salaam into his bourbon and water.

"Speaking of kissing on stage," Thelma had only been waiting for her opening, "do you know what happened in *House of Blue Leaves* on opening night?"

"Ah, *House of Blue Leaves*," Marge was remembering, "what a funny show. That was the one where the crazy wife thought the nuns were penguins."

"Yes, the husband was a songwriter and a zookeeper, and his wife was confused, depressed, insane, who knows?" Thelma, our historian, warmed to her story. "Near the end of the play, the zookeeper and his crazy wife have this dramatic kiss. They must have rehearsed it and it had been OK, but on opening night the actor playing the husband either forgot where he was or got carried away or was trying to send the actress playing the madwoman a message, who knows? Anyway, he french-kissed her, really slipped her the tongue. She didn't even hesitate. She stepped back and decked him with a right cross to the chin. Knocked him flat on his back and went right into her lines."

"My god," John Collins jumped up in mock terror, "you wouldn't do that to me, would you Tracy."

"Not if you keep your tongue in your mouth," Lori laughed.

Collins stuck out his tongue and waggled it ferociously at her.

Thelma went right on with her story as if she had a responsibility to keep these moments of stage lore alive.

"Well, the audience loved it. They just thought she was this crazy lady and it was all part of the show. Meanwhile, the husband is flat on the floor dazed, the crazy lady is circling his body like a vulture saying her lines, and he's not answering. So she starts her lines over, and as she walks by him she gives him a good kick. Well, the audience is laughing so hard the old ladies in the front row are peeing their pants. The actor's afraid he's gonna get kicked again so he tries to say his lines, but they just come out gibberish. So there's a kitchen onstage and the actress walks over to the counter, picks up a pitcher of water that's a prop, comes back downstage and pours it right on his head as he's trying to get up. The audience has lost it. They're laughing so hard some of them are starting to cough and choke, and it's not even in the play. Anyway, the water sort of offsets the effect of the punch and the zookeeper gets to his feet, takes one step on the wet floor, and goes straight up in the air in a pratfall that would make Chevy Chase green with envy, and comes down right on top of a small table that he smashes to matchsticks. By this time the audience is laughing so hard that tears are running down their faces. So the actor struggles to his feet, utterly dazed, and the actress, who has given up trying to get through the lines and is just leaning against the couch watching him stumble around, suddenly gets an inspiration. I swear she was doing a Mae West imitation. She says: 'Hey baby, ya wanna lay another kiss on me?' And the actor, the husband, just ran off the stage screaming.

I mean, the woman was brilliant. She just turned to the audience and shrugged, then walked off doing her crazy lady confused act. The audience gave them a standing ovation. You're right, it's a really funny play, but it was never as funny as it was that night."

"And the moral of that story," Harvey Winkins shook his forefinger in what was supposed to be sternness yet came out lewdness, "is that you can never have too much kissing rehearsal."

"No," Bill got up the courage to enter the conversation, "the moral is that maybe surprises on stage, a little reality in the midst of illusion, makes for good theater."

"I'll tell you one thing," Thelma always insisted upon having the last word when it came to her stories, "he never kissed her that way again and the play was never that good again. Go figure."

"Well," Marge addressed them in her best gym teacher voice, "let's not have any surprises like that in our show."

"Aw heck," John Collins mocked disappointment, "ya mean we gotta keep our tongues in our own mouths and pull all our punches."

Everyone laughed except for Marge.

The conversation swirled around the table. Harvey ordered another drink and had one of the pitchers refilled. Sam Wilcox finished his beer and left, waving goodbye.

"Going home to do his philandering no doubt," Harvey commented as, through the front window, we all watched Sam cross the railroad tracks to his car.

"You and Sam sure play off of each other well," Lori seemed genuinely appreciative.

"Of course, we've been doing it since Lyndon Johnson was the President."

"Now, was he before or after Lincoln?" Collins couldn't resist.

"No, he was the one right before Nixon," then Lori got it, wished she hadn't opened her mouth, reddened with embarrassment.

Harvey rode in to her rescue. "Young John boy here thinks everything began with disco. He dates history from the release of *Saturday Night Fever*."

Utterly nonplussed, Collins rejoined, "Harv was the one, you know, who asked, 'Besides all that, Mrs. Lincoln, what did you think of the play?' That's how long he's been in theater."

"Oh you two," Lori had formed a nice little triangle with Harvey and John, and was basking in their attentions. Bill sat beside her listening to their byplay and looking for some way to enter in.

"Remember the Ku Klux Klan costumes for *The Foreigner,* how somebody spotted an actor coming out of the shop in one and alerted the NAACP?" Thelma was launching into another of her stories."The police showed up for rehearsal the next night . . ."

"I was in that play," John Collins leaned toward Lori and Bill, "it was funny. I think the director thought they were going to tow his car."

" . . . and thought we were holding Klan meetings in the theater. Like we were planning a cross-burning or something."

"The man from the NAACP was really embarassed when he found out it was a theater and we were rehearsing a play that made fools of the Klan," Collins piped in.

"Dummy didn't even know it was a theater," Harvey scoffed. "Probably thought it was still an abandoned train station."

"The cop kept looking around sort of amazed. I think he figured that even if it wasn't the Klan it all still looked pretty suspicious."

"One of the actors," Collins was chuckling as he remembered it, "thought it was a dope raid. He ducked down the steps to the dressing room and flushed his drugs down the toilet. When he found out what it was really all about, boy was he pissed."

"You people really have a lot of fun," Lori just sort of said it on the general euphoria of the moment.

"That's why we do it," Harvey seemed serious, but wasn't, "that and the princely salaries they pay us actors."

"I've got a design project due on Monday," John Collins announced to explain his getting up to leave. "It's going to be a working weekend."

"And I've got a golf game at nine tomorrow," Harvey, fine actor that he was, picked right up on the cue line that Collins had given.

They departed together, standing out on Fifth Street (Lori and Bill watched them through the window) discussing one last thing for long minutes before getting in their separate cars and driving off.

Across the table, Marge and Thelma were deep in conversation about acquiring the furniture for the set.

"It doesn't look like Eddie is going to show," Lori said quietly, taking Bill by surprise.

"Eddie? Oh, your husband."

"He probably had a lot of paperwork he had to finish."

Bill was desperate, casting about for something to say. The beer was gone.

"I'm going to have another beer. Would you like one?"

"I should probably head home."

"It's Friday night and only eleven thirty. It's early."

The long-legged waitress had arrived at Bill's wave.

"OK," Lori didn't need much encouragement, "but I don't want another beer. How about a diet coke?"

Bill ordered her coke and a bottle of Mexican beer for himself.

Marge and Thelma demurred when he asked them if they wanted another drink. They got up to leave before the waitress returned. For reasons he had no desire to explore, was not yet ready to own up to, Bill was happy when they left him and Lori alone. He sensed that she regretted ordering the coke, hadn't planned on being left alone with him. He felt it was his job to put her at ease.

"I hope your husband doesn't come in now and catch us," *you idiot,* even as he said it he realized he couldn't have said anything less appropriate for making her relax in his company.

She gave a thin little laugh and said, "I doubt that he will."

"Well, there's no reason for me to go home. Martha's been asleep for hours."

An awkward little silence ebbed in between them, the sort that uncertainty causes.

"Last monday," she took the first plunge, "when we were introducing ourselves, you said this was your first Civic Theater production. I guess that makes us the rookies, doesn't it?"

"Yeah, I haven't been in a play since high school. You majored in theater in college, didn't you say?"

"Uh-huh. I really missed it. I guess that's one of the reasons I came for the audition."

"One of the reasons?"

"Well, yeah," but she didn't say what the others were, and he decided not to press her. "Why are you doing this acting thing if you haven't been in a play since high school?"

"Harvey asked me to."

"What do you mean?"

"He called me up and asked me to come to the audition, said he thought I'd be good for the part." One of those awkward little silences ebbed in again. He could tell that Lori was thinking something over. "Anyway, he called, and it seemed like a fun idea, and I came to the audition, and they gave me the part."

"It didn't seem to me like you had much competition. There just weren't any Dexters around."

"I think you're right. That's why they called me I think. 'Cause they didn't have anybody else."

"That sure wasn't the case with me. I think they tried everybody else they could find before they settled on me."

"But you are absolutely perfect for the part. That night of the audition, I went home and I was absolutely certain it was going to be you. You look like Tracy," he was carried away and his mouth was racing, "those gorgeous high cheekbones. You're gonna be beautiful onstage."

She didn't say anything. There was almost a look of shock on her face. He had given himself away. She realized that he had been thinking about her outside the confines of the play. *What am I doing here alone with this man in this bar?* the question taunted her mind, but she realized that she didn't want to leave, that what he had just said about her cheekbones, about how she was going to look on stage, had made her feel better than anything had made her feel in months.

"Well, you were a lot more confidant about it than me," she laughed off his compliment. "I really wanted the part and they seemed to keep bringing new Tracys in because they didn't want to give it to me."

"I was sure it was going to be you."

"I'm not so sure our director shares your confidence in me. It seems like I can't make a move without her bitching at me."

"It's just the first week. She reminds me of some Army sergeant. She loves to give orders. I'm enjoying it though. I'm glad Ol' Harv gave me that call."

"Is that the only reason you did it, because he asked you to?" It was a more personal question, and she knew it. Her voice lowered, signaling that the conversation was moving to a more intimate level.

"No, Harvey was just an acquaintance. We'd played golf a couple of times. I could easily have said 'no.' But the idea intrigued me. And I think he hit me at a good time. I was really bored. I was looking for something interesting to do." He stopped for a minute, marveling at the fact that he was opening up to this stranger, then realizing that it was more than just boredom that made him do it. "I think the idea of being someone else, of pretending I was Cary Grant, really pushed my

buttons. Sometimes we're all unhappy being who we are in real life."
Back off, you're getting too philosophical. he stopped himself. "So now
I'm C.K. Dexter Haven, what a great name!" he laughed it off and
took refuge in his beer.

"I sorta know what you mean," she wasn't put off by his introspec-
tion at all. She had actually listened to what he had said. He couldn't
remember the last time he'd had a real conversation with Martha. "I
think I just really wanted to get out of the house. With my husband
working nights, I was just sitting home by myself, with the cat, watching TV. Now that's really boring. And, you're right, I sorta like being
Tracy. I get in the car at night and it's like Cinderella or something.
On the way to the theater, I change into this rich Philadelphia chick."

"You're having fun with it then? Tracy looks like an awful lot of
work. All I've done this week is watch you guys work. I've only got a
few lines at the end of Act One."

"It sure beats sitting home watching TV," Lori answered, "but I'm
not sure fun is what I'd call it yet."

"You sure do have a lot of lines."

"Oh, it's not the lines. I've never had any trouble with the lines before. They just come when you say them enough times."

"Well, I don't have half as many lines as you do and I'm having a
hell of a time memorizing them."

"You oughta try tapes. Just make a tape of your scenes with everybody else's lines on it and leave gaps where your lines come. Then you
just pop it in and run lines with yourself whenever you want."

"Hey, I'm going to have another beer," he'd been playing with the
empty bottle for long minutes as they talked, "can I get you another
coke?"

"No, I really have to get home. It's been a long week. I've got to
work on lines for Act Two all weekend. You ought to make a tape.
We've got our big fight scene coming up monday and tuesday. Then
John and I have the drunk scene. I've never been a very good drunk.
Two beers and I get goofy."

"Can't you stay? I'm enjoying the conversation. It's still early." But
she was already up and fleeing.

"I can't. See you monday," and she was out the door, leaving him
sitting there alone with the abandoned pitchers, glasses and beer bottles.

I'll bet I could act the hell out of that drunk scene, he thought as he moved to a stool at the bar, *it's one of the few things I do really well.*

He sat at the bar drinking and listening to the sad sax of the background jazz. He was pretty sure he had scared her off. At the end of their conversation, all she could talk about was getting home to her husband. One beer, then another, and pretty soon his old romanticism was back. He was thinking about magic again. He knew that every time he started thinking about magic he ended up dreaming himself into something he couldn't really be, forcing fiction to take the place of reality. But his old confidence in magic had returned and it held such temptation. He knew this magic. When it showed up, he realized that he was the magician who could make his old self disappear and pull a whole new self out of his hat. When it showed up, he was usually helpless to resist its temptation. It was as if it was his responsibility to let the magic work its spell on him. He knew that there were different kinds of magic.

There was the magic of imagination that casts spells over a writer and lets the words flow out as if he is caught in some elegant current being carried away toward some all-accepting sea. That kind of magic used to come to him all the time, but he hadn't felt it lately.

There was the magic of meeting a woman and knowing that she was going to so twirl you and turn you that you would have to have her, be forced to tell her (words again) how she makes you feel. That was the magic of enchantment

Only two women had ever worked this magic on him. Martha when they were kids. A woman named Ellie back when he first started playing softball. It hadn't happened with Lori yet. He wondered if that was the kind of magic he felt bearing down upon him like the train that was suddenly rumbling down the middle of Fifth Street.

Then, there was the magic of those special moments of transcendence when everything is so perfect that you want it to go on forever. You want to hang suspended above the rim, or stretched flat out as you glove a line drive, or frozen in your follow-through with that fine feeling of solidity lingering in your hands as your drive flies true with just the slightest draw into the center of the fairway 260 yards off the smooth summer tee, or dancing in a sleek black tuxedo with a gorgeous woman in the moonlight (*like Cary Grant,* he thought).

"Arn'tchoo one o' the actors?" that slightly slurred female voice broke his reverie like a bird hitting the windshield. It came out of nowhere and, through no fault of his own, made him feel guilty. His head snapped up out of his beer. He caught sight of her in the mirror. She was standing expectantly like some ruffled bird of prey just off his right shoulder. "Frum Shivick Theaturrr, one o' the actors in The Phillerdelphia Shhhtory?"

"Well yes, I, uh . . ." he didn't really know what to say. He'd never been approached by a groupie before. At least that's the impression he got when he swirled around on the stool to face her. She had a hungry, suddenly alert, and hopeful look on her face, like a hawk floating effortlessly on the high currents who has just spotted a fat pigeon fly unsuspecting into range below. He recognized her immediately. "You're the, uh, costume mistress."

"Oh, 'mistress' issh hit," and she climbed up onto the stool next to him, somehow pushing it closer as she did, and, with a comic leer, elbowed him in the ribs, "I love that wurrd."

"Yes, it's a, uh, well, interesting word," he was trapped. He'd had too many beers and wasn't thinking quickly enough to deal with whatever this woman had in mind. He wasn't too drunk to see that she was pretty well ripped herself. But now she had him surrounded. She had already ordered them both a beer and was leaning close to begin a serious conversation. He could smell the evening's beer and cigarettes on her breath, and the cheap perfume on her neck. She wasn't at all unattractive. In fact, she had rather impressive breasts beneath a shiny black blouse open a full two buttons down which showed off the tops of her breasts right down to the lacy edges of her black bra. *No need for Jiffy Boob here,* he thought.

"Aren't those puppies great?" she laughed. She had caught him looking and could have cared less. "Barb Dwyer," and she clapped him lightly on the shoulder, "now isn't that a great name to go with those great tits?"

The bartender brought two beers. She paid him and pushed one over in front of Bill.

"Why thanks I . . . yes, I remember your name . . . I, uh . . ." he had no way to deal with the rest of what she had said. It was as if her aggressiveness had paralyzed him. "I was, a, just having a drink after rehearsal before I went home."

"I've been drinkin' shinssh I got off wurk at five. Shhhtarted at Presshton's, ate a shandwich therr, then went to Nick'shh, but the band wassh shit and the guys who assshed me to dance wurr either retards or shhhoww drunk they could barely shhtand up, shhhow I jussh gave up. Thissh is the most boring town. I deesshided to shtop in here for a drink before I went home too." She smiled brightly and abruptly stopped her monologue to light a cigarette, tossed her head to blow the smoke from the first deep drag up into the air, and then swooped back down upon him. "Musssht be the end of shhummer. Not menny people out in the bars tonight. Oh, the shhtudents are everywhere, but who cares about those little pricks. I think wenn they come back into town they scare the real people away from the bars. Whaddooyoo think?"

Bill didn't know what to say. He sat there staring dumbly at her. He had drunk too much and it had slowed him down. *Wow, she's been out looking for a man all night, and now it's almost closing time and she's got me,* he felt like that defenseless pigeon looking up and spotting the dark shadow of the hawk just as it whirls into its dive.

"How are the costumes coming?" was all he could think to say.

Barb Dwyer laughed and blew smoke in his face: "Honey, I haven't even shtarted on 'em yet. Christ, they'rre thirties clothes. The men's shhtuff I'll try to pick up in old clothes shhtores and garage shhales, but I'll haveta make the women's dreshhes." Then she leaned in closer and put her hand firmly on his knee: "But who cares about that to-night, huh? I'm glad I shhtopped in here. That's one o' the reasons I do Shhivic Theater. Ta meet new people."

"Well, I'm new to it, but I'm sure enjoying it so far." He'd had a lot to drink, but he wasn't slurring his words like she was.

"That's the way it's shhupposed ta be. Shhum people, like that dreckter o' yers, git too shheerious about this shhit."

"Yes, I could see that happening."

"Shhurr could. Yer shhupposed ta have fun."

Then Barb Dwyer leaned in even closer and, in a stage whisper, half conspiratorial, half drunkenly seductive, buried him alive in the point she had been leading up to: "I'm in it for the fun. Let'shh, you an me, have shhum fun. Letshh go back ta my playshh an fuck. For fun. Whatta ya shhay? No ushhe sittin' alone in a bar drinkin' when we could go home an have sum fun."

What bothered Bill the most was the indisputable logic of her proposition. There was absolutely no reason under the sun why he shouldn't get up, go with her, and enjoy the fun she promised. Except that she was stone drunk, and he was pretty drunk, and he didn't even know her, and he wasn't sure he could get it up no matter how wonderful her breasts were, and he was scared, of getting caught, of her wanting to see him again, of her, terrified in fact. He was flashing on images of Mae West.

She just looked at him through the smoke rising from her cigarette.

He clawed his way out from under her suffocating spell.

He stood up and shook her hand.

His first impulse was to tell her he was gay.

"I can't," he stammered. "I've drunk too much. I'm afraid I couldn't. Maybe a rain check." *Good lord, it sounds like you're talking about a baseball game,* he was frantic.

She gaped at him, the cigarette smoke curling.

"I'll blow you," she said.

"That's good of you, but I've gotta go. Really do, I'm late. Good night. Nice meet . . . uh, see ya," and he was out the door in full flight.

He calmed in the car driving home. In bed next to Martha, images of himself and Barb Dwyer in every conceivable position of perverse 'fun' swirled in his mind. The last conscious thought he remembered was: *Why didn't I do it? I'll never get a chance like that again.*

> Friday, Sept. 6
> Friday night and a bunch of us in the cast go out for beer at the Saloon. Funny people. Harvey Winkins tells great jokes and Thelma the office lady tells stories about funny stuff that has happened in earlier shows. I talked mostly to Tracy, I mean Lori. Something is bothering her. Maybe she's nervous about her role. I don't blame her. It's the one that carries the whole play. She gave me a good tip about how to memorize lines. Make tapes. Lori left. I wanted her to stay. I stayed because I felt like drinking. Big mistake. The costume mistress shows up. What a trip she is!

12 Frustration and Jealousy

"Tracy, don't stoop! Shoulders back, nose in the air. You're rich. You're Katherine Hepburn, for god's sake . . ."

"Look, Tracy, I've got to have triangles. . . ."

"You've got to get rid of your Hoosier twang on these line readings, Tracy. 'Ore-ange' is not 'orrnnnge.' 'Wash' is not 'warsh.' This is the Philadelphia Main Line, not Wabash City, Indiana . . ."

"For god's sake, kiss him. Kick your downstage foot up when you kiss him. Trust me, Tracy, it's an old movie convention. People will laugh . . ."

"Tracy, hold it a second. You're so stiff. You're drunk in this scene, remember. You don't care what you do. If your boobs fall out of your dress, you don't even care. . . ."

"Tracy, please, say the line on the cross, and when you flirt with someone you look right at them . . ."

"Dammit Tracy, get mad! He's just all but called you a spoiled little rich bitch and nobody talks to you that way . ."

"Tracy! Think! You're up on that line and crossing . . ."

"Don't stoop . . ."

"It's 'ore-ange' not 'orrnnge,' . . ."

"Kiss him hard, like you'd kiss your husband or lover."

"That's not mad, Tracy, that's pathetic . . ."

"No! No! No! You're drunk and you want to go skinnydipping with this man you don't even know. You're not shy anymore."

"Get mad . . ."

"Not 'warsh' . . ."

"Tracy, don't stoop . . ."

As far as she's concerned I can't do anything right, Lori was determined not to cry, at least not in front of the others. *She hasn't said a word to John about his line readings. That fat whale is only on me. I can't walk right, talk right, kiss right, even stand right. I don't stoop. You'd think I was a hunchback. What's wrong with her? Why did she cast me if she hates me. I'm doing the best I can. Why can't she see that? Eddie'd just love it if I quit. 'Bit off more than you could chew, huh?' he'd hang it over me. Is it me? Am I really so much worse than the others? Don't any of them make mistakes? How can she expect me to kiss him like I'd kiss my husband? I'm not stiff. All she does is yell at me . . . and no one else. They probably think I deserve it. Or maybe she just hates all lead actresses. She must have cast me because I was the only one who looked the part and now she's having second thoughts because I can't act. But I can act. None of the professors in school ever yelled at me the way she does. They all said I was a good actress, worked hard at it. What is with her? I can act. Ok, who am I kidding? She's right. I'm playing Tracy like some Midwestern sorority girl, like me. She isn't like me. She sure as hell doesn't live in some red-neck trailer park. I'm not Tracy, and that's why she's yelling at me. I can't do this. I'll never be Tracy. Eddie's right. I am in over my head. I wouldn't give that bitch the satisfaction. Who am I kidding? I hate being yelled at. I'm letting her get to me. A real actress wouldn't let all her criticism bother her. But why do I want to cry everytime she yells out my name. Tracy. Tracy. It wouldn't be so bad if she'd yell at some of the others once in a while, but it's only me. I should have just stayed home watching television with the cat. This would be great if only that cow would die right in the middle of rehearsal, keel over and croak right onstage. Then maybe they'd get a director who wouldn't just pick on me. Yikes! I'm actually wishing she was dead. Maybe it is me. Maybe I'm taking this all too seriously. But she only yells at ME! Everybody else is having fun, kidding around. Some of 'em aren't even off book for Act One. Dexter can't even touch me without either flinching or siezing up. He's the one who's stiff, not me. He almost gave me whiplash when he grabbed me at the end of Act One the other night. What does she say to him? 'Just relax' she says. I really don't deserve this. But I can do this part, make Tracy convincing. I know it. This is making me crazy.*

"Tracy, kiss him again. You're the aggressor. It's not so much a passionate kiss, but you're looking for an adventure. Think, Tracy, think about how your character feels . . ."

She feels terrible every time you open your mouth, Lori was still troubled and there was no sign of a let-up.

For the third night in a row Marge had opened rehearsal by spotlighting one of her litany of Lori's shortcomings. Dexter had one major scene in Act Two, his confrontation with his ex-wife Tracy, whom he

still loves but won't admit it. The rest of Act Two is pretty much all
Tracy and Mike the reporter doing their drunken antics. Marge the
director was starting to grate on Bill too. He found himself growing
jealous of Mike Connor the character's enviable position as the target
of all those kisses that Marge kept exhorting Tracy to make more real-
istic and passionate. Every time they were ordered to redo a kiss, Bill,
sitting in the theatre watching, felt this nagging envy for Mike Connor
the character onstage getting kissed. This vague jealousy was but one
of the conflicting emotions that nagged at him. Things on the set had
changed since last week, gotten heavier, more serious.

Monday, Sept. 9
Boy, was I lousy tonight. I sat around all evening waiting for the last two pages of Act One. It was our first
night off book on Act One. I knew my lines, but when
I got onstage, I made an utter fool of myself. I hate
to look stupid in public. I can't seem to get this short
exchange with Tracy right. I grab her as if she's a ragdoll, then I can't say my lines. She may be the first
actress ever to suffer from onstage whiplash is how the
director put it. I really wanted to shoot myself. Instead
I just went out and got drunk.

Tuesday Sept. 10
They've started working on the set. The builders have
put the stage part down. The front of the set is a patio
which is the flat stage floor, but the rest is the interior
of the mansion which is sloped for some reason. They
call it "raked." We all feel like we're walking uphill
all the time. Ah, Sisyphus, maybe theatre is what you
were really talking about. Everybody in the cast is getting more comfortable with each other. They're nice
people, and they're funny, and they're really dedicated
to this whole idea of theater. That's cool, because they
aren't getting paid a cent. Tonight I felt more comfortable with Tracy, I mean Lori, whatever. Putting
my arm around her at the end of Act One is no longer turning me into a blubbering idiot. Somehow she
keeps from laughing at how clumsy I am onstage. We

ran Act One again tonight before we started working the big scene in Act Two. Lori is amazing. She's
got almost every other line in Act One and she knows
them all. John and Sunny who play Mike and Liz are
real pros, and Harvey and Sam will get the biggest
laughs when they come onstage. They are really funny
together, like Laurel and Hardy. I sit and watch the
whole Act, waiting for my entrance in the last two
pages. It is really starting to look like a play. We spent
the second half of rehearsal working the two major
scenes in Act Two, the scene where Tracy and Dexter confront each other, and the drunk scene between
Mike and Tracy that ends with the kiss.

Bill sat in the darkness of the theatre, an audience of one to the
rehearsal progressing onstage. John Collins playing Mike the reporter
and Lori as Tracy were working their drunk scene while Thurman and
Ernie passed back and forth behind them installing a flight of three
steps down from the stage. The set builders had set about transform-
ing the theatre into a Main Line mansion over the weekend. What had
been a flat floor thrusting gently out into the audience had become,
using risers with different length legs, a rather steeply raked stage that
sloped upwards from front to back. All week Ernie and Thurman had
been fixtures at rehearsal, puttering around the stage making adjustments to the set. The major set construction took place on the weekends, but the small fine tunings were done by these two trying not to
interrupt the actors during rehearsal. Since John Collins had designed
the set, he was usually consulting with the two set builders whenever
he wasn't onstage rehearsing. As Mike watched from the audience,
Thurman and Ernie took a break from their shuffling and banging
backstage to watch the scene leading up to the kiss.

Mike Connor, the newspaper reporter, warily circled Tracy,
shrugged his hands in drunken disorientation, asked her ingenuous-
ly why she was so unhappy when she was so rich and so beautiful.
Tracy, tossing off yet another glass of champagne, perked up when
he offhandedly said she was beautiful. Thurman's and Ernie's heads
were peeping up over the back of the raked stage. Thurman must have
been standing on a box or something. When Mike Connor and Tracy

kissed to end the scene, Ernie turned to Thurman and said something that brought Thurman's hand to his mouth to stifle a laugh.

I'll bet they've got their perspective on all this nonsense. Bill thought. *How strange it must be building illusions out of wood. Set builders, actors, really do have their Sisyphus side,* he found a metaphor, *always trying to make real something that is never anything more than a fiction. Acting on a raked stage,* he grinned to himself, *always moving uphill.*

Bill sat there watching it all happen, and then it happened all over again. The director was really on Lori, badgering her to make Tracy more aggressive, more sensual. She would stop the two actors on almost every other line to correct them or make adjustments in their movements, their posture, their line readings. The scene was stuttering along at the slowest possible pace, and everyone concerned was ready for a break, but Marge kept at Lori.

She's only yelling at Lori, Bill realized. *She hasn't said a word to John about his characterization.*

Finally, after one last feeble attempt at a kiss, utterly lame because Lori's nerves were so frazzled by the barrage of criticism, the director called a ten-minute break. Lori immediately disappeared down the stairs to the dressing room.

"Watch this," John Collins said as he passed by Bill's seat in the audience, heading backstage.

Bill followed, curious.

Collins made a beeline for Thurman and Ernie.

"Hey Ernie," he always just ignored Thurman, which pissed Thurman off even more than Collins' mere presence did, "you know those pillars we were talking about?"

"What pillars?" Thurman went on point, suspicious of Collins the moment he walked within range.

"He wants pillars to make it look like a rich mansion," Ernie explained to Thurman.

"How many pillars?" Thurman was still suspicious.

"Two," Ernie promptly answered.

"No, twelve," John Collins corrected.

"Twelve!" Ernie almost choked.

"Twelve!" Thurman screamed. "Are yew out o' yer mind?"

"We want to overwhelm them," Collins was enjoying himself no end. "The whole back of the stage will be covered with magnificent carved Corinthian pillars. I'll get some books from the library to show you how to carve the tops out of styrofoam. It'll look like the Parthenon or the Lincoln Memorial."

"It'll look like shit," Thurman growled.

"Like the Parthenon," Ernie was all wide-eyed.

"Yeah," Collins ignored Thurman. "Maybe twelve is not enough. Maybe we need eighteen."

"You want the top of the stage to look like the Parthenon?" Ernie was already envisioning his most spectacular set. His voice had an awestruck sense of wonder in it.

"Parthenon, my ass! Ya know how long it takes to carve one o' those pillars out o' styrofoam. We did that for *My Fair Lady* and I swore I'd niver do it agin. No way."

"Now wait a minute, Thurm. We could do it. We'd have to git Wiley. He's super with styrofoam . . ."

"No way! We're not makin' no pillars out o' styrofoam or nothin' else."

"If you don't want to make them out of styrofoam, you could make them out of gingerbread," Collins took his own life in his hands.

"Gingerbread?" Ernie stared with the incomprehension of the eternal butt of all jokes.

"Ya see, Ernie, he's doin' it agin," Thurman had seen the light, "and yer lettin' him do it to yew. I told yew he does it on purpose. He's doin' it to us agin and yer takin' the asshole seriously."

"Asshole?" Somehow Collins had managed to keep a straight face all through this, but Bill could tell that the strain was beginning to tell and he was ready to burst.

"That's a nice word for you," Thurman shot back.

"Oh well," Collins turned back to Ernie "if Thurman doesn't think its a good idea . . . then maybe . . . let's see . . . instead of pillars maybe we could have ivy on a brick wall going all the way to the ceiling."

With his hands cupping his chin contemplatively, Ernie was considering the idea when Thurman stalked off muttering obscenely.

"The ivy would probably all die over the course of the play," Ernie was serious.

"You're right," Collins agreed. "Let's just leave it the way it is," and he left.

As Collins walked away, Lori emerged from the stairwell to the dressing rooms headed for the drinking fountain in the lobby. Bill noticed that her face was all red as if she was overheated. As she came abreast of him, she put both hands up to the sides of her face as if to hide her appearance.

"Are you OK?" Bill asked, his concern genuine.

But before Lori could answer, Marge bellowed: "All right people, let's get back to it. Tracy, Mike, let's work the drunk scene a couple more times."

"Sorry, gotta go," Lori fled to the stage.

Back in his seat in the darkness of the theater, *she's been crying*, Bill thought.

He watched closely as they did the scene. The director stopped Lori three times to make suggestions or demand different line readings. Each time the director spoke, Lori recoiled as if wounded. Then came the kiss. Bill thought they really did it well, too well. Lori was tense as Connor moved toward Tracy for the kiss, but once their lips met she seemed to melt into his arms with her hands rising up around his neck. They held it longer than they ever had before. When they broke off, Collins turned out to the dark theatre and mouthed "WOW!" in that exaggerated vaudevillian way of his.

"That was better," Marge intoned out of the darkness grudgingly. "Now let's do it again."

Bill watched them do the scene three more times to the point that he felt like a peeper outside someone's bedroom window. Each time as the kiss approached, a resentment rose within him. They would close in that long sensuous kiss and he would wish it was him kissing Tracy. He wished he had Collins' part so he could hold Tracy in his arms. As he watched her under the stage lights, he realized how much he was attracted to her. With one last lingering kiss, Marge gave up on that scene for the evening. *And its a good thing too,* Bill thought. He was getting more and more jealous of Collins. *How unprofessional,* he thought. *It's only acting, but he longed to be doing it.* Lori had his attention alright. He couldn't take his eyes off of her onstage.

"Thank god that's over," Collins joked. "My lips were getting numb."

"Gee, thanks a lot," Lori played mock angry. It was the first light moment for her in the whole rehearsal.

The way Lori collapsed into the theatre seat when she came off-stage you would have thought she had just gone fifteen rounds with the heavyweight champ.

"No rest for the wicked," Marge heavyhandedly tried to sound lighthearted. "Mike, Dexter, Tracy, let's try the fight scene after the drunk scene."

Lori was deflated. As she dragged herself up, he heard her mutter "shit!" under her breath.

"Now, Dexter," and Marge took him by the hand and led him to a downstage spot, "it's three in the morning and you're all alone on the veranda. Now, Mike and Tracy, you're both drunk, you've been skinnydipping in the pool, you've both got on terry cloth pool robes and nothing else. You'll do a quick change in the lobby cloak room. You'll drop your dress and just leave it there, Tracy. The costume mistress will get it for you. That puts you in bra and panties under the short robe. I'm going to want a lot of leg when Mike carries you onstage passed out. Wear some french-cut panties or something."

"If we've both been skinny dipping and we're both in robes, where does John change?" Lori asked innocently.

"Oh, you'll both change in the cloak room at the same time," Marge answered as if surprised the question was even asked.

"We're both going to strip down to our underwear in the lobby?" Lori said it slowly as if the reality of the concept was dawning in her mind. When it broke through, she threw her glance upon the mercy of John Collins.

He was no help. He raised his eyebrows lecherously in his best Groucho Marx leer.

Images of Lori's dress falling to the floor and her standing before him in a skimpy bra and french-cut panties crept into Bill's mind's eye and lit the short fuse of his irrational jealousy once again. *Man, he gets to kiss her, undress with her, what a deal.*

"Don't worry, honey," the director wasn't the least bit sympathetic, "you know what they say, there's no modesty in theatre."

Dirty pictures of Lori in bra and panties were still dancing like sugarplums in Bill's imagination.

"Now Mike, you and Tracy will enter down the aisle through the audience. You'll be carrying her in your arms. Tracy, you'll be almost passed out. I want a silly drunken grin on your face."

"And a lot of leg" Lori added with unenthusiastic sarcasm.

"Exactly," Marge was obtusely pleased with her easy acceptance of direction.

They blocked the scene. It was just a simple pass through for Tracy. She was carried on, the two men exchanged some lines, then she was carried off. Mike the reporter then returned to the stage to confront George, Tracy's jealous husband-to-be, and Dexter, Tracy's mischievous ex-husband.

When they tried the scene, Mike's entrance carrying Tracy was barely over when Marge stopped them.

"Tracy, you're too stiff. You're drunk! Your head should be lolling. You're limp as a ragdoll. There should be a stupid smile on your face. Now try that entrance again."

When rehearsal ended forty-five minutes later, Lori was sitting in the third row when Bill came offstage to pick up his script preparatory to going home. As he approached, she leaned over the seats and asked in a conspiratorial whisper: "Would you have time to go out for a drink? I need one."

"I've never turned down a drink in my life," Bill answered as a smile bloomed in his face.

Lori laughed, but even in the dim offstage light he could see that her eyes were red and irritated.

13 Triangles

"What is it with her? I'm working just as hard as I can. Can't she see that?"

They were sitting at a small table for two in the dim back of *The Hoosier Saloon*. The waitress hadn't even come for their order yet, but Lori wasn't in the mood for waiting. She needed to tell someone how frustrated she was.

"I think you're doing great," Bill meant it, and said it with feeling, but it made no impression on her.

"She thinks I'm terrible," Lori spit back.

"No, she doesn't," he tried to comfort her.

"Can't you see what she's doing. She's not yelling at anyone else. She's not giving anyone else acting lessons every minute they're onstage. It just me, me," and Lori burst into tears as the waitress arrived.

"Uh, two beers," Bill ordered, embarrassed, worried the waitress might think that he had made her cry. "Uh, light beers. Light, Lori?"

"Here honey," the waitress said through her gumchewing, and handed Lori two cocktail napkins.

One for her eyes and one for her nose? Mike watched as Lori used them as the waitress had surely intended.

"I want to quit," Lori's tears were in her voice.

"It's that bad, huh?" he was stunned at how upset she was.

"I'm the only one she criticizes," the napkins sat in a soggy wad in front of her, "every line, every move, every look on my face. I'm really trying and she hates me. I've always been told I was a good actress. What am I going to do?"

"Don't quit," there was desperation in his voice. "Please don't quit. I don't want you to." It was clumsy, but it seemed to cheer her.

"I don't know if I can take this for four more weeks of rehearsal," her eyes were finally beginning to dry up. Dirty mascara smudges had formed just above her wonderful cheekbones.

"Do you know what 'stress' is?" sudden inspiration had come to Bill.

"What?" Lori was confused, as if saying 'what the hell does that have to do with any of this?'

"Stress." he was going to cheer her up with a joke. "Stress is when one's mind overrides the body's basic desire to choke the life out of some moron who desperately needs it."

"What. Oh . . ." and she laughed, just a small giggle. "You're right, that's exactly what I'd like to do to Marge the Barge."

An awkward silence ebbed in between them. The beers came. They sipped dutifully. Lori swabbed at her face with a fresh cocktail napkin.

"It's just that," she stopped, as if looking for the right words or, perhaps, deciding if she wanted to go on, "that . . . I'm not whining, really . . ."

"I know," he lied. He didn't have a clue.

" . . . she's always on *me*. She criticizes, changes everything I'm doing onstage. And she never says anything to anyone else. It's not fair," and her voice broke again. Two large tears rolled out of the inside corners of her eyes, picked up speed down the sides of her nose and splashed spectacularly on her upper lip.

She looked so vulnerable that Bill felt this impulse to put his arms around her, but he knew he couldn't do that. That would really spook her.

"I'm really trying. I really am," she wiped her wet lip under her nose with her hand, "I've got to stop this crying. You must think I'm a big baby. Some liberated Eighties working woman, huh? Bawling her eyes out because some fat cow is carping at her? I'm sorry," and for the first time during this whole sob session she made solid eye-contact with him. When she did, she caught him thinking about her marvelous mixing of that cow and carp metaphor.

"For the last week and a half I've been sitting out in the audience watching you and, believe me, you are going to own the stage. You're the perfect Tracy. The audiences are going to love you. I mean, that's why you can't quit, because you're going to be so good. I can see it even now as I'm sitting there watching you in rehearsals. I can't take my eyes off of you." He stopped. His voice had dropped and he'd been talking to Lori softly, perhaps too seriously

Her eyes came up and fixed on his for a brief moment. They were still misty, but she wasn't crying anymore, and she gave him a feeble little smile.

"Thanks," she said, softly, simply, turning him into her manservant forever.

"I mean," he was suddenly a babbling idiot, "I told you the other night how great you looked onstage. And I can't believe you already know all your lines. You're gonna be great, great."

He stopped, lunged for his beer, took a long pull to calm himself down, puffed it out in his cheeks once like a chipmunk, then swallowed it. It calmed him down, stopped his directionless babbling, gave him a chance to think. It also gave her a chance to talk. She was much calmer now, her voice under control.

"I just don't know how long I can keep taking it from her." She laughed, big mood shift. "I'm afraid that one of these nights when she yells 'don't stoop' I'm just going to turn around and give her the finger and call her a fascist cow."

"Fascist cow?"

And they both laughed, bending their heads toward each other across the table.

The awkward little silence ebbed in again. Lori looked up at him again. He just wasn't used to looking right into a woman's eyes. He didn't know if her look was inquiring, expectant, come hither, or pleading. He didn't know how she felt or how he was supposed to feel. He still didn't know what he was doing with this woman fifteen years younger than him in this bar late at night telling her how beautiful she was. To tell the truth, he didn't know what he was doing at all, but he went on doing it nonetheless.

"When you stop and think about it," which is really why he had taken that pause that had drawn that curious look from her, "what she is doing is the smart thing. From her point of view . . . certainly not from yours, or mine, as actors who have to stand there and take it. But you are the whole play. Whether you like it or not, you're the star of this show. If you're not good, the show's not good . . ."

"Hey, who's side are you on?" She said it with a mocking grin.

"Yours, all the way. We're both in the same boat. That's why she's paying so much attention to you, because you're the one who makes this whole thing fly. Granted, she's not very tactful, and certainly not fair, but right now you're the one she's interested in. I had a basketball coach in high school who every year told us not to be thin-skinned or rabbit-eared because he was going to yell at us every chance he got. Then he said that the time to be worried was when he stopped yelling at us because that meant he'd given up on us, didn't care about us anymore."

"Yeah, maybe, but she's so ugly about it. I don't think she likes me at all, not as Tracy and not as me. She's a mean person."

"Hell, she probably thinks that actors are just cattle, objects she can do anything she wants with in order to make her play come out right."

"Is that what you meant when you said we're both in the same boat?"

"Sort of. I don't have near as big a part as Tracy's, but I can see how she'd be more worried about you and me."

"Why? I mean, she *wanted* you, *asked* you to audition, and I've got a degree in theatre. I've probably been on stage as much or more than anybody in this cast."

"I know. I know. But that probably doesn't make any difference. You've got the major role in her play and she doesn't know what you can do. Maybe she *should* be hyper about you and me. We're the rookies here. I'd sure be worried about me if I was her! I'm not even sure I can memorize all the lines."

"You're doing fine onstage. She never yells at you."

"Yes she does. Remember that first week when I was grabbing you by the shoulders to talk to you at the end of the first act. She said I was stiff as a Methodist minister."

"That *was* pretty funny. It was like you were scared of breaking me."

"See."

"Ok, I guess I'm feeling a little sorry for myself, but she's sure not doing anything to help my confidence. If she'd just say I did something right once in a while."

"You know something, I'm really glad you picked me to talk to about this."

"Why? What? You *like* people dumping all their insecurities on you?

"No, not that. It's just that, you and I, we're the outsiders on this show. All of these people know each other and we're the unknown quantities."

"Hey, John and Harvey and Sonny are really good actors, but I don't think they're any better than we are."

"Yeah, but don't you see, in *this* theatre they're the professionals and we're the amateurs."

"Then we've gotta stick together."

"There you go."

"Then let's have another beer. I can buy you one. I never paid for anything last Friday night."

"Hey, the dude's buyin,'" and he waved for the waitress whom he hoped when she came would notice that Lori was no longer crying and that he was the one responsible for her miraculous mood shift from moist despair to dry-eyed determination. "Two more," he placed the order, "and she's paying."

The waitress took away the soggy pile of cocktail napkins. When she left, Lori didn't say anything and Mike sneaked a look at her. She caught him, and smiled weakly, shaking her head.

"I guess I just can't stop thinking about it," she said. "That woman really got to me tonight."

"Lori, look," his voice was soft and serious again, "the object of all this is to have fun, isn't it?" An image of Barb Dwyer, voracious costume mistress, sitting next to him in this same bar proposing her version of 'fun' suddenly darted across his mind.

"Yes, you're right."

"Has it been fun for you? It has for me so far."

"It was fun for a while. It was exciting and competitive during the auditions, and then that first week it was fun meeting everybody, and getting back onstage again, and all, going out Friday night."

"It sure beats sitting home watching TV, doesn't it?"

"But this week she's just gotten me so uptight. No, it hasn't been much fun this week."

"They don't pay us enough and the hours are too long for it not to be fun. Hell, they don't pay us anything."

"You're right. I know that but . . ."

"Look, we're doing this for ourselves. It ought to be fun."

"And what I'm sayin' is it wasn't any fun at all tonight doing that silly kissing scene over and over with her yelling at me and John Collins standing there like a limp piece of fettucini."

Bill wanted to tell her how irrationally jealous it had made him feel all night watching her repeatedly kiss Collins. He wanted to tell her how different it would have been if she had been kissing him. He wanted to tell her that if they had already been kissing all evening they could be in a motel room right now. But he didn't tell her any of that.

"Limp piece of fettucini?" was all he could think to say. He and Lori caught the same image in each other's eyes. They both laughed hard out loud.

"I really didn't mean it that way," Lori protested.

"Oh yes, I think you did, and Freud thinks you did."

"Well, he's funny, John is, but he's sure not the sexiest hunk around. He's too tall and skinny and passive. I have to do all the kissing."

"Oh you poor pitiful thing, forced to stand there and kiss all the men in the cast."

"Oh stop it, you sound like my husband."

They were kidding each other like a couple of old cronies sitting over their beers in a bar. For Bill it was much more interesting than sitting in a bar with men, professors or softball players.

"What *does* your husband think of all this? Have you told him you're thinking of quitting?"

"Ha! Eddie? He could care less. He thinks this is all silly and a waste of time. Deep down, I even think he'd like seeing me fail."

"What do you mean? I mean, I can't understand that. For me it would be exciting watching my wife doing something like this. Having other people acknowledge her talent."

"He makes real sarcastic comments about 'kissing practice' and 'going to play little rich bitch again tonight?'"

"Maybe he feels threatened by you going outside the house in the evenings. Maybe he's jealous that you're kissing other men."

"Eddie, jealous? I wish. No, it's not that. Threatened, I don't think so. Threatened by what?"

"I don't know. By all the men in the cast, by all the men who are going to be looking at you onstage."

"What do you mean?"

All of a sudden, Mike was sorry he'd ever asked the question about her husband. *Dexter sure wouldn't sit still for this,* Bill thought, *he'd be making witty fun of Eddie.*

"Uh, I really don't know what I mean. I don't even know your husband. Just thinking out loud I guess. All I meant is I don't think you should quit and maybe he ought to be more supportive."

"'Supportive,'" Lori had become thoughtful, "that's a good word. I'll tell him that. God knows I've been supportive of him."

"What about your wife?" Lori asked.

"I don't think she cares one way or the other. She probably just thinks I'm off doing another stupid thing. She thinks I'm an arrested adolescent."

Lori finished her beer.

She's going to get up to leave now, Bill thought.

"Uh, Miss," she flagged the waitress on her way by, "could I have another light beer?"

Her order surprised them both.

Bill took it as a clear signal that she enjoyed being with him, didn't want their conversation, which was merging toward intimacy, to stop.

"I can't remember the last time I had three beers in one sitting," Lori smiled as she took her first sip from the new glass.

"Me neither," Bill said as he finished the one in front of him and ordered a fresh one before the waitress got away. "Just to keep us even," he assured her, "after all, I do have to walk you back to your car."

"Oh yeah," she remembered.

"You seem to be feeling better already," he raised his bottle to her. "Doctor Franklin prescribes three beers and some good talk as a perfect cure for the Wabash City blues."

"Thank you, doctor," Lori clinked her glass against his beer bottle, "you're right. It's working."

"Hey, here's to Marge the Barge," Mike proposed the toast, "whose relentless bitching made this all possible. Thanks to her insensitivity and tactlessness we're having this night on the town together. To Marge and her triangles."

"I'll tell you one thing," and Lori was right in the raucous, elbow-nudging spirit of Bill's toast, "Marge can take her triangles and put them where they'd have to send in an army of weight watchers with flashlights to find them."

"I'll drink to that."

"You know, I just don't think she's directing the way actors need to be directed," Lori set out to explore another undiscovered country.

"What do you mean?"

"Think about it. We're all volunteers. We all want to be good actors, do a good job. It's Civic Theater for god's sake! Why does she have to do that? Yell at us . . . check that, yell at me . . . on every line. I mean, she ought to be nicer. We're there because we want to be. That's all I'm saying."

"It's probably just her directing style."

"What? Naziism?"

Bill had to laugh. Lori was really quite funny on her third beer.

"Ok, but all I mean is I'll bet other directors direct in much different ways. I haven't had much experience with theater directors so I don't know. But I'll bet other directors are more sensitive to the actors."

"I had a couple of good directors in college. All she's doing is telling, telling, telling us what to do, I mean, down to the tiniest details, when she could be asking us what we think Tracy or Dexter would do here, what pose they'd strike, how their face and voice would react."

"If Dexter was here, he'd ask you to go sailing tomorrow."

"C'mon, I'm serious. Anyway, I have to work."

"Where do you work?"

"At Dibble, Dobel and Dunne, I'm a legal secretary."

"Great name."

"Not if you have to answer the phone with it forty times a day. I was starting to develop a stuttering problem. Duh, duh, D-D-Dibbbbble, duh, DDDobel, duh-DDunne, Good Duh-Day."

Bill laughed. *She really is funny,* he thought. She had been so upset and it all had been so awkward walking over to the bar and when they had first sat down. But now they were at ease with each other, like old friends. *I wonder what would happen if I could get one more beer into her,* he thought.

"I'm serious," Lori went back to her expedition into directing styles. "A director ought to give an actor some freedom to build a characterization."

"Marge would never do that." All he was doing was agreeing with her so that he could look into her blue eyes.

"You're right, she's a power freak." Lori was really caught up in her little psychoanalytic foray. Bill didn't know that she had minored in psychology in college. "She's trying to make me into a puppet so that whenever she pulls a string, my nose will pop up in the air and I'll jump for her. It's just not a good way to direct. You get dead, cold actors."

"But she's directing, and we have to live with it."

"I'm afraid you're right. You've been right about everything else tonight. What time is it?"

"Quarter to twelve."

"Aw hell, Eddie's not home yet. Let's have another beer."

Bingo!, lights started going off in Bill's mind, but for some reason he said: "Are you sure you can drive home? You said you couldn't remember the last time you'd had three beers." He could have kicked himself as soon as he said it.

"Do you have to go? We could just go."

"No. No. I didn't mean that. Martha's been asleep for hours. In fact, the last thing I want to do is go. No, I want to stay. In fact, I am going to have another beer. I'm used to it. I know I can get home."

"You're right. Do you think they'd have a pot of coffee going?"

"I'm sure they do."

Her coffee came. It was his fourth beer. It took that many for him to even feel the slightest effect. The whole evening was starting to smooth out like the soft wake of Dexter's yacht with the wind filling its sails.

"It'll get better, I know it will," he went back to giving Lori the pep talk she had so needed when they first sat down.

"Oh, I know it will," Lori seemed totally at ease, the dull mascara smudges the only surviving evidence that she had been crying. "She has to start yelling at some of the others sometime. I'll be OK. It really helped to talk about it. I didn't really want to quit, but she was driving me bats."

"Like I said, it sure beats staying home watching TV."

"I just wish we'd gotten a different director."

"So the director is a pain. She won't be the last. It's like sports coaches. I've had all kinds—football, basketball, baseball—I've dealt with my daughter's coaches in grade school, junior high, high school. Some are good. Some are morons. Ultimately the bad ones always go away. That'll happen with this director. I'm betting that in every play, the time comes when the director has to go away, and the play becomes the actors,' to do with what they will."

"My, my, aren't we becoming the analytic one."

"You should talk! You're the one who sounds like she's got a degree in psychology."

"I do. Well, a minor."

She finished her coffee and he sipped on his beer, and they talked of heiresses and yachtsmen, but mostly actors, mostly themselves. It was almost one when Lori reluctantly decided she had better head for home. She had never stayed out later than her husband.

"That's what coffee tells you to do," Bill kidded her, even though the coffee really had been his idea.

"Well, what do you want to do," she taunted him right back.

The moon was still full, and the night was still soft and warm, when they stepped out onto Fifth Street and crossed over the railroad tracks heading toward the theater. It was one of those lush Wabash City nights when the river breeze barely ruffles the air. It wasn't at all dark. In fact, the moonglow spread a whitish wash over the street as if they were walking in an old movie like *Casablanca*. They didn't talk as they walked. They both seemed comfortable in the silence. But, both of their minds were racing on the current of the evening toward something neither had either the power or the inclination to control.

What would she do if I took her hand, turned her toward me, and kissed her right here in the street, the idea crept up on him.

He's fifteen years older than me, Lori thought. *I want him to kiss me. I'm not a child. What would he do if I just took his arm as we walked, like I was afraid of the dark or something? He'd probably run like hell. He's not thinking of me that way. Why isn't he? Am I so ugly?*

I can't do this. I'm too old for her. I like her. We could be friends. I do that and I'll spook her, ruin the whole thing.

Why doesn't he say anything? Why is he so afraid to touch me? If he'd just kiss me goodnight. It's no big thing. He's been so nice about everything. He's too much of a gentleman. He'd probably never even think of kissing me.

I'd really like to kiss her, Bill fought that thought.

They reached the Civic Theater parking lot much too soon.

"I think I'm a little tipsy. Now that's something Tracy would say," Lori broke the silence of their short moonlit walk.

"You've been tipsy all evening ever since you and John-boy started doing that drunken scene in rehearsal," Bill teased.

"It feels good," she stopped beside her car and smiled up at him, "like floating."

"An unbearable lightness of being," he said softly, wistfully.

"What?"

"Oh, nothing, just something from a book."

The theater loomed dark behind them, monolithic, like the old stone train station that it was.

"You know," they had arrived at Lori's car, but she made no move to open the door and get in, "doing that silly scene with John over and over tonight takes all the fun out of it."

"Out of what?"

"Kissing. Kissing ought to be fun."

"Yes. It should."

Again he wanted to tell her how jealous he had felt as he'd watched her do the kissing scene over and over, how different it would have been if she were kissing him. But he didn't have to tell her any of that now.

Instead, she looked up into his eyes.

He met her look sheepishly, then caught its determination. *Wow!* he thought, *it's really going to happen.*

Her face came up and he took her in his arms as if they'd had months of rehearsal.

And they kissed.

Long and slow and soft, neither questioning why or wondering how, both just sailing on the gentle breeze, floating on the magic, of their first real kiss.

The train came clanking down the middle of Fifth Street as their lips parted and she buried her head in the soft down of his sweater as his arms held her close. The train pounded by, drowning out the pounding of their hearts. It wasn't the 9 o'clock Amtrak which had punctuated their first and only stage kiss. It was a long slow midnight freight rumbling through the center of the deserted town.

But she couldn't stay still in the comfort of his arms. Her hands were already up around his face, meeting behind his neck, as she rose up to take his lips once again, this time kissing him harder, more urgently. That first kiss had been a friendly kiss. After it, they should have stepped back out of each other's arms, got in their cars and gone home. But they didn't. They had stopped as if suspended in time, held each other close for a moment, looked into each other's eyes, and then really kissed, a lover's kiss. If Marge had been there directing, she would have applauded. "Now that's more like it," she would have growled.

The moonlight bathed them in its soft glow as they reveled in their long and breathless kiss.

The train rumbled through the town, pummeling the air.

They withdrew reluctantly from their kiss, and this time did step back.

"Wow," Lori looked right at him, but there was an almost dazed look on her face.

Bill just stared dumbly. He wanted her so badly that his whole being ached with the thought of it. He wanted to take her back into his arms and kiss her again and again until she never wanted to stop. Instead, he came to his senses and made a joke out of it.

"Every time we kiss, it seems like that train shows up," he grinned awkwardly.

"Maybe it's a good omen," Lori answered, and then she was back in his arms, kissing him even more hungrily, her mouth open, her tongue parting his surprised lips, her body curving insistently into his, moving firmly against him. Her mouth, her breasts, her hips, all speaking to him in a wondrous language of the body and the heart.

"Oh Lori, this is dangerous," he whispered into her hair as he pressed her even more tightly against him.

"I know, but it's the best I've felt in months," she was breathing in short quick gasps.

They kissed again, long and hard with a passion neither understood nor wanted to question. They were as one in that kiss, breathing through each other's beings.

Lori was the first to flee.

"I'm sorry, I didn't mean for this to happen. No, I did. Yes, I did. I'm sorry. I just don't know what I'm doing," and she pulled out of his arms and lunged for her car door.

"I'm not sorry," Bill pulled her back, held her wrists. "Look at me," he commanded her as he gently shook her wrists. "I've wanted to kiss you all night, since the first time you kissed John in rehearsal. I've wanted to kiss you. I feel jealous every time you kiss Collins. No, look at me. That's how I've felt all night. I've wanted to kiss you, and I want to kiss you again."

"No. We can't. This is crazy," Lori was panicked. "I've got to go. It feels too good. We shouldn't. Oh Jesus . . ." and she was back in his arms and this kiss sent them into a new world where they wanted to stay forever locked in the heat of their embrace, languishing in their gift of tongues.

14 Bill's Journal

Wednesday, Sept. 11

Last night it was not so much what happened during rehearsal but after. Tracy, at the end of rehearsal, asks if I want to go out and get a drink. As we walked to the bar, I figured something was bothering her. Next thing I know she is crying, threatening to quit the show, all because the director has really been on her. I agree, the director is singling Lori out for too much criticism, I'm listening to her, but I'm also looking at her. I tell her to have fun. I try to console her. But all the time I am thinking other things. I'm really starting to like her, and that's bad. The end of the evening got a little out of hand. Too many beers.

Thursday, Sept. 12

An uneventful rehearsal. The director is still yelling at Tracy, but it doesn't seem to be bothering Lori so much. I didn't get to rehearsal until an hour after it started, faculty meeting ran late. Tracy and Mike were onstage already. When I got there, Tracy was dismissed. A good sign. The director let her go home. Maybe the director sees how much stress Lori's under. Hopefully, we'll get a chance to talk tomorrow after rehearsal when we all go out. I need to apologize to her. I feel like I took advantage of a real vulnerable situation. We went too far. Collins and I worked the punch scene for an hour. My punch needs a lot of work. It really looks fake. I added a nice little piece of business though. After the punch I go down on one knee holding the knuckles of my hand and grimacing

in pain. The director ate it up. Let's hear it for small
satisfactions.

Friday, Sept. 13
TGIF, Friday the 13th. Watch out. Everyone is out
to have fun. Except Lori disappears after rehearsal
and doesn't come out to the bar with the rest of us.
Maybe she's avoiding me. Maybe she thinks what happened the other night might happen again. She probably thinks I'm some kind of dirty old man. But she
seemed a lot less tense on stage tonight. I couldn't take
my eyes off of her all evening. She was having fun and
it was Friday and the director let up on the actors. But
then she disappeared. We all went to the Saloon. I was
disappointed Lori wasn't there, but we still had a good
time. That's why we're doing this, to have fun.

"Have you ever met a dirty young man?" Harvey Winkins was leering
across the table at Barb Dwyer. "It takes seasoning, spice, to reach my
level of dessicated lechery."

"I've met a lot of dirty young men," Barb Dwyer piped up.

"I'll bet you have," Harvey assented without the slightest hesitation.

"Have you ever noticed how it's the fallen women who always get
picked up," John Collins entered the fray.

"What the hell does that mean?" Barb challenged him.

"Nothing. I think I saw it in a Woody Allen movie."

"Barbara Dear . . . fallen women, picked up, get it? Just a joke, a
joke," Harvey enjoyed his role as mediator.

They were all sitting around three small tables pushed together
near the front windows of *The Hoosier Saloon* on Friday, the 13th.
Almost the whole cast was there, except for the high school girls and
Lori, who had abruptly left after rehearsal. Her just taking off like that
had left Bill uneasy and wondering.

*Wednesday night, both a little tipsy, after we kissed we had both been
embarrassed. But it hadn't stopped us from kissing again . . . and again.*

Bill didn't know what to think. Lori had chosen not to join him,
them, at the bar on Friday night. *You're too old to be this confused,* he
thought.

Some of the cast had walked the two blocks down from the theater, crossing the tracks as they went. The others had driven, parking their cars in the small lot across the street, and the tracks, from the bar. They all arrived at about the same time. The walkers were waiting for the riders to cross the street when a rusty old freight rumbled down the tracks between them. Collins and Sunny and Thelma and Marge had all walked. They stood by the glass front door of the tavern waiting for the others to cross the street. Bill and Harvey and Barb Dwyer and Sam Wilcox had all driven. The train bore down as they were getting out of their cars and cut them off from the group waiting by the door of the bar.

John Collins, irrepressible cut-up, was the first to take advantage of the situation. He moved closer to the side of the passing train and started jumping up and down and flipping the bird between the interstices of the passing cars. Soon the others, even Thelma and Marge, were making faces, thumbing their noses, putting their thumbs in their ears and waggling their fingers at their cut-off colleagues. It was an astonishing display of purely adolescent silliness and Bill and Harvey and Barb Dwyer gave it back in kind. Sam Wilcox just stood there staring through the train at those mad dancers with that eternally bemused look on his face.

Bill was having a great time giving Marge the finger as the train clattered between them. The moving train gave their frenetic motions that look of people moving in a strobe light. Only parts of their antagonists, fragments of their gestures, passed through the moving interstices of the rumbling train. It struck Bill funny, this wall full of holes coming between the two halves of the zany company. For a flashing moment, he saw the train tracks as this barrier right down the middle of everything. *We're always stopped for trains,* he thought, *cut off from the other side of the tracks. There's always a barrier. It keeps reality and illusion separate. Constantly forces us to stop and think whether we want to cross over to the other side.*

"Let's moon 'em!" Barb Dwyer shouted above the din of the clanking freight cars.

"Barbara Dear. Please. Let me at least have a couple of drinks before I start exposing all my shortcomings in public," Harvey beseeched her.

"Oh, OK," Barb Dwyer left off reluctantly, sparing us all.

Through the train, Sunny was doing a wild chicken dance in tandem with Collins as Thelma and Marge, winded from their silly exertions, looked on.

Sam Wilcox stared sweetly through the train at them.

Barb Dwyer chicken danced back.

Harvey applauded them all.

Everyone had finally snapped.

It was a brief street theater, performed on both sides of a moving tattered curtain. Everyone was backstage and onstage and in the audience at the same time. The whole performance moved like strobing images in a frenetic magic lantern.

Then the red caboose with two trainmen smoking on its back porch scuttled by and the play stopped as abruptly as the street emptied. The two trainmen stared dully down at them as the train moved away and disappeared around a curve.

Final curtain, Bill thought, signifying nothing, *and suddenly there's nothing left between you and the audience. You have no choice but to go back to reality.*

Inside, the company pulled the tables together and ranged themselves in an intimate circle, relaxed by their street theater silliness. Thelma sat with them, taking it all in. She always showed up on Friday nights during rehearsals, never missed a cast party or actors' foray out into the Wabash City night. Recording their history was her job, and she kept to it with the dedication of a medieval monk over a manuscript.

Marge sat at the head and Thelma at the foot of their charmed circle. All four of the men ranged themselves down one side along the wall with the oversized figures of Lauren Bacall and Katherine Hepburn leaning over their shoulders. Sunny and Barb Dwyer failed to fill the aisle side of the table, and sat amused at the men opposite. This dancing school seating was probably because the men were afraid to sit next to the redoubtable Barb.

This was only his second occasion for joining the company in the bar, but Bill had already noticed how the conversations around the table never flagged. If Harvey wasn't telling a joke, then Collins was doing an impression, or Barb Dwyer was throwing a pass at one of the men, or they were talking as a group about the tricks and strategies of acting, or Thelma was telling a story.

On Friday the 13th Thelma told the story of the overenthusiastic dresser.

"It was about ten years ago and I think the play was called Norsemen or Vikings or something like that. It was a play about carpenters—honest!—and the whole cast was men."

"I remember that one," Harvey Winkins broke in. "I never saw so many hammers onstage. It was great! The only tools those carpenters carried were hammers."

"Anyway," Thelma ignored Harvey as a rule of thumb, "all three men in the cast had quick changes at one point or another, and during tech and dress rehearsal week the director sent out word that the show needed a dresser for the performances. A new volunteer showed up at rehearsal one night, a quite attractive woman in her thirties, Jean or Joan or Jeri or something like that. She said she'd heard they needed a dresser, and she'd always wanted to get involved with Civic Theater. Well, the director hires her on the spot, and tells her to come to dress rehearsal the next night to get used to the costumes and practice the changes with the actors. And this woman is great. The quick changes go like clockwork. After one rehearsal, all the actors are raving about her."

Thelma paused for a long pull of beer.

"She's a werewolf," Collins speculated.

"Phantom of the Opera," Sunny made her nomination.

"Backstage slasher," Marge chipped in.

"Nothing so gruesome," Harvey Winkins waved them off, "but intimidating nonetheless." He obviously had heard the story before, or, who knows, perhaps he had been in it.

"Everything went beautifully opening night and all through the first weekend's performances. It was the second weekend when our dresser made her move."

"This is good," Harvey Winkins nudged Bill.

"The woman had a habit of waiting on her knees when the actor came offstage so that she could work on the lower half of his body while he worked on the top half."

"AHA!" Collins said it so lasciviously, with a simultaneous thrusting of his upraised forefinger toward the revolving ceiling fan, that everybody jumped.

"Oh shut up, John." Thelma squelchedhim. "It was a great way for a dresser to work. She'd unlace their shoes and unbuckle their pants . . ."

"AHA!" This time it was Harvey Winkins jumping up, exclaiming, then sitting right back down.

Thelma just ignored him.

"That whole first weekend she did the changes without a single glitch. The actors loved her. She completely had their trust. There were three actors. A young man in his twenties. The kid's father in his forties. The kid's grandfather in his sixties. When she changed them they hardly even knew she was there. The second weekend, the Friday night performance, she started in on the young guy. He had a quick change early in the first act and when he came off for it she was waiting on her knees. Only, this time, she not only pulled his pants down, but yanked his underpants down around his ankles too and, instead of getting his other pair of pants for him to put on, she starts, well, fondling him . . . and worse."

"How worse? How worse?" There was a voyeuristic quickening in Collins' voice.

Harvey was chuckling to himself.

"Use your imagination, geek," Thelma snapped at Collins and proceeded to chug what was left in her beer glass.

"The poor kid knows he's got to get back on stage, but his dresser is doing something to him that he's only dreamed about in his college boy fantasies. But finally he hears his entrance lines and he jumps for his pants, barely gets them on, has to carry his shoes out on stage and put them on while he's delivering his lines. But he covers it all so well that when the next actor, the middle-aged guy, comes off, he hasn't got a clue. The kid tries to warn him as he's leaving, but they're onstage and he can't really get it across. When the second actor comes off, she's there on her knees waiting for him too with an angelic smile on her face"

"Why did we ever let her go? She should work every play. Is she still in town? Marge, you've got to get her for us."

It was just at this moment in Thelma's story that Bill first felt Barb Dwyer's unsheathed foot playing with his ankle above his running shoe.

"You're a pig," Sunny lobbed across the table at Collins, but her heart wasn't in it.

"Anyway, the father gets back on stage, late, and he's carrying his shoes too. The kid has been shuffling around the kitchen set playing with dishes to try to cover. Their eyes meet as they try to get the scene started and both go dead silent. Each knows that the other one knows. The next time they look at each other, they both start to giggle. They try to cover it with a cough that comes out a choke. By now, the scene hasn't even started, two of the three principles are hacking onstage, and the old man, the third actor in the show, doesn't know what the hell is going on."

At this point, knowing she had them all in her power, Thelma paused for effect, filled her beer glass from the pitcher, and took a sip.

Bill felt Barb Dwyer's foot beginning to move up his leg underneath the table.

"So the third actor, playing the grandfather, comes over to his two sons and asks, 'what's going on?' It's not a line in the script, but the audience doesn't know that."

"'You don't wanna know," the actor playing the father finally gets enough control of his face and voice to say. The kid is almost apoplectic he's trying so hard to keep from laughing.

"'Well, if you're not careful, you're going to blow this whole deal,' the old actor said, not realizing that he was throwing gasoline on the fire. With that, the father and son actors both completely lost it, burst out laughing. None of it was in the play. The audience didn't know what was going on, and it took about two minutes of struggling around the stage for the actors to get back on the scene."

Like a snake, that soft foot moved slowly up over Bill's knee and stopped. The toes moved playfully on the inside of his thigh. Across the table, Barb Dwyer was alternating laughing with the others over Thelma's story and smiling boldly right at Bill. Her foot began to move again, relentlessly.

"What happened when the old guy went for his quick change," Collins couldn't resist asking.

But instead of Thelma, Sam Wilcox answered: "He didn't have a costume change until the second act. They removed the dresser at intermission. Just my luck!" He said it in the same voice of lobotomized calm that characterized all of his infrequent speech.

"It was you?" Collins stated the obvious.

"Yes, I always seem to miss out on the fun things that happen around the theater," Sam said, as if eternally resigned to his fate.

Bill was squirming. Her foot was moving on him. Slowly his right hand went beneath the table into his lap and reached for her probing toes. She kicked playfully out at him and withdrew, but, as soon as his hand once again appeared above the table, her foot was back, moving insistently. He cleared his throat and glared at her, but she wasn't about to be intimidated with a look. She smiled sweetly back and pushed the plastic swizzle stick from her drink in and out of her mouth, rolling it on her tongue while all the while her toes moved relentlessly toward their target.

John Collins had taken the floor after Thelma and was holding forth on his favorite real and unreal names.

"In grade school, we had a nun that my buddy Lenny Egan always called Sister Mary Milk of Magnesia, but that wasn't really her name. My favorite was Regina Fornicus."

Bill's hand went down and slapped at Barb Dwyer's foot, but she was quick and pulled it back. She smiled and raised her eyebrows in coy acknowledgement. He saw that now it was game between them. She was enjoying teasing him, making him squirm, and he didn't know what to do about it.

"Her parents and the nuns always pronounced her name 'Regee-na,' but all the boys in the school called her 'Regeyena,' rhymes with 'vagina.' And then, I remember, my mom had this dried up old lady who had been a friend of my grandmother and her name was Myrna Pecker. Honest!"

Barb Dwyer's toes moved relentlessly.

Bill shifted his weight, but he couldn't escape. Her foot started moving again. He couldn't stand it any longer.

"Pussy Galore!" John Collins exclaimed.

Bill jumped up as if he had been sitting on a snapping turtle and made a dash for the men's room. Hardly anyone noticed. They were all listening raptly to Collins' list of outrageous names.

"In college there was a girl in one of my classes . . no lie . . . named Sally Sexauer.

Thelma was taking mental notes, adding it all to her store of Civic Theater backstage lore.

Sam Wilcox came in and took the urinal one down from Bill. "Barb Dwyer's a lot of fun in an under the table sort of way," Sam commented in that zombiesque monotone that he used everywhere but on the stage.

"Oh, you noticed," Bill shook himself.

"Let's just say that past experience leads one to observe things going on beneath the surface."

"So you've had the pleasure of sweet Barbara's horny foot before?"

"I never flinch and tell," Sam was sort of witty in his quiet dry way.

"I'll tell 'ya, that woman is hormones a go go."

"You ain't seen nothin' yet," Sam advised sagely. "You know Thelma's story. Did you see the look of envy on Barb's face. All that story did was give her ideas."

When Bill returned to the company, the table had turned. On the excuse of a draft from the opening and closing of the front door—it was, after all, a balmy September night—Barb had moved around and taken Bill's seat in the middle of the men. Flanked by Harvey Winkins on one side, she was stroking John Collins' pigeon chest for no reason that anyone could divine.

Bill took her vacated chair next to Sunny and listened in, relieved to be temporarily replaced as Barb's target. *She smells good,* Bill noticed Sunny's perfume. He hadn't really ever had a conversation with her in the two weeks of rehearsal. She was very attractive, much closer to his age than Lori, probably about 38 or 40, with thick blonde hair and striking green eyes. She seemed rather quiet, reticent almost, more reserved than most of the others who always seemed more than willing to talk about themselves. She was a terrific actress; it hadn't taken him long to observe that. She was doing the part of Liz with a mixture of wide-eyed innocence and cynical sarcasm.

"Is this your first play at Civic?" Sunny made a conversational opening.

"Yes. It is," Bill was a bit startled that she was talking to him.

"Are you enjoying it?"

"I sure am. I haven't done anything like this since high school, and it's fun."

"I know. Every time I think about doing a play I remember how much work it is, how hard a time I had learning my lines the last time, but then I get into it, and there is something to do every night, and the people are fun and uninhibited, like that thing with the train out there before we came in."

"Yeah, I know what you mean. My colleagues at the university are so boring compared to you guys."

"Hey," she laughed demurely, "I've met a couple of them and you've got that right. ."

Across the table Harvey Winkins was smoking one of Barb Dwyer's cigarettes. He actually was somewhat miffed that Barb wasn't paying more attention to him. Barb, meanwhile, was running her hand up and down John Collins' arm as he talked about his first acting role in college. He had one line—"You're smart, but you can't get away with that"—but when he got onstage it came out "Your smut can't be got here." When Barb caught Bill looking at her and eavesdropping, she flashed him a wicked pursed-lip grin and winked.

Smart, smut, slut, that string of disassociated alliteration tumbled end over end down through Bill's mind. Collins' story was one that every actor probably had a version of, and Barb Dwyer may not have been the most brazen woman in Wabash City, but both of them were new to Bill. He wished Lori were there. Sunny didn't make him as uncomfortable as Barb Dwyer did, yet he couldn't think of anything to say to her. Two nights before, he and Lori's conversation had raced. Now he was sitting next to this atractive woman who was trying to strike up a conversation and he couldn't think of anything to say. When Sam Wilcox got up to leave, Bill begged off also. He couldn't believe he wasn't going to stay and try. He'd had fun the Friday before. But it was different without Lori there.

"See you next week," Sunny said cheerily.

"Work on your lines," Marge intoned like a pinched school mistress or a big nurse.

"I've got some fittings ready for you," Barb threatened with an evil relish in her voice.

He fled like a frightened virgin.

15 Rehearsal Touches

Monday, Sept. 16
They have started building the set. The raked stage is
up. It is really strange to walk on. I'm glad I don't have
to walk at an angle in heels like the girls do. The director is not just yelling at Tracy anymore. She's starting to spread it around. You have to be sort of thin-
skinned in this acting business. I got a chance to talk
to Lori tonight.

"No. No. No. No," Marge jumped up and launched into her usual
unbelieving cavil as if it really was beyond her belief how bad we could
be. Then she took a short breath to calm her fury, singled out the felon,
and tried to cajole that unlucky actor into doing it the way she wanted
it done. "Dexter, look, say it like you mean it. You're in love with her.
It's the night before her marriage and you're trying to get her back. For
god's sake, you sound like you're talking to a tape recorder."

He had been saying this speech to a tape recorder for two weeks.
He'd gotten the words down perfect, but the speech didn't have any
flesh and blood, emotion. It was only voices on a tape. He looked at
Lori and felt sheepish. *At least she's not just yelling at her anymore,* he
thought. It was almost like he and Lori's conversation in the bar had
somehow exorcised the omnipotent Marge. She was yelling at everybody now.

The director was right. He was stiff like a machine. Lori, Tracy,
hadn't even been there in his imagination. He felt a need to touch her,
to make sure she was real. In fact, the director was right most of the
time. Grudgingly Mike had to admit that the director was working
hard and making a lot of sense to him (if not to Lori).

"Now do it again," Marge growled, "and put some feeling into it."

So he touched her. Lori, Tracy, was standing sideways to him looking at the director. He reached out and brushed his fingertips across
the back of her shoulder. He felt her tense, but she caught herself. Then
he really got bold. He let his fingertips slide down her bare arm to her
elbow and with his whole hand pivoted her toward him for the scene.
Real actors wouldn't think twice about this sort of incidental touching. Real actors are used to touching and being touched by perfect
strangers in all contexts. "There is no such thing as modesty in theater," Marge had quoted chapter and verse. But for Bill the initiation
of this touching was much more demanding and intimidating than
simply actors touching on a stage. He touched her at Marge's direction, Dexter demanding the attention of his ex-wife Tracy, but when
she turned at his touch it all came back, Lori and Bill alone in that
moonswept parking lot. It came back with all the heat that he had felt
just before they kissed, all the passion that had carried them away as
they kept on kissing. He wanted to kiss her again, right there on the
stage in front of everyone, to show that he was capable of feeling, but
it wasn't in the script and they had to do the scene. He looked into her
face and caught the soft tinge of a blush on her cheeks.

She's feeling it too, he thought.

They did the scene, and then they did it again, and Dexter, unable
to tell her that he still loves her, scolds Tracy for being so selfish, and
Tracy spits back selfishly like the spoiled little rich girl that she is. The
scene got better each time they did it. They really were two people
probing each other's shortcomings. There was starting to be some feeling in it. Both of them knew that the next time they did the scene
it would be even better, more real. The director called a ten-minute
break.

"I've got to talk to you," Bill cornered Lori backstage as everyone
was drifting off toward the dressing rooms, the rest rooms and the
parking lot to smoke cigarettes.

"I know," Lori looked as if she'd been dreading it, "but I'm not sure
I'm ready."

"Ready for what?"

"I guess I've just been hoping it would all go away, that you'd forget
about it, or pretend it didn't happen."

"I guess we got a little carried away."

"No, we didn't. That's the problem."

"I don't . . . what do you . . . ?"

"It's not going away for me at all. I wasn't that drunk. I knew what I was doing. I wanted it to happen."

"I can't stop thinking about it. Just now when we were onstage and I touched you, that whole night came back like a flood. I wanted to kiss you again."

"It's not going away for you either. What are we getting into?"

"I don't know."

"I need to think. I don't want to talk about this anymore right now."

"Lori I . . ."

"Oh Bill," she stopped him with a touch, a hand on his forearm as he took a step toward her, "you got me through that night. You really helped me cope. I'm not sure I wasn't just so grateful . . . I just don't know. The bad part is I'm dying to kiss you again too."

And she fled into the ladies restroom leaving him standing alone in the hallway.

> Tuesday, Sept. 17
> We tried to run Act II tonight. What a disaster! I messed up almost all my lines. I felt like a complete stumblebum onstage. I'm actually feeling sorry for Marge having to deal with an actor this bad. I didn't want to talk to anybody after rehearsal, not even Lori. I went to a bar all by myself to drink. I hate making a fool of myself.

"Dexter, c'mon . . ." the director paused, thinking, or maybe just trying to get control of herself before she said something she didn't want to say, "You're a playboy, a rich, aimless, playboy. You've got to loosen up. Relax. Let's start with your posture. How do you stand? Dexter doesn't take any of these pretentious people seriously. He's amused by it all. How does he stand? Think a moment, and then just be Dexter onstage without any lines or reference to the others, just with your body language."

Bill was embarrassed. Everything had stopped onstage and everyone was looking at him. He grinned nervously. He did think a moment, but his mind was racing. *How would Cary Grant stand?* He walked over to the proscenium wall and leaned against it with his shoulder, shoved his hands into his pants pockets, and jauntily crossed his right foot over his left ankle leaving the toe resting on the ground.

"Perfect!" Marge was so happy. "That's it! Perfect!" she blubbered, and they went back to the scene.

> Wednesday, Sept. 18
> What a difference a day makes. I got my haircut for the show and a dye-job to get rid of the grey. I'm supposed to be young Cary Grant. I also ran all my lines with the tape recorder before rehearsal and managed to relax onstage. It was fun tonight. We ran through Act I first and it is fine. Even the director is comfortable with it. Then we ran Act II. Tracy, I mean Lori, gets better each night. We've been rehearsing for almost three weeks and she has changed completely. Her posture has changed. She keeps her head up now, proud like the spoiled rich girl she's playing. I sit in the audience watching she and Collins do their drunk scene together and it is hilarious. Uncle Willie was sitting next to me watching it tonight and I whispered to him: "I wish I had a drunk scene." He agreed: "It's one of the few things you really do well."

"Dammit Tracy, get mad," Marge bellowed from somewhere back in the darkness. "You look at Dexter as if you're all smiles your neer-do-well ex-husband has shown up the day before your wedding. You should be so upset you're blistering the wallpaper."

It wasn't easy for Tracy to get mad at Dexter onstage when Lori spent so much time fantasizing about Bill offstage. It had started raining Wednesday morning. As she sat at her counter sipping her coffee alone (Eddie hadn't gotten in until two the night before and probably wouldn't be up until noon), watching the large drops run like tears down her kitchen window, the lingering taste of Bill's lips kept intruding. She tried to think about her schedule for the day, her need to leave for work, her not wanting to think about him the way she had been thinking about him for almost a week now.

Sitting at her word processor, she found it hard to concentrate. Images of she and Bill in each others' arms in that moonlit parking lot, of she and Bill in bed wrapped in each others' arms, of she and Bill in full costume backstage sharing a long deep kiss, kept coming up on her computer screen in place of the boilerplate wills and gibberish briefs that were her normal law office fare. She couldn't type or file him out of her mind. But she knew she had to deal with him somehow.

He's fifteen years older than you, she told herself, but it didn't work. His body hadn't felt fifteen years older when he'd held her in his arms in the moonlight.

He's got a Ph.D. He's too smart and sophisticated, but that argument didn't hold up either because she felt comfortable with him and they were equals onstage, both newcomers at Civic, both trying to find their way.

He's married, that should have clinched it. Everyone knew you never fooled around with a married man. But so are you, and she felt guilty because she didn't feel guilty. Here she was fantasizing about cheating on Eddie and she honestly didn't feel guilty about it at all. In fact, her fantasy life had been more interesting in the last week than it had been in months.

So why don't you do it, she asked herself. Fantasizing was one thing but actually committing adultery with an older man she hardly knew was quite another. Yet she didn't feel guilty about wanting to do it. In fact, the images of their doing it kept getting clearer and clearer, more detailed. It was as if in her daydreams she was no longer just wondering what it would be like to do it or if she really wanted to do it, but was actually planning how to do it.

You're a slut! She accused herself.

Hardly, she became her own defense lawyer. *It would all easier if you were. You'd have been in bed with him already.* She wished she could just once do some of the wild things she dreamed about doing.

You've never even thought of stuff like this before. What did he say Monday night? "We got a little carried away." No! That's the problem. I didn't get carried away enough. I want to be swept right out of my whole life, carried away, literally, like in a flood. She couldn't believe what she was thinking. The cursor on the computer screen was winking lewdly at her.

He wants to talk to me about it, about us, she thought driving home, and the prospect floated like a threat in the flood of confusion all around her. It hadn't stopped raining all day, steady, grey, heavy. She had to pay attention to keeping the car straight on the slippery road. For a moment she thought it was raining inside the car too. But it was tears blurring her vision and running down her cheeks. She pulled over to the side of the road about a mile from the trailer park gate. She just didn't know what to do.

> Thursday, Sept. 19
> Short rehearsal tonight. We had to work in the lobby of the theater because the set builders had to be onstage. They're building a low wall to separate the raked stage which is the mansion from the flat space right in front of the audience which is the terrace. Actually, all we did was a French line run of Acts I and II. It was pretty stuttery. Then the director wanted to run a couple of scenes from Act One where the younger daughter, Dinah, played by the red-headed high school girl—I think her name is Heather—is always teasing her older sister Tracy. She sent the rest of us home early with the command: "Work on your lines!" Yeah, right! Four of us—me, Collins, Harvey Winkins, and Sunny—went straight to the bar. Lori said she had to go home and didn't come with us. I wish she had. But we had a great time. Both John Collins and Harvey Winkins are really funny and tell hilarious stories. I just wish Lori had come along.

"People, people, we've only got two weeks until tech and dress and you don't even have your lines down for the first act," Marge was unhappy. But then, when was she ever happy? She was unhappy because the set builders were in the theater. She was unhappy because everyone didn't know their lines perfectly for Acts One and Two. Though Tracy and Collins and Harvey Winkins certainly did.

"You people go home and work on your lines. I want them perfect tomorrow night. We're going to run Act Two and it better be good." With that she dismissed her minions with a queenly wave and the scolding shake of a schoolmistressly finger, all done with her voice. That woman could gesture with her voice the way a sailor spoke in semaphore. Warning flags, permissions, declarations of war, and weather signals wig-wagged when she spoke. She gloried in both subtle and demonstrative changes in tone and inflection. She must have been quite an actress once.

It had been raining without let-up for a day and a half. As Bill drove through the splashing pools on Fifth Street toward *The Hoosier Saloon,* the water beat steadily on his windshield and he wondered if perhaps they all ought to be working on an ark rather than rehearsing a play. Earlier, driving across the Wabash River bridge on the way to rehearsal, he had checked out the river as everyone who lived in the twin towns did whenever the rainy season set in. It was just starting to overflow its banks, to edge toward the softball fields, the golf course and the junked car graveyard. It was still two full days of rain away from the high water mark and flood stage. *'Flood stage,'* he thought, *all the world's a stage. What an odd saying?* But though the river wasn't yet a threat, the current was running fast and deep. You could see it moving under the bridge. *Everything could just be carried away,* Bill thought, *on a flood.*

It had been a long day, and rehearsal had been a disappointment. They hadn't done anything but throw disembodied lines at each other, stumbling over them much of the time. Rehearsal usually perked him up, injected something fresh into his daily routine. But tonight he had been tired when he got there and bored while it was going on. He was ready for a couple of beers and a few heedless laughs.

Maybe, tonight, it is better that Lori didn't come, he thought. The pressure was off. The threat of her wouldn't be there. The guilt of what (against all his better judgment) he was planning for her wouldn't have to be faced. He was relieved that he could just relax, sit back, and not have to act. *Acting,* he thought, *onstage, in real life, it's all acting.*

He had taught two classes that morning, one on Eliot's novel *The Mill on the Floss* to his grad students and the second on the thirties musical *42nd Street* to his undergraduate film class. Then, he had sat in his office doing paperwork, reading student papers, and looking out the windows at the rain, wishing it would stop so he could sneak off to the golf course. Late in the afternoon, before Martha could come in from work and make him self-conscious, he ran his lines with the tape recorder, emoting out loud to the empty house. He and Martha had eaten a disinterested dinner together, their mutual fatigue hanging between them at the table like a ground fog. After dinner, they had hidden in silence behind their different sections of the newspaper. Each evening after dinner he found himself checking his watch, counting the minutes until he could kiss Martha 'good night' and head for the theater. But tonight rehearsal had been a disappointment and, as he parked across from the bar, he hoped that a few beers and a few laughs would salvage his day.

John Collins' car pulled up beside him and Sunny got out of the passenger-side door. Harvey pulled up in his Cadillac and parked one down from them. They all crossed the railroad tracks together.

"Did you hear the one about the one-legged Baptist preacher and the Polish dwarf with the glass-eye and herpes?" Harvey asked as soon as they sat down.

I'll deal with Tracy some other night, Bill listened for the punch line.

> Friday, Sept.20
> It's Friday. I had a hangover this morning from drink-
> ing with Harvey and John and Sunny last night. I
> think there might be something going on between
> those two. She's older than he is. I should talk. It has
> been a long week on Act II. It is the most important
> act. If we can set the characters and relationships and
> keep the audience with us through Act Two, then Act
> III will be like dessert. The director was really push-
> ing us tonight. They were excellent directions. We all
> know our lines and the blocking, now she is yelling
> at us about the little things. I know she almost bad-
> gered Lori into quitting, and she had the little red-
> headed high school girl in tears at least once tonight,
> but I really think she's doing an excellent job. The play
> is starting to come together. She's pushing and chal-
> lenging us. She's worked a whole sort of Pygmalion
> transformation on Lori. She's not a very nice human
> being, but she's a hell of a director. After rehearsal we
> all decided to go to the bar. Even Tracy, I mean Lori,
> came along. She must have figured there was safety in
> numbers.

"C'mon, give me a triangle! Dexter, cheat downstage of Tracy. Mike, cheat downstage of Uncle Willie. C'mon, you look like the Rockettes doing a kick line."

Marge was stopping them on almost every line. It was sadistic for a Friday night. It had been a long intense week of rehearsal. Any director should have seen the fatigue in the cast, their need for a break from their characters.

After being stopped four times in a row in the opening scene of Act Two, Heather, the pale, red-headed high school girl playing Dinah, the little sister, burst into tears and ran off the stage. Marge didn't even blink. "Michelle," she intoned out of the darkness of the theater's last row, "please play Dinah until Heather composes herself." Everyone but Marge was alarmed. The child could be doing anything down in the dressing room: crying her eyes out, tearing her script to tatters, hanging herself. But Marge never showed the slightest tremor of concern. Michelle jumped up and ran greedily onstage, and Marge bulled right on with her directing. Five minutes later, red as her hair, Heather resurfaced out of the backstage depths and watched Michelle taking the same abuse.

I wonder if she's ever even considered the possibility that actors might give better performances for a director who is nice than they would for a director who is a screaming shrew of a Nazi fascist bitch! Lori wondered.

She'd make an interesting character in a novel, Bill thought. *Every novel needs some kind of villain.* Yet he couldn't get past his perception that she really was a good director.

"No, no, Dexter, you're not even coming close to his chin. You've got to concentrate and make it look real. Make eye contact with your partner. Eye contact is absolutely essential to any stage combat." Collins was on one knee with his back to the seats as the Director unleashed her tirade upon the hapless Dexter. He was supposed to be knocked into that position by Dexter's punch, but the Director was right—the punch had been landing about two zip codes wide of its target. The whole time that Marge was venting her disdain upon Dexter, Collins was making faces at Bill who was fighting to keep his face straight. Collins eyes were bugging out, his mouth inflating like a frog, his tongue lolling and darting all the time that Marge was casting aspersions on Bill's masculinity. "You're close to the audience and we can't camouflage it," Marge came down a couple of decibels to reason with Dexter, "so you've got to work fairly close in. It's got to look like a real punch."

Dexter murmured something apologetic like "I'll try to do better" or "I'm sorry, I'll get it this time" that Marge ignored. He felt he had to say something. What he really wanted to do was kick Collins for making faces while he was getting chewed out. Instead, they tried the punch again and this time it was worse than it had ever been before.

"Oh god! You just got the biggest laugh of the play," Marge jeered from the dimness of the seats. "Go on, go on, that whole scene's hopeless anyway."

After the break, the director said that she was going to shut up and they were going to run Act Two straight through. "Now listen, please concentrate. Don't hurry yourselves. Articulate your words. Don't line up, give me triangles. Remember your posture, how your characters move and stand. Think rich. Now let's try and do it straight through."

Marge did pretty well. She let them go almost seven minutes before she stopped them. But she just made a blocking adjustment and sent them right on.

Tracy and Dexter did a pretty good confrontation scene, although Dexter did stumble over a couple of lines and had to be righted by Tracy.

Then Bill sat in the audience watching Tracy and the reporter do the drunk scene which always ended in the kiss that made him so envious.

Marge stopped them a few more times, but generally allowed them to get through it. Bill was determined to end the run-through on a high note, to do the punch right, to make eye contact and swing as close to Collins' chin as possible in order to make it look real.

All it is is concentration, Bill told himself, *like keeping your head down on a golf shot.*

The scene was a short one at the very end of Act Two, the tail-end of a long and drunken night before Tracy's wedding. Tipsy, not really sure she wants to get married, Tracy has gone skinnydipping with Mike Connor the reporter and has passed out. Dexter intercepts them as Mike is carrying her to her room. After Tracy is safely tucked away, the confrontation between the two men occurs, and the whole act ends with the punch that comes on the line "the lady is my wife, Mr. Connor."

Concentrate, Bill thought as the line approached.

Eye contact, Bill glared determined into Collins' unsuspecting eyes as the line began.

Close in, Bill coached himself as he began to swing.

"The lady is my husband, Mr. Connor," he said as he stepped in and swung for John Collins' chin. **THE LADY IS MY HUSBAND!** he realized what he had said.

The punch caught Collins perfectly on the point of the chin. It made a small cracking sound like a pencil breaking. Bill was holding his eye contact right through the swing like a good golfer so he had a close-up view of the look of shock on Collins' face that stage illusion had suddenly become reality right in the center of his face. The punch, which wasn't really that hard, sprung Collins off his feet, off the stage and into the first row of seats stage left.

"That's great," Marge bellowed out of the darkness, "but you can't fall offstage like that. People are sitting in those seats."

" You punched me," Collins moaned in awe.

"I'm so sorry John. Oh god, are you OK? I didn't mean to. I'm so sorry," Bill, utterly horrified, was helping Collins up. He hadn't punched anybody for years, not since that championship summer playing softball when they had gotten in the season-ending brawl.

The reactions of the cast moved in slow motion.

What great acting, they thought at first as Collins vaulted into the seats.

Then, *he really hit him,* they all realized.

Is he OK? they wondered as Collins picked himself up holding his chin.

It's really funny, they thought, but knew they couldn't laugh.

It's really funny, they choked back their laughter as Collins rotated his jaw.

"I think we've got to work some more on *that* baby," the irrepressible Collins finally declared, and the whole cast burst into laughter.

Even the director was laughing. "That's enough for tonight," she said. "Let's all go have a drink."

16 The Heartbreak of Adultery

When two people are thinking about committing adultery, it tends to show. One of the outward signs is stuttering indecisiveness.

"I really shouldn't tonight," Lori said to the assembled group milling around in the steady rain in the theater parking lot. The curtain had finally come down on their grueling Friday night rehearsal and they wanted her to join them in playtime at the bar.

"Aw c'mon. Let's go have a couple of drinks," came a chorus of scoffs.

"I should really get home," Lori hesitated. *But I really want to,* she was thinking.

"It's Friday night. Come on. We're all going."

"Well maybe just one."

"Alright, let's hit it," John Collins loped for his car. "It's raining out here."

"Ah, the temptations of demon rum," Harvey Winkins emoted as if doing a scene from *The Devil and Daniel Webster.*

Another outward tic of the potential adulterer is a chronic guilty nervousness.

Ever since that moonlit night of escalating kissing in the parking lot, Bill had found himself, whenever he was near Lori, furtively swiveling his head to see if anyone was watching them. Sitting across the table from her in the bar, even with all the others ranged around, he found himself shooting quick glances every time the front door opened to see if her husband was walking in.

But, perhaps the most telling sign of a contemplating adulterer is a tongue-tied shyness in the presence of the potential adulteree.

Neither Lori nor Mike seemed to have any idea what to say to each other offstage in the week that had passed since their first passionate indiscretion. Their conversations took the form of hieroglyphics, trailed off into avoidance.

"Hi Lori . . ."

"Bill" (alarmed, skittish).

"Good scene. You're doing great onstage."

"Thanks. I . . ."

"We . . ."

Not now. I've got to . . ."

"No, I just wanted to . . ."

"I know. Me too. I've been . . ."

"No big deal. I just . . ."

"Gotta go. My cue line . . ."

All the telltale signs were there, hanging between them like primitive messages scrawled on the walls of caves. Both of them could read the messages, but neither was courageous enough to take the plunge at deciphering them. For more than a week they had both been thinking about adultery, scripting it over and over to play on the stages of their secret thoughts. Neither, however, was ready to raise the curtain and really play the scene.

But that Friday night, when Lori consented to go to the bar, Bill's heart leapt up with expectation. *Something's going to happen,* he knew, but he had no idea what. This was real, and it excited and terrified him. Lori's car was the last one out of the theater parking lot. He watched her headlights in his rear-view mirror as they drove toward the bar. She caught the stop light at the corner, her headlights blinking through the rain. As the group parked and crossed the railroad tracks to go in, Bill hung back.

Lori parked and got out. She saw him waiting and, for the briefest moment, that frightening fact stopped her just on the other side of the tracks. A look of panic flooded across her face. The rain drummed rhythmically down. But she got up her courage and crossed over to him.

You're going to do it, his whole body sparked electric.

She smiled sadly as she came up to him, and he felt like he was rising off the ground.

"I, I really want to talk to you alone," he stammered like a schoolboy. There was nobody else there, but he was whispering as if the night was bugged.

"I know," she said with a soft serenity. "We will."

That was all, and they went in.

But his face was tingling with the excitement of it. He had to stop at the corner of the long oak bar to collect himself. She walked serenely back to join the others at the big round table. He wasn't used to a rush of feeling like this. He wasn't used to feeling at all.

They outwaited the others. He gave her credit for doing it because, after all, he was the one so intent upon talking about it, and she was the one who had been avoiding it all week. Their approaches, however, were different. Lori nursed the same beer the whole time.

She wants to be stone sober when she tells me to leave her alone, Bill figured. He, on the other hand, drank his usual four beers in under an hour to keep up his courage.

I wish I could drink beer like that, Lori envied him. *I'd spend the whole evening in that filthy ladies room.*

As they sat there outwaiting the others, Harvey Winkins told a few jokes: "Did you hear about the businessman going on a trip who approached the airline ticket counter and spotted the beautiful and extremely well-endowed ticket agent? (Chorus of 'no's.') He was momentarily flustered as he looked down at her generous endowment, but recovered himself and said, 'yes, could I please have a picket to Titsburgh?' Well, as soon as he said it, he wanted to pack himself into his own suitcase. He apologized profusely. His face got all red with embarrassment. But the airline agent just smiled and reassured him; 'It's OK. It's OK. Believe me I understand. Why just this morning a very similar thing happened to me. My husband and I have been talking about a separation and this morning at breakfast I asked him to pass the corn flakes and it came out, 'You son of a bitch you've ruined my life!'" (Cascade of laughter.)

Naturally, Bill tried to top Harvey's joke with "one of my students wrote in an essay last week that 'Socrates died of an overdose of wedlock.'" (Polite laughter.)

"Here's an academic joke, a university joke, for you," Harvey never let up. "An advanced grad student at the university spends Thanksgiving with his family on the Indiana family farm. After dinner, the kid and his aged grandfather, a farmer all his life, are sitting on the front porch rocking when the old man asks, 'so yore teechin' while yore gittin' that P-H-nnn-D, eh?' 'Yes sir,' answers the kid. 'Well, how menny hours you teech?' 'Three classes, nine hours.' The old man scratches his crotch and reflects a moment: 'Well, that's a long day, but it's easy work."" (Mike laughed heartily as did Collins; the others, unconnected to the university, didn't get it.)

When Harvey paused to sip at his Jack and water, Thelma, who always showed up near the end of rehearsals on Friday nights, jumped right in with a story about the college professor who auditioned for the part of George in Albee's *Who's Afraid of Virginia Woolf.* It seems the audition was so good that he was cast immediately over some more experienced Civic Theater actors who had also auditioned. But it turned out that the reason he took to the character of George so well was that he actually was George. By the second week, he was showing up for rehearsal drunk. He knew his lines, but as he weaseled at his wife in the play, Martha, he always called her Mildred. The director tried to get him to stop doing it, but he wouldn't. Then they found out that his wife's name in real life was Mildred and that the man hated her so much that he was having a nervous breakdown. They replaced him in the part during the third week of rehearsals."

Marge reminisced about some of the bad casting decisions she had made over the years: "When I did *On Golden Pond,* I think the whole cast had Alzheimers, the young ones and the old. Not only couldn't they remember their lines, but they didn't know stage right from stage left."

"By the way, speaking of not knowing stage left from right, I want to thank our expert in stage combat for loosening my bridgework." John Collins lifted his beer glass as if proposing a toast.

Bill acknowledged John's toast with a wiggle of his beer bottle.

Collins made them all laugh with some silly stories of his high school cut-ups before he and Sunny left together after about an hour. They were the first to go. Nobody else seemed to notice or think twice when Sunny asked, "Hey John, can I catch a ride across the river with you," but Bill suspected something was going on. Or maybe he was just more sensitive to the idea of people sneaking around.

Then the others left in small groups or one by one.

Mike and Lori outwaited them all, and finally they were alone.

They smiled nervously at each other. Lori sipped and Mike slugged at their respective beers. The silence grew awkward.

"Lori, I can't get you, that night, out of my mind."

"I know. I can't stop thinking about it either. It scares me."

"It scares the hell out of me."

"It scares me because it made me feel so good. I liked it so much."

"Maybe you'd had too much to drink."

"No. I thought about that at first. No way. I needed you that night. You got me through all that stuff about Marge and the play, and whether I could be Tracy. You really helped me out."

"Is that why you kissed me?"

"I thought you kissed me."

"Whatever."

"No, that's not why we kissed . . ."

"And kept on kissing?"

"Ok. It just . . . just . . . it made me feel good, I mean really good, to know that somebody, a guy I hardly even knew, cared about me, wanted to kiss me. Geez Bill, it really turned me on, and that scares me."

Bill reached across the table and put his hand on top of hers, then glanced quickly around to see if anyone had seen him do it.

That panicked look came back into her face, but she fought it off . . . and didn't take her hand away. In fact, she turned her hand up into his and closed her fingers around his. The slight pressure of her touch sent an almost electric shock all through him.

"For the last week, I haven't been able to take my eyes off of you onstage. Everytime you kiss Collins my neck muscles tighten with jealousy. And you're doing so well. You really *are* Tracy now. There's none of that indecision, that nervousness that you're going to get yelled at anymore."

"That's your doing. You talked me out of that."

"I can't take my eyes off of you onstage. I want to be the one kissing you." But he saw that the intensity of his grasp on her hand and his leaning over whispering these secrets was making her skittish. He dropped her hand, picked up his beer, slouched back in his chair, and tried to make a joke out of it. "Do you think it's too late in the play for me and John Collins to change roles?"

"Way too late, thank god," she laughed, and the tension was eased. They were just two friends talking again. "I'd be a nervous wreck if I had to kiss you onstage every night."

"Why?"

"Cause it wouldn't be acting. I'd be afraid everyone would see how much I was enjoying it. I mean, they'd all know," and then her voice got real quiet as his had been before. "I'd probably be shaking so bad I'd never be able to finish the scene."

"Does that mean you want to kiss me again?"

"Yes, I do."

"If we start, this time I'm not sure we'll be able to stop. I could hardly drive home after the last time."

"I'm not sure I'll want to stop."

There was a new agressiveness in her whisper, and a flirting grin on her face.

He leaned toward her, stopped, glanced guiltily around. They both smiled, then giggled.

"We probably shouldn't do it here," she laughed, and all that weight was lifted.

"No," he agreed and relaxed back in his chair, finishing his beer in one gurgle and waving for the waitress to order another. Lori got another too. They sipped in silence for a long moment.

"Have you ever cheated on your husband before?" Bill couldn't believe that it was his voice saying it.

"No," she said, almost as if she was embarassed.

"I'll tell you, it's a pain," he said.

"You have cheated on your wife before, I take it," she asked. It had all become a joke, a hypothetical game, the stuff of witty conversations and Cary Grant movies. They were no longer talking about their private adultery, but some general adultery of the sort that sophisticates traded witticisms about in the oak bars of Philadelphia Main Line hotels.

"Yes, but I've always been very selective about it," he joked.

"Selective?" she raised an eyebrow the way that Tracy would.

"I've never cheated on my wife with anyone who didn't have an advanced degree before."

"Well ex-cuuuse me," she replied in the spirit of the game.

"I've never cheated on my wife in the same city before," he escalated the hilarity of the game. "Hell, I've never cheated on my wife with anyone as young as you before. This is a really bad idea; you know that don't you?"

"I've never cheated on my husband at all before," and the way she said it brought the whole game to a somber stop. All of a sudden she looked as if she were going to cry.

"What's wrong, Lori?" he was walking gingerly now, uncertain what direction her mood would take next. But she perked up almost right away and looked him right in the eye.

"Nothing. I'm fine. It's just that it seems like such a rotten thing to do and you make it seem like such a joke or game."

"Joke? No, no way. Do you have any idea how hard this all is?" And he was joking again, drawing her back into the sophisticated verbal game of adultery. "How much you have to do? How many lies you have to tell?"

"I haven't had to tell any yet. Eddie hasn't asked me anything. He doesn't care about any of this. I don't think he cares about me any more."

"I mean, the logistics. It's like putting on a play. You've got to rehearse lies, arrange schedules, get motel rooms, pay with cash, all kinds of stuff to think of." He was trying to keep it light, make it all a joke, but he found himself being caught up in the intrigue. He was getting more serious and the challenge was starting to turn him on. *I can do this,* he started thinking. "Of course, we could go out to the Hort Park and make love on the grass. That's sexy, except for the grass stains on your ass. Try to explain that to your husband," and that line cracked her up. It was a good thing she didn't have any beer in her mouth. "Usually it's lipstick on your collar that tells the tale, but not if you're doing it in the Hort Park."

He had her laughing freely about it. Adultery was no longer some sinister thing lurking in the back of each of their minds.

"You know what really ticks me off?" he went on, grinning archly across at her. "Every time you kiss Collins at the end of that scene, you look like you're enjoying it."

"Hey, what can I say, I'm a great actress. You're the one who taught me good kissing on this play," she was grinning back at him. This light sparring was fun. They were talking about a subject that had put them both on edge for a week, and they were almost at ease with it. "Hey, the train's never shown up when I'm kissing John," she turned slightly serious. "The earth's not moving, believe me."

"I think it is for Sunny."

"What?"

"Nothing. Never mind. Just a stupid joke."

"You think they're doing the same thing we are."

"Yeah. Maybe. I don't know."

Suddenly Lori plummetted into one of her instant mood changes. "The only difference is," and there was a trace of bitterness in her voice, "they're not married."

"I don't know, are they?" Mike wanted to distract her from this despair which had intruded upon their joking. "I know Collins isn't."

"I don't know if Sunny is or not," Lori was just mouthing words as if they didn't mean anything to her and she didn't care anyway. It was too obvious for Mike to ignore or try to slough off with another joke.

"What is it? You look like you're going to cry."

"I'm OK. It's nothing."

"It doesn't look like it's nothing."

"It's just that I don't know how I feel. I feel like a ping-pong ball. One minute I'm thinking about you and what we did and how good it made me feel, how I like being with you." She stopped and leaned closer over the table toward him in the intensity of her feelings. "But sometimes Bill I just feel so rotten, like Judas, like my whole marriage, my whole life, is this big lie."

"But we haven't done anything," he realized that she was really bothered by this, that perhaps he wasn't taking what they were on the brink of as seriously as he should.

"Ha! Are you kidding?" and her mood jumped into bitter laughing sarcasm. "If Eddie had seen us kissing in that parking lot last week he'd of had a cat fit. First he'd call me a whore, then a lousy wife, then he'd ask me why I had to always do everything I could to make his life miserable like I was a nymphomaniac for the CIA or something."

Bill actually wanted to laugh at the melodramatic spin she was putting on the whole situation. *It was only two new friends kissing each other,* he thought, but then he realized that in his case it was really much more than that. An hour hadn't gone by in the last ten days when he hadn't felt the exhilaration of those kisses. *Had she been feeling the same need to feel that exhilaration again?*

When he didn't answer her, just sat there looking at her stupidly, that look of panic once again passed like a shadow over her face. She just shrugged her hands and shoulders, and gave him a tight-lipped little grin of despair.

He hid behind a long pull from his beer bottle.

"What would your wife say?" Lori finally broke the awkward silence.

"Martha thinks that just because we're married, 51% of the human race is ineligible for my friendship."

He hadn't meant to be funny, but it made her laugh. It was just a sarcastic offhand comment, but it had given her a whole new outlook on this feeling of betrayal that had so paralyzed her.

"You know, you're right," she said it almost defiantly. "We are friends, aren't we . . . and there's nothing wrong with that."

"No. There isn't."

Her momentary exhilaration subsided.

He sipped at his beer, wondering where this was going.

"It's good . . ." she started hesitantly, "to have a friend who isn't just somebody you work with or your husband. Somebody who's so different. I mean, we've only known each other three weeks and you've already been a good friend. I'd better go home, it's been a long night."

"Yeah, it has," he agreed, but neither made any move to get up. They knew they hadn't resolved a thing.

"Oh Bill," she seemed panic-stricken again, "I just wish I was someone else," she stared, crestfallen, and made that little shrugging gesture with her hands, "but I'm not."

He realized that she was telling him that their silly little charade was over. The only refuge he could find was in a wry and cynical chagrin: "Adultery is like that, I guess. If you're yourself, you'd probably never do it. But if you can just believe that you're someone else, in a different, private, special world, then it's a possibility. You're right, we better go."

It had stopped raining. When they came out of the bar and crossed the railroad tracks to their cars, the pavement beneath their feet glistened black and wet in the long diffusing yellow light of the street lamps. Their cars were parked three empty spaces apart. They crossed the street in silence, not touching. They split when they reached the parked cars, but stopped and turned back toward each other after only a step or two.

"Thanks for . . ."

"I really had a . . ."

They burst out with meaningless words both at the same time. The collision of their voices made them laugh and shrug.

"We better go home, I guess," he stated the obvious.

"Yeah, we better," she agreed. "I'll see you on Monday," and she gave him a silly stupid little wave.

"Yeah, see you then," he waved, just as stupidly, back across that five foot chasm of slick, shimmering street.

Like robots they turned and walked to their cars.

Mike pressed the door handle and pulled it open, then stopped, looked over for one last glimpse of her. She was standing beside the passenger door of her car, feet together, hands hugging herself, looking right at him.

When their eyes met, she launched herself into his arms and their mouths met in the hungry kiss that the whole evening had been but a prelude to.

And then they kissed again . . . again, her arms around his neck, in the middle of the black glisten of that shining street with the railroad tracks running by. Who knows, perhaps in the suspension of their kiss her right ankle even kicked up behind.

17 Foreplay

The middle weeks of rehearsal for any play are drudgery. The auditions and the first weeks are all discovery and innocent enthusiasm. Tech week is all desperation, panic, self-doubt, and despair. But the middle weeks are when all the heavy work really gets done. They move slowly, are based on repetition, and are rarely broken by hilarious laughter or triumphant shouts. John Collins was a veteran of many Civic Theater plays as both an actor and a set designer, and he knew all about the doldrums of the middle weeks of the rehearsal schedule. Therefore, as the designated cast clown, he felt it his duty to breathe some life into those dog days of drama. When he entered the theater, he was looking for trouble.

Collins moved stealthily and silently through the semi-darkened theatre onto the almost-built set. There were slight rustlings in the rafters. Three catwalks hung from the ceiling, crisscrossed above the matrix of light bars and the tangle of rubber cables all converging on the control booth against the back wall. One glaring flaw in the theater's design had always been the total lack of access from the control booth to the ceiling catwalks. In order to hang lights or anything else, like the crystal chandelier now suspended over Tracy's dining room, one had to wheel the biggest A-frame ladder available to a particular point on the left front of the stage, ascend into the snake pit of light cables, and swing up onto the catwalks from below. Once on the catwalks, one had a free run of the whole circuitry of the light bars and cable outlets above the stage.

When Collins tiptoed into the theater looking for trouble, Ernie and Thurman, were up on the catwalks puzzling over Collins' light plan. Their wheeled A-frame ladder stood invitingly unattended downstage left. Of course, unhesitating, incorrigible, Collins decided on the spot to steal it.

It was still a half hour until rehearsal began at 7:30 and Ernie and Thurman, as was their habit, planned to putter away until the director kicked them out.

As Collins stole to the base of the ladder, Ernie and Thurman, twenty feet above, using a flashlight in the darkness, were puzzling out Collins' light plot blueprint. They never heard nor saw him approach below. They never noticed as the top of their ladder rolled slowly away backstage. As they worked, they never realized that they were marooned and that Collins had gotten them again.

As for Collins, he blithely dumped backstage their only means of egress from their crow's nest, and headed down the steps to use the dressing room toilet. Barb Dwyer waylaid him as he came out of the rest room zipping up his fly.

"Oh honey, I'm so glad I caught you," she giggled as she appropriated his elbow and steered him through the unhung doorway of the men's dressing room. "Just slip out of your pants will you, I've got three different suits I want you to try on."

Collins hesitated, but Barb Dwyer didn't."Oh honey, don't be shy," she teased. "It is the divine right of every costume person, I've got it in my contract, to watch young men take off their pants. Believe me, honey, it's one of the few perks of this job. I mean, after a show goes on, how many theatergoers come up to me and say 'Gee honey, we sure did enjoy your costumes tonight?' Not many, I'll tell you." To his horror, she was already down on her knees in front of him unzipping his pants. "Am I makin' you nervous, sweetie?" she continued to tease as she pulled his pants down around his ankles. "Or am I makin' you something else?" at which point she stared speculatively right into the crotch of his boxer shorts.

"Uh, no, not at all," Collins stammered. He was trapped and intimidated. It had all happened so fast that he didn't have any idea of how he was going to extricate himself. But he was especially fearful that a particular ungovernable part of his body would send her a signal he most assuredly did not want to send.

"Here, try this one on first," Barb Dwyer was up off of her knees and getting a brown suit off the long closet pole set into the bottom of the overhead shelf against the wall.

Collins gratefully pulled himself into the pants. At least she's not going to rape me outright, he inwardly breathed a sigh of relief. But he may have spoken too soon. Barb Dwyer, before he had pulled on this suitcoat, was already back down on her knees shoving her tape measure as high up his inseam as she could.

"Just what I thought," she leered up at him.

"What's that?" he still didn't have complete control of his voice.

"About an inch longer than I thought it would be," she winked. "Take these off and we'll try another pair on."

This time, she let him take off the pants by himself, watching his every move hungrily from her post on her knees right in front of him.

"Here, this one," she jumped up and got him another suit, dark blue, off the rack. He was still extricating himself from the brown pants as she stood waiting. "I sure do like watching men take their pants off," she laughed.

Maybe it's all just kidding around to her, Collins hoped, just a game she plays with everybody. He pulled the pants on as she knelt back down in front of him and picked her tape measure up off the floor.

"Have you ever noticed that theater is all foreplay?" It sounded like a line Barb Dwyer had used on actors before.

"What?" Collins zipped himself up.

"Get it, 'foreplay,' before the play."

"Oh yeah," Collins nodded, stupidly, vainly hoping it was really just a coquettish little verbal game she was playing with him from her point of vantage on her knees.

"I like foreplay," Barb Dwyer knelt holding her tape measure speculatively.

It was as if, suddenly, she had grown tired of the game. She was looking at him as lewdly as anything he could ever imagine.

"No, we can't," he stammered. "I don't do foreplay. I mean, I mean, I've got to go and you've got to sew and where are my own pants?"

"Heeeere's Johnny," Sunny announced gaily as she barged into the dressing room. She had evidently heard his voice as she came down the steps and, probably thinking he was running lines by himself, decided to charge right in and surprise him. She was the one who got the surprise. What she saw was Barb Dwyer on her knees on the floor with her face about six inches from Collins' fly.

"Holy shit!" she came to a sudden halt in the doorless doorway.

Collins stood straight up with a look of utter horror flooding into his face.

Barb Dwyer turned to look up at her, raised her eyebrow and looked down her nose as if to say "what the hell is she doing here spoiling my fun."

It didn't take Sunny long to react, but her reaction caught Barb Dwyer utterly unaware.

"Stop that, you slut!" Sunny hissed, and, giving it a full roundhouse treatment, slapped Barb full in the face with her open hand. "He's mine." She made it sound as if she had caught the costume lady, mistress, slut, trying to steal her car.

It was all a bit melodramatic, but it certainly had its effect on Barb Dwyer. The blow spun her around off of her knees to a sitting position in the middle of the floor, her long blue gingham skirt spread out in front of her with her black boots peeking out from beneath.

Sunny stood over her, still feeling the tingle of the blow in her hand, shocked at the violence she had just done.

"Whoa!" Collins half-gasped as his wide-eyes swiveled from Sunny glaring angrily at him to the red flush coming up on Barb Dwyer's cheek on the floor and back to Sunny's evil intake of breath as she took a step toward him. His first inclination was to duck, but Sunny didn't take a swing at him.

"What in the hell is this?" Sunny spit the words out as if they tasted bad.

"It's not my fault," Collins whined. "She made me take off my pants. She's the one who started all the foreplay."

"Foreplay!" Sunny fired that word back at him like a broadside from a battleship.

Collins didn't know what to say. It is hard for a six-foot, two-inch able-bodied man to marshal a convincing argument that he has just been molested by a woman.

Luckily, they were both distracted by the whimpering sounds coming from Barb Dwyer on the floor. The costume mistress was crying tears the size of chandelier facets and was blubbering into her two hands cupped over her face as if she were trying to catch and drink her own tears. She wasn't doing a very good job. The tears were running down over her knuckles. Collins noticed she had long seamstresses fingers, but he didn't dwell on them because he was frantically swivelling his head in search of some avenue of escape from a situation gotten so far out of hand that he wanted to call for a cease fire.

"Oh my god," Sunny moved toward the wounded Barb Dwyer, and Collins instinctively stepped between the two women to prevent further escalation of the violence. "Oh, I didn't mean to hurt you." Sunny's voice was more motherly than murderous. "Get out of my way, you jerk," it turned back to murderous when she leveled it at him.

"DAMN IT, COLLINS! BRING THAT LADDER BACK!" Ernie and Thurman in a capella synch bellowed open his window of opportunity. He dove through it in someone else's pants like a philanderer surprised in a strange house with someone else's wife.

"Gotta go," he shrugged toward Sunny even as he fled for the steps to the stage.

"Are you OK?" Sunny went down on her knees beside Barb Dwyer who was still sobbing on the floor. "I just saw red. I didn't mean to hurt you, honest. Things have been so screwed up lately and I'm not coping very well and John's been the only good thing I've had going and I'm really sorry. I can't believe I slapped you," and, as fitting terminal punctuation to this torrent of words, Sunny burst into tears herself.

"I didn't know," Barb Dwyer wailed. "I didn't know, honest, you and him. Nobody did. I don't go after other women's men." she managed to get the words out between sobs.

The two of them sat there in the middle of the dressing room floor bawling their eyes out and blubbering out the petty narratives of their woes. Neither one was really listening to the other. They were talking pretty much at the same time. Just doing it to tell someone else, in hope they would understand, maybe forgive, Sunny her sudden violence, Barb her rapacious loneliness. What they were doing in their disconnected blubberings was consoling each other.

"Nobody knew. We couldn't tell anyone until my divorce is final. My ex-husband's a real prick when he gets mad and if he found out about John and me. It'd be trouble."

"You think I do this because I like sewing and altering other people's clothes? You think I like spending my nights off making clothes for other people to look good in? Get a grip. I do this for the parties and the sex, and I've been doing it for ten years. Every nine weeks there's a new set of men in here."

"I'm not really a violent person. I don't believe I hit you. The divorce has really got me on edge, and then sneaking around with John. It's all so . . . so . . . so . . ."

"Horny."

And they were both giggling now, like two schoolgirls comparing their boyfriends.

"I don't mind talking about it," Barb Dwyer was her old all-confiding self once again. "All the measuring is just foreplay. I'm just trying to have some fun. Usually, on every play, there's one guy who wants to have fun. But it's hard. The actresses, like you, always get first pick on the men. I guess that's why I push it a little. Everybody's entitled to some fun."

And they blow dried each other's tears with their laughter.

"I won't go near your boyfriend again, I promise. I meant no harm."

"I'm really sorry. I don't know what came over me. No man's worth hurting somebody like that."

"Amen to that, honey."

And they both got up, looked in the mirrors, looked at each other like two raccoons, the mascara forming muddy circles around their eyes, hiccuped another good giggle, and went to work on their make-up.

Upstairs the two high school girls wandered in for rehearsal as Collins wheeled the big ladder across the stage. First Thurman then Ernie descended from the catwalks.

Halfway down the ladder, Thurman started cussing Collins. On the first bellowed "YOU SON OF A BITCH!" the eyes of the two high school girls went wide and they stopped chewing their gum.

From backstage out of the stairwell up from the dressing rooms Sunny's voice—"YOU TELL 'IM THURMAN"—seconded that sentiment and popped the high school girls' eyes even wider.

"Now Thurman," Ernie was placating his partner even before he got off the ladder.

For just a single mad moment, Collins was sorely tempted to get the ladder rolling across the stage while they were still on it, take them for a Mr. Toad's Ride. But Thurman was much too mad for that idea to ever reach the stage of real silliness.

"We're gonna git you for all the deals you've pulled, Collins. You watch." The look in Thurman's eye said that this was no idle threat.

"Now Thurman," Ernie, ignoring Collins, continued to placate his sidekick.

It was all John Collins could do to keep from laughing. *For such a fun-loving guy,* he thought, *I sure am making a lot of enemies.*

Sunny emerged from the stairwell with a mock scowl on her face.

The school girls were watching it all like it was an afternoon soap opera.

Both of Collins' hands went up in the air in a gesture of surrender as if Sunny had him covered with a gun. "Honest, I didn't do a thing down there," he protested. "She jumped me."

"You dork!" Sunny laughed at him. "You sure weren't fighting very hard for your honor."

"You're the one who punched her. Is she OK?"

"She's not so bad," Sunny smiled, letting him know that she wasn't really mad about it. Taking her cue, Collins good humor pedaled back in.

"Not so bad," he scoffed. "Great, she's not always tearing your pants off!"

It took almost a full minute after that declaration for the high school girls to go back to chewing.

18 Gulag

Friday, Sept. 27

The end of the week and tonight we are supposed to know all our lines for Act III. I know all except the last two pages. I hope I can fake it so I don't screw up the others. I shouldn't have worried. They didn't know all of their lines either. The director was not happy. She demanded that at our next rehearsal all lines vill be known perfectly. There vill be no fooling around. There vill be no sitting in the audience watching the others work. Each actor before he or she goes onstage vill take five minutes to get into character. In other words, it is time to get serious, people! It sounds to me as if this nice little Civic Theater experience is about to turn into a gulag. None of the irrepressible cut-ups took her speech too seriously.

The fourth week of rehearsal had been a long and touchy one for the whole cast. Even John Collins' jokes hadn't made it any less of a slog. By the end of the week, everyone was thankful there were only two weeks left until opening. There were all sorts of reasons why that fourth week had been so bad. It all started on Tuesday with the blocking of Act III. That night became the longest and most frustrating rehearsal of the show. Then, on Thursday, Marge lost it with one of the high school girls and turned the whole cast into rebels.

As if that wasn't bad enough, she followed up on Friday with her "Gulag" speech, as it came to be known in *The Hoosier Saloon* gripe sessions. Nobody likes to work under a dictatorship, especially actors, who are already flakes balanced on the edge of anarchy.

Tuesday night's rehearsal had begun innocently enough with a read-through of Act III. Then, the Director started blocking. Everyone in the cast of 15 is onstage in Act III and blocking their comings and goings through the scene was like trying to move an army through a maze. The director was changing positions of rest and crosses so fast that every member of the cast felt like a helpless marionette dancing at a puppeteer's whim. Erasers flew as blocking was written, scratched out, rewritten, rubbed out, and rewritten again. After three hours and fifteen minutes, Marge finally completed blocking the play-ending bridal tableau. When she finally said, "Ok, that's it," Harvey Winkins rose from his seat in the second row, raised both arms like an Old Testament prophet, and dramatically intoned: "THUS ENDETH WAR AND PEACE!" Even Marge had to laugh at that one.

What happened Thursday night wasn't nearly so funny. The lead high school girl, playing Dinah, Tracy's little sister, was late for rehearsal. She had been stopped by a train for almost twenty minutes coming across town. By the time she got there, her understudy was already onstage doing her part and Marge was seething. She made the young girl sit in the audience the whole rehearsal watching the other girl play the role. Then, at the end, Marge dropped her bomb. After the cast was dismissed, she asked the two high school girls to stay behind for a moment.

Bill and Harvey, Lori and Sunny and John were loitering in the parking lot trying to decide whether or not to go have a drink, when the lead high school girl, whose name was Heather, came running out of the stage door and burst into tears right in front of them.

Harvey Winkins went all fatherly and consoling: "Heather honey, what is it? Don't cry now. It can't be that bad. Here, wipe your eyes." Courtly, he proffered one of his white linen handkerchiefs. Either Harvey was a real classy guy or he was merely warming to his dirty old man persona.

Since Lori's problem with being ridden too hard early on, things had been going pretty smoothly with the play, despite the small insensitivities of the director. But they all should have seen it coming. Marge was just wound too tight for conflicts not to arise.

Once Heather was able to talk through her tears, she told how the director had gone ballistic at her for being late, and how, as a punishment, she was taking Heather's last weekend of performances and giving them to the understudy.

"It's just not fair," the young girl sobbed. "I was stopped by a train. I would have been here on time."

Gathered around, they tried to console her. They stood in the parking lot for twenty minutes talking before Harvey decided she was capable of driving home. It was a bad scene when they got to the bar. They decided to talk to the director, and Bill was designated to present their case for the unfairness of it all. He didn't really want the job, but it was a consensus that Marge would listen to him better than to any of the others because he was in her best graces. They gave him their diplomatic portfolio.

Bill got to the theater early before rehearsal Friday night and lay in wait by his car in the parking lot for Marge to arrive. She pulled in right on schedule at 7:15.

"Marge, could we talk a second before we go in," he caught her getting out of her car and finishing off a Big Mac.

"Ah, Dexter, what is it?" As he moved close to her, he could smell the onions on her breath and track the last bulges of her wolfed sandwich down her throat.

"It's about Heather. She was really upset last night. I wondered if we could talk about it."

"There's really nothing to talk about," Marge's defenses went up immediately.

"A number of us think there is," he said with a smile, trying to be the diplomat they thought he was. "She just had a problem with one of those damn trains."

"That's what she said." It was clear the director wasn't really interested in this conversation.

"Don't you think it's a little harsh to take away her whole last weekend of performances?"

"Look, she's not showing the kind of commitment that is needed from an actor in the theater. Her understudy will do just fine in the role that weekend."

And that was it. Marge bustled off into the theater leaving Bill the diplomat standing in the parking lot like a poor supplicant outside the gate of a great lord in some feudal melodrama.

Before rehearsal began, Marge had the final say. Her little speech left no one in doubt about who was running the fiefdom.

"I've been told that some of you are upset about my decision to allow Wanda to step in for a few performances as Dinah," Marge began. "I'm sure that Heather is unhappy, but Wanda has been here for every rehearsal and has worked as hard as everyone else." Wanda, sitting with Heather on the side, looked embarrassed at having this attention drawn to her. "She is a good understudy and deserves the opportunity to perform." Marge was making herself sound like the picture of sensitivity. But she shattered that illusion forthwith. "And one other thing. I'll thank you people to let me do the directing. There has been altogether too much backstage directing on this show already. Now let's try to concentrate on our characters and stumble through Act III."

"Now what the hell does that mean?" Harvey Winkins whispered to Bill as they went backstage to their places. He didn't say it with his usual good natured irony either.

Marge was cool and aloof, and rehearsal was tense all evening. Lori was shaken, having trouble saying the lines that everyone knew she knew.

Harvey was storming around the stage barking his lines as if he was just waiting for the director to say something so that he could turn snarling and pounce.

Bill was trying hard, but couldn't concentrate. He couldn't get the sense of his diplomatic failure off his mind. When he made one exit offstage, he blundered right into Sunny curled protectively in John Collins' arms.

The two highschool girls were cowed and walking on eggs, both terrified at being yelled at by the director.

It was as if they had all fallen from grace and Marge sailed along above all the chaos of her own making as if nothing had happened and the whole issue was closed.

And then, at the end of rehearsal, she gave her "gulag" speech.

Everything had changed. Suddenly this was a job and they were employees, no longer willing amateurs having fun.

All that week the bar had beckoned them, but no more so than on Friday night. Almost every night after rehearsal they had gone drinking. Tuesday night out of exhaustion; Thursday night out of anger at the Director; Tonight, Friday, out of dismay at what a job their play had become. Each night they ended up in the bar because they had something they needed to talk about outside the confines of the theater. They gathered around their table hunched over their beers like rebels in the back of a cantina.

Lori had gone out drinking with them each night, had become a regular, and she always sat next to Bill who wondered if anyone noticed. He could have put his hand on her knee underneath the table, but he didn't. He still was uncertain. He didn't know what she would do. Tuesday night, after their marathon blocking session, when Bill had gotten up from the table to leave, pleading he had to teach an early class on Wednesday, Lori had also risen and gone out with him. Crossing the street, she took his hand and when they got to the cars she kissed him. It wasn't just a friendly actor-to-actor peck on the cheek, but a long and deep question followed by a studied raised eyebrow and a challenging smile. As she kissed him, he stood like a guilty man feeling the eyes of the others burning into them through the windows of the bar. The surprise of it paralyzed him. He almost didn't get his arms around her before the kiss ended. The others probably weren't even looking, but her tossing of caution to the winds threw him. *Where are we going with this?* Lori's aggressive kiss asked. *I've gotten used to this, so what do we do now?* Lori's kiss interrogated him. For some reason, she had decided that she was comfortable with their romantic flirtation. That unsolicited kiss, not instigated by any foreplay discussion together alone in the bar as all the others had been, put the ball solidly in Bill's court. What he didn't know is that Tuesday had been Lori's day off from work at the law office and her husband Eddie had slept through it, waking up only a half hour before he had to go to work.

Lori went to the bar with them on Thursday too, and Bill wondered if she would hold his hand right at the table. But everything was different that night. They were all shaken over Marge's treatment of Heather, the high school girl. After three angry beers and some heated discussion, they all left together like a caucus so there was no kissing at the car doors. Bill was surprised at the relief he felt at not having to field another of her pressing kisses. He liked Lori. She was beautiful. He was actively fantasizing an affair with her. But she was fifteen years younger. So far it had been an innocent flirtation, two actors exchanging meaningless stage kisses, but it was starting to go further. Lori didn't think twice about going to the bar with them after rehearsal anymore. Lori hadn't hesitated a second in kissing him right out there in the open on Tuesday night. Their mutual adultery was actually entering the realm of possibility. They were no longer just playing exciting romantic scenes on a somewhat expanded stage. Lori seemed ready.

On Friday night, Marge came to the bar as she always did, but the atmosphere was charged and Harvey Winkins, after glowering at her for long minutes while downing his Jack and water, finally, bluntly, just brought the whole issue right out in the open.

"I don't think you should take away that kid's performances Marge," he growled.

Marge must have been a great actor once. She knew we were all bothered by that issue, but she brushed it off like a cow's tail at a cat-bird.

"Wanda has worked hard and deserves a chance too," Marge smiled primly, utterly unscuffed by Harvey's surliness, claiming fairness for her side. "That's the way it's going to be. Now they'll both work harder on that part." She smiled serenely all around and took a dainty sip from her beer mug.

And that was it. Case closed. Marge had one drink and left. When poor Barb Dwyer got there later, the table was like a sullen encounter group of the depressed, nobody saying much. The whole episode had left a bad taste in all of their mouths. Doing this play just wasn't as much fun anymore, and the "gulag" was starting on Monday.

Lori left early that night and Mike stayed long after the others had left, drinking senselessly and writing out his journal entries on bar napkins. It was raining again when he left the bar at closing time. His car stood all alone in the empty street. Only one week before he and Lori had played their glistening romantic scene right here.

Driving over the Wabash River bridge, his wipers dashing back and forth between the clear window of reality and the blurring curtain of illusion, it was almost if he could sense the river rising in the rain. Only two weeks until the play opened, and so much was still up in the air.

19 Who's Afraid of an Aging Wolf

Their Saturday morning sex was proceeding as usual. It had started with drowsy rubbing. She stirred slowly, still half asleep, feeling the mild insistence of him stretching himself along her back. She rolled over and they wrapped each other in their arms, not kissing. Their hips ground into each other, and she felt the familiar scratch of the course hair of his chest scoring her skin. He kissed mechanically at her neck and cheek, avoiding her mouth. She stretched along his body. She felt his tongue moving down, as it always did at this point, into the hollow of her throat.

He glanced up at her face. Her eyes were half-open but blank, un-involved. He wished she would smile at him or bare her teeth like an animal or run her tongue over her lips hungrily as vamps did in movies, but she was still half asleep, or maybe just bored. The thought made him feel cruel, and that was the first thing that had truly excited him since they'd begun.

Her eyes were closed. Her mouth was pursed in a dreamy little grin. She seemed to be off somewhere else thinking about something sort of funny.

Maybe she's laughing at me, he thought, and that detonated his cruel streak once again.

But immediately she pulled back. He knew what he had done, maybe had even done it on purpose. It was the harsh scratch of the stubble of his beard on her vulnerable body that had shocked her out of her reverie. He pulled back.

"Go slow, sweetie. Slow. Your whiskers," she cajoled.

Her hands had come back around his head, caressing softly. . But he knew those hands were also there to control him, to yank him back by the hair if he hurt her again. He hadn't meant to scratch her skin. It was early in the morning, and he'd just awakened. He'd forgotten that he hadn't shaved yet. There was no way he could stop now. His body was well past the point of no-return.

He had to do it all her way . . . and he did.

This is all so boring, he thought. He wasn't nearly as excited now as he had been earlier. He was disappointed, then angry that she hadn't done anything for him to bring him to that verge, that glorious edge upon which she was so precariously balanced begging for him to push her over, that edge where she stopped being herself and became some other being—woman, animal, pure pulsar, whatever—and only wanted to move and feel and fly and explode. He resented the fact that he still knew what he was doing and she obviously didn't even care. He resented the fact that he was clearly responsible for her orgasm and she felt no responsibility for him at all. He resented her urgency, her disinterest in making it last, doing it differently. He felt like it ought to mean something, though he knew it never did. All of his resentments focused on her, and triggered his cruel intent.

Ok, he thought, *there, you've got what you want exactly when you wanted it, but there's not going to be anything romantic about the rest of this.*

Their routine rarely varied. When they reached a certain point, they always found a groove that controlled them as inexorably as tracks control the path of a train. Her litany began. He knew its words and rhythms as well as he knew the beating of his own heart. She recited her litany because she knew it excited him, helped pull him along into the vortex of her own arousal. Her litany was made up of well-rehearsed strings of coarse words, words that he mindlessly obeyed like a ball on a band pounding on a wooden paddle. He hated her for forcing such violence upon him. The violence of their sex had become such a regular thing that it too was beginning to bore him. He realized how fake it was. He wasn't a violent man, a rapist. He loved his wife, didn't want to rape her. He hated what he was doing. They weren't making love, yet he and she, were utterly powerless to stop it, change it, escape it. It was all anger and frustration. They did it the same way, always in the same place, usually at about the same time, once a week. Their motives had little to do with love, respect, or even passion or desire. When they were finished, she smiled up at him in a glazed sort of way, floating in her masquerade, murmuring something he couldn't hear, didn't care about. She seemed happy despite what he had just done to her.

It wasn't bad sex. They had both thrown themselves into it. If only it wasn't so predictable, so rehearsed. They were like actors in a long run, so comfortable in their blocking that on the same word every time they returned automatically to the same spot to utter the same next line. Their lovemaking, no matter how hot and sweaty, how coarse in its language, eloquent in its movements, violent in its intent, and seemingly satisfying, had become so somnolently familiar, something they acted out, simply did most Saturdays, like the summer gardening or the winter paying of bills. Maybe that's why Bill was so restless and his wife of nineteen years, Martha, so sluggish. Maybe that's why he sighed so deeply as he lay beside her trying to catch his breath.

"What is it, hon?" she read his sigh. She knew all his sounds. A sigh was unlike him. *He must be really depressed,* she thought.

"What?"

"You just sounded so sad," she whispered close in his ear, braiding her hand in the thick hair of his chest. "And after having so much fun with me too," she tried to tease him out of whatever had suddenly quieted him.

"Right," but he said it in an ugly sarcastic way that intimated that it hadn't been good for him at all. His tone put her off. And then he just laid there beside her, silent and sullen.

"Bill, sweetie, what's wrong?" She wanted to cheer him up. The day had only begun. The sun was streaming through the bedroom window and it promised to be a glorious fall Saturday. "You made me feel so good. What a great way to start the day."

But he wasn't interested, as if the sex hadn't been good for him. He lay there almost resentful.

"Dammit, Bill, what is wrong?" she repeated more insistently, demanding an answer, forcing him to deal with her.

"Nothing. Everything. Hon, the sex was great," but he sure didn't sound like he meant it. "I just have a headache, a little hangover I guess."

"I'm not surprised." She hadn't really meant anything by it. Sure, it had been said sarcastically, but she hadn't even thought about what she was saying. She was just sort of agreeing with his admission, with only the smallest hint of a hidden agenda, just the slightest trace of censure in her voice. She hadn't meant a thing by it really, but it turned him ugly in a mere instant.

"And what does that mean?" The words exploded out of the pent-up frustration of his boredom: with her, with their sex, with the absence of passion in their life, in his life (really none of these absences seemed to be bothering her). Maybe that was what made him even more angry.

She recoiled as if she'd been slapped. She had been joking. She really didn't mean anything by it, and he had exploded in anger. She didn't deserve this. She had just given him great sex, and now he was striking out at her. "Nothing. I didn't mean anything. What's wrong with you?"

"You're not surprised that I have a hangover, right? Are you surprised that sex with you bores the hell out of me? Huh, is that a surprise? Is it?"

"Hon, calm down. I'm sorry I said it. I didn't mean anything." Then she realized what he had just said about her, processed it, started to see red herself. *What a rotten thing to say,* she thought. *He sure seemed to be enjoying himself.* But she decided not to say anything.

"That's just it," his voice was bitter, "nothing means anything around here anymore. We don't do anything. We don't even talk. We just go on from day to day."

She didn't want to get into this fight. She had held her tongue when he had the gall to say that sex with her was boring. But he wasn't giving her any choice. Yet still she held back. It looked like such a nice day, and she didn't want to start it with a big fight over one of his stupid over-thought insecurities. She didn't say a word. She just lay next to him in their rumpled bed as the silence grew like an intentional snub between them.

"Good. Give me your silent treatment, you bitch!" he spat as he ripped himself out of the bed and bent down looking for his pajama bottoms.

She realized that he was looking for this fight. She had to answer, and somehow she knew that whatever she said would just make him madder.

"Bill, what is the matter with you? I didn't do anything. What do you want from me? I am not boring."

"Our whole life is boring."

That really angered her."How the hell would you know? You're never home. That's why we never talk. You're never home."

"Every night that I'm home you fall asleep on the couch at eight o'clock. It's a lot of fun sitting there watching TV and listening to you snore."

That really stopped her in her tracks. She hated to admit he was right. She didn't fall asleep every night.

"I don't snore."

"Right. And you don't fall asleep every night either, do you?"

"I work hard all day. I've got a real job."

"Now what does that mean?" He had found his pajama bottoms and was fumbling with the tie. "I don't work, right? Teaching isn't a job? Writing isn't a 'real' job?"

"I didn't mean it that way."

"It sure sounded like that's how you meant it."

"I just meant that I'm tired when I get home from work and, yes, watching TV does put me to sleep most nights."

"Every night."

She was trying to conciliate and he wasn't giving her any room for negotiation. He wanted to fight. He didn't want to talk. He wanted to ruin their whole weekend before it even began. It wasn't fair. *If he wants a fight,* she decided.

"How the hell would you know?" She was up, out of the bed, standing right up to him, stark naked. She made no attempt to cover herself. He stared unbelieving, realizing how angry she was, regretting suddenly that he had pushed her this far. "You're gone every night doing that silly play. You never come home afterwards. You're out drinking yourself senseless. That's why we never have a conversation, because you're never here."

Her tirade had drawn her up on her toes. All of a sudden, just as she finished, she realized she was naked and crossed her arms defensively over her breasts.

Bill remembered how when the play had just started she had encouraged him, thought it was a good idea. Now it was 'silly.' That angered him even more, but still he was momentarily cowed by the vehemence of her counterattack. *I've pushed this too far,* he thought. Not really knowing how to deal with her, he chose to become the offended party.

"What's wrong with the play. It's not 'silly.' A month ago you thought it was a good idea."

"I didn't know you'd be going out drinking 'til three in the morning every night."

"You thought it was a good idea because it would get me out of the house while you slept away your evenings."

"That's ridiculous."

"So why is it such a big deal if I stay out and have a few beers with the cast. You're still asleep."

"Why do you resent my resting so much. If you want to do something in the evening, we do it. If you wanted to have a conversation with me, I'd stay awake to talk. You don't even try."

"Can't you hear me? You're always asleep! You know what it's like being onstage, doing a play. You get offstage at ten or eleven at night and you're totally wired. It's exciting, and it just doesn't go away when you walk offstage. The first few nights I came home. You'd gone to bed. There was no way I was going to sleep. I'd just sit up drinking beer alone."

"Bill, I hate this. Let's not fight."

"No. No. Hear me out. What's wrong with me going out drinking with the cast. It's dead certain you're not gonna wait up for me. You probably can't wait 'til I leave the house so you can sack out on the couch."

"Is that why you're so excited about the play? Because it gets you out of the house away from me. Because I bore you so much."

"No. I didn't mean to say that."

"You said I bore you, even when we make love."

"It just came out. I didn't mean you. I meant our whole life."

"Great!"

"I'm excited about the play because it's new. It's a challenge. I wanna see if I can do it, do it well."

"It's juvenile. Just like your softball. You're too old Bill. You should have stopped playing softball ten years ago." She couldn't have said anything worse, and as soon as she said it she knew it. Her equivalent of a duck was to run into their walk-in closet on the pretense of putting on her robe.

He hated her. She always ran down the things he enjoyed the most in his life. He still played softball as well as the young guys on the team. Granted he couldn't run hardly at all anymore, and he couldn't make the long throw from third base where he'd always played before, and he hadn't hit one over the fence in three years, but he was a pitcher now, and he could still hit singles with the best of them. She could never understand that. And he sure wasn't too old to be an actor. He was playing a role in this very play written for a man ten years younger.

"What the hell is your problem? Now you hate softball too? I'm not allowed to do anything that takes me out of the house and away from the intense pleasure of watching you sleep, is that it?"

"That's not what I mean. I'm sorry I said that. I don't care if you play softball. You never come home after that either though, do you? It's always just a couple of beers with the guys on the team afterwards, isn't it?"

He knew she was right, but it made no difference. He was the wounded party now.

"So what?" he spat back at her. "Just so what. It's not like I'm out running around on you," and as soon as he said it, he regretted it. That was exactly what he was doing, and he'd never really faced up to it until now.

"I'm surprised you're not . . . since you're so bored with me," she wasn't counterpunching anymore. There was real hurt rather than anger in her voice. He'd all but told her that she wasn't attractive to him anymore. *I'm sort of like a habit he can't shake,* she thought, something familiar, like smoking or tying his shoestrings in bows, something he keeps doing just because he always has. *What a terrible way to live.*

She's like an itch I can't scratch, Bill thought, *at least without repercussions. She's there, and she's aggravating, but there's just no way to deal with her.*

She was crying, two tears running down her cheeks. He hated it when she cried. It made him angry, especially when he caused it. He had accused her of manipulating him with tears so many times that she had stopped crying, so these tears had to be real. Years ago she had stopped giving him the satisfaction of making her cry. Only something deeper could draw up her tears now. They told him that he had really gone too far this time and that he had to somehow pacify her.

"I'm not bored with you," he lied. "It's just everything, my whole life. I'm sick of sitting around waiting for something to happen because it won't. This play happened, and I like it. It's exciting pretending to be someone else."

"Is that why you do it?" she seemed genuinely interested. "It just seems like so much work for no pay." They were actually talking about something for a change.

"It beats the hell out of watching television every night, and it pays. It's fun. I don't know, the other actors say that when an audience likes you it's a real rush." He realized that he'd calmed her down, could handle her now. "I'm sorry hon," he lied. "I didn't mean any of that. I really didn't. I guess I just get frustrated."

She knew he was lying, that he had meant every word, but she chose to let things lie. It promised to be too nice of a Fall day. But the shadow of divorce was on her again. It had passed over like a huge predatory bird at other times in their marriage like when he fell in love with that that softball slut. Whenever it came, she wanted to run and hide. Nineteen years of marriage is a tough habit to shake.

How was your weekend?" Lori slid down in the seat next to him in the theater Monday evening. She looked terrible. Her eyes were all puffy, like she'd been crying for two days. "I missed you, thought about you a lot."

For a long moment, Bill didn't know what to say. Lori usually had to be given three beers and coaxed for two hours before she'd acknowledge that the attraction was there. Ever since that first night in the bar Lori had been fleeing their relationship, but now she seemed to be proffering an invitation. "Weekend? Uh, not good. . Martha and I had a big fight."

"You're lucky. At least your wife cares enough about you to fight about something. Eddie just comes home and falls asleep. He's always too tired for anything."

"Anything?"

"You got it, Dexter," and she raised her eyebrows and rolled her eyes to punctuate her complaint.

At that moment the director called for "places" and Bill could only wonder at the uncharacteristic aggressiveness of Lori's confidences, as if their having an affair was almost a done deal in her mind. It was a change in Lori's attitude. Their kissing so far had only been flirtation. They had talked about adultery the way ordinary people talked about renting a limo or booking on the Concorde, a neat elegant thing to do but much too expensive. Now there was something in her voice that said she was really getting ready to take the plunge. That troubled Bill because he wasn't sure that he wasn't just playing at adultery.

What had pushed Lori to the edge of adultery was the loneliness of her weekend. After rehearsal on Friday night and a quick drink with the others at the bar, she had gone back to the trailer and waited up for Eddie. She had gone home early expressly so she would be there when he came in. He usually got home about a quarter to twelve. She had put on the sexy lace see-through camisole and panties set from Victoria's Secret and was waiting and ready in bed at eleven thirty. The truth is, ever since her strange friendship with Dexter had erupted in those thoughtless, half-drunk kisses in the theater parking lot, Lori had been almost in heat, more than she could remember being since high school when she and Eddie had first started groping each other in the back seats of cars. But he hadn't come home. When he stumbled in at two, full of beer from a kareoke bar on the east side, she was so glazed with wanting that she didn't even notice his condition . . . at first. When he climbed into bed next to her, thinking she surely was asleep, he ignored the urgency of her sexual caresses.

"Aw jeez, hon, I'm toasted," he grunted, not apologizing at all, and rolled over to fall asleep in seconds.

The next morning, a gorgeous Saturday of his weekend off, he announced that he was going fishing overnight at a lake in Southern Michigan with two buddies he had met in the bar the night before. He didn't even remember that she had been awake and waiting when he came in. She had spent the rest of the weekend alone with the cat, crying and wishing that there was a rehearsal to go to.

When the director called their first break Monday night, Bill wandered out into the parking lot where Lori was standing with John Collins and Sunny under the single Victorian lamppost."You guys have a good weekend?" he asked innocently by way of just making conversation.

John and Sunny broke up in a torrent of giggles, but Lori just looked at him with an empty stare as, with a dirty rumble, the evening train dragged its weary length along Fifth Street.

20 "There's no modesty in theater"

Monday, Sept. 30

The director's gulag began today. This is the last week
of rehearsals before "Tech Week" the other actors tell
me, but I don't really know what "Tech Week" is, except it's the last week before we open when, I guess,
all the technical aspects of the play fall into place. A
lot of that stuff has come together already thanks to
those two set builders that John Collins spends all his
time playing jokes on. Tonight, when we came into
rehearsal, a power drill was whirring somewhere in
the theater. Collins immediately went to the orange
extension cord that snaked across the backstage floor
and unplugged it. "Hey, what the . . ." someone yelled
from the theater. Collins plugged the cord back in, the
power tool resumed its whirr, Collins waited a minute grinning evilly, then unplugged the cord again and
fled down the stairway to the dressing room. "Hey,"
the set builder shouted again, "dammit Collins, is that
you?" I fled back out to the parking lot before the man
worked his way backstage to plug his power tool back
in. The set is really beginning to look like a Main Line
mansion. Barb Dwyer —what a great name!—was
there in full force tonight with costumes for all of us
to try on. In one scene she's going to make me wear
an ascot under the collar of my white shirt, well la-
di-da! I guess one must put up with certain indigni-
ties if one is impersonating a Philadelphia millionaire,
yachtsman, polo player, playboy. Barb Dwyer warned
us that she'll be bringing in costumes every night this
week. All the men looked at each other, mostly in fear.

Rehearsal has changed. No one is allowed in the theater to watch. We have to stay in the dressing rooms (where we can hear what is going on onstage through the intercom) or backstage, and we must hit all our cues. It is starting to feel like we are doing a real play. Now that we know our lines, it sure is a pleasure to play scenes with Tracy. She knows exactly what she is doing. Our scenes together are going well. The director is fine tuning our movements, gestures, line readings—I like her suggestions. She's giving me good stuff to do. The cast is unhappy with her I know, but she's a pretty good director, I think.

Damn her, Lori silently cursed as she stomped down to the dressing room, *she's wrong. 'Trill that line.' What the hell does that mean? Tracy doesn't 'trill.' She snaps. She's sarcastic as hell. Tracy doesn't 'trill.'*

The doorless dressing rooms were empty and Lori knew she had a good long break with only a costume change to do. It was her only break of the play really, the only scene when Tracy wasn't onstage and the center of attention. They were running full acts now, not just scenes, and the actors were getting the timing of their entrances and exits and cues and costume changes and prop pickups and make-up touch-ups and all the little things that had to become automatic before opening night. Now that it was getting close, Lori resented even more the directions the director offered about her character, Tracy. Lori couldn't wait for performances to begin so that the director would drop out of the loop, and Tracy could just be herself.

Now, when Lori looked in the dressing room mirror, it really was Tracy looking back, Tracy who stood taller, whose proud face demanded the attention of everyone in the room, whose eyes sparked with wit and confidence. Lori looked in the mirror and didn't see an actress getting ready to make a costume change. Staring back was a proud young heiress about to snap her fingers for the maid to bring her wedding dress. In the mirror, Tracy was clad in the short terry cloth robe that she is wearing when they stagger back from the pool to the house after their drunken midnight skinnydip. "The robe is short so you can give the audience a lot of leg," the director said when she presented it to Lori. *And most of my ass,* Lori had thought at the time.

Lori untied the belt of Tracy's robe and let it fall open. Tracy would have had nothing on underneath, but Lori had kept on her bra and panties when she and Collins made their quick change in the coat room in the lobby. There may be 'no modesty in theater' as Barb Dwyer had said more than once, yet stripping all your clothes off in a public coat room where anyone could walk in anytime in the company of a man she barely knew who was also shedding his clothes was not something Lori was really used to yet.

With a slough of her shoulders, she let the swim robe fall to the floor. But she didn't move to pick it up. Instead, she stood looking at herself in the mirror, not really there, thinking that Tracy would be naked under her robe, drunk on champagne, not worried about John Collins seeing her body as they changed clothes in the cramped cloak-room. Tracy would be proud of her athletic body.

Bill was thinking about his scene—the punch still wasn't right, too fakey—as he slowly descended the steps to the dressing room. All the lights, except for two blue work lights that had been set up to help actors find their props, were off backstage. The stairwell down was little more than a dark tunnel with the bright dressing room lights at its end. As he neared the bottom of the stairs, he glanced up straight ahead through the doorless doorway of the ladies' dressing room into the wall-to-wall make-up mirror. What he saw stopped him in his tracks, then made him step back into the deeper darkness of the stair-well.

Lori, dressed only in a cream-colored bra and color-matched pant-ies, was standing before the mirror looking at herself, not moving, almost as if she was studying a painting in a museum, "Actress at her Mirror," like those ballet dancers or bathing nudes drying themselves by that French painter Martha liked so much, Degas. She was just standing there in her skimpy bra and panties looking at herself.

Bill had not really meant to become a Peeping Tom. He had as-sumed that position instinctively. He was truly captivated by her na-kedness, compelled to spy upon her. He tried to rationalize his step back into the darkness. *It's a reflection in a mirror,* he defended himself, *not the real thing.* But that mirror image had managed to utterly para-lyze him from his eyes all the way down to his conscience. She couldn't see him in the mirror. He was a secret sharer of her almost nakedness.

Then it got even better.

With one elegant movement, Lori's two hands, like a dancer's pir-ouette, moved between her breasts and unhooked her bra from the front, then teased it down off her shoulders until it hung limp in her right hand by her side. Strangely, however, she didn't move to quickly cover herself with a dress. Confident she was alone, pensive, she stood still a long moment, contemplating herself in the glass as if to reassure herself that she was real and not just an image in someone else's mirror.

Then it all ended for Bill, though he wanted it to go on forever., It was his own voice that betrayed him.

"Lori? You down here?" his moralistic traitor of a voice called out of the shadows of the stage.

She jumped in the mirror and protectively crossed her arms like a frightened doe.

"Uh, yes, yes I am," Lori answered, frantically darting her eyes for the open closet where all the costumes hung in search of the wedding dress for the last scene.

"Are you decent?" Bill emerged from the steps as if he had just walked down from backstage.

"No. I mean, not yet. Wait a minute, then I'll need you to zip up this damn wedding dress."

And that quickly it was over. In a mere second, they were just actors once again getting ready for the next scene.

"Ok, you can come in," Lori called gaily. She was hooking the top of the wedding dress behind her neck when he walked in upon her. She was Tracy, radiant in that gorgeous white wedding gown, all beadwork and chiffon. "Zip me up, will you?" Tracy commanded.

"I'm not sure you should be asking your ex-husband to be doing stuff like this on your wedding day," he teased her.

"Why Dexter," she put on her best Scarlett O'Hara voice, "ahh do buhleeeve yooo're jealous." His fingers fumbled nervously at the zip-per, but immediately got it caught in the fabric of the dress. He had to bend down to free it, bring his face, his eyes, uncomfortably close to the bare skin of her naked back.

"Nervous, Dexter honey?" she taunted him.

He got the zipper going again, and mourned as it rose, slowly clos-ing off access to the provocative expanse of her naked back.

"I don't think Dexter's nervous at all," Bill picked up her joking tone as the zipper rose to the top. "He knows he gets the girl in the end, but my hand is shaking like a leaf." Then, not really meaning to, but not able not to, he leaned slightly down and kissed her softly on the nape of her gorgeous long neck.

Lori couldn't believe what was happening. They were right in the dressing room. Anyone could walk in on them. Yet the touch of his lips on her neck was so delicious that she melted back against his chest without even thinking. He was a man who wanted her, wanted to touch and kiss her, thought she was beautiful, and, at that moment, she wanted him so badly that she could already feel the wonderful tightening in her body.

Melting back into his arms, the cool burn of his lips still on her neck, his hands joining around her waist, her typical impulse to flight wrestled with her brief shocking impulse to turn and kiss him back.

You slut, the thought strutted like a streetwalker in her mind. "Oh Bill, we can't, we shouldn't, not here . . ." she protested faintly even as she was turning in his arms to kiss him hard on the mouth. *You sound like one of those soap opera queens,* she chided herself. "Oh Bill, somebody could come in . . ." but then she was kissing him again.

"Oh , we shouldn't, don't . . ." she continued to protest in a throaty whisper even as her arms were up around his neck and she was kissing him once again.

"Places for Act Three," came the stage manager's call over the small squawkbox intercom peeping down at them from the corner of the dressing room ceiling. That intrusion of the play back into their real lives ripped them asunder.

"If anyone came, we'd just tell them we were rehearsing," Bill explained away her fears much too late for her even to remember what fears he was explaining away.

"Gotta go," she tossed over her shoulder as her original impulse to flight finally took hold with the help of that nagging voice over the intercom, and she fled for the stairwell up to the stage.

Wednesday, Oct. 2
The gulag is in full force. We are running acts straight through. Marge is taking notes and passing them on to us on little pieces of yellow paper. This week there is a solidarity in the cast. The director isn't getting any less bitchy, she's just doing it on paper. She even yelled at Ernie and Thurman yesterday when Thurman balked about making some minor adjustment in

the set. This cast has grown close (some much closer than others). I think we're starting to do some pretty good work onstage.

"Bill, this has got to stop. You are turning me into a nervous wreck. All the time I want to kiss you, but I'm married. I'm terrified of my husband finding out. But it's turning me into a horny little slut because all I think of is seeing you at the theater each night, hoping that we'll be alone, that you'll kiss me again, and worse."

Lori rehearsed this whole speech inside her mind all week, but she could never bring herself to deliver it. She and Bill had passed through the first kiss stage to this desperate kissing that neither had found time to understand. Now she knew they needed to talk. She needed to figure out for herself at just what stage they were. Stages, her whole life was on stages anymore. Each time she and Bill found themselves alone together, she found herself some reason not to deliver her speech. Instead, they talked about the play, or ran their lines.

"I think she's a good director," Bill served up an honest assessment for Lori to spike back at him.

"Oh great! So we're dealing with a talented bitch. That makes it all OK?" Lori flailed back.

"No, of course not," he was trying to be reasonable. He should have known better.

"I think we're all doing great work onstage, and she still isn't happy," Lori wasn't going to let him defend Marge no matter what.

They were sitting in the theater lobby where they had gone to run lines.

"It's as if she's the one whose butt is going to be on the line. But we're the ones who are going to be up there in front of all those people. Don't you see? It's our play, not hers."

"All I'm saying," Bill was in full retreat even though sitting down, "is that she's got us all acting our butts off. Whether that's out of hatred for her or because of her I don't know, but it's working. You're going to be a terrific Tracy, and all I'm saying is I think she's going to get good performances out of us."

"Ok, maybe you're right, but being onstage in a play has always been something I really liked, like it was the one time in my life when I was in control of who I was."

"But onstage you're always someone else."

"I know that, but you know who you are. Maybe that's why all of that woman's nagging has bothered me so much. I wanta be my Tracy not her Tracy."

Bill caught the passion in her voice. For him the play was a sort of escapist lark. But for her it was salvation and identity and power all rolled into one. Just looking at her really turned him on. But they were in the fishbowl of the lobby, glass doors all around, and he couldn't take her into his arms and kiss her.

> Friday, Oct. 4
> We're almost there. We open in one week. We've done all three acts straight through. The cast is eager to go. We need an audience, some reaction to all the things we're doing onstage. I was really on tonight. My big scene with Tracy really went well. But I know that during some performance my mouth will rebel and the words won't come, or the wrong ones will. Barb Dwyer found a shirt and a pair of slacks with pleats and cuffs, very Thirties, that fit me. After the little act I caught tonight after rehearsal, nobody will ever be able to accuse this cast and crew of not being friendly.

On Friday night, Bill and Lori decided to go to the bar after rehearsal to talk. It was Lori's idea. Strangely, none of the others seemed interested in drinking this night. It had been the hardest, most focused, week of rehearsals yet, with so much happening, what with being completely off book, and running the full acts, and the costumes, and the props, and the ugly little notes, and the set rushing to completion. Collins and Sunny disappeared as soon as the director let them all go. Lori, rather wistfully, watched them hop into John's car and race off together. *They probably can't wait to get somewhere private,* she thought. Harvey Winkins had to get one of his costumes fitted after rehearsal, but they presumed that he would join them at the bar. Marge begged off, and Thelma, for the first Friday night since the play began, just didn't show up. Lori wondered if she was sick.

"Let's go have a drink anyway," Lori wasn't ready to go home, "we can talk, just you and me." She said it quietly, thoughtfully, sort of like Tracy in the third act after she has been chastened.

"Great," Bill smiled with artificial enthusiasm, wondering if there was more kiss and run on the menu for the evening. He loved kissing Lori in those quick rushes of passion that were impelling her lately, but for weeks he had been thinking much more sinister thoughts that went far beyond her fleeing kisses.

They both drove down Fifth Street to the bar, angle parked side by side, crossed the tracks and went in. They ordered beers and were making smalltalk about what a rough week of rehearsal it had been when the waitress showed up with their order.

"Damn," Bill had reached into his pocket for his wallet and had come up empty, "I left it in the dressing room. I know just where it is."

"What?" Lori hadn't a clue what he was talking about.

"My wallet."

"Oh. I can pay for the drinks."

"Oh I know, but I better go back and see if I can get it before they close up. I'll need it for the weekend. I'll be right back."

"Wait. I don't want to sit here by myself. I'll go with you. Here," and she paid the waitress for the beers, "just set them here and we'll be right back," she ordered the girl like Tracy giving directions to one of her servants.

The waitress, however, in her black leather miniskirt and red bow tie, instead of saying "yes miss" and curtsying, just mumbled "no problem," cracked her gum, and left the drinks.

They drove back to the theater in Bill's car. There were a couple of cars still in the parking lot, but the theater was dark.

"I hope somebody's in there and the door is still open," Bill muttered more to himself than to Lori. "All the lights are off," Lori stated the obvious. "I'm going with you. It's dark out here."

But the stage door turned open to Bill's touch, and they entered a step or two into the pitch blackness of backstage. They both stopped just inside the door, to accustom their eyes to the deeper darkness. Backstage was littered with set building materials, tools, ladders, and props, and they would have to see something in order to pick their way across the back of the stage to the stairway down to the dressing rooms. They started to move slowly, Bill first feeling his way, Lori with her hand on his shoulder in the way you exit a blacked-out stage, but the sounds stopped them.

They were unmistakeable sounds, the coarse, gutteral grunts and bumps of two people making love, and they were coming from the stage. Lori and Bill stood there in the darkness, their eyes slowly adapting, unable to even make out shapes, two voyeurs listening to something they couldn't see, imagining. Lori and Mike were looking at each other in the backstage darkness, but neither of them knew it. The sounds from the stage had a kind of frantic regularity about them. They weren't anything resembling words. They were more like a primitive drum being beaten. They were dirty, sweaty, rough, working sounds of take and give, deep animal growls.

Bill was starting to make out the darkest shadows. Lori was only two feet away, but her shadow was but a few fragments of gray in the void of black where they stood eavesdropping. The sounds onstage were slowly building with a pounding rhythm toward a violent crescendo. Bill reached out toward Lori's silent shadow, found her hand. He led her step by step through the minefield of backstage to the swinging doorway at centerstage. It was where they made most of their entrances and exits, and he knew its location by instinct.

Bill cracked the swinging door in the middle to look through like an actor counting the house before a performance. A dim green light, the bleed from the two "EXIT" signs over the theater doors, hung like a thin mist over the stage.

"Get down! I wanna see too," Lori squeezed his hand as she whispered with the fierce urgency of someone afraid of missing an important historical event. Bill went to his knees and Lori leaned in over him from behind to look through the crack in the door. He could feel the front of her body straddling his head and back as she pressed forward.

Neither of them thought twice or even blinked in their voyeurism. The unmistakeable sounds had only quickened their lust to see what was going on.

In the eerie green mist floating over the stage, two dim figures were bent over the sofa moving in the violent coil and recoil of upright barnyard coupling. The thin quixotic silhouette of Harvey Winkins mounted upon his partner from behind was unmistakable. The object of his affections was bent over the back of the sofa, her feet planted firmly on the stage floor as Harvey's shining hips drove rhythmically into her.

It has to be Barb Dwyer, the thought came to both Bill and Lori simultaneously as they spied wide-eyed upon Harvey's mounting assault upon that happy bent-over backside.

Neither Lori nor Bill spoke.

Neither Lori nor Bill moved.

Neither Lori's nor Bill's eyes could pull themselves away from the fascination of that fierce animal encounter on the stage.

What great theater! neither of them consciously thought, yet both were drawn to it in exactly the way that a great performance or a riveting scene literally transports the audience out of itself and fixes their attention so firmly that they are no longer aware of being in a theater.

From what Lori could see, Harvey's waxed mustache certainly wasn't the only thing he could make stand up.

Bill remembered a line from an old blues song, the dirtiest line he'd ever heard in a song, "I'm a one-eyed jack peepin' in a seafood store,"

Suddenly, Barb Dwyer seemed to levitate into the air, her feet arching out behind her and around Harvey's straining hips as if she had just taken off into flight. At the same time Harvey went high up on his toes and suspended his whole body above her with a perceptible shudder. The two of them hung there in the joyful stretch and press of their meeting like two taut wires crossing and giving off sparks.

Bill realized that he had been holding his breath. He exhaled with a half-strangled "whoosh" into the wood of the door. Lori's knees, pressing hard into his back, suddenly relaxed as Harvey collapsed on top of Barb Dwyer and the two lovers rolled over the back of the couch and disappeared out of sight.

Bill looked at Lori whose shadow was already backing away in the blackness. Carefully, not wanting to make the slightest sound, he closed the crack in the door through which they had been spying and backed away on tense tiptoe. He realized that it would be much more compromising for he and Lori to be caught watching than it could ever be for Barb and Harvey to be caught doing what they were doing.

As they inched through the blackness of backstage toward the stairs down to the dressing rooms, they were both terrified of tripping over something, or bumping into something with an attendant crash, and giving themselves (and their kinky fascination) away. Suddenly, they were stopped by a whole new libretto of sounds from the dark quiet of the stage. Harvey's full-throated laugh of surprise was accompanied by a cascade of Barb's girlish giggles of joy and coquetry. It sounded as if the two were tickling each other and, under cover of their comical sound effects, Lori and Bill fled down the stairs where he grabbed his wallet on the run and they made their escape out the back door.

Up in the parking lot, scrambling into Bill's car, Lori suddenly burst out laughing, her hand over her mouth.

"Do you believe that?" Lori managed to squeeze the words through the cracks in her giggles.

"Yeah, wild, right on stage," Bill said it with admiration for the imagination and the recklessness of it.

"I'd be terrified of getting caught," Lori still couldn't keep a straight face. Small giggles kept forcing their way out of the sides of her mouth.

"They didn't seem afraid of anything. In fact, they looked like they were in orbit," Bill suddenly remembered the joke from Dickens he had made one night in the bar. *When I said "Winkins is willin,"* he thought, *I didn't know how right I was.*

"Boink heaven."

"What?"

"That's what Eddie calls it."

They were getting out of Bill's car in front of *The Hoosier Saloon.* He had just driven back there automatically without any consultation with Lori. After all, their drinks were still sitting on their table.

"Boink heaven? Actually that's pretty good," and the phrase started to dance in Bill's mischievous imagination, "but since he was boinking her from behind, this was a back-boink and they were in back-boink heaven."

Lori was laughing out loud. She took his arm as they crossed the tracks. They were like two schoolkids being silly as they careened into the bar. People looked up from their drinks at their hilarity, but Lori didn't seem to care. It all just struck her so funny. All her agonizing about her feelings toward Bill seemed so silly. Everybody else in the cast—Harvey and Barb Dwyer, John and Sunny—was having a wonderful, romantic, flirtatious time. *My husband doesn't even pay any attention to me anymore,* she thought as she looked across the table into Bill's eyes. He still couldn't resist the grin that kept pulling at his face.

"Ol' Harvey won't top that performance no matter how good he is in this play," Bill laughed out loud.

Ten minutes passed. They had successfully gotten themselves under control, and their second drink had just arrived when the night took yet another turn for the silly.

Harvey Winkins, hair meticulously combed, cheeks ruddy from being washed, pants a bit wrinkled but securely belted around his waist, zipper closed, golf sweater a bright blue with "Pebble Beach" blazoned on its chest, mustache waxed fully erect, walked in the front door alone and right up to Bill and Lori's table.

Lori saw him first and her eyes went wide.

Bill turned to look over his shoulder and stared stupidly as Harvey walked right up to them. *Wow!* Bill thought, *it looks like he just walked out of the locker room after a game of golf.*

"Harvey," Lori said.

"Harvey," Bill echoed.

They were both wondering where Barb Dwyer was.

"Harvey," Mike repeated in disbelief.

"Am I interrupting something?" Harvey was trying to find some explanation for their bizarre, wide-eyed greeting.

"No, no, not at all," Bill stammered, trying to cover up their surprise.

"No, Harvey, not us, interrupting, no," Lori tried to second Bill's denial of any wrongdoing on their part and overdid it. "We just thought everyone had gone home, from the theater. No, I don't mean from the theater . . . I mean after reahearsal, you know. Uh, would you like a drink?."

Harvey still had a puzzled look on his face, but he traded it for one of his winning smiles, shrugged his hands out to his sides, chuckled "Winkins is willin,'" the very words that had crossed Bill's mind only moments before, and sat down craning for the waitress' attention.

When Harvey said it, Bill choked on the sip of beer he was taking and spit half of it back into his glass with the rest running down his chin.

It was all Lori could do to choke back her own howls of laughter.

Harvey was looking for the waitress and missed their little incontinence. By the time he had turned back Bill had his cocktail napkin to his mouth and Lori had gotten herself under control.

"It looks like it's gonna rain yet tonight," she said.

"Yeah, we can't hardly stand anymore," Harvey answered. "Couple more good rains and that river will be at flood stage."

The word "stage" made Lori want to break out in giggles all over again.

21 Full Dress Revenge

It rained every day during Tech Week. That September dreariness just added to the impatience of the actors. Tech Week was the time when the actors become mere pieces of furniture for the lights to shine on, the sound to be timed to, the costume and prop people to hang things on.

The actor as coat rack, Bill thought on Monday night as Barb Dwyer shoved her third dyed ascot down his throat and stepped back to see how it looked in the lights.

Lori had phoned him from a pay telephone booth that afternoon to call it all off (whatever it was they had on). He was writing a diary entry about the play between working with the tape recorder on his lines when the phone rang. .

"Oh good, I was afraid you weren't there," her voice was rushed, almost desperate. "This is crazy. It can't go on. It's really screwing me up. I can't concentrate, thinking of you, us. I'm acting like Tracy. It's getting out of hand. I'm thinking about you all the time. I need to be thinking about the play. We're not going to do this anymore. Promise me you'll call it off. It's making me crazy," her words came in a flood.

The grey desultory rain was falling outside his study window as her torrent of words engulfed him. She was panicked. Everything was coming down on her at once. Their stolen kisses. Her anger at her husband. Her lust. Her guilt. Her uncertainty. But more stressful than any of these was the imminence of opening night, only four nights away. She was the lead and the pressure was pulling her down. He should have been sympathetic, understanding, tried to calm her down, as he had earlier in the play, but he wasn't feeling that way. What he was feeling, suddenly, was anger. The steady grey rain added to his impatience with her. All he could think of was how boring his life had been before the play and their little dance of flirtation. But nothing had happened yet. Here she was coming apart over the phone as if something had. It angered him. It was just more playacting, and he was sick of playacting. He wanted the real thing, or at least the real playacting, to begin.

"Call it off. Call what off?" His voice was level and cold. He was looking out into the sullen rain. "Lori, we haven't done anything yet."

"But, but . . ."

"Why couldn't you have told me this tonight, in person? Why the phone? I hate phones."

"I, I, it's . . . oh Bill, it's making me crazy." And she hung up, just left him hanging there looking out at the boring rain.

That night, when he drove into the theater parking lot, she was sitting on the back fender of her car with her script in her hand pretending to be working her lines. It was a break in the rain and the wet blacktop glistened in the autumn twilight. She was waiting for him. As he parked, she hopped down off her fender and skipped toward his car. His window was down and, as she approached, he caught her looking over her shoulder toward the stagedoor to see if anyone was watching. Feeling safe, she came right up to the car, put her head through the open window, and kissed him on the mouth. Then, she kissed him again, this time with her mouth open, her tongue probing provacatively.

Man, how does she expect me to go in and do my lines now, he thought.

"I'm sorry. Honest, I panicked," she was apologizing even as she was stepping back and casting a quick glance around to see if anyone had seen them. "It seemed like everything was caving in on me. You were right to tell me off. We haven't done anything, and you've been the one who's gotten me through all this. Oh Bill, I didn't mean to get stupid with you. You've been great. I just need to get it together for this week. I don't want to mess up Tracy. I think I've almost got her, and I need you, I need to touch you to make her work. And it all scares the heck out of me."

Getting out of the car, Bill realized that she was giving him no choice. *She's probably been rehearsing that speech ever since she hung up the phone this afternoon,* he thought. But what could he say? She was pleading for his steady, understanding presence which had coaxed her through those earlier rocky moments in the play.

"Calm down, Lori. I didn't mean to be so sharp on the phone this afternoon . . ."

"I didn't mean to be so stupid. You must think I'm . . ." her voice trailed off.

"I don't think you're anything, except about three different people trying to figure things out right now. I think you're worried about the play. You've got the biggest part and you're going to be great. Now let's get this play open, and then we'll worry about this other stuff."

"Oh Bill," and she started toward him, her arms actually reaching to pull his face down for a kiss, but she must have caught a glimpse out of the corner of her eye of Ernie and Thurman coming out of the stagedoor carrying a large styrofoam pillar.

"C'mon, let's go in," Bill took her arm and steered her toward the stage door. "Nothing happens until Tracy arrives."

Tuesday night the combination hairdresser and make-up person was there, and he put them all through their paces with bases and blushes and pencils and brushes. For actors, Tech Week is drudgery because the rehearsing is so fragmented. So little gets done. But all the other aspects of the play have to be fine-tuned. It seemed to take forever.

Bill and Harvey Winkins played golf the Tuesday afternoon of Tech Week. Bill hadn't played once since the play began, and when Harvey suggested it he leapt at the chance to take his mind off of opening night (which was fast approaching) and Lori (who seemed always running away). They played at the Elks Club course, green refuge of horned lodge brothers, which, like everything else in the Wabash Valley, butts up against the cornfields on the northern fringe of West Wabash. Harvey took his golf seriously. He hit his drive off the first tee up into a grey and theatening fall sky.

It's going to rain on us out here today, Bill thought confidently since it had rained a large part of every day since Friday.

"Never rains on a golf course," good ol' Harvey, as if reading Bill's mind, said as he stepped back to admire the high controlled hook he had hit out into the dismal sky.

Bill stepped up to his ball and sawed a low slice off the neck of his club into a clump of sapling pines in the right rough. But he was happy to be outdoors no matter how overcast it was. They were pretty much alone on the course. There was a twosome of bright orange and blue well off in the distance in a cart, probably a couple of Elk does who had started on the back nine so they wouldn't get in the way of the bucks.

This is a good idea, Bill thought as they walked up the first fairway. That was when good ol' Harvey sandbagged him.

"You sleepin' with that little blonde?" Harvey asked out of a clear blue sky unlike the one they were playing under.

"Uh, what? What blonde?"

"Don't give me that. You know. Tracy, Lori. The little blonde in the play. You are, aren't ya? You're porkin' her."

Bill laughed, back in control after the initial surprise of Harvey's probably innocent question. "I'm not . . . 'porkin' . . . her, as you so quaintly put it in that charming Hoosier way of yours." From the knowing grin on Harvey's face, Bill knew he wasn't buying it. "Honest, I'm telling you, we're just friends, just friends is all."

"Aha!" Harvey struck his most pompous Shakespearean pose, "methinks he doth protest too much."

Bill had to laugh at Harvey's fairway theatrics. "You can stop 'methinking' right now. I know it will disappoint you terribly, but I'm not sleeping with her."

"Not yet you aren't maybe," Harvey hooted knowingly as he peeled off toward his ball on the other side of the fairway.

Bill found his ball lodged in high grass between two adolescent pine trees. All he could do was chop it out sideways into the fairway where he was still away. He hit his shot, a half-topped seven-iron that rolled almost all the way to the green ending up at the bottom of a low bank just short.

"How about a two-dollar Nassau, press anytime?" Harvey called gleefully from across the fairway, knowing he was already probably one-up.

"Sure," Bill waved, "why not."

Harvey stepped up and hit a gorgeous high iron shot with that little hook right at the end that descended from the grey heavens to the dull Elk-trod green, fed softly left from its point of impact, and nestled nicely about eight feet below the pin right on line.

Harvey was happy, and Bill already knew he'd been had. He hadn't even asked for strokes or insisted upon match play rather than medal. *Oh, who cares,* he thought, *I can afford a couple o' bucks, and I can beat this guy.* In the annals of self-deception, that fleeting hope goes down with Napoleon thinking he could conquer the world, and with Bill thinking he and Lori weren't on a straight highway to "boink heaven."

The double bogey Bill took on the first hole, losing to Harvey's easy par, was but the first in a succession of catastrophes that Bill was destined to endure that day. As Harvey hit his friendly little hook into fairways and onto greens, Bill sprayed shots left and right and mostly short. His only salvation was his putting which kept his score from completely caving in. To add insult to ineptitude, the rain held off until they were trudging up the seventeenth fairway. It pelted down as they putted out on seventeen, and it dogged them all the way up the eighteenth fairway to the clubhouse.

"If I catch a cold, lose my voice, and can't say my lines on Friday, it's all your fault," Bill chided Harvey in the steam of the showers for insisting they finish in the rain so he could record his 77. Bill was eleven shots worse, barely breaking ninety, a score that ten years earlier would have horrified him. He paid Harvey the six dollars he had lost and considered it a pretty good purchase of time killed until the play opened on Friday.

Wednesday night was their last run-through before the full dress rehearsal on Thursday. "Work on serving your cue lines up to your fellow actors," Marge directed them before they began. "Work on listening to each other on stage. Work on being in character, on standing, walking, talking just the way your character would."

The set was almost fully dressed. All of the props, the telephone that rings, all of the furniture was in place. They all decided to wear their costumes, make their changes, but they didn't bother with make-up—that would be Thursday night's worry. Barb Dwyer was there in full force, still fiddling with their costumes. Rehearsal went rather well actually, not too many lines were mangled and no one got tongue-tied and had to be rescued. It all looked pretty natural, and Marge had to be pleased . . . until John Collins struck.

He waited until the final wedding scene and had, clearly, recruited Barb Dwyer as his accomplice. The cast had almost made it all the way through the play. The wedding was about to begin, and Tracy still hadn't decided whether she was going to go ahead and marry George or run off with Connor the newspaper man. All the while, C. K. Dexter Haven lurked devil-may-care in the background. Marge was sitting up in the darkness of the theater's last row.

Collins entered through the audience from the right and Dexter and Uncle Willie (Bill and Harvey) were the first to notice. They fought back their laughter for a moment, but couldn't control it once they looked at each other and then back at Collins. Bill tightened his lips and gritted his teeth, but couldn't hold the giggles back.

Then the laughter began to spread. Lips tightening and then cracking into burbling giggles rippled across the stage. Collins had gotten them again.

Marge was the only one who couldn't see what had cracked them all up, driven them out of character. She sat up in the darkness staring down at her whole cast suddenly fighting back full-blown laughter. It was as if a whole world she had created and controlled had suddenly collapsed right in front of her eyes.

"What the hell's going on?" she jumped up growling. But, as soon as she got to her feet, she could see what was going on and, bless her, couldn't help but laugh herself.

John Collins really hadn't done anything overt. He'd come on completely in character, saying his lines as if he meant them. He'd made his entrance down the aisle through the audience so that from a sitting position in the back of the house on the other side the lower half of his body was mostly blocked by the seats. He stopped just offstage to deliver his first line, and that is when everybody onstage started cracking up. As for Collins, he paid no attention, just went right on with his lines. He had on his character's elegant black tuxedo, but his black pants with their velvet stripes were perfectly hemmed and cuffed just below the knee. Over six-three and skinny, Collins looked like he'd put on a dwarf's tuxedo, was wearing pedal-pushers with black tie and cummerbund. But he hadn't stopped just at his munchkin re-tailoring. Protruding straight out from the fly of his abbreviated trousers was about a foot of the tail of his white starched evening shirt. And Collins just kept going on with his lines, keeping a straight face as if absolutely nothing was awry and the whole cast wasn't convulsing with laughter right in front of him.

Actually, the whole cast owed Collins a debt. He loosened them up, kept their minds off the mistakes they were still making, the nervousness that was beginning to build, all the possibilities for things to go wrong which were built into every play. The cast owed Collins a debt of laughter, but Ernie and Thurman owed Collins a lot more than that.

When the cast and crew arrived at the theater at seven on Thursday for full dress rehearsal at eight, Ernie and Thurman were clanking around up on the catwalks making some final necessary adjustments in the lights, everyone presumed. If any member of the cast had professed not to be nervous, he or she would have been immediately stoned for a liar. But they got into their costumes, did their make-up and hair, warmed up their voices, sipped their lemon juice, ran their lines and were in their places waiting to go on, at eight o'clock.

And then they were actually doing it.

There was no audience yet. That was the only ingredient to be added that would make it all real. But Marge was there, and Ernie and Thurman were sitting up in the darkness of the control booth, and full lights and sound were in place, and it was just like it was going to be when all the seats were full. Before they even knew it, it had begun. Tracy was out there whining about her stupid wedding presents, and her little sister was being charmingly obnoxious, and then Connor and his photographer Liz arrived from the big city, and then Uncle Willie made his marvelous entrance playing it for all its worth, and finally Dexter got to make his entrance down the aisle just before the end of Act One, and they were actually doing it, saying their lines and moving about the stage as if they'd lived in that grand house all their lives. And their confidence began to build and express itself in their carriage and their ease at delivering their lines. It had really happened. They had created another world in which they could live and move easily, comfortably, confidently. Tracy and Connor did their tipsy love scene, then Dexter and Connor made it through the punch on the veranda without mishap.

Reticent little Ernie was waiting for Collins as the whole cast came offstage at the end of Act II. They had about ten minutes to get into their costumes for the wedding finale and no one was in a hurry.

"John, we've got a problem," Ernie was almost breathless as he approached Collins backstage as they came off.

"What's wrong?" Collins was concerned.

"Could you just take a minute and take a look at it?" Ernie was all alone, which was unusual. Glowering Thurman was nowhere in evidence.

"Sure, what's up?" Collins followed Ernie around to the ladder up to the catwalks. "It's the way one part of the set is showin' up in the lights," Ernie climbed to the catwalk and beckoned Collins to follow. "We noticed it from up here earlier. It's weird. Thought you might want to do somethin' about it before we open."

"What is it?" Collins followed him trustingly up into the darkness. It was quiet up there. Thurman was waiting for them on the catwalk right over center stage.

"Places!" the assistant stage manager shouted in a whisper down the steps to the dressing rooms. The actors, all dressed for the wedding, scurried up to the blackness of backstage, and Act Three began.

Tracy's mother and father, and Uncle Willie and the obnoxious little sister, were onstage fidgeting at the beginning of the scene, then Dexter made his usual airy entrance, followed a page or two later by Tracy in full wedding dress sweeping through the high double doors at the back of the stage and taking it all over. Almost the whole cast was onstage when Liz wandered in holding her camera and looking sort of dazed. She looked around at them quizzically, and they looked at her. Something was wrong, but they didn't quite know what.

"I can't find Mike Connor," Liz finally said, trying to stay in character, but it was really Sunny begging for help.

That's not in the script, Bill thought.

All the actors, or characters, looked stupidly at one another.

"Well, where is he?" Tracy finally broke the awkward silence as if they were still following the script.

"I don't know," Liz shrugged, "he didn't show up back . . . uh, back, back there in the, uh, right wing."

"Well, he must be coming," Uncle Willie went upstage to the doors to look for him.

"He'll be here soon, I'm sure," Tracy's mother assured them.

"I think I'll go see where he is," Uncle Willie careened downstage then back upstage like an addled shuttlecock.

"Oh no you don't, you stay right here," Tracy cut off his escape.

They were re-writing the play, all gathered at center stage in a quandary, staying in character, but making it up as they went along, stalling in hopes that Connor would miraculously show up. It was turning into a bizarre high society version of *Waiting For Godot.*

"I hope he's okay," Dexter did his part. "I gave him a good pop in the eye last night. Hope I didn't hurt him."

Even as Dexter was delivering these lines (which he thought were surpassingly clever), he was sensing some object descending from above, or rather, being lowered toward them from the ceiling.

Collins, upside down, his hands and mouth duct-taped, his ankles bound together in a rope harness, wiggling feebly as if trying to escape, cleared the lights above the stage and descended toward their midst until he suddenly stopped in mid-air about two feet above their collectively astonished heads.

But Ernie and Thurman weren't done. They started to swing Collins like a pendulum side to side in the air in longer and longer swings until all that was needed was some circus music to complete the act.

The actors stared up at the careening Collins, mouths agape.

In the darkness of the theater, Marge was utterly speechless.

God only knows how avid and joyeous were Ernie and Thurman up on the catwalks operating their swinging engine of revenge. They had Collins exactly where they wanted him, and suddenly everyone understood. It was the practical joke to end all practical jokes. There could have been no more imaginative way to bring rehearsals to an end. For the second night in a row rehearsal broke up in uncontrollable laughter. But even in their convulsions of mirth and their tears of glee, as Collins swung helplessly at the end of his rope, they all realized that tomorrow was opening night and they had to get down to business.

22 Opening Night: Act One

The steady rain beat against Lori Martin's windshield as she crossed the Wabash River on opening night in quest of Tracy Lord.

The raindrops bounced like harmless popcorn off of Bill Franklin's fenders as he parked in the theater lot on opening night trying to imagine himself C. K. Dexter Haven, millionaire yachtsman.

By 7:15, everyone in the cast was fussing in the dressing rooms, working at make-up, twisting to get hair just right, pulling at costumes, running lines to themselves. The dressing room was festooned with cards and gifts. The Civic Theatre board always sent a boring card that said something smartly original like "Break a leg" or "Have a great show." But the board always sent flowers too, and the long shelves along the mirrors in both the men's and women's dressing rooms dripped with bud-vased roses and carnations and daisies and lilies, all reds and yellows and whites and greens in a springlike explosion. They bouyed the actor's spirits. There were cards from Thelma and Barb Dwyer for the whole cast, and they were funny and appropriate. Barb Dwyer's showed a snooty, high-hatted *New Yorker* magazine gentleman with his nose in the air on the front and the same gentleman with a baseball bat pounding on a mugger inside over the caption: "I say, old boy, knock them dead!" Thelma's was a "dogs playing poker" card, but it was quizzical monkeys in tuxedos holding champagne glasses with a caption inside that read: "So that's why they call them monkey suits?" Marge had taped a card and a single rose for everyone in a line across the dressing room mirrors. Each actor's card had a fervent "thank you" for all their effort and a final direction for improving their performance. She insisted on being the director to the end. Her card to Lori was addressed to Tracy and read: "Shoulders back, chin and nose up, and think rich!" Her card to Bill read: "Dexter, you're the troublemaker. Make trouble and have fun doing it." Bill thought it was a pretty good last bit of direction. The best opening night dressing room favor was from John Collins. He had drawn marvelous caricatures of each actor in the costume and setting of their character, and had them speaking in balloons one of their best lines from the play. Bill was caricatured in evening clothes saying "a writer: It's extraordinary. I thought all writers drank to excess and beat their wives. I expect at one time I secretly wanted to be a writer." Amidst the flowers and cards, in between the actors bumping into each other and checking each other's hair and tying each other's ties, there vibrated a tension of anticipation and fear and insecurity and panic and excitement and nausea and competitive desire. They all wanted to get it going, enter the lists. The theater was off-limits. Thelma was giving it its final vacuum cleaning before the house opened at 7:30.

"We're sold out tonight," Marge told them as she bustled about doing nothing more than offering utterly obvious last minute instructions: "Keep up the pace. Keep the cue lines clear and coming. Listen on stage. Think rich." There was no way she was going to set them free. Marge liked her position of control, and she would only take herself out of the loop begrudgingly.

Barb Dwyer made a quick pass through begging for any last minute buttons to be sewn or strings to be cut. She didn't seem to pay extra attention to Harvey. She had radiant opening night smiles and compliments on their appearance—"Oh, you look great!" and "My, you *are* handsome tonight!" Finally, finding next to nothing to do, she gave a little sideways wave with her scissors and, almost sadly, said: "Hey, break a leg guys."

On the squawkbox attached to the microphone that hung over the stage, the actors in the dressing rooms could hear the rustles and thumps and coughs and trips and murmurs of conversation of the audience coming into the theater. The whole company, as if at some unspoken cue, suddenly stopped their make-up dabbing and hair patting and line scanning as the sounds of the audience filing in wafted down and over them. They all went still for a short moment and listened. They looked at one another in the mirrors, stopped in a shock of realization. An audience. It was what they all had been waiting for, the only missing ingredient, the last thing needed to make their play-acting real.

"What has three teeth and an IQ of ten?" John Collins broke that tense moment of suspension. Everyone was pretty much dressed, and just waiting for the call to places. They looked at him with a blank stare as if collectively wondering *what the hell does this have to do with the alien that is eating my stomach and the biker who is strangling my vocal chords.*

"What has three teeth and an IQ of ten?" Harvey obligingly repeated Collins' question as the others shrugged.

"The front row at a Hank Williams Jr. concert."

Everyone laughed sort of tentatively, but Harvey Winkins, bound determined to support Collins as co-custodian of the company's opening night jitters, picked the theme right up: "Ok, what is asleep with their pantyhose rolled and their legs wide open?" Harvey chortled.

"Oh, I know that one," Sunny laughed out loud, remembering. "The front row of a Civic Theater Sunday matinee."

"Right you are," Harvey was doing his ringmaster's imitation, "give the little lady a kewpie doll." The whole company cracked up. And it helped. John and Harvey knew what they were doing. They were letting the air out of pressurized time. The sounds of the audience settling in murmured over the dressing room squawkbox, but weren't as intimidating as before.

"Places!" finally came the stage-whispered call out of the shadows of the stairwell from the assistant stage manager with her headset.

"Places," a number of the actors repeated with a kind of awe in their voices.

Places, each actor thought. *It's time,* each actor knew. *I have to do it now,* each actor realized. *Oh, I'm not ready for this,* each actor shuddered.

Places, Lori prayed to the patron saint of actors. . *Oh please let me be Tracy.*

One by one they touched each other—"Let's do it"—pecked each other on the cheek—"hey, here we go"—nodded—"break a leg"—and filed solemnly up the steps to the stage as if mounting a gallows. Barb Dwyer stood at the top of the steps to give each of them a squeeze as they entered the blackness of backstage. She really was such a good-hearted person despite all.

Bill followed Lori to her place in the wings and kissed her on the nape of the neck in the darkness. "You're gorgeous, Tracy," he whispered in her ear. "They are going to love you so much."

"Oh Bill, thanks," she whispered breathily.

"It's Dexter now," he joked as he faded away from her into the dark void of backstage.

"Places and holding for two," the assistant stage manager glided through the darkness whispering as if she had infra-red glasses on.

Places and holding, Lori thought, *the theater's own unique version of the water torture.*

"They're still seating people," the assistant stage manager tried to explain, but it didn't help. All anyone wanted to do was get on stage and somehow croak out their first line.

"Places and holding two more," the assistant stage manager had taken up residence right behind Tracy. "More latecomers," she tried to explain in deference to Lori having the lead role and thus being susceptible to the largest case of stomach loops.

But then the houselights went slowly down. The darkness of backstage spread out to possess the whole theater. The soft big band music of the Thirties came up, the mere hint of an overture, and they all knew that it was time.

"Take the stage. Take the stage," the assistant stage manager moved from side to side urgently whispering.

Lori felt herself walking through the doorway to the right corner of the couch where she would receive the first line of the play from Tracy's mother. In the two short beats as she stood in the blackness of the stage touching the corner of the couch, she felt the transformation take place. Her shoulders went back and stiffened, her head and nose came up, her lips pursed to pout, and, magically, just as the lights rushed up, she became Tracy Lord, petulent on the day before her wedding.

Bill had a much more difficult time of it. Dexter is the second to last character to take the stage in *The Philadelphia Story.* He comes on a half hour after everyone else in the last minutes of Act One. So Bill sat on a folding chair in the darkness of backstage and listened as each of his fellow actors took the stage and delivered those crucial first lines as their characters settled into their rhythms. The audience was quiet at first. *Attentive,* Mike thought. But then the first murmur of laughter, tentative, rippled over them, then another laugh, bigger, freer, happened. Soon the audience was reacting to the lines. Waiting in the wings, Bill could feel their gradual involvement in the play. When Uncle Willie took the stage (Harvey in his ridiculous knickers), tall and lanky like some wealthy Don Quixote doing his dirty old man hijinks, the audience exploded in laughter and all the actors had to wait for it to subside before they went on. *It's working,* Bill realized. *It's working.*

When Lori came offstage the first time and moved into the dim glow of the blue backstage worklight on the prop table, Bill moved to her and she was radiant in the excitement of it. Her smile flashed when she caught his movement toward her. She was a different person, suspended in that soft blue glow as if reality had withdrawn and she floated like some magical goddess risen out of the power of her own imagination.

"Oh Dexter, it's good," she gushed, "and they like it . . . they like it." She touched his cheek and the heat from her fingertips seemed to burn clear through him, and then she was gone, back into her enchanted world from where she had dropped in to touch his mere mortality.

Onstage, Tracy moved with a lightness of being she had never experienced before. The lines sang in her throat as if they had always been there just waiting to be sung. She picked things up and put things down with the confidence and elan of a young heiress secure in her beauty and wit and power over all whose eyes were riveted only upon her. She glided across the stage with the grace of a goddess bestowing her brilliance upon them. She had made the leap—what a plunge!—across time and space and class and beauty into another world which she completely controlled. She felt the power of Tracy in her skin, the glow on her cheeks, the fire in her fingertips. She was touching them all, and when she laughed they turned their heads to share in her joy.

And Bill waited in the wings . . . waited . . . listening for the lines that would draw him out of the gloom. And he waited on, while all the others romped like gods and goddesses out there in their charmed circle. He waited to go on, to step into life, to lose himself in the magic they had all created.

All the while he waited, the panic built. *They're doing so well. The audience is with them all the way, and all I can do is screw them up.* He felt a huge weight gathering in his stomach.

"Dexter, Dexter, go, go now," some voice whispering urgently in the darkness slapped him back to consciousness. It was the assistant stage manager. She loomed in the blue light like some martian with antennas protruding from her head. She was signaling his cue to take his place for his entrance.

He staggered up out of his chair, the sweat running off his face, and moved like a zombie out through the theater lobby to the closed doors of the theater. His entrance was through the audience, and there was a full page before he had to go on. He cracked the double swinging doors and peeked through, listening for his cue lines. On either side of the aisle he would enter down, the backs of the audience's heads swayed and bobbed like balloons at a carnival. The stage was so bright. The balloons floated in a pool of darkness that lapped up against that brilliant world of the stage. Every time Uncle Willie pranced across the stage, bony in his outrageous knickers, the audience howled and bobbed their shadowy heads.

His cue lines were coming, coming, ever closer, sinister and threatening.

Then Tracy asked whether it wasn't time for lunch, and Bill knew he had to go. His knees felt locked and heavy as he started to move. The fear hit him hard in the face as he stepped through the doorway and started down the aisle. The fear smashed into his whole body like a wall of water from a fire hose as he careened down the dark aisle toward the terrible bright light of the stage. The fear shot right through him as Tracy's little sister squinted out at that sea of bobbing heads and squeeked maliciously, "Oh look, it's Dexter." He hardly knew where he was as he struggled down the aisle against all those invisible obstacles. Everything suddenly was swirling in front of his eyes as he moved out of the darkness into light, lurching in grim imitation of Dexter's jaunty bouyant skip which he had practiced numberless times.

This time, however, he forgot that there was one small step up to the raked stage off the veranda that fronted on the audience. Then he remembered it at the last moment when it was too late. He tried to hop up onto the stage, but he caught the right toe of his patent leather shoe on the edge of the riser.

It was a classic trip. It catapulted him forward onto the brilliantly lit stage with his arms wildly windmilling and landed him flat on his face right at Tracy's feet. Everyone onstage was in shock, mouths agape, eyes wide and stunned.

The audience exploded in laughter, howled as he rolled onto his side and came to his knees. He looked up at Tracy and her hand was to her mouth trying to stifle a giggle. No one was mad at him for screwing up the scene. They all seemed inordinately, unpredictably happy. He realized they were enjoying his clumsiness. The audience, the cast, were all laughing uproariously at his pratfall as he groped desperately for his line. Just as the laughter began to subside, he found it. Smiling sheepishly from his unrehearsed blocking on the floor, he shrugged his hands into the brightly lit air, at Tracy, at the audience, at anyone willing to listen and delivered it.

"Hello friends and enemies," he grinned stupidly. "I just dropped in for lunch."

And the whole audience exploded once again in uproarious laughter.

Thus, perhaps, are comedians born out of clumsy actors. But he realized that he was really Dexter now and that the audience was on his side. He picked himself up off the carpet, dusted himself off just as Dexter would do, and began exchanging greetings with everyone on the stage. With the laughter of his entrance to bouy them up, the whole cast sailed into intermission.

"Wow, what a great bit," Collins was the first one to him as they flooded down into the dressing rooms at the end of the first act. "Vintage Chevy Chase. What a great idea! What a great laugh! Boy, we've got 'em now. Dexter, you're a genius."

"What? Genius?" Bill was dumbfounded by Collins' enthusiasm. "I didn't. . . . It was. . . . I'm sorry."

"You didn't plan it? It was real? You're kidding me?"

"No, honest, I was nervous and I tripped and I don't even remember how it happened."

"Talk about coming out smelling like a rose," Uncle Willie chimed in. "You got the biggest damn laugh of the whole act."

"It really was funny, Dexter," Tracy purred. "I couldn't help laughing myself right along with the audience.

"Well, I guess my debut was a success despite all," he answered with an embarrassed shrug. They had all been going on so professionally and suddenly this bumbling fool comes onstage and captures the attention of the whole audience with his sheer clumsiness. Somehow it just didn't seem fair. They had rehearsed so long and so hard to attain such precision and then the one totally unrehearsed happening of the evening works best.

"Drop in for lunch, indeed," Harvey laughed over his shoulder as he opened his make-up case. "What luck! Even the line fit. No wonder everyone likes Dexter. He leads a charmed life."

When he went back out onstage for the second act, he felt comfortable, as if that comical trip, disaster turning into magic, had exorcised all of his fears and self-consciousness. He lounged around the stage with all of Dexter's playful disdain. He delivered his speeches with the puckish nonchalance of a heedless millionaire. He stood on the stage feeling the fine new magic woven into the very fabric of the time and

space. He was aware of them up there in the darkness, rows of disembodied heads, all focused on him and Tracy and the others, caught up
in the illusion they had worked so hard to create.

All buying it, Bill thought, *all buying it.* Aware of them all up there
in the darkness, Dexter liked the feeling of actually doing exactly what
they had rehearsed. The most amazing thing was that, once it was
begun, it came so easy. What amazed him even more was how ready
he was and how exciting it became when it was all together—the audience, the lights, the music, the lines, the movements to and from each
other across the stage, the bringing it all to life. It made him realize
how special one's first opening night can be.

Lori wasn't nearly as emotional about it. In fact, after the first two
or three minutes of the performance, she was actually smug. Tracy
was there from the very beginning. Once that was established, Lori
knew that she was perfectly in control. She was a good actress. She had
proved that in college, and it isn't something that just goes away, fades
or gets lost, like love or the color of new jeans. Once Tracy spoke, Lori
knew that Tracy was going to walk the stage full blown, witty, imperi-
al and vulnerable that whole evening. Perhaps Tracy wouldn't be so vi-
brant and "there" in other performances, but this opening night Tracy
Lord strutted the stage with all the authority that her name bestowed.

It's magical, Lori thought, *and I, Tracy, made it happen. When she
said the final line of the play, they all clapped, and Dexter held her hand
and bowed with her, and she felt this glow of love coming over her.*

23 Opening Night: Act Two

For Bill Franklin, the applause was an aphrodisiac. All the women coming up in the lobby afterwards in the "meet and greet" receiving line to shake his hand and tell him how much they enjoyed the play, and how good he had been onstage, saying outrageous things like "when you tripped it was the funniest thing in the whole play, and looked so real" or "you're so handsome and so casual onstage, such a natural actor," all their adulation was an aphrodisiac. Just being at the center of so much attention all evening, from the flowers and cards in the dressing room to the howl of laughter when he made his head over heels entrance to the fervent applause of their curtain call, was an aphrodisiac. The whole affair had him walking on air and consumed with lust.

Martha wasn't coming to the cast party. She was her company's representative to the *United Way* and there was a dinner that night that she had to attend, so they decided she would come to see him on Saturday and they would go out afterwards.

The opening night cast party was at Thelma's spacious apartment. Bill had stopped for beer on the way, so almost everyone was already there. Lori was standing by the piano with a beer can in her hand talking happily to Marge.

Marge will probably claim that she directed me to my trippingly epic entrance, Bill thought as he deposited his twelve-pack in the refrigerator. *Hell, she'll probably want me to do it every night from now on.*

When he got back to the living room, Thelma, enthroned on the sofa, was just beginning a story. Lori was standing with John Collins and Sunny who were beaming like newlyweds.

"We were doing a play called *The Musical Comedy Murders of 1940*," Thelma began, "and Dottie Seacraft was playing the hostess of this fancy cocktail party. 'Dottie' was the perfect name for her character. She played this rich flaky old broad and was absolutely hilarious, reminded me of Margaret Rutherford. Oh never mind, you're all too young, except for Harvey who isn't listening, to even know who Margaret Rutherford is."

Bill had to chuckle to himself. He knew who Margaret Rutherford was, but he was pretty sure that Lori didn't.

"Anyway, it's opening night right in the middle of the first act with most of the large cast onstage, and Dottie's fixing herself a drink. When she turns upstage from the portable bar, her skirt catches on one of the ornamental curlicues and she pulls the whole thing over. Glass shatters, the martini pitcher spills all over the front of the stage, olives and twists of lemon are rolling out into the audience.

"Well . . . Dottie just looks at the havoc she's wreaked for a long moment. The rest of the cast onstage gives a collective gasp and gapes at her like a bunch of dopes. Dottie's hand goes to her mouth and in that startled little girl voice of hers she gives off one of her patented 'Oh my's' and says 'Oh my, this will never do.'

"With that, she flounces off to the kitchen door stage left and calls for the maid. 'Oh Helga, Helga, I've just made an awful mess.'

"This wonderful young actress from the university is playing Helga, the Nazi maid, and she stomps onstage in character wondering what in the hell is going on.

"'Oh, I've made a dreadful mess, Helga,' Dottie announces. 'Please clean it up,' and she points regally to the chaos at the front of the stage.

"Helga looks daggers at her, but stays brilliantly in character, surly and scowling, and starts cleaning up the mess with Dottie hovering over her and supervising the whole time like Perle Mesta."

"Who's Pearl Mesta?" Lori asked.

I know that name too, Bill realized.

"Never mind, it doesn't matter," Thelma was eager to get on with her story. "Anyway, Helga sets the bar upright and picks everything up, then stomps offstage to get a towel. When she returns, she gets down on her hands and knees to wipe up the stage, while all the time making murderous faces at her 'dotty' mistress who is still flouncing around blowing stupid remarks at everyone like kisses: 'Oh, how clumsy of me,' and 'Yes, that's good Helga, wipe it up,' and 'I just can't believe I knocked over that whole wonderful pitcher of martinis.' One of the men in the cast, right in character, leers around the piano at Helga and says 'Yes, she does good work on her hands and knees, doesn't she?'

"Finally, Helga finishes, and Dottie just shoos her away, steps back, takes a deep breath, and says, 'Now everyone, where were we,' and goes right into her cue line as pretty as you please as if nothing at all of a cataclysmic nature had even happened.

"The whole cast had gotten caught up in it. It was one of the most beautiful ensemble improvs I've ever seen. The audience never suspected that anything was wrong. They thought it was just all part of the show. And Dottie and Helga even got some good laughs out of it."

"That's great," Bill uttered his first words since joining the party, "but I sure hope we don't have to come up with any impromptu scenes in this play."

"Don' worry, sonny," Harvey was raising his drink glass, a high tumbler half full of an evil looking brown liquid, to proclaim, "I'll take care o' everthin' onstage. Just don'tchoo worry." Ol' Harvey must have gotten into the bourbon awfully quickly because he already seemed half-drunk.

Marge steamed across the living room at the sound of Bill's voice and cornered him by the fireplace to dump a full load of unsifted compliments on him.

"You did just a wonderful job tonight, Dexter. So relaxed, so natural. You're the perfect Dexter.

"Well thanks, actually I was having trouble breathing and I thought I was going to throw up the whole time I was onstage, but I'm glad you liked it," Bill answered, pulling Marge up short as she momentarily wondered whether he was serious or putting her on.

"You know, Dexter" Marge turned viciously serious without warning (re-enter the director), "that trip onstage . . ."

Here it comes, Mike chuckled to himself. *He'd already called this one.*

" . . . really got a good laugh. I mean, I know it was unrehearsed and totally unplanned—wasn't it?—well, whatever, but it *was* very successful."

No doubt about that, Bill grinned evilly.

"Yes, I guess it was," he agreed.

"Why don't we just leave it in. Do you think you could do it every night. It really did get a huge laugh."

"Sure, I can do it, but not nearly as well as I did it tonight," Bill nodded solemnly, but he just couldn't resist. "I do sort of see Dexter as a cross between Cary Grant and Chevy Chase, don't you?"

"Well, I guess so," Marge gave him a long look, still not knowing if she was being put on or not.

Bill escaped in the direction of Lori, Collins and Sunny. John Collins was waxing philosophical when Bill wandered up.

"You know," Collins was saying, "you can worry about homeless people, or soldiers getting killed, and all the drugs, but no matter how much you worry, or who you vote for, you still feel frustrated, like you can't change anything, then you get up on stage and you can be anybody, change anything. That's what's so cool about this."

Lori smiled when Bill joined them, as if she knew that he had been watching her from across the room.

"Guess what?" Sunny was beaming. "My divorce was final today. I don't have to worry about having a husband anymore. Now John and I can officially be an item, as if anybody in the cast hadn't already noticed."

"It did cross my mind that you two tended to disappear from the bar at the same time a lot," Bill teased.

"Oh it did, did it," Sunny beamed. "I guess all actresses are just natural sluts."

She's been into the booze too, Bill thought. *How did all these people get so far ahead of me? What? Are they doing shots?*

Lori, who was in the midst of taking a slug of her beer when Sunny delivered her "all actresses are sluts" line, almost choked, spewed little drops down the front of her dress.

"Well, not all actresses are sluts," Collins said archly, "except in Wabash City."

Sunny slapped him playfully across the back of the head, then put her arms around him and kissed him chastely. "Sluts have more fun," she laughed.

"Always have," Collins agreed.

"If I was a woman, I think I'd be a slut," Bill added offhandedly.

Something about John and Sunny suddenly being so openly lovers made him look quickly at Lori.

She wouldn't meet his eyes, as if she was embarrassed.

"We've got to go," Collins suddenly announced.

You two are too happy to live. I hope her ex-husband drops a piano on your bed, Bill thought.

"They certainly seem happy," Bill turned to Lori after the nauseating lovers had gone.

"Yes, don't they," and she sipped on her beer in lieu of having anything else to say.

"Probably because they're getting so much sex," Bill was trying to joke, but Lori wasn't laughing. Instead, she was actually fidgeting as if she was embarrassed. But he blundered on anyway like a true dolt:"Well, marriage will certainly cure that."

Lori *did* laugh at that, but weakly, falsely, as if her laughter was only camouflage for some other feelings that she really didn't want him to see

Suddenly, he realized that they hadn't all raced over to this party and started doing shots. They were all flying on the euphoria of having actually done the play . . . and done it well. He was feeling it himself, this irresistible urge to be outrageous and expansive.

Lori's reaction was utterly unpredictable.

"Bill, let's get out of here. I want to be alone with you."

"Uh, why . . . uh . . . I've got this beer . . . uh sure, uh yes . . ." all of his bravado deflated in the reality of her proposition, "uh . . . where's your husband?"

"At work. He's coming tomorrow night."

"Aha," Bill sipped desperately at his beer sensing that his bluff of their flirtation, their stolen parking lot kisses, their soul-sharing, was finally being called.

"Oh Bill, let's go someplace. I've never felt like this before. They loved the play. When I was onstage it was like I was a queen. It was an unbelieveable rush. I've never felt so wonderful. Oh Bill, I want you so much I could die."

"Wow," Bill cast a quick guilty glance back over his shoulder at the rest of the party, but no one was paying any attention to them. Thelma was telling another story about the time Count Dracula actually sank his fangs into his leading lady's neck and, by reflex, she kneed him square in the balls and he sang his lines soprano for the rest of the performance.

Lori stared solemnly over the top of her beer can: "John and Sunny are so happy. Why not you and me? It was so great being onstage and the audience laughing with us and clapping for us. I want to be alone with you tonight, Bill."

"We're going to do it, aren't we," he spoke his realization slowly, looking right into her excited face.

"Yeah, we are, aren't we," Lori smiled radiantly like a brilliant young heiress, utterly in control.

Bill felt like an inexperienced actor not quite able to work up enthusiasm for his character. He regularly dreamed of making love to women other than Martha, but when it happened, he was always surprised and terrified. It was as if he loved the idea of other women but was frightened of the idea made flesh.

"Let's leave separately," he submerged his misgivings in logistics. "Don't say anything to anyone, just leave. They won't miss us for a while and they won't know when we left. I'll meet you outside. I'll get a couple of beers to take with us."

She just nodded and did what he told her. He got four beers from the twelve pack in the refrigerator and let himself out the kitchen door.

"We'll take my car," he met her in the front yard, his hands bulging with beer cans.

"Fine. I don't care." She flung her arms around his neck and kissed him hard and long, grinding her hips against him as he stood utterly defenseless with his hands and mouth full.

He managed to back her to his car at the curb in front of the house with her still wrapped around his neck and kissing like a woodpecker in heat. He set the beer cans on top of the car, got the door open, and manuevered her into the front seat. Grabbing the sweating beer cans, he went around and got in the driver's side, but she was all over him once again as soon as he slid in beside her.

"I don't care," she said again as her arms clamped around his neck and her mouth moved in upon him. "I need to make love tonight," but there she stopped and looked almost murderously into his face, "no, I want sex tonight, hard sex," and her mouth closed over his, opened, her tongue lunging desperately.

He couldn't get his keys out of his pocket to start the car because she was kissing him and running her hands down his chest and stroking the front of his pants between his legs.

"Just wait a minute, Lori, we can't do it here."

"I don't care," she said again, and clearly meant it.

She kissed him even harder, moaning as he touched her breasts right through three layers of fabric, her sweater, her turtleneck, and her bra. It was the first time he had ever touched her carnally. His hands had held her face when he kissed her. His arms had encircled her neck. His fingers had chastely brushed the backs of her shoulders. But his hands had never had the nerve to roam freely over her body. He had just begun to explore when he came to his senses, realized where they were, what they were doing. Warming to her surprise attack, he had momentarily lost all touch with reality.

"We'll get a room," he gasped, when she finally freed his mouth.

Forcefully, he disentangled himself from her. She sank back onto the seat, gulping deep draughts of air with a wild look on her face.

He bent to the beer cans rolling around underfoot, but when he rose up to hand them to her, her hand was moving across his back, caressing him. "Lori . . . I've gotta drive . . . hold these . . . put 'em in the back seat. We'll be there in a minute," and he dumped them into her lap.

The beer cans were cold and wet, and they momentarily distracted her. In that brief surcease, he managed to get his car keys out, force ignition, and get into gear. She disposed of the beer cans somewhere— for all Bill knew, she could have thrown them out the window!—and cuddled back against him, her right hand wandering pruriently all over him as he tried to drive. To make matters worse, it was raining steadily again.

He drove her to *The Riverview Motel,* the only one in downtown Wabash City. There were a gaggle of motels out on the bypass near the interstate, but the Riverview was the only one close in. It was a scenic little place, perched right on the Wabash with its rooms overlooking the river. The rain was coming down harder when Bill pulled in and got out to get the room. He got number sixteen down on the end of the one-storey building, but all of the parking places in front were taken so he left Lori off with the key and drove down to the lower lot by the river to park the car. As he walked back up the slight incline to the room, he wondered if she would already be naked on the bed waiting for him, wondered if he really wanted to go through with this, thought of Martha and how long he had loved her, was tempted to turn tail and flee back down to the car and just drive off to the west to disappear and never see Lori, Martha, anyone ever again, but then he remembered that the show must go on the next night and that he truly was caught up in the adventure of it all.

Lori was not naked on the bed in the girlie magazine tableau he had briefly imagined. She was sitting demurely in one of the two chairs that flanked a ridiculously small round table beside the large double bed which filled seventy percent of the room. The rain was beating on the flat roof as he stood in the doorway looking down at her. She had turned on the bathroom light and it leaked a shadowy glow out through the partially open door.

"This is so romantic," Lori murmured as she rose to him in the shadow-light and put her arms around his neck for one of her long, lingering tongue kisses.

It's two married people getting a room to cheat on their spouses, Bill thought, his touch with reality returning and intruding uninvited, *hardly romantic.* But he kissed her back and tried to get a grip on his romantic leading man role.

Lori stepped back from their kiss, and his fantasy began. She pulled her sweater over her head with that particularly elegant and sexy move that only women use when taking off their pull-over shirts, crossing her arms at her waist and somehow pulling the whole garment up and over her head in one magical motion. In one more simple move, using only her right hand, she unhooked her black bra. He couldn't help a sharp intake of breathe as her breasts confronted him.

"I was in a Tennessee Williams play in school once," Lori whispered in the shadow-light. "'We're all in solitary confinement within our skins,' was one of the lines my character said."

"It's such beautiful skin," Bill reached out to touch her with his fingertips. He ever so slowly and gently rotated her until she was standing against him with her back to his body as he kissed the nape of her neck.

That was pretty romantic, he thought. He felt himself entering into his role.

"You are exquisite," he whispered in her ear from behind as he kissed her neck. "Your body is so beautiful. I've been fantasizing about you naked for weeks"

"Naked. I like that."

"I love to look at and touch your naked body. We've been kissing for so long."

"Kiss my body."

The rain ran in rivulets down the window panes as they undressed each other. From behind, he unzipped her skirt and it dropped to the floor when she simply shifted the subtle curve of her body.

What an elegant pirouette, he thought, as she stepped out of her skirt and turned, wearing only her black bikini panties.

Lori had fallen back onto the bed like a goddess entering her bath. She wore her near nakedness like a velvet cloak, flowing, begging to be stroked and opened up. Her eyes ordered Bill to strip for her as if he were her private slave.

Finally naked and standing before her at the foot of the bed, Bill was clearly ready to make love, but shyly hesitant about how to proceed.

Lori solved his dilemma. She arched her back and slowly slid her panties off, letting them hang a moment on her ankle, then kicking them jauntily away. The bed was a new stage and, secure now as the lead actress, she was taking it.

Thus encouraged, Bill, not functioning at high coordination, tried to join her in the bed but stubbed his toe hard on one of the legs. He let out a yelp of pain and fell back then jumped up and down holding his throbbing foot.

Lori giggled, and their heated romantic rendezvous veered off into farce.

Bill ducked into the bed like a schoolboy sneaking in late, then didn't know what to do with his hands. As he moved in beside her, Lori rolled to him, her arms going around his neck for another of her storybook kisses. He had kissed her before, but this time as her tongue raked his mouth, her whole skin was pressing upon him.

They kissed, and for the moment, all his misgivings and guilts retreated. He realized that she wasn't Martha and he wasn't who he had always been. He wanted to abandon himself to this experience, let it happen as if he really was a whole new person.

But he couldn't do it.

"I want to make you happy," he whispered, trying to camouflage his guilt, "what can I do to make you feel good."

Lord, you sound like Mister Rogers, he thought. *I just want to be your neighbor.*

"Everything," she answered in a breathy whisper.

So he made love to her until she arched like a lovely dolphin leaping toward the moon, rising out of the waves of fluid stretch which bore her body up and rythmically crested over her.

So far so good, Bill thought, *she's got to be happy, and she isn't laughing at me.* He lay his head upon her flat white stomach. .

"It's funny," he heard himself whispering, compelled to talk, to ruin it all with words, even though he didn't have the slightest idea of what he wanted to say.

"What's funny?"

"Us here," he tried desperately to give form to his feelings.

"Funny?"

"No, not funny, but, I mean, what's so good about all of this, us, the play, it's not so much *what* it makes you feel, but just *that* it makes you *feel,* like all this has brought me back from some limbo where I was just hanging around not feeling a thing."

"Yeah, I guess," Lori was stretching again for a kiss. "I'm feeling great," she whispered almost below the threshold of hearing. "Can we do it again," she ordered in that same low murmur of desire that made the words feel more like caresses.

Whoa, this is really scary, Bill thought. *She is really into this.*

Lori was utterly carried away by this role she had taken on of the wicked married woman. It was as if the play had gotten out of hand, as if their characters in play had taken over their real characters in life. Lori was a fine actress and she had accepted this new role without hesitation, but Bill was still just a bumbling amateur.

Lori was like some enchantress singing a siren song to lure heroes to exquisite death.

Bill, unfortunately, was no hero and already on the rocks. He worked doggedly to satisfy her but his most acute awareness was of a perverse and consistent dripping sound that seemed located right next to the bed.

Much to his surprise, Lori seemed utterly unaware and disinterested in his imagined dysfunction. She was once again riding the crest of her own stretch and wild thrash, moving upon Bill's partial indecision without the slightest concern for anything but the utter freedom and release she was feeling. What Lori was thinking was . . . nothing. She was only feeling, not thinking, and not emotionally feeling, but only physically feeling, feeling how good it felt, and how much she wanted it to last.

She's so excited, Bill thought, *if only I could get out of my mind and enjoy her.* But he couldn't.

Finally she fell back against the pillows. Her hair was all tangled, drenched with sweat and plastered to her forehead. Her eyes were dead and wide. Her lips gasped for breath.

"Oh Bill, that felt so good. Oh Bill, that was great. I haven't come twice in one night in two years. Oh Bill, thank you. That was so great."

It didn't make any sense. If sex was art, this had turned into a french farce . . . for him. She hadn't seemed to notice. She had created it all right out of her own imagination. All he had done was kiss her, tell her how exciting she was, and somehow it had worked . . . for her. He realized that all he wanted to do was escape back into the safety of his life with Martha, escape back to the make-believe of the stage where he didn't have to deal with these demands of reality.

As he lay there beside her, listening to her breathing as it slowed, he was still conscious in a detached way of a persistent dripping sound somewhere nearby. The dripping seemed to have magnified, seemed relentless. *The roof leaks and its coming in,* Bill thought. *But it's leaking right next to the bed.* Curiosity made him reach for the light on the bedside stand.

"Oh wow, that's bright," Lori protested, diving under a pillow when it came on.

Bill blinked three times, then spotted the leak right away. The heavy steady drip was coming from the tip of a large hanging udder that had formed in the latex ceiling paint just above the edge of their bed. He started to laugh. It was a ludicrous looking thing hanging precariously from the ceiling.

"What's so funny?" Lori asked from under her pillow.

"Look at this thing. You're not going to believe it," Bill coaxed her.

"Whoa, what is it?"

"The water is leaking through the ceiling, but it's all gathering underneath the rubber ceiling paint."

"It looks like . . ." Lori started to giggle.

"Yeah, it does."

"A big boob."

Staring up, they both cracked up. But, as if in retaliation, the weight of the water caused that large rubber boob to burst, and they were both drenched as if someone had doused them from a bucket.

"Boy, it must be raining hard out there now," Bill wondered. Then, like a wild man, he jumped out of bed and ran to the sliding glass door. Yanking aside the drapery and peering out into the darkness, he could see most of the lower parking lot where he had left his car. Even the little he could see confirmed his worst fear.

"Damn," he howled.

"What is it?"

"The river's flooding the parking lot. I've gotta get to the car before it's too late."

"What?"

"The car."

"What?"

"The river. The car."

He launched himself into his pants, not even thinking about his shoes. He was out the door before Lori had put any of it together.

How do I explain to Martha that my car is stranded underwater in the no-tell motel parking lot, panic drove him as he ran down the hill and into the rising water. It was already halfway up his ankles. Dirty little white caps bounced off his bare feet as he slogged through the flooding water.

I'm dead. She'll know I was here with another woman. She'll think I do this all the time. I'm dead. He must have stepped in a pothole in the blacktop and twisted his ankle because suddenly he was on his face in the rising water fighting to regain his feet. .

The water's not over the tires. I've still got a chance, he hoped as he pulled open his car door. It started right up just as if it were sitting high and dry in his driveway. *But can I drive it out?* he was suddenly rather calm as he sat there dripping on his vinyl seat, switching on his windshield wipers and lights, and peering out at the thirty yards of flooded blacktop between him and the driveway up the incline to the motel. *I'll really have a charmed life,* he thought, *if I get out of this one.*

He revved the motor for long seconds until it was running smooth and fast, then he quickly pulled it into gear hoping against hope that the tires would find purchase in the water, that the car would move and keep moving, that he could drive it out and save his marriage.

Never once did he think that he might be carried off on the flood in the car to drown and be found downriver tangled in a logjam.

Never once did he think that he was risking his life just to avoid embarrassment, to cover up a lie.

Never once did he think of Lori standing at the top of the driveway in only her dress getting drenched watching him flail his way through the flood.

He dropped it into gear and the wheels caught. It moved forward in a sudden leap then slowed to a sluggish trudge as the resistance of the rising water caught the spinning tires. He stepped down hard on the accelerator and the car actually picked up a little speed.

Only ten more yards to go, Bill prayed as he pressed the accelerator to the floor. The engine screamed, a plume of water shot out of the exhaust pipe behind, and the car leapt out of the flood and roared careening up the inclined driveway to skid to a halt in the glistening parking lot.

Thank god I made it, Bill thanked the deity who had been toying comically with him.

Lori was saying something through his closed window that he couldn't hear. Stupidly, he rolled the window down and the rain pelted in on his face.

"Let me in," Lori was shouting above the beat of the rain. "Are you OK?" There was genuine concern in Lori's voice as she scrambled in next to him.

"I think so."

"I thought you were going to drown. When you fell. I thought you were going to be carried away. What a dangerous night."

"Oh, it hasn't been so bad," he smiled in the euphoria of an escape artist. "Not bad at all. Parts of it have been absolutely exciting."

Sitting there relieved, all Lori and Bill could do was look at each other and laugh, survival laughs, the kind that people laugh when they've gotten away with being human once again.

24 Striking the Set

Bill and Lori both went home like two cats left out in the rain. Lori beat Eddie home and was already in bed when he stumbled in drunk. When Bill got home, Martha was already in bed and no questions had to be answered. Before he went to bed, he washed Lori and the river off in a hot shower and drank all four of the beers he had salvaged from the floor of his car. Neither of their spouses ever suspected. Two cars got stranded in the parking lot of *The Riverview Motel*. There was a picture of them half under water on the front page of *The Wabash City Journal and Courier*. .

I'll bet those guys had some explaining to do, Bill automatically assumed.

The play went on for eight more performances, all sell-outs except for two matinees. With each performance, the cast came closer together in an enchanted circle of perception, timing and cooperation. After a while, they no longer even knew that the audience was there. It was their magical realm.

Bill's tongue-tied follies in the eighth performance on the Saturday of the final weekend provided one of the highlights of the run. The play was going extremely well at a quick and witty pace when, on a throwaway line, Bill completely lost it.

The line comes at the beginning of Act Three, the morning of the wedding when everyone is trying to get over a hangover. "Uncle Willie's in the pantry doing wild and wonderful things," the line reads and it provides an exit direction for Connor, Liz the photographer and Tracy to all get offstage. But in that second to the last performance, under some unknown influence, probably the gods who plague adulterers and amateurs toying with him once again, Bill couldn't get that line out.

"Uncle Willie's in the pastry . . ." *no, that's not right!* Bill realized and stopped.

Collins and Lori and Sunny just stared at him and waited. A terrible embarrassing silence began to build.

"Uncle Willie's in the pastry . . ." he tried it again, and blew it again in exactly the same way.

"What?" Bill couldn't tell whether Collins' question was serious or he was just mugging trying to avoid another of those ferocious silences.

"I said," Bill slowed down, being careful this time, "Uncle Willie's in the pastry," and did it wrong a third time.

Collins and Sunny were fighting back their laughter and leaning toward their exit in the wings, but they couldn't go until they sorted out the lines. All they wanted to do was get offstage and his tongue-tied bumbling was holding them prisoner. Only Tracy had any presence of mind left. She was the only one able to retain any semblance of character.

"You mean the pantry, don't you Dex?" she prompted him.

"Yes, I do, I certainly do. The pantry, doing wet and wild things, or something like that."

Collins and Sunny fled the stage as if pursued by demons, and Tracy followed with a quizzical shrug. It may have been the longest exit line in history, but the audience never even noticed. They thought that Dexter was still drunk and his silly play on words was just another of his jokes.

At the very end of the last performance, as he stood behind her with his arms around her waist in the final tableau, Tracy in her flowing white wedding dress, Dexter smiling in triumph at having won back his ex-wife, Bill felt this strong urge to step up and kiss Lori, but it wasn't in the script. Lightly he brushed his cheek against her hair, and she felt it. Tilting her head back, she smiled radiantly up at him. It was the play's happy ending, and the lights went down with a rush.

Then they struck the set. Tracy's Philadelphia Main Line mansion came down under their common crowbars and hammers. One of the saddest realities of theater is that once the set is struck so are all the temporary relationships. The loves cool, the friendships fade, and the magical community steps out of their charmed circle and disbands. When the final curtain falls and the set is struck, real life takes over. For the actors, plays never have happy endings, they just end. But their endings are not sad either, just real. When a play finishes its run, both characters and actors die and are immediately reincarnated, not as jackrabbits in Wyoming as the old joke goes, but as real people once again. Sometimes it's somewhat of a shock.

So, they struck the set of *The Philadelphia Story* and, to everyone's delight, John and Sunny announced their engagement at the strike party. The real aftershock came six weeks later though when Harvey Winkins and Barb Dwyer eloped to Reno and got married. In later years, Harvey swore she abducted him at needlepoint and kept him in handcuffs the whole honeymoon.

They struck the set, but Thelma's favorite story from the play was always of Dexter falling onstage at his first entrance on opening night. She always told how Marge insisted he keep doing it and how it never was as good or got nearly as big a laugh again.

They struck the set, and they all walked away from each other and their magical illusion, but the fragile imagination has a certain tenacity. Bill and Lori went out to lunch a week after the play ended. As they toyed with their salads, he thought about suggesting they get a motel room, try to rekindle what they had that night before the rains came.

"I want to keep seeing you," he finally asked her in a whisper so tentative that she could hardly hear him.

"Bill, the play's over," she leaned toward him over her salad, all earnestness and practicality. "We're both married. It's time to go back to them."

"Why? Why can't we keep seeing each other? I want to have more of you."

"The play's over. We're not Dexter and Tracy anymore. We're just Lori and Bill."

"So? So what? We were in love with each other. We wanted each other."

"It wasn't us. It was them. They were rich and beautiful and free, and they could afford to fall in love all they wanted."

"So what we've been doing for the last three months was all only acting?"

"No, not for me. I wasn't acting. Being in bed with you was exciting, an imaginative thing. Eddie's my husband, my childhood sweetheart, and I love him. He's just having a tough time right now. But you're my first lover, and that is so special. You saw me totally differently than Eddie does, without all that past history. You treated me like a star, not just some little legal secretary from Wabash City,

Indiana. I mean, that's why we can't keep seeing each other. It's like Warren Beatty."

"Warren Beatty?"

"Yeah, he romances and falls in love with all of his leading ladies, but after they get done making the movie he always breaks it off."

"What does he have to do with . . ."

"He realizes that he was in love with someone else, a character in a play, not a real person. That's why he breaks it off."

"Fine, but I don't want to break it off. I don't want our illusion to end. Why does it have to? Why can't you be Tracy forever, and me Dexter? Why can't we make it last just a little longer?"

"Because we can't"

And she was right. They finished their lunch in that fancy restaurant, and they parted with smiles and chaste kisses on cheeks. He realized he wouldn't see much of her again, unless they happened to get into another play together. Six months later, she and her husband moved away. But years later, a strange miracle happened. A friend's daughter was getting married in a very fancy affair (by Wabash City standards) and Bill borrowed a black tuxedo from the *Civic Theater* costume shop for the event.

"How do I look?" he asked Martha when she came down gorgeous in her black beaded sheath.

"Just like Cary Grant, hon," she winked playfully.

At the reception he was standing at the bar waiting for a drink when he felt a tap on his shoulder. He turned and there she was, Tracy, in a drop-dead gorgeous strapless black cocktail dress beaming up at him, her smile so radiant that he felt momentarily blinded.

"Oh my god," he gasped. "It's you."

"I know," she literally glowed she was so beautiful, such a gift, "surprise."

And, for a brief moment as he held her to him in an old friend's hug, they were Tracy and Dexter all over again and his heart leapt up in the excitement of it.

But Martha was back from the powder room and at his side in a moment.

"You remember Lori Martin from *The Philadelphia Story,*" he stuttered, still overcome by Tracy's beauty.

In yet another breath Lori was leading them both over to say hello to Eddie who was sitting with some friends across the room.

The tiny miracle had only lasted a moment, but it attested to the power of the dream. Doing a play is like being Cinderella. You become a whole new person for a fine but finite while, but time always catches up with you. That's the whole problem with theater: the play ends and you have to go back to being yourself again.

About the Author

William J. Palmer is the author of the "Mr. Dickens" series of Victorian murder mysteries which have been selections of *The Literary Guild, The Book of the Month Club, The Mystery Guild* and *The Doubleday Book Club*. Two of these novels have also been optioned for feature film production. He has also written books on film history and novel criticism. He is a professor in the English Department at Purdue University and lives in West Lafayette, Indiana, in close proximity to the Wabash River.

www.ingramcontent.com/pod-product-compliance
Lightning Source LLC
Chambersburg PA
CBHW020242030726
47499CB00001B/25